Edward M. Hodges

Hodges American Bank Note Safe Guard

1862

Edward M. Hodges

Hodges American Bank Note Safe Guard
1862

ISBN/EAN: 9783742800978

Manufactured in Europe, USA, Canada, Australia, Japa

Cover: Foto ©Andreas Hilbeck / pixelio.de

Manufactured and distributed by brebook publishing software
(www.brebook.com)

Edward M. Hodges

Hodges American Bank Note Safe Guard

NEW ENGLAND MUTUAL LIFE INS. CO.,

All over and above the actual liens and charges against the Company, returned in cash to all the insured, every five years, thus making it purely mutual. Last Cash Dividend, 39 ℘ cent.

COMPANY'S BUILDING.

This Company has never failed to make large dividends, and pay them in cash. An uniform prosperity and economy have marked its course since its organization—a period of twenty years.

BOSTON & NEW YORK. ORGANIZED, 1843.

BRANCH OFFICE, METROPOLITAN BANK BUILDING,

No. 110 BROADWAY, N. Y.

CAPITAL - - TWO MILLIONS, ONE HUNDRED THOUSAND.
SURPLUS - - - - - - ONE MILLION.

Last dividend paid *in cash to all* the policy holders, 39 ℘ cent., amounting to over $400,000, and making nearly $1,000,000 thus paid since the company began business. The past year, 1861, notwithstanding the adversities of the times, was one of marked prosperity.

WILLARD PHILLIPS, Pres. B. F. STEVENS, Sec.

Economy, care in its risks, and prudent investments characterize this Company. The last report of the Insurance Commissioners, comparing this company with all the principal companies, makes this the *leading company in the United States, in surplus and economy.*

This Company being purely mutual, insures at the lowest possible rates; and, if the premiums paid exceed the *actual* cost, the surplus is returned to the parties insuring.

Every five years, at the time of declaring the dividends, the business is, as it were, closed, so that its actual position and solvency are made manifest at that time; and the surplus funds are divided *pro rata*, among all the insured. This guards the assured against any possible loss from inefficiency on the part of the Company, and is a sure guaranty as regards the future.

The terms of payment are peculiarly advantageous to the insured. Premiums can be paid annually, semi-annually, quarterly, or one half of the first five annual premiums on life policies loaned to the insured, if desired.

Insurances may be effected for the benefit of married women, beyond the reach of their husband's creditors. Creditors may insure the lives of their debtors.

Documents of an interesting character, showing the benefits of the mutual plan, explaining the different forms of policies and the manner of making payments, furnished gratis, upon application, by mail or otherwise, to

JOHN HOPPER,
Agent and Attorney for the Co.,
(Metropolitan Bank Building) 110 Broadway, New York City.

ENDORSEMENTS

Of the Leading Bank Note Engravers of the Country, in Favor of this Work.

OFFICE OF THE NATIONAL BANK NOTE COMPANY,
New York, December 10, 1861.

E. M. HODGES, Esq.: SIR—We have examined the copy of your "Bank Note Safe-Guard" submitted to our inspection, and cheerfully recommend it as a work of unquestionable utility, well deserving the patronage of bankers, merchants, and tradesmen, throughout the country. As the merits of your work are very apparent, it will, doubtless, receive the liberal patronage of all who have occasion to handle paper money.

Yours, &c.,
J. MACDONOUGH, SECRETARY.

OFFICE OF DANFORTH, WRIGHT & CO.,
New York, March, 1859.

E. M. HODGES, Esq.:

SIR—Your "Bank Note Safe-Guard" seems to possess unequalled merit, in the detailed description it gives of all Genuine Bank Notes; and combined with the "Journal of Finance and Bank Reporter," you certainly offer a work of great utility, as a protection against frauds in paper currency.

Respectfully yours,
DANFORTH, WRIGHT & CO.

OFFICE OF RAWDON, WRIGHT, HATCH & EDSON,
New York, March, 1859.

E. M. HODGES, Esq.:

SIR—Having examined the plan proposed in your "Bank Note Safe-Guard," for enabling the public to detect Spurious and Altered Bank Notes, by furnishing accurate descriptions of the Genuine Notes of all the Banks of the country, we take pleasure in expressing our approval of the same, as affording a simple and effectual protection against that species of fraudulent paper money.

Respectfully yours,
RAWDON, WRIGHT, HATCH & EDSON.

OFFICE OF WELLSTOOD, HAY & WHITING,
New York, March, 1859.

E. M. HODGES, Esq.:

SIR—We regard your "Bank Note Safe-Guard" as a work that should receive the most favorable attention from all who are accustomed to handle Bank Notes. The facility with which Altered, Spurious, or Counterfeit notes can be detected, is such that the most inexperienced can scarcely go astray. And we have no hesitation in commending the work to the public as one which is much required, and as fully accomplishing its object.

With best wishes for the success of your efforts to prevent imposition, through the medium of your publication,

We remain, truly yours,
WELLSTOOD, HAY & WHITING.

OFFICE OF THE NEW ENGLAND BANK NOTE CO.,
Boston, March, 1859.

E. M. HODGES, Esq.:

SIR—Allow me to express to you my unqualified opinion in favor of your "Bank Note Safe-Guard." The simplicity of it is what I most admire; the most inexperienced of the great mass, who are in the habit of taking Paper Currency can at once detect an altered or spurious note, which are much more dangerous than counterfeits, and more numerously in circulation.

You have my best wishes for its success, believing it to be the best work of its character ever published.

ISAAC CARY, Agent.

New York, March, 1859.

E. M. HODGES, Esq.:

SIR—We take great pleasure in endorsing Mr. Cary's opinion of your "Bank Note Safe-Guard," and in recommending it as a work of the greatest utility.

Respectfully yours,
TOPPAN, CARPENTER & CO.

OFFICE OF THE AMERICAN BANK NOTE CO.
New York, March, 1859.

E. M. HODGES, Esq.:

SIR—Attempts at literal imitation, or counterfeiting, in the present advanced state of Bank Note Engraving, are of unfrequent occurrence, most of the notes represented in Bank Note Detectors and Reporters being either Spurious or Altered Notes.

Spurious Bank Notes merely retain the name of the Bank and place of issue—not always using the true name of the President and Cashier, and are made up of devices unlike those of the genuine notes, a want of familiarity with which, on the part of the public, being counted on in perpetrating these frauds.

Your "Bank Note Safe-Guard," supplies a desideratum in a manner so simple and so easy of reference, that there can be no danger of suffering from Spurious or Altered Bank Notes, if brought to the test of comparison which it furnishes.

Respectfully yours,
JOCELYN, DRAPER, WELSH & CO.

☞ TERMS. ☜

The SAFE-GUARD sent by mail to all parts of the Country on receipt of........ $3 00
The Journal of Finance and Bank Reporter, including Hodges' Gold and Silver Coin Chart Manual, and Safe-Guard, Weekly Issue........ $4 00
Semi-Monthly........ $3 00
Monthly........ $2 50

INDEX

TO THE

BANK NOTE SAFEGUARD.

The Figures Enclosed in Brackets Denote the Denomination of Notes IMITATED AND PHOTOGRAPHED!

SPECIAL NOTICE.—In consequence of the removal of certain Banks, particularly in the Western States, some will be found differing from the Index bearing the *original* place of location. And a few banks part of the plates of which have the *original location*, while the remainder of the plates of the *same Banks* have the place of *removal* on them. The *Index* contains their place of location at the time of the publication of this work. For a complete list of all Broken, Worthless and Retired Banks see JOURNAL OF FINANCE AND BANK REPORTER.

MAINE.

NEW HAMPSHIRE.

VERMONT.

MASSACHUSETTS.

RHODE ISLAND.

CONNECTICUT.

NEW YORK CITY.

NEW YORK STATE.

NEW JERSEY.

PENNSYLVANIA.

PHILADELPHIA CITY BANKS.

PENNSYLVANIA COUNTRY BANKS.

DELAWARE.

MARYLAND.

DISTRICT OF COLUMBIA.

VIRGINIA.

NORTH CAROLINA.

SOUTH CAROLINA.

GEORGIA.

ALABAMA.

LOUISIANA.

OHIO.

INDIANA.

ILLINOIS.

KENTUCKY.

TENNESSEE.

MISSOURI.

MICHIGAN.

IOWA.

WISCONSIN.

FLORIDA.

CANADA.

NEW BRUNSWICK.

U. S. TREASURY.

THE

SAFE-GUARD.

This work is at length thoroughly completed, being now arranged GEOGRAPHICALLY AND ALPHABETICALLY, thereby obviating the only objection there ever was to it. The notes of each Bank are all on one page, and it is but the matter of a moment to find any note required. This work has cost us many years of toil and expense, and we now present it to the public, with the assertion that no work was ever published that is of greater utility for commercial purposes. It is of interest and importance to every individual, of every age, condition, or sex, who handles a dollar of the miscellaneous and precarious paper currency of our country.

The paper money of the United States is of such infinite varieties of design and execution, that the artful and accomplished counterfeiter can sport upon and defy the perception of the great majority of our people. And the frequent and cruel impositions so repeatedly practised upon the honest and credulous, have derived their impunity from the fact that other works and Detectors have only attempted to direct attention to the spurious and counterfeit, while, in our SAFE-GUARD ALONE, has the idea been developed of minutely describing the genuine Bank notes.

A new counterfeit, or spurious Bank note, is prepared by a rogue, who, with his numerous accomplices and confederates, distribute and circulate their issue simultaneously in different and distant localities. These notes (not being described in the Reporters and Detectors) being readily taken by the unsuspecting, and by the imperfect judges, in a short time obtain an extensive circulation; and days, weeks, and, in some instances, months have elapsed, before the VIGILANT Bank Note Reporters have informed the community that they have been fearfully victimized. Thus, being at last exposed, but not until he has reaped a rich harvest from his first issue, the counterfeiter again takes the plate to his hand and alters it to some other bank or denomination, and may do the same thing again and again, and each time with impunity and profit, before the Detectors can act as an efficient check on his proceedings.

But the SAFE-GUARD always, and in every case, acts as a check and preventative against these impositions and frauds, by describing every GENUINE Bank note, and every part of every note, dissecting and analyzing all denominations of all notes, of every Bank, organized and doing business in the United States and British North America, showing each note, made up of different designs, vignettes, &c.; each denomination differing so materially, that no one one of the notes could be altered to another and larger denomination, without the certainty of an immediate detection on reference to the fac-simile of the plates (in the SAFE-GUARD) of the particular bank on which such fraud has been perpetrated. Herein is exemplified the great superiority of the SAFE-GUARD over all Reporters and other Bank Note Detectors.

Spurious, altered, or *raised* notes are by far the most numerous class of bad money, and bear no resemblance to the genuine. They are detected at a glance by reference to the SAFE-GUARD, there being therein portrayed a perfect Daguerreotype of the genuine notes; the dress and design of which are as unlike the spurious as is light to darkness.

Counterfeits, or *fac-simile* notes, are comparatively rare. They are intended to resemble and imitate the true, and calculated to circulate where the genuine are well-known, but can be more easily detected, by close inspection, than any other class of bad bills. Very few of this description are in circulation. Nine-tenths of the bad bills in circulation being altered, raised, or spurious. On reference to our Reporter this will be seen.

Within a few years, photograph imitations have made their appearance. They can be detected by applying cyanide of potassium, which turns the bills white.

In a word, THE SAFE-GUARD detects all PAST, PRESENT, and FUTURE spurious, altered, and raised notes, and is of more value, protection, and security to the commercial interests of the country, than all the Detectors, Bank Note Lists, and other works which, up to this time, have been published. In fact, THE SAFEGUARD is almost indispensable, FOR IT GOES AHEAD OF, AND ANTICIPATES THE COUNTERFEITER, cutting off his success, while the Reporters and Bank Note Lists but follow AFTER, and to use a homely but forcible expression, "can only lock the stable after the horse is stolen."

We have herein endeavored to show the utility and importance of this work, and with the promise *that it shall be always correct to the date of its issue*, we are satisfied to send it forth to the public on its own merits.

☞ On another page will be found commendations from *all the first class* BANK NOTE ENGRAVING COMPANIES in the Union, endorsing HODGES' AMERICAN BANK NOTE SAFE-GUARD. This testimony, together with the approval and patronage of nearly every Banker and Broker in America, at once stamps it as the most valuable publication of the times—indispensable to every well-regulated counting room or business place.

☞ No Person is authorized to act as Agent, unless having the Publisher's Printed Receipts and written authority.

E. M. HODGES.

HODGES'

AMERICAN BANK NOTE

SAFE GUARD

MAINE.

Left	Centre	Right
Spread eagle and shield. 1	Portrait of Washington, two females, sickle and sheaf of wheat at the left; milkmaid and cows at the right. ALFRED BANK. Alfred, Me.	1 Female, eagle and shield.
Female. 2	ALFRED BANK, Alfred, Me. Harvest scene.	2 Portrait of Franklin.
Portrait of Webster. Three and 3	Locomotive and train of cars. ALFRED BANK. Alfred, Me.	3 Female seated on a bale.
V and Five Farmer sitting under a tree.	ALFRED BANK. Alfred, Me. Signing of the "Declaration of Independence."	V Female with sickle, and an Indian woman.
State Arms. X, 10, Ten	ALFRED BANK, Alfred, Me. Indian, spread eagle, and two horses; factories and steamboat in background.	10 Female drawing water at a well.
XX Milkmaid.	Man on horseback, farm-house and drove of cattle. ALFRED BANK, Alfred, Me.	20 Female, eagle and shield.
50	Title of Bank. Three female figures. Female	50

MAINE.

Left	Centre	Right
100 Two females; shield between.	ALFRED BANK, Alfred, Me.	100 C 100
1	Vig. Female on either side of a shield; steamboat on left, train of cars on right. 1 AMERICAN BANK Hallowell, Me	1 Female Portrait.
2 2	AMERICAN BANK Hallowell, Me. Ship building 2 Locomotive and car.	2 Cupid and a sea monster.
3 Female with balances in one hand, wreath in other, eagle by her side.	AMERICAN BANK, Hallowell, Me. Female and swan in water. 3	3 Two females
Female reclining; eagle, globe, &c., steamer and city on left. 5	5 AMERICAN BANK, Hallowell, Me.	5 Figure 5 and five females.
Female feeding an eagle from cup. X	Spread eagle, steamer on left; public building on right. AMERICAN BANK, Hallowell, Me.	10 Portrait of Washington.
Female. XX	Vig. Capitol at Washington. AMERICAN BANK, Hallowell, Me.	20 Man beside a capstan, and barrels behind.

MAINE.

Left	Centre	Right
50 [illegible]	Female. State Female. Arms. AMERICAN BANK, Hallowell, Me.	50 Female with pole, cap, shield, etc.
100 Man with grain cradle.	Vig. Ships, steamboats, vessels, &c., city in distance. AMERICAN BANK, Hallowell, Me.	100 Female with rake
1 Boy with rake, fork, and canteen; also dog.	AUBURN BANK. Auburn, Me. Train of cars, load of hay, men, cattle, &c.; in distance train of cars on bridge, city, &c.; in extreme distance city, bridge, water, &c.	1 Two females, one engaged at table, the other with horn in hand, chickens, &c.
Female reclining with scales. 2	Two men, horse, dog, cattle, and sheep. 2 AUBURN BANK. Auburn, Me. Loading hay.	Female erect with sword and scales.
Male portrait. 3	Wharf scene—train of cars, depot, horses and carts, canal boats, vessels, men, buildings, steamboat, &c. AUBURN BANK. Auburn, Me. Cow and calf.	3 Male portrait.
V Female portrait.	Five gold dollars with three cupids above them; hunter seated on right, Indian female on left; cars in distance. AUBURN BANK. Auburn, Me.	5 Female portrait.
Female portrait. 10	Female seated; on her right is ten gold dollars; in front of her nine cupids making offering to her; steamboat and cars in distance. AUBURN BANK, Auburn, Me.	X Female seated with sheaf.

20 XX	View of large public building; horses, carriages, mules, females, &c., in front. AUBURN BANK, Auburn, Me. Female seated.	20 Female portrait.
Female erect leaning on anchor; ship in storm in distance. FIFTY	Spread eagle; U. S. Capitol on right, and steamship on left. AUBURN BANK, Auburn, Me.	50 Female reclining with Balance, &c
C Portrait of a boy. 100	Blacksmith shoeing a horse, forge, &c.; a jackass tied to anvil; locomotive on left. AUBURN BANK, Auburn, Me. Two horses.	100 Portrait of Webster.
	AUGUSTA BANK, Augusta, Me. This Bank uses the old Perkin's stereotype plate, which has the denomination printed in fine letters all over the bill.	
ONE Mechanic and sailor with flag, quadrant and sledge, right.	1 Large ship. B'K OF COMMERCE, Belfast, Me.	1 Man chopping a tree. ONE
TWO Two females with arms extended, holding grain	Vig. Steamship. B'K OF COMMERCE, Belfast, Me.	2 TWO
3 Sailor seated with quadrant and spyglass, compass by his side, steamship and vessel on right. 3	Farmer and sailor on either side of a shield, representing commerce and industry. B'K OF COMMERCE, Belfast, Me. Goose.	3 Female seated on merchandise.
V FIVE	Vig. Spread eagle, on either side flags with the names of the different States. B'K OF COMMERCE, Belfast, Me. Geese.	5 Female.
X Dog's head.	Ship building. BANK of COMMERCE Belfast, Me. Female head.	10 TEN
TWENTY Indian with bow and arrow, sail boat near him; vessel in distance.	XX Two females with scroll, liberty pole and grain, cornucopia at their feet; cars crossing bridge on right; vessels on left. BANK of COMMERCE Belfast, Me. Female head.	20 Bridge.

1 Med. Head. 1	1 Female seated with right hand on wagon and left on shield safe by her side. BANK OF CUMBERLAND Portland, Me.	Large figure 1 and full length female.
1 Propeller. ONE	BANK OF CUMBERLAND, Portland, Me. Sailor and farmer on either side of shield on which is deer and tree.	1
2	Title of Bank. Female erect apparently rushing to three others seated.	2
2 Med. Head. 2	2 Female seated on safe with cornucopia &c.; farmer plowing on right; building &c., on left. BANK OF CUMBERLAND, Portland, Me.	Large figure 2 and full length female.
3	Steamboat and other vessels. Title of Bank.	3 Liberty.
3 Med. Head. 3	Figure 3 and three cupids thereon. Sportsman, female and child seated, train of cars on right; log house on left. BANK OF CUMBERLAND, Portland Me.	Large figure 3 and full length female.
5 Female seated with sledge; cog wheels &c., buildings in distance.	Female seated with sprig in left hand; eagle, shield, sheaf, train of cars, &c., on right, town ocean and vessels on left. BANK OF CUMBERLAND, Portland, Me.	5 Portrait of Washington.
Sailor with flag, bale, &c., anchor and quadrant. TEN	Shield on which is figures 10; on right females seated with sickle, and man on horseback, and negro driving drove of pigs; on left, female, rudder, safe and steamboat. BANK OF CUMBERLAND, Portland, Me.	10 Female Portrait.
XX Male portrait. 20	20 Vessels sailing, &c. XX BANK OF CUMBERLAND, Portland, Me.	20 Male portrait. XX
50 Male portrait. FIFTY	Steamboat, schooners, sloops, &c; Female seated with spear and shield. BANK OF CUMBERLAND, Portland, Me.	50 Male portrait. FIFTY

100 Portrait of Van Buren. 100	C Ship under full sail on ocean, two vessels in background. C BANK OF CUMBERLAND, Portland, Me.	100 Male portrait. 100
500 Portrait of Van Buren. 500	Vig. Same as hundreds. 500 BANK OF CUMBERLAND, Portland, Me.	500 Portrait of Jackson. 500
1000 Portrait of Jackson. 1000	Vig. Same as 20's. Female seated with spear and shield. BANK OF CUMBERLAND, Portland, Me.	1000 Portrait of Van Buren. 1000
Washington. 1	Farm yard scene, farmer and drover. BK. OF SOMERSET, Skowhegan, Me. Man plowing.	1 Goddess of Liberty, globe and Declaration of Independence.
Cattle, sheep, etc. 2	Maine logging scene in winter. Title of Bank. Female with scales, etc.; ship	2 Jefferson.
Clay. 3	Boot and Shoe manufacturing scene. Title of Bank.	3 State Arms.
Train of cars, city in distance. 5	Head of Webster. Title of Bank. FIVE	5 and FIVE Large 5, eagle and Goddess of Liberty; head of Washington and "FIVE."
Franklin. 10	Blacksmith shoeing a horse; train of cars in distance. Title of Bank. Blacksmith & locomotive.	10 Vulcan.
TWENTY Jackson. 20	Vig. Landscape; locomotive in background; city, train of cars, etc., in distance; farmer plowing, mill, etc. Title of Bank. Load of hay.	20 Female churning.
Goddess of Liberty, crown and wreath. 50	Indians and whites trading. Title of Bank. Man cradling grain.	50 Male portrait. FIFTY

Goddess of Liberty. 100 | Spread eagle; U. S. capitol; steamship in distance. Title of Bank. Agricultural implements. | 100 Male portrait.

1 Female with tablet. | Female portrait BANK of THE STATE of MAINE. Bangor, Maine. State Arms. | ONE Female by a [illegible] male.

2 Portrait of female. | Title of Bank. State Arms; with agricultural implements and products. | 2 Portrait of female.

3 Female gathering flowers | A man watering horses at a trough, and woman feeding swine; farmhouse and buildings. Title of Bank. State Arms. | 3 Boy gathering corn.

Female seated with sickle and figure 5. FIVE | Title of Bank. State Arms. | Female seated and holding out figure 5. FIVE

Ship, brig, and schooner. X | Portrait of Gen. Taylor. Title of Bank. | 10 State Arms 10

20 20 | Title of Bank. Female seated, eagle and globe and word "America" thereon. State Arms. | 20 Washington

30 Med. head. 50 | Title of Bank. State arms, female on either side; in distance steamboat and train of cars. | 50

C | Shipping; city in the distance. Title of Bank. State Arms. | 100 Spread eagle.

B'K of WINTHROP, Winthrop, Me. This Bank uses the old Perkins' stereotype plate, which has the denomination printed in fine letters all over the bill.

Indian standing erect with bow and arrow. | ONE Vig. Sail vessels; light house in back ground. BATH BANK, Bath, Me. Dog. | 1 Portrait of little girl.

TWO Dog's head. | Vig. Indian paddling canoe accompanied by two squaws, shrubbery and mountains in background. BATH BANK, Bath, Me. Ducks. | 2 Female reclining on bale of cotton.

3 Sailor and blacksmith. | 3 Vig. Eagle, and female partly disrobed. 3 BATH BANK, Bath, Me. Dog. | 3 Large sail vessel, other smaller ones, &c.

FIVE State arms. V | Vig. Large sail vessel; smaller ones on either side. BATH BANK, Bath, Me. Female head. | 5 Portrait of Webster.

TEN Portrait of boy. | Vig. Log-rolling; three persons, another felling a tree; cattle in background, &c. 10 BATH BANK, Bath, Me. Beehive. | TEN Group of three females representing Agriculture, Commerce, &c.

XX Sailor seated | Vig. Ship building; ships on stocks, &c. factory on left. BATH BANK, Bath, Me. Beehive. | 20 Miniature view of little girl.

50 Female gazing on ocean; vessel, &c. | BATH BANK, Bath, Me. State arms; sailor and farmer either side. | 50 Female with flower.

100 | One Hundred Dollars Sailor with trumpet on vessel. 100 BATH BANK, Bath, Me. | 100 Hunter drinking from brook.

ONE | Vessels. 1 BELFAST BANK. Belfast, Me. | ONE Female. ONE

2 TWO 2 | Ship and other vessels. 2 BELFAST BANK. Belfast, Me. | TWO Female. TWO

THREE | Sleeping scene. 3 BELFAST BANK. Belfast, Me. | THREE Steamer Figure 3, and word "Three."

FIVE | Female holding drapery over a figure 5. V BELFAST BANK. Belfast, Me. | 5 Ship under sail.

The word "Five" and letter "V." | Female holding rake and sickle; sheaf of grain, machinery, &c. Large V with female. BELFAST BANK, Belfast, Me. | 5 Washington

X | Signing the Declaration of Independence. X BELFAST BANK, Belfast, Me. | X Locomotive and car.

1 | Factory and train of cars. 1 BIDDEFORD BANK, Biddeford, Me. | 1 Female.

2 | Aurora and the hours. 2 BIDDEFORD BANK, Biddeford, Me. | 2 Steamship.

3 | Female seated. 3 BIDDEFORD BANK, Biddeford, Me. | 3 Head. THREE

5 | Man ploughing with horses. Female, cupid, V. BIDDEFORD BANK, Biddeford, Me. | 5 Female.

10 | Two ships under sail. Ship and X BIDDEFORD BANK, Biddeford, Me. | TEN Head of Washington. TEN

20 Female. | XX Eagle. XX BIDDEFORD BANK, Biddeford, Me. | 20 Ship.

FIFTY Female FIFTY	50 Man and horse. 50 BIDDEFORD BANK, Biddeford, Me.	FIFTY Female. FIFTY
The figures 100 with the words "one hundred" running across. Portrait.	Horses, wagon, wharf and shipping. BIDDEFORD BANK, Biddeford, Me.	The figures 100 with the words "one hundred" running across. Portrait.
ONE Indian crouching with gun.	Moonlight scene; fishing schooners, etc. BUCKSPORT BANK, Bucksport, Me.	1 Boy's portrait.
ONE Indian kneeling on the bank of river with gun in his hand. ONE	Drove of wild horses, two more prominent than others. BUCKSPORT BANK Bucksport, Me.	1 Portrait of a boy.
TWO Two females holding a bundle of grain over their heads, a sickle in the handle.	BUCKSPORT BANK, Bucksport, Me. 2 TWO 2	2 Ship; light-house and vessels seen in the distance.
THREE	Spread eagle over the banners of the different States. Head of a dog. BUCKSPORT BANK, Bucksport, Me.	3 Portrait of girl resting on right arm; left hand over her eyes to shield from light.
FIVE Sailor erect and blacksmith seated	Fleet of Vessels; light-house in the distance. BUCKSPORT BANK, Bucksport, Me.	5 V
TEN Female with sheaf.	Marine view; ship, schooner and other vessels under sail. Title of Bank.	X State Arms.
TEN Female with a sickle in right hand, left hand holding a bundle of grain on her shoulder.	Three ships on the stocks, steam mill, &c. BUCKSPORT BANK, Bucksport, Me.	X State Arms.
20	Light-house, small vessels, steam boat, and train of cars. BUCKSPORT BANK, Bucksport, Me. Bee hive	20 Sailor with quadrant in right hand.

L Three dogs.	BUCKSPORT BANK, Bucksport, Me. Santa Claus riding over the top of houses by moon light. Dogs.	50 Indian.
100 Man with his gun and dog in the woods by the side of a fire.	100 Indian, white man, woman and child in a canoe. BUCKSPORT BANK, Bucksport, Me. Head of Washington.	100 C
1 ONE 1	CALAIS BANK, Calais, Me. Male portrait; angel on left; cherub on right.	1 Female and fig. 1.
2 Farmer and sailor either side of shield	Saw mill; men seated on load of lumber drawn by two oxen. Title of Bank.	2 Male portrait
3 Sailor and State Arms.	Ship-yard scene in general. Title of Bank.	THREE 3 Male portrait
	☞ This Bank also uses the Perkins' stereotype plate which has the denomination printed in fine letters all over the face of the bill.	
1	Female seated, in the act of crowning eagle with wreath; ship on left, and drover, drove of cattle, and sheep, and train of cars on right, in distance. Head of Washington, figure 1. CANAL BANK, Portland, Me.	1 Indian Princess.
2	Same as ones. 2 CANAL BANK, Portland, Me.	2 Mechanic and work-bench.
3	Same as ones 3 CANAL BANK, Portland, Me.	3 Female Portrait.
5	Same as ones 5 CANAL BANK, Portland, Me.	5 Female Indian, seated with pole and cap, and shield.

10	Same as ones. X CANAL BANK, Portland, Me.	10 Female partly nude with pen and tablet; cog wheel on left.
20	Same as ones. 20 CANAL BANK, Portland, Me. XX	Female with sheaf of grain under left arm. 20
50	Same as ones. 50 CANAL BANK, Portland, Me. 50	Female Portrait. Med. Head.
100	Same as ones. 100 CANAL BANK, Portland, Me. 100	Female erect with sickle and sheaf of wheat
D	Same as ones. 500 CANAL BANK, Portland, Me. 500	Female figure erect, with flag; left hand on a warrior's shield.
	☞ All denominations have on the back of the bill, a locomotive and one passenger car; three men and dog.	
Block of stores. 1	Female and Merchandise; factory and shipping in background. CASCO BANK, Portland, Me.	1 Sailor with quadrant, ships in background.
Block of stores. 2	Female and vegetables; river and village in background. CASCO BANK, Portland, Me.	2 Female.
Block of stores. THREE	3 Female seated on a bale; steamship and train of cars in background. 3 CASCO BANK. Portland, Me.	Female and Merchandise. THREE
Boy's Head. 5	Landing of the pilgrims. CASCO BANK, Portland, Me.	5 Girl's Head.

Left	Centre	Right
Three female figures and anchor. TEN	State Arms. Female, scale, and sheaf of wheat. CASCO BANK, Portland, Me.	10 Portrait of Taylor.
Female with a rose. TWENTY	Family group at supper; Indians looking in at the door; dog barking at them. CASCO BANK, Portland, Me. 20 20	20 Male portrait
Female portrait. 50	Signing treaty with the Pilgrims. CASCO BANK, Portland, Me. FIFTY	50 Male portrait
100	Marine view—large steamship; city in background. CASCO BANK, Portland, Me. HUNDRED	100 Male portrait
Female Portrait. 500	CASCO BANK, Portland, Me. Hunter with gun overlooking rock; female behind him. D D FIVE HUNDRED	500 Male portrait
M	Wharf scene—steamboats, men on dock, horses, drays, men at work, city in background. Male portrait. CASCO BANK, Portland, Me. 1 0 0 0	1000 Sailor boy; two sailors in distance; ship seen in offing.
ONE Brig	Sailor reclining, anchor, capstan, cordage, &c; ship, brig and sloop in the distance. CITY BANK, Bath, Me.	1 ONE State Arms ONE
2	Train of cars, factories in distance. CITY BANK, Bath, Me.	TWO Sailor on rail of ship, spy glass in hand
3 State Arms. 3	Ship and steamship in full sail; schooner in distance. CITY BANK, Bath, Me.	3 THREE 3
5	Ship-yard—Ships building. Shield flag, and safe; anchor on left; factories in distance. CITY BANK, Bath, Me.	5 FIVE

Left	Centre	Right
Goddess of liberty, shield, eagle, &c.	10 Man seated, anvil, house; train of cars, hills, lake, buildings, &c. CITY BANK, Bath, Me.	10 Portrait of female.
	20 CITY BANK, Bath, Me. Sailor, two girls, anchor, cog-wheels, bale, &c., tall chimney, hills and town, near shore of lake, light-house, &c.	20 Stream trees &c.; woman & child bathing.
50 Man load of hay, hills in distance.	CITY BANK, Bath, Me. Three females; on left town and hills, bridge; train of cars going out.	50 Ship and brig, city in distance.
Female erect holding oval portrait; in left hand a winged wand	100 CITY BANK Bath, Me. Signing declaration of independence.	100
ONE Female feeding fowls.	ONE on fig. 1. CITY BANK, Biddeford, Me. Cherub rolling silver dollar; cars and bridge in distance.	ONE on fig. 1 Female and figure 1.
TWO Female with flowers.	Boot and shoe manufactory; men at work. CITY BANK, Biddeford, Me.	2 Santa Claus.
3 Washington	View of U. S. Capitol. CITY BANK, Biddeford, Me.	THREE on 3. Female seated by shield and fig. 3.
5 Portrait of a female.	CITY BANK, Biddeford, Me. Five cherubs and five silver dollars.	5 Sailor with quadrant; globe, bales, &c.
X State Arms. Sailor and farmer.	CITY BANK, Biddeford, Me. Nine cherubs, ten gold dollars, female, shield and cornucopia.	10 Portrait of a female.
20 Two children	Cattle, sheep, horse, dog and two men. CITY BANK, Biddeford, Me.	XX Female representing Agriculture.

Left	Centre	Right
Fountain 50	CITY BANK, Biddeford, Me. Three female representing Agriculture, Commerce and Manufactures; ship in distance.	50 Female churning.
C Female portrait.	CITY BANK, Biddeford, Me. Large spread eagle.	C Female portrait.
	COBBOSSEECONTEE BANK, Gardiner, Me. This Bank uses the old Perkins Stereotype Plate, which has the denomination printed in fine letters all over the bill.	
1 Indian female seated, with shield, &c.	Vig. Farmer and sailor on either side of a shield on which is a deer and tree; on right, ships; on left, mill, &c. EASTERN BANK, Bangor, Me. Spread eagle.	1 Female seated with pen and tablet.
2 Female portrait.	Vig. Farmer and sailor on either side of a shield on which is a deer and tree; on right, ships; on left, mill, &c. EASTERN BANK, Bangor, Me. Spread Eagle.	2 Female portrait.
3 Mechanic seated with mallet and chisel in right and left hand.	Vig. Farmer and sailor on either side of a shield on which is a deer and tree; on right, ships; on left, mill, &c. EASTERN BANK Bangor, Me. Spread eagle.	3 3
5 Spread eagle	Vig. Female leaning on anchor, merchandise, &c.; on right, sloop of war; on left, city, vessels, &c. EASTERN BANK, Bangor, Me. Horse.	5 Steamboat.
10 Portrait of Washington	Vig. Spread eagle, ships, &c. EASTERN BANK, Bangor, Me. Dog, key and safe.	10 Two females seated, one with scales and sword.
Female with sheaf of grain. TWENTY	Vig. Spread eagle on rocks; man of war on right, brig on left EASTERN BANK, Bangor, Me. Female seated, ship, &c.	20
50 Medallion Head.	Female reclining, shield, cage, cornucopia, liberty pole and cap, &c. EASTERN BANK. Bangor, Me. Agricultural implements.	50 Medallion head.

100 | Vig. Female seated; on right men loading wagon with hay; ship, steamboat, &c. | 100
Female portrait. | EASTERN BANK. Bangor, Me. Head of Indian. | Female Indian princess.

1 | Two farmers, one seated, apparently eating, the other smoking and holding a jug. | 1
Female Portrait. | FARMERS BANK, Bangor, Me. | Train of cars.
1

ONE | FARMERS' BANK, Bangor, Me. | 1
Female resting arm on fence. | Has the denomination in small words and letters all over the middle part of the bill. | ONE
ONE | | 1

2 | Man ploughing; village on right; on left steamboat in distance. | 2
Ships, &c. | FARMER'S BANK, Bangor, Me. Bee-Hive. | Female Portrait.

2 | Title of Bank. | 2
Men, horses, carts, buildings, etc. | Has the denomination same as ones. | TWO
TWO | | 2

3 | Cattle and sheep, two cows standing in water. | 3
Large figure 3, and three Cupids. | FARMER'S BANK, Bangor, Me. Agricultural Implements. | Female seated with flowers.

FIVE | Title of Bank. | 5
Vessel; name Gold Hunter on sail. | Has the denomination same as ones. | FIVE
FIVE | | 5

5 | Drove of cattle and hogs, two men on horseback, train of cars, village &c, in background. | 5
Large figure 5, & female. | FARMER'S BANK, Bangor, Me. Locomotive. | Ship, steamer, lighthouse, &c., in distance.

TEN | Title of Bank. | 10
Vessel on stocks. | Has the denomination same as ones. | TEN
TEN | | 10

Mill could [illegible] [illegible] & two [illegible]; cows, houses, trees, &c. in distance. | Female Portrait. | 10
10 | FARMER'S BANK, Bangor, Me. Steamboat. | Man sharpening scythe.

FARMERS BANK. Bangor, Me.
Use Perkin's stereotype plate for 5's, 10's, 100's and 50's which have the denomination printed in fine letters all over the surface of the bill.

20 | Female sitting with arms extended, scales in right hand, cap & pole in left; naked boy on one side and one partially draped on the other. | 20
Female with scales and sword; eagle, key & safe. | FARMER'S BANK, Bangor, Me. Steamship. | Female with sheaf of wheat.

50 | Two females seated with pieces of machinery, factories on right, ship in distance on the left. | 50
Female with sickle. | FARMER'S BANK, Bangor, Me. Engine & Tender. | Farmer gathering corn.
50

100 | FARMER'S BANK, Bangor, Me. Female reclining with One Cupid Hundred scattering fruits over a city in foreground. Machines. | 100
Sailor supporting a flag staff. | | Portrait of female.
| | 100

500 | FARMER'S BANK, Bangor, Me. Three females one seated the others reclining; train of cars & ship in the distance. Eagle. | 500
Female with bow & quiver surrounded by Coat of Arms of the different States. | | 500

FREEMAN'S BANK. Augusta, Me.
This Bank uses the old Perkins' Stereotype Plate, which has the denomination printed in fine letters all over the bill.

ONE | Vig. Sailing vessels. 1 | ONE
| FRONTIER BANK, Eastport, Me. | Female.
| | ONE

| Vig. Persons engaged with sheep; shrubbery and houses in the background; large figure "2" across the note and miniature view of four persons. | TWO
| | Miniature view of female.
2 | FRONTIER BANK, Eastport, Me. | TWO

| Vig. Farmers, farming implements, cattle, &c.; vig. on upper left corner. 3 | Figure 3 and word Three.
| | Miniature of Female.
3 | FRONTIER BANK, Eastport, Me. | THREE

Vig. Female in representation of agriculture, commerce, &c. shipping, houses, &c. | Large V and female. | 5
Letter V and word Five. | FRONTIER BANK, Eastport, Me. | Head of Washington.

X | Vig. Steamboat; sail vessels, &c. X | 10
Indian with bow and arrow. | FRONTIER BANK, Eastport, Me. | Female with sheaf of grain; forest in background.

20 | XX Vig. Spread eagle. XX | 20
Miniature view of female. | FRONTIER BANK, Eastport, Me. | Shipping.

FIFTY | 50 Vig. Man holding wild horse. 50 |
Female standing erect. | | Same as on opposite end.
FIFTY | FRONTIER BANK, Eastport, Me. |

Figure "100," with word "ONE HUNDRED" across. | Vig. Large covered wagon; horses, persons, &c.; shipping in background. | Figure "100," with word "ONE HUNDRED" across.
Male portrait. | FRONTIER BANK, Eastport, Me. | Portrait of Columbus.

| Vessels under sail; steamboat, &c. 1 | 1
1 | GARDINER BANK. Gardiner, Me. | Man and sheep.

| State Arms. 2 | 2
2 | GARDINER BANK. Gardiner, Me. | Ship under sail.

| Train of Cars, &c. 3 | 3
| | Female.
3 | GARDINER BANK. Gardiner, Me. | THREE

This Bank has also the Perkin's Stereotype Plate for all denominations except 50's.

20 | 2 Female. 0 | 20
| | Female.
Figure with helmet and spear. | GARDINER BANK, Gardiner, Me. XX | 20

50 | Male and Female Head. | 50
| | Cupid in sail boat.
Flowers. | GARDINER BANK, Gardiner, Me. 50 | 50

Left	Centre	Right
100 Vulcan	Spread eagle; train of cars, canal, &c., in background. GARDINER BANK, Gardiner, Me. 100	100 Female seated
500	Indians in canoe, trees and mountainous scenery in background. 500 GARDINER BANK, Gardiner, Me.	500 Female holding scales.
Female seated; train of cars and canal in distance. 1	Large figure 1, and five male figures. GEORGE'S BANK, Thomaston, Me.	1 Female and sheaf.
Farmers washing sheep. 2	Large figure 2, and five male figures. GEORGE'S BANK, Thomaston, Me.	TWO Female with wreath. TWO
Farmers and cattle; load of hay, &c. 3	3 GEORGE'S BANK, Thomaston, Me.	The word three and figure 3. Female with basket of flowers. THREE
FI 5 VE	Female with rake and sickle, various emblems representing Commerce, Agriculture, Mechanic Arts &c. V and Indian female. GEORGE'S BANK, Thomaston, Me.	5 Head of Washington.
X Indian with bow.	Steamboat and vessels. X GEORGE'S BANK, Thomaston, Me.	10 Female with sheaf of grain.
20 Minerva.	2 Female. 0 GEORGE'S BANK, Thomaston, Me. XX	20 Female seated with horn of plenty, &c. 20
50 Female with spear.	Female with rake, and male with sledge. GEORGE'S BANK, Thomaston, Me. 50	50 Cupid in sail boat. 50
100 Male with sledge.	Spread eagle; train of cars and canal in distance. GEORGE'S BANK, Thomaston, Me. C 100 C	100 Female with wand, &c.

Left	Centre	Right
	GRANITE BANK Augusta, Me. This Bank uses the old Perkin's Stereotype plate, which has the denomination printed in fine letters all over the bill.	
1 Sailor, quadrant, capstan, etc.	Ships under sail. INTERNATIONAL BANK, Portland, Me.	1
2 Boy's head	Female on bales of cotton; factory and farm in distance. Title of Bank.	2 Cooper making barrels.
3 State Arms.	Title of Bank. Scene on sea-shore; sailor, anchor, boat, etc.	3 Eagle on shield.
5 5	Railroad depot—cars leaving, etc. 5 Title of Bank.	5 Five figures, male and female and large V.
10 Female, ship and pillar.	Eagle. Sailor and mechanic seated, with State arms between; steamboat, wharf, factories. Title of Bank.	X
Female head 20	INTERNATIONAL BANK, Portland, Me. Man plowing with two horses; house, etc.	20 Female with flowers.
FIFTY	Title of Bank. Steamship and other vessels.	50 Girl's head.
100	Three females and cupid in water. Title of Bank.	100 Anchor, barrels, bales, etc.
D Five Hun Dollars	INTERNATION'L BK Portland, Me. Three females; shield; one crowning bust. dred Five	500 Hundred Dollars

Left	Centre	Right
Liberty with pole and cap resting on column on which is 1000.	M Washington INTERNATION'L BK Portland, Me.	1000
1 General Taylor.	Brig under sail. Spread eagle. Ship at anchor. KENDUSKEAG BK. Bangor, Me. Bee Hive.	1 Female seated and supporting figure 1.
2 Female seated with pole and cap.	Head of Marshall. Head of Clay. Ship under full sail. KENDUSKEAG BK. Bangor, Me. Horse.	2 Female seated.
3 Female portrait.	Female portrait. Dog & tr. on chest. Female portrait. KENDUSKEAG BK. Bangor, Me. Steamer.	3 Harrison.
FIVE Male and female. 5	Head of Columbus. Figure 5 in the air with horn of flowers. Portrait of Franklin. KENDUSKEAG BK. Bangor, Me. Vessel.	5 FI 5 VE 5
10 Washington.	Female seated. Loading hay, two men, oxen, cart, in distance train of cars. 10 KENDUSKEAG BK. Bangor, Me. Eagle.	TEN Female with sickle.
50 Vulcan with sledge, anvil &c.	KENDUSKEAG BK., Bangor, Me. Eagle and globe; female seated on right and Indian on left. 50	50
100 Portrait of La Fayette. 100	100 KENDUSKEAG BK. Bangor, Me. Female seated, a child and dog at her feet; plough, sheaf, &c. behind.	
Female figure holding scales of Justice. 1	Drove of cattle and sheep with man on horseback. LEWISTON FALLS BANK, Lewiston, Me.	1 Dairy maid churning.
TWO Females sight	Vig. Female feeding an eagle; horn of plenty in foreground; ship in the distance. LEWISTON FALLS BANK, Lewiston, Me.	TWO Cupid, &c., female erect supporting 2

Left end	Centre	Right end
3	View of Lewiston Falls on the Androscoggin river. LEWISTON FALLS BANK. Lewiston, Me.	3 Female and 3
5 Large V, with five male and female figures in and around it.	Vig. Ornamental figure 5, with five female figures around it; ship, steamer, locomotive, and factories in the distance. LEWISTON FALLS BANK. Lewiston, Me	5 Large figure 5, with five male and female figures in and around it.
X	View of Lewiston Falls on the Androscoggin river. LEWISTON FALLS BANK, Lewiston, Me.	10 Cotton mill.
Fountain. XX	Vig. Spread eagle and shield; steam ship and building in distance. LEWISTON FALLS BANK. Lewiston, Me	20 Head of Female.
Goddess of liberty feeding an eagle. 50	Vig. Female resting on cotton bale, and [illegible] wheel in foreground; manufacturing village in distance. LEWISTON FALLS BANK. Lewiston, Me.	50 Female, globe, shield, and Declaration of Independence.
Marble worker at labor. 100	Vig. National capital. LEWISTON FALLS BANK, Lewiston, Me.	100 Cupid and dolphin.
ONE 1	Farmer ploughing and farmer sowing; trees, &c. 1 LIME ROCK BANK, East Thomaston, Me.	1 Ship. ONE
TWO 2	Spread eagle on rock; train of cars on left in distance. 2 LIME ROCK BANK, East Thomaston, Me.	2 TWO Schooner.
THREE 3	Sailor, bales, casks, ship; wharves, drays, &c., on right, and on left vessels, warehouses, &c. 3 LIME ROCK BANK, East Thomaston, Me. Medallion. Medallion	3 THREE Train of cars.
5 Ship on stocks, water and skiff. 5	Head of female. Lime shed and kilns; Head of child. quarry on right, with casks and cooper, on left horse, man, vessel, &c. LIME ROCK BANK, East Thomaston, Me.	5 Steamship 5

Left end	Centre	Right end
5 Female seated; top sails of vessel in background.	State Arms. LIME ROCK BANK, East Thomaston, Me. Safe, dog, and boy.	5 Female
TEN Steamer and ship. TEN	Farmer with team; houses in distance. State Arms. Beehive and flowers. LIME ROCK BANK, East Thomaston, Me.	10 Farmer with rake and large load of grain, horse, &c. 10
10 Justice with sword and scales; spread eagle on a safe.	Ship under full sail at sea. Large X, with ten dollars on both sides. LIME ROCK BANK, East Thomaston, Me.	Medallion head of Female.
20 Female in partly nude state seated; sails, &c.	XX Eagle. XX LIME ROCK BANK. East Thomaston, Me.	20 Ship.
FIFTY Full length female, with wreath on head. FIFTY	50 Man and horse. 50 LIME ROCK BANK, East Thomaston, Me.	FIFTY Full length female. FIFTY
Same as on right. Bust of Male.	Wharf scene, wagon, men loading dray, vessels, &c. LIME ROCK BANK. East Thomaston, Me.	The words one hundred across figure 100. Male portrait.
Train of cars, house on right. 1	LINCOLN BANK Bath, Me.	1 Man in his shirt sleeves, with tools at his feet.
Man ploughing with two horses; tents of boats on the right. 2	Large figure 2 and a child. LINCOLN BANK, Bath, Me.	2 Female reclining.
Steamship, ships lying too. 3	LINCOLN BANK, Bath, Me.	3 Ship under full sail.
5 5	Schooner lying too; ship and brig. Large V, female and Cupid. LINCOLN BANK, Bath, Me.	5 Female with basket of flowers.

Left end	Centre	Right end
TEN Ship under full sail. TEN	Pilot boat, steamboat, shipping and a small boat with four men in it. LINCOLN BANK, Bath, Me.	10 Large X and a female.
XX Steamship.	Depot with engine and tender, man with wheelbarrow, steamboat at wharf, and also boat with two men. LINCOLN BANK. Bath, Me.	20 Ship under full sail.
50 Steamboat and pilot boat.	Farm house and out buildings, load of hay, two persons on top, man with rake in right hand, pail in left. LINCOLN BANK, Bath, Me.	L Female with sword in right hand.
100 Eagle. 100	C Neptune in car drawn by three horses. 100 LINCOLN BANK, Bath, Me.	C Head of Washington. C
ONE on 1 1	LINCOLN CO. B'K. ONE Sailor with trumpet. ONE ONE DOLLAR. Wiscasset, Maine.	1 Girl's head.
2 Man playing with dog.	LINCOLN CO. BANK. Farmer seated on grain; sailor leaning against capstan, boy, dog, &c. 2 TWO DOLLARS 2 Wiscasset, Me.	2 TWO on 2
3 THREE. 3	Girl's head. Hunter beside fire; deer on horse; dogs, etc. LINCOLN CO. BANK. THREE DOLLARS. Wiscasset, Me.	3 State Arms
1	Female, cars, &c. 1 LONG REACH BANK Bath, Me.	1 Female.
2	Men washing sheep. 2 LONG REACH BANK, Bath, Me.	TWO Female. TWO
3	Scene in a farm yard. 3 LONG REACH BANK Bath, Me.	THREE Female with basket of flowers. THREE

FIVE Female with rake, grain, machinery, &c. Female Indian seated in V. 5 LONG REACH BANK Bath, Me. FI V VE Washington	20 XX Spread Eagle. XX 20 LUMBERMAN'S B'K, Old Town, Me. Female seated. Ship.	C Eagle on bale; products, etc. 100 100 Man and boats. Title of Bank. Female with sickle and sheaf. 100 100
Signing Declaration of Independence. X 10 LONG REACH BANK Bath, Me. X Cars, man, buildings, etc.	FIFTY. 50 Man and horse 50 FIFTY. Female with wreath. Female. LUMBERMAN'S B'K, Old Town, Me. FIFTY FIFTY.	ONE Agricultural scene; farmer sowing; another in the distance harrowing. 1 1 Ship. 1 MANUFACTURERS BANK. Saco, Me. ONE
FIFTY 50 Three females, eagle, shield, ship, etc. FIFTY on 50 Grain and fruit. 50 LONG REACH B'K. Bath, Me. Man seated; anvil, horn, blast, &c.	100 C Wild horses and chariot. 100 C Eagle. Washington. 100 LUMBERMAN'S B'K, Old Town, Me. C	TWO Spread eagle; iron castings, cannon balls, machinery, &c. 2 2 TWO 2 Title of Bank. Schooner rigged boat.
C Eagle on bale of goods; anchor, sheaf, horn of plenty, etc. 100 100 Boat at rocky landing; another in distance. Female with sickle in her hand. C LONG REACH B'K. Bath, Maine. 100	ONE 1 Boy on horseback, horse, colt, sheep, cows, etc. 1 MAINE BANK, Brunswick, Me. Men catching cattle. 1	THREE Sailor; hat in hand, reclining against bales; in the distance are vessels, warehouses, dray, horse &c. 3 3 THREE 3 Title of Bank. Train of cars.
500 500 Scene in Shipyard. 500 Old man with musket; boy with a gun. LONG REACH B'K, Maine. 500	TWO Santa Claus in sleigh drawn by reindeers over roofs of houses. 2 TWO MAINE BANK, Brunswick, Me. 2 Cattle, hogs, sheep, etc.	FIVE Female resting upon her left knee, lifting veil from figure 5. 5 Title of Bank. Ship.
The word "one" and two cupids. Shield—Indian seated on left and woodchopper on right. 1 LUMBERMAN'S B'K, Old Town, Me. Bust of a Female. Dog. Female seated with pole and cap.	Farmer drinking; woman and child; load of grain; farmers mowing; cars, crossing bridge, etc. 3 THREE DOLLARS MAINE BANK, Brunswick, Me. 3 Three on 3.	Female seated, holding rake in left hand and sickle in right, ships, buildings &c. in backgro'd. Large V and Indian. 5 Title of Bank. Portrait of Washington.
TWO Spread eagle; ships in the distance. 2 TWO LUMBERMAN'S B'K, Old Town, Me. Sailor. Bust of a Female. Agricultural implements. Female seated.	FIVE MAINE BANK, 5 FIVE 5 FIVE DOLLARS Franklin. Brunswick, State of Maine. Female seated on bale with quadrant, etc., vessels, etc., in distance. FIVE	10 Vig. Man with oxen. 10 TEN X Title of Bank. Female figure with cornucopia of fruits and flowers. 10
3 Neptune with sea-car, &c. 3 LUMBERMAN'S B'K, Old Town, Me. Female erect surrounded with wreath with names of the States. Horn of Plenty, safe and key. Large 3, sailor, mechanic, and farmer. THREE	Male portrait. Ship yard scene; city in distance. 10 MAINE BANK, Brunswick, Me. X Male portrait.	20 XX Eagle. XX 20 Title of Bank. Female. Ship sailing.
FIVE Milk-maid and cows. 5 Large figure 5, female seated, and portrait of Washington. LUMBERMAN'S B'K, Old Town, Me. FIVE FIVE Horn of Plenty and anvil. FIVE	20 Female either side of anvil; building in distance. 20 Title of Bank. Sailor and farmer, either side of shield on which is a deer and tree. Washington.	FIFTY 50 Man and horse 50 FIFTY Female. Female. Title of Bank. FIFTY FIFTY
Vulcan, with sledge and anvil, train of cars in distance. X 10 LUMBERMAN'S B'K, Old Town, Me. TEN Man erect, with sickle and sheaf of wheat.	FIFTY 50 Three females seated; eagle, shield, vessel, etc. Fifty on 50. Agricultural products. Title of Bank. Vulcan seated; cars, buildings, etc., in distance. 50	Words one hundred and figures 100. Vig. Market scene; shipping on left. Words one hundred, and figures 100. Title of Bank. Male portrait. Male portrait.

Left end	Centre	Right end
Female seated, pass leading hay in distance. 500	500 D Title of Bank.	500
1	Interior of an iron foundry; six men at work, pouring metal, &c. 1 MAN. and TRADERS BANK, Portland, Me.	Word ONE and fig. 1. Portrait of sailor.
1 Washington	Female. 1 Female. MAN. & TRADERS' BANK, Portland, Me.	1 Portrait.
ONE	Water scene, ships, &c. 1 MAN. & TRADERS' BANK, Portland, Me.	ONE Female. ONE
2 2	Shield with bull's head thereon; on left female binding sheaves; on right man dressing leather; sails, &c. Figure 2 and State Arms Title of Bank.	TWO Sailor seated on ship railing with spy glass.
2 TWO 2	Water scene, ships, &c. 2 MAN. & TRADERS' BANK, Portland, Me.	TWO Female. TWO
2 Portrait.	Female with cornucopia. 2 Female with balance. MAN. & TRADERS' BANK, Portland, Me.	2 Portrait
THREE	Female with hat in hand, man swinging and another carrying grain. 3 MAN. & TRADERS' BANK, Portland, Me.	THREE Ship. The word three and figure 3.
THREE Figure 3 and portrait of Webster within.	MAN. and TRADERS' BANK. Portland, Me. Portrait of Washington; on either side female; on right train of cars, on left man at work, bots, steamboat &c.	Word THREE and figure 3. Male portrait
3 Washington and his horse.	Portrait of Female. 3 Portrait of Female. MAN. & TRADERS' BANK, Portland, Me.	3 Blacksmith, anvil &c.

Left end	Centre	Right end
FIVE	Female, &c. V MAN. & TRADERS' BANK. Portland, Me.	5 Ship.
Spread eagle. FIVE	Female with sceptre and horn of plenty, figure 5 and angel. MAN. & TRADERS' BANK. Portland, Me.	5 Female with hat and wreath in hands.
5 Female portrait.	MAN. & TRA. BANK, Portland, Me. Large letter V, and words Five Dollars.	5 Portrait of Girl.
10 Female. TEN	MAN. & TRA. BANK, Portland, Me. Letter X, and word Ten, shipping on right; haycart, trees, city and bridge on left.	10 Female. TEN
10 X 10	Oxen and men. 10 MAN. & TRADERS BANK, Portland, Me.	TEN Female with horn of plenty, &c.
TEN	Blacksmith seated, sledge in right hand resting on anvil; block and wheel behind him. X MAN. & TRADERS' BANK, Portland, Me.	10 Farmer with sheaf of grain and sickle.
TWENTY Female seated.	XX Eagle. XX MAN. & TRADERS' BANK, Portland, Me.	20 Ship.
FIFTY Female. FIFTY	50 Man and horse. 50 MAN. & TRADERS' BANK, Portland, Me.	FIFTY Female. FIFTY
The words one hundred and figures 100. Harrison.	Wharf scene, market wagon, drays, horses, oxen, vessels, &c. MAN. & TRADERS' BANK, Portland, Me.	Same as on left. Columbus.
500	Indian paddling in canoe; mountain, &c. 500 MAN. and TRADERS' BANK. Portland, Me. D D	500 Female figure holding sword and scales.

Left end	Centre	Right end
1 Webster.	Ships on the stocks. MARINE BANK Damariscotta, Me. Eagle.	1 Sailor.
2 Female	MARINE BANK Damariscotta, Me. Ship under full sail, and a small steamship.	2 Franklin.
3 Sailor with quadrant; small ship	Spread eagle; ship on right, and ship on left. MARINE BANK Damariscotta, Me. Indian head.	3 Female with spy glass.
5 Washington.	John Adams Spread Eagle Jefferson MARINE BANK, Damariscotta, Me. Steamer.	5 Ship under sail.
Indian and female; globe surmounted by an eagle between; State arms underneath. 10	Portrait of Jackson 10 MARINE BANK, Damariscotta, Me. Sloop.	Female. 10
20 Figure of Justice.	Female with extended arms; Cupid on either side. MARINE BANK. Damariscotta, Me. Steamship.	20 Female with sheaf of grain.
50 Female. 50	Two females seated; ship on right, and on left is rail cars and buildings. MARINE BANK. Damariscotta, Me. Locomotive.	50 Boy gathering corn.
100 Sailor with American flag.	MARINE BANK, Damariscotta, Me. 100 ONE Female HUNDRED with Cupid. Cog Wheels.	Female.
Female portrait. 1	MARKET BANK, Cupid riding silver dollar on railroad track; cars, steamboat and city in distance. Bangor, Me. Cow and calf.	1 Female Indian seated
Female reclining with scales in right hand. 2	Two cupids and two silver dollars; Cupids apparently in an engraving; train of cars, cattle, hills, city, &c. in distance. MARKET BANK. Bangor, Me. Two horses.	2 Bull's head.

THREE Female seated, fruits, &c.	Three cupids and three silver dollars, all engaged at some art. MARKET BANK, Bangor, Me.	3 3
5 Cattle. 5	Five silver dollars and five cupids. MARKET BANK, Bangor, Me. Man plowing with two horses.	5 Cattle; man seen on right
Female feeding horse. X	Two men, horse, dog and drove of cattle and sheep. MARKET BANK, Bangor, Me.	10 Boy's head.
Female portrait. 20	Drove of cattle and sheep; man on horseback. MARKET BANK, Bangor, Me.	20 Female churning.
50 State arms.	Female seated; barrels, bales, anchor, &c.; steamship on right, and ship on left. MARKET BANK, Bangor, Me.	50 Sailor with left hand on capstan; masts, blocks, &c.
Ornamental fountain. C	Female reclining on sofa; two females, cows, haystack, on right; train of cars, vessel, buildings, &c. on left. MARKET BANK, Bangor, Me.	100 State arms.
ONE Female with sheaf. ONE	State Arms, female and ships. MECHANICS' BANK, Portland, Me. Steamer.	1 Henry Clay.
2 Cupids.	Three Graces. MECHANICS' BANK, Portland, Me. Plough and sheaf.	2 Female balancing scales
THREE Fame seated on a globe blowing trumpet.	Eagle, with steamers and ships in distance. MECHANICS' BANK, Portland, Me. Dog, key and safe.	3 Girl playing a lute
5 Female with trident. 5	Steamship. MECHANICS' BANK, Portland, Me. Locomotive.	5 Female portrait.

10 Portrait of Washington.	Train of cars. MECHANICS' BANK, Portland, Me. Eagle.	10 Female in dian, shield and liberty cap.
Twenty (vertical, with 20)	Fame blowing trumpet; eagle and globe. MECHANICS' BANK, Portland, Me. Steamship.	20 Roman female.
50 Sailor with flag.	Female indian, eagle and flag. MECHANICS' BANK, Portland, Me. Plough.	50 Portrait of female.
Eagle. 100	Female portrait. MECHANICS' BANK, Portland, Me. Locomotive.	100 Sloop, &c.
Portrait of Franklin. 500	State Arms; two females, horse's head, &c. MECHANICS' BANK, Portland, Me.	500 Portrait of female.
ONE Bust of male ONE	Interior of a blacksmiths' shop; two men at work at anvil, forge, &c. 1 MEDOMAK BANK, Waldoboro, Me.	ONE Female. ONE
1 Female	Bull's head on shield; on right men dressing leather; on left female sewing shoes. MEDOMAK BANK, Waldoboro, Me. Incorporated in 1836.	ONE on 1. Female.
1	Female seated; train of cars, shop, and steamboat on right; on left canal, lock, &c. Large 1, and five men. MEDOMAK BANK, Waldoboro, Me.	1 Female leaning head on her hand
1 Male portrait	Portrait of female; on left female and farming scene; on right female, bale, barrel, steamboat Title of Bank. Incorporated in 1836.	1 ONE Female with a rake.
2 Female reaper.	Scene in an Iron Mill; men at work. Title of Bank. Incorporated in 1836.	2 Female with cornucopia.

2	Man and two boys; two sheep in water; drove on left, and buildings on right. Large 2 and five men. MEDOMAK BANK, Waldoboro, Me.	TWO Female seated. TWO
TWO Female. 2	2 Harvest scene; two men seated, one handing female drink; loading hay in background. 2 MEDOMAK BANK, Waldoboro, Me.	TWO Female. 2
Word Three and fig. Girl.	Rafting scene—men, women and children on raft. Title of Bank. Incorporated in 1836.	3 on Dollars. Female.
3	Man on horseback, cattle, dog, and man; load of hay entering barn, likewise three men; in distance city. 3 MEDOMAK BANK, Waldoboro, Me.	Word three and figure 3. Female seated with basket of flowers. THREE
THREE Farmer sharpening scythe. Word Three, and figure 3.	3 Female seated, entwining wreath around eagles' neck; flowers, fruits, &c. 3 MEDOMAK BANK, Waldoboro, Me.	THREE Sailor with hat in hand; horse and cart; ships, &c. Word three, and figure 3.
Word five, letter V, and figure 5. Female seated, right arm on shield; left hand pointing.	Train of cars; buildings, sloop, &c. MEDOMAK BANK, Waldoboro, Me. Incorporated in 1836.	5 Ship; steamboat on left.
FIVE Portrait of Webster.	MEDOMAK BANK, Waldoboro, Me. Three females in clouds; one with quadrant; the middle one with sickle. Incorporated in 1836.	5 Female leaning on railing.
10 Female portrait.	State arms on shield; indian, squaw and papoose on right; female and three children on left, with globe, &c. MEDOMAK BANK, Waldoboro', Me. Same as fives.	10 Female portrait.
20 Jenny Lind. TWENTY	Steamship and ship; men in boat, view of New York City and Governor's Island. MEDOMAK BANK, Waldoboro', Me. Same as fives.	20 Female portrait.
50 Female seated with sheaf and sickle; train of cars in distance on bridge.	State arms surmounted by an eagle; sailor and ship on right; indian and huts on left. MEDOMAK BANK, Waldoboro', Me.	50 Female portrait.

100 | MEDOMAK BANK, Waldoboro', Me. Female reclining, at her back eagle, city, train of cars, harvesting, &c., on left. | 100 Incorporated in 1836.
Female with shield and sickle.

Medallion head. 1 | Winged female blowing a trumpet. Spread Eagle. MERCANTILE BK., Bangor, Maine. | 1 Sailor with spyglass in hand.

TWO | State Arms: farmer and sailor either side; ship, etc. MERCANTILE B'K, Bangor, Maine. Winged female, &c. | 2 Ship. 2

3 Head 3 | Eagle, &c. MERCANTILE BK. Bangor. | 3 Females; vessels, &c.

FIVE 5 | State Arms: female either side, city, ship, &c. 5 MERCANTILE B'K. Bangor, Maine. | 5 Indian squaw.

10 | Steamboat, vessels, &c. X MERCANTILE B'K, Bangor, Maine. | 10 Female.

20 XX 20 | 20 Female, vessels, goods, &c. 20 MERCANTILE B'K, Bangor, Maine. | TWENTY

50 Female, steamboat, &c. | FIFTY DOLLARS and 50 MERCANTILE B'K. Bangor, Maine. | FIFTY

C Washington. C | 100 Man, vessel, &c. 100 MERCANTILE B'K. Bangor, Maine. | ONE HUNDRED

500 500 500 | 500 500 MERCANTILE B'K. Bangor, Maine. | 500 D 500

1 | Female, State arms, shipping and railroad. 1 MERCHANTS' BK., Bangor, Me. | ONE Female supporting figure 1. ONE

2 | Sailor, merchandise, and shipping. 2 MERCHANTS' BK., Bangor, Me. | 2 Portrait of female.

3 | Female, eagle and shield; factory and steamship in the distance. 3 MERCHANTS' BK., Bangor, Me. | 3 Sailor.

5 | Female and merchandise. Large V, female and sheaf of wheat. MERCHANTS' BK., Bangor, Me. Ship | FIVE Indian female with bow and arrow.

TEN | Farmer, dog and grain. Female and X on right. MERCHANTS' BK., Bangor, Me. | 10 Female.

20 Female with book. | Large Eagle. MERCHANT'S B'K. TWENTY. Bangor, Maine. | 20 Ship under full sail.

20 Female figure, with spear and globe. | 2 Female. 0 MERCHANTS' BK. Bangor, Me. XX | 20 Female. 20

50 Female figure. | Male and female seated. MERCHANTS' BK., Bangor, Me. 50 | 50 Cupid in a sail boat. 50

100 Vulcan the blacksmith. | Spread eagle standing on a tree; railroad and canal in background. MERCHANTS' BK., Bangor Me. 100 | 100 Female seated.

1 Sailor seated and holding flag. | View of the Custom House, Portland. MERCHANT'S BANK Portland, Me. | 1 Ship under full sail.

1 | Train of cars crossing a bridge; mountains in the distance; boat on river and three figures in the foreground railing. MERCHANT'S BANK Portland, Me. | 1 Female Portrait.

Figure with shield, pole and cap. 2 | Spread Eagle; on right, man-of-war, and on left, a brig. MERCHANT'S BANK Portland, Me. Locomotive. | 2 Female gathering flowers, &c.

Goddess of Liberty. 2 | View of the Portland Custom House. MERCHANT'S BANK Portland Me. | 2 Washington and his horse.

3 Large figure 3, and three Cupids. | Portrait of Daniel Webster; ship, steamship, &c. MERCHANT'S BANK Portland, Me. Agricultural Implements. | 3 Cooper at work.

Portrait of female. 5 | MERCHANT'S BANK Portland, Me. View of the Portland Custom House. FIVE | 5 Female with basket.

Female reclining on bales of goods; ships, &c., in distance. 10 | Portrait of female. MERCHANT'S BANK Portland, Me. Steamboat. | 10 Train of cars.

20 Portrait of Fillmore. | Spread Eagle, houses, &c. MERCHANT'S BANK Portland, Me. Indian Head. | 20 Portrait of Washington.

50 Female with scales. | MERCHANT'S BANK Portland, Me. Steamship, man-of-war, and brig. | 50 Female leaning on a pedestal, harp at her feet.

C 100 C | MERCHANT'S BANK Portland, Me. Female figure holding shield, pole and cap; on right, Capitol at Washington. | C 100 C

Agricultural scene; female seated pointing to sea-port. 500 | 500 D MERCHANTS' BK. Portland, Me. | 500

ONE Aerial figure and female reclining on the ground.	NEW CASTLE BK., New Castle, Me. ONE DOLLAR	1 Ship under full sail. Ship and steamboat in distance.
2 Eagle standing above the rising sun; female, anchor, &c.	NEW CASTLE BK., New Castle, Me. TWO DOLLARS.	2 Same as ones.
The word three and figure 3. Female seated with sword.	NEW CASTLE BK. New Castle. Me. THREE DOLLARS.	3 Three mechanics; man and two horses in background.
FIVE Five females, liberty cap, &c.	NEW CASTLE BK., New Castle. Me. 5 FI 5 VE 5	FIVE
Letter X and words ten dollars. Female bathing.	NEW CASTLE BK., New Castle, Me. Ship building, &c.; men at work.	10 Washington.
XX Signing the Declaration of Independence.	NEW CASTLE BK., New Castle, Me. TWENTY DOLLARS.	20 Washington.
50 Portrait of Jameson.	Ship under full sail; ship, steamer, schooner and boat at left; city on right. NEW CASTLE BK., New Castle, Me. Guinea hens.	50 Two sailors, flag, anchors, &c.
Goddess of liberty, eagle, shield, pole and cap.	NEW CASTLE BK., New Castle, Me. Spread Eagle. 100	100 State Arms. Three Indians, four white men, globe, &c., house in background.
ONE Female seated. ONE	Cupid & Figure 1 Cupid & Figure 1 Vig. Female seated, ship on right in distance. NORTH BANK. Rockland. Me.	ONE Female. ONE
2	Female seated with Portrait of Washington and eagle; steamer, shipping, &c., on right; large building and train of cars on left. 2 NORTH BANK. Rockland, Me.	2 Figure of Justice.

3 Female with wreath and basket; eagle and shield.	Three silver dollars and three Cupids. NORTH BANK. Rockland, Me.	3 Female seated; globe, shield, and "Declaration of Independence."
5	Sailor and Indian with word FIVE between them; two females seated on either side of a frame, surmounted by an eagle; bust between Indian and female, steamer, ship and canal lock in distance. Five at top of large figure 5 Title of Bank.	5 Female with pole and cap and shield.
10	Female seated on rocks; three Cupids sporting with sea monster in water. Large X's male Portrait. NORTH BANK, Rockland, Me.	X Female Portrait.
Farmer about to drink from jug. ONE	1 Corn husking scene in barn. NORTH BERWICK BANK, North Berwick, Me.	1 Female with sewing machine.
2 Female feeding fowls.	Title of Bank. 2 Female milking cow; one reclining man, ladder, dog, house, etc., on right.	2 Male portrait
5	Blacksmith shoeing horse; man at anvil Eagle. 5 Title of Bank	5 State Arms.
Female seated in chair. TEN	Title of Bank. Two females at work on looms.	10 Male portrait
Female eagle, sheaf of wheat 20	20 Female portrait. NO. BERWICK BK, Maine.	20 Franklin
FIFTY Flowers, grain, etc. 50	50 Three females, eagle and ship. NO. BERWICK B'K, Maine.	50 Vulcan
C Boat, fisherman, rocks, etc. 100	Eagle on bale, flowers, and anchor. 100 NO BERWICK B'K Maine	100 Female 100

	NORTHERN BANK, Hallowell, Me. This Bank uses the old Perkin's Stereotype plate, which has the denomination printed in fine letters all over the bill.	
ONE	Blacksmith, anvil, and forge. 1 OAKLAND BANK, Gardiner, Me. ONE	ONE
TWO	2 Steamboat. 2 OAKLAND BANK, Gardiner, Me.	TWO
THREE	Interior of an iron foundry. 3 OAKLAND BANK. Gardiner, Me.	THREE
FIVE Mechanic, sailor, and two females, city and harbor in distance.	OAKLAND BANK, Gardiner, Me. 5	FIVE Farmer, two females, and a yoke of oxen.
X and Ten Girl with a sickle.	OAKLAND BANK, Gardiner. Me. Figures 10 across words Ten Dollars.	10 Female with horn of plenty.
XX Portrait of female.	Figures 20 across words Twenty Dollars, and small figures 20 between words. OAKLAND BANK, Gardiner, Me. Schooner	XX Sailor
Male, female, two children, and a lamb.	OAKLAND BANK, Gardiner, Me. 50	50 Sailors.
ONE HUNDRED Female with spear and shield.	OAKLAND BANK, Gardiner, Me.	100 ONE HUNDRED
Word one, and figure 1.	Ship under full sail; ship, steamboat and pilot-boat; city in distance. ONE OCEAN BANK, Kennebunk, Me.	1 Female with arm on American shield.

2	OCEAN BANK, Kennebunk, Me. Foundry; workmen pouring out heated metal. TWO	2 Ship under full sail; steamboat in distance.
3	OCEAN BANK, Kennebunk, Me. Three persons in boat, one man rowing; female with spy glass. Word three and figure 3.	3 Blacksmith with hammer sitting; buildings in background.
FIVE 5 FIVE	OCEAN BANK, Kennebunk, Me. State Arms. Ship-yard; 2 vessels on stocks.	5 FI V VE 5
10 Tree; load of hay; train of cars on bridge with arches.	OCEAN BANK, Kennebunk, Me. Three females representing arts, agriculture and commerce.	10 Ships; city in back ground.
TWENTY	OCEAN BANK, Kennebunk, Me. Two male figures standing, one with a quadrant; Two females sitting and holding tablet; one with dividers; spinning-wheel and anchor, &c., light-house, mountains and city in background.	TWENTY 20 TWENTY
FIFTY Five female figures, two sitting and three reclining, one with liberty cap and pole.	OCEAN BANK, Kennebunk, Me. L 50 L	50 Man with spy-glass; boy with quadrant.
Liberty, with cap and pole in left hand, right on Am. shield; eagle.	100 Three female figures, left one representing agriculture, with horn of plenty; middle one with wings, joining hands with first; reaching an apple to third, which has quadrant in one hand. OCEAN BANK, Kennebunk, Me.	100
1 Blacksmith seated, implements around him.	Three females reclining and cupid. ORONO BANK, Orono, Me.	1 Portrait of General Taylor.
2 Female with basket of flowers.	Female, horn of plenty, shield, eagle, cars, &c.; [illegible] and steam boat in the distance. ORONO BANK, Orono, Me.	2 Portrait of Jackson.
3 Indian resting, his gun reclining.	State arms; ships in distance. ORONO BANK, Orono, Me.	3 Portrait of Henry Clay.

5 Female seated.	Curved rail road track. Cars in the foreground and in the distance near bridge; also further in the distance, cars going out of sight. ORONO BANK, Orono, Me.	5 Man erect with whip in hand. House and steamer in distance.
10 Same as threes.	Heads of Washington and Franklin in frame; four cupids and X. ORONO BANK, Orono, Me. Steamboat.	10 Portrait of W. H. Seward.
Two winged females holding figure 20, two cupids.	Spread eagle and shield. ORONO BANK, Orono, Me.	20 Female with sheaf of wheat.
50 Female in frame with sickle. 50	Two females seated; ship, factory buildings; train of cars crossing bridge. ORONO BANK, Orono, Me. Engine and tender.	50 Boy gathering corn.
100 Sailor seated with flag in hand.	Female and eagle over a map; water and vessels in the distance. ORONO BANK, Orono, Me. Cogwheel and cylinder.	100 Female Portrait. 100
Female and figure 1. One and 1.	Indian seated, holding fig. 1. PEJEPSCOT BANK, Brunswick, Me.	1 Female head.
Two females carrying grain. 2	State Arms with females seated each side. PEJEPSCOT BANK, Brunswick, Me.	2 Female holding a flag with an Indian seated.
Factory. 3	Ships and steamer. PEJEPSCOT BANK, Brunswick, Me.	Three and 3 Head of Indian.
5 Washington	Signing declaration of Independence. PEJEPSCOT BANK, Brunswick, Me.	5 Female head
X Head of Indian.	Capitol at Washington. PEJEPSCOT BANK, Brunswick, Me.	10 Indian seated

Female head XX	Capitol at Washington. PEJEPSCOT BANK, Brunswick, Me.	20 Indian's head
50 Sailor standing with cap in hand.	Vessels and steamer. PEJEPSCOT BANK, Brunswick, Me.	50 Webster.
C Female seated beside a basket holding sheaf of grain.	Engine, Depot and cars. PEJEPSCOT BANK, Brunswick, Me.	100 100
500	Indian paddling canoe. 500 PEJEPSCOT BANK, Brunswick, Me. D D	500 Female holding scales.
Reaper. 1	Female reclining; milk-maids, cows, factories, shipping, locomotive, &c., in background. PEOPLES' BANK, Waterville, Me.	1 Female in kneeling posture.
Two females. 2	Female, merchandise and shipping. PEOPLES' BANK, Waterville, Me.	2 Female.
State Arms, reaper and sailor. 3	Milkmaid and cows. PEOPLES' BANK, Waterville, Me. Loading hay	3 Female sitting on a plow, with sickle and sheaf of wheat.
Female feeding an eagle from a cup. 5	Indian sitting upon the ground, by the side of a slain deer. PEOPLES' BANK, Waterville, Me.	5 Five female figures and figure 5.
Farmer sharpening a scythe. 10	Scene at a railroad station. PEOPLES' BANK, Waterville, Me.	X Female and ten gold dollars.
Reaper and milkmaid. 20	Cattle and sheep. PEOPLES' BANK, Waterville, Me.	20 Indian woman.

Left	Centre	Right
Female portrait. 50	Three females representing Agriculture, Commerce and Manufactures. PEOPLES BANK, Waterville, Me.	50 Webster.
Jefferson. 100	Farming scene—men at lunch. PEOPLES BANK, Waterville, Me.	100 Jackson.
Indian. 1	Two ships and one steamship. RICHMOND BANK, Richmond, Me.	1 Female.
2 Head of Washington.	Spread eagle. Title of Bank. Dog's head.	2 Female.
3 Three persons supporting a globe.	Train of cars. Title of Bank	3 Angel.
5 Foul anchor.	Title of Bank. FIVE Sailor, ships and steamboats. DOLLARS	5 Female.
10 Male portrait	Milkmaid and cows. Title of Bank.	10 Female.
Sailor, anchor, etc. FIFTY	Steamship. Title of Bank.	50 Female holding a spy-glass.
100 Female.	Title of Bank. Male. C Female.	100 Portrait.
ONE	Female sitting on the ground, supporting a figure 1; steamboat and train of cars in background. 1 ROCKLAND BANK, Rockland, Me.	1 Portrait of a female.

Left	Centre	Right
TWO	Spread eagle, Capitol at Washington and steamship. 2 ROCKLAND BANK, Rockland, Me.	2 Sail-boat.
Steamboat. 3	3 ROCKLAND BANK, Rockland, Me.	THREE Fountain. 3
FIVE	Scene in a ship-yard. Female and large V. ROCKLAND BANK, Rockland, Me.	5 Indian girl
TEN	Ships. X ROCKLAND BANK, Rockland, Me.	10 Sailor.
20 Female with spear.	2 Female 0 ROCKLAND BANK. Rockland, Me. XX	20 Female reclining. 20
Sailor hoisting a flag.	20 Female embracing eagle and globe; ships in background. 20 ROCKLAND BANK, Rockland, Me.	Goddess of Liberty.
Female feeding an eagle from a cup. 50	Shipping and merchandise; female seated on a bale. ROCKLAND BANK. Rockland, Me.	50 Ship; city in distance.
100	Female sitting on the ground; merchandise and shipping in the background. ROCKLAND BANK, Rockland, Me.	100 Blacksmith, anvil and forge.
Female, oars, etc. 1	1 SAGADAHOCK BK., Bath, Me.	1 Female.
Man washing sheep. 2	2 Title of Bank.	TWO Female. TWO

Left	Centre	Right
Scene in a farm yard. 3	3 Title of Bank.	THREE Female with basket of flowers. THREE
5 Portrait of Washington. FIVE	View of City of Bath. Title of Bank.	5 Indian. FIVE
Eagle, shield anchor, etc. FIVE	V Title of Bank.	5 Girl.
10 Portrait of Washington. TEN	View of the City of Bath. Title of Bank.	10 Head of Indian.
Man and anvil, train of cars and village in background. TEN	X Title of Bank.	10 Man holding a bundle of wheat.
FIFTY Female. FIFTY	50 Male and horse. 50 Title of Bank.	FIFTY Female. FIFTY
ONE HUNDRED and figure 100. Portrait.	Covered wagon, shipping, etc. Title of Bank.	Same as on left side. Portrait.
Indian paddling canoe. 500	500 Title of Bank.	500 Female.
1 Female holding tablet and pencil.	Females working at loom. SANDY RIVER B'K. Farmington, Me. Eagle.	1 Portrait of Webster.
2 Male and female sitting.	Man standing against a fence with pipe in his mouth, another man lying on the ground. SANDY RIVER B'K Farmington, Me. Eagle.	2 Sailor with spyglass.

3 Female sitting and holding sheaf of grain.	Woman and cows in front, cows, trees, &c., in background. SANDY RIVER B'K, Farmington, Me. Beehive.	3 Female portrait.
5 H. Clay and his dog.	Cattle grazing, sheep to left of cattle. SANDY RIVER B'K, Farmington, Me. State Arms.	5 Female portrait.
10 Female sitting leaning on a shield.	Vig. Same as 5's. SANDY RIVER B'K, Farmington, Me.	10 Currier at work on bl leather.
20 Portrait of Pierce.	Men and women on a raft, buildings in left background, village on right, &c. SANDY RIVER B'K, Farmington, Me. Man and cow.	20 Portrait of Webster.
1 Head of Female.	Ship yard — two ships on the stocks —City in distance. SEARSPORT BANK, Searsport, Me.	1 Ship under full sail.
2 Washington.	SEARSPORT BANK, Searsport Me. Steamship.	2 Female leaning on bale.
THREE Sailor seated holding flag.	3 Men on horseback, drove of cattle & sheep SEARSPORT BANK, Searsport, Me.	3 Female with spy glass.
5 5	Spread eagle on rock; ship at right, and ship under sail on left. Head of Female. SEARSPORT BANK, Searsport, Me. Head of Indian	5 Bale of goods & anchor.
Group of 3 females, the [illegible] supported by the others. TEN	Ship under sail; in distance steamship and sail ship. SEARSPORT BANK, Searsport, Me.	10 Female with [illegible] seated in car of Neptune.
1 Female leaning on a figure 1. 1	[Old Plate.] ONE Female, horn of plenty, plow, schooners, &c. ONE SKOWHEGAN BANK Bloomfield, Me.	1 Eagle. 1

Female head. ONE 1	[New Plate.] SKOWHEGAN BANK Bloomfield, Me. Man ploughing with two horses.	1 Indian.
2 Female and eagle. 2	[Old Plate.] 2 Same as ones, old plate. 2 SKOWHEGAN BANK Bloomfield, Me.	2 Female with sickle. 2
Two females. 2	[New Plate.] SKOWHEGAN BANK Bloomfield, Me. Haying scene.	2 Indian.
3 Eagle. 3	[Old Plate.] 3 Same as ones, old plate. 3 SKOWHEGAN BANK Bloomfield, Me.	3 Female. 3
Boy's head. 3	[New Plate.] SKOWHEGAN BANK Bloomfield, Me. Female with milk pail and cows.	3 Indian.
5 MAINE Female with horn of plenty. 5	[Old Plate.] SKOWHEGAN BANK Bloomfield, Me.	5 State arms. 5
5 Figure 5, and five females surrounding it.	[New Plate.] SKOWHEGAN BANK Bloomfield, Me. Female; on right steamer, and on left steamer and cars.	5 Indian holding an ear of corn and a letter V.
Female leaning on bale and sheaf of wheat, scales in her hand. 10	[New Plate.] SKOWHEGAN BANK Bloomfield, Me. State arms, with eagle on top and female on either side; in distance, on right train of cars, on left steamer.	10 Bust of female. TEN
	The old plate of 10s and 20s are the same in every particular as the old plate of 5s, except the denomination.	
FIFTY Female. FIFTY	50 Man and horse. 50 SKOWHEGAN BANK Bloomfield, Me	FIFTY Female. FIFTY

Words one hundred and figures 100. Portrait of Harrison.	Scene on a wharf—wagons, shipping, &c. SKOWHEGAN BANK Bloomfield, Me.	Same as on left. Portrait of Columbus.
ONE 1	Agricultural scene; farmer sowing; another in the distance harrowing. 1 SOUTH BERWICK BANK. South Berwick, Me.	1 Ship. ONE
1 Farmer sharpening scythe.	SOUTH BERWICK BANK, South Berwick, Me. Female seated, holding vase; vessels in the distance.	1 Blacksmith, forge, anvil, &c.
2 Med. portrait of Franklin.	SOUTH BERWICK BANK, South Berwick, Me. 2 Female seated, having a child in her lap; hogsheads, compass, quadrant, &c. 2	2 Med. head of female
TWO 2	Spread eagle; iron castings, cannon balls, machinery, &c. 2 SOUTH BERWICK BANK, South Berwick, Me.	2 TWO Schooner rigged boat.
THREE 3	Sailor; hat in hand, reclining against bales; in the distance are vessels, warehouses, dray, horses &c. 3 SOUTH BERWICK BANK, South Berwick, Me.	3 THREE Train of cars
Med. portrait of Lafayette. 3	Female figure seated; sickle in right hand; train of cars, ship and steamer in the distance SOUTH BERWICK BANK. South Berwick, Me.	3 Med. portrait of a female.
5 Blacksmith and anvil. FIVE	Vig. Figure of Mercury, sheaf of grain, anchor &c.; vessel in the distance. V SOUTH BERWICK BANK, South Berwick, Me.	5 Child kneeling. FIVE
Vig. Two females seated; vessels on their right; wagon on their left. 5	SOUTH BERWICK BANK. South Berwick, Me.	5 Med. of Washington.
X Indian and bow.	Steamer, sail-boat, &c. X SOUTH BERWICK BANK, South Berwick, Me.	10 Female figure; [illegible] in right hand; sheaf of grain under her left arm

Left	Center	Right
10 Portrait of Hancock. TEN	SOUTH BERWICK BANK, South Berwick, Me.	10 Spread eagle, shield, olive branch, and arrows; ships approaching on either hand. TEN
Steamer. XX Train of cars.	Three female figures seated. 20 SOUTH BERWICK BANK South Berwick, Me.	XX Milkmaid; pail in her right hand; cradle in her left hand.
20 Figure of Justice.	Female figure seated; arms extended; Liberty cap and staff in left hand, balance in right; a child on each side; fruit, bales, &c. SOUTH BERWICK BANK, South Berwick, Me.	20 Female with sheaf of grain on her back.
50 Bust of female, with sickle in her right hand; hat on her head. 50	Two females seated; factories, train of cars and ship in background. SOUTH BERWICK BANK, South Berwick, Me.	50 Boy gathering corn.
100 Sailor with flag and staff in right hand; left hand raised, holding his hat.	SOUTH BERWICK BANK, South Berwick, Me. Female and Cupid in the clouds.	100 Med. head of female. 100
ONE Portrait of Pierce.	Cupid riding stive, roller on railroad track; cars, steamboat and city in distance. STATE BANK, Augusta, Me.	1 Indian female seated.
2 Male portrait.	Two cupids and two silver dollars; cupids apparently in an engagement; train of cars, cattle, hills, city, &c. in distance. STATE BANK, Augusta, Me.	2 Indian female erect with bow and spear.
Male portrait. Figure 3 surrounded by sailor mechanic and farmer.	Three cupids and three silver dollars, all engaged at some act. STATE BANK, Augusta, Me.	3 Cupid astride a sea-monster.
5 Male portrait.	View of the Maine State House. STATE BANK, Augusta, Me.	5 Figure 5 surrounded by females.
X Male portrait.	Vig. Same as fives. STATE BANK, Augusta, Me.	10 State Arms, sailor on right, farmer on left.

Left	Center	Right
Mercury seated between 2 and 0. XX	State Arms surmounted by an eagle; female on either side; on right in distance, train of cars and buildings; on left steamboat and vessels. Title of Bank.	20 Female reclining on cornucopia. TWENTY
Portrait of Webster. L	Train of cars leaving Depot, horses before carriage rearing, men, &c. STATE BANK, Augusta, Me.	50 Same as 10's.
Portrait of Washington. C	Spread eagle on shield; U. S. Capitol on right and steamship on left. STATE BANK, Augusta, Me.	100 Female seated, bales, &c., building in distance.
Indian princess. 500	Female reclining on safe; cattle and girls on right; wheat, vessels, hats, bales, locomotive on right. STATE BANK, Augusta, Me.	500 Indian portrait.
1 Washington.	Female. 1 Female. THOMASTON BANK, Thomaston, Me.	1 Franklin.
1 Barrels, bales, ship, &c. 1	ONE DOLLAR 1 Female seated beside bales; ship on left. 1 THOMASTON BANK, Thomaston, Me.	1 Agricultural implements. 1
1 ONE DOLLAR	THOMASTON BANK Thomaston, Me. Head of Washington.	1 ONE DOLLAR
2 Webster.	Spread eagle. Title of Bank.	2 Small die with 2s on it.
2 Male portrait.	Female. 2 Female. THOMASTON BANK, Thomaston, Me.	2 Male portrait.
2 Man on horse. 2	2 Female seated with fig. 2. 2 THOMASTON BANK, Thomaston, Me.	2 Man on horse. 2

Left	Center	Right
3 Female portrait.	Shipping scene. Title of Bank.	3
3 Washington and his horse.	Female. 3 Female. THOMASTON BANK, Thomaston, Me.	3 Vulcan with hammer.
Spread eagle on shield; ship and manufactories in distance. FIVE	Large V, female and child. THOMASTON BANK, Thomaston, Me.	5 Female with basket of flowers.
Vulcan seated, cars in distance. TEN	X THOMASTON BANK, Thomaston, Me.	10 Farmer seated.
20 Full length female figure with helmet and spear.	2 Female seated. 0 THOMASTON BANK, Thomaston, Me. XX	20 Female seated. 20
50	Vessels sailing on ocean. THOMASTON BANK, Thomaston, Me.	50 Dog's head.
50 Male figure with spear in right hand.	Female seated with rake; male seated with scroll. THOMASTON BANK, Thomaston, Me. 50	50 Cupid in sea-boat. 50
100	THOMASTON BANK, Thomaston, Me. Liberty with wreath, shield, etc.	100
100 Male figure seated.	Spread eagle on branch of a tree; train of cars, canal boats, bridge, &c. in distance. THOMASTON BANK, Thomaston, Me. 100	100 Female seated with rake.
	TICONIC BANK, Waterville, Me. This Bank uses the old Perkins Stereotype Plate, which has the denomination printed in small letters all over the bill.	

1 State Arms. ONE DOLLAR, in part circle. — Eagle on an arch; three females sitting, ship on left, cars on right. TRADER'S BANK, Bangor, Me. — 1 ONE

2 — Spread eagle, steamship on left, sail-ship on right. State Arms. TRADER'S BANK, Bangor, Me. TWO — 2 2

3 Maine Logging scene. — TRADER'S BANK, Bangor, Me. Portrait of Washington. — 3 3

FIVE Maine Logging scene. — FIVE DOLLARS TRADER'S BANK, Bangor, Me. Male Portrait. 5

X TEN — TRADER'S BANK, Bangor, Me. Three female figures sitting holding dividers, sickle and sextant. — 10 Ship under full sail, city and shipping in the distance.

State Arms, on the left an Indian and child, on the right female three children and globe. 20 — Male Portrait. TRADER'S BANK, Bangor, Maine. TWENTY—curved. — 20

Male Portrait. 50 — State arms with eagle on top, Indian and tools on left, sailor on right. TRADER'S BANK, Bangor, Me. FIFTY — 50

C on four strips of lathe work. — TRADER'S BANK, Bangor, Maine. Male portrait. — 100 Two females seated; one erect; on left a temple.

1 — Wood-choppers, cattle, and horse. 1 UNION BANK, Brunswick, Me. — 1 Female with sickle.

2 — Locomotive and train of cars. 2 UNION BANK, Brunswick, Me. — 2 Portrait. 2

3 — Three female figures; factories in back ground. 3 UNION BANK, Brunswick, Me. — 3 Sailor boy.

5 — Ship building. Large V, female, and sheaf of wheat. UNION BANK, Brunswick, Me. — 5 Ships.

TEN — Vulcan the blacksmith seated. X UNION BANK, Brunswick, Me. — 10 Reaper.

10 — Female seated with globe, distaff, quadrant, compass, etc.; railroad and steamship in distance. X UNION BANK, Brunswick, Me. — X Indian seated.

20 Female. — 2 Female. 0 UNION BANK, Brunswick, Me. XX — 20 Female 20

50 Female figure. — Male and female seated. UNION BANK, Brunswick, Me. 50 — 50 Cupid in a sail boat. 50

100 Vulcan the blacksmith. — Spread eagle standing upon a tree; railroad and canal in background. UNION BANK, Brunswick, Me. 100 — 100 Female seated.

Male portrait 1 — Saw mills. 1 Saw mills, dam, lumber raft, &c. VEAZIE BANK, Bangor, Me. — 1 Male portrait

Male portrait 2 — Ship. 2 Ship. VEAZIE BANK, Bangor, Me. — 2 Male portrait

Male portrait 3 — Washington on horseback. 3 Washington on horseback. VEAZIE BANK, Bangor, Me. — 3 Male portrait

Male portrait 5 — Eagle on promontory; ship in distance. Letter V. and Indian girl seated. Same as on left side. VEAZIE BANK, Bangor, Me. — 5 Male portrait

Likeness of Gen. Jackson 10 — Saw mills. X Saw mills, dam, &c. VEAZIE BANK, Bangor, Me. — 10 Male portrait

20 Female sitting; right hand resting on book; open book on lap. — XX Vig. Spread eagle standing on rock. XX VEAZIE BANK, Bangor, Me. — 20 Two ships, one in foreground, one in distance.

FIFTY Full length figure of female in right hand wreath, and bunch of flowers in left. FIFTY — 50 Vig. Man and horse; horse rearing. 50 VEAZIE BANK, Bangor, Me. — FIFTY Full length figure of female. FIFTY

Words one hundred running across figures 100. Male portrait — Dray cart, into which men are rolling barrels, horses, shipping, &c. VEAZIE BANK, Bangor, Me. — Words one hundred running across figures 100. Male portrait

500 — 500 D Vig. Female sitting, sheaves of grain at her feet; load of grain and men reaping in distance. VEAZIE BANK, Bangor, Me. — 500

Group of statuary. 1000 — THOUSAND Engine and cars. VEAZIE BANK, Bangor, Me. — 1000 Ship 1000

ONE Ship ; city in distance and other vessels. — 1 Train of cars stopping at station. VILLAGE BANK, Bowdoinham, Me. — 1 Wood cutter ONE

2 Indians on cliff ; city in distance. — Two oxen before load of hay, boy on top and another boy with fork. VILLAGE BANK, Bowdoinham, Me. Beehive. — 2 Webster.

THREE Male portrait — Cattle and sheep. VILLAGE BANK, Bowdoinham, Me. Hesperus. — 3 State Arms. 3

V Male portrait	Ship. Washington. VILLAGE BANK. Bowdoinham, Me. Female bathing.	5 Eagle. FIVE
X TEN X	Spread eagle on globe with flags for every State surrounding it. VILLAGE BANK, Bowdoinham, Me. Ducks.	10 Washington
TWENTY Indian seated, with bow and quiver.	XX Wild horses. VILLAGE BANK, Bowdoinham, Me. Dog.	XX 20
FIFTY Steamship and schooner	L VILLAGE BANK, Bowdoinham, Me. Ship yard scene in general.	50 Cars; tunnel, bridge, city, etc.
1 Indian seated on rock, gun beside him.	Two horses and a colt; farm houses in distance. WALDOBORO BANK Waldoboro', Me. Beehive.	1 Spread eagle
TWO William Penn (full length) with scroll in hand	Indian seated on rock with gun in right hand; city, steamer, steamboat, &c., in distance. WALDOBORO BANK Waldoboro', Me. Spread eagle.	2 Vessel at sea. TWO
THREE	Man-of-war with sails set; in distance steamship and vessel. 3 WALDOBORO BANK Waldoboro', Me. State arms.	THREE
5 FIVE	Three females floating in water, supporting a cupid. 5 WALDOBORO BANK Waldoboro', Me Head of sailor.	5 Female portrait.
10 Female portrait. TEN	WALDOBORO BANK Waldoboro', Me. X Spread eagle on rock at sea; ship on right and left.	10 TEN
Female seated with sword in right hand. TWENTY	Man with two horses (white and black); farm-house on right, train of cars, water, &c., on left. WALDOBORO BANK Waldoboro', Me Steamboat.	20 Female seated aloud to look through spyglass, vessel in distance.

50 50	WALDOBORO BANK Waldoboro', Me. Ship yard; men at work, buildings in background. Dog, key, and safe.	50 Man sharpening scythe, steamboat in distance.
100 Henry Clay seated, dog by his side.	WALDOBORO BANK Waldoboro', Me. Female seated in a shell with trident; ships in background. Indian.	100 Female milking cow, one lying down; girl on right
1 Bust of Washington.	Female. 1 Female. WATERVILLE B'K, Waterville, Me.	1 Bust of Franklin.
2 Bust of Columbus.	Female. 2 Female. WATERVILLE B'K, Waterville, Me.	2 Male portrait
3 Washington and horse.	Female Bust. 3 Female Bust. WATERVILLE B'K, Waterville, Me.	3 Blacksmith hammer and anvil.
FIVE	Eagle with spread wings on American flag, steamer on left. Large V, cupid and female. WATERVILLE B'K, Waterville, Me.	5 Female with basket of flowers.
TEN	Male figure seated on pile with balance on knee supported upright; buildings and cars in distance. X WATERVILLE B'K, Waterville, Me.	10 Full length portrait of man with sickle and bundle of wheat.
Steamship. XX Railroad cars and engine.	Group of three females Faith, Justice, Mercy; ship on right and eagle on left. 20 WATERVILLE B'K Waterville, Me.	XX Full length of female with milk-pail and stool
FIFTY Female full length with wreath in hand and on brow. FIFTY	50 Man and horse. 50 WATERVILLE B'K, Waterville, Me.	FIFTY Full length female with sceptre in one hand and flowers in other. FIFTY
Words ONE HUNDRED and figures 100. Bust of Harrison.	Market, wagon, men rolling in casks; horse and wagon on right; ship on left. WATERVILLE B'K, Waterville, Me	Words ONE HUNDRED and figures 100. Bust of Columbus.

	YORK BANK, Saco, Me. This Bank uses the old Perkins Stereotype Plate, which has the denomination printed in fine letters all over the bill.	
ONE Female figure.	AMOSKEAG BANK, Manchester, N. H. Vig. Indian reclining on frame, and motto "enterprise;" spread eagle, lake, mountains, and deer in background.	1 Portrait R. H. Ayer.
2 Portrait R. H. Ayer.	AMOSKEAG BANK, Manchester, N. H. Vig. Female on each side Coat of Arms, of New Hampshire; steamboat, train of cars, &c., in background.	2 Two females.
3 Male Portrait.	AMOSKEAG BANK, Manchester, N. H. Vig. Three females seated.	3 Small female figure reclining. Large figure 3, supported by three laborers.
5 Portrait R. H. Ayer	AMOSKEAG BANK, Manchester, N. H. Vig. Female seated; horn of plenty; books, &c., &c.; steamboat and merchandise on left; safe, harrow, rake, and train of cars on right.	5 Large figure 5, supported by 4 females.
Female figure reclining holding scales. 10	AMOSKEAG BANK, Manchester, N. H. Vig. Female reclining on safe; Pastoral scene on right; steam engine and merchandise on left; and commercial scene in background.	10 Portrait of Frank Pierce
20 Figure of Mercury between figures 20.	AMOSKEAG BANK, Manchester, N. H. Harvest scene; railroad bridge; train of cars; church, &c., in background.	20 Portrait of Frank Pierce
Male Portrait. 50	Vig. Female seated that in lap, beside dog; cattle in background. AMOSKEAG BANK, Manchester, N. H.	50 Portrait of Frank Pierce
100 Male portrait 100	Female with sand, cupids and dolphin sporting. AMOSKEAG BANK, Manchester, N. H.	100 Male portrait
Mountainous native scene, Indian in canoe. 500	500 AMOSKEAG BANK Manchester, N. H.	500 Female holding scales.

Left end	Centre	Right end
1 A man sitting cutting a log, gold dollar, a hat, traveling wagon in distance.	ASHUELOT BANK. Keene, N. H. 1	1 Female leaning on a fig. 1, sheaf at her feet.
TWO Female with spear, cap of liberty and scroll; shield at her feet.	ASHUELOT BANK, Keene, N. H. Milkmaid sitting with pail, cows; two gold dollars; man reclining with rake. 2	2 2
State arms. 3	ASHUELOT BANK. Keene, N. H. Farmer sitting with scythe, sailor sitting with spy glass, blacksmith sitting, and three gold dollars.	3 Female portrait.
5 Large figure 5, with five images with scales, shield spear, & cap of liberty.	ASHUELOT BANK, Keene, N. H. Three cupids, five gold dollars; sportsman sitting on right, female Indian sitting on left.	5 Female portrait reading.
Large X, with figures 10 across it.	ASHUELOT BANK, Keene, N. H. Harvest scene, females, female, dog, &c.; female sitting with a basket.	X Two females.
One figure with spear, shield, and helmet, and another with scales and sword. 20	Female in the clouds holding a shield; the American eagle flying with its back fastened to the shield. ASHUELOT BANK. Keene, N. H. Bell.	20 Two females, one with sword the other with sickle.
Female with spear, shield and helmet, and a book and globe at her feet. 50	Two men, boy and dog driving a flock of sheep across a stream, man in the foreground pushing a sheep into the stream. ASHUELOT BANK, Keene, N. H. Sheep, plough, rake, &c.	50 Female portrait.
Male with arms extended, sitting between two cupids riding on the back of an eagle. C	100 ASHUELOT BANK, Keene, N. H. A man shearing sheep; factory in the background.	100 Washington
1 Coat of Arms and two females. ONE	Head of Franklin. Female, sheaf of wheat, sickle and plough. Head of Washington. BK., OF LEBANON. Lebanon, N. H. Man sitting on a plow.	1 Female head
Female sitting with sickle. TWO	Female head. BK., OF LEBANON, Lebanon, N. H. Dog's head.	2 Cow and hogs.
Man sharpening scythe FIVE	V Railroad train. V BK., OF LEBANON, Lebanon, N. H. Sheaf of wheat.	5 Female head
Blacksmith with sledge and anvil. TEN	Female with horn of plenty between 1 and 0; male, boy, female on right. BK., OF LEBANON, Lebanon, N. H. Deer.	10 Two females with sickle; sheaf of wheat, &c
20 Roman warrior, globe, &c.	Female sitting, and large figures 20. BK., OF LEBANON, Lebanon, N. H. XX	20 Lady with horn of plenty; globe, &c. 20
20 Female with tablets; child at her feet.	Boy, child, cattle, etc. Red word TWENTY on either side. BANK OF LEBANON Lebanon, N. H.	20 Female with flower.
50 Roman warrior.	Two figures seated; horn of plenty. BK., OF LEBANON, Lebanon, N. H. 50	50 Cupid in a sail-boat. 50
50 Boy	Female either side of anvil; factories in distance. BANK OF LEBANON Lebanon, N. H.	50 Girl
Two children. C	Female seated; sheep, etc. BANK OF LEBANON Lebanon, N. H. 100	100 Boys head.
100 One Hundred Man sitting; hand on sledge.	Large eagle, wings stretched; railroad trains. BK., OF LEBANON, Lebanon, N. H. 100	100 One Hundred Female sitting; horn of plenty.
Female erect with emblems of liberty. ONE	1 Female seated on a rock; cupids playing with a dolphin. BANK OF NEW HAMPSHIRE, Portsmouth, N. H.	1 Portrait of female.
Figure of Justice. TWO	2 Agricultural scene; laborers seated, load of hay in distance Title of Bank.	2 Female seated with sheaves and sickle.
3 Artist with chisel and hammer.	Two ships on the stocks; vessels in distance. Title of Bank.	3 Figure 3, sailor, farmer and mechanic.
5 Eagle. V	Helmeted head. Female seated with shield. Helmeted head. Title of Bank	5 Ship under sail. V
5	Indian hunter overlooking deer; cabin and squaw in background. 5 BK OF NEW HAMPSHIRE, Portsmouth, N. H. Vessel	5 Female head
10 Fisherman.	Title of Bank. X Steamship sailing; men in boat. X	X Am. shield.
10 Head of male X	TEN TEN X Brig and schooner sailing. X Title of Bank Shield. TEN TEN TEN TEN	10 Head of male X
Girl with sheaf on her head; loading grain in distance. 20	Title of Bank. Steamboat; lighthouse in background.	20 Female with flowers.
TWENTY Neptune seated; ship in distance. TWENTY	TWENTY TWENTY TWENTY Title of Bank. Shield. TWENTY TWENTY	TWENTY 20 Mercury in clouds. TWENTY
50 Washington	Storm on the coast; sailors in surf boat; ship in distress in distance. Title of Bank.	50 Spread eagle on shield.
50 Two helmeted heads. 50	50 Ship and steamer in distance. 50 Title of Bank. Shield.	FIFTY
Reaper reclining by sheaves. HUNDRED.	One hundred One hundred Title of Bank.	100 Head of man 100

1	Female. 1 Female.	1
	BELKNAP CO. B'K, Meredith, N. H.	
Portrait of Washington.		Portrait of Franklin.

ONE	ONE Female with sword and scales; ship on the stocks.	1
Sailor hoisting a flag.	BELKNAP CO. B'K. Meredith, N. H.	Indian girl with bow and spear.

TWO	Spread Eagle. 2	2
	BELKNAP CO. B'K. Meredith, N. H.	TWO
2		Sail-boats.

Female.	Wood choppers, cattle and horse.	2
	BELKNAP CO. B'K, Meredith, N. H.	Girl with sheaf of wheat.
2		

3	Female 3 Flower girl	3
	BELKNAP CO. B'K, Meredith, N. H.	
Washington.		Vulcan the blacksmith.

3	3 Harvest scene 3	3
	BELKNAP CO. B'K, Meredith, N. H.	
Female with flowers.		Females raking hay.

Spread eagle	Large V, female and cupid.	5
	Title of Bank.	
FIVE		Flower girl

Female seated on a rock.	Female reclining, Milkmaids, cows; locomotive and factories in background.	5
	Title of Bank.	
V		Martha Washington

10	Cincinnatus standing by his plough. 10	TEN
X	Title of Bank.	
10		Female figure.

TEN	Capitol at Washington.	10
	Title o. Bank.	
Goddess of Liberty.		Washington

20	2 Female. 0	20
		Female
Female with spear.	Title of Bank.	20
	20	

FIFTY	50 Man and Horse. 50	FIFTY
Female.	Title of Bank.	Female.
FIFTY		FIFTY

50	Vulcan and a female.	50
		Cupid in a sail boat.
	Title of Bank.	
Female.	50	50

100	Spread eagle standing on a tree; railroad and canal.	100
Vulcan the blacksmith.	Title of Bank.	Female with a rake.
	100	

ONE	CARROLL CO. BANK. Sandwich, N. H.	1
	Three female figures floating in the air, partly covering the face of the bill,	
1	ONE ONE	Portrait.

Female.	2 Indian, squaw, and child; plough, sickle, and wheat. 2	Female.
	CARROLL CO. BANK Sandwich, N. H.	
Portrait of Z. Taylor.		2

3	Indian, squaw, and child; plough, sickle, and wheat.	THREE
Locomotive and train of cars.	CARROLL CO. BANK. Sandwich, N. H.	Portrait.
3		THREE

V	5 Vig. Same as 2s. 5	V
	CARROLL CO BANK. Sandwich, N. H.	
Dog and key.		Portrait of female.

X	10 Title of Bank. 10	X
Female.	Locomotive and train of cars.	Female.

20	CARROLL CO. BANK. Sandwich, N. H.	20
Portrait of Franklin.	Locomotive and train of cars,	Portrait.

50	CARROLL CO. BANK, Sandwich, N. H.	50
	Egyptian figure with wings seated beside globe, female, etc.	
50		50

	This Bank also uses an old plate, but they are rapidly retiring them from circulation.	

1	Train of cars.	1
Medallion head with wreath around it.	CHESHIRE BANK. Keene, N. H.	Woman with plow, sheaf of wheat and cornucopia.
	Ox.	

TWO	Cart load of grain; man on horseback; agricultural implements; mill house in distance.	2
Engine and cars.	CHESHIRE BANK, Keene, N. H.	Fancy medallion head.
TWO	Fort and ship.	

THREE	Spread eagle on a branch; train of cars and other boats in the lands.	3
3	CHESHIRE BANK, Keene, N. H.	Man shearing a sheep; woman standing by.
DOLLARS	Ploughing with horses.	

5	Medallion head. 5 Medallion head.	5
Eagle and shield, which bears the word five.	CHESHIRE BANK. Keene N. H.	Woman with bow and arrow.
	Plow.	

10	Medallion head of Franklin. X Medallion head.	10
Head of Washington.	CHESHIRE BANK, Keene, N. H.	Woman with cornucopia.
	Ox.	

20	Female with one hand resting on 2 and the other on 0.	20
	CHESHIRE BANK. Keene, N. H.	Small female with cornucopia, &c.
Roman soldier.	XX	20

50	Male and female figures seated, with cornucopia between them.	50
	CHESHIRE BANK, Keene, N. H.	Cupid in a sail-boat.
Roman soldier.	50	50

FIFTY	50 Three females, 50 on shield and scales.	Fifty
Grain and fruit.	CHESHIRE BANK, Keene, N. H.	
50		Vulcan.

ONE — 1 Three male figures; tree village, &c. 1 — CHESHIRE CO. B'K, Keene, N. H. — ONE

TWO — CHESHIRE CO. B'K, Keene, N. H. — TWO 2 — Female feeding fowls. — TWO

FIVE DOLLARS FIVE DOLLARS — 5 Anvil, plough, anchor, cogwheel, &c. — CHESHIRE CO. B'K, Keene, N. H. — Dog, key and safe. — 5

Word ten, figure 10 and letter X. Ship on stocks. — CHESHIRE CO. B'K, Keene, N. H. — Large X, and words ten dollars. — Ruling machine. — Word ten, figure 10 and letter X. Sailor at wheel.

XX — Female gathering wheat. — CHESHIRE CO. B'K, Keene, N. H. — Figure 20, across words twenty dollars. — 20 — Female with cornucopia.

Full length female with helmet, spear and shield. 50 — $50 Ship on stocks. 50 — CHESHIRE CO. B'K, Keene, N. H. — Fifty dollars. — Full length female. 50

Word one and figure 1. — Vig. Train of cars. 1 — CITIZENS' BANK, Sanbornton, N. H. — 1 Two females Indian grain, cattle, &c.

2 Female with quadrant, anchor at her side; eagle at top of shield on left. — Vig. Group of three females, with quadrant, chart, spy glass, globe, liberty pole and cap. — CITIZENS' BANK, Sanbornton, N. H. — 2 Female with shield and balances.

3 Indian with tomahawk and bow. — Vig. Drove of wild horses. — CITIZENS' BANK, Sanbornton, N. H. — 3 Squaw and papoose.

FIVE — CITIZENS' BANK, Sanbornton, N. H. — Vig. Drove of cattle, man plowing on left; farmers at work on right. — 5 Two horses; cars on left.

TEN — Female right hand resting on shield. — Pudding [illegible] iron hill. 10 — CITIZENS' BANK, Sanbornton, N. H. — TEN — Mechanic.

20 Two males and female with telescope in boat. — CITIZENS' BANK, Sanbornton, N. H. — 20 — 20 Male, two females, dog and cattle.

L 50 Dls — View of the U. S. Capitol — CITIZENS' BANK, Sanbornton, N. H. — L 50 Dls

100 Three females representing the Arts and Sciences. — CITIZENS' BANK, Sanbornton, N. H. — Female giving eagle drink. 100

1 Train of cars. — Ship on stocks. — CITY BANK, Manchester, N. H. — ONE — 1

2 Female and eagle. — Blacksmith at forge. — CITY BANK, Manchester, N. H. — 2 — TWO

3 Female. — Mechanic, forge, factory, cars, &c. — CITY BANK, Manchester, N. H. — 3 — 3

FIVE Female. — Three mechanics. — CITY BANK, Manchester, N. H. — FI 5 VE 5

Gen. Stark. TEN — X — CITY BANK, Manchester, N. H. — 10 Indian and two squaws; factory in distance.

20 — CITY BANK, Manchester, N. H. — Three females. — 20 F. Pierce.

L 50 — CITY BANK, Manchester, N. H. — Franklin. — 50 Harvest scene, male and female, cattle, dogs, &c.

C — Indian, squaw, and papoose on left of shield; female and three children with book and globe. — CITY BANK, Manchester, N. H. — 100 Washington.

D Suspension bridge, canal boats. 500 — Safe, female, ship on stocks, grain, sheep, &c. — CITY BANK, Manchester, N. H. — Mermaid. — 500 Two male and 1 female.

Female. 1 — CLAREMONT BANK, Claremont, N. H. — State Arms — 1 Portrait of Webster.

2 Two cows. TWO — CLAREMONT BANK, Claremont, N. H. — 2 Two females seated on each side of a frame on which is a vessel. — 2

THREE Female seated on a bale. — CLAREMONT BANK, Claremont, N. H. — 3 3 — Portrait of Washington. — THREE Female seated on a bale.

5 — Blacksmith shoeing horse; jackass tied to anvil, train of cars in background. Letter V and female. — CLAREMONT BANK, Claremont, N. H. — Wheels, bales, &c. — FIVE Figure five surrounded by five females.

X — Female reclining on bale; city on left. Letter X and female. — CLAREMONT BANK, Claremont, N. H. — 10 Two females.

20 — Drove of Cattle XX — CLAREMONT BANK, Claremont, N. H. — Sheaf of wheat and farming implements. — 20 Female holding sheaf and horn of plenty. TWENTY

Female with liberty cap. 50 — Man ploughing with a span of horses; train of cars on right; house on left. Cupid and figure 50. — CLAREMONT BANK, Claremont, N. H. — FIFTY Female with horn of plenty.

Left	Centre	Right
100 Female representing commerce.	CLARKMONT BANK, Claremont, N. H. Man with a sledge on his shoulder, factory in distance, cars crossing bridge; three cows drinking at the river.	100 Goddess of Justice.
1 Indian on rock with gun.	Two females at work on machines. COCHECHO BANK. Dover. N. H. Building.	1 Sheep at work.
1	Female seated train of cars and vessel on right, canal scene on left. 1 COCHECHO BANK, Dover, N. H.	1 Female resting arm on fence.
2	Man forcing sheep in water, another man reading; boy driving flock; buildings on right. 2 Title of Bank.	TWO Female seated. TWO
Sailor seated on bale with flag. TWO	Female on either side of a frame surmounted by eagle, on which is seen plow, steamboat and buildings in distance. Title of Bank. Building.	2 Female with sheaf of wheat over shoulder.
3	Man on horseback; cows and men; load of hay entering barn. 3 COCHECHO BANK, Dover, N. H	Word three and figure 3. Female with basket of flowers. THREE
3 Female seated, with sword and balance. THREE	Cattle and hogs; buildings in distance. COCHECHO BANK. Dover. N. H. Building.	3 Male portrait. THREE
FIVE	Eagle on shield; city and ships in distance. Large V, female and Cupid. COCHECHO BANK, Dover. N. H.	5 Girl with basket of flowers or fruit.
5	Female seated representing agriculture; boats, village, &c., in distance. Male portrait. COCHECHO BANK, Dover, N. H.	5 Indian seated.
Female seated, at work on machine. 10	Ships, steamship, &c.; city on left. COCHECHO BANK, Dover, N. H.	10 Female portrait.

Left	Centre	Right
TEN	Vulcan seated, with sledge and anvil; train of cars and buildings in distance. X COCHECHO BANK, Dover, N. H.	10 Farmer with sheaf and sickle.
20 Female seated, with sword and scales; eagle standing on safe.	Three human figures; centre female with outstretched arms. COCHECHO BANK, Dover, N. H. Steamer.	20 Female with sheaf of wheat on shoulder
50 Female with sickle. 50	Two females seated; on right, ship; on left, factories and cars. COCHECHO BANK, Dover, N. H.	50 Boy gathering corn.
100 Sailor with flag, and swinging his hat	COCHECHO BANK, Dover, N. H. Female and cherub arm in arm; cherub scattering flowers. Machinery.	100 Female portrait. 100
1	Stream of water and load of straw; mill in the distance. 1 CONNECTICUT RIVER BANK, Charlestown, N. H. Bundle of grain.	1 Justice with sword and scales.
2	Eagle on an old tree. 2 CONNECTICUT RIVER BANK, Charlestown, N. H. Ox.	2 Head of Washington.
Man representing agriculture, surrounded by axe, sickle, plough, harrow with the motto "Enterprise." THREE	Head. 3 Head. CONNECTICUT RIVER BANK, Charlestown, N. H. Man shearing a sheep.	THREE Minerva with helmet and spear leaning on her shield.
5 Female seated holding United States flag.	Female and eagle. CONNECTICUT RIVER BANK, Charlestown, N. H. Bundle of grain.	5 Bull.
10 Stream of water; load of straw; mill in the distance.	Two females seated. CONNECTICUT RIVER BANK, Charlestown, N. H. Bull.	10 Eagle, bale, barrel and shield.
Female portrait. 20	Female seated on a rock; three cherubs sporting with dolphin in water. CONNECTICUT RIVER BANK, Charlestown, N. H.	20 Two females.

Left	Centre	Right
Female seated. 50	View of U. S. Capitol. 50 Title of Bank.	Justice.
Soldier with sword. 100	Female seated on bale giving eagle drink, cornucopia and distaff at her feet; ship in distance. Title of Bank.	100 Female representing Agriculture.
1	Female seated; factories in distance; fig. 1 on right. DERRY BANK, Derry, N. H. Machinery.	1 Female with sheaf and basket of fruit.
Indian with bow and arrow. 2	Milkmaid and cattle; fig. 2 on left. DERRY BANK, Derry, N. H.	2 Female with sheaf.
3 Sea monsters. Steamship	Three females, each leaning on a fig. 1; fig. 3 on left. DERRY BANK, Derry, N. H	3 Three male figures.
Hunter with gun and game. 5	Webster supported by figure of Fame and cupid; 5 on right. DERRY BANK, Derry, N. H.	5 Justice and 5
TEN Justice and Minerva.	Woodcutter and oxen; figure 10 on left. DERRY BANK, Derry, N. H. Loading hay	X Server.
XX Female and bales.	Train of cars DERRY BANK, Derry, N. H.	20 Female
Female and agriculture. 50	50 Steamship. DERRY BANK, Derry, N. H. Man plowing.	50 Two females.
C Men, vessels, etc. 100	Eagle on bale; horn of plenty, grain, etc. 100 DERRY BANK, Derry, N. H.	100 Female with sheaf and sickle. 100

Left	Centre	Right
Female with sheaf of wheat. ONE	1 Ship on stocks. DOVER BANK, Dover, N. H. 1	1 Sailor.
Female seated on bale of goods with sheaf of wheat; cars, factory in distance. TWO	2 Ship on stocks. DOVER BANK, Dover, N. H. 2	2 Cattle
Female reclining; factories in distance. 3	3 Ship on stocks. DOVER BANK, Dover, N. H. Washington.	THREE Stone cutter
Washington	Ship on stocks and female either side 5 DOVER BANK, Dover N. H. Wheels.	5 Two females
TEN	Female illustrating industry. X Ship on stocks. DOVER BANK, Dover, N. H.	10 Blacksmith at his forge.
20 Female.	XX Eagle. XX DOVER BANK, Dover, N. H.	20 Ship sailing.
FIFTY Female. FIFTY	50 Man and horse. 50 DOVER BANK, Dover, N. H.	FIFTY Female. FIFTY
Word one hundred and figure 100. Male portrait.	Wharf scene—loading wagon, men, horses, shipping, &c. DOVER BANK, Dover, N. H.	Same as on left. Male portrait.
ONE 1 Female seated with right arm resting on figure 1, owl, &c.	FARMINGTON BK. Farmington, N. H. Vig. Spread eagle; on left, steamship; on right, Capitol at Washington.	1 ONE Female seated, liberty pole and cap, shield, globe, &c.
Female reclining with sickle in right hand. 2	Vig. Drove of cattle and sheep, herdsman, horse and dog. FARMINGTON BK., Farmington, N. H. Man ploughing.	2 Female erect, pole, cap and shield.

Left	Centre	Right
Mermaid holding horn out of which water is running. 3	Vig. Two men ploughing with horse and oxen; road, train of cars, horses, cows, &c., in distance is city on left, on right is a church, &c. FARMINGTON BK., Farmington, N. H.	3 Female portrait
FIVE Female seated, pole and cap, shield, flowers, &c.	FARMINGTON BK., Farmington, N. H. 5	5 Blacksmiths at work, horses, men, &c.
TEN Indian princess.	FARMINGTON BK., Farmington, N. H. Vig. Female Indian seated with left arm up lifted; on left a deer, trees &c. Man loading hay.	X Horses. X
20 Man seated with gun, train of cars on right.	FARMINGTON BK., Farmington, N. H. Vig. Female on the back of an eagle, soaring in clouds.	20 Indian female reclining.
L Female seated, portrait of Washington, eagle, train of cars, &c.	FARMINGTON BK., Farmington, N. H.	50 Female portrait.
Female feeding an eagle from cup. 100	FARMINGTON BK., Farmington, N. H. Train of cars, depot, steamboat, &c. on right. Dog.	100 100
ONE Liberty and squaw.	ONE on fig. 1. Indian squaw and papoose seated; city in distance. FAR. & MECH. B'K, Rochester, N. H.	1 Female representing Agriculture.
Females haying. 2	Men at work in boot and shoe manufactory. FAR. & MECH. B'K, Rochester, N. H.	2 Two females.
3 Female, eagle, shield, and fig. 3	Three cherubs and three silver dollars; mechanical and other implements. FAR. & MECH. B'K, Rochester, N. H.	THREE on 3. Female head.
Farmer with scythe. 5	5 Milkmaid milking cow; another cow on left. FAR. & MECH. B'K, Rochester, N. H.	5 Franklin.

Left	Centre	Right
TEN inverted. Female feeding fowls.	X Cattle and sheep, dog, men and horse. FAR. & MECH. B'K, Rochester, N. H.	10 Male portrait
TWENTY Officer with sword.	20 Female seated; locomotive and factory in distance. FAR. & MECH. B'K, Rochester, N. H.	20 Male portrait
Two children 50	Farmer seated; others at work in distance. FAR. & MECH. B'K, Rochester, N. H.	50 Washington
Fountain. 100	Battle of Niagara. FAR. & MECH. B'K, Rochester, N. H.	100 Large building
1 Head of Washington	Female sitting. 1 Female sitting. FRANCESTOWN B'K Francestown, N. H.	1 Head of Franklin.
2 Head of Columbus.	Female 2 Female. FRANCESTOWN B'K Francestown, N. H.	2 Male portrait.
3 Portrait of Washington	Female head. 3 Female head. FRANCESTOWN B'K Francestown, N. H.	3 Vulcan the blacksmith
Letter V with word five running across it.	Female with sickle and rake, sheaf of grain; steam engine, store house, and shipping in the distance. V and Indian. FRANCESTOWN B'K Francestown, N. H.	5 Head of Washington.
10 X 10	Pair of oxen and male standing by their side. 10 FRANCESTOWN B'K Francestown, N. H.	TEN Female with vase of flowers.
20 Female sitting.	XX Eagle. XX FRANCESTOWN B'K Francestown, N. H.	20 Ship, sails all set.

FIFTY Female FIFTY — 50 Man and horse. 50 FRANCESTOWN B'K Francestown, N. H. — FIFTY Female with vase of flowers. FIFTY

100 Eagle. 100 — C Four horses abreast driven by Neptune. 100 FRANCESTOWN B'K Francestown, N. H. — C Head of Washington. C

Word one and figure 1. Bust of female. — Harvest scene—farmers at lunch; female with child; men loading hay, and farm-house in distance. GRANITE STATE BK Exeter, N. H. — 1 Female with pole and cap, seated on safe, right hand on figure 1.

2 Bust of female. — State arms surmounted by an eagle, female on either side. GRANITE STATE BK Exeter, N. H. — 2 Two females erect, one with sickle and sheaf.

FIVE Letter V with three males and two females. — Milkmaid seated and two cows; three cows and farm house in distance. GRANITE STATE BK Exeter, N. H. — FIVE 5 and five females.

10 State Arms. — Drove of cattle and sheep; man on horseback GRANITE STATE BK Exeter, N. H. — 10 Female seated with sheaf and cornucopia.

20 State arms. — Female seated with portrait of Washington, and with her left hand crowning eagle with a wreath; anchor, hogshead, &c.; in distance factory and steamboat. GRANITE STATE BK Exeter, N. H. — 20 Female seated between 2 and 0.

50 Female holding wreath over eagle; in her left hand scales — Female seated holding in right hand emblems of wisdom; state arms on left also oak and pole; on right train of cars, bridge, and steamboat. GRANITE STATE BK Exeter, N. H. — 50 50

100 State arms. — 100 Female seated leaning on bales and looking at ships in distance; on her right train of cars, &c. GRANITE STATE BK Exeter, N. H. — 100 100

500 — Female seated among sheafs of grain, pointing to reapers and workmen loading grain. 500 D GRANITE STATE BK Exeter, N. H. — 500

Female seated; at her feet is a figure 1. ONE — Female seated with agricultural implements and products; in distance is train of cars and canal lock. GREAT FALLS BK., S. Somersworth, N. H. Female. — 1 Female portrait.

2 Female portrait — Female seated with mechanical implements around; train of cars, boat on stocks, and steamer in distance. Title of Bank. Dog's head. — 2 Female portrait.

THREE Farmer with sheaf of grain and rake. THREE — Two females seated. Title of Bank. Bull. — 3 Female erect

Two females erect; one with sword and balances — Large figure 5 and female, & Cupids sporting around it. Title of Bank. Eagle and shield. — 5 Two females seated; one with scales; shield between them. FIVE

Female erect in clouds. 10 — Female with key in left hand, is seated between 1 and 0; canal lock and train of cars in distance. Title of Bank. Agricultural implements. — 10 Female portrait.

20 Female with spear; globe, behind her. — 2 Female. 0 Title of Bank. XX — 20 Female reclining. 20

50 Female with spear; pedestal. — Male and female seated. Title of Bank. 50 — 50 Cupid in a sail-boat. 50

100 Vulcan the blacksmith. — Spread eagle on branch of tree; train of cars, canal boat, lock, etc. Title of Bank. 100 — 100 Female seated.

ONE 1 — [Old Plate.] Vig. Farmer sowing seed. 1 INDIAN HEAD B'K, Nashville, N. H. — 1 Ships. ONE

1 1 — [New Plate.] INDIAN HEAD B'K, Nashua, N. H. Indians welcoming white men to shore. — 1 Indian female and papoose.

TWO 2 — [Old Plate.] Spread eagle on rock, train of cars on right. 2 INDIAN HEAD B'K, Nashville, N. H. — 2 TWO Schooner and sloop.

TWO Indian Princess. — [New Plate.] INDIAN HEAD B'K, Nashua, N. H. Mechanic seated with sledge hammer, anvil, &c; train of cars and large building on left. — 2 Female Portrait.

THREE 3 — [Old Plate.] Sailor standing on wharf; ships, drays, &c. 3 INDIAN HEAD B'K, Nashville, N. H. — 3 THREE Train of cars.

3 Female seated. — [New Plate.] INDIAN HEAD B'K, Nashua, N. H. 3 Indian in canoe. 3 — 3 Figure 3, sailor, mechanic, and farmer.

Spread eagle; ships, &c., in distance. FIVE — [Old Plate.] Large letter V, and female and cupid. INDIAN HEAD B'K, Nashville, N. H. — 5 Girl with basket of flowers.

5 — [New Plate.] INDIAN HEAD B'K, Nashua, N. H. Indian reclining on shield, on which is inscribed word "Enterprise"; eagle, deers, Indians in canoe, &c. — 5 Figure 5, and five females surrounding it

TEN — [Old Plate.] Male seated with mechanical implements. X INDIAN HEAD B'K, Nashville, N. H. — 10 Man with sheaf of grain.

10 Female Indian seated. — [New Plate.] INDIAN HEAD B'K, Nashua, N. H. Train of cars; depot, steamer, &c., on left. — X Indian female seated

20 Full length figure of a female. — Female seated between figures 2 and 0. INDIAN HEAD B'K, Nashville, N. H. — 20 Female seated. 20

50 Full length female; pedestal, &c. — Vig. Male and female seated; flowers, &c. INDIAN HEAD B'K, Nashville, N. H. — 50 Cupid in sail-boat. 50

100 Male seated with sledge hammer.	Spread eagle on branch of tree; train of cars on left, canal boat, &c., on right. INDIAN HEAD B'K, Nashville, N. H.	100 Female seated with flowers.
500	Indians in canoe. 500 INDIAN HEAD B'K, Nashville, N. H. D D	500 Female holding scales.
Spread eagle and ship. 1000	1000 INDIAN HEAD B'K, Nashville, N. H. M M	1000 Female.
1 Man seated with scythe.	LAKE BANK, Wolfborough, N. H. Indian seated; deer; sailing vessel and steamboat.	1 Female seated with pails.
2 Two females seated.	Drover and cattle. LAKE BANK, Wolfborough, N. H.	2 Male portrait.
3 Man with grain cradle.	Farmer ploughing with horses; buildings and cars in distance. LAKE BANK, Wolfborough, N. H.	3 Female churning.
Large V, surrounded by two persons. 5	LAKE BANK, Wolfborough, N. H. Steamboat.	5 Head of female. 5
Portrait of female. X	LAKE BANK, Wolfborough, N. H. Ten gold dollars; nine cherubs; female seated.	10 Head of Frank Pierce. 10
Female with balances and sheaf of wheat. XX	Shoe and boot manufacturers. LAKE BANK, Wolfborough, N. H.	20 Portrait of Jackson.
Female seated. 50	Portrait of Washington. Cupid on right; winged female on left. LAKE BANK, Wolfborough, N. H.	50 Portrait of Webster.

Portrait of Cass. 100	Harvest scene; haying team hauling hay; female with child seated; pitcher, basket, &c. LAKE BANK, Wolfborough, N. H.	100 Indian seated.
1 Winged female with trumpet and wreath. Another female figure reclining and eagle.	LANGDON BANK, Dover, N. H. 1 Cupid rolling a silver dollar; village, train of cars, steamboat, in background.	1
Hunter resting on gun, game near him. 2	LANGDON BANK, Dover, N. H. Interior of shoe manufactory. Two horses.	2 Factory.
Man standing with sheaf of grain on left arm; female figure in sitting posture. 3	Three cupids and three silver dollars. LANGDON BANK, Dover, N. H. Load of hay.	3 Man resting on plow. THREE
Goddess of Liberty with scroll and shield.	LANGDON BANK, Dover, N. H. Winged female with wreath and trumpet. Portrait of Jackson. Cupid.	5 Female with sheaf and sickle, plow and basket of fruit.
Portrait of female. TEN X	Female and nine cupids and ten gold dollars. LANGDON BANK, Dover, N. H.	10 Female, globe, and shield.
XX Female portrait.	Harvest scene. LANGDON BANK, Dover, N. H. Cow and calf.	20 Sheaf of wheat. Female portrait.
Military officer, with left foot resting on gun-carriage. FIFTY	Goddess of Liberty, globe, eagle, ship, and steamboat. LANGDON BANK, Dover, N. H. Plowing scene.	50 Portrait of Washington. 50
100 Goddess of Liberty, shield, fruit, and grain.	Winged female. Portrait of Webster. Cupid. LANGDON BANK, Dover, N. H.	100 Female portrait.
ONE 1	Farmer sowing, two horses and man on right. 1 MANCHESTER BK., Manchester, N. H.	1 Ship. ONE

TWO 2	Spread eagle, with wheels, cogwheels, &c., on ground, on left train of cars in distance. 2 MANCHESTER BK., Manchester, N. H.	2 TWO Schooner and sloop.
THREE 3	Sailor standing by bales; vessels, wharf scene &c., on right; ships masts and building on left. 3 MANCHESTER BK., Manchester, N. H.	3 THREE Train of Cars.
FIVE	Female seated and in the act of raising drapery from off a figure 5. V MANCHESTER BK., Manchester, N. H.	5 Ship.
The word FIVE and letter V.	Female seated surrounded by mechanical and agricultural implements and products, on right vessels &c.; on left men, wagon, horses, buildings, &c. V and female. MANCHESTER BK., Manchester, N. H.	5 Head of Washington.
10 X 10	Male erect, behind him oxen. 10 MANCHESTER BK., Manchester, N. H.	TEN Female erect.
20 Female seated.	XX Eagle. XX MANCHESTER BK., Manchester, N. H.	20 Ship.
FIFTY Female. FIFTY	50 Man and Horse. 50 MANCHESTER BK., Manchester, N. H.	FIFTY Female. FIFTY
One Hundred and 10s. Portrait.	Wharf scene, wagons, horses, shipping, &c. MANCHESTER BK., Manchester, N. H.	Same as left. Portrait.
500	Indian paddling canoe. 500 MANCHESTER BK., Manchester, N. H. D D	500 Justice.
1 Female erect with shield and spear.	MECHANICS' B'K, Concord, N. H. 1 View of a street with bank and other buildings.	1

Left	Centre	Right
ONE Portrait of Washington 1	Child's head. Interior of a blacksmith's shop. Child's head. MECHANICKS' B'K, Concord, N. H.	1 Portrait. ONE
TWO Ship building. 2	2 Interior of a blacksmith's shop. TWO MECHANICKS' B'K, Concord, N. H.	2 Female, eagle and bust of Washington TWO
2 Same as vig. of ones.	2 MECHANICKS' B'K, Concord, N. H. 2	Justice erect
THREE Female, 3	3 Interior of a blacksmith's shop. THREE MECHANICKS' B'K, Concord, N. H.	3 Female and ships. THREE
3 Wheels and bales. 3	MECHANICKS' B'K, Concord, N. H. Same as ones.	3 Safe. 3
5 Pierce.	Same as ones. MECHANICKS' B'K, Concord, N. H.	5 Large fig. 5 surrounded by five females.
FIVE Portrait of Van Buren. 5	V Farmers, cattle and sheep. FIVE MECHANICKS' B'K, Concord, N. H.	5 Portrait of Jackson. FIVE
TEN Portrait of Jefferson. 10	X Farmer sowing seed. X MECHANICKS' B'K, Concord, N. H.	10 Portrait of Jackson. TEN
TEN Same as the X	MECHANICKS' B'K, Concord, N. H. vignette on ones.	10 Pierce. TEN
20 TWENTY Female portrait	MECHANICKS' B'K, Concord, N. H. Same as ones.	20 DOLLARS Male portrait

Left	Centre	Right
20 Portrait of Franklin. TWENTY	Female in foreground; harvest scene in background. Canal and boat. MECHANICKS' B'K, Concord, N. H.	XX General Washington 20
FIFTY Agricultural produce, etc. FIFTY	50 Three females seated, pole, cap, eagle, scales, ship, etc. MECHANICKS' BK., Concord, N. H.	FIFTY or 50. Vulcan seated by anvil.
FIFTY Female. FIFTY	50 Man and horse. 50 MECHANICKS' B'K, Concord, N. H.	FIFTY Female. FIFTY
Words One Hundred and figures 100. Portrait of Harrison.	Female on a wharf. MECHANICKS' B'K, Concord, N. H.	Words One Hundred and figures 100. Portrait of Columbus.
1 Boy with fruit.	MECH. & TRA. B'K. Portsmouth, N. H. Red fig. 1. Vessel sailing. Cogwheel, spindles, etc.	1 1
1 Head of Washington.	Female 1 Female. MECHANICS' AND TRADERS' BANK, Portsmouth, N. H.	1 Head of Franklin.
2	Female with sheaf; man reaping, house, etc. in distance. Red 2. Title of Bank. 2 2	2 Old man, child and bust of Washington.
2 Head.	Female. 2 Female. MECHANICS' AND TRADERS' BANK, Portsmouth, N. H.	2 Head.
3 Washington, full length.	Female head and bust. 3 Female head and bust. MECHANICS' AND TRADERS' BANK, Portsmouth, N. H.	3 Vulcan, full length.
3 Red word THREE	Title of Bank. Female, sheep, farmhouse, etc. Red 3 Eagle.	3 Two children

Left	Centre	Right
Eagle resting on United States shield and an anchor. FIVE	A large V, with female figure and child. MECHANICS' AND TRADERS' BANK, Portsmouth, N. H.	5 Female figure and basket.
Male figure seated on machinery; cars at distance. TEN	X MECHANICS' AND TRADERS' BANK, Portsmouth, N. H.	10 Male figure with sheaf in hand.
20 Female figure seated.	XX Eagle. XX MECHANICS' AND TRADERS' BANK, Portsmouth, N. H.	20 Ship with sails partly furled.
FIFTY Female figure holding a wreath. FIFTY	50 Man and horse 50 MECHANICS' AND TRADERS' BANK, Portsmouth, N. H.	FIFTY. Female figure holding horn of plenty. FIFTY
Figures 100 and words one hundred. Head of Harrison.	Wagon with horses and goods; ship at a distance. MECHANICS' AND TRADERS' BANK, Portsmouth, N. H.	Figures 100 and words one hundred. Head and bust of male.
ONE Female portrait. ONE	1 Farming plowing with two horses. MERRIMACK CO. BK Concord, N. H. Bull.	1 Female portrait.
TWO Washington TWO	Deers, Indians in canoe, hills, trees, &c.; on a rock on left, in words "Penny Cook, 1725." MERRIMACK CO. BK Concord, N. H. Agricultural implements.	2 Indian female with bow.
5 Female erect with sword and scales.	Female soaring with eagle; shield, pole and cap, and horn of flowers. MERRIMACK CO. BK Concord, N. H. Deer.	5 Farmer with sheaf on his knee.
10 Female.	Female seated, with eagle; pole, cap and sheaf; shield on safe, &c. MERRIMACK CO. BK Concord, N. H. Agricultural implements	10 Female on either side of a shield. 10
20 Female erect	Female seated on plow, with sickle, sheaf, &c.; on right, train of cars; on left, canal scene. 20 MERRIMACK CO BK Concord, N. H. Bull.	20 Figure with spear, shield and owl.

Left end	Centre	Right end
50 Female seated; sheaf, plow, &c., on her right.	Train of cars; two men in foreground. MERRIMACK CO. BK Concord, N. H. Agricultural implements and products.	50 Female seated, with spear and shield; ship on left.
100 Vulcan seated with sledge.	Spread eagle on branch of tree; cars and canal in background. MERRIMACK CO. BK Concord, N. H. 100	100 Female with rake.
1 Female operative drawing-in.	River, falls, locks, rows of old mills, island, village and hills in the distance. MERRIMACK RIVER BANK. Manchester, N. H.	1 Female portrait.
2 Two wheelwrights employed in mending farmers wagons.	Title of Bank. Vig. Same as ones.	2 Mill girl with shuttle, and shop boy with hammer and anvil. TWO
Three females on a cliff overlooking the ocean, one resting right hand on anchor; one with sheaf under her arm.	Title of Bank. Vig. Same as ones. 3	3
5 Indian overlooking the Falls.	Title of Bank. Female seated in large letter V with sheaf.	5 Portrait of female.
10 Mechanic with hammer and anvil.	Title of Bank. Bust of Washington, Continental soldiers, Indians, and figure of Liberty.	10 Figure of Liberty.
20 The Genius of Manufactures and Mechanics.	Title of Bank. Landing of Roger Williams among the friendly Indians.	20 Arms of the United States.
Design illustrating the tariff protecting American productions.	Title of Bank. American Eagle.	50 Dairy maid; farmhouse and village church.
100 Female resting on tablet; village in distance.	MERRIMACK RIVER BANK, Manchester, N. H.	100 Train of cars and village, lake and scenery in distance.

Left end	Centre	Right end
1 Head of Washington.	Female. 1 Female. MONANDOCK BANK. East Jeffrey, N. H.	1 Head of Franklin.
2 Head.	Female. 2 Female. MONANDOCK BANK. East Jeffrey, N. H.	2 Head.
3 Washington, full length.	Female head and bust. 3 Female head and bust. MONANDOCK BANK, East Jeffrey, N. H.	3 Vulcan, full length.
Spread eagle; city and vessels in distance. FIVE	Large V, female and Cupid. MONANDOCK BANK, East Jeffrey, N. H.	5 Portrait of a girl.
Vulcan seated; train of cars, &c., in distance. TEN	X MONANDOCK BANK, East Jeffrey, N. H.	10 Farmer with sheaf of wheat and sickle.
20 Female sitting, right hand upon a book.	XX Eagle. XX MONANDOCK BANK East Jeffrey, N. H.	20 Ship under sail.
FIFTY Female. FIFTY	50 Man and horse. 50 MONANDOCK BANK, East Jeffrey, N. H.	FIFTY Female. FIFTY
Words one hundred running across figures 100. Male portrait	Dog cart, into which men are rolling barrels, horses, shipping, &c. MONANDOCK BK. East Jeffrey, N. H	Words one hundred running across figures 100. Male portrait
ONE Girl and dog. 1	1 An Indian with bow and arrows. ONE NASHUA BANK, Nashua N. H	1 Girl with rake. ONE
TWO Milkmaid with pail and stool.	Reapers. TWO NASHUA BANK. N. H.	2 Girl knitting. TWO

Left end	Centre	Right end
THREE Full length figure of Justice with scales and sword.	3 Hall road cars and workmen with pick and wheelbarrow. THREE NASHUA BANK, Nashua, N. H.	3 Washington, standing by the side of horse. THREE
V 5	Eagle on limb of a tree, loaded canal boats, locomotive and cars in the distance; on right large V. NASHUA BANK, Nashua, N. H.	5 Portrait of girl with sprig in left hand.
TEN Head of Washington. 10	Female and Steamship, Mercury. NASHUA BANK, Nashua, N. H	10 Head of Lafayette. X
20 Woman with spear, globe, &c.	2 Female seated. 0 NASHUA BANK N. H. XX	20 Female seated. 20
50 Full length figure of female, pedestal, &c.	Male and female seated; flowers, &c. NASHUA BANK, N. H.	50 Cupid in small boat. 50
100 Male seated with sledge and hammer.	Spread eagle on branch of tree; train of cars on left, canal boat, &c., on right. NASHUA BANK. N. H.	100 Female seated, with flowers
Spread eagle, shield, Capitol at Washington. 1	1 NEW IPSWICH B'K. New Ipswich, N. H. 1	1 Milkmaid seated with pail.
Farmer, man and sheep; mills in distance. 2	Heads of Hancock and Adams. NEW IPSWICH B'K. New Ipswich, N. H.	TWO Woman with wreath. TWO
Man on horseback; another with scythe cattle. 3	NEW IPSWICH B'K. New Ipswich, N. H.	THR3EE Girl with flowers on shoulder. THREE
Washington. 3	Steamships and ship at sea. NEW IPSWICH BK., New Ipswich, N. H.	3 Webster.

Left end	Centre	Right end
Woman in the air holding shield, eagle beyond. 5	5 NEW IPSWICH B'K, New Ipswich, N. H.	5 State Arms.
Declaration of Independence; numerous heads. X	X NEW IPSWICH B'K, New Ipswich, N. H.	10 Locomotive, man with wheelbarrow
20 Woman with spear and globe.	2 Female sitting. 0 NEW IPSWICH B'K, New Ipswich, N. H. XX	20 20
50 Woman with balance, pillar.	Woman and man seated, flowers between them. NEW IPSWICH B'K, New Ipswich, N. H. 50	50 Cupid in sail boat. 50
100 Man seated hand on sword and scroll.	Eagle on branch of tree, cars and canal boat in distance. NEW IPSWICH B'K, New Ipswich, N. H. 100	100 Woman with flowers.
Indian in canoe. 500	5 0 0 NEW IPSWICH B'K, New Ipswich, N. H. D D	500 Woman with snake.
Ornamental work. Boy's head. ONE	1 Female seated on bales, with roll of cloth; factories, road, &c., on right; falls and village on left. 1 NEW MARKET B'K, New Market, N. H.	Ornamental work. Girl's head. ONE
2 Male portrait	Farmers harvesting grain, female and child in front; men loading hay cart in background. Cart. Title of Bank. Mechanical implements.	2 Female feeding chickens.
Cupid. 3	Female pouring water in trough; sheep drinking. NEW MARKET B'K, 3 N. H. 3	3 Old man, child, and bust of Washington.
5 Male portrait	Title of Bank. Declaration of Independence. Eagle.	5 Cass.
Ornamental work. 10	Portrait of Webster. Title of Bank. Farmer and drover bargaining for ox; barn yard scene. Horse.	10 Justice.
20 on ornamental work. Henry Clay	Two females with wings, and two Cupids entwined in fig. 20 in clouds. Figs 20 either side of vig. NEW MARKET B'K, N. H.	20 on ornamental work. Andrew Jackson.
Ornamental work. Female figure of Liberty; U. S. Capitol in distance.	50 Title of Bank. Large portrait of Washington.	50 Head of female.
Spread eagle, shield, etc. 100	Ship on stocks. Title of Bank.	100 Head of Indian female.
Eagle on shield. 1	PAWTUCKAWAY BANK, Epping, N. H. Horses with shield and Indian, shield surmounted by an eagle; steamboat, rail cars, and factories in distance.	1 Indian squaw and papoose.
Female 2	PAWTUCKAWAY BANK, Epping, N. H. On right two female figures, one kneeling with a sickle in hand; portrait of Washington; milkmaid and cows on left.	2 TWO 2
State arms. 5	PAWTUCKAWAY BANK, Epping, N. H. Large V and word five.	5 Portrait.
Female portrait. 10	PAWTUCKAWAY BANK, Epping, N. H. Shield; on left Indians; on right woman and children studying globe.	10 X 10
Portrait of Webster. XX	PAWTUCKAWAY BANK, Epping, N. H. Farming scene; sheaf of grain.	20 Two female figures.
Portrait of Cass. 50	PAWTUCKAWAY BANK, Epping, N. H. Female figure and iron chest; ship building, sheep, &c., on right	50 Female holding globe in right hand, staff in left.
Cupid—a fountain of water. 1	PENNICHUCK B'K, Nashua, N. H. Indian female seated.	1 Portrait of Washington.
Female erect with glass in hand. TWO	State Arms and eagle; female on either side; cars, factories, steamboat and man plowing in distance. PENNICHUCK B'K, Nashua, N. H. Man plowing with horses.	2 Portrait of Pierce.
Sailor with flag. THREE	Title of Bank. Three females seated with sickle, etc. Load of hay.	3 Portrait of Clay.
Sailor, Indian, female, etc. 5	Large V, female within. PENNICHUCK B'K, Nashua, N. H. Mechanic seated.	5 Portrait of Cass.
Male portrait. X	Female seated; cows, milkmaids, engine, ship, etc. PENNICHUCK B'K, Nashua, N. H.	10 Female with liberty cap and declaration of Independence.
Indian portrait. XX	Female with liberty cap; portrait of Washington; factories and vessels. PENNICHUCK B'K, Nashua, N. H.	20 Dam and water fall.
Female with calve seated 50	Man seated with elbow resting on a column; two men etc., team of horses. PENNICHUCK B'K, Nashua, N. H.	50 Portrait of Jackson.
Portrait of Webster. 100	Cattle, sheep and two men with horse and dog. PENNICHUCK B'K, Nashua, N. H.	100 Hunter with dog, gun and game.
ONE 1 Webster.	PETERBOROUGH BANK, Peterborough, N. H. Spread Eagle and shield.	1 ONE Washington
TWO DOLLARS 2	Horses running, man on horseback in distance. PETERBOROUGH Peterborough, N. H.	2 TWO DOLLARS

THREE	Men Loading Hay. 3 on Three. PETERBOROUGH BANK. Peterborough, N. H.	THREE
FIVE	PETERBOROUGH BANK, Peterborough. N. H. Drove of sheep, and dogs, man on horseback, mill in distance. FIVE	5 Pierce.
Ship on stocks. Word "Ten" letter "X," and figures "10."	PETERBOROUGH BANK. Peterborough, N. H. Female and raft, cotton mill in distance.	10 Woman drawing water, steamboat in distance.
20 Three female figures.	PETERBOROUGH BANK, Peterborough. N. H.	XX Clay.
50 Signing Declaration of Independence.	PETERBOROUGH BANK. Peterborough. N. H.	50 Jackson
ONE Female feeding fowls.	1 Man seated by basket of fruit and cradle; load of hay in distance. PINE RIVER BANK, Ossipee, N. H. ONE ONE	1 Child's head.
Justice erect and Minerva seated. Two dollars.	Cattle, sheep and colt; boy on horse. PINE RIVER BANK, Ossipee, N. H. TWO TWO	2 Female with flowers.
3 Man cutting down a tree.	3 Blacksmith shop; man shoeing horse; Jackass tied to Anvil; cars in distance. PINE RIVER BANK, Ossipee, N. H. THREE THREE	3 Boy's head.
Justice erect FIVE	Ox; house and cows in distance. PINE RIVER BANK, Ossipee, N. H. FIVE FIVE	5 Female churning.
Heaper X	Males and females, views, etc. PINE RIVER BANK, Ossipee, N. H. Ten Dollars Ten Dollars	10 Franklin.

Indian on a cliff.	Female on either side of shield, surmounted by an eagle; steamboat in distance. PINE RIVER BANK, Ossipee, N. H. TWENTY TWENTY	20 Male portrait 20
FIFTY Washington	L on American shield; eagle at top surrounded by flags. PINE RIVER BANK, Ossipee, N. H. FIFTY FIFTY	50 50
100 100	Female seated; letter C; factories and bridge in distance. PINE RIVER BANK, Ossipee, N. H. ONE HUNDRED	100 D. Webster.
1 Female with sickle. 1	Ship on stocks. Winged female seated holding fig. 1. Vessel bows, bales, &c. PISCATAQUA EXCHANGE BANK, Portsmouth, N. H. Male Portrait.	1 Female. 1
Large figure 2; Portrait of Washington and ship on stocks within.	Farmer plowing with two horses; houses, and steamboat in distance. PISCATAQUA EXCHANGE BANK. Portsmouth. N. H.	Large figure 2, Portrait of Franklin and vessels with in.
3 Sailor erect with quadrant. THREE	Vessels in stocks, men at work, &c.; sloop and city in distance. PISCATAQUA EXCHANGE BANK, Portsmouth. N. H.	3 Farmer whetting scythe. THREE
5 Med. Head. 5	Male Portrait. Letter V, and female with sheaf within. Portrait of Washington. PISCATAQUA EXCHANGE BANK, Portsmouth. N. H.	5 Ship on Stocks. 5
10 Female seated, shield, &c. 10	Med. Head of Franklin. Large letter X and portraits of 10 of the Presidents of the U. S. Med. Head. PISCATAQUA EXCHANGE BANK, Portsmouth, N. H.	10 Ship on Stocks. 10
20 Portrait of Washington. 20	Portrait of Wm. Penn. Female seated with kid on knee, two cows; female milking &c. Portrait of Franklin. Title of Bank. Spread Eagle.	20 Vessel on stocks. 20
100 Washington. 100	Vessels. Two female seated, buildings on right, ship on left. Vessel on stocks. PISCATAQUA EXCHANGE BANK. Portsmouth, N. H. Agricultural Implements.	100 Male portrait 100

1	Female seated; train of cars, sloop, and steamboat on right, on left canal, lock, &c. Large 1, and five men. PITTSFIELD BANK, Pittsfield, N. H.	1 Female bearing load on her head.
2	Man and two boys; two sheep in water; drove on left, and buildings on right. Large 2 and five men. Title of Bank	TWO Female seated. TWO
3	Man on horseback, cattle, dog, and man; load of hay entering barn, likewise three men; in distance city. 3 Title of Bank	Word three and figure 3. Female erect with basket of flowers. THREE
Spread eagle; city and vessels in distance. FIVE	Large V, female and Cupid. Title of Bank	5 Portrait of a girl.
Vulcan seated; train of cars, &c., in distance. TEN	X Title of Bank	10 Farmer with sheaf of wheat and sickle.
20 Female with spear.	2 Female. 0 Title of Bank XX	20 Female seated. 20
50 Female with spear.	Male and female seated. Title of Bank. 50	50 Cupid in boat. 50
100 Man with staff, anchor.	Vig. Spread eagle upon branch of tree; canal scene on right; train of cars crossing bridge on left. Title of Bank 100	100 Female with rake, seated beside cornucopia.
ONE Figure of Justice, holding sword and balance.	Train of cars. ROCHESTER BANK, Rochester, N. H. Carding machine.	ONE Washington standing by his horse. ONE
2 Eagle and shield. 2	Three female figures. TWO ROCHESTER BANK. Rochester, N. H. Dog, key and chest	2 Female; Goddess of Liberty, with shield and trident. 2

Left	Centre	Right
THREE Stone cutter 3	Female reclining; eagle; globe; ships in distance. ROCHESTER BANK, Rochester, N. H. Female and bee-hive.	THREE Blacksmith 3
5 Franklin. 5	Drover on horse, with cattle and sheep. ROCHESTER BANK, Rochester, N. H. Deer.	5 Washington. 5
10 Female head. TEN	Female with key on right; sheaf on left. ROCHESTER BANK, Rochester, N. H.	10 Female head. TEN
20 Minerva; Goddess of wisdom, with spear and helmet; an owl and globe.	Female sitting with rake; between 2 and 0. ROCHESTER BANK, Rochester, N. H. XX	20 Female reclining 20
FIFTY. 50	50 Three females seated, eagle on left; sheep on right. ROCHESTER BANK, N. H.	FIFTY on 50 Blacksmith; anvil, cars in distance, &c.
C Fisherman and boat. 100	Eagle on bale; grain, flowers, &c. 100 ROCHESTER BANK, N. H.	100 Female, sickle and grain. 100
500	Indian paddling a canoe. 500 ROCHESTER BANK, Rochester, N. H.	500 Justice, with sword and scales.
1000	Eagle on cliff; sea and ship in distance. 1000 ROCHESTER BANK, Rochester, N. H.	1000 Indian female warrior with bow and arrow.
1 Portrait of John Jay.	View of the U. S. Capitol. ROCKINGHAM B'K, Portsmouth, N. H. American eagle.	1 Sea nymph.
TWO Steamship.	Portrait of Taylor. Portrait of Fillmore. ROCKINGHAM B'K, Portsmouth, N. H.	2 Brigantine.

Left	Centre	Right
3 Portrait of Henry Clay.	ROCKINGHAM B'K. Portsmouth, N. H. Portrait THREE of DOLLARS Daniel Webster.	3 Portrait of John C. Calhoun.
5 Sailor leaning on a capstan.	View of war ships near the Navy Yard, Portsmouth, N. H. ROCKINGHAM B'K. Portsmouth, N. H.	5 Portrait of Mrs. Crittenden.
10 Portrait of girl.	View of a ship of the line, and merchant ship under sail. ROCKINGHAM B'K. Portsmouth, N. H.	10 Blacksmith near a forge.
Figure of a female representing Young America. 20	ROCKINGHAM B'K, Portsmouth, N. H. Portrait of Daniel Webster.	20 American eagle.
Sailor holding the American flag FIFTY.	Steamship of the Collins' line. ROCKINGHAM B'K, Portsmouth, N. H.	50 Figure of a female with horn of plenty, &c.
American eagle on a shield. 100	Portrait of Washington. ROCKINGHAM B'K. Portsmouth, N. H.	100
1 Washington.	Female 1 Female SALMON FALLS BK., Rollingsford, N. H.	1 Franklin.
2 Columbus.	Female 2 Female SALMON FALLS BK., Rollingsford, N. H.	2 Portrait.
3 Washington and horse.	Female Portrait. 3 Female Portrait. SALMON FALLS BK., Rollinsford, N H.	3 Vulcan at his forge.
Eagle on rock with wings extended. FIVE	Large V. Female and Cupid. SALMON FALLS BK., Rollingsford, N. H.	5 Female Portrait.

Left	Centre	Right
Vulcan the Blacksmith. TEN	X SALMON FALLS BK. Rollingsford, N. H.	10 Reaper.
20 Female sitting.	XX Eagle XX SALMON FALLS BK., Rollinsford, N. H.	20 Ship.
FIFTY Female standing. FIFTY	50 Man and Horse 50 SALMON FALLS BK., Rollinsford, N. H.	FIFTY Female standing. FIFTY
ONE HUNDRED and figures 100. Portrait of Harrison.	Loading baggage wagon, horse shipping at wharf. SALMON FALLS BK., Rollinsford, N. H.	ONE HUNDRED and figures 100. Portrait.
1	Farmers at lunch. 1 SOMMERSWORTH BANK, Sommersworth, N. H. Load of hay.	1 Sailor.
2	Farmers at lunch; dog and sheaf of wheat. 2 Title of Bank Blacksmith and anvil.	2 Sailor boy pulling oar.
3	Girls tending looms. 3 Title of Bank Cattle.	3 Eagle. Train of cars.
5	Man plowing with horses. 5 Title of Bank Man plowing	5 Portrait of Washington.
Portrait of a boy. X	Drove of cattle. Title of Bank. Horses. TEN TEN	X Men cradling wheat.
Female representing liberty, with eagle. XX	Artist drawing plans; stone cutters and tools in distance. Title of Bank. Bale and machinery.	20 Female head.

Left	Centre	Right
Blacksmith at anvil. 50	Mechanic in a sitting posture, leaning his arm upon a steam boiler; workmen in distance. Title of Bank Safe.	50 Factory building.
Female figure of Justice. 100	Female with shield, sheaf of wheat and horn of plenty. Title of Bank Anvil, hammer and boiler.	100 Stone cutter at work.
Female figure representing agriculture; reapers in distance. 500	500 D Title of Bank.	500
Laocoon and sons struggling with the serpent. 1000	THOUSAND Train of cars. Title of Bank.	1000 Vessels. 1000
Female with American shield. 1	SOUHEGAN BANK, Milford, N. H. Blacksmith shoeing a horse.	1 Male portrait
Indian female; Arms of 20 States for the border. 2	State Arms surmounted by an eagle, female on either side. SOUHEGAN BANK, Milford, N. H.	2 Portrait of Washington
3 Farmer.	SOUHEGAN BANK, Milford, N. H. Landscape.	3 Farmer's wife.
Female with scales and sheaf of wheat. 5	Figure 5, surrounded by five females. SOUHEGAN BANK, Milford, N. H. 5	5 Figure 5, and five females.
10 Female churning.	Train of cars. SOUHEGAN BANK, Milford, N. H.	X Female seated.
Fancy female head. 20	Farmers nooning. SOUHEGAN BANK, Milford, N. H. Loading hay	20 Fancy female head.

Left	Centre	Right
Female figure of Justice.	Boat making device; fig. 50 on left. SOUHEGAN BANK, Milford, N. H. Shield, bales, etc	50 Fancy female head.
Female reclining with tride 1. 100	Arms of the Union; eagle, letter U on shield. SOUHEGAN BANK, Milford, N. H. Liberty.	100 Female representing Agriculture.
Female reclining on bale with scales in right hand. 1	STATE CAPITAL BK. Concord, N. H. Female reclining with pole and cap; eagle and motto "E Pluribus Unum," on right; in distance on left, steamer and ship.	1 Female with sickle, leaning on ornamental figure 1.
2	STATE CAPITAL BK. Concord, N. H. Male at work on chart with compass; on right, three men, two horses and cart. TWO	2 Female sporting with a swan in water.
THREE Female erect with pole, cap and scroll in hands; shield scales, &c.	STATE CAPITAL BK. Concord, N. H. Milkmaid seated, with pail on lap; five cows on her left.	3 Female portrait.
5 Female portrait.	STATE CAPITAL BK. Concord, N. H. Five females; figure 5 between two of them, &c.; on left, vessel, &c.; on right building, locomotive and tender.	5 Figure 5 surrounded by five human figures.
Female seated on rock, with pole and cap. 10	Indian female crowning bust with wreath; on right of bust, female with pole and cap, bbl., bale, ship, &c.; sheaf, fruit, &c., on left of Indian female STATE CAPITAL BK. Concord, N. H.	X Man seated with rake; left arm resting on figure, on which is "Ten."
XX XX	STATE CAPITAL BK. Concord, N. H. Harvest scene; man, female and child; man with sickle—another sharpening scythe, and one reclining on ground; loading wagon on right.	20 Female barefooted, with sheaf of grain.
50 Blacksmith shoeing horse, colt present; anvil, &c.; steam engine.	STATE CAPITAL BANK, Concord, N. H. FIFTY	50 Female feeding horse from apron.
100 Portrait of Frank Pierce	STATE CAPITAL BK. Concord, N. H. Farmer, wife and children in sitting posture; farm houses; load of grain, dog, &c. One Hundred	Large letter "C." Cupid astride of a sea monster.

Left	Centre	Right
1 Head of Washington.	Cows, woman milking, another woman seated. STRAFFORD BANK, Dover, N. H.	1 Female scribe and Eagle.
2 Head of Franklin.	Dog and safe. STRAFFORD BANK, Dover, N. H.	2 Eagle.
3 Female bust	Female, plough, sheaf and sickle; cars in distance. STRAFFORD BANK, Dover, N. H.	3 Med. head.
5 Indian female seated.	STRAFFORD BANK, Dover, N. H. Fame with trumpet; globe and eagle. 5 5	5 Female leaning on a column.
10 Head of Judge Marshall.	Female leaning on bale of goods; men loading hay. 10 STRAFFORD BANK, Dover, N. H.	TEN Female with a sheaf. 10
20 Locomotive & building.	Female with her arms extended; boy on each side. STRAFFORD BANK Dover, N. H.	20 Female, sickle and sheaf
50 Female holding scale. 50	Two females; ship, buildings and cars in the distance. STRAFFORD BANK Dover, N. H.	50 Man standing among corn.
100 Sailor with hat off, holding a flag	STRAFFORD BANK, Dover, N. H. Female and cherub in a cloud over sky.	100 Ship. 100
500 Female.	STRAFFORD BANK, Dover, N. H. FIVE HUNDRED Three females, cars and vessel in the distance.	500 500
M Two females; ships; buildings and cars in distance. 1000	STRAFFORD BANK, Dover, N. H. ONE THOUSAND	1000 1000

Left	Centre	Right
1 Milkmaid. ONE	Harvest scene. SUGAR RIVER B'K. Newport, N. H.	1 Locomotive.
2 Eagle on top of shield; female on right with quadrant.	2 Harvest scene; man on horse. SUGAR RIVER B'K. Newport, N. H.	2 Squaw and pappoose.
THREE	SUGAR RIVER B'K. Newport, N. H. Commerce, Agriculture, and Manufacture.	3
FIVE	FIVE Sailor, mechanic, and farmer offering grain to Liberty; eagle on her right. SUGAR RIVER B'K. Newport, N. H.	5 Eagle and Liberty; shield and figure 5.
X Two men with rakes.	SUGAR RIVER B'K. Newport, N. H. Spread eagle and shield; on either side vessels.	10 Two females, one kneeling with sickle and grain.
Figure of Justice with shield.	20 Little girl; men plowing with oxen. SUGAR RIVER B'K. Newport, N. H.	20 Female, grain, and sickle.
Liberty with heavy drapery and shield.	Three females. SUGAR RIVER B'K. Newport, N. H.	50
Female giving eagle drink. 100	Shield with portrait of Washington, eagle at top; on either side Liberty, Truth, and Justice. SUGAR RIVER B'K. Newport, N. H.	100 Male head. 100
1 ONE	United States Capitol. Female head UNION BANK, Concord, N. H.	1 Female portrait
2 Male portrait TWO	UNION BANK, Concord, N. H. Medallion head on shield; Indian and two females on each; on left soldier.	2 Male portrait TWO

Left	Centre	Right
THREE 3 Wm. Penn.	Boys attempting to catch horse, dog, etc. UNION BANK, Concord, N. H.	3 Blacksmith and implements.
5 Battle scene—female loading gun; old man gazing at troops below.	Vessel at dock; cars, drays, &c. UNION BANK, Concord, N. H.	5 Male portrait
10 Washington	Launching of a steamship; city in background. UNION BANK, Concord, N. H.	10 Female feeding fowls.
20 Farmer, horse, dog, pigeons, etc.	Scene in blacksmith's shop; old man and boy hammering. Title of Bank.	20 Milkmaid, cow and calf.
50 Female seated with sheaf and sickle.	Title of Bank. Cattle, sheep, stream, etc.	50 Webster.
C Man and boy mending carts.	Title of Bank. Female in clouds with eagle, pole, cap, shield, etc. 100 on left.	100 Female portrait.
ONE Ship building scene. ONE	VALLEY BANK, Hillsborough, N.H. Boy, two horses, female, etc. at trough.	1 Female portrait
TWO Female with flowers.	Female with eagle, and shield; steamer, etc. VALLEY BANK, Hillsborough, N. H.	2 Child's head.
3	White and black horse; cattle, trees, etc. VALLEY BANK, Hillsborough, N.H.	3 Two Indians
5 Farmer with scythe	5 Female portrait 5 VALLEY BANK, Hillsborough, N.H.	5 Female with smoking urn and flowers.

Left	Centre	Right
10 Youthful portrait	Boy and child on bank; cattle in stream. VALLEY BANK, Hillsborough, N.H. 10	10 Child's head
Female with sword and shield. 20	Cattle, stream, etc. VALLEY BANK, Hillsborough, N.H.	20 Dog & safe.
100 THE 0	Female head. VALLEY BANK, Boy, child, cattle, sheep, etc. Hillsborough, N.H.	100 Youthful portrait.
ONE Medallion figure.	1 Two blacksmiths and anvil. 1 WARNER BANK, Warner, N. H.	ONE Figure of a girl. ONE
TWO Lady's head resting on her hand, elbows on table. 2	2 Haying scene. Girl standing with rake handing cup of water to two men seated on the ground. 2 WARNER BANK, Warner, N. H.	TWO Lady with a sickle resting over her shoulder. 2
FIVE	Spread eagle standing on a shield. V, female and cupid. WARNER BANK, Warner N. H.	5 Girl with Basket of Flowers in her hand.
TEN	Blacksmith seated hammer in his hand, resting on an anvil, wheel by his side on the ground. X WARNER BANK, Warner, N. H.	10 Man tying up a bundle of grain, sickle in his hand.
20 Lady seated looking over shoulder.	XX Eagle. XX WARNER BANK, Warner, N. H.	20 Ship
FIFTY Female. FIFTY	50 Man leading a rearing horse. 50 WARNER BANK, Warner, N. H.	FIFTY Female. FIFTY
ONE HUNDRED and figures 100. Male Portrait.	Wharf scene; team loading a covered team wagon, &c. WARNER BANK, Warner, N. H.	ONE HUNDRED and figures 100. Male Portrait.

Left	Centre	Right
ONE Female head. 1	Man on horseback with drove of cattle and sheep, &c. WEARE BANK, Hampton Falls, N. H.	1 Portrait of Gov. Baker. ONE
Portrait of Gov. Baker. 2	Man plowing with two horses. WEARE BANK, Hampton Falls, N. H. Loading hay.	2 Female with basket of fruits, sickle, sheaf of grain, sitting on a plough
Goddess of Liberty feeding eagle. 3	Husbandman sitting with sheaf of grain and a cradling scythe lying near; mowing and loading grain in the background. WEARE BANK, Hampton Falls, N. H. Cow and calf.	3 Portrait of Gov. Baker.
FIVE Justice standing with sword and scales; Mars sitting with spear and shield, book and globe near.	Two trains of cars. WEARE BANK, Hampton Falls, N. H.	5 Portrait of Gov. Baker. FIVE
Boy standing with sheaf of grain under his arm, and farm girl sitting leaning on pail. X	Two men with horse and dog, driving a drove of cattle part of them laying down. WEARE BANK, Hampton Falls, N. H.	10 Man sitting on plough. X
Man sharpening a cradling scythe. 20	Ganymede and the eagle; ship under sail in the distance; cornucopia lying in front. WEARE BANK, Hampton Falls, N. H. Two horses	XX Portrait of Washington.
Portrait of Jefferson. 50	Ceres sitting by cornucopia; ship under sail in distance on left. WEARE BANK, Hampton Falls, N. H. Man ploughing with two horses.	50 Female churning.
1	Female seated; train of cars, sloop, and steamboat on right; on left canal, lock, &c. Large 1, and five men. WHITE MOUNTAIN BANK, Lancaster, N. H.	1 Female seated with head on her hand.
ONE Two girls with sheafs.	Cupid rolling silver dollar on track; cars, steamboat, city, etc., in distance. WHITE MOUNTAIN BANK, Lancaster, N. H.	1 Cattle, sheep, hogs, etc.
TWO Female and squaw.	2 Santa Claus in sleigh drawn by reindeers over roofs of houses. Title of Bank.	2 Cars; bridge, cars, etc, in distance.
2	Man and two boys; two sheep in water; drove on left, and buildings on right. Large 2 and five men. WHITE MOUNTAIN BANK, Lancaster, N. H.	TWO Female seated. TWO
Three scenes 3. Female portrait.	Title of Bank. Man with scythe; loading hay on left.	THREE across fig. 3. Male portrait
3	Man on horseback, cattle, dog, and man; load of hay entering barn, likewise three men; in distance city. 3 WHITE MOUNTAIN BANK, Lancaster, N. H.	Word three and figure 3. Female seated with basket of flowers. THREE
Female giving eagle drink. 5	Female seated with spy glass shield and wheat; vessels, steamer, lighthouse, etc., in distance. Title of Bank.	5 Male portrait
FIVE	Spread eagle on shield; city and ships in distance. Female, cupid, and letter V. WHITE MOUNTAIN BANK, Lancaster, N. H.	5 Little girl with flowers.
TEN	Vulcan seated, anvil, sledge, &c.; train of cars and buildings in distance. X WHITE MOUNTAIN BANK, Lancaster, N. H.	10 Farmer with sheaf on his knee.
20 Female.	XX Eagle. XX WHITE MOUNTAIN BANK, Lancaster, N. H.	20 Ship sailing.
FIFTY Female erect with wreath. FIFTY	50 Man and horse. 50 WHITE MOUNTAIN BANK, Lancaster, N. H.	FIFTY Female erect FIFTY.
Word one hundred and figure 100. Male portrait.	Wharf scene—loading wagon, men, horses, shipping, &c. WHITE MOUNTAIN BANK, Lancaster, N. H.	Same as on left Male portrait.
ONE Female.	Man ploughing with span of horses. WINCHESTER B'K Winchester, N. H.	1 Female.
Blacksmith. TWO	Female. WINCHESTER B'K. Winchester, N. H.	2 Reaper.
Man cradling grain. THREE	Railroad cars. WINCHESTER B'K. Winchester, N. H. Man and plow.	3 Cattle and swine.
Female. FIVE	Female reclining. WINCHESTER B'K, Winchester, N. H. Shearing sheep.	5 Group of females.
10 Female. TEN	Female. WINCHESTER B'K, Winchester, N. H.	10 Female. TEN
20 Female.	2 Female. 0 WINCHESTER B'K. Winchester, N. H. XX	20 20
50 Female.	Male and female. WINCHESTER B'K. Winchester, N. H. 50	50 Cupid in sailboat. 50
100 Male figure.	Spread eagle on branch of tree; cars and canal boat in distance. WINCHESTER B'K. Winchester, N. H. 100	100 Female.
ONE State arms. ONE	Vig. Ploughman ploughing with oxen and girl by his side. ASCUTNEY BANK. Windsor, Vt. Steam engine.	ONE Head of Washington. 1
TWO Head of Franklin, Tower, &c.	2 Vig. Blacksmith; railroad train in distance. ASCUTNEY BANK. Windsor, Vt. Wheelbarrow, plough and sheaf of grain.	2 State arms. TWO
THREE Medallion head. State arms.	Vig. Two horses and man crossing in front of railroad train; on left, fig. 3. 3 ASCUTNEY BANK. Windsor, Vt. Man's arm, with hammer anvil and tools.	3 Female head. 3

Head with five upon helmet. Head of J. Q. Adams	5 Vig. Man on horseback, driving sheep, with dog; mill in distance; on left, fig. 5, with the word five on top. ASCUTNEY BANK, Windsor, Vt. Eagle.	
X Franklin. TEN	Signing of the Declaration of Independence. Jefferson. Title of Bank.	X John Adams. TEN
FIFTY Female seated; steamboat and ship in distance. 50	Man with gun and two Indians. Head and word "fifty" on helmet, either side. Title of Bank.	FIFTY Female seated. 50
Female with spear supporting ornamental fig. 1. ONE	1 Female seated with left arm on bale, spinning wheel on her right; city, bridge, &c. in distance. BANK OF BELLOWS FALLS. Bellows Falls, Vt. Cars	1
2	Train of cars; Cupid and depot, steam, and fig. 2 boat &c. on left. BANK OF BELLOWS FALLS, Bellows Falls, Vt. Ox and a tree.	TWO Female seated on bale, horn of plenty at her feet.
Large figure 5, in centre of which is portrait of Washington.	Female reclining on sheaf with sickle; in distance men loading wagon with sheaf and city. BANK OF BELLOWS FALLS, Bellows Falls, Vt. Agricultural implements.	5 State arms.
Large X with portrait of female and portrait of Franklin.	Man on horseback, drove of cattle and sheep. BANK OF BELLOWS FALLS. Bellows Falls, Vt.	10 Female with sword and scales.
Female with horn of plenty, pole and cap. 20	BANK OF BELLOWS FALLS. Bellows Falls, Vt. 20 Female seated with wagon, cows and house on left. 20 Cupid on back of reindeer.	20 Sheaf. 20
50 State arms. 50	Title of Bank. 50 Male seated with pole, mechanical implements; ship on left. 50 Spread eagle.	50 Two men and cattle. 50
1 Head of Washington. 1	Vig. Train of cars and two horses. BK OF BL'CK RIVER Proctorsville, Vt Fish.	ONE Female head ONE

TWO Female holding scale and sword. TWO	Vig. Farmers again, two oxen, cart, and men loading hay. BK OF BL'CK RIVER Proctorsville, Vt. Horse and bbl's.	2 Female in a sitting posture with a staff.
THREE Female seated on plow holding a sickle and sheaf of wheat. THREE	Train of cars, female with sickle in hand, two Indians, steamboat in distance. BK OF BL'CK RIVER Proctorsville, Vt Female head.	3 Female head. 3
FIVE Head of B. Franklin. FIVE	Man ploughing with two oxen and horse. BK OF BL'CK RIVER Proctorsville, Vt. Eagle.	5 Female head 5
10 Wharf scene with vessels on the ocean.	Female head. Indian female and child. BK OF BL'CK RIVER Proctorsville, Vt. Engine.	10 Two females holding scales; Seal of State; Freedom and Unity. TEN
TWENTY Male portrait. TWENTY	20 Two Females, one with basket of fruit; XX between. BK OF BL'CK RIVER Proctorsville, Vt. Wheelbarrow and sheaf of grain.	
Female erect holding staff with Flag of our Union; Eagle.	BK OF BL'CK RIVER Proctorsville, Vt. L Three females	50
1 Barrels, bales, ship, &c. 1	ONE DOLLAR 1 Female seated beside bales; ship on left. 1 BK OF BRATTLEBORO, Brattleboro, Vt.	1 Agricultural implements. 1
1 Portrait of Washington.	Female. 1 Female. BANK OF BRATTLEBORO, Brattleboro, Vt.	1 Portrait of Franklin.
2 Washington on horseback 2	TWO DOLLARS 2 Female seated beside fig. 2; flowers, etc. 2 Title of Bank.	2 Washington on horseback 2
2 Male portrait	Female. 2 Female. BANK OF BRATTLEBORO', Brattleboro, Vt.	2 Male portrait

2 TWO 2	Female 2 Female BANK OF BRATTLEBORO, Brattleboro, Vt.	TWO Female. TWO
3 Child's head. 3	THREE DOLLARS 3 Female seated beside fig. 3 3 Title of Bank.	3 Child's head. 3
3 Washington and his horse	Female. 3 Female. BANK OF BRATTLEBORO, Brattleboro, Vt.	3 Male figure
FIVE	Female. 5 BANK OF BRATTLEBORO. Brattleboro, Vt.	5 Ship.
10 X 10	Man and oxen. 10 BANK OF BRATTLEBORO, Brattleboro, Vt.	TEN Female.
X	Signing Declaration of Independence. X Title of Bank.	10 Cars, men, etc.
TEN	Blacksmith seated, sledge, anvil, etc Title of Bank	10 Farmer with sheaf and sickle.
20 Female	XX Eagle. XX BANK OF BRATTLEBORO, Brattleboro, Vt.	20 Ship.
FIFTY Female erect FIFTY	50 Man and horse. 50 BANK OF BRATTLEBORO, Brattleboro, Vt.	FIFTY Female erect FIFTY
Figures 100 and words one hundred Male portrait	Wharf scene, team loading wagon; shipping, &c BANK OF BRATTLEBORO. Brattleboro, Vt.	Figures 100 and words one hundred Male portrait

Left end	Centre	Right end
ONE Female head. ONE	Milkmaid with pail and cows. BANK OF BURLINGTON, Burlington, Vt. Locomotive and tender.	1 Portrait of female. ONE
TWO Portrait of female. TWO	Two females in sitting posture, one with sickle and sheaf; steamboat and sail vessel in distance. BANK OF BURLINGTON, Burlington, Vt. State arms.	2 Female in sitting posture with sheaf and sickle. 2
THREE Goddess of liberty with shield and eagle on right. THREE	Drover on horseback, with cattle and sheep. BANK OF BURLINGTON, Burlington, Vt. Safe, dog and key.	3 Female THREE
5 Portrait of female. FIVE	Side view of spread eagle on a branch; factory and cars in the distance. BANK OF BURLINGTON, Burlington, Vt. Carding machine.	FIVE Female in sitting posture, right hand elevating liberty cap. FIVE
TEN Train of cars on a curve approaching. TEN	Female sitting between 1 and 0; lake and steamer in the distance. BANK OF BURLINGTON, Burlington, Vt. Dog, key and safe.	TEN Young, vulcan at the anvil. X
20 Sheaf of grain. 20	20 Female sitting holding sword in right hand, left resting on pillar, with lion reclining at her left. 20 BANK OF BURLINGTON, Burlington, Vt. Indian in canoe.	TWENTY
50 Ship. 50	50 Female sitting; right hand pointing to vessel, left around a pillar. 50 BANK OF BURLINGTON, Burlington, Vt. Spread eagle.	50 Ship. 50
100 Portrait of Hamilton. 100	100 Female sitting and feeding eagle from urn. 100 BANK OF BURLINGTON, Burlington, Vt. Steamboat.	100 Eagle. 100
ONE Female writing on desk, the desk representing a large figure 1 ONE	1 Man with sheaf on his left shoulder, and cradle on his right arm, shoes dangling from the snath, on the right in the distance a farm house and trees and a flock of sheep before it. 1 B'K OF CALEDONIA, Danville, Vt. Spread eagle.	ONE
TWO Female with bundle of grain in her left hand raised over head forming top of figure 2, Cupid with sickle, &c. TWO	2 Man plowing with a span of horses; ship and steamboat on left and farm house on the right in the background. 2 Title of Bank. Sheaf of Grain and Agricultural Implements.	TWO

Left end	Centre	Right end
THREE Large figure 3 supported by a female and two Cupids. THREE	3 Two men on horseback with drove of cattle and sheep; a covered bridge and shop. 3 B'K OF CALEDONIA, Danville, Vt. Horse.	THREE
FIVE Commerce sitting on a bale of goods in a large V. 5	A large figure 5, supported by five winged Cupids. 5 B'K OF CALEDONIA, Danville, Vt. Indian's Head.	FIVE
TEN Girl with sheaf of grain on her head, basket on her arm; boy sitting with key in his lap dog team and load of grain. TEN	X Mythological scene; the goddess Mercury descending from her car in the clouds with her attendants; one drinking from a vase. X B'K OF CALEDONIA, Danville, Vt. Dove with a motto in its beak.	TEN DOLLARS
20 Man carrying grain; horse, dog, etc.	Cattle dealer selling cow to farmer. BK OF CALEDONIA, Danville, Vt. Boy on horseback.	20 Female portrait
20 Female sitting, right hand upon a book	XX Eagle. XX BK OF CALEDONIA, Danville, Vt.	20 Ship under sail
FIFTY Female figure with wreath of flowers in right hand. FIFTY	50 Man and horse. 50 BK OF CALEDONIA, Danville, Vt. FIFTY DOLLARS	FIFTY Female figure standing, globe in her right hand, flowers at her right FIFTY
50 Man, woman and child. FIFTY	Landing of Roger Williams; Indians, etc. BK. OF CALEDONIA, Danville, Vt.	50 Male portrait
100 Two farmers, woman and babe.	Female seated with bales, etc.; factories, dam and village in distance. Title of Bank.	100 Male portrait
Words One Hundred running across figures 100. Male portrait.	Dray cart, into which men are rolling barrels, horse, shipping, etc. BK OF CALEDONIA, Danville, Vt.	Words One Hundred running across figures 100. Male portrait.
ONE Male Portrait	[First Plate.] BANK OF LYNDON, Lyndon, Vt. Eleven Indians in council; a chief addressing them. Ducks.	1 Portrait of Webster.

Left end	Centre	Right end
ONE	[Second Plate.] Large Spread Eagle. BANK OF LYNDON, Lyndon, Vt. Female bathing.	ONE Three females, anchor, sickle, sheaf of grain
TWO Two females holding aloft sheaf of grain	Three Indians in a canoe, one a female; hills, trees, &c. BANK OF LYNDON, Lyndon, Vt. Dog.	2 Male Portrait
Word THREE and figure 3. Man on horseback.	Cattle scene, 4 cattle, 1 standing 3 lying down, 3 sheep 1 standing 2 lying. BANK OF LYNDON, Lyndon, Vt.	3 Little Girl shading her eyes with left hand.
V Train of cars	Wild horses running. BANK OF LYNDON, Lyndon, Vt. 5 5	5 Portrait of Jackson.
Large number of cattle and men entering and fording a river. 10	BANK OF LYNDON, Lyndon, Vt. Head of Washington.	10 Man on horseback and boy on foot driving sheep.
XX Portrait of an Indian, bow in right hand, left hand over right shoulder drawing arrow from quiver.	Female and Indian seated on either side of view of sunrise, wigwams, ship and city in back ground. BANK OF LYNDON, Lyndon, Vt. Woodman chopping tree.	20 Portrait of S. Houston.
50 Spread Eagle	2 cows lying down, 1 standing, 2 in background, 1 drinking. BANK OF LYNDON, Lyndon, Vt.	50 FIFTY DOLLARS. Portrait of Webster.
C Indian seated with gun and dog, warming his hands at a fire on ground.	1 male and 1 female Indians near wigwam watching and pointing to the approaching train. City, railroad bridge with cars on it, another train coming. BANK OF LYNDON, Lyndon, Vt. Ducks.	100 Portrait of Clay.
1 Washington. 1	1 Farmers and cattle. 1 BANK OF MIDDLEBURY, Middlebury, Vt. 1	1 Head of a Horse. 1
2 Farmers and cattle. 2	TWO TWO Title of Bank. Harvest scene.	2 Three cherubs. 2

Left	Centre	Right
3 Male and female. 3	3 Female with her arm resting upon a wheel. 3 Title of Bank. Female reclining.	3 Farmers and cattle. 3
5 Farmers and cattle. 5	5 Female, eagle and shield; ship in the distance. 5 Title of Bank	Female leaning upon an urn, bearing the name of E. Allen and McDonald; also, winged female with a trumpet. 5
TEN Ten Gold Dollars TEN	10 Vulcan the blacksmith and two females. 10 Title of Bank. Washington.	Child's face. X Child's face
20 Washington. 20	Male and female; sheaf of wheat; canal and reapers in background. Title of Bank. Female bust.	TWENTY
50 Female, eagle and scales; merchandise &c. 50	50 Officer mounted. 50 Title of Bank	FIFTY
100 Female.	Shepherd and sheep; village in the distance. Title of Bank.	100 Female with sheaf of wheat. 100
1 1	BK OF MONTPELIER Montpelier, Vt. Female seated and two cows, one standing and the other lying down. Steamboat.	1 Female.
2 Horse, train of cars in distance.	BK OF MONTPELIER Montpelier, Vt. Female portrait. 2	2 Female. TWO
Female and 3 THREE	3 Female head. BK OF MONTPELIER Montpelier, Vt.	3 Female seated, bales, &c.
State capital. 5	5 BK OF MONTPELIER Montpelier, Vt.	5 Washington.

Left	Centre	Right
State capitol 10	BK OF MONTPELIER Montpelier, Vt	TEN Female with sickle.
Female head. 20	State Capitol. BK OF MONTPELIER Montpelier. Vt. Plough.	20 Head of Pierce.
50 Female 50	Two females; ship, factories and railroad cars in distance. BK OF MONTPELIER Montpelier. Vt.	50 Young man harvesting corn.
100 Sailor with flag in one hand and hat in the other.	BK OF MONTPELIER Montpelier. Vt. Female and cupid over a city.	100 Female head. 100
	BK OF NEWBURY, Wells River, Vt. The 1s, 2s, 3s, 5s, and 10s, are a special stereotype plate with the words "Wells River," in fine letters throughout the upper part of the notes and the denomination in the same manner on lower half	
20 Female with spear.	2 Female. 0 Title of Bank XX	20 Female seated. 20
50 Female with spear.	Male and female seated. Title of Bank. 50	50 Cupid in head. 50
100 Man with sledge, anchor.	Vig. Spread eagle upon branch of tree; canal scene on right; train of cars crossing bridge on left. Title of Bank. 100	100 Female with rake, seated beside cornucopia.
1 Nude female. 1	BANK OF ORLEANS, Irasburg, Vt. 1 Safe and dog.	1 Ox. 1
ONE Head of Washington. ONE	1 Blacksmith's shop. 1 BANK OF ORLEANS, Irasburg. Vt.	ONE Female. ONE

Left	Centre	Right
2 Man with sledge on his shoulder. 2	BANK OF ORLEANS, Irasburg, Vt. 2	2 Milkmaid and two cows. 2
TWO Female. 2	2 Family group. 2 BANK OF ORLEANS, Irasburg, Vt.	TWO 2
3 Man with axe, oxen and cart. 3	BANK OF ORLEANS. Irasburg, Vt. 3 Man shearing sheep.	3 Two males, female and three children.
THREE Man with scythe. Word three and figure 3 across.	3 Female, eagle, anchor, &c. BANK OF ORLEANS, Irasburg. Vt (There is imitations of this plate.)	THREE Sailor. Word three and figure 3 across.
5 Cattle. 5	BANK OF ORLEANS. Irasburg, Vt. Ox.	5 Workmen and boiler. 5
FIVE	Female. V BANK OF ORLEANS, Irasburg, Vt.	Ship.
X	Signing the declaration of Independence. X BANK OF ORLEANS, Irasburg, Vt	10 Train of cars and man with wheel barrow.
X Agricultural scene — load of grain and man on horseback. X	BANK OF ORLEANS, Irasburg, Vt. X	X Two men and a woman in field. X
20 Female sitting, book in left hand, right hand on a box.	XX Eagle. XX BANK OF ORLEANS, Irasburg, Vt.	20 Ship, with buildings in the distance.
FIFTY Female with wreath of flowers on her head and in her hands FIFTY	50 Man and horse. 50 BANK OF ORLEANS, Irasburg, Vt.	FIFTY Female with flowers in her left hand FIFTY

Left end	Centre	Right end
100 Female with cornucopia. 100	100 100 BANK OF ORLEANS, Irasburg, Vt. 100 100	100 Waterfall and eagle. 100
Figures 100, with words one hundred across. Portrait of Harrison.	Covered wagon, wharf, ships, warehouses, truckmen, &c. BANK OF ORLEANS, Irasburg, Vt.	Same as on left end. Portrait of Columbus.
Female with pen, tablets, etc. ONE	1 1 BK of ORANGE CO., Chelsea, Vt. Old man with gun; female loading gun at his back.	Female with pole, cap, &c. ONE
2 TWO Cupid.	Eagle. Title of Bank. Apotheosis of Washington; soldier on left; female and two Indians on right. Fig. 2 on right of vig.	2 Female, cow, calf, fowls, etc.
Female portrait. THREE	Title of Bank. Man and boy plowing with two horses.	3 Agricultural implements and produce.
Title of 5	Bank. Portrait of boy. Man with bag, horse, colt, mill etc.; [illegible] bridge.	5 Female feeding fowls.
10 Man, horse, dog, pigeons, etc.	Title of Bank. Scene in the Arctic Regions; man steering boat; dog, icebergs, etc.	10 Blacksmith at forge.
20 Bull.	Title of Bank. Large portrait of Washington; small [illegible] side at bottom.	20 Two females one milking cows, etc.
50 Female, column, steamer, etc.	Title of Bank. Male, female, horses at trough, etc.	50 Male, female child, etc.
C 100	Title of Bank. Man and woman either side of shield; girl, dog, child, etc.	100 Indian on horse.

Left end	Centre	Right end
ONE Farmer plowing. ONE	1 Two females seated, one with sickle; on right cows, on left a building with large steeple. 1 BK. OF POULTNEY, Poultney, Vt. Agricultural Implements.	ONE Female seated with tub at her feet. ONE
TWO Farmer bare-headed with sheaf of wheat on left shoulder. TWO	2 Two females, one seated the other erect, the one erect has pail in her arms; on right out-house and female milking cow; on right farm house and trees. 2 BK. OF POULTNEY, Poultney, Vt. Horse.	TWO Female erect with cow, pails at her feet. TWO
V Female seated within large letter V. FIVE	5 Two females on either side of a frame, on which is tree, cow, &c., surmounted by head of reindeer. At bottom words "Vermont, Freedom and Unity." 5 BK. OF POULTNEY, Poultney, Vt. Dog's Head.	V Female seated within large figure 5. FIVE
State of X Head of Franklin.	(New Plate) Vermont. Train of cars; village in distance. Female portrait. B'K OF POULTNEY. State Arms of Vermont.	10 Indian female seated; pole, cap and shield.
20 Male with sledge on right shoulder; cog wheel, anvil, &c.	BK. OF POULTNEY, Poultney, Vt. Train of cars; village in distance. Dog's Head.	20 Factory buildings, men, horse and wagon, &c.
ONE Indian with bow, spear, &c.	Agricultural scene, cattle, &c. Female seated with sickle. BANK of ROYALTON, Royalton, Vt.	The word ONE and figure 1. Man seated with agricultural implements, and ONE on half shield.
Two females embracing each other. 2	Two farmers, one seated; female seated; load of hay in distance. BANK of ROYALTON Royalton, Vt.	2 Head of Jefferson.
Blacksmith and anvil. 3	Three females seated representing Agriculture, Manufactures and Commerce. BANK of ROYALTON Royalton, Vt.	3 Head of Henry Clay.
Large figure 5 and five females. 5	Head of Hon. Jacob Collamer. BANK of ROYALTON Royalton, Vt.	5 Female seated with globe, quadrant &c.
10 Female seated, with sheaf of wheat.	Boy pushing sheep into creek, man standing behind him; boy and dog driving sheep, &c. B'K OF ROYALTON, Royalton, Vt.	10 Indian girl holding ear of corn in right hand and X in left.

Left end	Centre	Right end
Mercury seated between 2 and 0 XX	Drover and drove of cattle and sheep. BANK of ROYALTON Royalton, Vt.	20 Female churning.
Female feeding a horse. 50	A farmer's family resting in hay field; load of hay &c. BANK of ROYALTON Royalton, Vt.	50 Head of Webster.
100 Head of Fillmore. 100	BANK of ROYALTON Royalton, Vt. Female seated crowning an eagle with wreath; small head of Washington on left of vig.	100 Load of straw drawn by oxen; man on horseback.
Cattle. 1	1 Vig. Farmers cutting grain. 1 BANK OF RUTLAND, Rutland, Vt. Eagle.	ONE Female sitting, with rake, &c. 1
Male portrait. Word one and figure 1.	View of stone-yard. BANK OF RUTLAND, Rutland, Vt. One dollar. One dollar.	1 Male portrait.
Portrait of Washington. 2	Drover and cattle; boy in water; trees and house in distance. BANK OF RUTLAND, Rutland, Vt. Two dollars. Two dollars.	2 Portrait of Martha Washington.
Female churning. 2	Portrait of Hamilton. Portrait of Washington. Vig. Farmers sowing grain. BANK OF RUTLAND, Rutland, Vt. Sheaf of wheat.	2 Farmer picking corn.
Female gathering wheat. Word dollars and figure 3.	BANK OF RUTLAND, Rutland, Vt. Blacksmith in shop.	3 Female with cornucopia.
Lafayette, full length; York Town monument. V	5 Female sitting with eagle, &c. 5 BANK OF RUTLAND, Rutland, Vt. Arm and hammer.	V Sheep shearing. V
Stone cutter. 5	BK OF RUTLAND, Rutland, Vt. 5 Farmer sharpening scythe; agricultural scene in the distance. 5 FIVE Dog. FIVE	5 Female portrait.

10 Cattle, &c. 10 — Washington. Franklin. Female sitting with sickle and sheaf, cattle, &c. BANK OF RUTLAND, Rutland Vt. Female and sheaf. — 10 Sheaf of corn, plow, &c. 10

10 Portrait of a General. — Spread eagle. BANK OF RUTLAND, Rutland, Vt. Tree and cow. — 10 Portrait of a General.

20 Farmer with scythe. — Title of Bank. Marble quarries; oxen drawing load of marble. — 20 Female with sheaf and scythe.

Washington full length. — 20 Vig. Three female figures sitting. 20 BANK OF RUTLAND, Rutland, Vt. Washington. — 20 VERMONT 20

50 VERMONT 50 — 50 State arms and two females. 50 BANK OF RUTLAND, Rutland, Vt. Washington. — 50 Female with scales, full length. 50

50 Female portrait. — Train of cars, etc. BANK OF RUTLAND Rutland, Vt. Dog's head. — 50 Female portrait.

100 Indian beside dead deer. — BANK OF RUTLAND, Rutland, Vt. C — 100 Indian female seated and pointing.

1 Portrait of McDonough. — BK. OF VERGENNES Vergennes, Vt. Agricultural scene—man ploughing, cattle, &c., spires in the distance. — 1 ONE and 1.

2 Man on horseback, cattle drawing, farm house, &c. — BK. OF VERGENNES Vergennes, Vt. Eagle. — 2 2

3 Hunting scene—dogs and birds. — BK. OF VERGENNES Vergennes, Vt. Train of cars; horses frightened. — 3 3

The word "five," letter "V," and figure "5." Medallion head. FIVE — BK. OF VERGENNES Vergennes, Vt. Man with rake on his shoulder, little girl running to meet him; female and boy rural scenery, &c. — V 5

X X — Three females, one with cornucopia, one with wings, and the other with quadrant. BK. OF VERGENNES Vergennes, Vt. — 10

Portrait of Washington 20 XX — BK. OF VERGENNES Vergennes, Vt. Steamship. — XX Horses and colt running.

Three figures, two seated; on left, factories, &c., on right, ship, boat and fish. 50 — L Man ploughing. L BK. OF VERGENNES Vergennes, Vt. Clasped hands. — 50 Female with balloon; eagle and shield; three of bids. 50

100 Female soaring in clouds with scroll in left and eagle on left. 100 — 100 Female seated with key in left hand. 100 BK. OF VERGENNES Vergennes, Vt. Eagle. — Same as on left of 50s. 100

1 — Cupid rolling silver dollar on railroad track, train of cars, and city in distance. Mechanical implements. BANK OF WATERBURY, Waterbury, Vt. — 1 Female, shield, and Declaration of Independence.

Goddess of Liberty, and eagle, drinking from cup; 2 — BANK OF WATERBURY, Waterbury, Vt. Two cupids, two silver dollars; train of cars, village, farm, &c., in distance. — 2 Female Indian.

THREE Female erect with pole and cap. — Farming scene; two males and female, dog, basket, &c.; in distance, men loading hay. BANK OF WATERBURY, Waterbury, Vt. — 3 Portrait of Washington.

FIVE A General erect, with sword in hand. — BANK OF WATERBURY, Waterbury, Vt. Female reclining, with pole and cap, eagle, globe &c., steamship, and ship on left. — 5

10 Spread eagle, U. S. Capitol on right; and steamer on left. — BANK OF WATERBURY, Waterbury, Vt. — X Farming implements and products.

TWENTY Female seated with pole and cap, flowers, &c. — Two men, horse, dog, and drove of cattle and sheep. BANK OF WATERBURY, Waterbury, Vt. — 20 Male Portrait.

50 50 — BANK OF WATERBURY, Waterbury, Vt. Boy reclining with compass in right hand, engaged on chart; on right 2 men and 2 horses before cart. — 50 Female erect with pole and cap, shield and scroll in right hand.

Female seated on rock. 100 — BANK OF WATERBURY, Waterbury, Vt. Large public building, horses, carriages, &c., in front. — 100 Train of cars.

ONE Portrait of Washington. 1 — Silkmaid sitting and case. 1 BATTENKILL BANK Manchester, Vt. — 1 Portrait of Lady Washington. ONE

2 State arms. TWO — Stone cutters. 2 BATTENKILL BANK Manchester, Vt. — TWO Head of Franklin. TWO on Medallion head.

5 State arms. FIVE — Portrait of De Witt Clinton. 5 Portrait of Abby Hutchinson. BATTENKILL BANK Manchester, Vt. — 5 Medallion head. 5

FIVE State arms. FIVE — BATTENKILL BANK Manchester, Vt. Female Large V Female and man with sickle. — 5 Medallion head.

10 State arms. TEN — Signing declaration of independence. Portrait of Washington and large X. BATTENKILL BANK Manchester, Vt. — X Female bust.

TWENTY State arms. TWENTY — 20 Two men, with oxen, loading hay, and three men in background. BATTENKILL BANK Manchester, Vt. 20 Eagle. 20 — 20 Goddess of Liberty with eagle and shield.

50 State arms. 50 — Man on horseback, and dog, driving sheep; mill in the distance. BATTENKILL BANK Manchester, Vt. 50 Female head. 50 — 50 Goddess of Liberty sitting; train of cars and buildings in distance. FIFTY

ONE — Two females with sword, spear, and shield.
Wood-chopper, one gold dollar; log cabin in background.
BRADFORD BANK, Bradford, Vt.
1 — Indian woman.

2 — Winged female. Female and eagle.
Farmer boy and milkmaid; also cows; two gold dollars.
BRADFORD BANK, Bradford, Vt.
2 — Fountain.

Female giving eagle drink. 3
BRADFORD BANK, Bradford, Vt.
Mechanic, sailor and farmer, with implements; three gold dollars.
3 — Reaper seated by Three

Farmer boy with sheaf of wheat, and milkmaid. 5
A hunter and Indian woman, and three cupids; five gold dollars.
BRADFORD BANK, Bradford, Vt.
5 — Portrait.

Two females. 10
Coat of arms surmounted; with female each side; steamboat and train of cars in distance.
BRADFORD BANK, Bradford, Vt.
X — Child and dolphin.

Female, XX
State arms, farmer and Indian.
BRADFORD BANK, Bradford, Vt.
20 — Agricultural imp. & profits

50
Female reclining; milkmaids and cows; locomotive, shipping, factories in background. Wheels, bale, etc
BRADFORD BANK, Bradford, Vt.
50 — Portrait of Webster.

100 — Female with scales.
State arms surmounted by an eagle, female on each side.
BRADFORD BANK, Bradford, Vt.
100 — Horses and load of hay.

1
Farming scene—haying and harvesting. 1
BRANDON BANK, Brandon, Vt.
Wheels and shafts, representing the mechanic arts.
1 — Female with sickle in left hand and a head of grain in right hand. ONE

TWO
Washing sheep. 2
BRANDON BANK, Brandon Vt.
Bundle of grain, plough.
2 — Blacksmith, hammer in hand; anvil.

3
Horses ploughing; house, steamboat and other vessels in the distance. 3
BRANDON BANK, Brandon, Vt.
Train of cars.
3 — Man chiseling marble, with mallet and chisel in hand.

FIVE
Farming scene—oxen ploughing, drove of cattle; cars moving in distance. 5 Seal of State.
BRANDON BANK, Brandon, Vt.
5
5 — Full length female with a flag. Three cherubs representing Agriculture, Mechanics, &c.

TEN
Farming scene—oxen and cart with load of grain; house in the distance. X
BRANDON BANK, Brandon, Vt.
Dog's head.
10 — Two female figures erect.

20 — Full figure of a female.
2 Female. 0
BRANDON BANK, Brandon, Vt.
XX
20 — Female reclining. 20

50 — Male figure standing.
Female and male seated.
BRANDON BANK, Brandon, Vt.
50
50 — Cupid in a sail-boat. 50

Figures 100, and words one hundred. Male figure sitting.
Large spread eagle on a limb of a tree; cars, canal, and boats in distance.
BRANDON BANK, Brandon, Vt.
100
Same as on left end. Female sitting.

1 — Head of Washington. ONE
Train of cars.
COMMERCIAL B'K. Burlington, Vt.
State Arms
1 — Head of Female. 1

TWO — Head of Franklin. TWO
Three females and eagle.
COMMERCIAL B'K, Burlington, Vt.
State Arms
TWO — Girl with rake and bouquet of flowers. TWO

THREE — Eagle, ship, and female. THREE
Indian with spear and horse; cars in distance.
COMMERCIAL B'K., Burlington, Vt.
State Arms
3 — Indian and female with sickle and sheaf of grain.

5 — Head. State Arms.
Vessels, steamboat and city.
COMMERCIAL B'K., Burlington. Vt.
Eagle,
5 — Head of Washington. FIVE

Head. State Arms. TEN
TEN on Head. Declaration of Independence.
COMMERCIAL B'K., Burlington, Vt.
Blacksmith arm and anvil.
X — TEN on Head. 10

TWENTY
COMMERCIAL B'K., Burlington, Vt.
Mechanics, 2 females sitting, city in distance.
Anchor, anvil, &c.
20 — Farmer, two females, dog and oxen.

50 — Head. FIFTY
State Arms and two horses; factory, cars and steamboat in background.
COMMERCIAL B'K., Burlington, Vt.
50 — Head of Female. FIFTY

100
COMMERCIAL B'K., Burlington, Vt.
Three Females, anchor, sickle, &c.; train cars, vessels and city at distance.
100
100

1 — Female erect left arm resting on basket
EXCHANGE BANK, Springfield. Vt.
Male Portrait. One dollar above.
1 — Mechanic reclining holding hammer in right hand houses in background.

TWO 2 TWO — Male Portrait TWO
EXCHANGE BANK, Springfield, Vt.
Masons at work building house, man on ladder, with hod of bricks.
TWO 2 TWO — Portrait of Gen. Jackson TWO

THREE 3
EXCHANGE BANK, Springfield. Vt.
Picture of a Mechanic, hammer resting on his shoulder.
THREE 3

Figure 5 and medallion head. Portrait of Webster.
Portrait of Washington, on right two females, one seated the other standing, on left three females, one in center holds a sickle.
EXCHANGE BANK, Springfield, Vt.
Figure 5 and medallion head. Male Portrait

10 Medallion head. TEN Portrait of Franklin. X Medallion Head.
Shield and letter X in center; on right woman and child, round globe, on left Indians [?].
EXCHANGE BANK, Springfield. Vt.
TEN TEN
[illegible] Medallion head. 10 Head. Portrait of Henry Clay TEN on right. Double Medallion head. X Head.

XX 20
EXCHANGE BANK, Springfield. Vt.
Two horses, eagle overhead, tree, sow and sheaf of wheat in background, steamboat on right, cars and houses on left.
20

L | EXCHANGE BANK. Springfield, Vt. Large spread eagle resting on a limb of a tree; train of cars on right; house and small boat on left. | 50 | 50 | 50

Female figure hovering over earth; steamboat, houses, cars, &c., beneath her. | Houses, stream of water, &c. FARMERS BANK Orwell, Vt. Farming scene—men gathering corn; large white 1 across | 1

Two girls under shed; one churning the other making cheese; cattle, etc. on right. | 2 Title of Bank. Man and girl gazing at boy playing with dog; farming scene on right. Large white 2 across. | 2

5 Eagle and serpent. 5 | (First Plate.) V Vig. female seated; V one arm resting on sheaf of grain; agricultural scene. FARMER'S BANK, Orwell, Vt. Man's head. | 5 Female reclining against a monument V

FIVE Statue of Washington; cloak wrapped about him. FIVE | (Second Plate.) FARMER'S BANK, Orwell, Vt. 5 Vig. Two females. 5 V Canal boat about passing a lock. | FIVE Female erect FIVE

FIVE Female; sheaf of grain; sickle plough, rake, hoe, &c. V | (Third Plate.) V Neptune in chariot, pursuing an angel upon the sea; ship. fig. 5 on right FARMER'S BANK. Orwell, Vt. Horse head. | FIVE

TEN Franklin. TEN | FARMER'S BANK, Orwell, Vt. X Cottage scene; shearing a sheep, with family around. Eagle. | TEN Justice. 10

XX Eagle; Stars and Stripes. 20 | FARMER'S BANK, Orwell, Vt. Sheaf of grain; plough and harrow. Horse. | 20 Steam ferry boat and canoe, with two men. 20

FIFTY | 50 FARMER'S BANK. 50 Orwell, Vt. Vig. Sheep, ships, and mountain in the distance; man making fence. Dog's head, safe, and key. | FIFTY

1 Figure of Justice. | (New Plate.) FAR. & MECH. B'K. Burlington, Vt. Bee Hive. | 1 ONE 1

Man and sheep. 1 | (Old Plate.) 1 Man and horse; cattle, sheep, &c. 1 FAR. & MECH. B'K. Burlington, Vt. Dog and safe | Blacksmith seated. 1

Two dollars. Sheep. Two dollars. | 2 Harvest scene; two 2 full length figures and dog. FAR., & MECH., BK., Burlington, Vt. | Two dollars. Cattle. Two dollars.

2 2 | Train of cars; river and mountains in distance. FAR., & MECH., BK., Burlington, Vt. Steamer. | 2 2

3 THREE 3 | Female seated; fruit and grain lying around; vessels in distance. FAR., & MECH., BK., Burlington, Vt. Eagle. | 3 THREE 3

THREE Milkmaid. 3 | 3 Blacksmith seated, with sledge hammer; cars in distance. FAR., & MECH., BK., Burlington, Vt. Dog and safe. | THREE Reaper and dog. 3

5 Eagle. | Steamer and vessels. FAR., & MECH., BK. Burlington, Vt. Sheaf of wheat. | Head of female. 5

Female and child seated on a plough; mowers in distance. 10 | 10 FAR., & MECH., BK., Burlington, Vt. Eagle. | Steamboat and vessels. 10

20 Female. | Steamer and vessels. FAR., & MECH., BK., Burlington, Vt. Wheat. | Blacksmith. 20

FIFTY Female reaper. | Spread eagle. FAR., & MECH. BK., Burlington, Vt. Locomotive. | 50

100 Portrait of Washington. 100 | Spread Eagle. FAR. & MECH. B'K. Burlington, Vt. Dog and safe. | 100

ONE Female portrait. | Man sitting holding sledge; train of cars, factory, &c. in background. 1 FRANKLIN CO. B'K. St. Alban's Bay, Vt. Cogwheel, bale, &c. | Female standing behind pillar. ONE

TWO Female and shield, spear in right hand, branch in left. | Female reclining on bale of goods; canal boat, train of cars, town, shipping, &c. in background. FRANKLIN CO. B'K, St. Alban's Bay, Vt. Sale. | 2 Female sitting. TWO

FIVE Female Indian, bow, spear, &c. in right hand, quiver of arrows on back. | 5 Female portrait, eagle, shield, &c.; steamer, sail vessel, train of cars, factory &c. in background FRANKLIN CO. B'K, St. Alban's Bay, Vt. Steamer. | FIVE Sailor, capstan, hogshead, &c.

10 Portrait of Franklin. 10 | Steamboat; wharf buildings, sail vessels, &c. in background. FRANKLIN CO. B'K, St. Alban's Bay, Vt. Horn of plenty. | 10 Locomotive and cars. 10

20 Locomotive. 20 | Female, sheaves of grain, &c. FRANKLIN CO. B'K, St. Alban's Bay, Vt. Sail vessel. | 20 Steamship. 20

Shed, flowers on the roof; two women, one churning, one turning cheese, poultry and cattle, part in the water. | ONE Oxen, cart and hay; man lying, and man with fork on his shoulder. LAMOILLE CO. BK., Hyde Park, Vt. | 1 Mechanics' arm.

TWO Woods, stream and Indian creeping with gun. | LAMOILLE CO. BK., Hyde Park, Vt. Woman, eagle, sword, &c. Geese. | 2 Two deers, one feeding; rocks, meadow, &c.

THREE | LAMOILLE CO. BK., Hyde Park, Vt. Cattle and sheep. Female bathing. | 3 Lady with veil.

V Woman blowing horn, table and crockery; load hay in distance, man on load, man with rake, another with scythe sitting. | LAMOILLE CO. BK., Hyde Park, Vt. Wild horses running. | 5

Santa Claus driving four reindeers. TEN | Female with hand over her eyes. LAMOILLE CO. BK., Hyde Park, Vt. | 10 Village scene, coaches, load of hay, riding horseback, driving cattle, &c.

Left	Center	Right
TWENTY 20 Three dogs.	Indian tent, squaw and two Indians, houses, train of cars. Portrait of Webster. LAMOILLE CO. BK., Hyde Park, Vt. Dog	20 XX 20
L	LAMOILLE CO. BK., 50 Hyde Park, Vt. Two females, train of cars, ship, bundle of grain, &c. Head of Washington.	FIFTY Two soldiers, one seated with pipe.
100 Jackson.	LAMOILLE CO. BK., Hyde Park, Vt. Female seated, rooster, two cows, &c.; trees and shed	100 Clay.
Three females with anchor; partly sitting, partly standing. ONE	Train of cars; village in the distance. MERCHANT'S BK., Burlington, Vt. State arms.	1 Female with spy glass, sitting beside a bale; ships in the distance.
Female head. 2	Female sitting by a bale; hayin scene, and train of cars in the distance. MERCHANT'S BK., Burlington, Vt. State Arms.	2 Engine, depot, &c.
Portrait of McDonough. 3	Female seated with a basket containing ears of corn, melons, fruit, &c., by her side; lake, sails, village, mountains, &c., in the distance. MERCHANT'S BK., Burlington, Vt. State arms.	3 Female portrait.
Portrait of Madison. 5	[First Plate.] Three females with basket of fruit, trident and spear; ship in background. MERCHANT'S BK., Burlington, Vt. State Arms.	5 Sailor with spy glass.
FIVE Female with spear, shield and branch. FIVE	[Second Plate.] 5 Female with horn of plenty and trident, sitting beside barrels, and sheaf of grain; bridge, cars, village and ship in the distance. MERCHANT'S BK., Burlington, Vt. State Arms.	5 Portrait of Harrison.
TEN Female with spear, standing beside a globe.	10 Female, globe, book; factory in the background. MERCHANT'S BK., Burlington, Vt. State Arms.	10 Portrait of Franklin. TEN
20 Female seated with spear, shield, &c. beside a globe.	Female seated between figures 2 and 0. MERCHANT'S BK., Burlington, Vt. XX	20 Small figure of a female 20

Left	Center	Right
50 Female with spear and shield.	Male and female seated; horn of plenty. MERCHANT'S BK., Burlington, Vt. 50	50 Cupid in a sail boat. 50
100 Male seated.	Eagle upon a branch; bridge, and train of cars passing over it. MERCHANT'S BK., Burlington, Vt. C C 100	100 Female with rake, and horn of plenty.
1 Man with scythe.	MISSISQUOI BANK, Sheldon, Vt. Large spread eagle.	1 Female representing Agriculture.
1	Female seated; train of cars and vessel on right, canal scene on left. 1 MISSISQUOI BANK, Sheldon, Vt.	1 Female resting arm on knee.
Female portrait. 2	Female in clouds reclining on eagle. MISSISQUOI BANK, Sheldon, Vt.	2 Female portrait.
2	Man forcing sheep in water, another man erect; boy driving flock; buildings on right. 2 Title of Bank.	TWO Female seated. TWO
Indian head. 3	Female reclining on a chest; two females and cows on right; cars and ship on left. MISSISQUOI BANK, Sheldon, Vt.	3 Indian head.
3	Man on horseback; cows and men; load of hay entering barn. 3 Title of Bank.	Word three, and figure 3. Female with basket of flowers. TH 3REE
FIVE	Eagle on shield; city and ships in distance. Large V, female and Cupid. Title of Bank.	5 Girl with basket of flowers or fruit.
TEN	Vulcan seated, anvil, sledge, &c.; train of cars and buildings in distance. X Title of Bank.	10 Farmer with sheaf on his knee.

Left	Center	Right
20 Female sitting, with book.	XX Eagle. XX Title of Bank.	20 Ship under sail.
FIFTY Female with wreath. FIFTY	50 Man and Horse. 50 Title of Bank	FIFTY Full length female, globe, Rake, &c. FIFTY
100 Eagle. 100	C Europe and Vermont, Female 100 Title of Bank.	C Washington. C
Milkmaid, cows, etc. 1	MUTUAL BANK, Castleton, Vt. Boy and two horses; house and train of cars in background.	1 Female with hen and chickens in her arms.
Two children 2	Title of Bank. Two men and horse; city in distance.	2 Two men, one husking corn, the other with basket on his shoulder.
Vulcan with anvil, sledge, wheel, etc. FIVE	Title of Bank. Bust of Washington and three female artists.	5 Cattle, cars, bridge, etc.
Washington. 10	Title of Bank. Spread eagle on shield; city, ships, etc., in distance.	10 Castleton Seminary and grounds.
State Arms. 20	Title of Bank. Cars passing under bridge; two Indians, etc. Female bathing.	20 Bust of a Boy
1 Portrait of Frank Pierce	Farmer sitting; oxen. NORTHFIELD B'K, Northfield, Vt. Beehive.	1 Train of cars
ONE Tree, &c. Cupid and L.	NORTHFIELD B'K., Northfield, Vt. Four males, two females, child, dog; horses, load of grain and men in distance. Boxes, bble., &c.	1 Male portrait

Left	Centre	Right
2 Factory girl at work.	NORTHFIELD B'K. Northfield, Vt Blacksmith's shop; Blacksmith shoeing horse.	2 Female head.
Treas. &c.	Mechanic seated by a boiler; men at work on boiler in distance. Male portrait NORTHFIELD BK, Northfield, Vt. Agricultural implements.	2 Cupid and 2
Treas. &c. 3	Milkmaid seated with pail; cars in distance. NORTHFIELD BK, Northfield, Vt. Dog's head.	3 Male portrait
3	Horse market. Female head. NORTHFIELD B'K. Northfield, Vt	3 Dairy maid milking.
Treas. &c. 5	NORTHFIELD BK., Northfield, Vt. Five gold dollars; three Cupids, hunter and Indian; cars in distance. Cog-wheels, &c.	5 Male portrait
5 Indian	Train of cars. NORTHFIELD B'K. Northfield, Vt	5 Female head.
10 Female head.	Load of hay, train of cars and packet boat. NORTHFIELD B'K. Northfield, Vt State Arms.	10 Vulcan.
TEN Treas. &c. 10	Train of cars; steamboat and houses in distance. NORTHFIELD BK, Northfield, Vt. Mechanics arm.	10 Male portrait
20 Henry Clay sitting, dog at his feet.	Cow and sheep, church in background. NORTHFIELD B'K, Northfield. Vt	20 Male portrait.
50 Vulcan, sledge on right shoulder, wheel in left hand.	NORTHFIELD B'K. Northfield, Vt Men on horseback, watering horse at trough; two boys and dogs.	50 Male portrait.

Left	Centre	Right
100 Vulcan.	NORTHFIELD B'K. Northfield, Vt. Elliott preaching to the Indians.	100 Portrait of Gov. Paine.
ONE	PASSUMPSIC BANK, St. Johnsbury, Vt. Cattle and sheep. 1	1 Blacksmith and anvil.
TWO	PASSUMPSIC BANK, St. Johnsbury, Vt Man with sledge on his shoulder; factory and cars in distance. 2 State arms.	2 Two Indians
THREE	PASSUMPSIC BANK, St. Johnsbury, Vt. Female with horn of plenty, barrels, &c.; ships, factories and train of cars. 3 Head of dog.	3 Head of Webster.
5	PASSUMPSIC BANK. St. Johnsbury, Vt. Drove of cattle and sheep; man on horseback. 5	FIVE Indian erect with bow and spear.
TEN	PASSUMPSIC BANK, St. Johnsbury, Vt. Train of cars. X Boy's head.	10 Female with pole and cap.
20	PASSUMPSIC BANK, St. Johnsbury, Vt. Female seated on sheaf of grain; men loading grain in distance.	10 Female with scales and sword.
Eagle upon shield, bale and barrel, with anchor, sheaf of grain, &c.; falls and factory in distance. 50	PASSUMPSIC BANK, St. Johnsbury, Vt. Imp. and products	50 Female with sheaf and sickle.
100	PASSUMPSIC BANK, St. Johnsbury, Vt. Female and eagle soaring in the air Dog and safe.	100 Female with basket of flowers.
ONE	Two horses; farm-house in distance. 1 PEOPLES' BANK. Derby Line, Vt.	ONE Boy gathering corn. ONE

Left	Centre	Right
1 Portrait of Washington.	Female. 1 Female. PEOPLE'S BANK. Derby Line, Vt.	1 Portrait of Franklin.
2 Male portrait.	Female with horn of plenty. 2 Female PEOPLE'S BANK, Derby Line, Vt.	2 Male portrait.
2 Female picking fruit.	Man watering three horses; female feeding pigs; farm house in distance. Title of Bank.	2 Farmer with scythe.
3 Washington standing by his horse.	Child. 3 Child. PEOPLE'S BANK, Derby Line. Vt.	3 Blacksmith with hammer and anvil.
Eagle on shield with manufacturing village in distance. FIVE	Large V with female with horn of plenty and a child. PEOPLE'S BANK. Derby Line, Vt.	5 Child with basket.
5 Washington.	Drove of cattle and sheep. Title of Bank.	5 Train of cars.
10 Four small portraits of Ex Presidents. 10	10 Three farmers and female at lunch; horses, etc. Title of Bank	X Indian seated
Blacksmith with hammer and anvil. TEN	X PEOPLE'S BANK. Derby Line, Vt.	10 Reaper with bundle of grain and sickle.
20 Man with helmet and spear, globe and an owl at his feet.	2 Female. 0 PEOPLES' BANK, Derby Line. Vt XX	20 Female. 20
50 Man with helmet and spear standing beside a broken column.	Vig. Female holding a rake sitting, man sitting holding a scroll, foot resting on an anchor. PEOPLE'S BANK. Derby Line, Vt. 50	50 Cupid in a sail boat. 50

100. Man sitting, holding a scroll, foot resting on an anchor. — Vig. Eagle on a branch of a tree, train of cars, locks and two canal boats. PEOPLE'S BANK, Derby Line, Vt. 100 — 100. Female sitting holding a rake.	2. Head of Abby Hutchinson. 2 — Train of cars; city and mountains in distance. STARK BANK, Bennington, Vt. Nymph bathing. — 2. Head of Gen. Stark.	2. Female sitting down with sword and scales; stars in distance. — Portrait of Franklin. UNION BANK, Swanton Falls, Vt. TWO 2 DOLLARS — 2. Female sitting down with cap of liberty on a pole; church and houses in distance.
1. View of Street, cattle and men, load of hay; town in distance. — ST. ALBANS' BANK, St. Albans, Vt. Vig. Selling Cattle. — 1	FIVE. Head of Gen. Stark. — 5 Drover on horseback with dog, driving sheep; mill in distance. STARK BANK, Bennington, Vt. Wheelbarrow and sheaf. — 5. Head of Washington.	2. Portrait of Columbus. — Portrait of female with flowers. 2 Portrait of female with sword and scales. UNION BANK, Swanton Falls, Vt. — 2. Male portrait.
2. Sailor leaning on capstan, merchandise and anchor on right, ships masts on left. — ST. ALBANS' BANK, St. Albans, Vt. Vig. Catching Horse. — 2. Mechanic and tools.	X — STARK BANK, Bennington, Vt. Head of Gen. Stark. Winged female with cornucopia; female with quadrant. State arms and two females. — 10	3. Indian sitting down with bow; hut in distance. — UNION BANK, Swanton Falls, Vt. III 3 — 3. Sailor sitting on bale of goods; steamship in distance.
3 — ST. ALBANS' BANK, St. Albans, Vt. Blacksmith's shop; men at work, smith shoeing horse. Squaw. — 3. Female and grain.	20. Female with sheaf, sickle, &c. — Head of Gen. Stark supported by Liberty, Justice, and Truth; ship in background. STARK BANK, Bennington, Vt. — 20. Head of Webster.	3. Washington standing beside his horse. — Portrait of female. 3 Portrait of girl. UNION BANK, Swanton Falls, Vt. — 3. Man standing with sledge.
Three females on a rock with anchor, spy-glass, &c. FIVE — Three females and Cupid. ST. ALBANS' BANK, St. Albans, Vt. Eagle. — 5. Female.	Female seated. 50 — Signing the Declaration of Independence. STARK BANK. Bennington, Vt. — 50. Head of Gen. Stark.	FIVE — Female kneeling against a shield. V UNION BANK. Swanton Falls, Vt. — 5. Ship.
10. Male portrait. — Train of cars; view of river and town; cars crossing bridge. ST. ALBANS' BANK, St. Albans, Vt. Farming implements. — 10. Farmer gathering grain.	Red 1. Cattle, load of hay. — STATE BANK, Montpelier, Vt. State House. — Red 1. State Arms.	Five on V. Drover on horseback with cattle and sheep. 5 — Title of Bank. FIVE 5 DOLLARS — Five on V. 5
20. Female. — Three females with wand, cornucopia, sword and balances; vessels on right. ST. ALBANS' BANK, St. Albans, Vt. — 20. Female artist; around her mechanical tools.	Red 2. State Arms. — State House, separating the words "State Bank," and small female head on right. — Red 2. Farmer gathering corn.	X. Hunter and dog by fire. — Drove of wild horses. UNION BANK, Swanton Falls, Vt. — 10. Girl.
50. Female. — ST. ALBANS' BANK, St. Albans, Vt. Portrait of Washington. — 50. Train of cars; village in background.	Female portrait. Red 5. — State House. State Arms. Title of Bank. — Red 5. Female feeding fowls.	X. Indian with bow and arrows. — Steamboat and sail vessels; wharf and buildings in distance. X Title of Bank — 10. Female with sheaf of grain under her arm; hat in her hand.
100. Soldiers with fife and drum. — U. S. Capitol at Washington. ST. ALBANS' BANK St. Albans, Vt. — 100. Portrait of Webster.	1. Washington. — Female 1 Female UNION BANK, Swanton Falls, Vt. — 1. Franklin.	Cattle and sheep; one of each standing, the rest reclining. XX — Female portrait. UNION BANK, Swanton Falls, Vt. — 20. Hunter drinking from a brook.
Goddess of Liberty with cap and shield and eagle. — 1 Female with cornucopia. STARK BANK, Bennington, Vt. — 1. Head of Gen. Stark.	1. Farmer with sickle and sheaf of grain; cars and canal boat in distance. — Portrait of Washington. UNION BANK, Swanton Falls, Vt. Large figure 1, with words one dollar running across it. — 1. Indian with bow sitting down; boat and animals in distance.	20. Female with book in left hand, right hand on a bust. — XX Eagle. XX UNION BANK, Swanton Falls, Vt. — 20. Ship, with buildings in the distance.

FIFTY Female with wreath of flowers on her head and in her hands. FIFTY	50 Men and horse; 50 Title of Bank.	FIFTY Female with flowers in her left hand FIFTY

Fig. 100 with words one hundred across. Harrison.	Covered wagon, wharf, ships, warehouses, truckmen, &c. Title of Bank.	Same as on left end. Columbus.

ONE State Arms. ONE	Cows; and man ploughing. VERMONT BANK. Montpelier, Vt.	1 Portrait of a lady. ONE

2 Head of Franklin. TWO	State Arms, surmounted with a stag's head; lady on left; man on right; fruit, &c., below. VERMONT BANK. Montpelier,	2 Head of Washington. TWO

THREE Locomotive and cars.	State Arms, with female; churn and pail on the right; man with plough and rake on the left. VERMONT BANK. Montpelier,	3 Female with bow and arrow.

5 Female with sheaf of wheat and sickle. FIVE	Agricultural scene; haymaker's and team; female seated on left; farmer's loading hay, on right. VERMONT BANK. Montpelier,	5 State Arms; female figure each side. FIVE

10 Lady's Portrait 10	Man ploughing; cattle grazing; cars passing under bridge; and in the distance, on left, village and train of cars. VERMONT BANK. Montpelier,	10 State Arms; female figure each side. TEN

20 Full length female, holding a spear; globe standing partly behind the female.	2 Female. 0 VERMONT BANK. Montpelier. XX	20 Female sitting; horn of plenty, and bales. 20

50 Full length female figure holding a spear in right hand; left hand rests on a shield.	Male and female seated. VERMONT BANK. Montpelier. 50	50 Cupid in a sail-boat. 50

100 Man sitting, holding a scroll.	Eagle on a tree; canal boat and cars in background. VERMONT BANK. Montpelier. 1 0 Vermont	100 Female seated, holding a rake, fruit, &c.

Two females standing. 1	Cupid rolling silver dollar on railroad track; cars, city, &c. in distance. WEST RIVER B'K. Jamaica, Vt.	1 Female seated clasping figure 1 in her arms.

Two men bearing Goddess. 2	Two Cupids and two silver dollars; cars cattle, &c. in distance. WEST RIVER B'K. Jamaica, Vt. Cow and calf.	2 Female churning.

Female sitting holding sickle; sheaf of grain. 3	Three cupids and three silver dollars. WEST RIVER B'K. Jamaica, Vt. Man ploughing.	3 State arms. THREE

Female head. V	Five cupids and five silver dollars. WEST RIVER B'K. Jamaica, Vt.	5 Sailor and Indian seated; five on shield between them

X Goddess erect holding trumpet Female seated holding liberty cap, eagle, &c.	Goddess and cherub holding portrait of Washington between them. WEST RIVER B'K. Jamaica, Vt.	10 Stonecutter at work.

XX Female erect with shield and spear	Female seated by shield, sheafs, &c.; lighthouse and ships in distance. WEST RIVER BANK Jamaica, Vt. TWENTY	20 Female representing Agriculture.

Justice FIFTY	Female and eagle soaring. WEST RIVER BANK Jamaica, Vt. FIFTY	50 Jackson.

1	Female representing Commerce. Man in top of 1. WHITE RIVER BK., Bethel, Vt.	1 Female with grain; fence, etc.

1 Washington.	Female. 1 Female. WHITE RIVER BK., Bethel, Vt.	1 Male Portrait

2 Male Portrait.	Female. 2 Female. WHITE RIVER BK. Bethel, Vt.	2 Male Portrait.

2	Sheep washing scene. Man in top of 2 WHITE RIVER B'K. Bethel, Vt.	TWO Female with garland of flowers. TWO

3	Man on horse; cattle, dog, load of hay, &c. 3 WHITE RIVER B'K. Bethel, Vt.	3 Female with basket

3 Washington and his horse.	Female. 3 Female. WHITE RIVER BK., Bethel, Vt.	3 Vulcan the Blacksmith.

Spread eagle on shield; village and ship in distance. FIVE	Large V, female and child. WHITE RIVER BK., Bethel, Vt.	5 Little girl with basket.

Vulcan the blacksmith seated, factory and building in distance. TEN	X WHITE RIVER BK., Bethel, Vt.	10 Man tying up bundle of grain.

20 Female seated.	XX Eagle. XX WHITE RIVER BK., Bethel, Vt.	20 Ship.

FIFTY Female erect. FIFTY	50 Man and Horse. 50 WHITE RIVER BK., Bethel, Vt.	FIFTY Female erect. FIFTY

The figures 100 with the words "one hundred" Portrait of Harrison.	Wharf scene, wagons, horses, men, vessels, &c. WHITE RIVER BK., Bethel, Vt.	Same as on the left. Male Portrait,

ONE	WINDHAM COUNTY BANK, Brattleboro, Vt. Man and three horses at mill; grain; sheep, hounds, etc. 1	1 Indian apparently asleep.

2 Farmer sowing. TWO	Title of Bank. Cattle, farming scenes, etc., in distance.	2 Female with sheaf and sickle. 2

VERMONT.

3 Bulls head. THREE.	WINDHAM COUNTY BANK, Brattleboro, Vt. THREE 3 Farmers operating with reaping machine.	3
5 Indian head.	Title of Bank. Horse on either side of a shield, on which is an eagle, tree, cow, etc.; cars, building, etc. in distance.	Five and 5. 5
X 10	Title of Bank. Three females and bust representing the Arts and Sciences.	10 X
XX inverted. Milkmaid and cows.	Title of Bank. TWENTY DOLLARS on dies.	20 inverted. Two females on right of a shield, on it agricultural implements and products cars, building, etc., in distance.
50 Milkmaid; cows and house in the distance.	Title of Bank. Mechanic erect with anvil and hogshead; buildings in distance.	50 Liberty seated.
100 Washington	Title of Bank. Female on either side of a beehive.	100 Martha Washington
ONE Blacksmith with anvil; cars in distance.	One on 1. Cattle, sheep and a colt; boy on horse. WOODSTOCK BANK, Woodstock, Vt.	1 ONE
Two men carrying female on their shoulders. ONE	Agricultural scene; man reaping, and female with sheaf in her arms. WOODSTOCK BANK, Woodstock, Vt. Female.	1 State Arms. ONE
TWO Two children	Two females seated with cornucopia; shield between them; factory in distance. WOODSTOCK BANK, Woodstock, Vt.	2 Female portrait.
Man with sheaf of grain on his knee.	2 Female seated on plow with sheaf and sickle; train of cars on right. 2 WOODSTOCK BANK, Woodstock, Vt. Sheaf, plow, &c.	Milkmaid seated.

MASS.

Female with scales, bale. THREE	3 Female reclining on cornucopia; ship in distance. WOODSTOCK BANK, Woodstock, Vt.	3 Three on 3.
Female with horn of plenty at her feet, figure 3 on shield. THREE	Forest scene with deer. WOODSTOCK BANK, Woodstock, Vt. Man plowing	3 Indian Queen
5 Portrait of Washington.	State Arms; on either side female and cupid. WOODSTOCK BANK, Woodstock, Vt. Sheaf, plow, &c.	5 Female Portrait.
10 Med. head and word TEN. Horse cars	State Arms, on left female seated with pole and cap; on right eagle. WOODSTOCK BANK, Woodstock, Vt. Bull.	10 Male and female; male shearing sheep; mill in back ground.
Female erect and capstan. 20	Portrait of Washington surrounded by all the State Arms and implements of war. WOODSTOCK BANK, Woodstock, Vt. Bull.	20 Cupid in sail boat. 20
50 Female erect with spear and shield.	Female and eagle soaring in clouds with shield between them. WOODSTOCK BANK, Woodstock, Vt. Man plowing with two horses. Scene dog's head	50 Female erect with hand on capstan.
Female.	Cherub reclining holding an American coin; scene eagle, box, barrels, &c. WOODSTOCK BANK, Woodstock, Vt. Bull.	Two males carrying a female. 100
1	Train of cars. 1 ABINGTON BANK. Abington, Mass. State Arms.	1 Female figure and cherubs
2	Cattle, village and train of cars in the background. 2 ABINGTON BANK. Abington, Mass. Female head.	2 State arms.
THREE	State arms with a female on either side Cupid and 3. ABINGTON BANK. Abington, Mass. Wheels, bale, etc.	THREE Female. THREE.

MASS.

5	Female eagle and shield. V Female and sheaf of wheat. ABINGTON BANK. Abington, Mass. Wheels, bale, etc.	FIVE Female and 5.
10	Female, eagle and safe. X ABINGTON BANK. Abington, Mass.	TEN Portrait of Adams.
20 Female.	2 Female with safe. 0 ABINGTON BANK, Abington, Mass. XX	20 Female 20
50 Female figure.	Male and female. ABINGTON BANK, Abbington, Mass. 50	50 Cupid in a sail boat. 50
100 Vulcan	Eagle, train of cars and canal. ABINGTON BANK, Abington, Mass. 100	100 Female.
Female giving eagle drink. 1	Cherub rolling silver dollar; city, cars, bridge and train of cars in distance. ADAMS BANK, North Adams, Mass.	1 Indian seated with fig. 1.
1 Portrait of Washington.	Female. 1 Female. ADAMS BANK, North Adams, Mass.	1 Portrait of Franklin.
ONE 1	Farmer sowing grain. 1 ADAMS BANK, North Adams, Mass.	1 Ship. ONE
2 Portrait of Columbus.	Female. 2 Female. ADAMS BANK, North Adams, Mass.	2 Portrait.
Two females. 2	Two cherubs and two silver dollars; cars in distance. ADAMS BANK, North Adams, Mass.	2 Sailor and Indian on either side of TWO on shield.

Left end	Centre	Right end
TWO 2	Spread Eagle. 2 ADAMS BANK. North Adams. Mass.	2 Sail boats
3 Gen. Washington.	Portrait of female. 3 Portrait of female. ADAMS BANK. North Adams, Mass.	3 Man with sledge.
THREE 3	Wharf and shipping. 3 on right ADAMS BANK. North Adams, Mass.	3 Train of cars.
Indian with bow. V	5 Vulcan and two female figures. 5 ADAMS BANK. North Adams, Mass.	V Train of cars V
10 Train of cars. 10	X Archimedes. X ADAMS BANK. North Adams. Mass.	Female 10
20 Female with apron.	Female between figures 2 and 0. ADAMS BANK. North Adams, Mass. XX	20 Female. 20
50 Female figure.	Male and female. ADAMS BANK. North Adams. Mass. 50	50 Cupid in a sail boat. 50
100 Vulcan with implements.	Spread eagle, railroad and canal. ADAMS BANK. North Adams, Mass. 100	100 Female with rake.
Two males and female. ONE	Female supporting the figure 1. 1 AGAWAM BANK. Springfield, Mass. Deer	1 Portrait of a female
2	Indian with figure 2, deer and canoe. AGAWAM BANK. Springfield, Mass. State Arms.	2 Reaper.

Left end	Centre	Right end
Two females. 3	3 AGAWAM BANK. Springfield, Mass. Cow	3 Portrait of a boy.
A party of Indians receiving a company of white men. 5	V and female. AGAWAM BANK. Springfield. Mass.	FIVE Female. 5
Female with sickle and sheaf of wheat. X	X AGAWAM BANK. Springfield Mass. Products and implements	10 Portrait of a girl.
20 Cupid in a sail boat. 20	Steamship. AGAWAM BANK. Springfield, Mass. Products and implements	20 Spread eagle and shield.
50 Indian girl with bow and arrows.	Female and eagle 1. on shield. AGAWAM BANK. Springfield, Mass. Cow	50 Female.
100 Female resting her hand upon a capstan.	Load of grain crossing a bridge. 100 AGAWAM BANK. Springfield, Mass. Deer	100 Milk maid.
ONE Drove of cattle. ONE	(Old Plate.) 1 Train of cars. 1 AGRICULTURAL BANK, Pittsfield, Mass.	ONE
ONE on 1 Female instructing children.	(New Plate.) Farming scene. AGRICULTURAL BANK, Pittsfield. Mass.	1 Indian woman and child.
TWO	(Old Plate.) 2 Milk maids; vessels in the distance. AGRICULTURAL BANK, Pittsfield. Mass. State Arms.	2 Man ploughing with horse.
Two female figures.	(New Plate.) Farming scene; female in foreground. TWO in 2 on right AGRICULTURAL BANK, Pittsfield, Mass.	2 State arms.

Left end	Centre	Right end
Female with sickle and horn of plenty; ship in distance. Three on 3	AGRICULTURAL BK. Pittsfield. Mass. Vig. White and black horse facing each other, Indian on shield surmounted with eagle between them, at right of black horse a steamboat, on left of white horse canal boat, cars and manufacturing establishment	3 Milk maid; cars and house in distance.
Female with sickle 3	State arms and 2 horses; factories, railroad and steamboat in distance. AGRICULTURAL BANK, Pittsfield, Mass.	3 Milk maid.
FIVE Man and agricultural implements. 5	5 View of Pittsfield. 5 AGRICULTURAL BANK, Pittsfield, Mass. State Arms	FIVE
FIVE Train of cars passing under a bridge.	Female reclining with her arm upon a chest; factories in background. AGRICULTURAL BK. Pittsfield, Mass.	5 Wood cutter.
10 X 10	Man and oxen. Large 10 at the right of Vig. AGRICULTURAL BANK, Pittsfield. Mass.	TEN Female figure.
10 Portrait of Webster.	Train of cars. AGRICULTURAL BK. Pittsfield, Mass.	Ten, X, 10. Hay makers.
20 Female.	XX Eagle. XX AGRICULTURAL BANK, Pittsfield. Mass.	20 Ship
TWENTY Farmer grinding scythe, stone being turned by negro. 20	XX AGRICULTURAL BANK, Massachusetts. TWENTY DOLLARS Pittsfield.	TWENTY Horses drinking at trough; boy, woman, &c. 20
Female figure holding plate, on which is written "Incorporated A. D. 1818."	FIFTY DOLLARS. 50 Agricultural Implements AGRICULTURAL BANK. FIFTY DOLLARS on FIFTY.	50 Dog on safe
1 Female with sickles.	Train of cars. ANDOVER BANK Andover Mass. Eagle	1 Portrait of Samuel Farrar.

Left	Centre	Right
TWO Female with the American flag.	Three female figures. ANDOVER BANK Andover, Mass. Indian head	2 Portrait of Samuel Farrar.
3 State arms.	Three female figures. ANDOVER BANK Andover, Mass. Cog wheels, etc.	3 Portrait of Samuel Farrar.
Three female figures. FIVE	Spread eagle. ANDOVER BANK Andover, Mass. Girl's head.	5 Portrait of Samuel Farrar.
10 Portrait of Samuel Farrar.	Winged female blowing a trumpet. ANDOVER BANK Andover, Mass. Imp. and produce	10 Female hiding Besice
20 Portrait of Samuel Farrar.	Farming scene. ANDOVER BANK Andover, Mass	20 Female
Female with sheaf of wheat. 50	Landing of Columbus ANDOVER BANK Andover, Mass.	50 Portrait of Female.
100	Female seated with eagle, shield, flags, etc. Female portrait. ANDOVER BANK, Andover, Mass.	100 Female portrait
500 Indian princess.	Title of Bank. Three females; ship and cars in distance.	500 500
M 1000	Title of Bank. Two females seated; shipping and cars in distance.	1000 1000
ONE Eagle with shield in talons; and ONE on shield.	Vig. Blacksmith blowing at forge, wheel behind him; anvil in front. 1 APPLETON BANK, Lowell, Mass.	1 Farmer with sickle and bundle of grain.

Left	Centre	Right
2	Vig. Sheep washing scene. 2 APPLETON BANK, Lowell, Mass. Cow and fence	2 Locomotive and cars.
3	Vig. Blacksmith's shop, man and horse, smith at anvil; dog at his feet, and boy at forge 3 APPLETON BANK, Lowell, Mass. Dog	3 Male portrait.
5	Vig. A person driving horses in chariot, accompanied by train of people; an angel above horses. 5 APPLETON BANK. Lowell, Mass.	FIVE Medallion head 5
X	Vig. Large house, train of cars; man with wheelbarrow; and steeple of church in distance. X APPLETON BANK, Lowell, Mass.	TEN Indian female. TEN
20 Woman sitting, with left hand on an open book	XX Eagle XX APPLETON BANK, Lowell, Mass.	20 Ship.
XX Female with tablets; child at her feet.	APPLETON BANK, Lowell, Mass. Title of Bank TWENTY	20 Boy and two horses at trough.
L Washingt'n	APPLETON BANK, Lowell, Mass. Title of Bank 50 DOLLS	50 Martha Washingt'n
FIFTY A woman with a wreath in her left hand. FIFTY	50 Vig. A man with his right hand on the mane of a wild horse. 50 APPLETON BANK, Lowell, Mass.	FIFTY A woman with a bunch of flowers in her left hand. FIFTY
C Female, cog wheels, etc.	APPLETON BANK Lowell, Mass. Title of Bank One Hundred Dollars	100 Female spinning wheel; factories, etc.
Same as right Portrait of Harrison	Vig. A wharf with a large covered waggon, into which two men are rolling a hogshead. APPLETON BANK, Lowell, Mass.	One Hundred and 100, Male portrait.

Left	Centre	Right
D Dog & safe.	APPLETON BANK, Lowell, Mass. Title of Bank. 500 DOLLS.	500 Eagle.
500	Vig. Woman sitting, pointing with her left hand to men reaping, and a man on horseback. 500 D APPLETON BANK, Lowell, Mass.	500
Female. ONE	View in Essex street, Salem. ASIATIC BANK Salem Mass	1 Elephants. ONE
TWO Elephants. TWO	View in Essex street, Salem, ASIATIC BANK Salem, Mass	TWO Female. TWO
THREE Female. THREE	View in Essex street, Salem. ASIATIC BANK Salem, Mass.	3 Elephants. THREE
Female. FIVE	View in Essex street, Salem, ASIATIC BANK. Salem, Mass.	V Elephants. FIVE
TEN	10 View in Essex street, Salem X ASIATIC BANK Salem, Mass.	10 Female.
20 Man ploughing with Horses. 20	20 Party of milk maids. ASIATIC BANK Salem, Mass.	20 Ship. XX
20 Female.	XX Eagle XX ASIATIC BANK Salem, Mass	20 Ship
20 Female.	Female seated between fig. 2 and 0. ASIATIC BANK, Salem, Mass. XX	20 Female. 20

FIFTY. Female with wreath. FIFTY.
50 Man and horse. 50
ASIATIC BANK
Salem, Mass.
FIFTY. Female. FIFTY.

50 Female figure.
Male and female.
ASIATIC BANK
Salem Mass.
50
50 Cupid in sail boat. 50

Same as right. Portrait of Harrison.
Scene on a wharf.
ASIATIC BANK
Salem, Mass.
One Hundred and 100. Portrait of Columbus.

100 Vulcan.
Spread Eagle train of cars and canal.
ASIATIC BANK
Salem Mass.
100
100 Female.

500
Female seated painting in reapers and load of hay.
500 D
Title of Bank.
500

Laocoon and serpents. 1000
THOUSAND Cars and laborers.
Title of Bank.
1000 Vessels. 1000

1 Portrait of Taylor on large l
ATLANTIC BANK,
Boston, Mass.
Spread eagle and ships above this.
1 Female with spy glass.

1 State Arms.
I Two sailors, anchor, rope, vessels, etc.
ATLANTIC BANK,
Boston, Mass.
1 Female seated with spy glass; vessels, etc.

2 Eagle, shield, etc.
Indian female, eagle, shield, steamer, etc.
2
Title of Bank.
TWO Same as ones.

2 Portrait of Taylor. TWO
Steamship and other vessels.
ATLANTIC BANK,
Boston, Mass.
TWO Female with spy glass. TWO

Female seated with spy glass, vessels, etc. THREE
Title of Bank.
3 Sailor erect with spy glass beside capstan on vessel. 3
3 Female portrait.

Female with spy glass. 3
3 Indian with gun and female with sickle. THREE between and eagle at top.
ATLANTIC BANK,
Boston, Mass.
3 Sailor seated on a bale.

FIVE Winged female with trumpet.
Portrait of Taylor with Title on right.
V
FIVE Male and female. 5

Female. X
Portrait of Taylor.
ATLANTIC BANK,
Boston, Mass.
TEN Female with spy-glass.

20 Two females.
ATLANTIC BANK,
Boston, Mass.
20 Female reclining with quadrant, globe, etc. 20
20 Pilot boat 5; vessels, etc.

L 50 on reddie. FIFTY
Title Girl's head.
Female erect with pen and fasces; shield at her feet. 50 on red die.
50 on red die. Man purchasing paper of news boy; bale, steamer, etc.

100 Sailor, mechanic, vessels, etc.
C Two children C
ATLANTIC BANK,
Boston, Mass.
100 Female

D Five Hundred 500
Title of Bank.
Sailor, farmer, boy, dog, capstan, anchor, ocean view, etc.
500
500 Five Hundred 500

1 ONE 1
ONE Atlas supporting the globe on his shoulders. 1
ATLAS BANK,
Boston, Mass.
ONE DOLLAR

2 TWO 2
TWO Vig. Same as ones. 2
ATLAS BANK,
Boston, Mass.
TWO DOLLARS

3 THREE 3
THREE Vig. Same as ones. 3
ATLAS BANK,
Boston, Mass.
THREE DOLLARS

5 FIVE 5
V Vig. Same as ones. 5
ATLAS BANK,
Boston, Mass.
FIVE DOLLARS

10 TEN 10
X Vig. Same as ones.
ATLAS BANK,
Boston, Mass.
TEN DOLLARS

20 TWENTY 20
XX Vig. Same as ones. 20
ATLAS BANK,
Boston, Mass.
TWENTY

50 FIFTY 50
FIFTY Vig. Same as ones. 50
ATLAS BANK,
Boston, Mass.
FIFTY DOLLARS

100 100 100
C Vig. Same as ones. 100
ATLAS BANK,
Boston, Mass.
ONE HUNDRED

This Bank also issues 500s and 1000s; they have the same vignette as all other denominations.

1
Vig. Locomotive and train of cars; village in the distance.
1
ATTLEBOROUGH BANK,
Attleborough, Mass.
1 Drover and cattle. ONE

2
Vig. Farmer on horseback; load of hay entering barn; hay-makers, cattle, &c. 2
ATTLEBOROUGH BANK,
Attleborough, Mass.
2 Female with bundle of grain and sickle. TWO

3
Female with grain under left arm, compass, dwelling house and mill in the background. 3
ATTLEBOROUGH BANK,
Attleborough, Mass.
3 Spread eagle. THREE

Left	Centre	Right
5 Reaper sitting with a sickle in his hand. 5	Medallion head. Vig. Two females and three cherubs surrounding the figure 5. ATTLEBOROUGH BANK, Attleborough, Mass.	5 Man harvesting corn.
10 Portrait of J. Q. Adams.	Vig. Female and Eagle. ATTLEBOROUGH BANK, Attleborough, Mass. Man at work; house and bridge in background.	10 Farmer cradling grain.
20 Spread eagle. XX	Vig. Two females sitting, plough and eagle between them; factory, man ploughing, steamboat and train of cars in the distance. ATTLEBOROUGH BANK, Attleborough, Mass. Dog.	20 Male portrait. XX
50 Female bust. 50	ATTLEBOROUGH BANK, Attleborough, Mass. Vig. Eagle bearing aloft person with arms extended; cherub under each arm. State Arms.	50 Female sitting. 50
Female sitting.	100 Vig. Male and female sitting; horn of plenty between 100 ATTLEBOROUGH BANK, Attleborough Mass. A deer.	Reaper with sickle and grain
Milk Maid. 1	(Old Plate.) Cattle, sheep and hogs; scene in Brighton on a market day. B'K OF BRIGHTON, Brignton, Mass.	1 General Washington. ONE
1 ONE 1	View of Cattle fair hotel. B'K OF BRIGHTON, Brighton, Mass.	1 A bulls head. ONE
TWO Female. 2	(Old Plate.) Cattle, sheep and hogs; a scene in Brighton on a market day. B'K OF BRIGHTON, Brighton, Mass.	2 TWO
2 TWO 2	(New Plate. View of cattle fair hotel. B'K OF BRIGHTON, Brighton, Mass.	TWO on 2. Yoke of oxen
3 Portrait. 3	(Old Plate.) Cattle, sheep and hogs; a scene in Brighton on a market day. B'K OF BRIGHTON, Brighton	3 Cattle. THREE

Left	Centre	Right
3 THREE 3	(New Plate.) View of Cattle fair hotel. B'K OF BRIGHTON, Brighton, Mass.	3 THREE Cattle.
5 Portrait of Franklin.] 5	(Old Plate.) Cattle, sheep and hogs; scene in Brighton on a market day. B'K OF BRIGHTON, Brighton. Mass.	5 Female. V
5 V and FIVE 5	(New Plate.) View of Cattle fair hotel, B'K OF BRIGHTON, Brighton, N. Y.	FIVE, 5, V, Cattle and sheep.
10 Portrait of Washington. 10	(Old Plate.) Cattle, sheep and hogs; a scene in Brighton on a market day. B'K OF BRIGHTON, Brighton, Mass.	10 Female. TEN
X Portrait of Webster. TEN	(New Plate.) View of cattle fair hotel. B'K OF BRIGHTON, Brighton. Mass.	10 Locomotive.
TWENTY Female.	(Old Plate.) Cattle, sheep, and hogs; a scene in Brighton on a market day. B'K OF BRIGHTON, Brighton, Mass.	20 Train of cars. XX
XX Portrait of Washington.	(New Plate View of cattle fair hotel. B'K OF BRIGHTON, Brighton, Mass.	20 Female and shield.
Portrait of Washington. 50	Drove of cattle. B'K OF BRIGHTON, Brighton, Mass.	50 Locomotive.
Female with flowers. 50	B'K. OF BRIGHTON, Brighton, Mass. Boy running after horses; sheep, cattle, trees, etc.	50 View of a street and bank building.
100 Street and bank building.	B'K. OF BRIGHTON, Brighton, Mass. Drover and cattle, boy in water; trees and farm house in distance.	100 Man dressing leather.

Left	Centre	Right
Female. 100	Drove of cattle. B'K OF BRIGHTON, Brighton, Mass.	100 Portrait of Franklin.
Female seated with shield on which is figs. 500.	B'K. OF BRIGHTON, Brighton, Mass. State Arms; horse on either side with eagle at top, cars on right; building on left.	500 Large building
ONE Sailor, bbl. bales; top of masts of vessels.	Schooners and sloops; men fishing; various vessels and lighthouse in distance. B'K OF CAPE ANN, Gloucester, Mass.	1 Boy with rabbits.
2	BANK OF CAPE ANN Gloucester, Mass. Vig. Same as ones.	2 Liberty, left arm on shield; train of cars and factory in distance.
Man with scythe in field; village in distance. 3	Two females; one feeding chickens; the other milking cow; cow, haystack, house, &c. BANK OF CAPE ANN Gloucester, Mass.	3 Female.
5 Female with chickens.	Vig. Same as ones. B'K OF CAPE ANN, Gloucester, Mass.	Figure 5, word five on either side. Indian female, left hand resting on rock.
10 Female portrait.	Launching boat in sea, men in it apparently going to rescue passengers from ship that has stranded. B'K OF CAPE ANN, Gloucester, Mass.	X Shield in scroler work with motto E Pluribus Unum.
Spread eagle on shield. 20	B'K OF CAPE ANN, Gloucester, Mass. Large Ship, steamship, and other ships in distance.	20 Sailor seated on rock with telescope.
50	Steamship; ships in distance. Female with cornucopia and sheaf of wheat. B'K OF CAPE ANN, Gloucester, Mass.	50 Two males, one holding plan of pillar, the other looking at it building a house.
100 Three female figures with pole and cap, and horn of plenty, &c.	B'K OF CAPE ANN, Gloucester, Mass.	C Indian seated on rock with bow.

Left	Centre	Right
1 Male portrait.	Brig, merchant and man of war; light house on left, steamship in distance. B'K OF CAPE COD. Harwich, Mass. Codfish.	1 Female with spy glass seated on cask; ship in distance.
2 Sailor seated with stars and stripes; anchor, cask, quadrant.	B'K OF CAPE COD. Harwich, Mass. Landing of Pilgrims at Provincetown. Codfish.	2 Portrait of Girl.
Portrait of female. 3	B'K OF CAPE COD. Harwich, Mass. Three sailors, one standing against wharf post, pipe in mouth, another standing at his right; third seated on anchor with spy glass and pipe; casks, ships, &c. Codfish.	3 Portrait of Girl.
Portrait of a boy. 4 FOUR	B'K OF CAPE COD. Harwich, Mass. Signing Declaration of Independence. Codfish.	4 Female seated in sea shell, trident in hand; ships in distance.
5 Male portrait FIVE	B'K OF CAPE COD. Harwich, Mass. Vig. Signing the first constitution in the cabin of the May Flower in Cape Cod Harbor in 1620.	5 Male portrait
10 Sailor leaning on capstan; cask, bale and shipping.	Signing the first constitution on board the May-flower, 1620; Indian princess on right, with bow and quiver. B'K OF CAPE COD. Harwich, Mass. Codfish.	10 Portrait of J. Q. Adams TEN
20	B'K OF CAPE COD. Harwich, Mass. Vig. Scene on Marshfield farm; cattle and sheep grazing.	20 Portrait of Dan. Webster.
Portrait of female. 50	B'K OF CAPE COD. Harwich, Mass. Vig. Sailor standing against vessels rail; steam ships and shipping in distance. Codfish.	50 Anchor and chain; box, bales, cask; ships.
Sailor with flag; female with horn of plenty, bale, anchor, &c.	100 100 B'K. OF CAUE COD Harwich, Mass. Portrait of Washington. One Hundred.	Female figure of justice; ensign with stars, covering her lap.
ONE State Arms.	BK OF COMMERCE, Boston, Mass.	1 Male portrait

Left	Centre	Right
1 Portrait.	Train of cars. BK. OF COMMERCE, Boston, Mass. Indian girl	1 Portrait.
2 Portrait.	Spread eagle and shipping. BK. OF COMMERCE, Boston, Mass. Ship	2 Female portrait.
2 Ship.	BK OF COMMERCE, Boston, Mass.	2 Male portrait
3 Portrait.	Spread eagle with view of State street and Faneuil Hall. BK. OF COMMERCE, Boston. Mass. Arms	3 Female figure.
THREE Sailor, capstan, anchor, etc.	BK OF COMMERCE, Boston, Mass.	3 Male portrait
5 Male Portrait.	Spread eagle with view of State street, and the Market House. BK. OF COMMERCE, Boston, Mass. Steamer	5 Male Portrait
Three female figures. TEN	Steamship and sailing vessels. BK. OF COMMERCE, Boston, Mass. Female, etc.	10 Male Portrait
Male Portrait. 20	View of the Boston Custom House. BK. OF COMMERCE, Boston, Mass. Vessels	20 Goddess of Liberty.
50 Sailor with flag.	Female with trumpet eagle, globe, etc. BK. OF COMMERCE, Boston, Mass. Locomotive and tender	50 Washington.
Male Portrait. C	Three female figures vessels, etc. BK. OF COMMERCE, Boston, Mass. Ship	100 Female portrait

Left	Centre	Right
Male portrait D	Squaw reclining; shield, eagle and flags; steamship in distance. BK. OF COMMERCE, Boston, Mass. Beehive.	500 Female
Female reclining; shipping scene. 1000	Male portrait BK. OF COMMERCE, Boston, Mass. Steamship.	1000
ONE	1 Columbus. 1 BANK OF THE METROPOLIS, Boston, Mass. State Arms.	ONE
2 State Arms.	Head of Franklin. Title of Bank.	TWO TWO TWO
THREE	State Arms. View of the State House, in Boston. 3 Title of Bank	THREE
FIVE	Title of Bank. Signing the Declaration of Independence.	5 State Arms.
TEN	Large public building, horses, carriages, pedestrians, &c. Title of Bank.	10 State arms.
Red 20. TWENTY XX	Title of Bank. State Arms.	Red 20. TWENTY XX
Red 50. State Arms.	Title of Bank. Three sailors, one looking through telescope.	Red 50. Eagle.
Red C. State Arms.	Title of Bank. Anchor, bales, barrels, masts, etc.	Red 100. Girls' portrait.

Left	Center	Right
Red 500	Horse Eagle Title of Bank Ocean scene; vessels, etc.	Red 500 State Arms
	BANK OF MUTUAL REDEMPTION, Boston, Mass. ☞ This Bank uses the Perkins' stereotype plate, which has the denomination in fine print all over the face of the bill. They intend shortly to use a different plate.	
1	Female seated and leaning on a bale; cars and canal; shipping in distance. 1 BK. OF NORTH AM., Boston, Mass.	Female and 1 ONE
Female reclining on bale. Canal, cars, ships, &c. 1	1 BANK OF NORTH AMERICA, Boston, Mass	1 Indian female, trees, rocks, &c.
2	Sailor and shipping. 2 BK. OF NORTH AM., Boston, Mass.	2 State Arms.
Sailor with spy glass in hand. Bale, barrels and compass. Ships under sail. 2	2 BANK OF NORTH AMERICA, Boston, Mass.	2 Goddess of liberty, shield, scales, &c.
THREE.	Two female figures and bust of Washington. 3 on right BK. OF NORTH AM., Boston, Mass.	3 Female holding flag and 3 on pieces
3	Two female figures and bust of Washington. 3 surrounded by small 3s. BANK OF NORTH AMERICA, Boston, Mass.	THREE. Sailor aloft with spy-glass in left hand, right hand hold of stay.
FIVE Female.	Spread Eagle. Cupid either side holding fig. 5. BK. OF NORTH AM., Boston, Mass.	FIVE Female.
FIVE Female.	Two females seated on bale of cotton. Factories; cotton field, &c. BANK OF NORTH AMERICA, Boston, Mass	5 Seal of the City of Boston.

Left	Center	Right
TEN	Train of cars. 10 BK. OF NORTH AM., Boston, Mass. State Arms	TEN Squaw with bow and spear.
Female with scroll, child at feet. TEN	Female seated, resting on shield. Eagle, steamship, &c. BANK OF NORTH AMERICA, Boston, Mass.	10 Eagle.
20 Female.	Two female figures either side of shield BK. OF NORTH AM., Boston, Mass.	20 Sailor.
20 Female seated on rock.	Two female figures either side of shield. BANK OF NORTH AMERICA, Boston, Mass	20 Goddess of liberty resting on shield.
Male and female.	50 Female, eagle and shield. 50 BK. OF NORTH AM., Boston, Mass.	Sailor and female.
100 Female.	Steamship and vessels. BK. OF NORTH AM., Boston, Mass.	100 Female.
500 Female, eagle and shield.	BK. OF NORTH AM., Boston, Mass. FIVE HUNDRED Female, eagle and shield.	500 Squaw and papoose.
Red 1 Auditors' die	BANK OF THE REPUBLIC, Boston, Mass. Vig. Early settlers at worship; dog; Indians at door.	1 Eagle.
Red 2 Auditors' die	Title of Bank. Fleet of fishing vessels at anchor, catching fish.	2 Sailor, capstan, anchor
Red 3 Auditors' die THREE	Sailor on beach; anchor, boat, etc. Title of Bank.	3 Liberty with State Arms.

Left	Center	Right
Red 5 Auditors' die	Capitol at Washington. Title of Bank.	5 Ship, pilot boat and steamboat.
Red X Auditors' die	Shipping, wharves, etc. Title of Bank.	10 Table with bust of Washington; old man and child.
20 on red edged die. State Arms. TWENTY	Female erect with sword and eagle on shield, etc., building in distance, with part of Title above and on sides. Washington on left and Martha Washington on right. 20 20	20 on red edged die. Sailor erect beside capstan.
50 State Arms.	Title of Bank. Title of Bank. 50 Dolls. in red.	50 Two children
C with words "One Hundred Dollars" around it. State Arms.	Title of Bank. Title of Bank. 100 Dolls. in red.	100 Franklin.
500 State Arms.	Title of Bank. Title of Bank. 500 Dolls. in red.	500 Male portrait.
ONE Female reclining on a fence, sheaf of wheat ONE	Ship. Ship cutting in a whale. Vig. Eagle standing on shield, bundle of arrows in talons. 1 1 BARNSTABLE BK. Yarmouth, Mass.	ONE Vessel and lighthouse. ONE
2 Sailor seated on bale of goods. TWO	Eagle on shld. TWO Eagle on shld. 2 2 BARNSTABLE BK, Yarmouth, Mass.	2 Ship and stern of another.
3 Sailor standing by capstan, ship, bales, &c.	View of street with bank and other buildings. BARNSTABLE B'K, Yarmouth, Mass. Ship.	THREE on 3. Male portrait
FIVE Sailor one hand on another; ships' masts seen in back ground. FIVE	Vig. train of cars; church on left; factory on right in distance. V V BARNSTABLE BK, Yarmouth, Mass	5 Schooner discharging her cargo into a flat boat. 5

10 | TEN TEN | 10
Jackson. Vig. Steamboat; ship on right, schooner on left. Sailor at helm.
10 | X X BARNSTABLE B'K, Yarmouth, Mass. | 10

20 | BARNSTABLE B'K, Yarmouth, Mass. | 20
TWENTY. Same as three. Liberty seated with globe and shield.
Male portrait.

XX | Sailor leaning against anchor stock smoking; stern of vessel on left. Vig. Ship and brig in foreground, pilot boat on left, and one on extreme right; two ships in the distance, between ship and brig. | 20 Steamboat and ship to bird.
XX | BARNSTABLE B'K, Yarmouth, Mass. Anchor and fish-spear. | 20

FIFTY | L L Vig. Female leaning on anchor by sea-side; ship in distance wrecked. | 50
BARNSTABLE B'K, Yarmouth, Mass. Boats and two men. | 50

50 | Same as three. | 50
BARNSTABLE B'K, Yarmouth, Mass. Male portrait.
Sailor boy's head. Barrels. FIFTY

ONE HUNDRED | BARNSTABLE B'K, Yarmouth, Mass. C C Vig. Female with grain on left, offering a part to a figure sitting on right with liberty pole and cap; ship in distance. Anchor and fish spear. | 100 Two ships and a part of another seen on right. 100

100 | BARNSTABLE B'K, Yarmouth, Mass. | 100
Vig. Same as three. Female portrait.
Male portrait. Ship.

ONE | Vig. Female reclining; on her left ships; on right houses, hills, &c. | 1
State Arms. BAY STATE BANK, Lawrence, Mass. Indian with liberty cap, shield and quiver on back.

TWO | Vig. Dog and safe; bags of specie, &c. | 2
State Arms. BAY STATE BANK, Lawrence, Mass. | TWO 2

THREE | Vig. Mechanics at work, one with sledge upraised, and the other holding chisel; steam mill and other buildings in background. | 3
State Arms. BAY STATE BANK, Lawrence, Mass. Medallion head.

FIVE | Portrait. BAY STATE BANK, Lawrence, Mass. | 5
State Arms. Vig. Commercial scene; boxes and men at work; horse and dray with a load of barrels; Navy yard crossing street; houses and hills in the background.

10 | BAY STATE BANK, Lawrence, Mass. | 10
Medallion head. Vig. Carpenter at his bench, plane behind him on bench. State Arms.

20 | BAY STATE BANK, Lawrence, Mass. | 20
Mechanic with sledge on his shoulder, anvil at his side. State Arms. Indian with liberty cap, shield and quiver on his back.

FIFTY | BAY STATE BANK, Lawrence, Mass. | 50
State Arms. Vig. Horses and chariots; men holding horses, and one horse drinking; persons on the right.

100 | BAY STATE BANK, Lawrence, Mass. | 100
State Arms. Spread eagle.

D | BAY STATE BANK, Lawrence, Mass. Vig. Female with shield, sitting on bale of goods; barrel on right, sheaf of wheat on left. 500 in dead letters. | 500 State Arms.

1 | 1 Child, dog, and safe; ship in distance. 1 BEDFORD COMMERCIAL B'K, New Bedford, Mass. | ONE

ONE | Steamship and other vessels. | 1
Sailor heaving log. BEDFORD COM B'K, New Bedford, Mass. ONE Female. ONE

2 | Female seated with telescope by shield; ship in distance. Fig. 2 on right. Title of Bank. | Ship and other vessels.
Female with flowers. TWO

2 | 2 Female seated, sea shore, ship in the distance. 2 BEDFORD COMMERCIAL B'K, New Bedford, Mass. | TWO

THREE | Spread eagle, capitol at Washington and steamship. | 3
Female. BEDFORD COMMERCIAL B'K, New Bedford, Mass.

5 | 5 Spread eagle, canal and railroad. 5 | FIVE
Indian sitting under a tree. FIVE | BEDFORD COMMERCIAL B'K, New Bedford, Mass. Female.

10 | X Spread eagle and ship. X | TEN DOLLARS.
Medallion head. 10 | BEDFORD COMMERCIAL B'K, New Bedford, Mass.

(New Plate.) Ship and steamship. | 20
20 Cupid. BEDFORD COMMERCIAL B'K, New Bedford, Mass. Wheels.

(Old Plate.) 20 | 20 Female sitting on a bale, ship in distance. | 20
Portrait of Wm. Penn. 20 | BEDFORD COMMERCIAL B'K, New Bedford, Mass. House.

FIFTY | Female, child and merchandise; ship in distance. | 50
Female. FIFTY | BEDFORD COMMERCIAL B'K, New Bedford, Mass. Building.

100 | Ships, city in the distance. | 100
Penny piece. Steamship. BEDFORD COMMERCIAL B'K, New Bedford, Mass. Justice.

Indian in canoe. | 500 BEDFORD COMMERCIAL BANK, New Bedford, Mass. | 500
500 | D D | Justice.

1 1 1 BERKSHIRE BANK, South Adams, Mass. | 1
Female seated with sickle and sheaf. Boy, girl, cattle, sheep, trees, etc. Farmer cutting corn stalks.

Cupid with sheaf. | 2 Title. 2 | Cupid with cornucopia.
Two females at work on machine. 2 | Mechanic at work at vice.

Left	Centre	Right
5 Girls head.	Title of Bank. White and black horse; cattle and trees. V 5 V	5 Two children
10 Franklin in his study.	Title of Bank. Female with pen and tablets; child at her feet. TEN either side of vig. X X	10 Female with globe.
1	Female, train of cars and canal. BEVERLY BANK, Beverly, Mass.	1 Female.
Female One, cupid.	BEVERLY BANK, Beverly, Mass. Shipping.	1 Female.
2 2	BEVERLY BANK, Beverly, Mass. Female and eagle ships in distance. 2	2 Two females.
Farmers washing sheep. 2	2 BEVERLY BANK, Beverly Mass.	TWO Females. TWO
Three female figures. 3	Portrait of Webster. BEVERLY BANK, Beverly, Mass.	3 Shipping.
Farming scene. 3	BEVERLY BANK, Beverly, Mass.	3 Female. THREE
FIVE Sailor and flag.	BEVERLY BANK Beverly, Mass. Group of females factory and shipping.	5 Portrait of Washington
Spread eagle, FIVE	V and female. BEVERLY BANK. Beverly Mass.	5 Girl

Left	Centre	Right
Vulcan the the blacksmith. TEN	X BEVERLY BANK, Beverly Mass.	10 Negro.
10 Female merchandise and shipping.	BEVERLY BANK, Beverly, Mass. TEN	X 10 Cupid.
20 Female.	XX Eagle XX BEVERLY BANK, Beverly, Mass.	20 Ship.
20 Fowls.	Cows in brook; boy, girl, etc. BEVERLY BANK. TWENTY DOLLARS. Beverly, Mass.	20 Female with grain.
Farmer seated on grain, sailor leaning on capstan; boy, dog, etc. 50	Beverly. 50 BEVERLY BANK. FIFTY DOLLARS. Massachusetts.	50 Dog, safe, &c.
FIFTY Female. FIFTY	50 Man and horse 50 BEVERLY BANK, Beverly, Mass.	FIFTY Female. FIFTY
100 Female beside State Arms, holding out wreath.	BEVERLY BANK, Beverly, Mass C Washington 100 C ONE HUNDRED DOLLARS.	100 Female reclining, globe, quadrant, &c.
Same as right. Harrison.	Scene on a wharf. BEVERLY BANK. Beverly, Mass.	One Hundred and 100. Columbus
1 Vessels.	Ship yard scene—men at work, etc. BLACKSTONE BANK Boston, Mass.	1 Mechanic with sledge.
1	View of Haymarket Square. 1 on 1 on right BLACKSTONE BANK Boston, Mass.	ONE Indian female with bow and spear.

Left	Centre	Right
TWO	Vig. Same as ones. 2 BLACKSTONE BANK Boston, Mass.	2 Sailor.
Two inverted. Sailor with female, vessels, etc., above him. TWO	Title of Bank.	2 Boy and rabbits.
3	Vig. Same as ones. 3 BLACKSTONE BANK Boston, Mass.	3 Ship under full sail.
Washington. 3	Shoemakers at work; female attending to household duties in background. Title of Bank.	3 Female, fig. 3
FIVE	Vig. Same as ones. 5 BLACKSTONE BANK Boston, Mass.	5 State Arms.
5 Female with flowers.	Title of Bank. Large public building	5 Cooper at work on bbls
X Washington.	Title of Bank. State Arms, or Indian and lone star.	10 Female with Ten on shield
10	Vig. Same as ones. Head of female on X on right. BLACKSTONE BANK Boston, Mass.	10 Female.
20 Female, eagle and shield.	Vig. Same as ones. BLACKSTONE BANK Boston, Mass.	20
20 Female with dove.	Eagle, building and steamer. Title of Bank.	20 Cars.

50 | Vig. Same as ones. 50; Cupid with L on shield on right. BLACKSTONE BANK Boston, Mass. | FIFTY Female.

---

50 Sailor, steamer, &c. | General railroad scene at depot. Title of Bank. | 50 Female portrait.

C Female portrait. | Female seated by side of shield, safe, etc.; steamer on right; cars and steamboat on left. Title of Bank. | 100

Female. 100 | Vig. Same as ones. BLACKSTONE BANK Boston, Mass. | 100 Female.

---

500 | Ocean scene. D Title of Bank | 500 Franklin.

---

1 Ox. | Horse Eagle BLACKSTONE BANK Uxbridge, Mass. 1 Female with sword & shield. 1 | 1 Girl's head.

---

1 Portrait of Washington. | Female. 1 Female. BLACKSTONE BANK Uxbridge, Mass. | 1 Portrait of Franklin.

Female resting arm on bale; cars, vessel, anvil, &c. 1 | Large figure 1 with five heads in miniature view on it. BLACKSTONE B'K. Uxbridge, Mass. | 1 Female with sheaf.

---

2 Portrait of Columbus. | Female. 2 Female. BLACKSTONE BANK Uxbridge, Mass. | 2 Portrait.

Worki[ng] shore; houses in distance. 2 | Large figure 2, with five heads on it. BLACKSTONE B'K Uxbridge, Mass. | TWO Portrait of female. TWO

Two on 2 Two girls with sheafs. | BLACKSTONE BANK Uxbridge, Mass. Old man, child and bust of Washington. Words Two Dollars on 2 either side. | 2 Female portrait.

Farming scene. 3 | Large figure 3 across the bill. BLACKSTONE B'K. Uxbridge, Mass. | Fig. 3, word three. Female with basket of flowers. THREE

---

3 Washington. | Female. 3 Female. BLACKSTONE BANK Uxbridge, Mass. | 3 Vulcan the Blacksmith.

---

3 Girl's head. | BLACKSTONE BANK Uxbridge, Mass. 3 Man oiling machinery 3 3 | 3 Man at vice.

Spread eagle. FIVE | V BLACKSTONE BANK Uxbridge, Mass. | 5 Girl.

Five on 5. Male portrait. | BLACKSTONE BANK Uxbridge, Mass. Female either side of anvil; buildings in distance. | 5 Girl's head.

---

10 Girl's head. TEN | Train of cars. BLACKSTONE BANK Uxbr[illegible] | 10 Male head.

Vulcan the blacksmith, train of cars, factories in the backgr'd TEN | X BLACKSTONE BANK Uxbridge, Mass. | 10 Reaper.

---

20 Female. | XX Eagle. XX BLACKSTONE BANK Uxbridge, Mass. | 20 Ship.

TWENTY 20 TWENTY | White and black horse, cattle, etc. Male head. BLACKSTONE BANK Uxbridge, Mass. | 20 Dog swimming with body of child

---

50 Female with name of Bank on scroll; child at her feet. | BLACKSTONE BANK Uxbridge, Mass. L Male portrait. L | 50 Youthful portrait.

Same as right Portrait | Scene on a wharf. BLACKSTONE BANK Uxbridge, Mass. | One Hundred and 100, Portrait of Columbus.

Male portrait 100 | BLACKSTONE BANK Uxbridge, Mass Three females reclining; vessel in distance 100 C 100 | 100 Sailor boy; sailors, vessels, etc.

---

1 Female portrait. 3 | View of a street with bank and other buildings. BLUEHILL BANK, Dorchester, Mass. | 1 Cows.

ONE 1 | Farmer sowing seed. 1 BLUE HILL BANK Dorchester, Mass. | 1 Ship. ONE

---

2 Portrait of a female. | Same as ones. BLUEHILL BANK, Dorchester, Mass. Horses. | 2 Female.

TWO 2 | Spread eagle. 2 BLUE HILL BANK Dorchester, Mass. | 2 TWO Sailboats.

---

3 Stone-cutter | Same as ones. BLUEHILL BANK, Dorchester, Mass. | 3 Female.

THREE 3 | Wharf and shipping. 3 BLUE HILL BANK Dorchester, Mass. | 3 THREE Train of cars.

---

5 Liberty. FIVE | Same as ones. BLUEHILL BANK, Dorchester, Mass. | 5 Female representing Agriculture.

FIVE Spread eagle. Large V near the centre. 5 BLUE HILL BANK, Dorchester, Mass. Girl.	1 1 Shipping, etc. 1 1 Indian with bow. ONE BOSTON BANK, Boston, Mass. Ship. ONE	M 1000 Shipping. Female, eagle, wreath and scales. BOSTON BANK, Boston, Mass. 1000
X Same as cut. 10 Farmer with scythe. BLUEHILL BANK, Dorchester, Mass. Two females.	2 2 Shipping, etc. 2 2 Mercury. TWO BOSTON BANK, Boston, Mass. State Arms. TWO	Portrait of Washington; steamer and locomotive. Same as right. ONE BOYLSTON BANK, Boston, Mass. Female fig.. ONE
Vulcan the blacksmith; train of cars and factories in the background. Large X near the centre. 10 TEN BLUEHILL BANK Dorchester, Mass. Reaper.	3 3 Shipping, etc. 3 3 Justice. Female. BOSTON BANK, Boston, Mass. Shield with fig. 3 on it. Female.	TWO Vulcan. TWO Eagle on fig. 2. TWO BOYLSTON BANK, Boston, Mass. Eagle on fig. 2. TWO
20 2 Female. 0 20 Female figure. BLUE HILL BANK Dorchester, Mass. 20	5 5 Shipping, etc. 5 5 Reapers. FIVE BOSTON BANK, Boston, Mass. Shipping. FIVE	Steamship and sailing vessels. THREE Eagle on 3. THREE BOYLSTON BANK, Boston, Mass. Indian and 3.
20 Three men, dog in grist mill—corn grinding scene. 20 Boy, dog, horses. BLUE HILL BANK, Dorchester, Mass. Two children.	Female and X on shield. X 10 BOSTON BANK, Boston, Mass. 10	V on Five. Eagle. 5 Same as right. BOYLSTON BANK, Boston, Mass. Man, boy and sheep on V.
50 Boy on horse which is drinking from stream; dog, trees, etc. 50 Man carrying leather. FIFTY BLUE HILL BANK, Dorchester, Mass. Dog & safe.	Deck of a ship; sailor at the wheel: 10 on right 20 BOSTON BANK, Boston, Mass. TWENTY	X Portrait of Columbus. X Portrait of Washington. 10 Farming scene. BOYLSTON BANK, Boston, Mass. Wharves, carmen and horses.
50 Farming scene 50 L Steamboat and sail vessel. BLUE HILL BANK Dorchester, Mass. Female, sword and scales.	50s and 100s, of the Perkins' Stereotype Plate, which has the denomination printed in fine letters all over the bill.	20 XX Eagle. XX 20 Female seated. BOYLSTON BANK, Boston, Mass. Ship.
100 Spread eagle, Railroad and canal. 100 Vulcan the blacksmith. BLUE HILL BANK Dorchester, Mass. Female.	50 Nautical scene in front of city. 50 either side. 50 State Arms. BOSTON BANK, Boston, Mass. Female with view of town and music	20 TWENTY TWENTY 20 BOYLSTON B[illegible]NS. Bost n Mass Female stepping into broad. Female portrait. Twenty on 20 Dollars on 20 Female portrait
Man, two horses, and pig at pump; cattle and barn in background. C 100 100 BLUE HILL BANK, Dorchester, Mass. C Female, spinning wheel, factories, etc.	100 C Nautical scene in front of city C 100 Sailor with trumpet on vessel. BOSTON BANK, Boston, Mass. Beehive.	FIFTY 50 Man and horse. 50 FIFTY Female. FIFTY BOYLSTON BANK, Boston, Mass. Female. FIFTY
D BLUE HILL BANK, Dorchester, Mass. 500 Wharf scene. Indian princess. Man at vice filing.	D 500 Shipping. Sailor standing by capstan. BOSTON BANK, Boston, Mass. 500	BOYLSTON BANK, Boston Massachusetts State Arms 50 Express wagon loading goods. FIFTY 50 Fifty Dollars Female figure leaning against column, [illegible] in hand.

Left	Centre	Right
Words one hundred and figs. 100. Male portrait	Wharf scene—loading wagon, men, horses, shipping, &c. BOYLSTON BANK, Boston, Mass.	Words one hundred and figures 100. Male portrait
100 Female figure beside ocean	BOYLSTON BANK, Massachusetts. Sailor & soldier, flags, fort cannon, shot, &c. One Hundred Dollars.	C Female seated, with shield, on which is city of Boston.
D Landing of the Pilgrims. D	Girl's head. BOYLSTON BANK, Boston, Mass. Five Hundred Dollars.	500 Female seated, with globe, book, &c.
Figs. 500.	Harvest scene; female seated pointing to sea-port. 500 D BOYLSTON BANK, Boylston, Mass.	500
1 Female ONE	Street in Brighton; droves of cattle. BRIGHTON MARKET BANK. Brighton, Mass.	1 Female and shield and fig. 1
Two female figures. 2	Street in Brighton; droves of cattle. BRIGHTON MARKET BANK, Brighton, Mass.	2 Sailor and Indian and TWO on shield
3 Cattle. THREE	Same as above. BRIGHTON MARKET BANK. Brighton, Mass. Man plowing	3 Farmer sailor and black smith, and fig. 3
5 Portrait of female 5	Same as above. BRIGHTON MARKET BANK. Brighton, Mass.	5 Female shield and globe.
Farmers washing sheep. X	Farming scene. BRIGHTON MARKET BANK, Brighton, Mass. Loading hay	10 Train of cars.
Female, 20	Farming scene BRIGHTON MARKET BANK. Brighton, Mass Farmer cradling	20 Cattle.

Left	Centre	Right
Female with a rake. 50	BRIGHTON MARKET BANK, Brighton, Mass Cattle. Imp. and products.	50 Female and sheep.
Female holding 50. FIFTY	Horse running; boys attempting to stop; dog, horses, houses, etc. BRIGHTON MARKET BANK, Brighton, Mass.	Female holding 50. FIFTY
C C	BRIGHTON MARKET BANK Brighton, Mass. Female reclining locomotive, factories, shipping and cattle in background. Two horses	100 Portrait of Webster. 100
C 100	Boy and horses at trough; female, pail, ducks, etc. Youthful portrait with cap. Title of Bank	100 Female, cow, calf, ducks, etc.
Boy's head. 500	BRIGHTON MARKET BANK, Brighton, Mass. 500	500 Washington; female on left; Cupid on right.
1 Blacksmith, anvil, hammer, &c.	View of Taunton green. BRISTOL COUNTY BANK, Taunton, Mass.	1 Female.
TWO Male and female. 2	Iron workers; factory in background. BRISTOL COUNTY BANK, Taunton, Mass. Eagle	2 Portrait of Fillmore.
3 2 Cupids and fig. 3	View of Taunton green. BRISTOL COUNTY BANK. Taunton, Mass. Agricultural implements	3 Portrait of Clay.
5 Female	Interior of an iron foundry. BRISTOL COUNTY BANK, Taunton, Mass.	5 Train of cars.
10 Shipping and merchandise.	River, Railroad and train of cars. BRISTOL COUNTY BANK. Taunton, Mass.	10 Portrait of Webster

Left	Centre	Right
20 Soldier loading gun	Settlers at their devotions; table, dog, etc. Indians entering door. BRISTOL COUNTY BK Taunton, Mass.	20 Two children.
50 State Arms.	BRISTOL COUNTY BK Taunton, Mass. Greetings of the Pilgrims at their landing in America.	50 Female at work at sewing machine.
C Two children.	BRISTOL COUNTY BK Taunton, Mass. Cattle in stream; children on bank under tree.	100 Female
Liberty giving eagle drink. 500	D Party of males and females viewing Niagara Falls. BRISTOL COUNTY BK Taunton, Mass.	500 D
1	Machinery, etc. BROADWAY BANK, Boston, Mass.	1 Indian female.
2	BROADWAY BANK, Boston, Mass. Machinery, etc.	2 Wheels, bale, TWO
3 Female THREE	BROADWAY BANK, Boston, Mass. Machinery, etc.	3
5 5	BROADWAY BANK, Boston, Mass. Machinery, etc.	5 Female and State Arms.
X Female and State Arms.	BROADWAY BANK, Boston, Mass. Machinery, etc.	X X
20 XX	BROADWAY BANK, Boston, Mass. Machinery, locomotive, etc.	20 Anchor, bales, barrels, etc.

50 Ship and bales. FIFTY | BROADWAY BANK, Boston, Mass. Machinery, etc. | 50

C | BROADWAY BANK, Boston, Mass. Machinery, etc. | 100 Sailor seated on a bale.

500 Machinery, locomotive, etc. | Title of Bank. Female and swan. | 500

1 Female resting her arm upon an urn, bearing the inscription of "Washington." ONE | BUNKER HILL B'K. 1 Bunker Hill Monument. 1 Charlestown Mass. | 1 Gen. Washington. ONE

1 | BUNKER HILL BK., Charlestown, Mass. Signing Declaration of Independence. Eagle. | 1 Milkmaid, cow and calf.

Sailor and Indian either side of a red, white and blue shield surmounted by eagle. 2 | Female, column, steamer, etc. Title of Bank. | 2 Girl's portrait.

2 Female. TWO | BUNKER HILL B'K. 2 Bunker hill Monument. 2 Charlestown, Mass. | 2 Gen. Warren. TWO

3 Gen. Warren. THREE | BUNKER HILL B'K. 3 Bunker hill Monument. 3 Charlestown, Mass. | 3 Eagle and shield. 3

3 3 | Title of Bank. Launch of the Adriatic. | 3 Eagle and shield.

V Female portrait. | Landing of William Penn; whites and Indians. Title of Bank. | 5 Fowls.

FIVE Female. | BUNKER HILL B'K. Bunker hill Monument. Charlestown Mass. | 5 Gen. Warren. FIVE

X Gen. Warren. X | BUNKER HILL B'K. Bunker hill Monument. Charlestown Mass. | 10 Female.

Female portrait 10 | BUNKER HILL BK., Charlestown, Mass. U. S. Capitol. | 10 Female seated in a shell.

20 Anchor, etc. | BUNKER HILL BK. Charlestown, Mass. Female, two Indians and old soldier gazing at portrait of Washington. 20 each side. | 20 Jefferson.

20 Female. | XX Eagle XX BUNKER HILL B'K. Charlestown, Mass | 20 Ship.

50 Female head. | Title of Bank. Man with gun; female loading gun. | 50 Adams.

FIFTY Female. FIFTY | 50 Man and horse. 50 BUNKER HILL B'K. Charlestown, Mass. | FIFTY Female. FIFTY

Same as right. Portrait of Harrison. | Scene on a wharf. BUNKER HILL B'K. Charlestown, Mass. | One Hundred and 100. Portrait of Columbus.

C Boy's portrait. | Angel blowing trumpet; eagle, globe, flags, etc. Title of Bank. C | 100 Indian on shield.

D Soldier and drum. | BUNKER HILL BK. Charleston, Mass. Landing of the Pilgrims. 500 on Five Hundred. | 500 Female portrait.

M Washington. | Marine view. BUNKER HILL BK. Charleston, Mass. One Thousand. 1000 | 1000 Franklin.

ONE Man and boy carrying sheep. | Vig. Blacksmith shop; three men, horse, dog, &c. 1 CABOT BANK, Chicopee, Mass. | 1 Man whetting scythe.

Female resting on figure 2, with sheaf. | Vig. Man watching sheep. 2 CABOT BANK, Chicopee, Mass. | 2 Beehive, flowers, &c.

THREE Man holding sheafs and sickle. 3 | Eagle. 3 CABOT BANK, Chicopee, Mass. | 3 Indian enclosed in a shield.

FIVE 5 | Vig. Cars, &c. V CABOT BANK, Chicopee, Mass. | FIVE Blacksmith with hammer resting on figure 5. FIVE

10 | Vig. Spread eagle, canal boats, and cars. X CABOT BANK, Chicopee, Mass. | TEN Cars. TEN

20 Female with chest and money bags. | XX Eagle. XX CABOT BANK, Chicopee, Mass. | 20 Ship.

FIFTY Female with flowers. FIFTY | 50 Man holding a horse. 50 CABOT BANK, Chicopee, Mass. | FIFTY Female with flowers. FIFTY

The words one hundred, with the figures 100 running across. Male portrait. | Vig. Wharf scene; men loading waggon; ships, &c. CABOT BANK, Chicopee, Mass. | The words one hundred with the figures 100 running across. Male portrait.

ONE Blacksmith, engine; factory. | View of Bank and street in Cambridge, with pedestrians, horses, etc. CAMBRIDGE BANK, Cambridge, Mass | 1 Boy.

Female with scales, etc. 2	Vig. Same as above ones. Title of Bank.	2 Cattle; cars passing over bridge, etc.
3 Two females.	Vig. Same as above ones. Title of Bank.	3 Female, globe, shield, pole and cup.
	CAMBRIDGE BANK, Cambridge Mass. This Bank uses the Perkin's stereotype Plate, which is the denomination printed in fine letters all over the bill.	
5 Female portrait.	Vig. Same as above ones. Title of Bank.	5 Franklin.
TEN Washington.	Vig. Same as ones. Title of Bank.	10 Blacksmith at forge, etc.
TWENTY Female feeding fowls.	Vig. Same as ones. Title of Bank.	20 XX
50 50	Vig. Same as ones. Title of Bank.	50 Webster.
100 Sailor, barrels, etc. C on 100.	Vig. Same as ones. Title of Bank.	100 Female portrait.
500 D 500	Street scene in Cambridge. CAMBRIDGE BANK, Cambridge, Mass.	500 500 500
Female and fig. 1 1	CAMBRIDGE CITY BANK, Cambridgep't, Mass. Man chopping trees, cabin and wagon. One gold dollar. ONE	1

Female feeding an Eagle from a Cup. 2	CAMBRIDGE CITY BANK. Cambridgeport, Mass. Farmer with rake, milk-maid and cows, farm house in back ground. Two gold dollars. TWO TWO	2 Two Dollars. Train of Cars.
3	Farmer, Sailor, and Mechanic, Female 3 gold dollars. CAMBRIDGE CITY BANK. Cambridgeport, Mass.	3 Farmer, Sailor, and Mechanic, and figure three.
5	Man with gun, Indian woman, 2 cupids and 5 gold dollars. Steamship CAMBRIDGE CITY BANK. Cambridgeport, Mass.	5 Group of Females, and figure five.
X X	CAMBRIDGE CITY BANK. Cambridgeport, Mass. Train of cars. TEN TEN	X Load of Grain.
XX Man holding fig. 20.	CAMBRIDGE CITY BANK. Cambridgeport, Mass. Female in foreground, R. R. and steamboat in background. Twenty Twenty	20
50 Female.	Spread eagle, capital at Washington and steamship in background. CAMBRIDGE CITY BANK. Cambridgeport, Mass. Fifty Fifty	50
Femal, spear and shield. Hundred	CAMBRIDGE CITY BANK. Cambridgeport, Mass. Female, Eagle and globe shipping in the backgrounds. One Hundred	100 A hunter.
1 Bull's head.	Figure 1 and cupid. Cows and sheep. CAMBRIDGE MARKET BANK, Cambridgeport, Mass.	ONE Female
TWO Female.	Figure 2 and cupid. Cows and sheep. CAMBRIDGE MARKET BANK, Cambridge, Mass.	2 Cattle and hogs.
Female. THREE	Man on horseback, cattle and sheep. CAMBRIDGE MARKET BANK, Cambridge, Mass.	3 Farmer, sailor, Mechanic and figure three.

Eagle. Female figure FIVE	Man on horseback, cattle and sheep. CAMBRIDGE MARKET BANK, Cambridge, Mass. FIVE	5 Mass. Spread Eagle. FIVE
Man plowing with horses. X	10 CAMBRIDGE MARKET BANK, Cambridge, Mass.	TEN Female with scales.
20 Cattle.	Train of cars. CAMBRIDGE MARKET BANK, Cambridge, Mass.	20 Female.
50 Female figure.	Cattle, houses in the distance. CAMBRIDGE MARKET BANK, Cambridge Mass.	50
100 Cattle	Spread eagle on shield; U. S. Capitol on right; steamship on right. CAMBRIDGE MARKET BANK, Cambridge, Mass. 100	100 Bull's head.
D Five hundred. 500	CAMBRIDGE MARKET BANK. Scene in woods; loading coal drawn by oxen. Massachusetts. 500	500 Five hundred. 500
Female sitting with pen and scroll. ONE	Vig. Female, dog and child; plough, sheaf, &c; railroad and vessels. CENTRAL BANK, Worcester, Mass.	1 Head of female.
Indian sitting on rock; waterfall. TWO	Vig. Mechanic sitting with one hand resting on wheel; female standing; mechanical implements scattered around; ship on right. CENTRAL BANK, Worcester, Mass.	2 Female with sheaf on shoulder.
Female with flowers in her apron. 3	Title of Bank. Female sitting, sickle in hand, shield on her right, fruit, flowers &c on the ground; railroad bridge on the right.	3 Female head.
Female with sickle, holding figure 5. FIVE	5 CENTRAL B'K. 5 Worcester, Mass. Horse at full speed; train of cars in the distance.	Female sitting on bale, holding the figure 5. FIVE

10 | Vig. Three female figures, one on the left with horn of plenty; ship on the extreme right. Title of Bank. | TEN | Female with sickle and sheaf.

20 | CENTRAL BANK, Worcester, Mass. | Winged figures supporting the figures 20 | 20

50 | Vig. Cows standing in water, sheep on the bank lying down. | CENYRAL BANK, Worcester, Mass. | Small female head. | 50 | Head of Washington.

100 | Vig. Female with shield; capital in the distance. Title of Bank. | Horses at water trough. | 100 | Head of Webster.

D | Vig. Female leaning on bale; ship on right. | CENTRAL BANK, Worcester, Mass. | 500 | Eagle and shield.

1 | ONE | View of Harvard College. | CHARLES RIVER BANK, Cambridge, Mass. | 1 | Portrait of Judge Story. | ONE

2 | Genl. Washington. | TWO | View of Harvard College. | CHARLES RIVER BANK, Cambridge, Mass. | 2 | Portrait of Judge Story. | TWO

3 | Female with sword and scales. | THREE | View of Harvard College. | CHARLES RIVER BANK, Cambridge, Mass. | 3 | Portrait of Judge Story. | THREE

Female. | FIVE | View of Harvard College. | CHARLES RIVER BANK. Cambridge, Mass. | 5 | Portrait of Judge Story. | FIVE

10 | Portrait of Franklin. | TEN | View of Harvard College. | CHARLES RIVER BANK. Cambridge, Mass. | Male seated | 10 | Portrait of Judge Story. | TEN

20 | Female. | Spread eagle; shipping and R. R., in background. | CHARLES RIVER BANK, Cambridge, Mass. | TWENTY | Female with sheaf of wheat. | 20

Medallion head. | 50 | State arms, female on either side, also spread eagle on the top. | CHARLES RIVER BANK, Cambridge, Mass. | 50 | Medallion head.

Female. | 100 | CHARLES RIVER BANK. Cambridge, Mass. | Horses, chariot and female figure. | 100

1 | Train of cars. Horse and 1. | CHICOPEE BANK, Springfield, Mass. | 1 | Spread Eagle. | ONE

2 | Farmer, horses, & harrow & old Pynchon house. 2 | CHICOPEE BANK, Springfield, Mass. | 2 | Loading hay. | TWO

3 | Medallion Head | THREE | Tubal the Blacksmith. 3 | CHICOPEE BANK, Springfield, Mass. | Three and 3. | Gen. Washington.

5 | Portrait of Washington. | Large V and reaper. | CHICOPEE BANK, Springfield, Mass. | 5 | Female. | 5

X | Female. | TEN | Man ploughing with horses. | CHICOPEE BANK, Springfield, Mass. | 10 | State arms with female on either side. | TEN

Goddess of Liberty eagle & shield. | XX Signing the declaration of Independence. | CHICOPEE BANK, Springfield, Mass. | 20 | 20 | 20

50 | Medallion head. | Man on horse back, flock of sheep. | CHICOPEE BANK, Springfield, Mass. | 50 50 | 50 | Medallion head.

100 | Medallion head. | 100 | Female reclining and horn of plenty. | CHICOPEE BANK, Springfield, Mass. | 100 | Medallion head.

State Arms. | 500 | CHICOPEE BANK, Springfield, Mass. | 500 | 500

Female figure and 1. | ONE | Female supporting the figure 1. Railroad & Steamboat. | CITIZENS BANK, Worcester, Mass. | 1 | Blacksmith & anvil.

2 | Portrait of Z. Taylor. | Farmer, dog & grain. | CITIZENS BANK, Worcester, Mass. | 2 | Cherub and dolphin. | TWO

3 | Sea monster. | Steamship. | Man resting a sledge upon his shoulder, factories & stream of water in the background. | CITIZENS BANK, Worcester, Mass. | 3 | State arms.

FIVE | 5 Juno & Mercury, also a griffin standing upon a safe. | 5 on right | CITIZENS BANK, Worcester, Mass. | Canal Locks | V | Female with a rake. | V

TEN | X Cupid X | CITIZENS BANK, Worcester, Mass. | Jupiter, Juno and Mercury. | 10

TWENTY | 20 Female & eagle, portrait of Washington. 20 | CITIZENS BANK, Worcester, Mass. | Ches | Jupiter. | 20

Female warrior. | 50 | L Train of cars L | CITIZENS BANK, Worcester, Mass. | 3 Female figures. | 50

Indian shooting an arrow. | 100 | 100 Neptune. 100 | CITIZENS BANK, Worcester, Mass. | Statue of Washington. | 100

Left	Centre	Right
1 Steamship.	View of Boston and the harbor. CITY BANK, Boston, Mass.	1 Ship under full sail.
2 Medallion.	Vig. Same as ones. CITY BANK. Boston, Mass.	2 Medallion.
3 Medallion. 3	Vig. Same as ones. CITY BANK, Boston, Mass.	3 Medallion.
5 Med head FIVE	Vig. Same as ones. CITY BANK, Boston, Mass. Indian on shield	5 Medallion.
TEN Word Ten on med. head.	Vig. Same as ones. CITY BANK, Boston, Mass.	10 Medallion.
	The 20s, 50s, 100s, and 500s, are of the Perkins' Stereotype Plate, which has the denomination printed in fine letters all over the bill.	
Figure 1 with a s s running across it	View of Lynn Common. CITY B'K OF LYNN Mass.	ONE on 1. portrait.
2	View of Lynn Common. CITY B'K OF LYNN Mass	2 Sailor on shipboard.
3	CITY BANK, Lynn, Mass. Yacht race; on the beach various males and females. 3	THREE on 3. Two males.
Female. 5	View of Lynn Common 5 CITY BANK 5 of Lynn, Mass.	V Ship. FIVE

Left	Centre	Right
FIVE 5 FIVE	View of Lynn Common. CITY B'K OF LYNN Mass.	5 The word "five" with a large V running across. 5
10 State arms	View of Lynn Common. CITY B'K OF LYNN Mass.	10 X 10
20	CITY B'K OF LYNN Mass. State Arms. Female on each side	TWENTY 20 TWENTY
50	Train of cars. CITY B'K OF LYNN Mass.	50 Portrait of Webster.
C	CITY B'K OF LYNN Mass. Three cherubs, one turning a screw, one splitting a block with wedge, the other lifting rock with lever. C 100 C	100 Ship
1 View of a large building.	CITY BANK, Worcester, Mass. Mechanic at work in machine shop.	Word one and figure 1 Same as above.
2 Same as on ones.	CITY BANK Worcester, Mass. Three farmers loading wheat, one on top of load another pitching up sheaf and the other holding horses. TWO	Word two and figure 2 2
3 Same as on ones.	Female reclining machine in centre of vine; sheep and sheafs of wheat on right, safe on left. CITY BANK Worcester, Mass.	3 Large figure 3
Word five and letter V	A Bull head man dressing leather and female sewing boots. CITY BANK Worcester, Mass.	V 5
Male portrait. X on Ten	CITY BANK, Worcester, Mass. Worcester city seal.	10 City bank building

Left	Centre	Right
XX 20	CITY BANK, Worcester, Mass. Three females.	20 City bank building.
50 50	CITY BANK, Worcester, Mass. Portrait of J. C. Calhoun.	50 City bank building.
100 C	CITY BANK, Worcester, Mass. City Bank building.	100 Portrait of Webster. 100
D	Title of Bank. City Bank Building. Five Hundred Dollars.	500 Clay.
1 Washington. 1	COLUMBIAN BANK, Boston, Mass. 1 Two blacksmiths, anvil, &c. 1	1 Female. 1
Female bust. 1	COLUMBIAN BANK, Boston, Mass. Female; ONE on 1 either side.	1 Male Portrait.
2 Female. 2	COLUMBIAN BANK, Boston, Mass. 2 Harvest scene. 2	2 Female. 2
Indian. 2	COLUMBIAN BANK, Boston, Mass. TWO Ships. DOLL'S.	2 Male Portrait.
Female. THREE	3 3 COLUMBIAN BANK, Boston, Mass. 3 Portrait. 3	Female. THREE
3 Harvest scene. 3	COLUMBIAN BANK, Boston, Mass. 3 Female, eagle, &c. 3	3 Sailor, roll of rope, &c. 3

Left	Centre	Right
Portrait. 5	Ship building. COLUMBIAN BANK, Boston, Mass.	5 Female in 5
5 Washington. 5	COLUMBIAN BANK, Boston, Mass. 5 Female, Landing of Columbus; city in distance. 5	5 Male portrait 5
10 Portrait of Washington. 10	COLUMBIAN BANK, Boston, Mass. Ten, large X, Ten across the note.	10 Portrait of Columbus. 10
Three females with anchor. TEN	Two females tending looms. COLUMBIAN BANK, Boston, Mass.	10 Male portrait
20 Female.	Spread eagle and ships. COLUMBIAN BANK, Boston, Mass.	20 Female.
50 Female 50	Steamship. COLUMBIAN BANK, Boston, Mass. Imp. and products.	50
C Portrait of Washington.	Female, eagle, shield and liberty cap. COLUMBIAN BANK, Boston, Mass.	100 Portrait of Columbus.
500 Man with crucible. 500	Landing of Columbus. COLUMBIAN BANK, Boston, Mass. FIVE HUNDRED	DOLLARS
1 State Arms.	COMMERCIAL BK., Salem, Mass. Hunter killing buffalo.	1 Male portrait
1 Female. ONE	Eagle and shipping. ONE COMMERCIAL B'K. Salem, Mass.	1 Female. ONE

Left	Centre	Right
2 Two Indians, city, etc.	Female with cloth, pointing to mills and rural scene on right; on left village and hills. Title of Bank. Eagle.	2 Female with sprinkling vessel, etc
TWO Ship. TWO	2 Female, cornucopia, and a ship in distance. 2 COMMERCIAL B'K. Salem, Mass.	TWO Head of an Indian. TWO
3	Two horses before load of hay, man on one, woman and child on top; boy, girl, dog, blacksmiths and shop. Title of Bank.	3 Portrait of officer
3 Male figure. THREE	THREE Indian seated on a rock. THREE COMMERCIAL B'K. Salem, Mass.	3 Ship. THREE
FIVE Justice. FIVE	5 View of steamboat, schooner, mill, bridge, etc. 5 COMMERCIAL BK, Salem, Mass.	FIVE State Arms. FIVE
5 Cattle. FIVE	Female. River, steamboat, ship and bridge. V COMMERCIAL B'K. Salem, Mass.	5 Cattle. FIVE
5 Male head.	Two sailors and nautical instruments; vessels, steamer, etc. Title of Bank.	5 Female with globe, tablets, etc.
10 Ship. TEN	10 Whale ships. Large X, female and horn of plenty. COMMERCIAL B'K. Salem, Mass.	10 Ship. TEN
20 XX 20	(Old Plate.) 20 Female, merchandise, ship in distance. 20 COMMERCIAL B'K. Salem, Mass.	TWENTY
20 Female, spear, and globe.	(New Plate.) 2 Female. 0 COMMERCIAL B'K. Salem, Mass.	20 Female. 20

Left	Centre	Right
Female and eagle. 20	Word "TWENTY" Female across figs. 20. Title of Bank.	20 Franklin.
50 Female figure.	(New Plate.) Male and female. COMMERCIAL B'K. Salem, Mass.	50 Cupid in a sail boat. 50
FIFTY Female. FIFTY	(Old Plate.) 50 Man and horse. 50 COMMERCIAL B'K. Salem, Mass.	FIFTY Female. FIFTY
50 Sailor, capstan, etc. on deck.	50 Man buying newspaper of boy; bldgs etc COMMERCIAL BANK Salem, Mass. 50	50 Cooper at work.
100 Eagle. 100	(Old Plate.) C Phœbus in the chariot of the sun. 100 COMMERCIAL B'K, Salem, Mass.	C Portrait of Washington. C
100 Vulcan the blacksmith.	(New Plate.) Spread eagle, railroad, and canal. COMMERCIAL B'K, Salem, Mass.	100 Female.
C Man and boats. 100	Eagle on bale; agricultural products, etc. 100 Title of Bank.	100 Female representing Agriculture. 100
100 inverted. Female figure erect.	100 COMMERCIAL BANK Salem, Mass. Large green C with small "C" at bottom. Sailor, farmers, vessels, etc.	100 100 inverted
500	Female seated pointing to papers and load of hay. 500 D Title of Bank.	500
Sampson in escape. 500	COMMERCIAL BANK, Salem, Mass. D 500 D	500 Female figure of Justice

Left	Centre	Right
	CONCORD BANK, Concord, Mass. This Bank uses the old Perkin's stereotype plate, which is the denomination printed in fine letters all over the bill.	
1 State Arms.	Man, two horses, and pig at pump; cattle and barn in distance. CONTINENTAL BK, Boston, Mass	1 Portrait of Continental soldier
2 State Arms.	CONTINENTAL BK. Boston, Mass. White and black horse, cattle, trees, etc	2 Washingt'n
3 State Arms.	Scene in Arctic regions; white bear attacking sailors in boat. CONTINENTAL BK, Boston, Mass.	3 Continental soldier.
5 State Arms.	Man, sailor, boy, dog, vessels, fort, boats, etc. Fig. 5 either side. CONTINENTAL BK, Boston, Mass	5 Franklin.
10 State Arms.	CONTINENTAL BK, Boston, Mass X Old man with gun; female loading gun. X	10 Soldier loading gun
Word Massachusetts across XX State Arms.	CONTINENTAL BK, Boston, Mass. Surrender of English General to Washington	20 Continental soldier with gun.
50 State Arms.	CONTINENTAL BK, Boston, Mass. Washington on horse; officers, tents, etc.	50 Male portrait
100 State Arms.	CONTINENTAL BK Boston, Mass. Figs. 100, Title & words One Hundr'd Dollars on green die.	100 Soldier with medallion head on shield.
500 State Arms.	CONTINENTAL BK Boston, Mass. Female erect with sword and shield. 500 on green die.	500 Eagle

Left	Centre	Right
Farmer sowing seed. ONE	ONE Man on horseback, flock of sheep. CONWAY BANK Conway, Mass Ducks	1 Female.
2 Mechanic and sailor	CONWAY BANK. Conway, Mass. TWO DOLLARS	TWO Two females supporting a sheaf of wheat.
3	Man driving a drove of cattle across a river. 3 CONWAY BANK, Conway, Mass.	3 2 females and sheaf of wheat.
V Negro with a basket of cotton.	CONWAY BANK. Conway, Mass. Females weaving at factory looms.	5 Portrait
TEN Indian.	Three Indians in a canoe. CONWAY BANK. Conway, Mass.	10 Portrait of a boy.
XX Indian.	Santa Claus in a sleigh drawn by reindeer over the roofs of houses. CONWAY BANK. Conway, Mass	20 Fancy piece.
L Hunter warming himself; gun, dog, etc.	CONWAY BANK. Conway, Mass. Female in clouds with sword, scales, eagle, etc.	50 Female binding shoes; child.
C Portrait.	Men cutting timber in a forest. CONWAY BANK. Conway, Mass	100 Rip Van Winkle smoking a pipe.
1 Portrait.	Farmer eating dinner in the open field DANVERS BANK. Danvers, Mass.	1 Portrait.
2 Portrait.	Milk maid and cows. DANVERS BANK. Danvers, Mass.	2 Portrait.

Left	Centre	Right
3 Portrait.	Female resting upon a bale; manufacturing village in distance. DANVERS BANK. Danvers, Mass.	3 Portrait.
5 Portrait.	Farmer ploughing with horses. DANVERS BANK. Danvers, Mass	5 Portrait.
10 Portrait.	Spread eagle, capitol at Washington, and steamship in distance. DANVERS BANK. Danvers, Mass	10 Portrait.
20 Portrait.	TWENTY TWENTY Portrait surmounted by an eagle, female on either side. DANVERS BANK. Danvers, Mass	20
Portrait. 50	DANVERS BANK, Danvers, Mass. FIFTY State arms. DOLLARS.	50 Portrait.
100 Portrait.	100 Three female figures. 100 DANVERS BANK. Danvers, Mass	100 Portrait.
1 Portrait of Fisher Ames. ONE	ONE Interior of a blacksmith shop. ONE DEDHAM BANK. Dedham, Mass.	1 Portrait of Washington. ONE
2 Portrait of Fisher Ames. TWO	TWO Spread eagle. TWO DEDHAM BANK. Dedham, Mass.	2 Portrait of Washington. TWO
3 Portrait of Fisher Ames. THREE	Female seated, farmers gathering grain. Factories and a machine. DEDHAM BANK. Dedham, Mass.	3 Portrait of Washington. THREE
5 Portrait of Fisher Ames FIVE	Man on horseback, cars and on foot. Train of Cattle. DEDHAM BANK. Dedham, Mass. Dog, key, safe	5 Portrait of Washington. FIVE

10 Portrait of Fisher Ames. TEN — Train of cars passing, barn of plough through a [illegible] gap. DEDHAM BANK, Dedham, Mass. Dog, key, safe — 10 Portrait of Washington. TEN

20 — Vig. two females at again; to the right a child's head either side of XX. DEDHAM BANK, Dedham, Mass. — 20 Female and sewing machine.

20 Female and a chest. — XX Eagle XX DEDHAM BANK. Dedham, Mass. — 20 Ship.

FIFTY Female. FIFTY — 50 Man and horses. 50 DEDHAM BANK. Dedham, Mass. — FIFTY Female. FIFTY

50 Female with book. — DEDHAM BANK Dedham, Mass. Female, shield, eagle, vessel, etc. — 50 Eagle

One Hundred and 100. Portrait of Harrison. — Scene on a wharf. DEDHAM BANK. Dedham, Mass. — Same as left. Portrait of Columbus.

C Female with cab[illegible]; child at [illegible]. — DEDHAM BANK. Dedham, Mass. Franklin. — 100 Female with C on shield.

D 500 — DEDHAM BANK, Dedham, Mass. Two females, owl, building, steamer, etc. D — D 500 State Arms.

1 Interior of a blacksmith's shop. ONE — Spread eagle. 1 EAGLE BANK, Boston, Mass. — 1 Man and horse. ONE

2 Flower girl. TWO — Spread eagle. TWO EAGLE BANK, Boston, Mass. — 2 TWO Female with sickle.

5 — Spread eagle. V, cupid either side. EAGLE BANK, Boston, Mass. Ceres — FIVE Female.

X — Spread eagle, building, safe, dog and key. EAGLE BANK, Boston, Mass. — 10 Female at well.

20 — Spread eagle Cupid either side of XX. EAGLE BANK, Boston, Mass. — 20 Female

L Steamboat. 50 — Spread eagle; bust of female. EAGLE BANK, Boston, Mass. — 50 Reapers. L

100 Female. 100 — Spread eagle. EAGLE BANK, Boston, Mass. — 100 Female. 100

The 500s, are of the Perkins' Stereotype Plate, which has the denomination printed in fine letters all over the bill.

1 — Eliot preaching to the Indians. Portrait of Pierce. ELIOT BANK, Boston, Mass. Female head — ONE Dog's head ONE

2 — ELIOT BANK, Boston, Mass. Eliot preaching to the Indians. 2 — TWO Sailors on board of a ship.

3 Boston Female. — Vig. Same as ones. ELIOT BANK, Boston, Mass. — 3 Portrait of Webster.

FIVE Boston Indian. — Female head Vig. Same as ones. ELIOT BANK, Boston, Mass. — 5 5

TEN Hunter seated by a fire in the woods. — TEN X X Title of Bank. — TEN Hunter seated by a brook.

20 — Ship under full sail. Portrait of Webster. ELIOT BANK, Boston, Mass. — 20 Female with sickle and sheaf.

FIFTY Sailor and mechanic. — L Portrait of J. Q. Adams. 50 ELIOT BANK, Boston, Mass. — FIFTY Three females.

100 inverted Indian erect, with bow and arrow — Indians on cliff contemplating the progress of civilization. ELIOT BANK, Boston, Mass. — 100 C

Indian with bow. — C Large Steamship. ELIOT BANK, Boston, Mass.

D — Wreckers scene; ship wrecked in distance. ELIOT BANK, Boston, Mass. — 500 D

Female sitting on the ground supporting the figure 1, train of cars and steamboat. 1 — 1 ESSEX BANK. Haverhill, Mass. — 1 Female.

2 — Two female figures, steamboat in the distance. 2 ESSEX BANK, Haverhill, Mass. — 2 Female.

Train of cars. THREE — 3 ESSEX BANK, Haverhill, Mass. — 3 Blacksmith and sailor, and figure 3

5 — Two females and [illegible] liberty, factory, steamship and train of cars in the distance. 5 ESSEX BANK, Haverhill, Mass. — 5 Group of females and figure

Two females, bust and shield ship in the distance. X 10 TEN ESSEX BANK. Haverhill, Mass. State Arms	Twenty on 20 Female with scales, shipping, locomotive and State Arms, cupid, etc. Twenty on 20 EXCHANGE BANK, Boston, Mass. Portrait of Columbus. Portrait of Washington.	20 XX Eagle XX 20 EXCHANGE BANK. Salem, Mass. Female. Ship
20 Ship, etc. 20 ESSEX BANK, of Haverhill, Mass. Anchor, bales, etc. Eagle. Sailor boy vessel, etc.	View of the Boston Custom House. 50 50 EXCHANGE BANK, Boston, Mass. FIFTY on 50 Franklin.	50 EXCHANGE BANK. 50 Fifty Dollars. Massachusetts. Male portrait. Salem. 50 State Arms.
50 ESSEX BANK. of Haverhill, Mass. 50 Horse. Three females. Female head.	Female, canal, train of cars and shipping. Hundred on 100 EXCHANGE BANK. 100 Boston, Mass.	100 Two females seated on bale, factories &c in distance. 100 EXCHANGE BANK. Salem, Mass. Man dressing limbus. One Hundred Dollars. Two Children.
100 ESSEX BANK, of Haverhill, Mass. 100 Female with sewing machine. Two horses, cattle, trees, etc. Girl's head.	Steamship and other vessels. 500 EXCHANGE BANK, Boston, Mass. 500 Dog's head. Female.	Female head in large circular die. EXCHANGE BANK. D Dog on Safe. D D Salem. Mass. 500 Five Hundred Dollars. 500
100 Spread eagle, rail road and canal. 100 ESSEX BANK, Haverhill, Mass. Vulcan the blacksmith. Female.	EXCHANGE BANK 1000 Boston, Mass. Female seated by horn of plenty and shield; ships, steamship, cars, bridge and city in distance. 1000	Large figure 1 across each end of bill with a female on the body of it. Ships and steamboat. Justice on a fig. 1. FAIRHAVEN BANK. Fairhaven, Mass. ONE ONE
State Arms. 1 1 EXCHANGE BANK, Boston, Mass. 1 Girl.	1 1 Female seated upon a rostrum with spear and shield, water, vessels, and mountains, in the background. 1 1 Portrait. Female. ONE EXCHANGE BANK. Salem, Mass. 1	Large 2 and female bust. Whale fishing. Same as left FAIRHAVEN BANK. Fairhaven, Mass. TWO TWO
Steamship. Female on 2 2 EXCHANGE BANK, Boston, Mass. 2 Female.	2 2 Same Vig., as above. 2 TWO Female, spear and shield. EXCHANGE BANK. Salem, Mass. Female and ships. TWO 2	3 Female and motto "enterprise." 3 FAIRHAVEN BANK. Fairhaven, Mass. Sailor and captain. Farmer, sailor and mechanic, and figure 3 THREE THREE
3 Steamship and sailing vessels. 3 Eagle at its bottom. EXCHANGE BANK, Boston, Mass. Sailor. THREE THREE	3 3 Same Vig., as above. 3 III Justice EXCHANGE BANK Salem, Mass. Female and ship in distance. THREE 3	5 Eagle and shield. V FIVE Female FAIRHAVEN BANK. Fairhaven, Mass. Medallion head. 5 5
5 Spread eagle. Female and cupid on V. EXCHANGE BANK, Boston, Mass. Female. 5	5 5 Same Vig. 5 FIVE Female. Female with stoke and sword, EXCHANGE BANK Salem, Mass. V 5	Female grain va., rail road and canal in background. 10 TEN Medallion head. FAIRHAVEN BANK. Fairhaven, Mass. X 10
Female figures, horses and chariot. 10 X Steamship. EXCHANGE BANK, Boston, Mass. 10 TEN	10 Same Vig. TEN Portrait of Washington. EXCHANGE BANK. Salem, Mass. Portrait. TEN 10	20 2 Female. 0 20 Female. FAIRHAVEN BANK. Fairhaven, Mass. Female with spear. 20 XX

Left	Centre	Right
Female and eagle. 20	TWENTY on 20. Female FAIRHAVEN BANK Fairhaven, Mass.	20 Franklin.
20 Female with basket, etc.	Female supporting shield on which is State Arms; nautical scene in distance. FAIR HAVEN BANK Fair Haven, Mass.	20 Sailor.
FIFTY 50	50 Three females, eagle and shield. Title of Bank.	50 Mechanic and factory.
50 Boy, girl, child, horse, etc.	FIFTY DOLLARS Medallion head. Boy, child, cattle, sheep, etc. FAIR HAVEN BANK Fair Haven, Mass. L	50 Female feeding fowls.
50 Female with spear.	Male and female. FAIRHAVEN BANK Fairhaven, Mass. 50	50 Cupid in a sail boat. 50
C Grain and [illegible]. 100	Eagle on tail. 100 Title of Bank.	100 Female with sickle. 100
100 Vulcan the blacksmith.	Spread eagle, R. R. and canal. FAIRHAVEN BANK. Fairhaven, Mass 100	100 Female.
C 100	Sailor, farmer and boy; depot, anchor and grain. FAIR HAVEN BANK Fair Haven, Mass.	100 Dog and safe.
Agricultural scene; female planting in [illegible]. 500	500 D Title of Bank.	500
1 Female figure and ship.	Females wearing at factory house. FALL RIVER BANK Fall River Mass.	1 Portrait of female.

Left	Centre	Right
2 Men, cattle and horses on a plank road.	Female leaning on a bale; ships in back ground. FALL RIVER BANK Fall River Mass. Steam boat	2 Train of cars.
3 Anchor.	FALL RIVER BANK, Fall River, Mass. Sailor, shipping in background.	3 Portrait of female
5 Blacksmith anvil &c.	FALL RIVER BANK. Fall River, Mass. Shipping.	5 Portrait of Female.
10 Sailor.	Steamship. FALL RIVER BANK. Fall River, Mass.	10 Female figure.
TWENTY. Male and female seated; two children and lamb.	FALL RIVER BANK, Fall River, Mass. Word Twenty in a semi-circle. Dollars on figs. 20 on a die. Double male head either side.	20 Male portrait
Two girls in large circle. L	FALL RIVER B'K. Fall River, Mass Boy watering two horses at trough. Female with pitcher and pail.	50 Oval male portrait
C Girls' head.	Steamboat Title of Bank.	100 Male portrait
500 Female.	Title of Bank. Three females; shipping, cars, etc., in distance.	500 500
M Shipping and two females seated. 1000	FALL RIVER BANK, Fall River, Mass. ONE THOUS	1000 AND 1000
Portrait of Washington.	Female. 1 Female. FALMOUTH BANK, Falmouth, Mass.	1 Portrait of Franklin.

Left	Centre	Right
1 Sailor at wheel.	FALMOUTH BANK. Falmouth, Mass. One on 1 Vessels on ocean, etc. One on 1 1	1 Female portrait
1 Box, bale, anchor, ship, etc. 1	1 Female seated, bales, box, [illegible], vessels, etc. 1 FALMOUTH BANK, Falmouth, Mass.	1 Agricultural implements, etc. 1
2 Two females.	2 Sailor on beach, anchor, boat, steamer, vessels, etc. 2 FALMOUTH BANK, Falmouth, Mass.	2 Man with corn stalks.
2 Portrait of Columbia.	Female. 2 Female. FALMOUTH BANK. Falmouth, Mass.	2 Portrait.
2 Man on [illegible]. 2	2 Female seated with fig. 2. 2 Title of Bank.	2 Man on horse. 2
3 Genl. Washington.	Female. 3 Female. FALMOUTH BANK Falmouth, Mass.	3 Vulcan the blacksmith.
3 Child's head. 3	3 Female and fig. 3 on shield. 3 Title of Bank.	3 Child's head. 3
3	Scene in Arctic regions; white bear attacking sailors in boat. Female portrait. FALMOUTH BANK, Falmouth, Mass.	3 Indian princess.
Female with sword and scales. FIVE	FIVE Female and cherubs. FALMOUTH BANK, Falmouth, Mass. Ship	5 Female.
10 Two female figures.	1 Female, chestnut bay. 0 FALMOUTH BANK, Falmouth, Mass.	10 2 females.

20 Female.	Eagle and shield, factories and falls in back ground. FALMOUTH BANK, Falmouth, Mass.	20 Female.
50 Female portrait. 50	Bullock between man with axe, and hunter with gun. Title of Bank.	50 Portrait.
100 Female. 100	C Shipping. C FALMOUTH BANK, Falmouth, Mass.	100 Female. 100
100 Sailor, mechanic, vessels, etc.	FALMOUTH BANK, Falmouth, Mass. Sailor, two farmers; agricultural and nautical scene. Green C either side.	100 Cooper at work.
1 Female and 1.	View of Faneuil Hall and other buildings. FANEUIL HALL BK. Boston, Mass.	1 Female with flag and cupid.
2 Washington.	Vig. Same as ones. FANEUIL HALL BK. Boston, Mass.	2 Female.
3 Female.	Vig. Same as ones. FANEUIL HALL BK. Boston, Mass.	3 Mechanic, sailor and farmer and fig. 3
5	Vig. Same as ones, with Cupid on V on right. FANEUIL HALL BK. Boston, Mass.	5 Five female figures and 5
TEN	View of Quincy Market. X FANEUIL HALL BK. Boston, Mass.	X Drove of cattle.
Ship. 20	Milkmaid and cows. FANEUIL HALL BK. Boston, Mass.	20 Female.

50 Female.	Cows and sheep. FANEUIL HALL BK. Boston, Mass.	50 State Arms.
100 Train of cars.	Farming scene. FANEUIL HALL BK. Boston, Mass.	100 Drove of cattle.
500 Washington and his horse	Female reclining on bale with distaff in her hand; ships, city, canal, boats, and high, cars, &c., in distance. FANEUIL HALL BK. Boston, Mass. 500	500 500
1	Train of cars. 1 FITCHBURG BANK, Fitchburg, Mass.	ONE Medallion head. ONE
2	Spread eagle, railroad and canal. 2 FI[illegible] BANK, Fitchburg, Mass.	TWO Female. TWO
3	Man on horse back, and drove of cattle. 3 FITCHBURG BANK, Fitchburg, Mass.	3 Blacksmith, anvil and forge.
Female. FIVE	Canal and inclined railway, buildings on each side. Train of cars. FITCHBURG BANK, Fitchburg, Mass. Agricultural implements	5 Portrait. FIVE
TEN Portrait, Mr. Van Buren. 10	State arms. Wharf, shipping and merchandise. Sailor in foreground. FITCHBURG BANK, Fitchburg, Mass.	10 Milk maid.
20 Female.	(1st. Plate.) XX Eagle. XX FITCHBURG BANK, Fitchburg, Mass.	20 Ship.
20 Female with spear and shield.	(2d. Plate.) 2 Female. 0 FITCHBURG BANK, Fitchburg, Mass. XX	20 Female. 20

XX	(New Plate.) FITCHBURG BANK, Fitchburg, Mass. Female seated on a bale, holding a sheaf of wheat.	20 Female.
FIFTY Female. FIFTY	50 Man and horse. 50 FITCHBURG BANK, Fitchburg, Mass.	FIFTY Female. FIFTY
FIFTY Grain, &c. 50	50 Three females seated with liberty pole and cap, eagle shield &c; ship in distance. FITCHBURG BANK, Fitchburg, Mass.	Fifty on 50. Male seated with mechanical implements.
50 Eagle on Shield.	FITCHBURG BANK, Fitchburg, Mass. 50 Male Portrait. 50	50 Dog and safe.
100 Eagle. 100	(Old Plate.) C Phaeton in the car of the Sun. 100 FITCHBURG BANK, Fitchburg, Mass.	C Portrait of Washington. C
100 Ox, woods, &c.	FITCHBURG BANK, Fitchburg, Mass. Male Portrait.	100 Small State Arms.
C Sailors and boat. 100	Spread eagle, grain &c. 100 Title of Bank.	100 Female with sickle, grain. 100
Same as right Portrait of Harrison.	Scene on a wharf. FITCHBURG BANK, Fitchburg, Mass.	One hundred and 100. Portrait of Columbus.
ONE Portrait of Webster.	Cows, farmer ploughing and train of cars. FRAMINGHAM B'K Framingham, Mass. 1	1 2 females
1 Female figure. 1	ONE Female ONE sitting on a bale with a horn of plenty. Shipping in back ground. FRAMINGHAM B'K, Framingham, Mass.	1 Eagle 1

Female with sickle and sheaf of wheat. Factory and train of cars. TWO	2 Cattle and hogs. FRAMINGHAM B'K. Framingham, Mass. 2	2 Blacksmith, anvil and forge.
2 Female and eagle. 2	2 Female sitting on a bale with horn of plenty. Shipping in background. 2 FRAMINGHAM B'K Framingham, Mass.	2 Female figure. 2
3 Male standing upon a rock overlooking the sea. 3	3 Female sitting upon a bale with horn of plenty. Shipping in background. 3 FRAMINGHAM B'K Framingham, Mass.	3 Female figure. 3
3	Farming scene. 3 FRAMINGHAM B'K Framingham, Mass. Machinery and bale	3 Portrait of Washington.
5	Farmers gathering corn. 5 FRAMINGHAM B'K Framingham, Mass.	FIVE 3 [illegible] and 2 female figures and a large V.
	5s, 10s, 20s, 50s, and 100s old plate of Perkins stereotype.	
X	Milk maid and cows. [illegible] FRAMINGHAM B'K Framingham, Mass.	10 Female with flag, and 2 cherubs.
FIFTY Female. FIFTY	50 Man and horse. 50 FRAMINGHAM B'K Framingham, Mass.	FIFTY Female FIFTY
ONE	Castle, farmer ploughing, train of cars in the distance. 1 FRANKLIN Co. BANK. Greenfield, Mass. 1	1 Portrait of Washington.
Farmer, ploughing, with horses steamboat in the distance. TWO	2 FRANKLIN Co. BANK, Greenfield, Mass. 2	2 Portrait of Franklin.

Farmer, smith and mechanic, 3 gold dollars. 3	FRANKLIN Co. BANK. Greenfield, Mass.	3 Portrait of Webster.
Farming scene. 5	5 FRANKLIN, Co. BANK, Greenfield, Mass. Imp. and products	FIVE Female. FIVE
Female, eagle and shield, portrait of Washington. TEN	X FRANKLIN Co. BANK. Greenfield, Mass.	10 2 females.
20 TWENTY Male portrait.	FRANKLIN CO. B'K Greenfield, Mass.	20 Male portrait.
50 Female with scroll on which is words "Fifty Dollars," child at her feet.	FRANKLIN CO. B'K Greenfield, Mass. Male portrait. FIFTY DOLLARS.	50 FIFTY Dog & safe.
C State Arms.	FRANKLIN CO. B'K Greenfield, Mass. C Male portrait. C	100 Eagle.
ONE Sailing vessel. 1	Battle of Bunker Hill. ONE on right. FREEMANS' BANK, Boston, Mass. Sheep, etc.	1 Female. ONE
TWO Girl. 2	Washington on horseback—ship builders. FREEMANS' BANK, Boston, Mass. Imp. and products	2 Franklin. TWO
THREE Female. 3	Steamboat landing and sailing vessels. THREE FREEMANS' BANK Boston, Mass. Sheep	3 Washington and horse. THREE
5 Wharf and shipping. FIVE	View of Quincy Market. FREEMANS' BANK, Boston, Mass. [illegible]	5 Female.

TEN Interior of a blacksmith's shop. 10	X Ships TEN FREEMANS' BANK, Boston, Mass.	10 Male and female. TEN
XX Female. 20	Cows. Female making hay. FREEMANS' BANK, Boston, Mass.	20 Ships. XX
FIFTY Female. FIFTY	50 Man and horse. 50 FREEMANS' BANK, Boston, Mass.	FIFTY Female. FIFTY
50 City seal.	FREEMAN'S BANK. Boston, Mass.	50 Male Portrait.
Words one hundred and figs. 100. Male portrait.	Wharf scene—loading wagon, men, horses, shipping, &c. FREEMANS' BANK, Boston, Mass.	Words one hundred and figures 100. Male portrait.
C Male Portrait.	FREEMAN'S BANK, Boston, Mass. FREEMAN'S BANK.	100 Arms of State.
D D Small State Arms. D D	FREEMAN'S BANK, Boston, Mass. D Male Portrait. D FIVE HUNDRED.	500 Vessel under sail.
ONE 1 ONE	GLOBE BANK, Boston, Mass. The title of this bank is repeated twice on the note—a special plate like Perkins', which has the denomination in fine letters all over the bill.	1 ONE 1
TWO 2 TWO	GLOBE BANK, Boston, Mass. Same as one.	2 TWO 2
THREE 3 THREE	GLOBE BANK, Boston, Mass. Same as one.	3 THREE 3

FIVE 5 FIVE
GLOBE BANK, Boston, Mass.
Same as ones.
5 FIVE 5

TEN X TEN
GLOBE BANK, Boston, Mass.
Same as ones.
10 TEN 10

FIFTY 50 FIFTY
GLOBE BANK, Boston, Mass.
Same as ones.
50 FIFTY 50

C 100 C
GLOBE BANK, Boston, Mass.
Same as ones.
100 C 100

GLOBE BANK, Boston, Mass.
500s and 1000s, same as ones except in the denomination.

ONE
Wharfs and shipping. ONE
GLOUCESTER BANK, Gloucester, Mass.
Horse and dray.
1
Sailing vessel.
ONE

2 TWO 2
Wharfs and shipping. TWO
GLOUCESTER BANK, Gloucester, Mass.
Ship, bbls., etc
2
Horse, cart and barrels.
2

THREE
Wharfs and shipping.
GLOUCESTER BANK, Gloucester, Mass.
3
Ship.

FIVE
Wharfs and shipping.
GLOUCESTER BANK, Gloucester, Mass.
5
FIVE
Horses and wagon. Merchandise.

TEN
Wharfs and shipping.
GLOUCESTER BANK, Gloucester, Mass.
10
Sail boat.
X

20
Eagle.
Wharfs and shipping. 20
GLOUCESTER BANK, Gloucester, Mass.
XX
Sail vessels.
20

50
Wharfs and shipping. 50
GLOUCESTER BANK, Gloucester, Mass.
50
Sailor, merchandise and shipping.
FIFTY

100
Wharfs and shipping.
GLOUCESTER BANK, Gloucester, Mass.
100
Sail vessels.

ONE
Farmers and load of hay. Portrait.
GRAFTON BANK, Grafton, Mass.
Female bathing
1
Portrait of H. Clay.

TWO
Portrait of Webster.
Female wearing at factory loom.
GRAFTON BANK, Grafton, Mass.
Dog
TWO
Portrait.

Female plowing a horse, also farmers and load of hay.
GRAFTON BANK, Grafton, Mass.
THREE
3
Portrait.

V
Portrait.
(New Plate.)
Scene in shoemaker's shop.
GRAFTON BANK, Grafton Mass.
5
Portrait.

V
Interior of a shoemakers shop.
GRAFTON BANK, Grafton, Mass.
Portrait. V Portrait.
5
Female sewing, her child resting upon her lap.

X
Portrait of W. Penn.
Wild horses running across a plain.
GRAFTON BANK, Grafton, Mass.
10
Portraits.

XX
Train of cars.
Female seated with bale, box, barrel, etc.; vessels and streamships in distance.
GRAFTON BANK, Grafton, Mass.
20
Male portrait.

Indian, erect.
FIFTY.
L Milkmaid and cows.
GRAFTON BANK, Grafton. Mass.
50
Portrait.

Female in clouds with eagle, etc.
100
Male portrait.
Title of Bank.
C
Female binding shoes; child.

1
Male and female.
ONE
1 Steamboat and sailing vessels. 1
GRAND BANK, Marblehead, Mass.
1
Female figure.
ONE

2
Ship.
2
Female resting her arm upon fence; dog.
2
GRAND BANK, Marblehead, Mass.
2
Agricultural implements.
2

Eagle.
FIVE
5 Allegorical figures 5
GRAND BANK, Marblehead, Mass.
Statue of Washington.

10
Sailor, his foot resting on a windlass.
10
X Ship. X
GRAND BANK, Marblehead, Mass.
10
Bee hive.
10

20
Female figure.
2 Female. 0
GRAND BANK, Marblehead, Mass.
XX
20
Female.
20

Steamboat
XX
Train of cars.
2 female figures, eagle and shield. 20
GRAND BANK, Marblehead, Mass.
XX
Milk maid.

20
TWENTY
Sailor.
Steamship and other vessels at sea
GRAND BANK, Marblehead, Mass.
Twenty Dollars on Twenty.
20
TWENTY
Pilot-boat under full sail.

Massachusetts.
50
Marblehead.
Ships, etc. 50
FIFTY
GRAND BANK.
Fifty Dollars.
L
50
Male portrait.

1 on ONE Ship. ONE	Female with scales, and motto, "Industry the means, plenty the result;" shipping and railroad in distance. ONE GRANITE BANK, Boston, Mass.	1 on ONE. Bee hive. ONE
2 Ship. TWO	Vig. Same as ones. TWO GRANITE BANK, Boston, Mass.	2 Bee hive. TWO
3 Ship. THREE	Vig. Same as ones. THREE GRANITE BANK, Boston, Mass.	3 Beehive. THREE
5 Ship. FIVE	Vig. Same as ones. FIVE, vessels on right; 5 merchandise, etc., on left. GRANITE BANK, Boston, Mass.	5 Bee hive. FIVE
10 Ship. TEN	Vig. Same as ones. TEN, vessels, 10 on right; 10, merchandise etc., on left. GRANITE BANK, Boston, Mass.	10 Bee hive. TEN
20 Ship. TWENTY	Vig. Same as ones. TWENTY GRANITE BANK, Boston, Mass.	20 Bee hive. TWENTY
FIFTY Female. FIFTY	50 Man and horse. 50 GRANITE BANK, Boston, Mass.	FIFTY Female. FIFTY
100 Vulcan seated.	Spread eagle on branch of tree; city and canal in distance. GRANITE BANK, Boston, Mass.	100 Female seated.
Words one hundred and figs. 100. Portrait of Harrison.	Scene on a wharf. GRANITE BANK, Boston, Mass.	Same as on left. Portrait of Columbus
ONE Large figure 1 with female on it.	Farmers driving sheep across a stream of water. GREENFIELD BANK Greenfield, Mass.	ONE Large figure 1 with female on it.

Factory and train of cars. 2	Large figure 2 with Indian. GREENFIELD BANK Greenfield, Mass.	2 Female with fruit basket upon her arm.
State arms. 3	Train of cars. GREENFIELD BANK Greenfield, Mass.	THREE Portrait Z. Taylor THREE
FIVE Farmer sowing seed. 5	5 Cluster of buildings. 5 GREENFIELD BANK Greenfield, Mass.	FIVE Vulcan the blacksmith, and fig. 5.
TEN Cattle. TEN	10 Cluster of buildings. 10 GREENFIELD BANK Greenfield, Mass.	X Female raking hay.
20 Female.	2 Female. 0 GREENFIELD BANK Greenfield, Mass. XX	20 Female. 20
50 Female.	Male and female. GREENFIELD BANK Greenfield, Mass. 50	50 Cupid in a sail boat. 50
100 Vulcan with implements.	Spread eagle on bush of tree; canal and railroad GREENFIELD BK., Greenfield, Mass. 100	100 Female with rake
Youthful portrait with cap. 1	HADLEY FALLS BK., Holyoke, Mass. Hunter killing buffaloes. Dog.	1 Female portrait
1 Portrait of female.	Female sitting on a bale also two sheaves, shipping and train of cars in background. 1 HADLEY FALLS BANK, Holyoke, Mass.	1 Indian woman and child
2	American flag and shield surmounted by an eagle; at right is female instructing children; at left an Indian woman and child 2 on right. HADLEY FALLS BANK. Holyoke, Mass.	TWO 2 Anvil and hammer.

THREE. Female feeding an eagle from a cup. THREE.	3 Three men. 3 HADLEY FALLS BANK. Holyoke, Mass. Girl swimming.	3 Sailor and dog; shipping in background.
FIVE Female drawing water from a well. FIVE	5 Man at work at lathe. HADLEY FALLS BANK. Holyoke, Mass. FIVE	5
5 Portrait of two children.	HADLEY FALLS BANK. Holyoke, Mass. 5 Husking scene; seven figures, dog, &c.	5 Male portrait.
5 Boy and girl.	Title of Bank. Corn husking scene—males and females in barn. Female bathing.	5 Male portrait
Male portrait. 5	Title of Bank. Steamship at sea. Indian boy's head.	5 Female portrait.
5 Female beside coming steamer, etc.	Title of Bank. Man on horse, colt, dog, sheep; man on fence.	5 Boys' portrait.
10 X	HADLEY FALLS BANK. Holyoke, Mass. View of Hadley Falls; mountains in background.	10 X
XX Female with scales and sword.	State arms and two horses, Factory, train of cars and steamboat. HADLEY FALLS BANK. Holyoke, Mass.	20 Female
Indian princess seated; shield, &c. 50	HADLEY FALLS BK., Holyoke, Mass. Portrait of Daniel Webster; female each side; ships and farmer in distance. 50 Horse. 50	50 A Blacksmith seated.
C River, train of cars crossing a bridge; city in distance.	HADLEY FALLS BANK Holyoke, Mass. Three female figures	100 Ship; city in distance.

Left end	Centre	Right end
ONE Dust. ONE	Eagle. 1 Eagle. HAMILTON BANK, Boston, Mass.	ONE Male Portrait. ONE
2 Male Portrait. TWO	Ship. 2 Ship. HAMILTON BANK, Boston, Mass.	2 Male Portrait TWO
THREE Male Portrait. THREE	Washington on his horse. 3 Washington on his horse. HAMILTON BANK, Boston, Mass.	THREE Male Portrait. THREE
	The 5s, 10s, 50s, and 100s, are of the 'Perkins' Stereotype Plate, which has the denomination printed in fine letters all over the bill.	
20 Male Portrait. XX	XX Portrait. XX HAMILTON BANK, Boston, Mass.	20 Male Portrait. XX
Figs. 500. Male portrait. Figs. 500.	Female either side of leaning on shield. HAMILTON BANK, Boston, Mass.	Figs. 500. Vessels.
ONE Female with sickle and sheaf of wheat ONE	1 Hampden bank building, store and Hotel. 1 HAMPDEN BANK, Westfield, Mass.	ONE Farmers mowing. 1
Female erect with sword and scales. ONE	HAMPDEN BANK, Hampden, Mass. General view of street and buildings.	1 Franklin.
TWO Female with sheaf and sickle.	Title of Bank. Vig. Same as above ones.	2 Washington.
2 Female, sheaf of wheat.	2 Same vignette as above 2 HAMPDEN BANK, Westfield, Mass. Steamboat	2 Train of cars

Left end	Centre	Right end
THREE Female figure. THREE	3 Same as above. 3 HAMPDEN BANK, Westfield, Mass. Ship	3 Men and sheep. THREE
5 Youthful portrait with cap.	Title of Bank Vig. Same as above ones.	5 Female portrait
FIVE Milk maid. FIVE	Same as above HAMPDEN BANK, Westfield, Mass.	FIVE Eagle and 5
TEN Portrait of Franklin. TEN	Same as above HAMPDEN BANK, Westfield, Mass.	10 Female with wreaths.
TWENTY	20 Street scene. HAMPDEN BANK, Westfield, Mass	TWENTY on 20. Washington.
FIFTY Medallion Head. 50	Same vig. as the others. HAMPDEN BANK, Westfield, Mass.	50 Portrait. FIFTY
100	C View of buildings, country inn, pedestrians, etc. HAMPDEN BANK, Westfield, Mass. Dog, safe and building.	100 Female Med head.
1 Portrait of female. ONE	View of Ware village HAMPSHIRE MANUFACTURERS BANK Ware, Mass.	Cupids supporting the fig. 1 ONE
Large figure 2; Portrait of Washington, and Portrait of Franklin.	View of Ware village HAMPSHIRE MANUFACTURERS BANK Ware, Mass. Eagle	2 Indian girl with bow and arrows
3 Female.	View of Ware village. HAMPSHIRE MANUFACTURERS' BANK Ware, Mass. Clay	3 Cupids in large 3.

Left end	Centre	Right end
	5s 10s 20s 50s all of the Perkins Patent Stereotype steel plate.	
100 Eagle. 100	C Phœbus in the car of the sun. 100 HAMPSHIRE MANUFACTURERS BANK Ware, Mass	C Portrait of Washington C
1 ONE State Arms.	View of Harvard College; pedestrians, trees, etc. HARVARD BANK, Cambridge, Mass. ONE 1 ONE	1 Male portrait
TWO State Arms.	HARVARD BANK, Cambridge, Mass. Male portrait. 2 View of Harvard College, etc. Two Dollars	Fig. 2 with name of Bank either side.
5 State Arms.	HARVARD BANK, Cambridge, Mass. View of Harvard College, pedestrians, etc. FIVE	5 Male portrait.
10 State Arms.	HARVARD BANK, Cambridge, Mass X Male portrait X	10 Female with State Arms on shield
20 State Arms.	View of Harvard College, pedestrians, etc. HARVARD BANK, Cambridge, Mass	20 TWENTY 20
50 State Arms.	State Arms HARVARD BANK, Cambridge, Mass Male portrait	50 50
1 Children sailing boats in a tub. ONE	Steamboat, sail vessels. Plough and sheaf of wheat HAVERHILL BANK Haverhill, Mass	1 Blacksmith, anvil and forge. ONE
ONE Female with flowers in apron.	View of a street. HAVERHILL B'K Haverhill, Mass. One Dollar One Dollar.	Word one and figure 1. Portrait of Webster.

Hunter loading his gun, deer at his feet.
TWO
Word Two and $ mark. View of a street.
HAVERHILL B'K.
Haverhill, Mass.
Two Dollars Two Dollars
2
Female gathering wheat.

2
Indian with bow.
TWO
Train of cars passing through a gap. Female and shield.
HAVERHILL BANK,
Haverhill, Mass.
2
Vessel.
TWO

3
View of a street. Word three and figure 3.
HAVERHILL B'K.
Haverhill, Mass.
Three Dols. Three Dols.
3
Female with cornucopia.

3
Ship building.
THREE
Farmer sowing seed. Cattle.
HAVERHILL BANK,
Haverhill, Mass.
3
Indian.
THREE

FIVE
Milk maid.
State arms. Farming scene. State arms.
HAVERHILL BANK,
Haverhill, Mass.
5
Female.
FIVE

Man with child on his knee; female, boy, dog, hen and chickens.
FIVE
HAVERHILL B'K.
Haverhill, Mass.
View of a street.
Five Dols. Five Dols.
5
Female binding shoes; box of shoes, etc.

Two men, horse, boy and negro holding bull by nose; cows, etc; barn, trees, etc, in back ground.
Word Ten and letter X.
Word Ten and letter X.
HAVERHILL BANK,
Haverhill, Mass.
10
Female feeding fowls.

10
Female.
TEN
TEN Cattle, man TEN on horseback.
HAVERHILL BANK
Haverhill, Mass.
10
Female
10

20
Female figure.
2 Female 0
HAVERHILL BANK
Haverhill, Mass.
20
Female.
20

XX
General street view in village.
HAVERHILL BANK,
Haverhill, Mass.
TWENTY
20
Same as on left end.

50
General street view in village.
Title of Bank.
Words "Fifty Dollars" across red figs. 50.
50
Indian erect.

50
Female figure.
Male and female.
HAVERHILL BANK
Haverhill, Mass.
50
Cupid in a [illegible].
50

100
Vulcan the blacksmith.
Spread eagle, R. R. and canal.
HAVERHILL BANK
Haverhill, Mass.
100
Female.

500
Male figure with a stylus and tablet.
Washington. Two females and beehive.
HAVERHILL BANK
Haverhill, Mass.
500
Martha Washington.

1
Indian erect and lone star.
Hunter on horseback catching wild bull.
HIDE AND LEATHER BANK,
Boston, Mass.
ONE
1
Sailor.

TWO
Indian on horse hunting buffaloes. Boston
Title of Bank.
TWO
2
Head of bull.

3
Female with shield, cornucopia, &c.
Fig. 3 on die; men dressing leather on right; female sewing shoes on left.
Title of Bank.
THREE
3

V
5
Scene in a leather manufactory; men dressing leather, etc.
Title of Bank.
5
5

Man shaving leather.
10
HIDE & LEATHER BANK, BOSTON,
State of Massachusetts
Title of Bank again and X on end die.
10
Steamship.

XX
Cattle.
Title of Bank.
Title of Bank again and 20 on red die.
20
Old man, boy and dog.

50
Three men rowing; vessels in distance.
Title of Bank.
50
Red letter L.

ONE HUNDRED
Title of Bank.
Three females—two seated, one erect reading from book.
100

Female seated with book on lap.
500
Title of Bank.
500
Ship in red circular die.

Goddess of Liberty erect.
Title of Bank.
1000 1000
1000
Cupids with grain between them.

ONE and 1
Sailor, quadrant, capstan, steamer.
Schooners, etc.
HINGHAM BANK,
Hingham, Mass.
1
Female portrait.

ONE
Steamboat and sail vessels. 1
HINGHAM BANK
Hingham, Mass.
ONE
Indian girl with bow and arrow.
ONE

2
Title of Bank.
Males, female, house, well, dog, horse at trough, etc.
2
Female portrait.

2
TWO
2
Ships 2
HINGHAM BANK
Hingham, Mass.
TWO
Female drawing water from a well.
TWO

3
Men haying, etc.
Title of Bank.
THREE
Milkmaid seated; boy pouring.

THREE
Reapers. 3
HINGHAM BANK
Hingham, Mass.
THREE
Steamboat.
3

Left	Centre	Right
FIVE, partly inverted. 5	Scene on sea shore. HINGHAM BANK, Hingham, Mass.	5 Sailor boy rowing.
FIVE	Spread eagle, shield and anchor, village and shipping in background. Large V and female within. HINGHAM BANK Hingham, Mass.	5 Girl
Vulcan the blacksmith. TEN	X HINGHAM, BANK Hingham, Mass.	10 Reaper.
10 Machinist at work.	Steamboat. Title of Bank.	10 Railroad train.
20 Female.	XX Eagle. XX HINGHAM, BANK Hingham, Mass.	20 Ship.
20	Scene in Arctic regions—white bear attacking sailors in boat. 20 HINGHAM BANK, Hingham, Mass.	20 Franklin in his study.
50 Boy, dog, house.	HINGHAM BANK, Hingham, Mass. 50 Sailor, two farmers, vessel, etc. Dog's head.	50 50
Words One Hundred on figs. 100	HINGHAM BANK, Hingham, Mass. Vessel under full sail. C Barrels. C	100 Eagle.
ONE HUNDRED on fig. 100	HINGHAM BANK, Mass. C C Barrels and bales	100 Eagle.
100 across words One Hundred. Male portrait	Wharf scene; loading wagons; ships, &c. HINGHAM BANK, Hingham, Mass.	Same as on left end. Male portrait

Left	Centre	Right
ONE Portrait.	Milk maid and cows. HOLLISTON B'K Holliston, Mass.	1 Portrait of Clay.
TWO Portrait.	HOLLISTON BANK Holliston, Mass. Two females supporting a sheaf of wheat above their heads.	2 Female.
3 Portrait of Charles Sumner.	HOLLISTON BANK Holliston, Mass. Females weaving at factory looms	3 Boy
V Portrait.	HOLLISTON BANK Holliston, Mass. Train of cars.	V 5 V Portrait of Webster.
TEN Portrait of General Cass.	Spread Eagle. HOLLISTON BANK Holliston, Mass.	X Portrait.
20 Portrait of J. Q. Adams.	Train of cars and railroad station. HOLLISTON BANK Holliston, Mass.	20 Female and child
50 Portrait of Charles Sumner.	Cattle. HOLLISTON BANK Holliston, Mass.	50 Portrait of Washington
C Farmer sowing seed.	Indians in a canoe. HOLLISTON BANK Holliston, Mass.	100 Portrait of Charles Sumner
1 Machinist & implements.	Man whittling stick beside horse, cow, sheep, boy on gate; boy in distance. HOLYOKE BANK, Northampton, Mass.	1 Buildings in background, bridge and buildings in foreground.
TWO Same as on right end of 1	Two females, spinning wheel; cattle scene on left; buildings on right. Title of Bank. Dog.	2 Female, cow, calf, ducks, etc.

Left	Centre	Right
5 Eagle.	V View in street; buildings, church, etc. V Title of Bank.	5 Female portrait.
10 Clay.	X Settlers at their devotions; Indians entering door; dog. X Title of Bank.	Ten on X. Male portrait
Female with liberty cap and pole.	20 Female sitting on the ground, with horn of plenty HOLYOKE BANK Northampton, Mass. Eagle	XX Female figure flying in the air.
Female eagle and shield.	HOLYOKE BANK Northampton, Mass. 50 on red head Three female figures. Yacht and steamer	50
100 on red head River, train of cars cross a bridge, city in distance.	HOLYOKE BANK Northampton, Mass. Three females. 100	100 on red head Ships and city in the distance.
1 Interior of a boot manufactory. 1	HOPKINTON BANK Hopkinton, Mass. Large figure 1 with words "ONE DOLLAR" running across. Dog's head	1 Portrait of Lee Claflin.
2 Interior of a boot manufactory. 2	HOPKINTON BANK Hopkinton, Mass. Large figure 2, with the words "TWO DOLLARS" running across. Dog's head	2 Portrait of J. P. Hale.
5 Same as ones and twos. 5	HOPKINTON BANK Hopkinton, Mass. Large figure 5, with the words "FIVE DOLLARS" running across. Dog's head	5 Portrait of Lee Claflin.
X Same as ones, twos and fives 10	HOPKINTON BANK Hopkinton, Mass. Large X, with the words "TEN DOLLARS" running across. Dog's head	X Portrait of J. P. Hale.
50 Male head.	HOPKINTON BANK Hopkinton, Mass. Boot makers at work.	50

C HOPKINTON BANK Hopkinton, Mass. 100
Boot makers at work. Wheels, bale, etc.

1 (Old Plate.) ONE
Medallion head. 1 Indian woman and canoe. 1 Female.
1 HOUSATONIC B'K Stockbridge, Mass. ONE

ONE (New Plate.) 1
Portrait of Taylor. Man with an axe and Indian with an ear of corn. Figure 1 each side.
ONE HOUSATONIC B'K Stockbridge, Mass. Safe. Stone cutter.

2 (Old Plate.) 2
Female. 2 Female, anchor, and spinning wheel. Factories and train of cars in background.
2 HOUSATONIC B'K Stockbridge, Mass. Medallion head.

TWO (New Plate.) 2
Two female figures and eagle, ship in distance. Fig. 2 each side. Female
Farmer sharpening a scythe. HOUSATONIC B'K Stockbridge, Mass. Wheat, &c. TWO

FIVE DOLLARS (Old Plate.) Indian.
5 Female feeding an eagle from a cup. 5
HOUSATONIC B'K Stockbridge, Mass. Drovers, cattle, &c. 5

FIVE (New Plate.) 5
V Train of cars. V
Indian. HOUSATONIC B'K Stockbridge, Mass. Mechanics arm. Two female figures, fig. 5, scales, bale, etc.

FIVE 5 Men plowing with two horses. 5
HOUSATONIC BANK Stockbridge, Mass.
Blacksmith with sledge and anvil. Mechanics' arm. Two children.

10 (Old Plate.) TEN
X Archimedes raising the world with a lever. X
Portrait of Washington. Portrait.
10 HOUSATONIC B'K Stockbridge, Mass. Female with wheat. TEN

Female and eagle. (New Plate.) 10
10 Farmers and cattle.
TEN HOUSATONIC B'K Stockbridge, Mass. Horses. Indian woman and X.

Two female figures. 20 Female sitting upon a rock also three cupids sporting with a dolphin in the water. 20
HOUSATONIC B'K Stockbridge, Mass. 2 Female. 0

50 Vig. sailor and Indian on either side of a shield; shipping in distance; two females on either side of shield, surmounted by an eagle, canal boats and locks in distance. Winged female with trumpet, another female at her feet with pole and cap; eagle and cornucopia.
Portrait of female. HOUSATONIC BANK, Stockbridge, Mass. Loading hay.

ONE Drovers on horseback and cattle. 1
HOWARD BANK, Boston, Mass.
Justice. Portrait of officer.

2 Med. head on shield surmounted by eagle; Continental soldier, cannon, etc., on right, female with pole and cap on left. 2
Youthful portrait with cap. Title of Bank. Sailor and capstan.

3 Title of Bank. 3
Three females in clouds; vessels in distance.
THREE Portrait of officer.

V Sailor on bench with anchor, etc.; steamer and vessels in distance. 5
Title of Bank.
Man dressing skins. Female with V on shield.

10 Title of Bank. 10
Female, cal-umet, steam-er, etc. Portrait of officer.

Marine view; ship under sail. 20
HOWARD BANK, Boston, Mass.
20 Male portrait.

50 HOWARD BANK, Boston, Mass. 50
Marine view, ships under sail, city in distance.
L Indian female on the ground.

100 HOWARD BANK, Boston, Mass. C
Steamship and ship under sail. HUNDRED.

500 HOWARD BANK, Boston, Mass. 500
Female, globe, chart, ship, &c.
500 Female head.

1 JOHN HANCOCK B'K Springfield, Mass. 1
View of the U. S. armory at Springfield also spread eagle. Portrait of female.

2 JOHN HANCOCK B'K Springfield, Mass. 2
Portrait of female. View of the U. S. Armory at Springfield also spread eagle.

3 JOHN HANCOCK B'K Springfield, Mass. 3
Train of cars.
Females. Female.

5 JOHN HANCOCK B'K Springfield, Mass. 5
Female eagle and shield, steamer in distance. Portrait of J. Hancock. Female and 5 on a shield.

Female, sickle and sheaf of wheat. 10 Three female figures ships in the distance. 10
JOHN HANCOCK B'K Springfield, Mass.
TEN Eagle. Female.

20 Female representing fame blowing trumpet; eagle, globe, flag, &c. 20
John Hancock. JOHN HANCOCK BK, Springfield, Mass.
TWENTY State arms.

50 Scene in a farm yard. 50
JOHN HANCOCK B'K Springfield, Mass.
Female and harvesters. Female and shield.

Indian female with eagle, globe, &c. 100 on large die. 100
Title of Bank.
100 Dog's head. Farmer with scythe; cars, mill, etc., in distance.

Female sitting on the ground supporting the figure 1. 1 Portrait of Franklin. 1
ONE LAIGHTON BANK, Lynn, Mass. 1 Portrait of a boy.

Left	Centre	Right
2	Blacksmith shoeing a horse. 2 LAIGHTON BANK, Lynn, Mass. State Arms	2 Female.
3	Female and eagle. 3 Portrait of Washington. LAIGHTON BANK, Lynn, Mass	THREE Indian woman and child.
5	State arms, female on each side. 5 LAIGHTON BANK, Lynn, Mass. Wheels, bales, etc.	5 Portrait of Webster.
TEN Female.	Farming scene. LAIGHTON BANK, Lynn, Mass Wheels bales, ect.	10 Portrait of Adams.
20 Leather Dresser.	LAIGHTON BANK, Lynn, Mass. 20 Male Portrait. 20	20 Female at work on sewing machine.
20 Female.	2 Female. 0 LAIGHTON BANK. Lynn, Mass. XX	20 Female. 20
50 Eagle on Shield.	LAIGHTON BANK, Lynn, Mass. Male portrait.	50 Child's head.
50 Female.	Male and female. LAIGHTON BANK, Lynn, Mass. 50	50 Cupid in a sailboat. 50
C Female seated on box, ship, schooner & goods.	LAIGHTON BANK, Lynn, Mass. Male portrait.	100 Sailor standing holding quadrant in left hand, right resting on capstan; ships & merchandise.
100 Male figure.	Spread eagle, railroad and canal. LAIGHTON BANK, Lynn, Mass. 100	100 Female.

Left	Centre	Right
D	LAIGHTON BANK, Lynn, Mass. Small eagle. Male portrait. D Interior of shoemakers shop; two men and one woman at work.	500
500	Indian paddling a canoe. 500 LAIGHTON BANK, Lynn, Mass	500 Justice.
State arms. ONE	Milk maid and cows. Cupid and 1 on right. LANCASTER BANK Lancaster, Mass	ONE Female figure.
Female. TWO	Female sitting upon the ground leaning upon a bale, factory, village in background. LANCASTER BANK Lancaster, Mass.	2 Indian woman and child.
FIVE	Female figure. V LANCASTER BANK Lancaster, Mass.	5 Ship.
FIVE Female sitting on a bale.	5 Cupid Cows, farmer ploughing, also a train of cars. LANCASTER BANK Lancaster, Mass.	FIVE Indian girl with bow, spear and arrows.
10 X 10	10 Man on [illegible]. LANCASTER BANK Lancaster, Mass.	TEN Female figure.
10 Female figure.	Farming scene. LANCASTER BANK Lancaster, Mass.	TEN A bull's head.
20 Female.	XX Eagle. XX LANCASTER BANK Lancaster, Mass.	20 Ship.
20 Man and girl at well, man drinking.	LANCASTER BANK, Lancaster, Mass. XX Dog on safe. XX	20 Eagle.

Left	Centre	Right
FIFTY Female. FIFTY	50 Man and horse. 50 LANCASTER BANK Lancaster, Mass.	FIFTY Female. FIFTY
50 Small State arms.	LANCASTER BANK, Lancaster, Mass. Boy and child, seated under tree, cows and sheep.	50 Indian, woman, rock, &c.
Same as right. Portrait of Harrison	Scene on a wharf. LANCASTER BANK Lancaster, Mass	One Hundred and 100. Portrait of Columbus
Female leaning on pillar, full length figure. 100	LANCASTER BANK, Lancaster, Mass. Goddess of liberty, holding wreath over small state arms.	100 Portrait of boy.
ONE Female	Railroad, and Cambridge bridge, train of cars, vessels, and East Cambridge in distance. LECHMERE BANK East Cambridge, Mass.	1 Portrait of Winchester.
2 Portrait of female.	LECHMERE BANK East Cambridge, Mass. Same vig.	2 Portrait of Winchester.
3 Same Vig.	LECHMERE BANK East Cambridge, Mass.	3 Portrait of Winchester.
5	Same vig. Portrait of female. LECHMERE BANK East Cambridge, Mass	5 Portrait of Winchester.
Female 10 TEN	LECHMERE BANK East Cambridge, Mass. Portrait of Winchester.	10 Female TEN
20 Sailor leaning upon a capstan.	LECHMERE BANK East Cambridge, Mass. Blacksmith shoeing a horse.	20 Portrait of Winchester.

50 | LECHMERE BANK East Cambridge Mass. Capitol at Washington, female and shield in foreground. | 50
State arms. | Portrait of John Hancock.

100 | Three female figures. LECHMERE BANK East Cambridge, Mass. | 100
Portrait of female. | Portrait of Winchester.

D | Vig. View of the Capitol at Washington. LECHMERE BANK East Cambridge, Mass. Eagle. | 500
Portrait of Washington. | Male portrait.

D | U. S. Capitol. LECHMERE BANK, East Cambridge, Mass. | 500
Washington. | Male portrait.

1 | LEE BANK, Lee, Mass. 1 Girl with dove. 1 | 1
Washington. | State Arms.

ONE Female. ONE | 1 Female, also eagle and shield surrounded by the several state arms; ship in distance. 1 LEE BANK, Lee, Mass. State Arms. | ONE Portrait of Washington. ONE

2 | LEE BANK, Lee, Mass. Three females and bust of Washington. TWO | TWO
Female portrait. | Large fig. 2 and 2 in top.

TWO Female. TWO | 2 Female each side of figure 2 in centre, city in background. 2 LEE BANK, Lee, Mass. State Arms. | Female figure, and large figure 2.

5 Blacksmith, anvil and forge. FIVE | Male figure and anchor, shipping and a city in background. V LEE BANK, Lee, Mass. | 5 Girl. FIVE

5 Female. 5 | 5 Female. 5 LEE BANK, Lee, Mass. State Arms. | Cupid in a cloud, with a basket of flowers upon his head.

5 | 5 LEE BANK, Lee, Mass. | 5
Female. | Female.

10 | LEE BANK. Lee, Mass. Two female figures seated; owl, barrels, bust, globe, &c.; steamship on left; buildings on right. | 10
Figure of Justice with sword and scales, seated on box. | Female head.

10 X 10 | Man and yoke of oxen. 10 LEE BANK, Lee, Mass. | TEN
Female.

10 | (New Plate.) X LEE BANK, Lee, Mass. Beehive. | 10
Female. | Squaw.

XX | Title of Bank. Female on either side of anvil; building in distance. | 20
Portrait of Indian female. | Two children.

20 | XX Eagle. XX LEE BANK, Lee, Mass. | 20
Female. | Ship.

FIFTY Female. FIFTY | 50 Man and horse. 50 LEE BANK, Lee, Mass. | FIFTY Female. FIFTY

Justice erect. | 50 Title of Bank. Three females representing Commerce, Manufactures and Agriculture; vessel in distance. | 50 FIFTY Male portrait.

100 | Title of Bank. Female resting on bale on which is letter C; city, etc., in distance on left. | 100
State Arms. | Male portrait.

Female seated pointing to coming scene. Fies. 500. | 500 D LEE BANK, Lee, Mass. | 500

1 | State arms with female on each side, mountains and train of cars in background. 1 LEICESTER BANK Leicester, Mass. | 1
Female.

TWO 2 Portrait of Fillmore. | Female with sword and scales, also shipping and bay. 2 LEICESTER BANK Leicester, Mass. | 2 Portrait of Webster.

3 THREE Clay. | Farmer and milkmaid. 3 LEICESTER BANK, Leicester, Mass. | 3 Taylor.

5 Portrait of Washington. | Reindeer running across a plain bearing a female upon his back. Large V, female within. LEICESTER BANK Leicester, Mass. | 5 Female with a flag, also three clouds.

Large X; with figure 10 running across. | Female with horn of plenty and key sitting, figures 1 and 0. LEICESTER BANK Leicester, Mass. | X Female.

20 | (Old Plate.) XX Eagle. XX LEICESTER BANK Leicester, Mass. | 20
Female. | Ship.

20 | (New Plate) 2 Female. 0 LEICESTER BANK Leicester, Mass. XX | 20 Female, 20
Female.

20 TWENTY XX | 20 Female, shield, eagle, hat, trees, &c. LEICESTER BANK, Leicester, Mass. | 20 Female portrait.

FIFTY Female figure. FIFTY | 50 Vig. A wild horse. 50 LEICESTER BANK, Leicester, Mass. | FIFTY Female figure. FIFTY

50 Figure of Liberty. | Vig. Two figures a male and female, the female holding a rake in one hand and in the other a handful of grain, male figure with a scroll in hand, his feet resting on an anchor, cog wheel, &c. LEICESTER BANK, Leicester, Mass. | Cupid in a boat. 50

Left	Centre	Right
50 Boy, dog, house.	Horses in field; brook, cows, &c. LEICESTER BANK. Leicester, Mass.	50 Female reclining with basket of fruit and flowers.
100 Male figure, cog wheel, &c.	Vig. Spread eagle on branch of tree; train of cars, canal boat, &c. LEICESTER BANK. Leicester, Mass.	100 Female with cake, fruit, &c.
One Hundred and 100. Portrait of Harrison.	Vig. Shipping, horses, waggon and merchandise. LEICESTER BANK. Leicester, Mass.	Same as left Portrait of Columbus.
Men loading express wagon. C	Small eagle. LEICESTER BANK. Leicester, Mass.	100 Female portrait.
Two females in sitting position. D	LEICESTER BANK. Eagle on rock. Leicester, Mass.	500
Female ONE	View of the city of Lowell. LOWELL BANK. Lowell, Mass Dog and safe.	Female. 1
TWO Female. 2	Same Vig. as ones. LOWELL BANK. Lowell, Mass Bales, bbls., etc.	TWO Female. 2
THREE Female. 3 on THREE	Same Vig. as ones. LOWELL BANK. Lowell, Mass Men and horses	THREE Female 3 on THREE
	5s, 10s, all of the Perkins Stereotype Steel Plate	
20 State Arms.	State of Mass. TWENTY. LOWELL BANK Twenty Dollars Lowell.	20 Girl beside spinning wheel.

Left	Centre	Right
20 Female.	XX Eagle. XX LOWELL BANK, Lowell, Mass	20 Ship.
50 Figure of Justice with sword and scales.	State of Mass FIFTY. LOWELL BANK. Fifty Dollars. Lowell.	50 Spread Eagle.
FIFTY Female. FIFTY	50 Man and horse. 50 LOWELL BANK, Lowell, Mass.	FIFTY Female. FIFTY
100 Mechanic beside Anvil.	State of Mass. ONE HUNDRED. LOWELL BANK. One Hundred. Lowell.	100 Dog and safe.
One Hundred and 100. Portrait of Harrison.	Scene on a wharf. LOWELL BANK. Lowell, Mass.	Same as left. Portrait of Columbus.
Female figure leaning against column, with torch in hand. 500	State of Mass. 500 LOWELL BANK, Five Hundred. Lowell.	500 Eagle on rock.
Female seated pointing to reapers. 500	500 D LOWELL BANK, Lowell, Mass.	500
Two females, one kneeling.	1 Two females on right of shield, on which is farming utensils; factory in distance; on left, cars and bridge. LYNN MECHANICS' BANK, Lynn, Mass.	1 Female.
1 Portrait of Washington.	Female. 1 Female. LYNN MECHANICS' BANK, Lynn, Mass	1 Portrait of Franklin.
Female with flowers. 2	State Arms with eagle at top; horse each side; cars, bridge, city and building in distance. Title of Bank.	2 Female with cornucopia.

Left	Centre	Right
2 Portrait of Columbus.	Female. 2 Female. LYNN MECHANICS' BANK, Lynn, Mass.	2 Portrait.
3 Gen. Washington.	Female. 3 Female. LYNN MECHANICS' BANK. Lynn, Mass.	3 Vulcan the blacksmith
3 Fremont.	Man watering three horses from trough by side of well; goat, kid and sheep; cattle and house in distance. Title of Bank.	3 Two cherubs soaring with distaff and sheaf.
5 Justice	Title of Bank. Three females sculpturing bust of Washington.	5 on FIVE. Female seated.
FIVE	Female. V LYNN MECHANICS' BANK, Lynn, Mass.	5 Ship.
X Five cupids, globe and anvil.	Title of Bank.	10 Five cherubs with rake and tablets.
10 X 10	Man, and yoke of oxen. 10 LYNN MECHANICS' BANK, Lynn, Mass.	TEN Female.
20 Female.	XX Eagle. XX LYNN MECHANICS' BANK. Lynn, Mass.	20 Ship.
XX Man dressing leather	LYNN MECHANICS' BANK, Lynn, Mass. Male portrait; female and children on right; Indian family on left.	20 Female portrait.
L Female with dove.	Title of Bank. Hunter shooting deer; dog, water, trees, etc.	50 Indian seated.

FIFTY. Female. FIFTY.
50 Man and horse. 50
LYNN MECHANICS' BANK, Lynn, Mass.
FIFTY. Female. FIFTY.

100. Eagle. 100.
C Phoebus in the chariot of the sun. 100
LYNN MECHANICS' BANK, Lynn, Mass.
C. Portrait of Washington. C.

Same as right. Portrait of Harrison.
Scene on a wharf.
LYNN MECHANICS' BANK, Lynn, Mass.
One Hundred and 100. Portrait of Columbus.

C. Two medallion heads.
Title of Bank.
Three females seated and one standing reading to others.
100. Two medallion heads.

500. Male seated with tablets.
Washington. Justice and Manufactures seated in alcove; beehive between them.
Title of Bank.
Machine.
500. Lady Washington.

Female. ONE.
Male and female. 1
MACHINISTS' BANK Taunton, Mass.
Man seated on plow.
1. Female with scales.

TWO.
Female, anvil, wheel &c.; ship building and train of cars in background. 2
MACHINISTS' BANK Taunton, Mass.
Indian in canoe.
2. Reaper.

THREE.
Female with a gun in her right hand, her left resting on a globe. 3
MACHINISTS' BANK Taunton, Mass.
Indian.
3. 2 females.

FIVE.
Train of cars. Large V with female in the centre.
MACHINISTS' BANK Taunton, Mass.
5. Female.

TEN.
Spread eagle, railroad and canal.
MACHINISTS' BANK Taunton, Mass.
10. Female.

20.
MACHINISTS' BANK Taunton, Mass.
Sailor by side of vessel with trumpet. Twenty on fig. 20 each side.
20.

FIFTY. Female with tablets; child at her feet. FIFTY.
FIFTY DOLLARS
L Cars, etc. L
MACHINISTS' BANK Taunton, Mass.
50. Sailor, mechanic, vessel, etc.

50. Female figure.
Male and Female.
MACHINISTS' BANK Taunton, Mass.
50
50. Cupid in a sailboat. 50.

100. Female gazing out on ocean on which is steamer.
State Arms.
MACHINISTS' BANK Taunton, Mass.
100.

100. Female on rock gazing on wreck—anchor at her feet.
[illegible]
MACHINISTS' BANK. Taunton, Mass.
One Hundred Dollars on ONE HUNDRED.
100.

500. D.
MACHINISTS' BANK. Taunton, Mass.
Vignette, sailor seated on gun-carriage, soldier resting on gun, flags, fort in distance, &c.
500. D.

ONE. Female.
Female sitting on the ground supporting the figure one.
MAHAIWE BANK, Gt. Barrington, Mass.
State Arms.
1. Cattle and hogs.

2. Female.
Man driving sheep across a brook.
MAHAIWE BANK, Gt. Barrington, Mass.
State Arms.
2. Stone-cutter.

Female borne in the arms of 2 males. THREE.
Train of cars. 3
MAHAIWE BANK, Gt. Barrington, N. Y.
State Arms.
THREE. Female figure. THREE.

Two Indian women, one of them stepping from a precipice into ravine below.
State Arms.
MAHAIWE BANK, Gt. Barrington, Mass.
5. Five female figures and 5.

Deer. 10. Farmer sitting upon a plough.
TEN TEN
Female sitting upon a bale with sickle and sheaf of wheat; train of cars and factory in background.
MAHAIWE BANK, Gt. Barrington, Mass.
State Arms.
10. Indian woman holding X.

20. Female figure.
2 Female. 0
MAHAIWE BANK, Gt. Barrington, Mass.
XX
20. Female. 20.

50. Female figure.
Male and female.
MAHAIWE BANK, Gt. Barrington Mass.
50
50. Cupid in a sailboat. 50.

100. Man seated.
Eagle on tree; canal and cars in distance.
MAHAIWE BANK, Gt. Barrington, Mass.
100
100. Female with cake.

Female erect with pole and cap.
1 MALDEN BANK, Malden, Mass.
Farmer seated with cradle, etc.
1. Two children.

1. Female.
Train of cars.
MALDEN BANK Malden, Mass.
Arm and hammer.
1. State arms.

Indian girl with bow and spear. TWO.
Man sitting upon the ground, anvil hammer, &c., factory and train of cars in background.
MALDEN BANK Malden, Mass.
Whole bale, cut.
2. Child and dolphin. TWO.

Female. THREE.
Farming Scene.
MALDEN BANK Malden, Mass.
3. Female and cherubs.

5. Portrait of female. FIVE.
Female leaning upon a bale, factory village in background.
MALDEN BANK Malden, Mass.
State Arms.
FIVE. Portrait of Z. Taylor. FIVE.

10. Blacksmith anvil and forge.
1 Female bag and horn of plenty. 0
MALDEN BANK Malden, Mass.
Cars.
10. Female.

20 Female.	Female, Eagle, and shield; factory, and ships in background. MALDEN BANK Malden, Mass	20 2 Female. 0
50 Female figure.	Mohawk Female. MALDEN BANK Malden, Mass 50	50 Cupid in a sail boat. 50
100 Vulcan the blacksmith	Spread Eagle R. R. and Canal. MALDEN BANK Malden, Mass. 100	100 Female.
C Vessels.	MALDEN BANK, Malden, Mass. Boy, child, cattle, etc.	100 Girl's head
1 ONE Fowls, pump, etc.	1 Boy on horse, colt, female, trough, etc. MARBLEHEAD B'K Marblehead, Mass.	1 One on 1. 1
1 Portrait of Washington.	Female 1 Female MARBLEHEAD B'K Marblehead, Mass	1 Franklin.
2 Man carrying leather.	Shoemakers at work; female at domestic duties. MARBLEHEAD B'K Marblehead, Mass.	2 Female and sewing machine.
2 Washington on horse. 2	2 Female and fig. 2 2 MARBLEHEAD BK Marblehead, Mass	2 Washington on horse. 2
2 Portrait of Washington.	Female 2 Female MARBLEHEAD B'K Marblehead, Mass.	2 Portrait
3 General Washington, and horse.	Female 3 Female MARBLEHEAD B'K Marblehead, Mass	3 Vulcan the blacksmith

Spread eagle FIVE	Large V; Female and Cupid. MARBLEHEAD B'K Marblehead, Mass.	5 Girl.
Five on 5 Locomotive	MARBLEHEAD B'K Marblehead, Mass Sailor, vessels, etc.	5 Schooner under sail.
Washingt'n 10	MARBLEHEAD B'K Marblehead, Mass Battle scene on shipboard.	10 Male portrait.
Vulcan the blacksmith. TEN	X MARBLEHEAD B'K Marblehead, Mass.	10 Reaper.
20 Female.	XX Eagle XX MARBLEHEAD B'K Marblehead, Mass.	20 Ship.
Two children. TWENTY	Twenty Twenty Man-of-war vessels, etc. MARBLEHEAD B'K Marblehead, Mass.	20 Indian princess
FIFTY Female with tablets; child at her feet. FIFTY	Man and two horses at pump, pig, cattle etc. MARBLEHEAD B'K Marblehead, Mass	50 Female with dove.
FIFTY Female FIFTY	50 Man and horse. 50 MARBLEHEAD B'K Marblehead, Mass	FIFTY Female. FIFTY
100 Franklin in his study.	MARBLEHEAD B'K Marblehead, Mass. Large C with small c at bottom.	100 Old man, child and bust of Washingt'n
1	Shipping 1 MARINE BANK, New Bedford, Mass.	1 Female.

2	Shipping Female and 2. MARINE BANK, New Bedford, Mass.	2 Whale fishing.
Steamship and sail vessels. THREE 3	MARINE BANK, New Bedford, Mass 3 THREE	3 Girl.
5 FIVE 5	V Eagle, anchor, merchandise, & shipping in background. V MARINE BANK, New Bedford, Mass	5 FIVE 5
Wharf and shipping. 5	V MARINE BANK, New Bedford, Mass.	5 Sailor, merchandise and shipping. FIVE
X Indian with bow	Shipping and wharf MARINE BANK, New Bedford, Mass.	10 Female and sheaf of wheat.
Female, seal and State Arms shipping and train of cars in background. TEN	X MARINE BANK, New Bedford, Mass.	10 Female.
20	Vig. Female, train of cars and canal in background. 20 MARINE BANK, New Bedford, Mass.	XX Portrait of Columbus.
50 FIFTY	Spread eagle, Railroad and canal. 50 MARINE BANK, New Bedford, Mass.	50 Ship.
100 Portrait of Washington.	Ship and steamship. MARINE BANK, New Bedford, Mass.	100 Large C with female within it
Shipping. 500	D MARINE BANK, New Bedford, Mass	500 Sailor at helm

Left	Centre	Right
Female, sheaf, etc. 500	500 D MARINE BANK, New Bedford, Mass.	500
1 Sailor with bundle.	Scene in ship-yard—men at work. MARKET BANK, Boston, Mass.	1 Portrait.
Horses and cart. ONE Farming scene.	1 Indian on 1 1 MARKET BANK, Boston, Mass.	Man on horseback; cattle. ONE Horses and traders with view of Quincy Market.
2 Basket of corn.	Forest scene—deer grazing MARKET BANK, Boston, Mass	2 Male portrait
Vase of flowers. 2	TWO 2 TWO MARKET BANK, Boston, Mass.	Ship. 2
3	Scene in harbor—steamboat, ships, &c. MARKET BANK, Boston, Mass.	3 Male portrait
3 Indian seated on rock.	Two females either side of anvil. MARKET BANK, Boston, Mass.	3 3
3 Vase of flowers.	Bust of Washington. 3 Female. MARKET BANK, Boston, Mass	3 Vase of flowers.
Train of cars FIVE	Portrait of Lady Washington. 5 Portrait of Washington. MARKET BANK, Boston, Mass Bull	5 Eagle and five on shield.
5 FIVE	Merchandise, shipping and Quincy Market. V MARKET BANK, Boston, Mass.	5 Cows. FIVE
X	Ship under full sail. X MARKET BANK, Boston, Mass. Bull	10 Female Portrait. TEN
10 Female. TEN	X Merchandise, shipping and Quincy Market. X MARKET BANK, Boston, Mass.	10 Ship. TEN
20 Washington TWENTY	Spread eagle on branch of tree; cars and canal in distance. MARKET BANK, Boston, Mass. Steamship.	20 Male portrait TWENTY
50	Steamship. 50 MARKET BANK, Boston, Mass.	FIFTY Portrait of Columbus. FIFTY
100 Neptune. 100	Steamship. MARKET BANK, Boston, Mass.	100 Franklin. 100
500 Med. head. 500	Female seated with sheaf, boat and cars in distance. MARKET BANK, Boston, Mass.	500 Portrait of Washington
1	MARTHA'S VINEYARD BANK, Edgartown, Mass. Shipping. Steamship.	1 Female, globe, and shield.
2	MARTHA'S VINEYARD BANK, Edgartown, Mass Haymakers at the left, and females preparing dinner at the right; two trains of cars and a city in background.	2
Deer hanging on limb of tree; dog on ground. THREE	Mechanic, sailor and farmer seated with implements; three gold dollars. MARTHA'S VINEYARD BANK Edgartown, Mass.	3 Female seated with fig. 3.
Sailor boy. V	Hunter, Indian woman, three cupids, and five gold dollars. MARTHA'S VINEYARD BANK, Edgartown, Mass.	5 Female reclining; ships in distance.
Female. 10	Goddess of Plenty and cherubs, representing the gathering of the harvest. MARTHA'S VINEYARD BANK, Edgartown, Mass.	10 Ships.
Female. XX	Shipcarpenters and architect. MARTHA'S VINEYARD BANK, Edgartown, Mass.	20 Sailor.
Sailor. 50	An Indian with bow and arrow; eagle flying; in the background is a lake; Indians in a canoe, wild deer, &c. MARTHA'S VINEYARD BANK, Edgartown, Mass	50 Two female figures.
C Female with sword and scales.	State arms surmounted by an eagle; female on each side. MARTHA'S VINEYARD BANK, Edgartown, Mass.	100 Spread eagle. 100
1 on Med. head. ONE 1 on med. head	Indian sitting on the ground; mountains in distance. MASSACHUSETTS BANK, Boston, Mass.	Same as left
1 ONE	MASSACHUSETTS BANK, Boston, Mass. State arms; words "One Dollar" across fig. 1 each side.	1 Massachusetts. ONE
TWO 2 TWO	Title of Bank. 2 State Arms. 2 TWO DOLLARS MASS.	TWO 2 TWO
TWO	Ships. MASS. BANK, Boston, Mass.	TWO
V Washington. 5	State Arms. MASS. BANK, Boston, Mass.	5 Male portrait. V
X Washington 10	State Arms. MASS. BANK, Boston, Mass.	10 Male portrait X

Left	Center	Right
MASSACHUSETTS BANK	20 20 State TWENTY Arms. DOLL'S MASS. BANK, Boston, Mass. 20 20	TWENTY
MASSACHUSETTS BANK	50 Fifty Dollars 50 State Arms. 50 MASS. BANK, Boston, Mass. 50 50	FIFTY DOLLARS
MASSACHUSETTS BANK	100 100 ONE HUNDRED State Arms. MASS. BANK, Boston, Mass. 100 100 100	ONE HUNDRED
FIVE HUNDRED	Five Hundred Dollars Indian on shield, farming utensils around; ship in distance MASS. BANK, Boston, Mass.	500
MASSACHUSETTS BANK 1000	1000 1000 ONE THOUSAND State Arms. Title of Bank. 1000	1000 MASSACHUSETTS BANK
Large figure 1, in the centre of which is an Indian ONE	Vig. A large factory, and train of cars. MASSASOIT BANK, Fall River, Mass.	Large figure 1, in the centre of which is an Indian ONE
2 Figure 2; spread eagle.	Steamboat. Bust of Indian. Locomotive. MASSASOIT BANK, Fall River, Mass.	2 Figure 2 and spread eagle.
3 Farmer with scythe, etc.	MASSASOIT BANK, Fall River, Mass. Train of cars, harvesting scenes, etc.	3 Two females preparing dinner.
Indian, dog, and dead deer 5	V MASSASOIT BANK, Fall River, Mass.	Eagle. 5 FIVE
X Washington, and his horse	Female head X Female head. MASSASOIT BANK, Fall River.	10 Indian springing bow.

Left	Center	Right
Two Indians, and a steamboat. 20	20 MASSASOIT BANK, Fall River.	XX Female with liberton her head.
FIFTY Female figure. FIFTY	50 Horse and groom. 50 MASSASOIT BANK, Fall River.	FIFTY Female figure. FIFTY
The figures 100, with the words one hundred across. Portrait,	Vig. Baggage wagon, and men loading it. MASSASOIT BANK, Fall River.	The figures 100, with the words one hundred Portrait
Indian in a canoe. 500	500 MASSASOIT BANK, Fall River.	500 Female with scales.
Female. ONE	Steamship and sail vessels. MATTAPAN BANK, Dorchester, Mass	1 Sailor.
Two Indian women, one stepping from a precipice into a ravine below. TWO	Train of cars. MATTAPAN BANK, Dorchester, Mass	2 Female.
3 Cattle.	Female seated with cornucopia; factories, bridge, canal and cars in distance MATTAPAN BANK, Dorchester, Mass.	3 Cattle.
3 Large figure 3 Mechanic, farmer and sailor.	Man sitting upon the ground, with a hammer upon his shoulder; train of cars and factory in the background. MATTAPAN BANK, Dorchester, Mass	3 Female.
Indian FIVE	Ships and steamship. MATTAPAN BANK, Dorchester, Mass. Wheels, bale, etc	5 Two female figures and 5
10 Stone cutter.	Spread eagle, ship and Steamship. MATTAPAN BANK Dorchester, Mass.	10 Indian woman.

Left	Center	Right
20 Female figure.	2 Female. 0 MATTAPAN BANK. Dorchester, Mass. XX	20 Female 20
20 Washingt'n	MATTAPAN BANK, Dorchester, Mass. Whites and Indians.	20 Girl's head
L 50	Female with shield—50 fifty on it; vessels, etc. 50 50 MATTAPAN BANK, Dorchester, Mass.	50 State Arms.
50 Female figure.	Male and female. MATTAPAN BANK. Dorchester, Mass 50	50 Cupid in a sail boat. 50
100 Shipwright.	Three sailors, coast and ocean scene. C MATTAPAN BANK. Dorchester, Mass. C	100 Female feeding fowls.
100 Vulcan the blacksmith.	Spread eagle, railroad and canal MATTAPAN BANK. Dorchester, Mass. 100	100 Female
One on 1.	Ship building and city in distance. MAVERICK BANK, Boston, Mass.	1 Female.
2 TWO 2	MAVERICK BANK, Boston, Mass. Ship building and city in distance.	2 Sailor.
3 Ship, bales, cars, etc. 3	MAVERICK BANK, Boston, Mass. Ship building and city in distance. Three 3 Three	3
5 V	East Boston ferry landing. MAVERICK BANK. Boston, Mass.	5 Portrait of Webster.

10 X	East Boston Ferry Landing. MAVERICK BANK, Boston, Mass.	10 Sailor and Indian. Pen on shield between.
XX	MAVERICK BANK, Boston, Mass. Winthrop block and street in East Boston.	20 Sailor.
50 FIFTY	MAVERICK BANK, Boston, Mass. Winthrop block and street in East Boston.	50 Ship and ship house in Navy Yard.
100 Female. HUNDRED	Winthrop block and street in East Boston. MAVERICK BANK, Boston, Mass.	100 Female and ship.
Five hundred Washington 500	MAVERICK BANK, Boston, Mass. D Winthrop block and a street in East Boston.	500
1 Vulcan seated with anvil and hammer.	MECHANICS' BANK, Boston, Mass. Wood cutter; gold dollar; log hut and wagon in distance.	1 Ships.
Statue of Washington	Fishing vessels Female MECHANICS' BANK, Boston, Mass.	1 ONE 1
2	Interior of a TWO black-smith's shop. TWO MECHANICS' BANK, Boston, Mass.	2 Female portrait. 2
2 Blacksmith anvil and forge.	MECHANICS' BANK, Boston, Mass. Farmer boy with rake; milkmaid with pail; two gold dollars; farm house and cows in distance.	2 Locomotive.
THREE Washington and staff on Dorchester Heights. THREE	Ship building. Steamboat. MECHANICS' BANK, Boston, Mass.	3 Man on horseback; cattle THREE

3 Female.	MECHANICS' BANK, Boston, Mass. Farmer with scythe, sailor with spy-glass, blacksmith, hammer and anvil; three gold dollars.	3 Stone cutter.
FIVE Female with pole and cap, shield at her feet.	MECHANICS' BANK, Boston, Mass. Indian female on left, hunter on right, three cupids in centre; five gold dollars; cars in distance.	5 Portrait of Webster.
FIVE	Washington and staff on Dorchester Heights; evacuation of Boston, 1776. MECHANICS' BANK, Boston, Mass.	5 Washington.
Wharf and shipping. 10	Steamboat landing and sail vessels Washington on horse on right. MECHANICS' BANK, Boston, Mass. B[illegible] scene	10 Train of cars. TEN
XX Female with pail and stool.	Man on horseback, and man [illegible] cattle, sheep and dogs. Cars MECHANICS' BANK, Boston, Mass.	20 Boy and girl sailing boat in tub.
MECHANICS' BANK, Boston, Mass. Engine. 50	Sailor with telescope &c. on yard-arm. FIFTY 50	50 DOLLARS
FIFTY Female. FIFTY	50 Mechanic's house 50 MECHANICS [illegible], Boston, M	FIFTY Female. FIFTY
100 Female seated with shield, on which is city of Boston.	MECHANICS BANK. Scene in Shipyard. One Hundred Dollars. Boston, Mass.	100 Mechanic at work.
Words one hundred and figs. 100. Portrait of Harrison.	Scene on a wharf MECHANICS' BANK, Boston, Mass.	Same as on left. [illegible] of [illegible]umbus
500 Mechanic beside column, on top of which is bust.	Steamship and other vessels at sea. MECHANICS BANK Five Hundred Dollars. Boston, Massachusetts.	500 State Arms.

1	Whale fishing. MECHANICS BANK New Bedford, Mass. Indian head	1
2 Stone cutter.	Sailor, merchandise, and ship in distance. MECHANICS BANK New Bedford, Mass. Cars	2 Dog and safe.
3 Two children	3 Ships 3 MECHANICS' BANK, New Bedford, Mass.	3 Sailor, barrel capstan, quadrant, etc
5	Whale fishing MECHANICS BANK New Bedford, Mass. Three female figures	5
10 Blacksmith anvil and forge.	City, R. R. Station and train of cars. MECHANICS BANK New Bedford, Mass. Ship.	10 Sailor with spy glass.
20 Medallion. 20	20 Child dog and safe. MECHANICS BANK New Bedford, Mass. Ships.	20
50 Medallion 50	New Bedford City Hall. 50 MECHANICS BANK New Bedford, Mass. Head	50
Indian in canoe. 500	500 MECHANICS' BANK, New Bedford, Mass. D D	500 Justice.
Train of cars and factory. 1	MECHANICKS B'K Newburyport, Mass.	1 Sailor at the wheel
Shipping and ship building. 2	2 and female head MECHANICKS B'K Newburyport, Mass.	2 Large figure 2 and eagle

Large steam-boat and landing. 3 — MECHANICKS B'K Newburyport, Mass. — 3 Blacksmith and forge.

Train of cars. 5 — Full length. MECHANICKS B'K Newburyport, Mass. — 5 Portrait of Franklin.

Ship and steamship. 10 — MECHANICKS B'K Newburyport, Mass. — 10 Portrait of Washington.

20 Female. — XX Eagle XX MECHANICKS B'K Newburyport, Mass. — 20 Ship.

20 TWENTY 20 — White bear attacking sailors in boat; Arctic regions scene. MECHANICKS' B'K Newburyport, Mass. — 20 Female portrait.

50 Two children. — FIFTY DOLLARS. Two sailors, bales, anchor, vessels, etc. MECHANICKS' B'K Newburyport, Mass. 50 — 50 Female blowing at flower.

FIFTY Female. FIFTY — 50 Man and horse. 50 MECHANICKS B'K Newburyport, Mass. — FIFTY Female. FIFTY

100 Vessels. — Cars. MECHANICKS' B'K Newburyport, Mass. Large green C — 100 Sailor with telescope at side of vessel.

Five Hundred and 100. Portrait. — Scene on a wharf. MECHANICKS B'K Newburyport, Mass. — Scene at sail. Portrait of Columbus.

1 Portrait of Washington. ONE — Blacksmith anvil and forge. MECHANICS BANK Worcester, Mass. Machine. — ONE and 1. Female, eagle and shield. ONE

TWO Portrait of Franklin. TWO — Female. Man on horse back; flock of sheep. Female. MECHANICS BANK Worcester, Mass. 2 Arms 2 — 2 Female. TWO on mail head

THREE Portrait of John Adams. THREE — State arms surmounted by an eagle; three females. MECHANICS BANK Worcester, Mass. 3 Female 3 — 3 Girl. 3

5 Female sickle and sheaf of wheat. 5 — MECHANICS BANK Worcester, Mass. State Arms. Boy, sheaf of wheat, and sheep, ship in background. Female. 5 Eagle. 5 — 5 Portrait of Webster.

Female, eagle and shield. — 10 Man and anvil, train of cars and village in background. MECHANICS BANK Worcester, Mass. X Arms. X — 10 Portrait of Z. Taylor.

XX Portrait of J. Q. Adams. — MECHANICS BANK Worcester, Mass. Three female figures. Female. — 20

Two males and two females. — 50 Farmer ploughing. MECHANICS BANK Worcester, Mass. — 50

100 Portrait. 100 — State arms, Two horses, factories, and train of cars and steamboat. MECHANICS BANK Worcester, Mass. — 100 Portrait. 100

D — MECHANICS' BANK, Worcester, Mass. Female seated with book and mechanical implements; factories on right and steamboat on left. Dog, key and safe. — 500

1 — Vessels, etc. 1 MERCANTILE B'K Salem, Mass. — 1 Female, emptying urn and flowers. ONE

ONE 1 — Farmer sowing seed. 1 MERCANTILE B'K. Salem, Mass. — 1 Ship. ONE

TWO 2 — Spread eagle. 2 MERCANTILE B'K. Salem, Mass. — 2 TWO Sail boat.

Female with tablets; child at her feet. TWO — MERCANTILE B'K Salem, Mass. Three females reclining; vessels in distance. — 2 Childs head.

THREE 3 — Sailor, wharf and shipping. 3 MERCANTILE B'K. Salem, Mass. — 3 THREE Train of cars.

5 Sailor, and mechanic, vessels, etc. — Female with shield, eagle, etc., steamer in distance. MERCANTILE B'K Salem, Mass. — 5 FIVE Sailor, capstan, bales, vessels, etc.

The word five with large V across. — Female, also emblems of agriculture, commerce &c. Large V and Indian girl. MERCANTILE B'K. Salem, Mass. — 5 Portrait of Washington.

10 Pilot boat under full sail. — MERCANTILE B'K. Sailor seated with telescope, etc. TEN DOLLARS Salem, Mass. — 10 Female portrait.

TEN — Vulcan the blacksmith. X MERCANTILE B'K. Salem, Mass. — 10 Reaper.

20 Female. — XX Eagle. XX MERCANTILE B'K, Salem, Mass. — 20 Ship.

50 Figure of Justice with sword and scales. — Scene on deck; men rolling barrels from ship, etc. MERCANTILE B'K. Salem, Mass. — 50 Two Sailors.

FIFTY Female. FIFTY — 50 Man and horse. 50 MERCANTILE B'K. Salem, Mass. — FIFTY Female. FIFTY

Left	Centre	Right
C Female figures, with foreg. &c.	Female seated; harvest, keys, coins bags, &c. MERCANTILE B'K, Salem, Mass One Hundred Dollars.	100 State Arms. 100
Female at right Portrait.	Horses, wagons, wharf and shipping. MERCANTILE B'K, Salem, Mass.	One Hundred and 100. Portrait.
500	Female seated pointing to reapers and load of hay. 500 D MERCANTILE BK., Salem, Mass.	500
Cupid on V. Female on safe with sword and scales.	View of Merchant's Bank and other buildings, street scene. MERCHANTS' BK., Boston Mass.	FIVE Fig. 5 on which is eagle, female and Washington. FIVE
5 Portrait of Franklin. V	View of the Merchants Bank and other buildings. V and cupid either side. MERCHANTS BANK, Boston, Mass. Cupid on V.	FIVE Female, eagle, Washington, on 5 FIVE
TEN Sailor leaning on capstan, with quadrant. TEN	Goddess of Liberty; female either side with shield. MERCHANT'S B'K, Ten Dollars. Boston, Mass. TEN	10 Steamship at sea.
Medallion head. X	10 Boston custom House. 10 MERCHANTS BANK, Boston, Mass. 10	TEN Female, with spear and shield. TEN
20 TWENTY. 20	MERCHANT'S B'K, Boston, Mass. United States Capitol. TWENTY.	20 Sailor boy holding his hat.
20 Female with flag. TWENTY	Ship of war and sail boats. MERCHANTS BANK, Boston, Mass. Washington.	20 Spread eagle and shield. TWENTY
Female in kneeling position. 50	Female, sickle and sheaf of wheat; factory and Railroad in distance. MERCHANTS BANK, Boston, Mass. Cornucopia, etc.	L Cupid in sail boat. 50

Left	Centre	Right
Female sickle and sheaf 100	Vig. Female &c. MERCHANTS BANK, Boston, Mass. Steamer	C State Arms.
Figs. 500. Eagle. Figs. 500.	Sailor, vessels, bales, clerk, men, buildings, etc. 500 Title of Bank.	Figs. 500. Ship. Figs. 500.
D 500 D Eagle D D	MERCHANTS' BANK Boston, Mass. 500 on green die.	D 500
1000 Eagle	MERCHANTS BANK Boston, Mass. Letter M and figs 1000 on green die.	1000 Female, child, sword pole & cap.
1000 Eagle. 1000	Vig. Same as 500s. Title of Bank.	1000 Female with figs. 1000. 1000
1	Female leaning upon a bale; streams of water, factories, railroad and shipping in background. 1 MERCHANTS BANK. Lowell, Mass.	1 Female.
TWO Ship. 2	Two females. 2 MERCHANTS BANK. Lowell, Mass.	2 Female and figure 2.
Female. 3	Large figure 3 and Three female figures; factory in background 3 on right. MERCHANTS BANK. Lowell, Mass.	3 Portrait
5 Female and ship. 5	Female and eagle; ship in distance 5 MERCHANTS BANK. Lowell, Mass	5 Ship. FIVE
10 Bales and barrels. TEN	Female, eagle and globe; ships in background. MERCHANTS BANK. Lowell, Mass.	10 Female.

Left	Centre	Right
20 XX	XX Portrait of female. XX MERCHANTS BANK, Lowell, Mass.	20 XX
50 Female.	Shipping; city in the background. MERCHANTS BANK Lowell, Mass.	50 Portrait of Washington.
100 Portrait C	Railroad depot, train of cars, wharfs, shipping, merchandise &c. MERCHANTS BANK. Lowell, Mass.	100 C
D State Arms.	MERCHANTS' BK. FIVE HUNDRED Dollars. Lowell, Mass.	500 Male portrait
D State Arms	MERCHANTS' BANK Lowell, Mass.	500 Justice seated on bale
ONE State Arms.	Male and female; train of cars and ship in background. MERCHANTS BANK, New Bedford, Mass. Locomotive	1 Female.
2 Female. TWO	Female sitting on bale; factory in background. MERCHANTS BANK, New Bedford, Mass Steamboat	2 Ship. TWO
3	Two females in foreground, shipping, train of cars in background. 3 on right. MERCHANTS BANK, New Bedford, Mass Beehive	3 Portrait of female.
5 Female.	MERCHANTS BANK, New Bedford, Mass Female sitting on a bale; ships and light house in background, 5 each side. Wheat, &c.	5 Female.
10 State arms	(New Plate.) Female, child, dog, and axe. 10 MERCHANTS BANK New Bedford, Mass Eagle	TEN Female with sheaf of wheat 10

Left end	Centre	Right end
TEN Ship building 10	(Old Plate.) 10 Interior of blacksmith shop. X MERCHANTS BANK, New Bedford, Mass.	10 Whale ship. TEN
20 Female.	(Old Plate.) XX Eagle. XX MERCHANTS BANK, New Bedford, Mass. 20 State Arms 20	20 Ship.
TWENTY Female with sickle and sheaf of wheat.	(New Plate.) Eagle. Indian, female and public building. MERCHANTS BANK, New Bedford, Mass. Female and ship	20 Ship.
Portrait of female. 50	Three females, train of cars and ship in background. MERCHANTS BANK New Bedford, Mass. Building	50 Portrait of female.
100 Portrait of Washington. 100	Female sitting on a bale. MERCHANTS BANK, New Bedford, Mass. House	100 Female and anchor; city in the background.
500 Male and female. D	MERCHANTS BANK, New Bedford, Mass. State Arms; female on each side; eagle at top; steamboat on right; houses on left. Bank Building.	500 Female. 500
1 Ships. ONE	ONE Whale ships and a whale. 1 Female. MERCHANTS BANK, Newburyport, Mass	1 Ship. ONE
TWO Train of cars. TWO	2 Ships. 2 MERCHANTS BANK, Newburyport, Mass.	2 Male figure 2
THREE Steamboat. THREE	Female Ship building. Sailor MERCHANTS BANK, Newburyport, Mass.	3 Ship. 3
Eagle. FIVE	Ship Washington and his troops crossing the Delaware. 5 MERCHANTS BANK, Newburyport, Mass.	Ships and merchandise FIVE

Left end	Centre	Right end
10 Surrender of Lord Cornwallis. TEN	Ship. Phoebus in the car of the Sun. Ship. MERCHANTS BANK, Newburyport, Mass.	10 Washington crossing the Delaware. TEN
TWENTY Female erect with sword and scales.	Vig. rural scene, cows and sheep. 20 MERCHANTS' BK., Newburyport, Mass.	XX Female with sheaf of wheat.
FIFTY Male figure. 50	FIFTY Steam boat, city in the distance. Female MERCHANTS BANK, Newburyport, Mass	50 Cart. FIFTY
100 Statue of Washington.	Battle of Bunker Hill. Three female figures. MERCHANTS BANK, Newburyport, Mass'	100 Female.
ONE Sailor boy. ONE	MERCHANTS BANK, Salem, Mass. Has the title, denomination and place of issue in red letters—The words Merchants' Bank, Salem, and "One Dollar" all over the middle part of bill in fine letters.	1 ONE 1
TWO Vessel on stock. TWO	MERCHANTS BANK Salem, Mass. Same as ones with denomination changed only.	2 TWO 2
FIVE Vessels. FIVE	MERCHANTS BANK, Salem, Mass. Same as ones with denomination changed only.	5 FIVE 5
TEN Vessels. TEN	MERCHANTS BANK, Salem, Mass. Same as ones with the denomination changed only.	10 TEN 10
FIFTY Steamboat. FIFTY	MERCHANTS BANK. Salem, Mass. Same as ones with the denomination changed only.	50 FIFTY 50
100 Sailor and shipping. 100	MERCHANTS BANK, Salem, Mass. Same as ones with the denomination changed only.	100 C 100

Left end	Centre	Right end
	MERCHANTS BANK. Salem, Mass. The plates of the 50's, are of the general Plate of the N. E. Bank Note Co.	
ONE	Phoebus in the chariot of the Sun. Dog, safe and building. MERRIMACK B'K. Haverhill, Mass.	1 Female.
2 TWO 2	Female figure and cupid TWO MERRIMACK BANK, Haverhill Mass.	2 Ship building.
THREE	Horses, wagons, wharf and shipping. 3 MERRIMACK BANK. Haverhill, Mass.	Female.
5 FIVE Female.	Train of cars. MERRIMACK BANK, Haverhill, Mass.	5 Fancy piece
X Steamboat.	Man on horseback, cattle and sheep. MERRIMACK BANK Haverhill, Mass.	10 Female. X
20 Female.	XX Eagle XX MERRIMACK BANK. Haverhill, Mass.	20 Ship.
Pilot boat, tug and vessel. 20	Female seated with sickle, sheaf; farmhouse, etc. MERRIMACK BANK Haverhill, Mass.	20 Old man, child, bust of Washington
Two children 50	50 Blacksmiths at work on anvil. Title of Bank.	50 Female with sewing machine.
FIFTY Female. FIFTY	50 Man and horse. 50 MERRIMACK BANK, Haverhill, Mass.	FIFTY Female. FIFTY

Left end	Centre	Right end
One Hundred and 100. Portrait.	Horses, waggons, wharf, shipping, &c. MERRIMACK BANK, Haverhill, Mass.	Same as left. Portrait.
C. Men and boats. 100	Single standing on bale of goods, etc. 100 MERRIMACK BANK, Haverhill, Mass.	100 Female with sickle, and bundle of grain.
Indian in a canoe. 500	500 MERRIMACK BANK, Haverhill, Mass.	5 0 Female holding hat [illegible] in right hand.
ONE Indian.	Indian, Indian woman and child in a canoe, the Indian throwing a harpoon at a fish. METACOMET BANK Fall River, Mass.	1 Portrait.
TWO Portrait.	Steam boat and sail vessels. METACOMET BANK Fall River, Mass.	2 Indian.
3 Portrait.	Steamboat and sail vessels. METACOMET BANK Fall River, Mass.	3 Indian in a canoe.
V FIVE	METACOMET BANK Fall River, Mass. Same vig as one's.	5 Portrait.
10	10 Same vig as ones. METACOMET BANK Fall River, Mass.	X Portrait.
XX XX	Steamboat and sail vessels. METACOMET BANK Fall River, Mass.	20 Indian in a canoe.
L 50	Same vig as ones. METACOMET BANK Fall River, Mass.	L Portrait.

Left end	Centre	Right end
100	Steamboat "Bay State," yachts and forts in distance. METACOMET BANK, Fall River, Mass.	C Indian in canoe spearing porpoise.
500 500	Indian, squaw and child in canoe; Indian is spearing porpoise. Title of Bank.	D Male portrait.
1000	Vig. same as above 100s. Title of Bank.	Letter M in circle and words "One Thousand" around. Indian.
ONE Indian seated by fig. 1.	Female seated; cars, factory and house in distance. 1 MILLBURY BANK, Millbury, Mass.	1 Blacksmith with anvil.
ONE Portrait of Washington. ONE	1 Interior of blacksmiths shop. 1 MILLBURY BANK, Millbury, Mass.	ONE Female. ONE
2 Catching wild bull.	Females tending machines. MILLBURY BANK, Millbury, Mass.	2 Franklin.
2	(New Plate.) Farmers driving sheep across a brook. 2 and 4 men. MILLBURY BANK, Millbury, Mass.	TWO Female. TWO
TWO Female. 2	(Old Plate.) 2 Farming scene. 2 MILLBURY BANK, Millbury, Mass.	TWO Female. 2
3 Man cutting down a tree.	Steamship at sea. MILLBURY BANK, Millbury, Mass.	THREE on 3. 3
3	Farming scene. 3 MILLBURY BANK, Millbury, Mass.	3 Female. THREE

Left end	Centre	Right end
FIVE Female crowning a bust of Washington. Made. 5	5 Interior of a blacksmith's shop. V MILLBURY BANK, Millbury, Mass.	5 Ship building.
TEN Washington and horse. 10	X Farming scene. 10 MILLBURY BANK, Millbury, Mass. Canal Locks.	TEN Portrait full length.
20 XX 20	20 Female holding scales; ship in background. 20 MILLBURY BANK, Millbury, Mass.	TWENTY
50 Female. 50	FIFTY DOLLARS 50 MILLBURY BANK, Millbury, Mass.	FIFTY
50 50	MILBURY BANK. Fifty on L Officer on horse, back receiving Anquietas. Dollars on L Milbury, Mass. 50	50 General Scott.
100 C	Scene in farm yard; farmer, horse, pig, cows, sheep, ducks, &c. MILBURY BANK. HUNDRED on One Hundred Dollars.	100 Daniel Webster.
1 A female. ONE	Vig. Interior of boot shop, with men at work. ONE on 1 on right. MILFORD BANK, Milford, Mass. Locomotive and tender.	1 Washington on horseback.
Portrait of Henry Clay.	Vig. Same as ones. MILFORD BANK, Milford, Mass. Job waggon and two horses.	2 Portrait of Gen. Taylor.
Portrait of Gen. Jackson.	Vig. Dairy scene, maid milking, female looking on, &c. MILFORD BANK, Milford, Mass.	3 Large figure three, and three cupids.
FIVE Male and female. FIVE	MILFORD BANK, Milford Mass. Vig. Girl with a sheaf of grain in large V.	5 Portrait of Daniel Webster.

Left	Centre	Right
X Portrait of female. 10	Vig. Large spread eagle. X MILFORD BANK, Milford, Mass. Job waggon and two horses.	10 Male portrait
20 Railroad depot and locomotive and tender.	Vig. Female, arms extended; cupids on either side. MILFORD BANK, Milford, Mass. Ship and steamboat.	20 Girl with a sickle in her hand and a sheaf of straw.
50 Portrait of female. 50	Vig. Two females sitting; ship on left, and houses on right. MILFORD BANK, Milford, Mass. Locomotive and tender.	50 Boy picking cotton.
100 Sailor with flag.	MILFORD BANK, Milford, Mass. Vig. Female and Cupid hovering over city.	100 Vessel under sail 100
500 Portrait of female.	MILFORD BANK, Milford, Mass. Vig. Three females, and Railroad trains. Eagle	500 Barrel and ship 500
Two females.	MILLERS' RIVER BANK. Athol, Mass. ONE DOLLAR.	1 ONE 1
2 Stream of water, bridge and train of cars.	MILLERS' RIVER BANK, Athol, Mass. TWO DOLLARS.	2 Indian woman and child.
3 Male, female and children.	MILLERS' RIVER BANK, Athol, Mass. THREE	3 THREE 3
FIVE 5 FIVE	MILLERS' RIVER BANK. Athol, Mass. Blacksmith's shop. FIVE DOLLARS.	V
10	MILLERS, RIVER BANK, Athol, Mass. Two females.	10 Portrait of Washington.

Left	Centre	Right
TWENTY Farmer, mechanic and sailor.	Female and eagle. Portrait of female. MILLERS' RIVER BANK. Athol, Mass.	20 Train of cars.
FIFTY Group of females.	MILLERS' RIVER BANK. Athol, Mass. L	50 Spread eagle.
ONE Full length female figure with sword.	MONSON BANK, A Monson, Mass. 1 Vig. Indian seated looking down upon a city; bow and arrows in hand 1	1 Female portrait.
ONE Girl with sheaf of grain on her head. ONE 1 ONE	Harvest field, farmers at work. B MONSON BANK. Monson, Mass. Vig. Female together, holding shield, laurels and tablets; cars and ship in background.	1 Locomotive horse, &c.
Female portrait. 2	Vig. Two men, one a farmer holding horse under a tree, factories several tall chimneys. MONSON BANK, Monson, Mass.	2 Shield, scroll E Pluribus Unum.
3 Male portrait.	MONSON BANK, Monson, Mass. 3 Vig. Three figures, liberty pole and cap, cornucopia, anvil and hammer 3	3 Blacksmith making horse shoe.
5	MONSON BANK. A Monson, Mass. Vig. Train of cars.	FIVE 5 FIVE Female Indian standing.
5 B Portrait of Washington.	Vig. Locomotive and train of cars also second train going towards village in distance. MONSON BANK, Monson, Mass.	5 5
FIVE C Farmer seated, sheaf of grain on either side, sickle in right hand.	MONSON BANK, Monson, Mass. 5 Vig. Two Females, one spinning. Train of cars in distance.	5
Vig. Drove of oxen, horses in front, farmers loading wheat.	10 MONSON BANK, Monson, Mass. X X	X Justice leaning on shield, scroll at feet, vessel, cars and lighthouse.

Left	Centre	Right
Full length female holding cornucopia. TWENTY	Vig. Two cows, mill, water, &c, in distance. MONSON BANK, Monson, Mass.	20 Male portrait
50 Medallion head. 50	MONSON BANK, Monson, Mass. Vig. Dogs chasing an elk.	50 Franklin.
1 Drummer boy and two soldiers seated.	Vig. Battle of Bunker Hill. Scene is the death of Warren. MONUMENT BANK, Charlestown, Mass. 1	1 Bunker Hill Monument.
2 Portrait of Warren.	MONUMENT BANK, Charlestown, Mass. Vig. Same as ones.	TWO Bunker Hill Monument.
THREE Bunker Hill Monument.	MONUMENT BANK, Charlestown, Mass. 3 Vig. Same as ones	3
5 5	Vig. Same as ones MONUMENT BANK, Charlestown, Mass.	5 Bunker Hill Monument.
10 Two soldiers throwing up a breastwork, officer giving orders	MONUMENT BANK, Charlestown, Mass. X Portrait of Washington. X	TEN Same as fives
L Bunker Hill Monument. FIFTY	MONUMENT BANK, Charlestown, Mass. 50 Surrender of Cornwallis at Yorktown.	50
C Bunker Hill Monument.	MONUMENT BANK, Charlestown, Mass. Spread eagle on shield; on the left is Charlestown with a view of the monument; on right a schooner sailing. Rail cars in front.	100 Portrait of Webster.
FIVE HUNDRED	MONUMENT BANK, Charlestown, Mass. Vig. Two angels, one woman and little boy scattering gold coin on city below.	500 Bunker Hill Monument.

Left	Centre	Right
1 State Arms.	MOUNT VERNON BK. Boston, Mass. Male portrait. View of the home of Washington.	1 1
TWO State Arms. TWO	Man buying newspaper of boy; hhds, etc. Mad Lead. MOUNT VERNON BK. Boston, Mass. 2	2 Female seated with shield on which is view of city and motto
3 State Arms.	Battle scene of the revolution. 3 MOUNT VERNON BK. Boston, Mass.	3 Soldier loading gun
Five on 4 State Arms.	MOUNT VERNON BK. Boston, Mass. View of the home of Washington. 5	5 Male portrait.
X State Arms.	Three men loading boats with bales. MOUNT VERNON BK. Boston, Mass. 10	10 Old man, child, and bust of Washington.
20 State Arms.	MOUNT VERNON BK. Boston, Mass. 20 TWENTY DOLLARS	20 Half length female
50 State Arms. FIFTY 50	Wharf scene in general. MOUNT VERNON BK. Boston, Mass.	50 Half length female
100 State Arms.	C State Arms. C MOUNT VERNON BK. Boston, Mass.	100 Male portrait
500 State Arms.	MOUNT VERNON BK. Boston, Mass. Female dressed in robes	500 Male portrait.
1 ONE Portrait of J. Q. Adams	MOUNT WOLLASTON BANK. Quincy, Mass. Interior of a shoe makers shop.	1 Dog. ONE

Left	Centre	Right
2 Portrait of J. Q. Adams. TWO	MOUNT WOLLASTON BANK. Quincy, Mass. Stone cutters.	TWO Church.
3 3	Portrait of Cha's F. Adams. Stone cutter. MOUNT WOLLASTON BANK. Quincy, Mass.	3 3
V Church.	View of the old mansion of J. Q. Adams. MOUNT WOLLASTON BANK. Quincy, Mass.	5 Portrait of C. F. Adams.
TEN Dog. TEN	Sailing vessel. MOUNT WOLLASTON BANK. Quincy, Mass.	X Church.
XX Hunter warming himself by a fire in the woods.	House. Female. House. MOUNT WOLLASTON BANK. Quincy, Mass.	20 Portrait of J. Q. Adams.
50 Dog. L	Train of cars. MOUNT WOLLASTON BANK. Quincy, Mass.	50 Female.
C	Spread eagle and American flag. MOUNT WOLLASTON BANK. Quincy, Mass.	100 Indian.
ONE Soldier holding a flag.	Wood cutter, gold dollar; house and wagon in distance. NATIONAL BANK, Boston, Mass.	1 Female and fig. 1.
Female. 2	Man with rake, female with pail; two gold dollars; horses, barn and cows. NATIONAL BANK, Boston, Mass.	2 Sailor with spy glass.
3 Mermaid and merman. [illegible]	Farmer with scythe, sailor with telescope and blacksmith with sledge, also three gold dollars. NATIONAL BANK, Boston, Mass.	3 Washington

Left	Centre	Right
FIVE Liberty.	Three Capitols, five gold dollars, hunter and Indian female. NATIONAL BANK, Boston, Mass.	5 Capitol at Washington.
X	Capitol at Washington. NATIONAL BANK, Boston, Mass.	10 Franklin.
Female giving eagle a drink. XX	View of building NATIONAL BANK, Boston, Mass.	20 Female feeding a horse.
Fountain. 50	Ship and two steamships. NATIONAL BANK, Boston, Mass.	50 Female bust.
100 Female with spear and shield.	Spread eagle and shield; capitol at Washington on right, steamship on left. NATIONAL BANK, Boston, Mass.	C Portrait.
D	Female seated by shield, steamship, cars, bridge and city in distance. NATIONAL BANK, Boston, Mass.	500 Female portrait.
M	1000 on a shield, surmounted by eagle; female each side, steamboat and cars in distance. NATIONAL BANK, Boston, Mass.	1000 Female with grain.
ONE Interior of railroad depot. ONE	1 Street in Salem. 1 NAUMKEAG BANK. Salem, Mass. Cars.	1 Indians. ONE
ONE Indian and dead deer. ONE	View of a street in Salem. NAUMKEAG BANK. Salem, Mass. Cars.	1 Cars, passengers, etc. ONE
TWO Indians. 2	Street in Salem. NAUMKEAG BANK. Salem, Mass. Shipping scene.	2 Man smoking, and shipping. TWO

THREE Ships. 3	3 Street in Salem. 3 NAUMKEAG BANK. Salem, Mass Vessels.	3 Indian and female. THREE
FIVE Indians. FIVE	Street view in Salem. Title of Bank. Boats, men, etc.	5 FIVE Female. Massachu'ts.
V Ships. V	5 Street in Salem. NAUMKEAG BANK. Salem, Mass Vessels	5 Man with dog and gun
5 FIVE 5	NAUMKEAG BANK. Salem, Mass. Street in Salem. Anchor, etc.	5 FIVE 5
Ship building. Sampson discharging a Box.	Street in Salem. NAUMKEAG BANK. Salem, Mass Anchor, &c	10 Train of cars. 10
Steamboat. XX Train of cars.	(Old Plate.) Three female figures and eagle. 20 NAUMKEAG BANK. Salem, Mass	XX Milk maid
20 Female.	(New Plate.) XX Eagle. XX NAUMKEAG BANK. Salem, Mass	20 Ship.
XX Indian princess.	Two females, scroll, building, etc. NAUMKEAG BANK, Salem, Mass.	20 Squaw.
FIFTY Sailor with female, vessels, etc. above him. FIFTY	Title of Bank.	50 Indian female rainbow, falls, etc.
FIFTY Female. FIFTY	50 Man and horse 50 NAUMKEAG BANK. Salem, Mass	FIFTY Female. FIFTY

50 Schooner and steamboat	Men with rake, load of hay, reapers, etc. 50 Title of Bank.	L Female with sword and scales.
100 Arm with scimitar. Mass State Arms.	NAUMKEAG BANK, Salem, Mass. Indian squaw, boy and papoose on cliff viewing city, etc.	100 Load of grain.
Same as right Portrait.	Horses, waggons, and shipping. NAUMKEAG BANK. Salem, Mass	One Hundred and 100. Portrait.
100 Eagle. 100	C Phebus in the chariot of the sun. 100 NAUMKEAG BANK. Salem, Mass	C Portrait of Washington. C
ONE Bust. ONE	(Old Plate.) 1 Interior of a blacksmith's shop. 1 NEPONSET BANK. Canton, Mass	ONE Female. ONE
ONE Female figure.	(New Plate.) Farming scene. NEPONSET BANK, Canton, Mass.	1 Spread eagle and shield. ONE
Female figure. TWO	(New Plate.) Female, train of cars, and steamship in background. NEPONSET BANK. Canton, Mass	2 2 females
TWO Female. 2	(Old Plate.) 2 Farming scene 2 NEPONSET BANK, Canton, Mass.	TWO Female 2
3 Female portrait. THREE	Cattle and sheep, man on horseback. NEPONSET BANK. Canton, Mass	3 Blacksmith, farmer, and sailor. THREE
FIVE Stone cutter. 5	Viaduct of the Boston & Providence railroad. NEPONSET BANK. Canton, Mass	5 Indian. FIVE

10 Portrait of Washington. X	Viaduct of the Boston & Providence railroad. NEPONSET BANK, Canton, Mass	10 Portrait TEN
20 Female.	XX Eagle. XX NEPONSET BANK. Canton Mass	20 Ship.
20 Boy, girl, child, horse, etc.	NEPONSET BANK. Canton, Mass. TWENTY DOLLARS	20 Two children.
FIFTY Female. FIFTY	50 Man and horse 50 NEPONSET BANK. Canton, Mass	FIFTY Female. FIFTY
50 Girl with pitcher and basket.	NEPONSET BANK, Canton, Mass. Title of Bank L	50 Dog & safe.
C Child's head.	NEPONSET BANK. Canton, Mass. One Hundred Dollars Title of Bank.	100 State Arms.
Same as right Portrait.	Horses, waggons and shipping. NEPONSET BANK. Canton, Mass	One Hundred and 100. Portrait
1 on large 1	Stone cutter. NEW ENGLAND BK. Boston, Mass. Eagle	Same as left
2	Portrait of Washington and Franklin on large 2. NEW ENGLAND BK. Boston, Mass.	2
Title and locomotive on large 3.	Female with a roll of cloth; factories and steamboat in distance. Indian head	3 Ship.

Left end	Centre	Right end
5	Female seated on bale; city in distance. Fig. 5 running the entire length of the note. NEW ENGLAND BK. Boston, Mass. Female head	5
TEN DOLLARS	Ten Dollars. Spread eagle on rock, overlooking the sea; ship in distance. NEW ENGLAND BK. Boston, Mass.	10 Female with spear and shield.
20 TWENTY DOLLARS 20	Twenty Dollars. Vig. Same as tens. NEW ENGLAND BK. Boston, Mass.	20 Female and 20 on shield.
Indian in canoe. 50	Fifty Dollars 50 NEW ENGLAND BK. Boston, Mass.	FIFTY
100	ONE HUNDRED 100 Indian in a canoe; mountains in distance on upper left. NEW ENGLAND BK. Boston, Mass.	100
FIVE HUN. D	FIVE HUNDRED DOLL'S. Title of Bank. Female seated; boxes and bales at her back; ships in distance.	500 NEW ENGLAND BK.
Indian seated. 1000	Various vessels; city in distance. NEW ENGLAND BK. Boston, Mass. Locomotive.	1000 Portrait of Washington.
1	Vig. The apostle "Eliot" attended by three others, with Bible in hand, preaching to seven Indians on a hill. Head of Franklin. 1 NEWTON BANK, Newton, Mass. Cog wheels resting on bale of cotton.	1 Head of J. Q. Adams. ONE
2	Vig. Same as ones. 2 NEWTON BANK, Newton. State Arms.	2 Head of Washington. TWO
3	Vig. Same as ones. 3 NEWTON BANK, Newton. Agricultural implements, and horn of plenty.	3 Female holding bow, arrows and quiver. THREE
5	Vig. Same as ones, on right side, head and 5. NEWTON BANK, Newton. Engine, tender, and car.	5 Cattle, sheep and swine. FIVE
10	Vig. Same as ones. X NEWTON BANK, Newton. Farmer sitting on plough.	10 Female Indian, left hand resting on an[illegible] X
Female seated, holding horn of plenty; shield with the word TWENTY on it. 20	Vig. Same as ones. NEWTON BANK, Newton. Engine and cars.	20 State Arms.
50 Female holding spear in right hand.	Vig. Male and female figures seated with horn of plenty; rake, anchor, &c., representing Agriculture, Commerce, &c. NEWTON BANK, Newton. 50	50 Cupid in a sail boat; using an oar as a rudder. 50
50 Whites treating with Indians.	50 50 NEWTON BANK, Newton, Mass. Words fifty twice, Dollars and Massachusetts on green die. L	50 Male portrait.
100 C	C Train of cars. NEWTON BANK, Newton, Mass. Whites treating with Indians.	100 Male portrait.
100 Male figure seated, representing Commerce, &c.	Vig. Eagle on a branch of tree over canal, on which are loaded boats; train of cars in backgr'nd. NEWTON BANK, Newton. C 100 C	100 Female figure seated, representing agriculture.
500	Vig. Female seated, sheaf at her feet, farmers reaping and loading grain in the distance. 500 D NEWTON BANK, Newton.	500
1 Female and 1.	(New Plate.) Female, electric machine and portrait of Franklin; Franklin drawing lightning from the clouds with a kite; telegraph, train of cars and State House in distance. NORTH BANK, Boston, Mass.	1 Female with sickle and fig. 1.
1 Female. 1	(Old Plate.) View of the State House and Boston Common. NORTH BANK, Boston, Mass.	1 Ship. 1
TWO Female feeding an eagle from cup.	Vig. Same as new plate of ones. NORTH BANK, Boston, Mass.	2 Washington.
2 Ship. 2	Female. Three females. Vig. Same as old ones. NORTH BANK, Boston, Mass.	2 Ship. 2
3 Eagle and shield. THREE	Vig. Same as ones, new plate. NORTH BANK, Boston, Mass.	3 Female
3 Reapers. 3	Vig. Same as old ones with word three on either side. NORTH BANK, Boston, Mass.	3 3
5 Male portrait	Vig. Same as ones, new plate. NORTH BANK, Boston, Mass.	5 Five females, and 5.
5 Ship. 5	FIVE FIVE Vig. Same as ones, old plate. NORTH BANK, Boston, Mass.	5 Female. 5
10 10	Ship. Female, spear and shield. Vig. Same as old ones. NORTH BANK, Boston, Mass.	10 Agricultural implements.
10 inverted Portrait of Fillmore.	Vig. Same as new ones. NORTH BANK, Boston, Mass.	10 inverted Sailor boy.
20 Female seated with eagle and shield.	Vig. Same as ones new plates. NORTH BANK, Boston, Mass.	20 Female portrait.
20 Female seated.	XX Eagle. XX NORTH BANK, Boston, Mass.	20 Ship.

Steamboat. XX Train of cars.	20 Three females; one with liberty cap; one with scales and the other with book; eagle and shield; ship in distance. NORTH BANK, Boston, Mass.	XX Milkmaid with pail and stool.
50 Female portrait.	Vig. Same as ones, new plate. NORTH BANK, Boston, Mass.	50 Female.
C Female with scales and sheaf.	Vig. Same as ones, new plate. NORTH BANK, Boston, Mass.	100 Female.
II inverted Sailor erect, leaning on capstan.	Vig. Same as ones, new plate. NORTH BANK, Boston, Mass.	500 inverted Female erect with cornucopia.
M Female seated with trident.	Vig. Same as ones, new plate. NORTH BANK, Boston, Mass.	1000 Female portrait 1000
Female seated, barrel, &c. guns and vessel in distance. 1	Fig. 1 with six male heads in centre of it. NORTHAMPTON BK, Northampton, Mass.	1 Female with grain.
ONE Bust. ONE	1 Interior of a blacksmith's shop. 1 NORTHAMPTON BK, Northampton, Mass.	ONE Female. ONE
1 Portrait of Washington.	Female. 1 Female. NORTHAMPTON BK, Northampton, Mass.	1 Portrait of Franklin.
1 Same as right.	NORTHAMPTON BK Northampton, Mass. Female with words "Incorporated 1833," on tablets; child at her feet.	1 One, 1, and One Dollar on green die
2 Stone cutter TWO	NORTHAMPTON BK Northampton, Mass. Two on 2 Boy, child, cattle, sheep, etc. Two on 2 Horse.	2 Dog & calf.

Washing sheep. 2	Large 2; five men in small circular frame. NORTHAMPTON BK Northampton, Mass.	TWO Female with wreath. TWO
TWO Female. 2	2 Farming scene 2 NORTHAMPTON BK. Northampton, Mass.	TWO Female. 2
2 Portrait.	Female. 2 Female. NORTHAMPTON BK, Northampton, Mass.	2 Portrait.
Farmer on horse; boy, barn, load of hay, plough, &c. 3	Cattle; city, &c. in distance. 3 NORTHAMPTON BK Northampton, Mass.	3 across three. Girl with flowers. THREE
THREE Man sharpening a scythe. 3	3 Female and eagle. 3 NORTHAMPTON BK, Northampton, Mass.	THREE Sailor. 3
5 FIVE 5	V Spread eagle; shipping in background. V NORTHAMPTON BK, Northampton, Mass.	5 FIVE 5
FIVE	Spread eagle and shield; village in distance. Large V, female and cupid. NORTHAMPTON BK, Northampton, Mass.	5 Girl.
5 Female seated, resting on wheel. FIVE	5 Small State arms. NORTHAMPT'N B'K, Northampton, Mass.	5
10 X 10	Man and oxen. 10 NORTHAMPTON BK. Northampton, Mass.	TEN Female
TEN	Vulcan the blacksmith; train of cars and factories in the background. X NORTHAMPTON BK, Northampton, Mass.	10 Reaper.

NORTH Old man, child, bust of Washing 10	AMPTON BANK, Northampton, Mass. ton on table. Eagle. Massachusetts.	10
20 Female.	XX Eagle XX NORTHAMPTON BK, Northampton, Mass.	20 Ship.
20 TWENTY 20	NORTHAMPTON BK Northampton, Mass. 20 TWENTY DOLLARS	20 TWENTY 20
FIFTY Female. FIFTY	50 Man and horse. 50 NORTHAMPTON BK. Northampton, Mass.	FIFTY Female. FIFTY
50 L 50	NORTHAMPTON BK Northampton, Mass. 50 FIFTY DOLLARS	50 L 50
Words One Hundred on figs. 100.	NORTHAMPTON BK Northampton, Mass. C One Hundred Dollars C	100 C 100
Words one hundred and fig. 100. Male portrait	Wharf Scene. Title of Bank.	Words one hundred and fig 100. Male portrait
1	NORTH BRIDGEWATER BANK, N. Bridgewater, Mass. A street in N. Bridgewater. Portrait.	1
2	A street in North Bridgewater, Train of cars. NORTH BRIDGEWATER BANK, N. Bridgewater, Mass. Female.	2 Portrait.
Female. 3	Street in North Bridgewater. NORTH BRIDGEWATER BANK, N. Bridgewater, Mass. Cow and calf.	3 Portrait.

Left	Centre	Right
5 Portrait.	NORTH BRIDGEWATER BANK. N. Bridgewater, Mass. A group of females; ships and factories in background.	FIVE Group of females and large figure 5.
Bill inverted 10	Train of cars. NORTH BRIDGEWATER BANK. N. Bridgewater, Mass. Loading hay	10 Female and X.
Female with a basket of fruit and flowers. XX	Female reclining; milk maids, cows, locomotive and factory in background. NORTH BRIDGEWATER BANK. N. Bridgewater, Mass. Female	20 2 Female 0 TWENTY
Female.	50 50 NORTH BRIDGEWATER BANK. N. Bridgewater, Mass. State arms, eagle and two females; steamboat and train of cars in the background.	Female.
Portrait of female. 100	View of the capitol at Washington. NORTH BRIDGEWATER BANK. N. Bridgewater, Mass.	100 Blacksmith, anvil and forge. 100
1 Portrait. ONE	Train of cars. NORTHBOROUGH BANK Northborough, Mass.	1 Female seated on plough with sickle &c.
2 Portrait.	Female reclining, train of cars, factories, and shipping, milk maids and cows in background. NORTHBOROUGH BANK Northborough, Mass. Man plowing	2 Interior of shoe maker's shop.
3 Male portrait	Man pressing horse in corn press; basket of horns, etc. NORTHBOROUGH BANK, Northborough, Mass	3 Farmer, sailor, blacksmith and fig. 3.
5 Farmer with scythe.	Portrait, a winged female with trumpet at the left of portrait and cupid at the right. NORTHBOROUGH BANK Northborough, Mass. Implements	5 Group of females, large figure 5.
10 Portrait.	A female figure and nine cherubs. NORTHBOROUGH BANK Northborough, Mass.	X Female, globe, and shield.

Left	Centre	Right
XX Portrait of Washington.	Female reclining also eagle and globe, ships in distance. NORTHBOROUGH BANK Northborough, Mass. Imp. and products	20 Cattle.
L Male portrait	Drove of cattle and sheep; man on horseback. NORTHBOROUGH BANK. Northborough, Mass. Horses.	50 Female standing.
100 Portrait of Z. Taylor. HUNDRED	Blacksmith at work; boy and horse. NORTHBOROUGH BANK, Northborough, Mass. Cows.	100 Building.
	OCEAN BANK, Newburyport, Mass. This Bank uses Perkins' Patent Stereotype plate, which is the denomination printed in fine letters all over the bill.	
1 Female figure holding sceptre and shield. ONE	1 Landing of the Pilgrims in 1620. 1 OLD COLONY BANK, Plymouth, Mass.	1 Portrait of Washington ONE
TWO Female with scales and sword. TWO	2 Landing of the Pilgrims in 1620. 2 OLD COLONY BANK. Plymouth, Mass.	2 Female figure. TWO
3 Portrait of Washington. 3	THREE Landing of the Pilgrims in 1620. 3 OLD COLONY BANK. Plymouth, Mass.	THREE
Statue of Washington.	5 Landing of the Pilgrims in 1620. 5 OLD COLONY BANK. Plymouth, Mass.	Eagle standing upon a rock over-looking the sea. FIVE
Eagle standing upon a rock over-looking the sea. TEN	10 Landing of the Pilgrims in 1620. X OLD COLONY BANK, Plymouth, Mass.	Female figure TEN
20 Indian.	Landing of the Pilgrims in 1620. OLD COLONY BANK. Plymouth, Mass.	20 Portrait of Washington XX

Left	Centre	Right
Indians.	Landing of the Pilgrims in 1620. OLD COLONY BANK. Plymouth, Mass.	50 Train of cars FIFTY
100 Reaper.	Landing of the Pilgrims in 1620. OLD COLONY BANK, Plymouth, Mass.	100 Female and eagle.
ONE Eagle. ONE	1 Farming scene. ONE OXFORD BANK, Oxford, Mass.	1 Female figures 1
2 Female with scales and sword. 2	Cattle and sheep, man on horseback. 2 OXFORD BANK, Oxford, Mass.	TWO General Washington. 2
3 Female. 3	THREE Surrender of Lord Cornwallis. 3 OXFORD BANK, Oxford, Mass.	THREE Agricultural implements. 3
FIVE Female.	V Battle of Bunker Hill. 5 OXFORD BANK, Oxford, Mass.	FIVE Portrait of Washington. 5
Statue of Washington.	10 Washington crossing the Delaware. 10 OXFORD BANK, Oxford, Mass.	TEN Portrait. X
20 Two children and butterfly	Three Indians reclining, city, etc. OXFORD BANK, Oxford, Mass	20 American shield.
Steamboat. XX Train of cars.	Three female figures and eagle. 20 OXFORD BANK, Oxford, Mass.	XX Milk maid.
50 Steamboat and sail boat.	Farming scene 50 OXFORD BANK, Oxford, Mass.	L Female with scales and sword.

Left	Center	Right
50 State Arms.	OXFORD BANK. Cows in brook. Oxford, Mass. Boy, girl, etc. Fifty Dollars.	50 Woman with sewing machine.
100 Boy drinking from pail; girl, well, etc.	Massachusetts. Two horses startled at flash of lightning; cows in water on right. OXFORD BANK. One Hundred Dollars.	C 100
100 Eagle. 100	C Phaeton in the car of the sun. 100 OXFORD BANK. Oxford, Mass.	C Portrait of Washington. C
Ships and car stations. 1	PACIFIC BANK Nantucket, Mass	ONE Whale, fishing. ONE
	The Pacific Bank also use the Perkins stereotype plate.	
Whale fishing. 2	PACIFIC BANK Nantucket, Mass	2 Ship.
Ships. 3	PACIFIC BANK Nantucket, Mass.	3 Farmers and sheep.
5 Female. FIVE	Neptune and three female figures. PACIFIC BANK Nantucket, Mass.	5 Sailor
10 Sea nymphs Steamship	Spread eagle, ships in distance. PACIFIC BANK Nantucket, Mass. State Arms	10 Female. TEN
20 Cupid in a sail boat. 20	Medallion. Neptune. Medallion. PACIFIC BANK Nantucket, Mass.	20 Female.

Left	Center	Right
50 Medallion. 50	Medal lion. Neptune. Medal lion. female figure. PACIFIC BANK Nantucket, Mass.	50 Portrait of a girl. FIFTY
100 Ship building. 100	C Two females shipping in background. C PACIFIC BANK Nantucket, Mass	100 Ships.
1 Portrait of female. ONE	Stream of water R. R. train of cars. PEMBERTON BANK Lawrence, Mass.	1 Portrait of Webster. ONE
2 Female.	PEMBERTON BANK Lawrence, Mass. Female weaving at factory looms.	2 Portrait of Washington.
3 Female.	Three female figures and cupid upon the water. PEMBERTON BANK Lawrence, Mass.	3 Portrait of Jackson. THREE
FIVE	White men in a boat and Indians on shore receiving them. PEMBERTON BANK Lawrence, Mass.	5 Portrait of Calhoun.
X Three female figures. TEN	Female, state arms and ships in background. PEMBERTON BANK Lawrence, Mass.	10 Blacksmith anvil &c.
20 Sailor leaning upon a capstan	Men and cattle. PEMBERTON BANK Lawrence, Mass.	20 Washington on horse back
50 Portrait of Clay.	PEMBERTON BANK Lawrence, Mass. Female and shield; capitol in distance.	50 Portrait of Female.
C Anchor, bale, etc.	Female seated with shield, pole, cap, eagle, etc. PEMBERTON BANK, Lawrence, Mass.	100 Eagle.

Left	Center	Right
500 Dorchester Heights.	Landing of the Pilgrims. Title of Bank.	500 Massach'sts D
ONE Female. ONE	Farming scene. PEOPLES BANK Roxbury, Mass.	Large figure one, female within. ONE
TWO Female.	Train of cars. PEOPLES BANK Roxbury, Mass.	TWO 2
THREE Indian girl with bow and arrow. THREE	Spread eagle R. R. and canal. PEOPLES BANK Roxbury, Mass.	THREE General Washington. THREE
FIVE Female.	Eagle and steamship. V PEOPLES BANK Roxbury, Mass.	5 Portrait.
Horse, elephant and a group of female figures. 10	PEOPLES BANK Roxbury, Mass.	TEN Portrait of Washington TEN
20 Female.	XX Eagle. XX PEOPLES BANK Roxbury, Mass.	20 Ship.
50 Soldier loading gun.	PEOPLE'S BANK. Female seated; eagle, shield, etc. Fifty Dollars. Roxbury, Mass.	50 Male portrait
FIFTY Female. FIFTY	50 Men and horse. 50 PEOPLES BANK Roxbury, Mass.	FIFTY Female. FIFTY
C State Arms.	Landing of the Pilgrims. PEOPLES BANK. Roxbury, Mass. One Hundred Dollars.	100 Benjamin Franklin

 MASS. MASS.

One Hundred and 100. Portrait.	Houses, wagons, shipping &c. PEOPLES BANK Roxbury, Mass.	Same as left Portrait.
D Washington	Boy with two horses, cattle, farm house &c. in distance. PEOPLE'S BANK Roxbury, Mass. Five Hundred Dollars.	5 0 Eagle on rock.
1 Stone cutters.	PITTSFIELD BANK, Pittsfield, Mass.	ONE Portrait.
Farm yard, horses, pump, man, pig, cows, barn. 1	Small State Mass arms. PITTSFIELD BANK, Pittsfield, Mass.	1 Male Portrait.
TWO Portrait.	Interior of a shoe makers shop PITTSFIELD BANK, Pittsfield, Mass.	2 2
Male Portrait. 2 on TWO	PITTSFIELD BANK, Pittsfield, Mass. Two children. TWO DOLLARS. TWO DOLLARS. 2 surrounded by 2's.	2 Male Portrait.
Male portrait 5	PITTSFIELD BANK, Pittsfield, Mass. Two females, spinning wheel, cattle scene on left; buildings on right. Female bathing.	5 5
FIVE V	Spread eagle and flags bearing the name of each State in the Union. PITTSFIELD BANK, Pittsfield, Mass.	5 Portrait.
5 Male Portrait.	PITTSFIELD BANK, Pittsfield, Mass. Words "FIVE DOLLARS" on figure 5, and word FIVE.	5 Male Portrait.
X Indian.	Portrait. Steamship PITTSFIELD BANK, Pittsfield, Mass.	X TEN

X Male Portrait.	Man cutting stick, horse, sheep, boy on gate, &c. PITTSFIELD BANK, Pittsfield, Mass.	10 Male Portrait.
20 Indian.	Santa Claus in sleigh, drawn by reindeer over roofs of houses. PITTSFIELD BANK, Pittsfield, Mass.	20 Portrait.
L	PITTSFIELD BANK, Pittsfield, Mass. Faust, Guttenburg and Schoeffer.	50 Portrait.
Cupids supporting the fig. 1	Landing of the pilgrims 1620. PLYMOUTH BANK Plymouth, Mass.	1 Female bust, have ships under sail.
2 Benj'n Franklin.	Landing of the Pilgrims, 1620. PLYMOUTH BANK, Plymouth, Mass.	2 Two cupids in figure 2
5 Portrait of Washington. FIVE	Landing of the pilgrims 1620. PLYMOUTH BANK Plymouth, Mass. Indian	5 Female, sickle and sheaf of wheat, in fig. 5. FIVE
10 10	Landing of the pilgrims 1620. X PLYMOUTH BANK Plymouth, Mass.	10 Female.
20 20	Landing of the Pilgrims, 1620. XX PLYMOUTH BANK, Plymouth, Mass.	20 Twenty on Medallion. Head.
Female, sickle and sheaf of wheat.	50 PLYMOUTH BANK Plymouth, Mass. Landing of the Pilgrims, 1620.	50
The figures 100 with the words one hundred running across. Female, ship in distance.	Landing of the pilgrims 1620 PLYMOUTH BANK Plymouth, Mass Eagle	100 100

ONE	Indian queen of Pocasset, crossing river on raft. Figure 1 with one running across. POCASSET BANK.	1 Silver dollar
Two on 2 Indian female.	POCASSET BANK. Word Rhode on 2 Cow, calf, sheep, stream, &c. Word Island on 2	2 Two children.
Figure 2, with two running across.	POCASSET BANK. Vig. Same as ones. Clasped hands.	2 Two silver dollars.
FIVE Five silver dollars.	5 POCASSET BANK, Vig. in centre of right end, same as ones. State arms.	Figure 5 with five running across. FIVE
10 Stonecutter at work; men hoisting in distance.	POCASSET BANK. Vig. in lower right corner same as ones.	10
20 Indian queen on raft.	Twenty dollars. 20 Vig. Female soaring with wreath in right hand; river scene, steamboat, &c. POCASSET BANK, State arms.	20
50	POCASSET BANK. Vig. Scythe hanging in tree, female standing; man sitting, dog lying down, water scene, steamboat, &c. 50	50 Indian queen on a raft. 50
100 Ship.	POCASSET BANK. C Vig. Indian queen on raft; C on right.	100 Man whetting his scythe.
500 Ship of war under full sail; ship in distance.	POCASSET BANK, D Vig. Indian Queen on raft.	500
Vig. Indian Queen on raft 1000	POCASSET BANK. M	1000 Indian seated smoking pipe, canoe on left, dog on right, squaw and wigwam, &c.

Left	Centre	Right
ONE	View in the streets of Salisbury. POWOW RIVER B'K, Salisbury, Mass.	1 Farmers and sheep.
2 Interior of blacksmiths shop. TWO	View in the streets of Salisbury. POWOW RIVER B'K, Salisbury, Mass.	2 Sail boats. TWO
THREE Female feeding poultry.	(New Plate.) View of bank and stage coach drawn by four horses passing. POWOW RIVER B'K, Salisbury, Mass.	3 Andrew Jackson.
5 Indian. FIVE	View of the town of Salisbury. POWOW RIVER B'K, Salisbury, Mass.	5 Farmers mowing. FIVE
10 Justice guarding the Treasury.	(New Plate.) View of bank and stage coach drawn by four horses passing. POWOW RIVER B'K, Salisbury, Mass.	10 Henry Clay.
20 Boy's head.	POWOW RIVER B'K, Salisbury, Mass. L 20 Dolls in red.	20 View of bank stores, &c.
Ship at sea. 50	Female seated, with grain, shield, &c. L POWOW RIVER B'K, Salisbury, Mass. Fifty Dollars.	50 Banking house.
FIFTY Female. FIFTY	50 Man and horse. 50 POWOW RIVER B'K, Salisbury, Mass.	FIFTY Female. FIFTY
100 Female with sickle, dog, &c.	POWOW RIVER B'K C Female seated; factories in distance. C One Hundred Dollars Massachusetts.	100 State Arms.
One Hundred and 100. Portrait.	Horses, waggons, shipping, &c. POWOW RIVER B'K, Salisbury, Mass.	Same as left Portrait.

Left	Centre	Right
1	Two females, train of cars and steamboat in background. 1 PRESCOTT BANK, Lowell, Mass.	1 Female.
2	Man sitting on the ground with hammer on his shoulder; factory and train of cars in background. Cupid and die X. PRESCOTT BANK, Lowell, Mass.	TWO Female.
3	Farmers ploughing, man on horseback, train of cars passing under a bridge. 3 PRESCOTT BANK, Lowell, Mass.	THREE Two females.
5	Female reclining; a stream of water and factories in background. 5 PRESCOTT BANK, Lowell, Mass.	FIVE Female, lion shield.
5 with small 5's above and below it.	Figure of America seated, with wreath, shield, bundle of rods, &c. Interior of cotton factory, man, girl, boy, and machinery. PRESCOTT BANK, Lowell, Mass. FIVE DOLLARS.	5 In die with small 5's on it.
TEN	Female, eagle and shield. Also portrait of Washington. X PRESCOTT BANK, Lowell, Mass.	10 State Arms.
Herd of Deer grazing in forest. Waterfall in back gro und, trees, &c. 10 On die with words ten.	PRESCOTT BANK, Lowell, Mass. TEN DOLLARS.	1) On die with words ten. Head of Girl.
20 Female.	2 Female. 0 PRESCOTT BANK, Lowell, Mass. XX	20 Female. 20
20 Female portrait.	PRESCOTT BANK, Lowell, Mass. Female reclining with chart, dividers, quadrant, globe, etc.	20 Male head.
FIFTY Female with globe, etc.	PRESCOTT BANK, Lowell, Mass. FIFTY DOLLARS Title of Bank. FIFTY in red.	50 Male head.

Left	Centre	Right
50 Female.	Male and female. PRESCOTT BANK, Lowell, Mass. 50	50 Cupid in a sail boat. 50
100 Vulcan the blacksmith.	Spread eagle, railroad and canal. PRESCOTT BANK, Lowell, Mass. 100	100 Female.
C Male portrait.	PRESCOTT BANK, Lowell, Mass. Title of Bank. 100 DOLLS. in red.	100 Dog and safe.
500 D	PRESCOTT BANK, Lowell, Mass. Male portrait; D each side of bottom. FIVE HUNDRED	500 D
500	Female seated pointing to papers and load of hay. 500 D PRESCOTT BANK, Lowell, Mass.	500
1 Man chopping down a tree. ONE	Ships. PROVINCETOWN BANK, Provincetown, Mass.	1 Girl.
2 Church.	Ships. PROVINCETOWN BANK, Provincetown, Mass.	2 TWO
3 Sailor and mechanic seated on bale of goods his hand resting on sledge hammer.	PROVINCETOWN BANK Provincetown, Mass. Ornamental figure 3	3 Vig. Large ship and small boats in distance; on right is a steamship, and ships on left.
Female and eagle. V	Portrait of Webster. PROVINCETOWN BANK, Provincetown, Mass.	FIVE Boy.
Female.	TEN Ships. PROVINCETOWN BANK, Provincetown, Mass.	10 X

XX Portrait of J. Q. Adams.	PROVINCETOWN BANK, Provincetown, Mass. Sailors on shore, throwing a rope with a mortar to a ship wrecked in the sea.	XX 20
L Portrait of female.	Female seated on a bale; steamship and sail vessels in the distance. PROVINCETOWN BANK, Provincetown, Mass.	50
C	Large Ship. PROVINCETOWN BANK, Provincetown, Mass. Large C in the middle of the bill printed in red.	100 Sailor leaning upon a capstan.
ON 1 E	Train of cars. 1 PYNCHON BANK, Springfield, Mass. 1	1 Head and shoulders of a man with hammer.
2 on TWO Old Pynchon House. TWO	Female; farming scenes in the background. 2 PYNCHON BANK, Springfield, Mass.	TWO Female.
3 A bull's head. THREE	Two horses and eagle; train of cars, factory and steamboat in background. PYNCHON BANK, Springfield, Mass.	3 THREE
Large figure 5, female and shield. FIVE	PYNCHON BANK, Springfield, Mass. 5 Three boys and ship. 5	5 Old Pynchon House. 5
X, 10, Ten Old Pynchon House. TEN	Man ploughing with yoke of oxen and horse. PYNCHON BANK, Springfield, Mass. X	10 Two females.
20 Portrait of Webster.	Indian and plough, log cabin &c. 20 on right. PYNCHON BANK, Springfield, Mass. XX	XX Female.
Female.	50 Signing of the Declaration of Independence. PYNCHON BANK, Springfield, Mass.	50 Portrait of Washington.
100 Female.	PYNCHON BANK, Springfield, Mass. C Female leaning upon a chest; old Pynchon House in the distance.	100
1 Head of John Adams. ONE	Vig. A scene in Quincy; houses, fence, stream of water, and sloops. QUINCY STONE BK. Quincy, Mass.	1 Head of John Hancock. ONE
TWO Head of John Hancock. 2	Vig. Same as ones. QUINCY STONE BK. Quincy, Mass.	2 Head of John Adams. TWO
THREE John Adams. 3	Vig. Same as ones. QUINCY STONE BK. Quincy, Mass.	3 John Hancock. THREE
5 John Hancock. FIVE	Vig. Same as ones. QUINCY STONE BK. Quincy, Mass.	5 John Adams. FIVE
X John Hancock. TEN	Vig. Same as ones. QUINCY STONE BK. Quincy, Mass.	10 John Adams. TEN
20 John Adams. TWENTY	Vig. Same as ones. QUINCY STONE BK. Quincy, Mass.	20 John Hancock. TWENTY
FIFTY Female with wreath in hand. FIFTY	50 Vig. Man and horse. 50 QUINCY STONE BK. Quincy, Mass.	FIFTY Female with horn of plenty. FIFTY
Stone quarry, oxen, wagon, man, railroad, &c. 50	L QUINCY STONE B'K. Quincy, Mass.	50 Male Portrait.
100 Eagle. 100	C Vig. Horses and man with truck, &c. 100 QUINCY STONE BK. Quincy, Mass.	C Head of Washington. C
Same as right. Hercules.	Scene on wharf. QUINCY STONE BK., Quincy, Mass.	One Hundred and 100. Columbus.
C State arms.	QUINCY STONE B'K. Quincy, Mass. C Franklin in study. C	100 Female Portrait.
500	Indian paddling in canoe. 500 Title of Bank. D D	500 Female with sword and scales.
500 D	QUINCY STONE B'K. Quincy, Mass. D Eagle. D	500 D
1000	Spread eagle on promontory, ship in distance. 1000 QUINCY STONE B'K. Quincy, Mass.	1000 Indian female with bow and arrows.
Head of female. 1	Vig. Church, court-house, dwellings, trees, men on horseback, carriages, &c., which is a view of Main street, Worcester. QUINSIGAMOND BANK, Worcester, Mass.	1 Portrait of male.
2 Plank road same.	Vig. Same as ones. QUINSIGAMOND BANK, Worcester, Mass. Female Head.	2 Houses in distance; railroad train, &c.
Mason at work. 3	Vig. Same as ones. QUINSIGAMOND BANK, Worcester, Mass. Eagle.	3 Female with bundle of grain under her arm.
5	Vig. Same as ones. Male Portrait. QUINSIGAMOND BANK, Worcester, Mass.	5 Female with flowers.
Wm. Penn. TEN	QUINSIGAMOND BK. Worcester, Mass. Street in Worcester.	10 Indian seated.

Left end	Centre	Right end
10 X 10	Vig. Cincinnatus at his plough, oxen &c. 10 QUINSIGAMOND BANK, Worcester, Mass.	TEN Full length female and horn of plenty.
State Arms. 20	Vig. Female figure with wings, blowing trumpet; eagle with arrows, &c. in his talons. QUINSIGAMOND BANK. Worcester, Mass.	20 Portrait of J. Q. Adams.
50 Head of Washington.	QUINSIGAMOND BANK. Worcester, Mass. Vig. Two cows in water, one lying down; two sheep resting and one standing.	50
100 Figure of justice with scales and sword.	Vig. House and cattle in distance; dairy maid, pail and two cows QUINSIGAMOND BANK. Worcester, Mass.	100 Head of Franklin.
500 Three heres, balances, female, dog, basket, bottle, &c.	QUINSIGAMOND BANK. Worcester.	500 Medallion head of Washington.
	RAILROAD BANK, Lowell, Mass. This Bank uses Perkins' Patent Stereotype plate, which is the denomination printed in fine letters all over the bill.	
1 Female. 1	ONE Female seated portraying on shield, engines, buildings, machinery, &c. 1 THE RAILROAD BK. Lowell, Mass.	ONE
TWO Archimedes 2	2 Vig. same as $1 note. 2 THE RAILROAD BK. Lowell, Mass.	TWO
3 Vulcan. 3	THREE Female locomotive, buildings, etc. 3 RAILROAD BANK, Lowell, Mass.	THREE
Male portrait 5	View of depot, cars, church, etc. RAILROAD BANK, Lowell, Mass.	5 Five females surrounding ...
10 X	View of buildings, pedestrians, etc. Title of Bank.	X Male portrait
XX 20	RAILROAD BANK, Lowell, Mass. Male portrait	20 Factory girl with wheel.
50	Factories, etc. Title of Bank.	50 Male portrait
100 Female seated holding spool of cotton; factories	Title of Bank. Factories, etc.	100 Male portrait
500 500	Railroad depot, cars, church, etc. Male portrait Title of Bank.	500 Indian chief erect on shield.
Two farmers, one tying up grain. 1	1 Bee hive. RANDOLPH BANK, Randolph, Mass.	1 Boots and shoes. ONE
TWO Boots and shoes. 2	2 Vig. Drover on horseback, cattle dogs, &c.; cattle lying down RANDOLPH BANK, Randolph, Mass. Dog and safe.	2 Portrait of Franklin.
THREE Portrait of Jefferson. 3	THREE Spread eagle. THREE RANDOLPH BANK, Randolph, Mass. Farmer's reaping.	3 Washington and his horse. THREE
5 Female child.	Vig. Three females, one with liberty pole and cap; Eagle on left of vig; and ship on right. V RANDOLPH BANK, Randolph, Mass. Dog and safe.	5 Boots and shoes. FIVE
TEN Female in the act of pouring water from a pitcher.	10 Vig. Blacksmith shoeing horse, and man holding horse by the head. X RANDOLPH BANK, Randolph, Mass Bundles of grain.	10 Boots and shoes.
20 Minerva	2 Female figure with rake. 0 RANDOLPH BANK, Randolph, Mass XX	20 Female with horn of plenty; globe and trident. 20
Female with flag and shield; Indian female at her feet	20 Two shoemakers at work; female at household duties in background. RANDOLPH BANK, Randolph, Mass.	20 Cattle, telegraph; cars on bridge.
50 Minerva.	Vig. Male and female figure; horn of plenty between them; rake on female's right, grain on left. State Arms. RANDOLPH BANK, Randolph, Mass. 50	50 Cupid afloat 50
FIFTY Female representing Agriculture. 50	50 Farmer seated with implements and products; load of hay, buildings, etc., in distance. 50 Title of Bank.	50 Female portrait
100 Female portrait.	Two females seated; steamer, etc. in distance on left; buildings, monument, etc., on right. Title of Bank	100 Train of cars bridge and dam in distance.
100 Male sitting, with scroll in right hand.	Vig. Spread eagle on branch; canal boats and lock; railroad train in distance. RANDOLPH BANK, Randolph, Mass 100	100 Female sitting with rule in right hand, and grain in left, resting on horn of plenty.
Female figure; cornucopia laden with grain. 500	500 D RANDOLPH BANK, Randolph, Mass.	500
1 Man carrying leather	1 REVERE BANK. Male portrait. Boston, Mass.	1 State Arms.
2 Blacksmiths boy at forge.	Male portrait. Stonecutter and man with plan. Title of Bank.	2 State Arms.
3 Sailor boy, etc.	Title of Bank. Male portrait.	3 State Arms.

5 Steamship, tug, city, etc. 5
Title of Bank
State Arms. Male portrait.

10 General scene in moulding shop; men, wheels, machinery, etc. 10
Title of Bank.
State Arms. Male portrait.

20 REVERE BANK, Boston, Mass. 20
State Arms. 20 DOLLS. in red. Male portrait.

50 Title of Bank. 50
Male portrait.
State Arms. L L Mechanic, sailor, steamer or vessel [illegible]

100 Title of Bank. 100
Male portrait. C
State Arms. Surveyor at work.

500 Title of Bank. 500
Hog-head, bales, rope, wheels, keel, etc.; steamboat in distance.
State Arms. Male portrait.

[illegible] Female, [illegible] [illegible] the [illegible], steamboat and train of cars in the background. 1
1 ROCKLAND BANK Roxbury, Mass. Farmer, plough [illegible] and ONE [illegible] half dollar.

Portrait of female. Farmers and sheep. 2
2 ROCKLAND BANK Roxbury, Mass. Female [illegible]

3 ROCKLAND BANK. Roxbury, Mass. 3
Farmer with scythe, sailor with spy glass, [illegible] mechanic, anvil, hammer, &c., at [illegible] three gold dollars. THREE A dog's head.

5 ROCKLAND BANK Roxbury, Mass. 5
Portrait. A man with gun, Indian woman, three angels hail five gold dollars.
FIVE

X ROCKLAND BANK, Roxbury, Mass. X
Two females. Farming scene. Portrait of Washington.

State Arms. Farmer ploughing; cattle and horses in pasture; city in distance. 20
XX ROCKLAND BANK, Roxbury, Mass. Portrait.

50 ROCKLAND BANK. Roxbury, Mass. 50
Ships, and city in the background.
Land Cupid 50

C ROCKLAND BANK, Roxbury, Mass. 100
Farming scene, men, women and children.
Fountain. Portrait of Jefferson.

D ROCKLAND BANK, Roxbury, Mass. 500
Female and horse. 500 Female reclining, eagle, globe, ship and steamship in distance. 500

ONE Vig. Wool scene, man sowing grain; oxen. 1 1
Full rigged ship.
1 ROCKPORT BANK, Rockport, Mass. ONE

Blacksmith, sledge and anvil. Team of oxen, stone quarry, &c. 1
ROCKPORT BANK, Rockport, Mass.
1 Man plowing. Stone cutter.

Sailor and capstan, [illegible] bales and boxes. Same as ones. 2
ROCKPORT BANK, Rockport, Mass.
2 Loading wagon. Two females.

TWO Vig. Spread eagle, steamboat, bell; ring whistle; Goddess of Liberty [illegible] 2 2
TWO
2 ROCKPORT BANK, Rockport, Mass. Schooner and sloop in a storm.

THREE Vig. Sailor, bales of goods, shipping, houses, horse, dray, &c. 3 3
THREE
3 ROCKPORT BANK, Rockport, Mass. Train of cars.

THREE Same as ones. 3
ROCKPORT BANK, Rockport, Mass.
Knickerbocker. Eagle. Female [illegible]

Man with cradle. Same as ones. 5
ROCKPORT BANK, Rockport, Mass.
5 Female.

Vig. Eagle standing on shield and anchor; town in distance; boundaries, &c. Female and child in large figure five. FIVE
FIVE ROCKPORT BANK, Rockport, Mass. Girl holding basket.

Soldier with squad. Same as ones. 10
ROCKPORT BANK, Rockport, Mass.
TEN Female portrait.

Vig. Man sitting holding sledge; train of cars crossing bridge. X 10
TEN ROCKPORT BANK, Rockport, Mass. Man holding sickle and sheaf of grain.

20 20
XX Eagle XX
Female sitting, book in her lap. ROCKPORT BANK, Rockport, Mass. Full rigged ship.

Female. Same as ones. 20
ROCKPORT BANK, Rockport, Mass.
XX Cow and calf. Male portrait.

Franklin. Same as ones. 50
ROCKPORT BANK, Rockport, Mass.
50 Shield. Male portrait.

FIFTY FIFTY
50 Vig. Man taming horse. 50 Female.
Female. ROCKPORT BANK, Rockport, Mass. FIFTY

Male portrait. Same as ones. 100
ROCKPORT BANK, Rockport, Mass.
100 Dog's head. Webster.

Left	Centre	Right
The figures 100, with the words one hundred across. Portrait of Harrison.	Vig. Loading covered waggons with merchandise. ROCKPORT BANK, Rockport, Mass.	The figures 100, with the words one hundred across. Fancy portrait.
ONE	Female seated on the ground; factory village in the distance; 1 on right. ROLLSTONE BANK, Fitchburg, Mass. Wheels, bale, etc	1 Female and 3 cherubs.
2	Female riding upon the back of a reindeer. 2 ROLLSTONE BANK, Fitchburg, Mass Oats	TWO Two females
3	Milk maid and cows. 3 ROLLSTONE BANK, Fitchburg, Mass.	3 Portrait of female. THREE
5	Train of cars. Female in large V. ROLLSTONE BANK, Fitchburg, Mass. State Arms	5 Females, chest and horn of plenty and 5.
TEN	Female with sickle, farmers gathering grain in the background. X ROLLSTONE BANK, Fitchburg, Mass Female head	10 Female figure.
20 Female.	2 Female. 0 ROLLSTONE BANK, Fitchburg, Mass. XX	20 Female. 20
50 Female.	Male and female. ROLLSTONE BANK, Fitchburg, Mass 50	50 Cupid in a sail boat. 50
100 Vulcan the blacksmith	Spread eagle, railroad and canal. ROLLSTONE BANK, Fitchburg, Mass 100	100 Female.
100 Female with tablets; child at her feet.	ROLLSTONE BANK, Fitchburg, Mass. C Male portrait. C	100 Female, child, pole and cap.

Left	Centre	Right
ONE	Three females floating in water supporting cupid. SAFETY FUND BK, Boston, Mass.	1 State Arms.
2 Female erect beside pedestal; steamer in distance.	Scene in the Arctic Regions; men chasing bear; dog, icebergs, etc. Title of Bank.	2 State Arms.
THREE on 3.	Scene in Printing office, Faust, Guttenberg and Schoeffer. Eagle. Title of Bank.	3 State Arms 3
State Arms. 5	Title of Bank. Apotheosis of Washington; soldier on left; female and two Indians on right. Red V each side.	5 Dog, key and safe.
10 Franklin at work at printing case	State Arms. Two females, owl, buildings, steamer, etc. Title of Bank. Eagle.	10 Sailor with anchor.
20 State Arms	Three females, safe, etc. SAFETY FUND BK., Boston, Mass.	20 City
50 Boy and rabbits.	Female on left of view of city, boats, shipbuilding, etc., 50 on stone and Indian in canoe on right; steamboat in distance. SAFETY FUND BK., Boston, Mass.	50 State Arms.
C State Arms.	Title of Bank. Four females on globe. One Hundred Dollars.	100 Male portrait.
500 Female seated on bale; globe, steamboat, etc.	SAFETY FUND BK Boston, Mass. Auditors. Die. Five Hundred Dollars.	500 Old man, child and bust of Washington on table.
1 Three female figures. 1	Machinery and factories. Ship. Bee hive. SALEM BANK, Salem, Mass.	1 Portrait of Washington 1

Left	Centre	Right
2 Masts, cornstalks, fruit, &c. 2	TWO Ship. Female figure. Farming scene. SALEM BANK, Salem, Mass.	2 Female crowning a bust of Washington. 2
THREE	Female sitting on the ground; also anchor and bale; ship in distance. 3 Female, anchor, merchandise and ships. SALEM BANK, Salem, Mass.	3 Portrait of Washington. 3
5 Female. 5	5 Female figure and ship. 5 FIVE SALEM BANK, Salem, Mass.	5 Female and sickle. 5
10 X 10	(Old Plate.) Man and oxen. 10 SALEM BANK, Salem, Mass.	TEN Female
10 Portrait of female. TEN	(New Plate.) 1 Female with key and horn of plenty. 0 SALEM BANK, Salem, Mass. TEN	10 Portrait of female. TEN
20 Female	2 Female 0 SALEM BANK, Salem, Mass. XX	20 Female. 20
50 Female figure	Male and female. SALEM BANK, Salem, Mass. 50	50 Cupid in a sail boat. 50
FIFTY Grain, fruit, &c. 50	50 Three female fig's, ship, eagle, etc. SALEM BANK, Salem, Mass.	Fifty on 50. Vulcan seated with implements.
100 Vulcan the blacksmith.	Spread eagle, railroad and canal. SALEM BANK, Salem, Mass. 100	100 Female.
Letter C. Men and boats. 100	Spread eagle on bale; products, etc. 100 SALEM BANK, Salem, Mass.	100 Female. 100

Left end	Centre	Right end
500	Indian paddling canoe. 500 in red across fight 500. Title of Bank. D D	500 Justice.
ONE View of Merchants' Row. 1	Indian seated on a rock; ship in distance. SHAWMUT BANK, Boston, Mass. Boat and men	1 View of Boston from the harbor. ONE
2 Same as ones TWO	Vig. Same as ones. SHAWMUT BANK, Boston, Mass. Men in boat, etc.	2 Same as ones TWO
THREE Same as ones on right end THREE	Vig. Same as ones. SHAWMUT BANK, Boston, Mass. Eagle	3 View of Merchants' Row
5 View of Boston from the harbor. FIVE	Vig. Same as ones. SHAWMUT BANK, Boston, Mass. Anchor, etc	5 Same as 2s
10 Same as fives 10	Vig. Same as ones. SHAWMUT BANK, Boston, Mass. 10	10 Same as fives 10
View of Merchants' Row. XX	Vig. Same as ones. SHAWMUT BANK, Boston, Mass.	20 View of Boston from the harbor. 20
50 Same as 20s. 50	Vig. Same as ones. SHAWMUT BANK, Boston, Mass.	50 Same as 20s. 50
C View of Boston from the harbor. C	Vig. Same as ones. SHAWMUT BANK, Boston, Mass.	100 View of Merchants' Row. 100
FIVE HUNDRED	Spread eagle, shield, etc. SHAWMUT BANK, Boston, Mass.	Figs. 500. Male portrait Figs. 500.

Left end	Centre	Right end
1000	Spread eagle shield and motto "E Pluribus Unum," etc. Title of Bank.	1000 Washington. 1000
Female erect by fig. 1. ONE on 1.	View of Shelburne Falls. SHELBURNE FALLS BANK, Shelburne Falls, Mass.	1 Female churning.
2 Farmer with scythe.	Farmers mowing; others loading wagon in distance Title of Bank.	2 Female representing Agriculture.
3 Blacksmith; anvil.	View of Shelburne Falls. 3 Title of Bank.	Liberty
5 Washington	Mechanic seated with hammer; cars, factory, bridge and cattle in distance. Title of Bank.	5 Female with grain.
X	Female seated before shield, reclining on chest; milkmaid and cows in distance on right; Two men, cars and ships on left. Title of Bank.	10 Female with shield, cornucopia and Anchor.
50 Female with flowers.	View of Shelburne Falls. Title of Bank.	50 Male portrait
100 Female portrait.	Three females representing Agriculture, Commerce and Manufactures. Title of Bank.	100 Franklin.
1 Man dressing leather. ONE	Shoe and Leather Dealers Store, horses, wagon, wharf and shipping. SHOE & LEATHER DEALERS' BANK, Boston, Mass.	1 Interior of shoemaker's shop. ONE
2 Interior of a shoemaker's shop. TWO	Vig. Same as ones. Title of Bank.	2 Morocco dressing. TWO

Left end	Centre	Right end
3 Cows THREE	Vig. Same as ones. Title of Bank.	3 Interior of a shoemaker's shop. THREE
5 Morocco dressing.	Vig. Same as ones. Title of Bank.	5 Justice.
10 Washington and his horse TEN	Vig. Same as ones. Title of Bank.	10 Shipping. TEN
XX Indian with bow. 20	Vig. Same as ones. Title of Bank.	20 Eagle. XX
FIFTY Washington 50	Vig. Same as ones. Title of Bank. Some have fig. 50 on vig.	50 Franklin. FIFTY
Words one hundred and figs. 100. Male portrait	Wharf scene—loading wagon, men, horses, shipping, &c. Title of Bank.	Words one hundred and figures 100 Male portrait
100 Justice seated.	Shoe and Leather Dealers store; horses, wagon, men wharf and shipping SHOE & LEATHER DEALERS BANK, Boston, Mass.	100 Female portrait.
500	Same as 100s. Title of Bank.	500 Cows
1	Vig. A man ploughing with two horses, and another sowing, two or three baskets, in the fore ground; cars in the distance. 1 SOUTHBRIDGE BK, Southbridge, Mass.	1 Spread Eagle. ONE
2	Vig. A large building, train of cars, man with wheelbarrow, and church in the distance. 2 SOUTHBRIDGE BK. Southbridge, Mass.	2 Man pitching hay

Left	Center	Right
3	Vig. Train of cars, church and village at the left in the distance; and a building with cupola. 3 SOUTHBRIDGE BK, Southbridge, Mass.	3 Female with a basket in her hands
FIVE	(Old Plate.) FIVE Two female figures and eagle, train of cars and ship in background. FIVE SOUTHBRIDGE B'K, Southbridge, Mass.	5 Portrait. FIVE
FIVE	Vig. Female sitting; a hand spinning wheel on the right of the scene, factory buildings in the distance. 5 SOUTHBRIDGE BK, Female head	5 Bust of a female FIVE
10 Portrait. 10	(Old Plate.) X Spread eagle. X SOUTHBRIDGE B'K, Southbridge, Mass.	10 Female.
TEN	Vig. A female sitting between the digits 1 & 0, holding [illegible] in her left hand, a cornucopia at her right hand. X SOUTHBRIDGE BK, Southbridge, Mass. Shield.	10 General Taylor. TEN
20 Female sitting.	XX Eagle XX SOUTHBRIDGE BK, Southbridge, Mass.	20 Ship
20 Female with flowers.	SOUTHBRIDGE B'K Southbridge, Mass. Female seated; sheep, etc.	20 Boy
50 Female and anchor, steamboat in distance. 50	FIFTY DOLLARS 50 SOUTHBRIDGE B'K, Southbridge, Mass.	FIFTY
FIFTY Large female figure, wreath in right hand FIFTY	50 50 Vig. A man holding a horse which is apparently trying to break away. SOUTHBRIDGE BK, Southbridge Mass.	FIFTY Female standing, her left elbow resting on a column. FIFTY
50 Two females.	SOUTHBRIDGE B'K Southbridge, Mass. Cattle scene, drovers, farmers, etc. L	50 50

Left	Center	Right
THE 100	SOUTHBRIDGE B'K Southbridge, Mass. Female at work on looms. C 100	100 Female, spinning wheel, factories, etc.
Words one hundred across the figure 100. Bust of Gen. Harrison.	Market wagons men and team. SOUTHBRIDGE BK, Southbridge, Mass.	Words one hundred across the figure 100. Bust of Kosciusko
500	Vig. Agricultural scene, female among sheaves, men in the distance reaping. 500 and D on right SOUTHBRIDGE BK, Southbridge, Mass.	500
Female and fig. 1. 1	Cupid rolling a silver dollar upon a Railroad track, train of cars and village in the distance. SOUTH READING BK South Reading, Mass	1 Portrait.
Female. 2	Two cherubs and two silver dollars, train of cars and cattle in the background. SOUTH READING BK South Reading, Mass.	2 Portrait.
3 Portrait.	Three cherubs and three silver dollars. SOUTH READING B'K South Reading, Mass	3 Blacksmith anvil and forge.
5 Portrait. 5	Five cherubs and five silver dollars. SOUTH READING BK South Reading, Mass.	5 Female and fig. 5
Farmer with basket of fruit and a cradle 10	Portrait. SOUTH READING BK South Reading, Mass.	X Female and anchor.
XX Female.	Female reclining, locomotive and factory, milk maids and cows in background. SOUTH READING BK South Reading, Mass	20 Portrait.
Girl with sheaf of grain. 50	Female sitting on a rock, and cupids sporting with a dolphin in the water. SOUTH READING BK South Reading, Mass	50 Portrait.

Left	Center	Right
Female feeding an eagle from a cup. 100	Capitol at Washington. SOUTH READING BK South Reading, Mass	100 Portrait.
ONE The arm of a man holding a hammer.	Factory. SPICKET FALLS B'K, Methuen, Mass.	1 Portrait of Webster.
TWO	Factory. Portrait of J. Q. Adams. SPICKET FALLS B'K, Methuen, Mass.	2 2
3 3	Train of cars and railroad station. SPICKET FALLS B'K. Methuen, Mass	3 Blacksmith.
5 Female sewing.	Interior of a shoemakers shop. SPICKET FALLS B'K, Methuen, Mass.	V Dog
TEN Indian.	Farmers, and horse and sled gathering grain, SPICKET FALLS B'K, Methuen, Mass.	X X
XX A hunter warming himself by a fire.	20 SPICKET FALLS B'K. Methuen, Mass.	20 Portrait of Lewis Cass.
50	Cattle. SPICKET FALLS B'K. Methuen, Mass.	50 Female with sickle and sheaf of wheat.
100	Santa Claus in sleigh drawn over the roofs of houses by a reindeer. SPICKET FALLS B'K. Methuen, Mass.	C Santa Claus sitting at a fire place,
1 Cattle. ONE	Man and dog in a forest. SPRINGFIELD B'K Springfield, Mass. Vessel.	1 Portrait of Jenny Lind.

Left	Centre	Right
Female. TWO	Man and dog in the forest. SPRINGFIELD B'K Springfield, Mass. Bales and boxes.	TWO 2 Hay makers.
	The Springfield Bank uses the old sterotype plate for all other denominations.	
1 Ship.	Winged female with scales and sword and fig. 1. STATE BANK, Boston, Mass. Steamer	1 State Arms.
2 State Arms.	Female and child, bale and boxes; steamboat on right, and vessels on left. STATE BANK, Boston, Mass. Machinery	2 Cupids and 2.
3 Cupids and 3	Spread eagle and ships. STATE BANK, Boston, Mass. Steamer	3 State Arms.
Female. 5	Female portrait. 5 Female portrait. STATE BANK, Boston, Mass.	5 State Arms.
10 Portrait of Washington.	State Arms; female and factories on right; female and shipping on left. X on right. STATE BANK, Boston, Mass.	10 State Arms.
20 State Arms.	Two females; shipping railroad and canal. STATE BANK, Boston, Mass. Dog's head	20 Med. head.
State Arms 50	Three females. STATE BANK, Boston, Mass. Horse	50 Sailor with telescope.
State Arms. 100	Female seated on a bale; ships and light-house in distance. STATE BANK, Boston, Mass.	100 Two females, eagle and globe.

Left	Centre	Right
500 Med. head. 500	STATE BANK, Boston, Mass. Female seated representing Commerce; ship and rainbow in distance. Steamship.	500 State Arms. 500
Justice seated. 1000	Spread eagle on limb of tree; ships in distance. STATE BANK, Boston, Mass. Ships	1000 State Arms.
1 Washington and his horse	Female portrait. 1 Female portrait SUFFOLK BANK, Boston, Mass.	ONE Eagle. ONE
TWO Washington and his horse TWO	2 2 2 SUFFOLK BANK, Boston, Mass.	TWO Female. TWO
Female.	THREE 3 THREE SUFFOLK BANK, Boston, Mass.	3 Dog, safe and building. 3
5 Two females. V	Winged female with trumpet. On right portrait of Columbus. On left portrait of Washington. SUFFOLK BANK, Boston, Mass. Keys	5 State Arms. V
Washington	10 Female, eagle and shield. SUFFOLK BANK, Boston, Mass. Building	10 Bust.
XX Female portrait. XX	Female on rock, cupids and dolphin sporting in water. SUFFOLK BANK, Boston, Mass. TWENTY TWENTY	20 Dog's head. XX
	☞ The Suffolk Bank formerly used the Perkins' Stereotype Plate, and still continue to use it for 50s and 100s, 500s and 1000s.	
50 Female with sword and shield.	FIFTY DOLLARS. SUFFOLK BANK, Boston, Mass. Fifty in block letters across face. L	50 Eagle. FIFTY

Left	Centre	Right
100 100 100	One Hundred Dollars SUFFOLK BANK, Boston, Mass. Words One Hundred in large block letters across face. C	100 100 100
500 Female with pole and cap and view of Boston.	500 SUFFOLK BANK, Boston, Mass Five large block letter D's across face. D	500 Female and Indian with bow and shield
1000 Justice.	One Thousand Dollars SUFFOLK BANK, Boston, Mass. 1000 M	1000 Letter M and words One Thousand Dollars. 100
Girl's head. 1	Train of cars at depot One Dollar. TAUNTON BANK, Taunton, Mass.	1 Female head
1 Reaper. ONE	Reaper gathering grain. 1 Shipping. TAUNTON BANK. Taunton, Mass	1 Vulcan the blacksmith.
TWO Indian 2	Eagle. 2 Washington on horseback. TAUNTON BANK. Taunton, Mass.	2 Train of cars
3 on ornamental die. Female portrait	Three children in circular die, reading book. TAUNTON BANK, Taunton, Mass. THREE DOLLARS.	3 on ornamental die. Male portrait
THREE	Female with a sheaf of wheat, reapers in the background. TAUNTON BANK. Taunton, Mass.	3 Male figure
Ornamental die, on which is name of bank 8 times & one large and eight smaller 5s.	View of Factory, Train of cars, etc. 5 in ornaments die. FIVE DOLLARS. TAUNTON BANK Taunton, Mass.	Ornamental die on which is name of bank 8 times & one large and eight smaller 5s.
5	Female seated; railroad and canal in background. V TAUNTON BANK. Taunton, Mass	FIVE Five and Eagle FIVE

Left end	Centre	Right end
10	State Arms, also a train of cars crossing a bridge. X TAUNTON BANK. Taunton, Mass.	10 Reaper
20 Female figure.	2 Female. 0 TAUNTON BANK. Taunton, Mass. 33	20 Female. 20
50 Female figure.	Male and female. TAUNTON BANK, Taunton, Mass. 50	50 Cupid in a sail boat. 50
One Hundred and 100. Portrait.	Horses, waggons, shipping &c. TAUNTON BANK. Taunton, Mass.	Same as left. Portrait.
ONE and 1 Merchandise. 1	TOWNSEND BANK. Townsend, Mass. Cupid rolling a silver dollar upon the railroad track; train of cars and city in distance, Farmer cradling	1 Two females.
2 Two females and eagle.	Two cupids and two silver dollars. TOWNSEND BANK. Townsend, Mass.	2 Female and large figure 2.
3 Portrait. 3	TOWNSEND BANK. Townsend, Mass. Three cupids and three silver dollars. Mechanic seated	3 Female reading.
Female feeding an eagle from a cup. 5	Five cupids and five silver dollars, TOWNSEND BANK. Townsend, Mass.	5 Group of females and large figure 5.
10 X	TOWNSEND BANK, Townsend, Mass. Farming scene	X Female.
TWENTY Indian woman with bow and spear.	TOWNSEND BANK, Townsend, Mass. Indian sitting on the ground beside a slain deer.	20 Farmer-boy and XX on half shield.

Left end	Centre	Right end
50 Female.	Capitol at Washington. TOWNSEND BANK, Townsend, Mass	50 Female feeding a horse
C Female, arm resting on a tub.	TOWNSEND BANK Townsend, Mass Vig. Blacksmith shoeing a horse.	100 Farming scene; load of grain, &c.
1 Ship building ONE	Wharf and shipping; view of Boston in distance; 1 on right, TRADERS' BANK, Boston, Mass.	1 Male and female. ONE
2 Boy and girl sailing boats in a tub. TWO	Vig. Same as ones. 2 TRADERS' BANK, Boston, Mass.	2 Girl. TWO
3 Interior of a blacksmith's shop. THREE	Vig. Same as ones. 3 TRADERS' BANK, Boston, Mass.	3 Female in a forest THREE
FIVE Justice.	Vig. Same as ones. 5 TRADERS' BANK, Boston, Mass.	5 Portrait of Webster. FIVE
TEN Female.	Vig. Same as ones. X TRADERS' BANK, Boston, Mass.	10 Female. TEN
20 Female. XX	Vig. Same as ones. TRADERS' BANK, Boston, Mass.	20 Justice XX
50	Vig. Same as ones. 50 TRADERS' BANK, Boston, Mass.	50 Covered wagon and merchandise.
Vig. Same as ones. 100	ONE HUND TRADERS' BANK, Boston, Mass.	Hundred on 100 Washington

Left end	Centre	Right end
500	Vig. Same as ones 500 TRADERS' BANK, Boston, Mass.	500 Eagle and shield.
Female with a spear and shield, holding a pillar in the form of a figure one ONE	Vig. View of Chelsea; ferry boat going into slip. TRADESMAN'S BK. Chelsea, Mass.	1 State Arms
TWO	Vig. Same as ones. 2 TRADESMAN'S BK. Chelsea, Mass.	2 Figure of Justice.
THREE	Vig. Same as ones. 3 TRADESMAN'S BK. Chelsea, Mass.	3 Blacksmith and anvil.
Figure 5 formed by an eagle and horn of plenty; likeness of Washington in the scroll or finish.	Same as ones. TRADESMAN'S BK. Chelsea, Mass. FIVE	5 Portrait of Gen. Taylor.
TEN	Vig. Same as ones. X TRADESMAN'S BK. Chelsea, Mass.	10 Female with horn of plenty in right hand, left hand on anchor.
20 Indian girl with bow and arrows.	Vig. Same as ones. TRADESMAN'S BK. Chelsea, Mass. TWENTY Machinery.	20 Female with 2 in right hand, and on her knee, and 0 under her left.
50 Female in the act of stepping into the water, an urn in her left hand.	Vig. Same as ones. TRADESMAN'S BK. Chelsea, Mass. FIFTY	50 Female holding a flag; three children representing Agriculture &c. all floating in the air.
100 Sailor and ship in the distance.	Vig. Same as ones, TRADESMAN'S BK. Chelsea, Mass. 100	100 Figure of a Stone cutter
500 Ship on stocks 500	Vig. Same as ones. TRADESMAN'S BK. Chelsea, Mass. 500 State Arms	500 Steamboat 500

ONE — Liberty. — ONE
Neptune; on right, Boston in 1859; on left Boston in 1630.
TREMONT BANK, Boston, Mass.
1 — Female

1 — ONE — 1
View of Street.
TREMONT BANK, Boston, Mass.
Word one, fig. 1 and I inside. — Male portrait

2
View of a street. 2
TREMONT BANK, Boston, Mass.
Word two and fig. 2 and II. — Two females.

Female surrounded by the names of the States. — TWO
Vig. Same as first ones.
TREMONT BANK, Boston, Mass.
2 — Two females.

3 — THREE — 3
3 View of a street.
TREMONT BANK, Boston, Mass.
Word three and fig. 3 and III. — Three females.

3 — Female seated on a barrel.
Vig. Same as first ones.
TREMONT BANK, Boston, Mass.
3 — Blacksmith, sailor and farmer.

All other notes of the Tremont Bank are of the Perkins' Stereotype Plate, which has the denomination printed in fine letters all over the bill.

1 — Portrait of Fillmore.
State Arms; female and man on right; female and steamboat on left.
UNION BANK, Boston, Mass.
Female and I. — ONE

The Union Bank also used the Stereotype Plate for 1s, 2s, and 3s, and still use it for 500s.

TWO — Indian female with bow and spear.
Female seated, leaning on bale; railroad, ships and city in distance.
UNION BANK, Boston, Mass.
2 — Gen. Taylor.

3 — Female
Spread eagle and ships.
UNION BANK, Boston, Mass.
3 — Webster

5 — Washington
Three females. Figure 5 running the entire length of the bill.
UNION BANK, Boston, Mass.
5

10 — 10
Sailor with flag; ships. Letter X running the entire length of the bill.
UNION BANK, Boston, Mass.
10 — 10

XX — State Arms
20 Female and eagle. 20
UNION BANK, Boston, Mass.
Steamer
XX — Portrait — XX

50 — Indian female with bow and arrow.
State Arms with female on each side.
UNION BANK, Boston, Mass.
Clasped hands
50 — Portrait of J. Q. Adams.

100 — State Arms.
Portrait of Washington surrounded by arms of the States.
UNION BANK, Boston, Mass.
Steamer
100 — Cupid in a sail boat. — 100

ONE
State Arms supported by two females. 1 Head of Franklin
UNION BANK, Haverhill, Mass.
Eagle
1 — Female. — ONE

TWO
Farming scene; female and four males prominent; load of hay. 2
UNION BANK, Haverhill, Mass.
Clasped hands
2 — Boy.

THREE
Female with horn of plenty; ships on left in distance; on right manufacturing scene. 3
UNION BANK, Haverhill, Mass.
Wheel, bale, etc
3 — Squaw and child.

5
Two females supporting an oval, with head of female enclosed; eagle on top; head of Washington on right hand corner, enclosed in large fig. 5. 5
UNION BANK, Haverhill, Mass.
Imp. and produce.
5

TEN
Horse shoeing scene. Female on X.
UNION BANK, Haverhill, Mass.
State arms
10 — Female and three children.

20 — Female with helmet and spear.
2 Female. 0
UNION BANK, Haverhill, Mass.
XX
20 — Female, globe and horn of plenty. — 20

Man holding fig. 20. — 20
Female reclining on cornucopia with distaff, ship in distance.
UNION BANK, Haverhill, Mass.
20 — Sea monsters — Steamship

50 — Female.
Male and female.
UNION BANK, Haverhill, Mass.
50
50 — Cupid in boat — 50

Horse and dolphin. — 50
Squaw seated; deer and hills in distance.
UNION BANK, Haverhill, Mass.
50 — Justice seated.

100 — Male seated
Female on brow of tree; cars and canal scene in distance.
UNION BANK, Haverhill, Mass.
100
100 — Female seated.

State Arms — 100
Indian reclining; deer.
UNION BANK, Haverhill, Mass.
100 — Female representing Agriculture

Agricultural scene; female prominent. — 500
500 D
UNION BANK, Haverhill, Mass.
500

Laocoon and serpents. — 1000
THOUSAND
Cars
Title of Bank.
1000 — Ship. — 1000

ONE — Bust of Washington. — ONE
(Old Plate.)
1 Interior of a blacksmith's shop. 1
UNION BANK OF WEYMOUTH AND BRAINTREE, Weymouth, Mass.
ONE — Female. — ONE

Left	Center	Right
1 Female with sickle and sheaf of wheat; reapers and farm house in back-ground.	(New Plate.) UNION BANK OF WEYMOUTH AND BRAINTREE, Weymouth, Mass. Portrait of Washington. Train of cars.	ONE 1
TWO Female. 2	(Old Plate.) 2 Farming scene. 2 UNION BANK OF WEYMOUTH AND BRAINTREE, Weymouth, Mass.	TWO Female. 2
TWO TWO	(New Plate.) UNION BANK OF WEYMOUTH AND BRAINTREE, Weymouth, Mass. Spread eagle and several flags bearing the names of the States.	2 Portrait of Z. Taylor.
THREE Farmer sharpening his scythe. 3	(Old Plate.) 3 Female and eagle. 3 UNION BANK OF WEYMOUTH AND BRAINTREE, Weymouth, Mass.	THREE Sailor. 3
I I I 3	(New Plate.) UNION BANK OF WEYMOUTH AND BRAINTREE, Weymouth, Mass. Two females, train of cars and ship in background.	3 Portrait of J. Q. Adams.
5 FIVE 5	(Old Plate.) V Eagle and shipping. V UNION BANK OF WEYMOUTH AND BRAINTREE, Weymouth, Mass.	5 FIVE 5
FIVE V	(New Plate.) UNION BANK OF WEYMOUTH AND BRAINTREE, Weymouth, Mass. A street in Weymouth.	V Webster V
10 X 10	(Old Plate.) Man and cars. 10 UNION BANK OF WEYMOUTH AND BRAINTREE, Weymouth, Mass.	TEN Female
TEN	(New Plate.) UNION BANK OF WEYMOUTH AND BRAINTREE, Weymouth, Mass. A street in Weymouth.	X Portrait of Washington.
20 Female.	(Old Plate.) XX Eagle. XX UNION BANK OF WEYMOUTH AND BRAINTREE, Weymouth, Mass.	20 Ship.

Left	Center	Right
XX Portrait of Franklin.	(New Plate.) UNION BANK OF WEYMOUTH AND BRAINTREE, Weymouth, Mass. A street in Weymouth.	20
FIFTY Female. FIFTY	50 Man and horse. 50 UNION BANK OF WEYMOUTH AND BRAINTREE. Weymouth, Mass.	FIFTY Female. FIFTY
100 across One Hundred. Portrait.	Horses, wagons, shipping &c. UNION BANK OF WEYMOUTH AND BRAINTREE, Weymouth, Mass.	100 across One Hundred. Portrait.
Female seated pointing to reapers. 500	500 D UNION BANK OF WEYMOUTH AND BRAINTREE. Weymouth, Mass.	500
Laocoon and sons strangled by serpent 1000	Train of cars THOUSAND. Title of Bank.	1000 Female. 1000
1	Cattle and large village in the background. 1 VILLAGE BANK, North Danvers, Mass.	ONE Female.
2 Ship and steamship.	2 VILLAGE BANK, North Danvers, Mass.	Female. TWO
3 Portrait of Fillmore.	Train of cars. VILLAGE BANK, North Danvers, Mass.	3 Female.
Female and sickle. FIVE	5 VILLAGE BANK, Danvers, Mass. Female and wheel, train of cars and steamship in background.	5 Female.
Female with sheaf of wheat. X	Cattle and sheep, man on horseback. VILLAGE BANK. North Danvers, Mass.	10 Washington on horseback.

Left	Center	Right
20 Female, eagle, chest, &c.	Female figure and two cherubs. VILLAGE BANK, North Danvers, Mass.	20 Female.
20 Female holding grain in right hand.	VILLAGE BANK. Danvers, Mass. Figures 20, XX, and the word Twenty.	20 Man plowing with two horses.
50 Female with sickle. 50	Two females, factories and ship in background. VILLAGE BANK. North Danvers, Mass.	50 Farmer gathering corn.
50 Horses and grain at well, man, etc.	VILLAGE BANK, Danvers, Mass. FIFTY	50 Male portrait.
100 Female portrait.	VILLAGE BANK, Danvers, Mass. 1 0 0 C	100 Two merchants at desk.
100 Sailor and flag.	VILLAGE BANK. North Danvers, Mass. Female and cupid floating in the air, over a city.	100 Portrait of female. 100
D Three females, two seated, one erect with open book.	VILLAGE BANK, Danvers, Mass. Round red die on which is figs. 500 and words Five Hundred.	500 Female holding ornaments and flowers.
Sailor hoisting a flag	WALTHAM BANK, Waltham, Mass. Female reclining, locomotive and factories, milkmaid and cows in background.	1 Cupid. 1
2 Females raking hay.	WALTHAM BANK, Waltham, Mass. A mechanic designing, also stone cutting.	2 Farmer, rake and plough.
3 Farmer with scythe.	WALTHAM BANK, Waltham, Mass. Female reclining on bales, barrels; factory in distance.	3 Mechanic, sailor and farmer with fig. 3.

Left	Centre	Right
Female. 5	WALTHAM BANK, Waltham Mass. Men, women and children; farming scene.	5 Female.
10 Female.	WALTHAM BANK, Waltham, Mass. Indian; river, canoe, deer in background.	10 Female.
20 Two females with sickle, grain, &c.	TWENTY. Boy watering two horses at trough; woman, &c. WALTHAM BANK. Twenty Dollars. Waltham, Mass.	20 Female beside spinning wheel
20 Female figure.	2 Female 0 WALTHAM BAN, Waltham, Mass. XX	20 Female. 20
Factories, &c. 50	Two females seated on bale. FIFTY State Arms. WALTHAM BANK. Fifty Dollars.	50 Mechanic at work.
50 Female.	Male and female. WALTHAM BANK, Waltham, Mass. 50	50 Cupid in a sailboat. 50
100 Sailor, mechanic, ships, machinery, &c.	WALTHAM BANK. C Two children at foot of tree; cows, sheep, &c. C Waltham One Hundred Dollars Massachusetts.	100 Public Building.
100 Vulcan the Blacksmith.	Spread eagle, railroad and canal. WALTHAM BANK, Waltham, Mass. 100	100 Female.
D Five Hundred Dollars.	WALTHAM BANK, Massachusetts. Sailor and soldier, flag, fort, cannon, shot, &c. Five Hundred.	500 Five Hundred Dollars.
1 Indian with bow and hatchet.	Brick layers. 1 WAMESIT BANK Lowell, Mass.	1 Stone cutter.

Left	Centre	Right
TWO, II, 2 Indians.	Carpenter at work. 2 WAMESIT BANK Lowell, Mass. Female bathing	2 Man sitting on the ground, factories in background.
3 Indians upon a cliff overlooking a city. THREE	Large figure 3 with State Arms top—Title across 3.	3 Hay maker.
FIVE Train of cars passing under a bridge.	Large V with five at top. Man with sickle and sheaf of wheat, at bottom. WAMESIT BANK Lowell, Mass.	5 Cattle, train of cars in distance.
TEN Two males and two females, city in background.	10 WAMESIT BANK Lowell, Mass. TEN	TEN A male and two females, also a yoke of oxen.
20	Male, female, two children and a dog. State Arms. 20 WAMESIT BANK Lowell, Mass.	Female. TWENTY
FIFTY	DOLLARS 50 Four female figures so arranged as to extend across the entire length of the bill. WAMESIT BANK Lowell, Mass. Female bathing	50
100 Two men loading wagon with sheaves; man holding horse.	WAMESIT BANK, Lowell, Mass. ONE HUNDRED Female bathing	100 Squaw and female
D	WAMESIT BANK, Lowell, Mass. Three females in clouds with quadrant, sickle, compass and cornucopia.	Female erect with shield and spear. 500
ONE Female erect both sides.	Indian reclining; deer behind him; gold dollar. WAMSUTTA BANK, Fall River, Mass.	1 Indian head.
2 Female representing Agriculture.	Male and female seated, two gold dollars; cattle, trees and house in distance. WAMSUTTA BANK, Fall River, Mass.	2 Squaw seated

Left	Centre	Right
3 Female portrait.	Mechanic, sailor and farmer seated with [illegible] and three gold dollars. WAMSUTTA BANK, Fall River, Mass.	THREE Liberty and a squaw.
V Farmer with scythe.	Five gold dollars, three cherubs, hunter and Indian, cars in distance. WAMSUTTA BANK, Fall River, Mass.	5 Female portrait.
10 Indian head.	Nine cherubs, ten gold dollars, female, cornucopia, shield, &c.; cars and steamboat in distance. WAMSUTTA BANK, Fall River, Mass. Mechanic.	X Cherub and dolphin.
FIFTY Female with shield and spear.	Indian, squaw and papoose seated; city in distance. WAMSUTTA BANK, Fall River, Mass.	50 Female portrait.
Deer and dog. HUNDR'D	Female seated on rock, three cherubs sporting in water with dolphin. WAMSUTTA BANK, Fall River, Mass.	100 Indian head.
1	Female feeding and shipping. 1 WAREHAM BANK Wareham, Mass.	1 Female.
1 Man and machinery.	View of Tremont Iron Works, buildings, horse and chaise, cars, &c. WAREHAM BANK, Wareham, Mass. ONE DOLLAR.	1 Male Portrait.
2	Farm, cows and sheep. 2 WAREHAM BANK Wareham, Mass.	TWO Female. TWO
Boy whittling under tree, child lying down, cows, sheep, &c. 2	WAREHAM B'K. Wareham, Mass. Eagle poised on rock. TWO DOLLARS.	TWO on 2 Male Portrait.
3	Farming scene. 3 WAREHAM BANK Wareham, Mass.	3 Female. THREE

FIVE — Spread eagle and shield; village in distance. Large V; female and cupid within. WAREHAM BANK Wareham, Mass. — 5 Girl.

V 5 5 — WAREHAM BANK V Small State arms. V Wareham, Mass. Sailor aloft with spy glass in hand, other hand on stay. — 5 Male Portrait.

X — Signing of the Declaration of Independence. X WAREHAM BANK Wareham, Mass. — 10 Train of cars.

TEN — Vulcan the blacksmith. X WAREHAM BANK Wareham, Mass. — 10 Reaper.

TEN Female, anchor, steamship, and light house. — Small arms of State. WAREHAM B'K, Wareham, Mass. TEN. Male Portrait. — 10 TEN

20 Female. — XX Eagle. XX WAREHAMBANK Wareham, Mass. — 20 Ship.

View of Tremont Nail Works 20 — WAREHAM B'K. Wareham, Ms. — 20 Male Portrait.

FIFTY Female FIFTY — 50 Man and horse. 50 WAREHAM BANK Wareham, Mass. — FIFTY Female. FIFTY

FIFTY DOLLARS. State arms. 50 FIFTY DOLLARS on FIFTY. — WAREHAM BANK Wareham, Mass. Male Portrait. Interior of an Iron Foundry. — 50

One Hundred and 100. Portrait. — Horses, waggons, shipping, &c. WAREHAM BANK Wareham, Mass — Same as left. Portrait.

View of Tremont Iron Works. 100 — WAREHAM B'K, Wareham, Mass. ONE HUNDRED DOLLARS. — C Male Portrait. Dog and safe.

Portrait 1 — WARREN BANK, Danvers, Mass. Large portrait. ONE — 1 Female

Portrait. 2 — WARREN BANK, Danvers, Mass. Large portrait. TWO — 2 Female and fig. 2

Fema . 3 — WARREN BANK, Danvers, Mass. Large Portrait. — 3 Indian, woman.

5 Two females. — WARREN BANK, Danvers, Mass. Large portrait. — 5 Portrait

10 Indian, woman. — WARREN BANK, Danvers, Mass. Large Portrait. — 10 Female.

xx inverted Justice. — WARREN BANK, South Danvers, Mass. Large portrait of George Peabody red 20 each side. — 20 Milkmaid churning.

FIFTY Peasant girl. — Title of Bank. Same as above 20s. — FIFTY Goddess of Liberty with cap, pole, shield and scroll.

100 Farmer and dog. — Title of Bank. Same as above 20s. — 100 Female portrait.

1 Washington. — Spread eagle; capitol at Washington on right; steamboat on left. WASHINGTON B'K., Boston, Mass. — Merchandise 1 Train of cars

ONE Washington and his horse ONE — 1 Indian in a canoe. 1 WASHINGTON B'K., Boston, Mass. — ONE Bust of Washington. ONE

1 Drummer and soldiers. — Washington reading paper; man writing on drum head; horse, negro, cannon, men, etc. WASHINGTON BK., Boston, Mass. — 1 Portrait with frilled cap.

Cupid and 2. 2 — Title of Bank. Washington on frame; female, soldier, Indians, TWO either side. — 2 and Cupid. 2

2 Portrait of Washington. — View of the State House. WASHINGTON B'K., Boston, Mass. — 2 State Arms.

TWO TWO — 2 Shipping. 2 WASHINGTON B'K., Boston, Mass. — TWO Washington and his horse TWO

3 — Washington on horse; officer submitting plans; other officers, cannon, horses, etc. Title of Bank. — 3 Washington.

Female THREE — Large steamships and sail vessels. WASHINGTON B'K., Boston, Mass. Washington — 3 Sailor.

5 Washington and his horse — View of the State House. WASHINGTON B'K., Boston, Mass. — 5 Female.

TEN Washington and his horse — Train of cars. WASHINGTON B'K., Boston, Mass. State Arms — 10 Steamship. TEN

TWENTY Square with box and spring. — XX Spread eagle and shield; Capitol at Washington on right; steamship on left. WASHINGTON B'K., Boston, Mass. Washington — 20

50 | Female seated, leaning on a bale; ships on right; railroad and canal on left. WASHINGTON B'K, Boston, Mass. Shell | 50
Washington. | | 50

100 | 100 Sailor seated on the ground. WASHINGTON B'K, Boston, Mass. | 100
Washington and his horse | | 100

Bunker Hill Monument. | WEBSTER BANK, Boston, Mass. Portrait of Webster. ONE DOLLAR | 1
ONE

Bunker Hill Monument. | WEBSTER BANK, Boston, Mass. Portrait of Webster. TWO DOLLARS | 2
TWO

Bunker Hill Monument. | WEBSTER BANK, Boston, Mass. Portrait of Webster. 3 DOLLARS | 3
THREE

Bunker Hill Monument. | WEBSTER BANK, Boston, Mass. Portrait of Webster. FIVE DOLLARS | 5
FIVE

5 | WEBSTER BANK, Boston, Mass. 5 Full length figure of Webster. 5 | 5

Bunker Hill Monument, X on left. | WEBSTER BANK, Boston, Mass. Portrait of Webster. TEN DOLLARS | 10 X
TEN

XX | WEBSTER BANK, Boston, Mass. Portrait of Webster. | 20
Twenty on XX | TWENTY DOLLARS | View of Faneuil Hall.

50 | WEBSTER BANK, Boston, Mass. Portrait of Webster. | 50
FIFTY | FIFTY DOLLARS | View of Faneuil Hall.

100 | WEBSTER BANK, Boston, Mass. Portrait of Webster. | C
100 | ONE HUNDRED DOLLARS | View of Faneuil Hall.

500 | WEBSTER BANK, Boston, Mass. Portrait of Webster. | 500
500 | | View of Faneuil Hall.

M | WEBSTER BANK. Boston, Mass. Portrait of Webster. | 1000
1000 | | View of Faneuil Hall.

ONE | Indian sitting on a rock, also plough and log cabin. 1 | 1
Portrait of Z. Taylor. | WESTFIELD BANK Westfield, Mass. | ONE on Medallion head.
1 | Female. | ONE

2 | Two females; farming scene in background. 2 | TWO
State arms. | | Indians.
TWO | WESTFIELD BANK Westfield, Mass. Fish. | TWO

THREE | WESTFIELD BANK Westfield, Mass. | 3
Dogs. | Three men. | Female teaching children.
THREE | Dog, boy and safe. | THREE

Two males and three females. | FIVE Westfield Green. WESTFIELD BANK Westfield, Mass. | 5

10 | Westfield Green. WESTFIELD BANK Westfield, Mass. | X
Train of cars and vessel. | Locomotive | Medallion head. 10

TWENTY | Westfield Green. WESTFIELD BANK Westfield, Mass. | 20
Female drawing water at a well. | Load of hay. | on med head. Blacksmith shop.

50 | WESTFIELD BANK Westfield, Mass. Westfield Green. | 50
Cattle. | | Female and ship machine.

1 | WOBURN BANK Woburn, Mass. | 1
1 | Female reclining, train of cars, milk maids and oats in background. Wheels, bale, etc. | Child and Dolphin.

Farmer, milk maid and cows. | Train of cars. WOBURN BANK Woburn, Mass. | 2
2 | | Females raking hay.

Female eagle, and ships. | WOBURN BANK Woburn, Mass. | 3
3 | | Cupid and figure 3.

Female feeding an eagle from a cup. | WOBURN BANK Woburn, Mass. | 5
5 | FIVE | Five females and fig. 5.

TEN | WOBURN BANK Woburn, Mass. | 10
Female. | Train of cars. TEN | Horses and load of hay.

20 | Portrait of Washington. WOBURN BANK Woburn, Mass. Spread eagle, Capitol at Washington and steamship in background. | 20
| | TWENTY

50 | WOBURN BANK Woburn, Mass. Two females, factories, steamship and train of cars in background. | 50
| | Female, vessel, etc. FIFTY

100 | WOBURN BANK Woburn, Mass. | 100
State Arms | 100 Capitol at Washington. |

1 | Large figure 1 with portrait of Washington. WORCESTER BANK, Worcester, Mass. | 1
Female. | | Carpenter at his bench.

2 | Portrait of Washington, and large figure 2. WORCESTER BANK, Worcester, Mass. | 2
Farmer sharpening a scythe. | | Dog and safe.

3 — Large figure 3 and portrait. — 3
WORCESTER BANK, Worcester, Mass.
Portrait. — Female.

5 — Portrait of female. 5 Portrait of female. — 5
WORCESTER BANK, Worcester, Mass.
Female Indian. — Female.

10 — Female; farmers loading hay; train of cars. — 10
WORCESTER BANK, Worcester, Mass.
Blacksmith. — 10 — Stone cutter

Female with sheaf of wheat. — Indian and female. — 20
WORCESTER BANK, Worcester, Mass.
20 — Farmer sowing seed.

L — Shepherd boy and sheep. — 50
WORCESTER BANK, Worcester, Mass.
50 — Female.

100 — [illegible] Winged female with a trumpet, also globe and eagle. — C
Female, sickle and sheaf of wheat. — WORCESTER BANK, Worcester, Mass. — Female. C

500 — Spread eagle on shield, cars, city, vessels, &c., in distance. — D
WORCESTER BANK, Worcester, Mass.
Red head — D — Red head

Female, Railroad and canal. — (Old Plate.) 1 — 1
WORCESTER CO. B'K Blackstone, Mass.
1 — Female.

1 — (New Plate.) Man sitting on the ground, anvil, hammer &c. Factories and train of cars in background. — 1
Portrait of Webster. — WORCESTER CO. B'K Blackstone, Mass. — Indian woman.

2 — Farmer and sheep, stream of water. 2 — TWO
WORCESTER CO. B'K Blackstone, Mass. — Female
TWO

2 — (New Plate.) WORCESTER CO. B'K Blackstone, Mass. — 2
Two females, and bust of Washington, ship in distance
Female. — Portrait of Washington.

Farming scene 3 — 3
WORCESTER CO. B'K Blackstone, Mass. — Female.
3 — THREE

(Old Plate.) — 5
Spread eagle and shield. Large V; Female and cupid.
FIVE — WORCESTER CO. B'K Blackstone, Mass. — Girl.

5 — (New Plate.) WORCESTER CO. B'K Blackstone, Mass — 5
Female reclining, train of cars, shipping, mill, masts and city in background.
Train of cars. — Arms

X — WORCESTER CO. BK Blackstone, Mass. — 10
Three females representing Agriculture, Commerce and Manufactures.
Squaw. — Cupid and dolphin

Vulcan the blacksmith. X — 10
WORCESTER CO. B'K Blackstone, Mass — Reaper.
TEN

20 — 2 Female. 0 — 20
WORCESTER CO. B'K Blackstone, Mass. — Female
Female — XX — 20

20 — WORCESTER CO. BK Mass. — 20
Three 20s and words Twenty Dollars on green die.
Ox's head. — Cattle, telegraph, bridge, cars etc

50 — WORCESTER CO. BK Mass. — 50
Green die with fig. 50, words Fifty, Fifty Dollars and Massachusetts on it.
Two children. — Clay.

50 — Male and female. — 50
WORCESTER CO. B'K Blackstone, Mass. — Cupid in [illegible] boat.
Female. — 50 — 50

C — WORCESTER CO. BK Mass. — 100
Green die with fig. 100, words One Hundred Dollars and Massachusetts on it.
Franklin — Dog & safe.

100 — Spread eagle, Railroad and canal. — 100
WORCESTER CO. B'K Blackstone, Mass.
Vulcan the black smith — 100 — Female

C — Eagle on bale of goods, &c. 100 — 100
Men fishing. — WORCESTER CO. BK. Blackstone, Mass. — Female with sickle and grain.
100 — 100

Female, train of cars and canal in background. 1 — 1
WRENTHAM BANK Wrentham, Mass.
1 — Female

1 — Man shoeing horse; man sitting on log and man standing. — 1
Soldiery, boy [illegible] — WRENTHAM BANK, Wrentham, Mass. — Two children.

Farmer and sheep, stream of water. 2 — TWO
Female.
2 — WRENTHAM BANK Wrentham, Mass. — TWO

2 — Man [illegible] boy on [illegible] — 2
WRENTHAM BANK, Wrentham, Mass.
[illegible] — Portrait of Webster.

Farming scene. 3 — 3
WRENTHAM BANK Wrentham, Mass. — Female.
3 — THREE

Blacksmith at forge. — WRENTHAM BANK, Wrentham, Mass. — 3
Female seated holding urn, ship, stove, goods, etc. — Boy, child and sheep.
THREE — THREE

FIVE — (Old Plate.) — 5
Female. 5
WRENTHAM BANK Wrentham, Mass. — Ship.

MASS.

Left	Centre	Right
Large V with five running arrows.	Female with sickle rake &c, shipping in background. Large V with Indian girl. WRENTHAM BANK Wrentham, Mass	5 Portrait of Washington.
5 Female seated, dogs, etc.	Two horses in field. WRENTHAM BANK, Wrentham, Mass	5 Portrait.
10 X 10	(Old Plate.) Man and [illegible] 10 WRENTHAM BANK Wrentham, Mass.	TEN Female.
X	Signing of the declaration of Independence. X WRENTHAM BANK Wrentham, Mass	10 Train of cars
10 Continental soldier; small State arms	Female seated holding cloth, factories, steamboat, &c. WRENTHAM BANK Wrentham, Mass.	10 Old man seated, child, bust of Washington on table.
20 Female.	XX [illegible] XX WRENTHAM BANK Wrentham, Mass.	20 Ship.
20 Two men at work on wagon.	Small eagle WRENTHAM BANK, Wrentham, Mass.	20 Female feeding horse, hens, old hens & ducks.
50 Steamboat and sail vessel.	Farming scene. 50 WRENTHAM BANK Wrentham Mass	L [illegible]
WRENTHAM BANK, Wrentham Mass 50 Female seated, arm resting on shield; eagle and steamboat. 50		50 Gen. Scott.
One Hundred and 100. Portrait.	Horses, wagons, shipping &c. WRENTHAM BANK Wrentham Mass.	Same as left. Portrait.

R. ISLAND.

Left	Centre	Right
100 Female Portrait.	Man cutting stick, horse, cow, sheep, boy on fence. WRENTHAM BANK, Wrentham, Mass	100 Female Portrait.
1 Female erect holding tablet upon pillar with left arm, pen in right hand.	[New Plate.] Female seated resting arm upon shield and quiver; view of niagara falls upon left; trees in background upon right. AMERICAN BANK, Providence, R. I.	1 Male portrait.
1 Men in boat, sloops in distance 1	[Old Plate.] 1 Female seated beside steam engine factory with water wheel in distance on left. 1 Title of Bank. State Arms.	1 Steamboats upon river 1
2 Spread eagle grasping arrows and shield in talons. 2	[Old Plate.] 2 Three females seated representing commerce, agriculture, &c. 2 AMERICAN BANK, Providence, R. I. State Arms.	Same as on left.
Male portrait 2	[New Plate.] View upon East River, large steamer sailing on right of note, ships, sloop, small steamboat, &c. AMERICAN BANK, Providence, R. I.	2 Female seated resting right arm upon shield.
3 3	AMERICAN BANK, Providence, R. I. Scene in a factory; females at work with machines, &c. 3	3 Male portrait
3 Portrait of Washington. 3	Portrait of female. Vig. Indian in canoe, paddling past high rocks; forest scenery around. Portrait of male. AMERICAN BANK, Providence, R. I. State Arms.	3 Male portrait 3
5 Male portrait	Vig. Nautical view; large steamship in foreground; sailing vessels on either side. AMERICAN BANK, Providence, R. I. Spread Eagle.	5 Female seated by large urn, nautical figure. 5
FIVE Hunting wild cattle.	AMERICAN BANK, Providence, R. I. Female seated by fig. 5; ships in distance.	5 Farmer feeding hogs.
5 Portrait of a girl with curls.	AMERICAN BANK, Providence, R. I. Large spread eagle.	5 Female portrait. V

R. ISLAND.

Left	Centre	Right
5 Portrait of Washington. 5	5 Vig. Washington crossing the Delaware. 5 AMERICAN BANK, Providence, R. I State Arms.	5 Portrait of Franklin. FIVE
5 Two girls carrying sheafs.	Five silver dollars and five cherubs. AMERICAN BANK, Providence, R. I.	5 Female portrait.
Male portrait. 10	AMERICAN BANK, Providence, R. I X Vig. State Arms; on right, resting right arm upon it female with liberty pole and cap; steamship in distance on left; female seated with sickle in right hand; locomotive &c., in distance.	10
10 Red. head. 10	TEN Vig. Locomotive and train of cars; forest scenery in background. TEN AMERICAN BANK, Providence, R. I. State Arms.	10 Red. head 10
20 Indian on ground, dead deer, scenery etc.	AMERICAN BANK, Providence, R. I. Female on eagle soaring in clouds. Red 20	20 Squaw seated.
50 Female seated, cornucopia in left hand. 50	Steamboat. Vig. Steamboat. Head of Washington in circular shield, surmounted by eagle on half globe; female on either side; vessels in distance. AMERICAN BANK, Providence, R. I. State Arms.	50 Same as left end. 50
100 Female erect holding balances in right hand, sword in left. 100	100 Vig. Two females; one with wings, wreath and book seated on right; the other standing with sword and scales; sun breaking through dark clouds over their heads. 100 AMERICAN BANK, Providence, R. I. State Arms.	100 Same as left end. 100
500 Male portrait	Vig. Indian girl seated upon ground; on left shield, spread eagle upon globe, drum, flag, liberty pole and cap, battle axe, &c.; on right ship in distance. Title of Bank State arms.	500 D
1000	Vig. Spread eagle upon shield. Male portrait AMERICAN BANK, Providence, R. I. State arms.	1000 M
American shield in which is figure 1. Spanish dollar.	Vig. State arms on either side, male figure; locomotive and cars on left; Indian huts and canal on right. AQUIDNECK BANK, Newport, R. I. Old stone mill.	1 Female sitting upon figure 1.

2
Express wagon.
2
AQUIDNECK BANK,
Newport, R. I.
Death of King Philip.
Old Stone Mill.
2
Spanish and American Dollar.

FIVE
Two Spanish and three American dollars.
AQUIDNECK BANK,
Newport, R. I.
Vig. Steamboat ferry, and view of the city of Newport on left.
Old stone mill.
5
Cars, Indians and ornamental figures.

10
State arms on either side of a female.
AQUIDNECK BANK,
Newport, R. I.
Letter X and figures 10 across; on left lighthouse; on right sailor with spy glass; man in boat.
10
Indian looking at the sea on which a vessel is dimly seen.

20
Female child.
20
AQUIDNECK BANK,
Newport, R. I.
Old mill; Indian squaw and pappoose in a canoe.
20
Female;
20

50
Large steamship.
Portrait of Webster.
AQUIDNECK BANK,
Newport, R. I.
State arms.
50
Ship under sail.

C
Two females and shield; steamship on right.
ONE HUNDRED
100 Head of Columbus. 100
Old mill.
AQUIDNECK BANK,
Newport, R. I.
C

ONE
1 View of Arcade city of Providence. 1
ARCADE BANK,
Providence, R. I.
State Arms.
Beehive.
Portrait of Female.
American shield.

TWO
2 Same as Ones. 2
ARCADE BANK,
Providence, R. I.
State Arms.
Beehive.
Female seated with liberty pole and cap.
Shield.

THREE
3 Same as Ones. 3
ARCADE BANK,
Providence, R. I.
State Arms.
Female with sickle, sheaf of grain, &c.
THREE

Female with her right hand resting on desk, and her left holding a pen.
5 Vig. Same as ones. 5
ARCADE BANK,
Providence, R. I.
State arms.
Eagle on limb.

Male portrait.
10
Male portrait.
10 Vig. Same as ones. 10
ARCADE BANK,
Providence, R. I.
State arms.
Male portrait.
TEN
Male portrait.

XX
Female.
XX
Vig. Three females seated, with beehive on the right, and sheaf of grain on the left. 20
ARCADE BANK,
Providence, R. I.
Do.
20
Drover and cattle.
20

Full length male figure.
50 Vig. Figures, globe, ship, scroll, &c.
ARCADE BANK,
Providence, R. I.
State arms.
50
Male portrait.
50

100
Portrait.
100
100 Vig. Men on horseback. 100
ARCADE BANK,
Providence, R. I.
State arms.
100
Portrait.
100

500
Vig. Indian paddling a canoe. 500
ARCADE BANK,
Providence, R. I.
500
Female with a sword and scales.

1000
Vig. Eagle standing upon a rock overlooking the sea, upon which a ship is dimly seen. 1000
ARCADE BANK,
Providence, R. I.
1000
Indian girl seated upon a rock, with bow and arrows.

ONE
Male seated, [illegible]
Indian seated with bow; plough, sickle, sheaf, hut, trees, &c. on left.
ASHAWAY BANK,
Ashaway, R. I.
1
Female portrait.

2
Two horses (white and black); train of cars on left.
ASHAWAY BANK,
Ashaway, R. I.
2
Two males erect, and a female seated.

Two females, one erect with spear, and the other kneeling with sprigs of wheat in right hand.
Word Dollars and figure 3
Two females seated, one with sickle [illegible], below, are vessels in distance on right.
ASHAWAY BANK,
Ashaway, R. I.
3
Two men with fork and rake, and dog; two males in background coming forward.

Webster.
5
Man on horseback, drove of cattle, boy in water, man with whip; house in background.
ASHAWAY BANK,
Ashaway, R. I.
5
Squaw and pappoose; forest scene in background.

Portrait of Indian.
X
ASHAWAY BANK,
Ashaway, R. I.
Female reclining on a box [illegible] at [illegible] view of city; sheep on right.
10
Female drawing water from a well; steamboat in distance.

FIFTY
Head of Liberty surmounted by stars.
50
ASHAWAY BANK,
Ashaway, R. I.
50
50
50

ONE
Two females erect, one with sickle and sheaf.
ONE
Steamship, sail vessels &c.; man in boat pulling toward steamship.
ATLANTIC BANK,
Providence, R. I.
Female Head
1
Spread eagle on shield.
ONE

ONE
Two females.
ONE
Steamer and other vessels.
ATLANTIC BANK,
Providence, R. I.
Girls' head.
1
Eagle on rock in ocean
ONE

2
TWO
Small figure with cornucopia.
ATLANTIC BANK,
Providence, R. I.
Female seated with left arm resting on shield; on her right, sheaf of wheat, fruit, and cars crossing viaduct in distance; on left ship and steamboat.
Head of Female.
2
TWO
Small figure with cornucopia.

2
TWO
Cupid.
Title of Bank.
Female and State Arms; vessels, cars, &c., in distance.
Girls' head.
2
TWO
Cupid.

Large V with word FIVE running across it.
Two figures seated.
5
ATLANTIC BANK,
Providence, R. I.
Steamship and three vessels, largest of which is in the foreground.
Female Head
FIVE
Sailor seated among bales; ship in distance.
5

10
Large X with figures 10 upon it; lighthouse on right, two sailors, one with spy glass, other in boat.
ATLANTIC BANK,
Providence, R. I.
Large ship under full sail.
Female Head
10
Female erect standing on rock, ship below under sail.

5
Female seated with sword in right hand, balances in left.
50
FIFTY
Female seated with sheaf and sickle, sailor with spy glass and quadrant on right; Artisan with hammer in hands on left.
ATLANTIC BANK,
Providence, R. I.
Female seated.
50
Sailor erect

[illegible] seated, locomotive, steamship and vessels in distance.
100
Sailor seated, bales, &c.
ATLANTIC BANK,
Providence, R. I.
Sailor in circular [illegible], on either side small figure.
Female Head
100
Female erect holding sheaf on her head with right hand, sickle in left.

Left	Center	Right
1 Ornamental Fountain.	Cupid riding silver dollar; locomotive and city in distance on right. ATLAS BANK, Providence, R. I. Goddess of Liberty.	1 Wants class with boy of toys on each
Hunter leaning upon rifle. 2	ATLAS BANK, Providence, R. I. Female seated, dog and pail beside her on right; cattle on left.	2 Female with sheaf of grain.
3 Indian girl seated.	Female floating on water; cupids on left and sea monster. ATLAS BANK, Providence, R. I.	3 Cupid astride of sea monster.
FIVE Female erect with spear and shield, eagle at feet	Locomotive and cars; Depot on left. ATLAS BANK, Providence, R. I. Dog's Head.	5 Portrait of Female. 5
Sailor leaning upon capstan, spy glass in hand. 10	Artisan seated beside machinery; factories on right in distance. ATLAS BANK, Providence, R. I. Landing Hay.	10 Female seated upon anchor, ship in distance.
Sailor boy in attitude of rowing. 20	State Arms surmounted by eagle; female with sword and scales on right; female with spear and cornucopia on left; locomotive on right in distance; steamboat on left. Title of Bank.	20 Goddess of liberty with pole cap and shield beside globe.
Female with spear and shield 50	ATLAS BANK, Providence, R. I. Female with sword and scales reclining upon shield, view upon it, Cupid soaring on right.	50 Indian girl seated upon ground, forest scenery in distance
Female portrait. 100	Vig. Female resting arm upon shield; safe, sheaf, plough, and city in distance on right; large steamship on left. ATLAS BANK, Providence, R. I.	100 Atlas drying up globe.
1 Male portrait.	Vig. Female seated between two pillars, shield, spread eagle, cars crossing bridge on right; anchor, &c.; city in the distance on left. BANK OF AMERICA, Providence, R. I.	1 Female bearing sheaf on shoulder.
2 Female holding tablet on pillar.	Vig. Female reclining upon bales; ships on right; vessel on left. BK. OF AMERICA. Providence, R. I	2 TWO Male portrait

Left	Center	Right
3 Female seated, holding sword and scales.	Vig. Portrait of Indian girl in ornamental shield, surrounded by drums &c. BK. OF AMERICA. Providence, R. I. Spread eagle between sig.	3 Ship under full sail.
5	Vig. Spread eagle upon shield, looking to left. Portrait of Washington BK. OF AMERICA, Providence, R. I. Steamship.	5 State Arms.
10	BK. OF AMERICA, Providence, R. I. Vig. Female seated, holding American shield; liberty pole and cap laying across lap; United States Capitol in background.	10
20 Locomotive, &c.	Vig. Female seated, holding scales in right hand; pole and liberty cap in left; small figure on either side. BK. OF AMERICA, Providence, R. I. Steamship.	20 Female with sickle and grain.
50 Portrait of female with sickle. 50	Vig. Two females seated; factories and cars crossing bridge on right; ship in distance, on left. BK. OF AMERICA, Providence, R. I. Locomotive.	50 Boy holding ears of corn in either hand.
100 Full length sailor; American flag in right arm; cap in left hand.	BK. OF AMERICA, Providence, R. I. Vig. Female and Cupid soaring in air, above city. Cog-wheel, &c.	100 Large ship under full sail. 100
ONE 1	1 Vig. Indian seated upon ground, bow in right hand 1 BANK OF BRISTOL, Bristol, R. I.	RHODE ISLAND.
II 2	2 Vig. Same as ones. 2 BANK OF BRISTOL, Bristol, R. I.	RHODE ISLAND
3 III	3 Same as ones, 3 BANK OF BRISTOL, Bristol, R. I.	RHODE ISLAND
V 5	5 Same as ones. 5 BANK OF BRISTOL, Bristol, R. I.	RHODE ISLAND.

Left	Center	Right
X 10	10 Same as ones. 10 BANK OF BRISTOL, Bristol, R. I.	RHODE ISLAND
XX 20	20 Same as ones. 20 BANK OF BRISTOL, Bristol, R. I.	RHODE ISLAND
30 XXX	30 Same as ones. 30 BANK OF BRISTOL, Bristol, R. I.	RHODE ISLAND.
50 50	50 Same as ones. L BANK OF BRISTOL, Bristol, R. I.	RHODE ISLAND.
1 Sailor erect on ship's iron, holding spyglass	Vig. Female seated reclining on bale; ship on right; factories in distance on left. B'K OF COMMERCE, Providence, R. I	1 Female erect holding tablet in left arm, pen in left hand.
Indian seated upon rock, rifle resting upon right leg. 2	B'K OF COMMERCE, Providence, R. I 2 Vig. Large ship under sail at sea, another large vessel following her; schooner on left. 2	2 Female with sheaf of grain under right arm.
3 Female seated, holding sickle in right hand; bundle of grain in left.	Vig. Spread eagle upon shield, overlooking sea upon which ship is dimly seen BK. OF COMMERCE, Providence, R. I.	3 Indian seated, holding gun in right hand.
FIVE Large steamship in foreground; vessels on either side in distance.	Vig. Portrait of Henry Clay BK. OF COMMERCE, Providence, R. I. Ornamental star.	5 Female seated, holding cornucopia.
10	Vig. A number of vessels upon water opposite a city. B'K OF COMMERCE, Providence, R. I.	TEN Female seated holding scales in left hand, sword in right.
50 Small cupid with cornucopia under left arm.	Vig. Female seated, resting left arm upon [illegible]; ship on right; cars leaving station on left. BK OF COMMERCE Providence, R. I. State arms.	50 Small figure holding sheaf under right arm.

100	BK. OF COMMERCE, Providence, R. I. Vig. Female leaning upon anchor, resting against bale; brig and steamboat on right; city, with vessels laying at wharfs.	100

D	Vig. Female seated, with either hand resting on pillar; spread eagle, locomotive, and train crossing viaduct on right; town and vessels upon water, in distance on left. Portrait of Washington BK. OF COMMERCE, Providence, R. I.	500

	BK. OF COMMERCE, Providence, R. I. Vig. Large steamship in foreground; ships on either side. 1000	1000

1 Female with shield, sword etc.	Female seated with cloth; bale, factory, etc. BANK OF KENT, Coventry, R. I.	1 Anchor and word "Hope"

ONE	Inside of a weaving room; females and looms. 1 on left. 1 BANK OF KENT, Coventry, R. I.	ONE Male Portrait ONE

2	Man driving cows; factory and village. 2 BANK OF KENT, Coventry R. I. State arms	TWO Head of Franklin. TWO

2 Female with dove.	Two females seated; buildings in distance. Title of Bank.	2 Mechanic at work at vise.

5	White and black horse, cattle, stream, etc. 5 Title of Bank.	5 Female spinning wheel, factory.

5	Forest and factory standing back. 5 BANK OF KENT, Coventry' R. I. State arms.	FIVE Head of Washington. FIVE

10 X 10	Yoke of oxen and man. 10 BANK OF KENT, Coventry, R. I. State arms.	TEN Female erect

20 Female seated	XX Eagle. XX BANK OF KENT, Coventry, R. I.	20 Ship, &c.

FIFTY Female erect FIFTY	50 Man and horse. 50 BANK OF KENT, Coventry, R. I.	FIFTY Female erect FIFTY

100 Eagle 100	C Horses and men in a chariot, in the clouds. 100 BANK OF KENT, Coventry, R. I.	C Head of Washington. C

Indian erect with bow and arrow. ONE	1 View of railway station; [illegible] upon the water before it steamer. 1 B'K OF N. AMERICA, Providence, R. I. Dog's Head.	Medal. Head with word ONE across

1 Female seated blowing trumpet	Goddess of liberty seated on globe; eagle on her right and small figure with cornucopia on her left. B'K OF N. AMERICA, Providence, R. I. Female and anchor.	1 Male portrait

2 Female seated on globe; eagle on the right and a small figure with cornucopia on left.	Male portrait BANK OF NORTH AMERICA, Providence, R. I.	2

TWO	B'K OF N. AMERICA, Providence, R. I. 2 Goddess of liberty leaning upon shield TWO Dog's Head.	2 Word TWO upon Medal Head.

3	Indian princess surrounded by flags, drums, etc. 3 BANK OF NORTH AMERICA, Providence, R. I.	THREE Farmer with sickle and sheaf. THREE

FIVE Female seated, pole, cap, &c.	Vig. 5 with word five running across it. Vig. Sailor in boat; city in extreme distance. B'K OF N. AMERICA, Providence, R. I. Steamship.	5 Portrait of Franklin.

TEN Female seated with box, [illegible] in left hand, [illegible] with [illegible] right.	B'K OF N. AMERICA, Providence, R. I. 10 Vig. Three male figures, representing commerce, agriculture and mechanics; ship on their left in distance; locomotive and town on their right. 10 Clasped hands.	

50 Indian female seated with bow and arrows.	B'K OF N. AMERICA, Providence, R. I. State arms. 50	50 Female seated.

100 Small figure holding cornucopia. 100	B'K OF N. AMERICA, Providence, R. I. Vig. Spread eagle upon shield, sailing vessels on right, steamship on left.	100 Small figure holding cornucopia. 100

500 Spread eagle on shield. 500	Vig. Goddess of liberty seated, with her left hand on shield. D B'K OF N. AMERICA, Providence, R. I. Anchor in shield.	500 Figure erect with left hand on shield, at whose feet is a female with globe and compass.

Female soaring in the air, olive branch in left hand, sword in right. 1000	B'K OF N. AMERICA, Providence, R. I. Vig. Portion of the globe showing the continent of North America, and extending in a half circle across the face of the note.	Female soaring in the air, [illegible] flowers with right hand, cornucopia in her left. 1000

ONE State arms, upon which is mounted an eagle. ONE	1 Vig. View of water and large ship; also smaller vessels, row-boats, &c. 1 BANK OF RHODE ISLAND, Newport, R. I. Bust of female.	ONÉ Bust of Commodore Perry. 1

2 [illegible] seated; on right public buildings; on left scrolls of paper. TWO	2 Vig. Female seated with wand in right hand, holding on right, and holding key in left hand. 2 B'K OF R. ISLAND, Newport, R. I. Steamboat.	2 Female seated on ocean side, eagle on left, also small portrait of Washington. TWO

Female reclining on anchor, looking over the sea. 3	3 Clinching Buildings 3 B'K OF R. ISLAND, Newport, R. I. Head of Franklin.	3 Laughing vessel. 3

FIVE Female seated with eagle on her lap. 5	5 Man seated with mechanical tools &c., ship on left. 5 B'K OF R. ISLAND, Newport, R. I. Head of Lion.	FIVE View of city in distance. Male raising the world. 5

TEN Female seated, with [illegible] in left hand looking up to male figure. 10	10 Vig. Ship. 10 B'K OF R. ISLAND, Newport, R. I. State Arms.	TEN Old Stone Mill. X

XX Washington.	Military officers and warlike implements. BANK OF RHODE ISLAND, Newport, R. I.	20 Clay

XXX Justice seated	Landing of the Pilgrims. Title of Bank.	30 Male portrait
L Washington.	Military officers and warlike implements. Title of Bank.	50 Franklin.
FIFTY	State Arms. B'K OF R. ISLAND, Newport, R. I. 50	50 L
C Male portrait	View of a battle. Title of Bank.	100 Male portrait
100 DOLLARS	State Arms. B'K OF R. ISLAND, Newport, R. I. 100	100 Letter C.
1 Portrait of Washington. 1	1 Vig. Winged figure with trumpet, globe and eagle on her right, flags on left. BLACKSTONE CANAL BANK, Providence, R. I. State arms.	1 Male figure head. 1
2 Male portrait.	Vig. Female seated upon bale, figure at her feet; locomotive, canal, &c. in distance on right of vig.; ships, town, &c. on left. BLACKSTONE CANAL BANK, Providence, R. I. State arms.	2 Indian girl seated with shield, pole and liberty cap.
5 Female seated, olive branch in left hand, spear in right	Vig. State arms, female figure on either side, schooner, locomotive and cars in distance on right; bales, barrels, steamboat and ship on left. BLACKSTONE CANAL BANK, Providence, R. I. Bale and cogwheels.	5 Female seated, spindle in right hand, wand in left.
10 Female portrait.	Vig. Mechanic seated, sledge hammer resting on his left shoulder; factories, &c., on right. 10 BLACKSTONE CANAL BANK, Providence, R. I. State arms.	TEN Indian erect with bow and spear in her right hand.
50 FIFTY 50	50 Vig. Female seated, reclining upon bale; ships in background. BLACKSTONE CANAL BANK, Providence, R. I. State arms.	50

100 HUNDRED 100	100 Vig. Female seated beside anchor, hogshead, &c., with horn of plenty. 100 BLACKSTONE CANAL BANK, Providence, R. I. Steamship.	ONE HUNDRED
D Mason at work, level in his hand	Vig. View of the Capitol at Washington. BLACKSTONE CAN'L BANK, Providence, R. I.	500 Locomotive
M Two large ships under full sail.	Vig. Large steamship under full sail at sea; ships on either side. BLACKSTONE CAN'L BANK. Providence, R. I.	1000 Anchor, bales, bbls., &c.; ship in background.
Male portrait 1	BUTCHERS & DROVERS' BANK, Providence, R. I. Drove of cattle, hogs, &c.; two men on horseback; cars crossing viaduct in distance.	1 Female portrait.
2 Male portrait TWO	Title of Bank. Drove of oxen and sheep; man on horseback; trees, etc., in distance.	2 Female portrait. TWO
Small figure 5 5	Vig. Three females floating through water, supporting Cupid. BUTCHERS' & DROVERS' BANK, Providence, R. I. Ox.	5 Male portrait
10 Drovers, cattle, hay, &c.	Vig. Two females seated on either side of state arms, steamship on the right, locomotive and cars on the left. Title of Bank. Beehive.	10 Portrait of Andrew Jackson.
50	Vig. Female reclining on bale of goods. Portrait of Henry Clay BUTCHERS' & DROVERS' BANK, Providence, R. I.	50 Anchor on a bale of goods
Indian looking in distance. 100	Vig. Steamship and other vessels. BUTCHERS' & DROVERS' BANK, Providence, R. I.	100 Male portrait.
1 Indian reclining, looking over rock.	Vig. [illegible] and bags of money. CENTREVILLE BK., Warwick, R. I. Shield and anchor.	1 Farmer erect, with sheaf of wheat, and scythe. [illegible]

2 Female seated, with scales and sword.	Vig. Large eagle and shield CENTREVILLE BK., Warwick, R. I. Wheel and rollers.	2 Female with spy glass; ships on left, in distance.
3 Female reclining, with sickle in left hand; she holds grain.	Vig. Female, shield, anchor, sheaf of wheat, plough, &c.; female holds sickle in left hand; cars and bridge on right. CENTREVILLE BK., Warwick, R. I.	3 Indian reclining.
5 Male Portrait	CENTREVILLE BK., Warwick, R. I. Vig. Horse, boys and dog; the boys are trying to catch the horse; one boy is laying on ground	5 Male Portrait.
10 Male Portrait.	CENTREVILLE BK., Warwick, R. I. Vig. Blacksmith shoeing a horse; two men on left, one seated on log; wagon and wheel on right.	10 Male Portrait.
	☞ The 20's., 50's., and 100's., are of the Perkin's stereotype plate, which has the denominations prints in fine letters, all over the bill.	
50 Male portrait	CENTREVILLE BK., Warwick, R. I. Man gathering and loading cart with corn, etc., etc.	50 Male portrait
100 Male portrait	Title of Bank. Horses in fields.	100 Male portrait
1 Washington.	Female. 1 Female. CITIZENS BANK, Cumberland, R. I.	1 Male.
1 ONE	CITIZENS' BANK, Woonsocket, R. I. Female seated with wheat in her hand; town in the distance.	1 ONE
2 Male.	Female. 2 Female. CITIZENS BANK, Cumberland, R. I.	2 Male.

2 Eagle. | Two females. CITIZENS BANK, Woonsocket, R. I. | 2 Bull's head. TWO	2 Sailor with flag, female at his feet. | Clay. Ancient Puritans around table. CITIZENS' UNION BANK, Scituate, R. I. | 2 Male and female seated.	Female standing erect in large ornamental figure 2. | 2 Vig. Scene upon the ocean; capturing whale in foreground, boat and ship in background. 2 CITY BANK, Providence, R. I. | TWO Cupid in sail boat. TWO
3 Washington and horse. | Female. 3 Female. CITIZENS BANK, Cumberland, R. I. | 3 Blacksmith with sledge.	TWO 2 | Spread eagle, iron castings, cannon balls, machinery, &c. 2 Title of Bank. | 2 TWO Schooner, pilot boat.	Female with sickle; dog's head. 2 | CITY BANK, Providence, R. I. Boy, child, cattle, etc. | 2 Building.
3 Train of cars. 3 | CITIZENS BANK, Woonsocket, R. I. Three females. | 3 Cabin. THREE	3 Same as 1's. | Fame in clouds blowing trumpet; eagle, globe, &c. CITIZENS' UNION BANK, Scituate, R. I. | 3 Three Cupids and fig. 3.	Sailor, mechanic, vessels, etc. THREE | CITY BANK, Providence, R. I. 3 Mechanic and boilers. 3 | 3 Dog & safe.
Eagle. FIVE | V CITIZENS BANK, Cumberland, R. I. | 5 Female with basket of flowers.	5 Female seated with sheaf of grain. | Figure 5, and five females; ship on right; building on left. CITIZENS' UNION BANK. Scituate, R. I. Agricultural implements. | 5 Indian Princess.	5 Portrait of female with sheaf in hand. 5 | 5 Vig. Female with shield, eagle, &c., seated in ornamental V, covering centre of note. 5 CITY BANK, Providence, R. I. | FIVE Female seated with staff and cap in left hand. V
Two males and two females. | 5 Anchor. 5 CITIZENS BANK, Woonsocket, R. I. | Female and eagle. FIVE	10 Washington. 10 | William Tell and boy on right; man on horseback surrounded by six others. X X CITIZENS' UNION BANK, Scituate. State Arms. | 10 Military officer on horseback. 10	Pilot boat 5, and other vessels. 5 | CITY BANK, Providence, R. I. Sailor with trumpet on vessel. | 5 Female and V on shield.
10 Female. TEN | 1 Female. 0 CITIZENS BANK, Woonsocket, R. I. | 10 Female. TEN	20 Spread eagle. 20 | 20 Washington on horseback, receiving gift from a female supporting pole and cap of liberty. 20 Title of Bank. Dog, &c. | 20 Lafayette. 20	10 10 | CITY BANK, Providence, R. I. Sailor and farmer either side of anchor on shield. | 10 Child's head.
20 Female with spear. | 2 Female. 0 CITIZENS BANK, Woonsocket, R. I. XX | 20 Female. 20	FIFTY | L Agricultural scene, buildings, load of hay, laborers with rakes, forks, &c. L Title of Bank. Engine and car. | 50 Man and cattle. 50	10 Female seated with grain in left hand. X | Vig. Ships, steamboat and other vessels. X CITY BANK, Providence, R. I. Ship under sail. | 10 Female with shield and scales in right hand, barrels in rear. X
50 Female with spear. | Male and female seated. CITIZENS BANK, Woonsocket, R. I. 50 | 50 Cupid in boat. 50	100 Female, steeple, man and a pair of horses in distance. 100 | C Steamboat filled with passengers; ship and sloop on left. C Title of Bank. Ornamental star. | 100 Three females seated.	L 50 | CITY BANK, Providence, R. I. L Sailor, two farmers, etc. L | 50 State Arms.
100 Man with sledge, anchor. | Vig. Spread eagle upon branch of tree; canal scene on right; train of cars crossing bridge on left. CITIZENS BANK, Woonsocket, R. I. 100 | 100 Female with pole, scales beside, cornucopia.	1 | CITY BANK, Providence, R. I. Female with shield and eagle; steamer, etc. Schooner, etc. | 1 Girl's head.	50 Female with left hand resting upon shield, right arm upon the neck of eagle. FIFTY | CITY BANK, Providence, R. I. Vig. Large steamship under full sail. | 50 Female seated, sickle in right hand, horn of plenty in left, sheaf, horse, &c. FIFTY
1 Female seated on bale; ship in distance. 1 | Female seated with left arm on shield; pole and cap, eagle, coin, &c. CITIZENS' UNION BANK, Scituate, R. I. Head of female. | 1 Female seated with sickle and sheaf on right shoulder. ONE and fig. 1.	ONE Female portrait. ONE | 1 Vig. Spread eagle upon limb; cars crossing canal on left, canal scene on right. 1 CITY BANK, Providence, R. I. Steamship. | ONE Farmer shearing sheep, woman standing behind him. ONE	100 Male portrait. 100 | Vig. Ship building; ship on stocks; ship's wheel on right; ship under sail in distance on left. CITY BANK, Providence, R. I. Cornucopia, anchor, wheel, &c. | 100 Portrait of female holding dish of fruit. 100

C
100
CITY BANK,
Providence, R.I.
C Female with sheaf and shield; vessels in distance. C
100
Eagle.

Franklin.
500
CITY BANK,
Providence, R.I.
Indians receiving whites in boat.
500
D

500
Indian paddling canoe; forest in back-ground.
CITY BANK,
Providence, R.I.
D D
500
Female with sword and scales.

1000
CITY BANK,
Providence, R.I.
Spread eagle on rock; vessel in distance.
1000
Indian female seated.
C

Washington
1000
CITY BANK,
Providence, R.I.
Female with cornucopia, vessel, etc.
1000
M

ONE
1
Agricultural scene; farmer resting, another in the distance harrowing.
1
COMMERCIAL BANK
Bristol, R.I.
1
Ship.
ONE

TWO
Male in grain field.
TWO
2 Naval engagement, ships of war, men in boat, &c. 2
Title of Bank
Anchor and word "hope" on shield.
2
Male portrait

THREE
3
Sailor, hat in hand, reclining against bales; in the distance are vessels, warehouses, dray, horses &c.
3
Title of Bank
3
THREE
Train of cars.

Spread eagle, city and vessels in distance.
FIVE
Large V, female and Cupid
Title of Bank
5
Portrait of a girl.

Village and depot, train of cars, &c., in distance.
TEN
X
Title of Bank
10
Farmer with sheaf of wheat and sickle.

20
Female sitting, with book.
XX Eagle. XX
Title of Bank
20
Ship under sail.

FIFTY
Female.
FIFTY
50 Man and horse. 50
Title of Bank.
FIFTY
Female
FIFTY

100
Small spread eagle.
100
C Vig. Man in chariot 100 with four horses abreast driving through air, clouds beneath.
Title of Bank.
Letter C.
Portrait of Washington
Letter C.

ONE
Western boy with ears of corn in left hand holding cornstalk in right.
ONE
1 Deck of ship with sailor at wheel steering. 1
COMMERCIAL B'K.
Providence, R.I.
ONE
Portrait of Indian female with bow in hand, quiver on back.
ONE

1
Steam at sea; steamship, vessels, etc.
COMMERCIAL BANK
Providence, R.I.
Bales.
1

2
Two Dollars
COMMERCIAL BANK
Providence, R.I.
Harbor scene—steamship, steamboats vessels, etc.
Barrels.
2
Two Dollars

2
Male portrait
COMMERCIAL B'K,
Providence, R.I.
Man-of-War and other vessels.
2
Commercial scene, sailor with quadrant, right hand on capstan.

THREE
Female with basket of grapes in right hand.
THREE
3 Two females sitting, at right [illegible] tree team and wagon in distance; on left bale of goods, ship and steamer in distance.
COMMERCIAL B'K.
Providence, R.I.
THREE
Sailor on deck of ship with telescope, ship in distance.
THREE

5
Female seated holding roll of cloth in left hand, machinery on right.
5
Vig. Steamboat Boston.
5
Three medallions in frame with words "Five Dollars" running across.
Title of Bank
Cupid mounted on Stag.
FIVE

5
Male portrait.
COMMERCIAL B'K,
Providence, R.I.
Commercial scene group of three sailors; one seated with spyglass.
5
Child's Head

10
Interior of a blacksmith shop, smith at work.
COMMERCIAL B'K,
Providence, R.I.
Commerce and Manufacture, shield with anchor and hope, female on right, female with scroll and scales on left.
10
Male portrait

10
Ship under full sail.
10
Female seated left arm resting on vase; in right hand pitcher pouring water in basin, spread eagle on left.
COMMERCIAL B'K,
Providence, R.I.
Anchors, barrels, and ship in distance.
10
Shield with view of mill on left; female with pole and cap on right; Indian with rifle.
X

20
Female erect with pole and cap, shield with view of mill on right.
20
20 Neptune in car drawn by sea horses; on right ship in distance. 20
COMMERCIAL B'K,
Providence, R.I.
Indian in canoe.
20
Female seated with sword and balances, resting with left arm on column.
20

50
Female with cornucopia in right hand, left arm resting on shield with view of house.
50
Title of Bank.
Shield; view of machinery on shield, eagle surmounting; on right female with sword and balances, on left female with spear and helmet, bridge and ship in distance.
50
FIFTY
FIFTY

Female erect with hand supporting anchor on right.
100
100 Shield with eagle holding small shield in talons on large shield; on left female seated with pole and cap; ship in distance, on right, cog wheel, anvil, &c. 100
Title of Bank
Female reclining.
Female erect holding [illegible] on right
100

Full length statue of Washington.
500
500 500
COMMERCIAL B'K,
Providence, R.I.
Female supporting shield in right hand, pole and cap in right, on left spread eagle all resting on globe.
Spread swan [illegible]
Full length figure of female, left arm resting on [illegible], right hand scroll.
500

1
Anchor, bales, &c.
Locomotive and train of cars, another train crossing bridge, water vessel &c., in background
CONTINENTAL B'K,
Providence, R.I.
Spread eagle.
1
Portrait of Female.

2
Same as One.
Portrait of Webster.
CONTINENTAL B'K,
Providence, R.I.
Sheaf and Plow.
2
Spread eagle and shield.

Three females upon rock, one erect with hand on anchor, stock.
THREE
CONTINENTAL B'K,
Providence, R.I.
Child seated upon the shoulder of a man, at whom woman [illegible] is gazing.
3 3
3
Female seated, leaning on bales; ship in background.

5
Indian with gun, seated upon rock.
Surrender of Lord Cornwallis.
CONTINENTAL B'K,
Providence, R.I.
Sheaf and Plow.
5
Portrait of Washington.

Male portrait Medal Head.	CONTINENTAL B'K, Providence, R. I. 10 Goddess of liberty with scale and globe. X	10 Male portrait
20 Female seated with spool factory in background.	Ornamental figures 20, with winged females on either side, two small figures in the middle of large 2 & 0. CONTINENTAL B'K, Providence, R. I.	20 Female seated in shell with trident.
50 Ship under sail.	Female seated leaning on bale, barrels, &c.; ship on right, factory in distance on left. CONTINENTAL B'K, Providence, R. I.	50 Portrait of Fillmore.
100 Female portrait.	Vig. Spread eagle on rock, large ship on either side. CONTINENTAL B'K, Providence, R. I.	100 Female erect holding tablet on pillar, cogwheels, &c. around.
500 Portrait of Henry Clay.	Vig. Steamship under full sail, ships on either side. CONTINENTAL B'K, Providence, R. I.	500 Sailor on ship's deck, with spy-glass in hand.
1 Female seated upon bale of goods with spool of yarn, factories in the background.	Three females seated, centre one lower than other two, ships in the distance on the right. COVENTRY BANK, Anthony Village, R. I. State Arms.	1 Washington on horseback.
Three females on a cliff overlooking the ocean, one resting right hand upon anchor, and with sheaf of wheat under her arm. TWO	Female seated resting one arm upon the State Arms of R. I. on seashore with ships in the background. Title of Bank. Mechanic Emblems.	2 Medal head of Franklin.
5 Male figure resting one arm upon a short column palette, pallet, &c. at her feet.	Female seated on a safe, child playing with a dog at her feet; cars with ship in the distance at the right, agricultural emblems on the left. Title of Bank. Sheaf of wheat, plow, &c.	5 Female fig. resting right arm on shield, pole with cap of liberty in her hand, bunch of arrows at her back.
5 Female seated with pen, scroll, harp, etc.	Eagle and shield. COVENTRY BANK, Anthony Village, R. I.	5 Indian princess.
10 Male seated.	Female seated with agricultural implements at her left; Female in medallion; on right, blacksmith shop in background on right. Title of Bank. Dog beside a Safe.	10 Two females erect.

20 Train of cars entering a city, seen in the background.	Female seated with extended arms, scales in one hand, pole with cap of liberty in the other, child upon each side. Title of Bank. Steamship.	20 Female with sheaf of wheat and sickle in her hand.
50 Female Portrait. 50	Two female figures seated; view of factories; cars and ship in the background. Title of Bank. Locomotive.	50 Man picking corn in a field.
100 Sailor with American flag.	Title of Bank. Female with child scattering flowers over a city. Mechanic emblems.	100 Ship under sail. 100
1 Portrait of Washington.	Female 1 Female CRANSTON BANK, Cranston, R. I.	1 Portrait of Franklin.
TWO Two Indians reclining, one smoking, falls in background. TWO	2 Three females, two erect and one seated, plow, &c., ship on stocks, &c. 2 CRANSTON BANK, Cranston, R. I. Cattle.	TWO Washington. TWO
THREE	Farmer in field of wheat. Spread eagle, shield, &c. 3 CRANSTON BANK, Cranston, R. I. Old fashioned cars and locomotive.	THREE Portrait of Female. 3
5 Franklin.	Female. Three female Cupids seated; vessel on right, eagle on left. CRANSTON BANK, Cranston, R. I. River scene, &c.	5 Washington and his horse.
X Indian in act of shooting with bow.	Steamboat, vessel, &c., buildings on right. X CRANSTON BANK, Cranston, R. I.	10 Female with hat and sheaf.
20 Female seated with book on lap.	XX Eagle. XX CRANSTON BANK, Cranston, R. I.	20 Ship
FIFTY Female. FIFTY	50 Man and horse. 50 CRANSTON BANK, Cranston, R. I.	FIFTY Female erect FIFTY

Words ONE HUNDRED, and figures 100. Portrait of Harrison.	Wheat scene, loading wagon with bbls., men, houses, shipping, &c. CRANSTON BANK, Cranston, R. I.	Same as on left. Male portrait
ONE	Vessels, &c. 1 CUMBERLAND B'K, Cumberland, R. I.	ONE Female Indian. ONE
2 TWO 2	Vessels, &c., 2 CUMBERLAND B'K, Cumberland, R. I.	TWO Female with rope in hand. TWO
THREE	Farmers reaping, on right female with hat in hand and sheaf under arm. 3 CUMBERLAND B'K, Cumberland, R. I.	THREE Steamboat with masts. Word THREE and fig. 3.
FIVE	Female raising drapery from a fig. 5 on shield. V CUMBERLAND B'K, Cumberland, R. I.	5 Vessel.
10 X 10	Man, oxen and plow. 10 CUMBERLAND B'K, Cumberland, R. I.	TEN Female erect with horn of flowers in left hand.
20 TWENTY	XX Eagle. XX CUMBERLAND B'K, Cumberland, R. I.	20 Ship.
FIFTY Female erect FIFTY	50 Man and horse. 50 CUMBERLAND BK, Cumberland, R. I.	FIFTY Female. FIFTY
	All other denominations are of the General Plate of the New England Bank Note Co.	
ONE	EAGLE BANK, Bristol, R. I. Vig. Indian chief, squaw and child upon back, gazing below them from rock. Eagle.	1 Female seated, eagle beside her on shield.

Left end	Centre	Right end
Goddess of Liberty erect with pole and cap in right hand; shield. 2	Spread Eagle. Vig. Female reclining upon cornucopia. EAGLE BANK, Bristol, R. I. Female swimming.	2. Female soaring in air, holding ornamental figure.
Goddess of liberty erect with pole and cap in right hand; shield, eagle.	5 Vig. Farmer driving drove of sheep, mill in distance. EAGLE BANK, Bristol, R. I.	FIVE. Indian erect resting hand on tomahawk.
50. Female erect leaning on a rock, cornucopia. 50	50. EAGLE BANK, Bristol, R. I.	FIFTY
C. Portrait of Washington. C	100 Vig. figure pouring water from vessel; ship on right. 100. EAGLE BANK, Bristol, R. I.	ONE HUNDRED
Spread eagle.	1 Portrait of female harp on right; book, scroll and globe on left. 1. EAGLE BANK, Providence, R. I. State Arms.	Portrait of Washington.
1. Machinist, bust of Watts, machinery, &c.	EAGLE BANK, Providence, R. I. Eagle on rock. 1 1	ONE. Two children.
TWO. Locomotive and cars crossing bridge. TWO	2 Portrait of female, resting left arm, on pail; agricultural implements around. 2. EAGLE BANK, Providence, R. I. State Arms.	TWO. Steamboat. TWO
Full length figure of America.	2 EAGLE BANK, Providence, R. I. Eagle on rock. 2	2. 2
Spread eagle on limb of tree.	3 Two females seated; safe and ship on right; steamer in distance on left. 3. EAGLE BANK, Providence, R. I. State Arms.	Portrait of female.
FIVE	5 Female seated on small globe, spread eagle by her side on left. V. EAGLE BANK, Providence, R. I. Anchor.	RHODE ISLAND

Left end	Centre	Right end
5. 5	Title of Bank. Vig. Large V. in centre of note, on right female seated, bales, barrel, &c., at her back; river and sheep in background before her; on left man reclining, two men seated on rocks, dray with man and two horses in background on his right. Female seated.	5. 5
FIVE. Female resting on wheel.	EAGLE BANK, Providence, R. I. 5 Portrait of Abe Lincoln. 5	5. Eagle on rock.
TEN	10 Vig. Neptune in car, drawn by two horses. X. EAGLE BANK, Providence, R. I. Anchor.	RHODE ISLAND
X. X	Title of Bank. Vig. Large X in centre of note; on right goddess of Liberty reclining, eagle behind her, globe, ship, and steam-ship on her left; on left of X female seated on bale, resting on hogshead; anchor, bale, and ship on her left; steamship in distance on her right. Dog.	X. X
RHODE I	20 Vig. Ship sailing, 20 shore, on which is anchor upright, and motto in scroll, "In God we hope." Title of Bank. Anchor.	TWENTY
RHODE ISLAND	50 Vig. [illegible] 50 of [illegible]; sloop sailing ahead of her. Title of Bank. Anchor on shield.	FIFTY
RHODE ISLAND	100 Vig. Spread 100 eagle upon anchor leaning against rock, overlooking sea, on which ship is seen; upon the rock is a scroll and motto, "In God we hope." Title of Bank. Anchor upon shield.	ONE HUNDRED
1. Head of Webster. ONE	View of Elmwood Village. ELMWOOD BANK, Cranston, R. I. Elm Tree.	ONE. Large figure 1 with male supporting it.
2	View of Elmwood village. Head of Franklin Pierce. ELMWOOD BANK, Cranston, R. I. Elm Tree.	II. Female supporting large figure 2.
FIVE. Figure representing a man sailing, woman talking and dog watching; high bluff of land water in distance.	5 View of Elmwood village. ELMWOOD BANK, Cranston, R. I. Elm Tree.	5. Figure of Justice with scales. FIVE

Left end	Centre	Right end
TEN. Female supporting large X. 10	ELMWOOD BANK, Cranston, R. I. View of Elmwood Village. Elm Tree.	10. Letter X covered with vines; female with pail and cow.
50. Female Head.	ELMWOOD BANK, Cranston, R. I. View of Elmwood Village. 50.	Figures 50 supported by three men representing agriculture, manufactures and commerce.
100. Ornamental letter C surrounding wheat and head of female.	ELMWOOD BANK, Cranston, R. I. Two females with scythe and shield. Tree.	100. View of village. 100
1. Locomotive and cars. ONE	Vig. Group of females, representing calling scene. Steamboat. EXCHANGE BANK, Providence, R. I. State arms.	1. Female bathing. ONE
ONE. Female supporting ornamental fig. 1. ONE	Male portrait with cupid on either side. EXCHANGE BANK, Providence, R. I. State arms.	ONE. Vig. Boy, sheep, dog, basket, &c.; cars crossing bridge. 1
2. Vessel and steamboat on river opposite town.	TWO. Vig. Female seated holding key in right hand, receiving cornucopia from winged figure on right, safe and griffin on left. EXCHANGE BANK, Providence, R. I. State arms.	2. Female with state arms on right, sailor on left. TWO
2. Portrait of Daniel Webster.	Male portrait. Vig. Two females, mechanic, safe and anvil; ship on right; cars on left. EXCHANGE BANK, Providence, R. I. State arms.	2. TWO
Female seated on bales, with cornucopia; 5 at her feet. FIVE	EXCHANGE BANK, Providence, R. I. Large V; female seated, sheaf, &c.	5. Female portrait.
10	Vig. Human figure with sickle in right hand; plough, rake &c. on right; sheaf of grain on left. 10. EXCHANGE BANK, Providence, R. I. State arms.	10. Two male figures supporting female with wreath of flowers.
Female soaring in air, with ear of corn in left hand. FIFTY	50 Male portrait. 50. EXCHANGE BANK, Providence, R. I. State arms.	Female soaring in air, sickle in right hand, grain in left. FIFTY

Left end	Centre	Right end
100 Cupid. C	EXCHANGE BANK Providence, R. I. Vig. New York Crystal Palace. State arms.	100 Cupid Mul porte A.
Sailor sitting upon bale of goods with spy glass; also ship in rear. 500	EXCHANGE BANK Providence, R. I. Vig. Male portrait with cupid on either side. State arms.	500 D Female with sword in right hand, seated in left, oars on left.
M	Steamship Massasoit. Male Portrait EXCHANGE BANK, Providence, R. I. State Arms.	1000 Sailor throwing the lead.
ONE Ships on the ocean. 1	[illegible] in left Indian seated; on right, sailor seated, holding quadrant; in distance ship. EXETER BANK, Exeter, R. I. Female with sickle and sheaf.	ONE Female seated, left arm resting on State Arms. 1
TWO Female seated, right arm resting above figure 2. 2	2 Cupid holding figure 2, in front of a block of stone. 2 EXETER BANK, Exeter, R. I. Eagle and small urn.	Female seated left arm resting on stone pillar. TWO
3 Portrait of Washington. 3	3 Female giving eagle drink. 3 EXETER BANK, Exeter, R. I. 3	3 Portrait of De Witt Clinton.
FIVF Female seated, watering eagle. V	5 Female seated, with sickle; cows standing, and farm house in distance. 5 EXETER BANK, Exeter, R. I. Indian in canoe.	FIVE
10 Female head and State Arms. 10	TEN Agricultural implements; beehive, cornucopia, tree, sheaf of wheat, wheel, &c. TEN EXETER BANK, Exeter, R. I. Cupid on the back of a deer.	10
1	Man on horseback, boy standing with left hand over eye, three other cows standing around on left of man, also houses in distance. Large figure 1, view of sea monster standing on rock on right. FALL RIVER UNION BANK. Tiverton, R. I. Steamboat and vessel.	ONE Full length figure of Indian with bow and arrow. 1
2	Train of cars; Depot and men on right; on left pier steamship, sail vessels, &c. Large figure 2, with portrait of female on right. Title of Bank	2 Washington standing beside horse; battle in distance. TWO

Left end	Centre	Right end
FI V VE	Vig. Indian in canoe; sloops and other sail vessels in distance on right; on left, house, trees, &c.; large letter V, extending across bill. FALL RIVER UNION BANK, Tiverton, R. I. Dog and safe.	5 Spread eagle holding shield in talons, on which is figure 5.
X	Vig. Blacksmith sitting on boiler, blowing bellows; forge, anvil, and bench with tools at right; wheel on left, large ornamental X extending across bill. Title of Bank.	TEN Large portrait of Washington. TEN
20 Female sitting; right hand resting on chest; open book on lap.	XX Vig. Spread eagle standing on rock. XX FALL RIVER UNION BANK, Tiverton, R. I.	20 Two ships, one in foreground, one in distance.
FIFTY Full length figure of female in right hand wreath, and bunch of flowers in left. FIFTY	50 Vig. Man and horse; horse rearing. 50 FALL RIVER UNION BANK, Tiverton, R. I.	FIFTY Full length figure of female. FIFTY
Words one hundred running across figures 100. Male portrait	Dray cart, into which men are rolling barrels, horses, shipping, &c. FALL RIVER UNION BANK, Tiverton, R. I.	Words one hundred running across figures 100. Male portrait
500	500 D Vig. Female sitting, sheaves of grain at her feet; load of grain and men reaping in distance. FALL RIVER UNION BANK, Tiverton, R. I.	500
1	Female seated, steamer in the distance. Large figure 1 and portrait of five men. FRANKLIN BANK, Chepachet, R. I.	1 Female with sheaf of wheat.
ONE	Vessels. 1 FRANKLIN BANK, Chepachet, R. I.	ONE Female. ONE
2	Agricultural scene. Large 2, and portraits of five men. FRANKLIN BANK. Chepachet, R. I.	TWO Female. TWO
2 TWO 2	Vessels. 2 FRANKLIN BANK. Chepachet, R. I.	TWO Female. TWO

Left end	Centre	Right end
THREE	Agricultural Scene. 3 FRANKLIN BANK, Chepachet, R. I.	Word THREE and fig. 3. Female. THREE
THREE	Man with sickle cutting grain; on right female with sheaf of wheat. 3 FRANKLIN BANK, Chepachet, R. I.	THREE Steamer. Word THREE and fig. 3.
FIVE	Eagle on shield V, female and anchor, and child, buildings, vessels, &c. FRANKLIN BANK. Chepachet, R. I.	5 Girl with basket of flowers.
FIVE	Female. 5 FRANKLIN BANK. Chepachet, R. I.	5 Female.
X Indian with a bow.	Steamer and sailing vessels. X FRANKLIN BANK, Chepachet, R. I.	10 Female holding bonnet, and sheaf of wheat.
Vulcan seated; anvil, &c. around him; in distance buildings, train of cars, &c. TEN	X FRANKLIN BANK, Chepachet, R. I.	10 Farmer with sheaf on his knee.
10 X 10	Oxen and man [illegible] 10 FRANKLIN BANK, Chepachet, R. I.	TEN Female.
20 Female seated, with book on lap.	XX Eagle. XX FRANKLIN BANK. Chepachet, R. I.	20 Ship
Steamer. XX Fer' &c.	Figure of a female seated with spear and balances; eagle on left. 20 FRANKLIN BANK. Chepachet, R. I.	XX Female.
FIFTY Female. FIFTY	50 Man and horse. 50 FRANKLIN BANK. Chepachet, R. I.	FIFTY Female. FIFTY

Left	Centre	Right
50 Vessels.	Agricultural scene. 50 FRANKLIN BANK, Chepachet, R. I.	L Female.

Left	Centre	Right
100 Eagle. 100	C Fairies. 100 FRANKLIN BANK, Chepachet, R. I.	C Washington. C

Left	Centre	Right
Words One Hundred, and figures 100. Portrait of Harrison.	Wharf scene; men loading wagon with bales; horses, drays, men, shipping, &c. FRANKLIN BANK, Chepachet, R. I.	Same as on left. Male portrait

Left	Centre	Right
1 RHODE ISLAND 1	1 1 Spread eagle on rock, olive branch and arrows in talons. FREEMANS' BANK, Bristol, R. I. ONE	1 ONE 1

Left	Centre	Right
2 RHODE ISLAND 2	2 2 Same as ones. Title of Bank. TWO	2 TWO 2

Left	Centre	Right
3 RHODE ISLAND 3	3 3 Same as ones Title of Bank. THREE	3 THREE 3

Left	Centre	Right
FIVE	Spread eagle on shield; city and ships in distance. Female, eagle, and letter V. Title of Bank.	5 Little girl with flowers.

Left	Centre	Right
Male figure seated on machinery; cars at distance. TEN	X Title of Bank.	10 Male figure with sheaf in hand.

Left	Centre	Right
FIFTY Female figure standing, globe in her right hand, flowers at her right. FIFTY	50 Man and horse. 50 Title of Bank.	FIFTY Female figure with wreath of flowers in right hand. FIFTY

Left	Centre	Right
Words one hundred, and figures 100. Male portrait	Vig. Wharf scene; hauling wagon, drays, horses, shipping, &c. Title of Ba[illegible]	Words one hundred, and figures 100. Male portrait

Left	Centre	Right
1 Ornamental vase and cupid with horn of plenty.	GLOBE BANK, Providence, R. I. Male supporting the world on shoulders on which he four females representing the nations; female reclining on left; and male representing time on right; cars and steamship in distance.	1 Same as left.

Left	Centre	Right
2 Same as ones	GLOBE BANK, Providence, R. I. Same as ones.	2 Same as ones

Left	Centre	Right
3 Same as ones	GLOBE BANK, Providence, R. I. Same as ones.	3 Same as ones

Left	Centre	Right
FIVE	Five Globe Dollars with three females around it, and male at bottom. GLOBE BANK, Providence, R. I. Shield.	Word five, and figure 5. 5 Word five and figure 5.

Left	Centre	Right
Female seated on rock with trident. FIVE	Nautical scene—ships, man of war, steamship, &c. GLOBE BANK, Providence, R. I. 5	5

Left	Centre	Right
FIVE	GLOBE BANK, Three females around globe; male at bottom. Providence, R. I. Anchor on shield.	Five on 5. 5 Five on 5

Left	Centre	Right
TEN	Title of Bank Same as above fives. Anchor on shield.	X 10 X

Left	Centre	Right
X 10 X	Ten Vig. Dollars Same as fives. GLOBE BANK, Providence, R. I. Shield.	TEN

Left	Centre	Right
10 Sailor with hand on capstan; bale, Cupid, mast, &c. behind.	Female reclining on bale with wand; city and vessels on right; cars, canal boat, lock, &c., on left. GLOBE BANK Providence, R. I.	10

Left	Centre	Right
50 Female erect with young child.	Male and female seated. GLOBE BANK, Providence, R. I. 50	50 Cupid in sail boat. 50

Left	Centre	Right
Large figure 50 surrounded by numerous small 50s.	FIFTY DOLLARS Female resting with quadrant, globe, etc. GLOBE BANK, Providence, R.I. 50	Same as left end.

Left	Centre	Right
100 Vulcan seated with sledge.	Spread eagle on limb of tree; train of cars on left, and canal scene on right. GLOBE BANK, Providence, R. I. 100	100 Female seated with rake.

Left	Centre	Right
One Hundred across 100. Male portrait	Wharf scene—men, horses, wagons, carts, etc. GLOBE BANK, Providence, R. I.	Same as on left end.

Left	Centre	Right
100 Anchor, bales, etc.	State Arms; female either side. GLOBE BANK, Providence, R.I.	100 Female

Left	Centre	Right
500 Washington	GLOBE BANK, Providence, R I. Two females seated on bale; factories in distance.	500 Female, spinning wheel; factories, etc.

Left	Centre	Right
Female figure seated, holding balances in right hand. 1	GLOBE BANK Smithfield, R. I. View of a public building.	1 Male portrait

Left	Centre	Right
THE GLOBE BANK. The word TWO in extreme corner and partly lengthwise.	Ocean scene: steamships and sail vessels.	2 Female with bunch of flowers and grass in left hand.

Left	Centre	Right
Female seated, with liberty pole and cap in left hand. 3	GLOBE BANK Smithfield, R. I. Group of hay makers, with female and children sitting and laying on ground; load of hay, with horses in background.	3 3

Left	Centre	Right
Water spouting from fountain. 5	Two steamships and sail vessel. GLOBE BANK Smithfield, R. I.	5 Female portrait.

Left	Centre	Right
Two females standing. 10	GLOBE BANK Smithfield, R. I. TEN Landscape scene; load of cultivated wheat. TEN	10 Female figure standing; ear of corn in right hand, and letter X to left.

20
GLOBE BANK
Smithfield, R. I.
Globe with Neptune seated in a shell; steamer and sail vessel in background.
XX
Squaw

50
GLOBE BANK
Smithfield, R. I.
Globe with Heathen God, and two cherubs astride an eagle.
L
50
Portrait of Webster.

C
GLOBE BANK
Smithfield, R. I.
Harbor and shipping.
C
100
Female with a bundle of wheat.

Wild scenery; Indian in canoe.
500
500
GLOBE BANK
Smithfield, R. I.
D D
500
Female with balances and sword.

Spread eagle standing on rock near water; sail vessel under full sail
1000
1000
GLOBE BANK
Smithfield, R. I.
M M
1000
Indian female, with bow and arrow.

1
Head of Washingt'n
Female 1 Female
GRANITE BANK,
Pascoag, R.I.
1
Head of Franklin

2
Head.
Female 2 Female
GRANITE BANK,
Pascoag, R.I.
2
Head.

3
Washingt'n full length.
Female head and bust. 3 Female head and bust.
GRANITE BANK,
Pascoag, R.I.
3
Vulcan full length.

Eagle resting on United States shie'd and an anchor.
FIVE
Large V, with female figure and child.
GRANITE BANK,
Pascoag, R.I.
5
Female figure and basket.

Male figure seated on machinery; cars in distance.
TEN
X
GRANITE BANK,
Pascoag, R.I.
10
Male figure with sheaf in hand.

20
Female with spear.
2 Female 0
GRANITE BANK,
Pascoag, R.I.
XX
20
Female seated.
20

50
Female with spear.
Male and female seated
GRANITE BANK,
Pascoag, R.I.
50
50
Cupid in boat.
50

100
Man with sledge, anchor.
Vig. Spread eagle upon branch of tree; canal scene on right; train of cars crossing bridge on left.
GRANITE BANK,
Pascoag, R.I.
100
100
Female with rake, seated beside cornucopia.

1
ONE on fig. 1
GREENWICH BANK
East Greenwich, R. I.
Sailor reclining with implements; ships in distance.
1 Stockholders, etc. 1
1
Train of cars

2
TWO DOLLARS
[illegible] female, boy, girl, dog, hen and chickens.
2 on shield on right is female instructing children; on left is Indian, squaw and papoose.
GREENWICH BANK
East Greenwich, R. I.
Red 2. Red 2.
2
Squaw and female.

5, V & FIVE.
State Arms.
FIVE
Signing Declaration of Independence.
Washington.
GREENWICH BANK
East Greenwich, R. I.
Red 5. Arm. Red 5.
5 on med. head
Male portrait

X
Liberty, eagle and shield.
GREENWICH BANK
East Greenwich, R. I.
View of buildings, trees and park.
Stockholders, etc.
10
Female portrait.

Female with pail.
XX
Title of Bank.
Train of cars coming from under arch; two laborers.
Stockholders, etc.
20
Man plowing with two horses.

50
Sailor, mechanic, two females, city, lighthouse, chimney, hills etc.
50
Title of Bank.
State Arms.
Fifty inverted.
Plow boy, two females, dog, oxen, sheafs, etc.

1
Two cattle; one standing other lying down.
ONE
GROCERS' AND PRODUCERS' BANK,
Providence, R. I.
Vig. Two females seated, one on right holding bale of goods upon her lap, factories in distance behind her; steamboat in extreme distance on left.
1
Female on either side of state arms.

2
Blacksmith leaning over anvil.
TWO
GROCERS' AND PRODUCERS' BANK,
Providence, R. I.
Female seated in large ornamental 2.
2
Portrait of little girl.
TWO

5
male.
State Arms; Indian seated upon right, farmer with sickle upon left; canoe upon river on right; cars in distance on left.
Title of Bank
Figure 5 with word FIVE.
Portrait of Sailor.

10
Large X with 10 on it;
glass on right light house on left.
GROCERS' AND PRODUCERS' BANK,
Providence, R. I.
State Arms, eagle upon globe surmounting it; female on either side.
10
Large ship at sea.

50
Title of Bank.
Two females seated; one on left supporting shield with sheaf upon its face, one on right holding wand in left hand; portrait of Franklin on right; steamboat vessel, &c., on right in distance, wagon crossing bridge over &c., on left in distance.
50
State Arms
50

100
Female seated supporting shield, with cog and hammer upon it; cars, steamship, &c., on right.
GROCERS' AND PRODUCERS' BANK,
Providence, R. I.
100
Boy with basket seated among sheep; cars in distance upon left.
100

D
Small Cupid holding cornucopia.
500
Title of Bank
Large steamboat sailing past city in background.
500
Farmer erect sharpening scythe, mill, bridge in distance.
500

ONE
1
Farmer sowing.
1
HIGH STREET B'K,
Providence, R. I.
1
Ship.
ONE

1
Portrait of Washington.
Female 1 Female
HIGH STREET B'K,
Providence, R. I.
1
Portrait of Franklin.

1
Clay.
HIGH STREET BK.
Providence, R. I.
Washington reading despatches; man writing resting on drum; horse, cannon, soldiers, &c.
1
Eagle on Shield.

2
Female, bales, horn of plenty, etc.
Title of Bank.
Cows in brook; children on bank; tree, etc.
2
Franklin.

Left	Centre	Right
TWO 2	Eagle on a rock. 2 HIGH STREET B'K, Providence, R. I.	2 TWO Vessels.
2 Male portrait.	Female. 2 Female. HIGH STREET B'K, Providence, R. I.	2 Male portrait.
3 Blacksmith at work.	HIGH STREET BK. Providence, R.I. Washington.	3 Man dressing leather.
THREE 3	Sailor with hat in hand; bales of merchandise, shipping, &c. 3 HIGH STREET B'K. Providence, R. I.	3 THREE Train of cars.
3 Washington and his horse.	Female. 3 Female. HIGH STREET B'K, Providence, R. I.	3 Male figure.
FIVE	Eagle on shield; V, female buildings, and child. and anchor; vessels, &c. HIGH STREET B'K, Providence, R. I.	5 Girl with basket of flowers.
FIVE	Female. 5 HIGH STREET B'K, Providence, R. I.	5 Ship.
10 X 10	Man and oxen. 10 HIGH STREET B'K, Providence, R. I.	TEN Female.
TEN	Vulcan seated; factory and cars in distance. X HIGH STREET B'K, Providence, R. I.	10 Farmer with sheaf on his knee.
20 Female.	XX Eagle. XX HIGH STREET B'K, Providence, R. I.	20 Ship.

Left	Centre	Right
Female erect with wand, eagle, etc. 20	20 Female portrait. HIGH STREET BK, Providence, R. I.	20 Franklin.
FIFTY Agricultural products. 50	50 Three females, city, vessel on left. HIGH STREET BK, Providence, R. I.	Word FIFTY and fig. 50. Vulcan seated with anvil, hammer, etc.; cars on left.
FIFTY Female erect. FIFTY	50 Man and horse. 50 HIGH STREET B'K, Providence, R. I.	FIFTY Female erect. FIFTY
Figures 100 and words one hundred. Male portrait.	Wharf scene; man loading wagon; shipping, &c. HIGH STREET B'K, Providence, R. I.	Figures 100 and words one hundred. Male portrait.
Male portrait. 1	Two trains of cars, another crossing bridge in distance. HOPE BANK, Warren, R. I.	1 Female portrait.
ONE	Vig. Scene upon water; sailing vessels &c. 1 HOPE BANK, Warren, R. I.	ONE Indian girl erect with bow and arrows. ONE
Male portrait. 2	Two cherubs with swords and two silver dollars; cars, hills and steamboat in distance. HOPE BANK, Warren, R. I.	2 Female portrait.
2 TWO 2	Vig. Ships sailing upon water, &c. 2 HOPE BANK, Warren, R. I.	TWO Female drawing water from a well. TWO
THREE	Vig. Farmers [illegible], female with sheaf under her arm, on right. 3 HOPE BANK, Warren, R. I.	THREE Steamboat. THREE with figure 3 across it.
3 Male portrait. THREE	Milkmaid milking cow; another lying down. HOPE BANK, Warren, R. I.	3 Female portrait.

Left	Centre	Right
Soldier with sword. FIVE	State and female portrait. 5 HOPE BANK, Warren, R. I.	Justice erect. FIVE
FIVE	Vig. Female raising drapery from shield, upon which is figure 5. V HOPE BANK, Warren, R. I.	5 Ship at sea with signals flying.
Five with V running across it.	Vig. Female with rake in left hand, sickle in right; ship, on right; man, team, &c. on left. V and [illegible] on queensware, &c. on HOPE BANK, Warren, R. I.	5 Portrait of Washington.
Female portrait. X	Bales and barrels. Female seated representing Commerce; ship in distance. HOPE BANK, Warren, R. I.	10 Indian princess.
10 X 10	Pair of oxen with a man standing by an ancient plow. 10 HOPE BANK, Warren, R. I.	TEN Female erect holding our weight in left hand, barometer in right.
50 Vessel and steamboat sailing.	Vig. Farming scene, loading waggon with grain, man with rake in right hand on right. 50 HOPE BANK, Warren, R. I.	L Female kneeling with sword and scales.
50 Female erect, arm resting upon shield on pillar.	Vig. Male and female seated, cornucopia between them. HOPE BANK, Warren, R. I. 50	50 Cupid in a sailboat. 50
100 Spread Eagle. 100	C Vig. Mercury in car with torch, drawn by four horses. 100 HOPE BANK, Warren, R. I.	C Portrait of Washington. C
100 Vulcan seated, hammer and scroll.	Vig. Spread eagle upon branch of tree, canal scene on right; train of cars crossing bridge on left. HOPE BANK, Warren, R. I. 100	100 Female with rake, seated beside cornucopia.
1 Drummer, two men seated.	JACKSON BANK, Providence, R. I. 1 Large Portrait Gen. Jackson. 1	1 Blacksmith by anvil.

2 — View of battle field, throwing up entrenchments. | JACKSON BANK. Providence, R. I. 2 Same as ones 2 | 2 — Soldier erect holding flag beside cannon.

5 — Scene upon prairie, Indians hunting Buffalo. | JACKSON BANK. Providence, R. I. Vig. Small portrait of Jackson | 5 — Country scene, two children, oxen in foreground, man felling tree on right of them.

X — Portrait of Gen. Taylor. | Vig. Jackson and staff on horseback overlooking battle field of New Orleans. JACKSON BANK. Providence, R. I. Spread eagle. | 10 — Portrait of Gen. Scott.

C — C | Vig. View of Harbor of N. Y. ships and steamships sailing off city. JACKSON BANK, Providence, R. I. State Arms. | 100 — Portrait of President Jackson.

1 — State arms. — 1 | 1 Vig. Landing of the Pilgrims. 1 LANDHOLDERS B'K. Kingston, R. I. State arms. | Female figure on large figure 1.

TWO — Head of Washington. — TWO | 2 Female figure. 2 Figure of Justice. 2 LANDHOLDERS B'K, Kingston, R. I. State arms. | 2 — Female sitting, sheaf of wheat &c. — 2

3 — Female head. — 3 | 3 Vig. Train of cars; houses in back-ground. 3 LANDHOLDERS B'K, Kingston, R. I. State arms. | THREE — Head. — 3

V on FIVE | Female seated with agricultural implements; factories, shipping, etc. Indian girl in V. LANDHOLDERS' BANK. Kingston, R. I. | 5 — Washington.

10 — X — 10 | Pair of oxen with a man standing by an ancient plow. 10 LANDHOLDERS B'K. Kingston, R. I. | TEN — Female figure with cornucopia of fruits and flowers.

Mercury with wand and eagle. — 20 | Twenty on 20 Female portrait. LANDHOLDERS B'K. Kingston, R. I. | 20 — Benjamin Franklin

FIFTY — Grain, fruit, flowers, etc. — 50 | 50 Three females seated with pole, cap, scales, book, eagle, ship. Title of Bank | Fifty on 50 — Blacksmith seated with implements.

C — Men and boats. — 100 | Eagle on bale. 100 Title of Bank. | 100 — Female with sickle. — 100

1 — Hunter with rifle in hand, dog beside him. | LIBERTY BANK. Providence, R. I. 1 Vig. Large horse running in foreground, boys trying to stop him, one with cap in hand on right; factory in distance; one boy fallen down, one running, on left; dog and horses in distance. 1 | 1 — Portrait of child.

2 — TWO — 2 | LIBERTY BANK. Providence, R. I. Female erect with sword and shield. Horse alarmed at lightning, cows in distance. TWO TWO | 2 — Portrait of female.

2 — Female portrait. | LIBERTY BANK, Providence, R. I. Vig. Drover buying cattle of farmer; sheep and two men on left. | 2

5 — Full length sailor looking to right of note. | LIBERTY BANK, Providence, R. I. 5 Vig. Landing of Roger Williams on Slate Rock. 5 | 5 — Female portrait.

10 — Anchor leaning upon bales; ship in background. | Vig. Goddess of Liberty with pole and cap, shield; spread eagle on left. Portrait of Indian girl with bow and quiver. LIBERTY BANK, Providence, R. I. Spread eagle. | 10 — Portrait of Washington. — TEN

50 — ...le portrait. | Vig. Spread eagle upon shield, scroll in beak, "E pluribus unum" upon it; vessels on right; cars and city in distance on left. LIBERTY BANK, Providence, R. I. Spread eagle. | 50 — Indian seated resting right hand upon shield, with pole and cap, quiver on her shoulder.

100 | Vig. Surrender of Lord Cornwallis to George Washington. LIBERTY BANK, Providence, R. I. | 100 — Spread eagle upon shield looking to left of note.

1 — Two sailors on spar reefing. — ONE | LIME ROCK BANK, Providence, R. I. Sailor and Indian either side of State Arms surmounted by eagle. | 1 — Male portrait.

2 — Old man with son; female loading gun. | Girl's head. TITLE. Red 2. Man and boy plowing with two horses. | 2

Three females erect supporting figure 3. | Vig. sailor seated among bales, with spy glass in his left hand; ship in distance on left of vig. Title of Bank. | 3 — Wild horse upon the prairie fleeing from locomotive.

5 — 5 | Vig. Mechanic seated on ground, surrounded with wheels, tools, &c.; hay making in distance. 5 Title of Bank. Dog's head. | FIVE — Goddess of Liberty erect — FIVE

X — 10 | Vig. Female seated upon ground, corn, fruit, &c.; vessels upon stream in distance on left. Title of Bank. Spread eagle. | 10 — Mason at work, level in his hand.

20 — Female erect; spear in left hand; small globe at her feet. | Vig. Female seated between ornamental figures 2 and 0. Title of Bank. XX | 20 — Female seated, cornucopia, etc. — 20

50 | Steamship sailing out of harbor, steamboat, sail vessels, etc. LIME ROCK BANK, Providence, R. I. | 50 — Female portrait.

Female portrait | Title of Bank. Marine view; man-of war and other vessels under sail. | 100

1 | Female seated with rod on left of shield on which is Hope and anchor; train of cars on right, buildings on left. 1 MANUFACTURERS' BANK, Providence, R. I. | ONE — Female Portrait.

2 | Same as 1's. 2 MANUFACTURERS' BANK, Providence, R. I. | TWO — Female Portrait.

2 — Portrait of a girl. | Fig. 2 on shield; eagle on right and female with pole, cap, bales, etc. on left. TWO MANUFACTURERS' BANK, Providence, R. I. | 2 — Female portrait.

3 Female erect with hand on capstan.	THREE Female reclining with pole and cap in left hand; right arm resting on bale, cornucopia, &c.; steamboat on left; Sheep on right. Title of Bank.	3 Female erect holding aloft scales; sword in left hand.
5 Male seated in an arm chair. FIVE	FIVE Female seated with pen in right hand and left resting on globe, &c., building, locomotive and tender on left; vessel on right. Title of Bank.	5 Female with spear; globe and owl at her feet.
10	View of bridge, coach and four crossing it; buildings in background; canal scene in front. X MANUFACTURERS' BANK. Providence, R. I.	TEN Female reclining on edge boat; pedestal or column in rear. 10
TWENTY	Female seated with arm around column, pointing to ship on water, behind her sheaf, rake, &c. XX MANUFACTURERS' BANK, Providence, R. I.	20 View of bridge, &c., same as vig. 10's. XX
Rhode Island 50	Canal boat loaded with bales of cotton; factory and other buildings in distance; water falls; schooner, men, &c. FIFTY MANUFACTURERS' BANK. Providence, R. I.	50 Male with tablet, resting on cog wheel, &c.
100 Female. 100	Vig. Same as 50's. MANUFACTURERS' BANK, Providence, R. I.	100 Vulcan with sledge; right arm pointing.
500	Female seated pointing to [illegible]. 500 D MANUFACTURERS' BANK, Providence, R. I.	500
[illegible] statue; [illegible] around human figures. 1000	THOUSAND Train of cars. MANUFACTURERS' BANK, Providence, R. I.	1000 Vessels. 1000
ONE Sailor with flag.	Shipping; navy yard in background. MARINE BANK, Providence, R. I.	1 Anchor and bales.
Sailor with flag and female figure of Agriculture.	2 Whaling scene. MARINE BANK, Providence, R. I.	2 Female with glass looking seaward.

Three females representing Agriculture, Commerce and Manufactures.	Steamship; city in distance. MARINE BANK, Providence, R. I.	3 Female figure of Commerce.
5 Sailor leaning on capstan.	Launch of the Adriatic. MARINE BANK, Providence, R. I.	5 Head of Fulton. FIVE
RHODE ISLAND 10 X	MARINE BANK, Providence, R. I. Female, anchor and word "Hope" in a frame; on right, female, vessels, &c.; on left female and view of Niagara Falls. TEN DOLLARS	10 RHODE ISLAND X
50 Fancy female head.	Steamboat landing and railroad depot; city view, etc. MARINE BANK, Providence, R. I.	50 Eagle on a shield.
100 Sailor leaning on capstan.	Fame blowing trumpet; eagle, globe, etc. MARINE BANK, Providence, R. I.	100 Washington
Mechanic, anvil, cog-wheel, sledge, &c. ONE	Vig. Spread eagle American shield, &c. MECHANICS' BANK, Providence, R. I. State arms.	1 Male portrait
ONE	1 Two Eagles with State Arms in centre. 1 MECHANICS' BANK, Providence, R. I.	ONE
2 Male portrait	Female resting upon State Arms, schooner in distance on right, and buildings on left. Title of Bank Blacksmith's Arm.	2 Male portrait
TWO	2 Two Eagles with State Arms in centre. 2 MECHANICS' BANK, Providence, R. I.	TWO
FIVE	5 Woman, eagle resting on Globe on left. 5 MECHANICS' BANK, Providence, R. I. Cogwheel.	FIVE

FIVE	5 Two Eagles with State Arms in centre. 5 MECHANICS' BANK, Providence, R. I.	FIVE
10 Mechanics Arm and sledge.	Two females with State Arms between them, with eagle resting upon State Arms. Title of Bank	10 Portrait of Washington.
20 Male portrait	Mechanic with tools and pieces of machinery. MECHANICS' BANK, Providence, R. I. State Arms.	20 Portrait of Franklin.
FIFTY Female with wreath. FIFTY	50 Man and Horse. 50 MECHANICS' BANK, Providence, R. I.	FIFTY Full length female, Globe, Bale, &c. FIFTY
Words one hundred and figures 100 Male portrait.	Vig. Marine scene; shipping on left. MECHANICS' BK., Providence, R. I.	Words one hundred, and figures 100. Male portrait.
Female seated, with factory at work in distance. 500	500 D MECHANICS' BK., Providence, R. I.	500
1000	THOUSAND Locomotive and cars. Vig. In upper left corner of note, which is [illegible]—a classical scene. MECHANICS' BK., Providence, R. I.	1000 Ship. 1000
1 Female seated resting her arm on shield.	MECH'S & MAN. BK., Providence, R. I. Vig. Santa Claus in sleigh drawn by deer.	1 Female leaning on ornamental figure 1, sickle in her right hand
ONE Female erect writing in book resting on ornamental figure 1. ONE	1 Vig. Two females, one kneeling, the other standing; bales, ship, and steamer on right; fruit, tree, wagon, &c., on left. MECH'S & MAN. BK., Providence, R. I.	ONE Female erect with sickle beside ornamental fig. 1. ONE
2	Vig. Two females representing Justice and Liberty; ornamental figure 2 between them. MECH'S & MAN. BK., Providence, R. I.	2 Female seated with sheaf of grain.

Left	Centre	Right
TWO Female portrait in circular die. TWO	2 Vig. Female with compass and book; cog wheel and anvil on right; plough, yoke, screw, hammer, &c., on left. MECH'S & MAN. BK., Providence, R. I.	2 Female seated, child beside her, cornucopia at her feet. 2
Portrait of Webster. 3	MECH'S & MAN. BK., Providence, R. I. 3 Vig. Figure 3 resting on book; two females reclining, one with arm on book on right; one female seated on left with wand in hand; factory in distance behind her.	3 3
5	Vig. Figure 5, Justice standing behind it holding scales; on either side of the 5 are two female figures, locomotive and factory on right of vig.; ships, bales, &c., on left. Title of Bank. Dog's head.	5 Head of boy
5 Female seated in large V. FIVE	5 Vig. Large 5 with five figures around it. 5 MECH'S & MAN. BK. Providence, R. I.	5 Female with sheaf of grain seated in large figure 5. FIVE
X Bales, cogwheels, &c. X	MECH'S & MAN. BK. Providence, R. I. Vig. Large Indian with bow, arrow, and quiver, reclining upon shield; three deers, woods, and water, on his right; deer, Indians in canoe, and soaring eagle on his left.	10 Female portrait.
10 Farmer sowing grain. TEN	Vig. Jupiter erect, with sickle, shield, sheaf, bags, bales and barrels; ship and steamer in distance, on right; coaches, factory, &c., on left. On right of vig., divided by a small space, is a scene on canal. MECH. & MAN. BK. Providence, R. I.	10 Ship and other vessels sailing by a light-house. TEN
XX Portrait of female.	MECH. & MAN. BK. Providence, R. I. Vig. Female kneeling beside globe; quadrant, compass, paper, &c., before her; sailing vessel and steamship on her right.	20 Bales, anchor, &c.
Steamer. XX Locomotive and cars.	Vig. Three females representing liberty, justice and hunting; ship on right; eagle on left. 20 MECH. & MAN. BK. Providence, R. I.	XX Female erect, with ball under right arm; steel in left hand.
50 50	MECH. & MAN. BK. Providence, R. I. Vig. Scene in a boiler yard; men working on boilers in background; in foreground, man seated with tools in his hands, leaning on piece of steamer's pipe.	50 Female portrait.
50 Steamer and schooner.	Vig. Harvesting scene; loading wagon with hay; farm-house in view. 50 MECH. & MAN. BK. Providence, R. I.	L Female kneeling, with sword and balance.

Left	Centre	Right
100 Ornamental fountain.	MECH. & MAN. BK. Providence, R. I. Vig. Female seated with pole and liberty cap; eagle behind her; globe, ship, and steamship on left.	100 100
100 Spread eagle. 100	C Vig. Four horses drawing chariot through the air, in which is erect figure with torch. 100 MECH. & MAN. BK., Providence, R. I.	C Portrait of Washington. C
500	Vig. Indian paddling canoe, forests in the background. MECH. & MAN. BK., Providence, R. I. D D	500 Female with sword and scales.
1000	MFG. AND MANUFACTURERS' BK. Providence, R. I. Spread eagle upon a rock overlooking the sea, on which a ship is dimly seen.	1000 Indian maiden seated.
1 Portrait of female.	MERCANTILE BANK Providence, R. I. Figure of sailor; ships in distance.	1 Female figure.
2 Figure of mechanic.	MERCANTILE BANK Providence, R. I. Train of cars, male and female figures.	2
3 Female figure.	Scene in blacksmith's shop; man shoeing horse, &c. MERCANTILE BANK Providence, R. I.	3 Male figure.
5 Sailor leaning on capstan.	Steamship, sailing vessels, &c. MERCANTILE BANK Providence, R. I.	5 Female reaper with bundle of grain.
10	Rural scene—cows; church in the distance. MERCANTILE BANK Providence, R. I.	10 Portrait of female.
20 Anchor, boxes, barrels, &c.	Ships, &c., sailing. MERCANTILE BANK Providence, R. I.	20 Train of cars, village in the distance.

Left	Centre	Right
50 Jupiter (God of Thunder) in his chariot.	MERCANTILE BANK Providence, R. I.	50 Man with arms full of corn stalks.
Portrait of Columbus.	MERCANTILE BANK Providence, R. I. Head of Franklin; on either side cupid. Head of Washington; on either side cupid. 100	100
500 Portrait of Webster.	MERCANTILE BANK Providence, R. I. Figures of mechanic and sailor, bale of goods; ship in distance.	500 Portrait of Washington.
1 RHODE ISLAND 1	1 One Dollar. 1 MERCHANTS' BK., Newport, R. I. 1	1 ONE 1
	1 View of paper mill and eagle. MERCHANTS' BK., Newport, R. I.	Cupid supporting figure 1.
1 Sailor and capstan.	Female reclining and supporting figure 1; train of cars on right; steamboat on left. MERCHANTS' BK. Newport, R. I.	1 Female seated on safe, pole, liberty cap and figure 1.
	2 View of a stone mill. MERCHANTS' BK., Newport, R. I.	
2 RHODE ISLAND 2	Two Dollars. 2 MERCHANTS' BK., Newport, R. I. 2	TWO
TWO Indian with bow and arrow.	Farmers washing sheep. MERCHANTS' BK., Newport, R. I.	2 Two females
3 RHODE ISLAND 3	3 Three Dollars. 3 MERCHANTS' BK., Newport, R. I. 3	THREE

3 — Female with anchor.
Three male figures, and three gold dollars; scythe and sheaf of grain on left; ship and factory on right.
MERCHANTS' BK., Newport, R. I.
3 — Female giving eagle drink.

V RHODE ISLAND V
5 Five dollars. V
MERCHANTS' BANK Newport, R. I.
V
FIVE

RHODE ISLAND
5 5 View of State House.
MERCHANTS' BANK Newport, R. I.
FIVE

5 — Female portrait. — FIVE
Female reclining with wand in right hand; steamship on right, and locomotive and bridge on left.
MERCHANTS' BANK Newport, R. I.
5 — Group of females supporting figure 5.

X RHODE ISLAND X
10 Words ten dollars. X
MERCHANTS' BANK Newport, R. I.
X
TEN

10 — Tritons supporting cornucopia. — Steamship.
Female with spear reclining on state arms, sheaf of grain, safe, plow, and rake; cars in distance on right; steamship on left.
MERCHANTS' BANK Newport, R. I.
10 — Spread eagle — TEN

TWENTY — Two Indians.
MERCHANTS' BANK Newport, R. I.
TWENTY
Twenty Twenty
Squaw and female. — 20

50 — Four females globe, &c.
View of steamship and ship.
MERCHANTS' BANK Newport, R. I.
50 — Locomotive.

RHODE ISLAND
50 Title of Bank. 50
Med. head of Com. Perry.
FIFTY

100
Train of cars.
MERCHANTS' BANK Newport, R. I.
Ship.
Female portrait. — 100

1 — Portrait of Franklin. — ONE
Large ship at sea under sail; ship in distance on left.
MERCHANTS' B'K, Providence, R. I.
State Arms.
1 — Sailor erect holding spy glass in left hand, hat in right.

1 — On die with words ONE. — Bust of Female with handkerchief on her head.
Ocean view, ships, &c.
MERCHANTS' B'K, Providence, R. I.
ONE DOLLAR on ornamental die
1 — On die with words ONE. — Female, plow, barrow, &c.

2 — Portrait of Washington. — TWO
Spread Eagle on limb of tree; cars crossing bridge over canal on left; canal scene on right.
MERCHANTS' B'K, Providence, R. I.
State Arms.
2 — Female erect representing Justice with scales and sword.

2 — On die with words TWO.
MERCHANTS' B'K, Providence, R. I.
Shipping.
Bust of Female in green die. Bust of female in green die.
TWO DOLLARS.
2 — On die with words TWO.

Vulcan erect sledge over right shoulder, left hand on cog wheel. — 3
Indian and female seated; miniature view of city between them, over which is globe with spread eagle upon it.
Title of Bank
3 — Portrait of Indian female holding bow in right hand.

Three females upon bales, one erect with hand upon anchor stock — FIVE
Vig. A number of ships opposite a city.
MERCHANTS' B'K, Providence, R. I.
5 — Portrait of female.

Sailor standing erect holding staff in flag; at his feet a female reclining against a cornucopia, bale, anchor, &c.
Vig. Female seated resting left arm on shield representing state arms; ship and steamship on right; ships in extreme distance on left.
MERCHANTS' B'K, Providence, R. I.
10 — Indian female seated, holding shield, liberty pole and cap with right hand.

Female supporting 50, holding sickle in right hand. — 50
50 Portrait of Henry Clay. 50
MERCHANTS BANK, Providence, R. I.
State arms.
Female seated supporting 50. — 50

ONE HUNDRED
100 Female seated 100
ships on right; schooner in extreme distance on left.
MERCHANTS' B'K, Providence, R. I.
Ship.
ONE HUNDRED

500
Vig. Large ship under full sail in the foreground; sailing vessel on right; steamship and vessel in extreme distance, on left. Portrait of Franklin
MERCHANT'S BK., Providence, R. I.
500

1000
MERCHANT'S BK., Providence, R. I.
Vig. Female seated, with right arm resting on cog wheel; steamship on right; locomotive and depot on left. 1000
ONE THOUSAND

ONE — 1
Farmer plowing with two horses; man sowing, train of cars in background. 1
NARRAGANSETT BK Wickford, R. I.
1 — Indian erect with bow and spear.

2
Female on right of a shield on which is an anchor, cupid on left, and ships; on right in background train of cars. 2
Title of Bank
2 — Same as one.

Medallion head. — 3
Spread Eagle on shield, buildings and vessels in distance. 3
Title of Bank.
THREE — Same as one.

FIVE
5 Letter V on shield; Indian seated on right, with gun in hand; female on left erect, with spear. 5
Title of Bank.
Hope, anchor and shield.
FIVE

10
10 Female seated holding eagle and twig; vessels in distance. X
Title of Bank.
Head of Indian.
TEN — Full length Female.

TWENTY
20 Two females seated with wand, cornucopia, &c., on left, wharf scene, vessels, bbls., &c., on right, steamboat; sails of a vessel seen at their back. 20
Title of Bank.
Clasped hands
XX — Steamboat — 20

FIFTY
L Female seated receiving horn of plenty from two floating figures; train of cars, bbls, &c. on right; on left, griffin on safe, vessels, &c. L
Title of Bank.
Train of cars.
50 — Steamboat. — 50

1 — Female reclining on ornamental pillar.
Spread eagle, overlooking sea; ships on right, and ships on left.
NATIONAL BANK, Providence, R. I.
State Arms.
1 — Female Indian with shield, liberty pole, cap, &c.

1 — Female gathering flowers
Vig. Spread eagle with ships on right and left.
NATIONAL BANK, Providence, R. I.
State Arms.
1 — Sailor with spy glass.

Left	Centre	Right
ONE Spread eagle, American shield, &c. 1	NATIONAL BANK Providence, R. I. Vig. Naval engagement. State Arms.	1 Spread eagle, American shield, &c. ONE
1 Clay.	1 Eagle on shield; oxen on right; town on left. NATIONAL BANK, Providence, R. I. ONE	1 Washington
2 Spread eagle overlooking sea, with ships on left.	Vig. Large ship, with vessel on right, steamship on left in distance. NATIONAL BANK Providence, R. I. State arms.	2 Spread eagle, American shield, ship on right.
Male portrait	NATIONAL BANK, Providence, R. I. 2 Vig. Female and safe on left; locomotive and safe on right. 2 Dog, safe and key.	Portrait of Franklin.
2 Female seated on safe with sword and scales.	NATIONAL BANK, Providence, R. I. 2 Three officers; one on horse, cannon, etc. 2	2 Eagle and shield.
2 Spread eagle, shield, &c.	NATIONAL BANK, Providence, R. I. Vig. Two females; ships on right; also, female with wand in right hand; American shield and public buildings on left.	2 Spread eagle and shield.
THREE	3 Vig. Large spread eagle, 3 on a rock, overlooking the sea. NATIONAL BANK, Providence, R. I. State Arms.	THREE
FIVE	5 Vig. Large spread eagle 5 on a rock, overlooking the sea. NATIONAL BANK, Providence, R. I. State Arms.	FIVE
5 Indian upon rock, with bow in left hand.	5 Vig. Steam-boat and sail-boat on right; ship and row-boat on left. 5 NATIONAL BANK, Providence, R. I.	Indian with left hand holding on tree, overlooking precipice. 5
10 Male portrait.	(New Plate.) Vig. Large spread eagle standing on anchor; cog-wheel and vessels on right; vessels on left. NATIONAL BANK, Providence, R. I. State Arms.	10 Portrait of Washington.

Left	Centre	Right
Soldier erect with flag in right hand. FIFTY	Male Portrait. NATIONAL BANK, Providence, R. I.	50
100	Female seated holding shield; U. S. Capitol in distance. Washington. NATIONAL BANK, Providence, R. I.	100
500 Justice.	NATIONAL BANK, Providence, R. I. Spread Eagle on shield—Letter D on each side of vig.	500 Goddess of Liberty.
Female, shield, liberty pole and cap, starry drapery across her lap; U. S. Capitol in rear. 1000	Portrait of Washington. NATIONAL BANK, Providence, R. I.	1000
1 Head of Washington.	Female. 1 Female. NEW ENGLAND COMMERCIAL BANK Newport, R. I.	1 Head of Franklin.
2 Head.	Female. 2 Female. Title of Bank.	2 Head.
3 Washington full length.	Female head and bust. 3 Female head and bust. Title of Bank.	3 Vulcan full length.
Eagle resting on United States shield and an anchor. FIVE	A large V, with female figure and child. Title of Bank.	5 Female figure and basket.
Male figure seated on machinery; cars at distance. TEN	X Title of Bank.	10 Male figure with sheaf in hand.
FIFTY Female figure standing globe in her right hand, flowers at her right. FIFTY	50 Man and horse. 50 Title of Bank	FIFTY Female figure with wreath of flowers in right hand. FIFTY

Left	Centre	Right
Figures 100 and words one hundred. Head of Harrison.	Wagon with horses and goods; ship at a distance. Title of Bank.	Figures 100 and words one hundred. Head and bust of male.
ONE	1 Two farmers seated at lunch; female pouring drink; dog; man reaping on left. N. E. PACIFIC BANK N. Providence, R. I. State arms.	1 Female erect holding aloft sabre.
TWO	2 Female seated on left of frame; representing Agriculture and Manufacture; train of cars and steamboat. 2 N. E. PACIFIC BANK N. Providence, R. I. State arms.	2 Indian female with bow, &c. 2
THREE	3 Male and females, six in all, cows, &c.; house on left, vessels on right. 3 N. E. PACIFIC BANK N. Providence, R. I. State arms.	3 Female portrait. 3
FIVE	Spread eagle on shield; buildings and vessels in distance. V, female, and cupid. N. E. PACIFIC BANK N. Providence, R. I.	5 Girl with basket of flowers.
TEN	Vulcan seated with sledge, anvil, &c.; cogs, buildings, &c. in distance. X N. E. PACIFIC BANK N. Providence, R. I.	10 Man with sheaf on his knee.
20 Female with spear.	2 Female. 0 N. E. PACIFIC BANK N. Providence, R. I. XX	20 Female seated. 20
50 Female erect with spear and shield.	Male and female seated. N. E. PACIFIC BANK N. Providence, R. I. 50	50 Cupid in a sail boat. 50
100 Vulcan seated with sledge.	Spread eagle on limb of tree; canal scene on right; train of cars on left. N. E. PACIFIC BANK N. Providence, R. I. 100	100 Female seated with rake.
Female seated pointing to farming scene. 500	500 D N. E. PACIFIC BANK N. Providence, R. I.	500

ONE
Med. head.
ONE
1 Vig. View of factory, river, &c.; female Indian and canoe; small deer on right. 1
NEWPORT BANK, Newport, R. I.
State arms.
1
1

TWO
Med. head.
TWO
2 Vig. 2; on either side a female, one with liberty pole and cap, the other with sword and balances; railroad cars and bridge and view of view of city in distance. 2
Title of Bank.
State arms.
2
2

5
Med. head with five across it.
V
Vig. Steamship and other vessels.
NEWPORT BANK, Newport, R. I.
State arms.
FIVE
View of Ocean House, Newport.
FIVE

10
Med. head.
TEN
Vig. Large spread eagle upon shield; United States Capitol on right; steam ship, &c., on left.
NEWPORT BANK, Newport, R. I.
State Arms.
Deer, &c.
10
Buffalo.

50
Med. head.
50
Vig. View of sea and rising sun, vessels, &c.; cupid on right; female with sword and balances on left.
NEWPORT BANK, Newport, R. I.
State arms.
FIFTY
Female in ornamental figure, with shield in left hand, and spear in right hand.
50

100
Med. head.
100
View of city in distance, shipping, &c.
NEWPORT BANK, Newport, R. I.
State arms.
100
Spread eagle
100

ONE
State Arms; on either side a female, one with scales and the other with shield.
1
Female reclining on State Arms; Neptune in chariot drawn by sea monsters.
EXCHANGE BANK, Newport, R. I.
1
Two figures, one holding wand.
1

TWO
Female seated; ship on left.
TWO
2 Female with wand; ship in distance on left. 2
EXCHANGE BANK, Newport, R. I.
Indian with bow and arrow.
TWO

Female seated, one looking at sea with cupids seated upon her lap.
3
3 Vig. Steamboat. 3
EXCHANGE BANK, Newport, R. I.
THREE
Female seated with balls, eagle on left and miniature portrait of Washington.
3

FIVE
Female, sheaf of wheat and sickle.
5
5 Female, eagle and miniature of Washington. 5
EXCHANGE BANK, Newport, R. I.
FIVE
Flying female with wand.
5

10
Cupid with scroll figures 10 engraved
10
Ships. Bust of Com. Perry. Female sitting, on right State Arms upon which is engraved an eagle and shield; ship &c., on left.
Title of Bank.
X
Female State Arms on right, upon which is mounted an eagle.
10

TWENTY
XX Neptune and female riding in sea car. XX
EXCHANGE BANK, Newport, R. I.
20
Cupid and basket of flowers.
20

50
Eagle feeding her young.
50
Female seated with wand in right hand. Same as on left.
Indian and native American seated, between them the arms of one of the States, upon which is mounted an eagle.
Title of Bank.
50
Eagle feeding her young.
50

1
Vig. Two Indians on horseback, train of cars in distance. American silver dollar.
NIANTIC BANK, Westerly, R. I.
1
1
Portrait of Webster.
ONE

Figure 2 with word two across it.
Female seated holding ornamental figure 2.
Vig. Drover and cattle.
NIANTIC BANK, Westerly, R. I.
Clasped hands.
2
Farmer sharpening scythe.

Ship under full sail.
Figure 3 with word three running across it.
Vig. Two females seated, canal boat and factory on right; bales, steamboat and sloop on left.
NIANTIC BANK, Westerly, R. I.
State arms.
III
Large fig. 3 in centre of which is lighthouse, female seated in the 3.

V
Indian queen seated with bow and arrows.
Vig. Indians and squaw in a canoe.
NIANTIC BANK, Westerly, R. I.
Moonlight scene.
5
Farmer carrying basket of corn.

10
Ornamental X with figs. 10 and lighthouse on its left; sailor with glass in hand on right.
NIANTIC BANK, Westerly, R. I.
Vig. Goddess of liberty and justice reclining on right of shield; spread eagle; ship in distance on left.
Dog.
10
Female erect, light house above her.

Figures 50 upheld by three full length figures representing commerce, agriculture and mechanics.
NIANTIC BANK, Westerly, R. I.
L Vig. Portrait of Henry Clay. L
FIFTY
50
Indian hunter upon brink of precipice looking down upon ship at sea.

ONE
Mercury.
Female and State Arms; ships, etc., in distance.
NORTHERN BANK, Providence, R. I.
1
Female with sheaf, cow and sickle

TWO
Female figure of Mechanics and the Fine Arts.
Spread eagle on shield.
NORTHERN BANK, Providence, R. I.
2
Farmer carrying stalks.

THREE
Justice.
Steamship and other vessels.
NORTHERN BANK, Providence, R. I.
3
Female feeding fowls.

FIVE
V
Dr. Kane and party in the Arctic Regions.
NORTHERN BANK, Providence, R. I.
5
Milkmaid, cow and calf.

X
Hen and chickens.
NORTHERN BANK, Providence, R. I.
Puritans at prayer surprised by Indians.
10

50
Beaver.
Mowing—farmer, two horses, etc.
NORTHERN BANK, Providence, R. I.
50
Dog and game.

100
Deer.
A party of surveyors.
NORTHERN BANK, Providence, R. I.
100
Men building railroad.

500
Bull.
Horses at trough, and girl filling basket.
NORTHERN BANK, Providence, R. I.
500
Indian.

1000
Indian on horseback.
Signing the first Constitution on board the Mayflower.
NORTHERN BANK, Providence, R. I.
1000
Dog and chest.

ONE
Schooner.
ONE
1 Female seated representing Agriculture and Commerce; train of cars, steamboats, &c., in distance. 1
NORTH KINGSTON BANK, Wickford, R. I.
Female, eagle, &c.
ONE
Female.
ONE

TWO
Vessels, &c.
TWO
2 Two females seated; wharf scene and vessel on left; steamboat on right, and ship at the female's back. 2
NORTH KINGSTON BANK, Wickford, R. I.
Arm, hammer, &c.
TWO
Female seated with shield on which is anchor.
TWO

Left end	Centre	Right end
THREE Vessels, and men in row-boats. 3	3 Male and female in air drawn by two sea horses; ships and steam-boat in distance. 3 NORTH KINGSTON BANK, Wickford, R. I. Schooner.	THREE Female seated with cornucopia, book, eagle and portrait of Washington. 3
5 Train of cars.	Sea god and goddess in chariot drawn by sea horses and attended by followers. NORTH KINGSTON BANK, Wickford, R. I. State Arms.	5 Cattle.
10 Female with sickle, eagle, etc. 10	X Female seated by shield on which is eagle, etc. 10 Title of Bank. Head of Dog.	TEN Ten cents lapped. TEN
50 Pelican and its young. 50	Indian; eagle on shield; male figure on right. Female with wand etc., on either side of vignette. Title of Bank. Steamboat.	50 Pelican and its young. 50
100 Female with torch, eagle, Washington, &c. 100	100 Washington. 100 Title of Bank Eagle.	100 Vessels. 100
ONE Female leaning on altar. ONE	1 Indian erect with gun, dog, and body of a deer; Indian and forest scene on left. 1 NORTH PROVIDENCE BANK, N. Providence, R. I. Female portrait.	ONE Female holding key and eagle. ONE
Female with sheaf and sickle. 2	Three females seated; eagle on left, vessel on right. 2 N. PROVIDENCE BK. N. Providence, R. I. Cars.	TWO Canal scene buildings in distance. TWO
FIVE	5 A naval engagement, men in row-boat, &c. 5 N. PROVIDENCE BK. N. Providence, R. I. Beaver.	5 Waterfall, building, &c. 5
10 and X across. Female seated, at her side sword, &c.; ship in distance.	Steamer, vessels, row-boat, buildings, hills, &c. N. PROVIDENCE BK. N. Providence, R. I. Hope, shield, and anchor.	X Female seated with sickle, surrounded by grain.
20 XX 20	20 Female seated with scales, sheaf, bales, &c.; on left men plowing; on right ship. 20 N. PROVIDENCE BK. N. Providence, R. I.	TWENEY

Left end	Centre	Right end
50 Female erect; steamboat in distance. 50	FIFTY DOLLARS 50 N. PROVIDENCE BK. N. Providence, R. I.	FIFTY
Words one hundred and figures 100. Portrait of Harrison.	Wharf scene, loading wagon with bale, men, houses, horses, shipping, &c. N. PROVIDENCE BK. N. Providence, R. I.	Same as on left. Male portrait.
500	Indian paddling in a canoe. 500 N. PROVIDENCE BK. N. Providence, R. I. D D	500 Female with scales and sword.
1000	Spread eagle on promontory; ship on ocean in distance. 1000 N. PROVIDENCE BK. N. Providence, R. I.	1000 Indian female with bow and arrows.
1	Vig. State arms; Indian on left, man with axe in left hand on right. 1 PAWTUXET B NK, Providence, 1 I. Plough and sheaf.	1 Bull's head.
2	Vig. Spread eagle behind shield, female on left, holding portrait of Washington, staff and cap; cars in distance; steamship in distance on right. 2 Title of Bank. State arms.	TWO Large ship under sail at sea; vessel on either side.
THREE Farmer erect with sheaf under left arm, female with pail at his feet. 3	Vig. Ornamental figure 3, medallion head on either side. PAWTUXET BANK, Providence, R. I. State arms.	3 Portrait of Indian girl with bow and arrow in hands.
Steamboat and three sailing vessels; city in distance. FIVE	Vig. Female with sheaf of grain seated in large ornamental V. PAWTUXET BANK, Providence, R. I. State arms.	5 Sailor erect, leaning upon binnacle, spy glass in left hand.
10 Head of girl with long hair. TEN	Female seated between ornamental 1 and 0. PAWTUXET BANK, Providence, R. I.	10 Female head TEN
10 X 10	Yoke of oxen, male figure stand beside them. Large ornamental 10. PAWTUXET BANK, Providence, R. I.	TEN Female erect holding horn of plenty in left hand, grain in right.

Left end	Centre	Right end
20 Female seated, back on two logs, left hand resting upon it.	XX Spread eagle standing upon rock. XX PAWTUXET BANK, Providence, R. I.	20 Large steamship under sail.
50 Female erect resting left hand upon shield, spear in right hand.	Vulcan seated beside female holding cake on left, cornucopia between them. PAWTUXET BANK Providence, R. I. 50	50 Cupid in sailboat. 50
100 Vulcan seated with sledge in left hand.	Spread eagle upon limb of tree; cars on left crossing canal, canal scene on right. PAWTUXET BANK, Providence, R. I. 100	100 Female seated with sickle in right hand, grain in left.
Washington. 1	State Arms with females. PEOPLES BANK, N. Providence, R. I.	1 ONE Female with sickle, wheat, &c.
Male head. TWO 2	Two females, wheat, sickles &c.; ship in background. PEOPLES BANK, N. Providence, R. I.	2 Female, eagle and shield.
5 Eagle and female.	Three females. PEOPLES BANK, N. Providence, R. I. The denomination across the bill in red letters.	5 Locomotive.
X F. Pierce. 10	State Arms. PEOPLES BANK, N. Providence, R. I.	10 Telegraph wires, cattle, &c.
20 Female with spear.	2 Female. 0 PEOPLES BANK, N. Providence, R. I. XX	20 20
50 Female with spear, &c.	Female figure with rake. Male figure with scroll in right hand. PEOPLES BANK, N. Providence, R. I. 50	50 Cupid in sailboat. 50
100 Male figure with anvil and staff.	Eagle on branch of tree, train of cars and canal in distance. PEOPLES BANK, N. Providence, R. I. 100	100 Female, rake, &c.

Left	Centre	Right
Indian in canoe. 500	500 PEOPLES BANK, N. Providence, R. I. D D	500 Female, scales, sword, &c.
Single ship in back ground. 1000	1000 PEOPLES BANK, N. Providence, R. I. M M	1000 Female Indian with bow & arrow.
1	Two females sitting by Coat of Arms; steam engine, &c. PEOPLES' EXCHANGE BANK, Wakefield, R. I. ONE	1
2	Three male figures, cart and horse, farming scene. 2 on right. PEOPLES' EXCHANGE BANK, Wakefield, R. I. TWO	2 2 Female
3	Three male figures sitting, farming scene. fig. 3 on right. PEOPLES' EXCHANGE BANK, Wakefield, R. I. THREE	3 Three horses, &c. 3
5	Female sitting: steamboat, rail car, steamer, &c. PEOPLES' EXCHANGE BANK, Wakefield, R. I. FIVE	5 2 females, &c. 5
10	Female figure with pail and cows, &c. PEOPLE'S EXCHANGE BANK, Wakefield, R. I.	10 TEN
20	Four figures, load of hay, team and farming implements. PEOPLES' EXCHANGE BANK, Wakefield, R. I. TWENTY TWENTY	20 Female figure standing.
50	Agricultural Cattle scene, team, carts, railway, cars, &c. PEOPLES' EXCHANGE BANK, Wakefield, R. I. TWENTY	50 Hull Stack.
100 Fig. of Male with bag of dollars.	Three men washing sheep, village, &c. PEOPLES' EXCHANGE BANK, Wakefield, R. I.	100 Girls with rake, making hay.

Left	Centre	Right
1 Female seated; cars in distance.	Vig. Spread eagle upon rock, overlooking the large ship on either side. 1 PHENIX BANK, Providence, R. I. Phenix.	1 Female seated; eye glass in hands.
2	Vig. Three females, one on right with sword; one on left with cornucopia; ships in distance on right. 2 PHENIX BANK, Providence, R. I. Phenix	2 Vulcan with sledge on right shoulder.
3 Female seated, with pen and scroll.	Vig. Female reclining on bale; ships on right, under sail. 3 PHENIX BANK, Providence, R. I. Phenix.	3 Portrait of Henry Clay.
FIVE Female with sheaf of grain in left arm. 5	Vig. Spread eagle upon shield. 5 PHENIX BANK, Providence, R. I. Phenix.	5 Goddess of Liberty, with shield, liberty pole and cap.
X Portrait of Washington 10	10 Vig. Female seated, liberty pole and and cap on her lap; her right hand upon shield; her left upon cornucopia; spread eagle on right. PHENIX BANK, Providence, R. I. Phenix.	10 Female seated, reclining on bale.
20	State Arms, female with shield on right; and cars crossing bridge, plow, corn, grain, scenery, &c., on left. Title of Bank. Steamboat.	20 Portrait of Fillmore.
50 Portrait of Gen. Taylor. FIFTY	Female seated, arm resting on bale; farm scene, loading hay, locomotive and cars in distance on right. Title of Bank. Locomotive and Tender.	50 Female bearing sheaf of grain
C	Female leaning upon anchor, resting against bale, of Franklin, steamer and ship. &c. boat in distance on right; city with ships at wharfs in distance on left. Title of Bank. Spread eagle	100 Portrait of Franklin.
Large ship under sail at sea. D	PHENIX BANK, Providence, R. I. Figures 500 on Circular shield. Head of Female.	Sailor seated on bale, spy glass in right hand 500
1 Portrait of Washington. 1	Female with sheaf of wheat; right hand uplifted, with straw of wheat therein; plow, female, locomotive, &c. PHENIX BANK, Westerly, R. I. Phenix with spread wings	1 Square 1

Left	Centre	Right
2 Portrait of J. Q. Adams. 2	Steamship, with a sail vessel before and aft. PHENIX BANK, Westerly, R. I. Phenix with spread wings.	2 Female with paper and dividers. 2
3 Female. V	Female figure and Indian chief; the former holding stems of grain in one hand, and sickle in the other; both reclining against a globe, on which stands a spread eagle. PHENIX BANK, Westerly, R. I. Phenix with spread wings	3 Portrait.
5 Portrait of Henry Clay. 5	Male and female figure with machinery; ship on right, and locomotive and train on left. PHENIX BANK, Westerly, R. I. Phenix with spread wings	5 Female head V
10 Indian Princess with implements of war.	Spread eagle holding the American flag in its talons. PHENIX BANK, Westerly, R. I. Phenix with spread wings	10 Female in a sitting posture, holding scales over eagle, one of whose wings are extended over American Flag.
20 TWENTY	Female in a sitting posture, with one arm thrown over an eagle, which stands on a segment of the globe, labelled "America." PHENIX BANK, Westerly, R. I. Phenix with spread wings	20
Female with sheaf of grain, whose feet rest on the figures below, 50	Three females in a group; one holding scales; ships on the right. PHENIX BANK, Westerly, R. I. Phenix with spread wings	50
1 ONE	PHENIX VILLAGE BANK, Phenix, R. I. View of bridge, water falls, houses and trees. Male portrait ONE	1 1 ONE
2 TWO	Title of Bank. Vig. Same as ones.	2 2 2
3 THREE	Title of Bank. Vig. Same as ones.	3 THREE 3 THREE
FIVE	5 Title of Bank. Man tending large machinery. 5	5 Male portrait

X TEN	Man at work in an iron mill. X Title of Bank.	10, X and Ten. Male portrait.
50 on red die	Title of Bank. View of factories, cars, water, hills, etc.	50 on red die
100 and C on red die.	Title of Bank. Male portrait	100 and C on red die.
Shield, female, starry drapery, liberty pole and cap.	Eagle. Indian viewing the improvement of the white man. 1 PRODUCERS' BANK, Woonsocket, R. I. Female bathing.	1 Mechanic's arm, anvil and hammer.
TWO Franklin. TWO	Liberty, justice and truth, eagle at top of shield; bridge and cars on right; ship on left. PRODUCERS' BANK, Woonsocket, R. I. Dog, safe and key.	TWO Female with rake. TWO
3 Washington.	PRODUCERS' BANK, Woonsocket, R. I. Two horses and train of cars. Farming implements.	3 Female.
5 Locomotive. FIVE	Horse on either side of shield; eagle at top; steamboat on right; factories, canal scene and cars crossing bridge, on left. PRODUCERS' BANK, Woonsocket, R. I.	5 Drove of cattle.
X [illegible] 10	Female seated be- [illegible] PRODUCERS' BANK, Woonsocket, R. I. Machinery.	10 Two female [illegible] bow, and arrows.
Female with liberty pole and cap. TWENTY	20 Man ploughing with oxen; little girl on right. PRODUCERS' BANK, Woonsocket, R. I	20 Female, grain, and sickle.
Female with shield; right hand holds [illegible] head, which rests on pillar.	50 Spread eagle on American shield. PRODUCERS' BANK, Woonsocket, R. I.	50 Washington.

100 Man seated instructing a little child.	PRODUCERS' BANK, Woonsocket, R. I. C	100 Med. head. 100
500 Artist at work.	Washington. Two females on either side of a beehive. PRODUCERS' BANK, Woonsocket, R. I. Machinery.	500 Portrait of Mrs. Washington.
ONE 1 ONE	Vig. Man seated on rock; ship under full sail on right. PROVIDENCE BANK Providence, R. I State arms.	1 State arms; Indian on left; female on right. 1
1 Female sitting on bale of goods, with [illegible] in left hand.	Vig. State arms supported by female reclining on ground, with left arm resting on bale of goods; factory and cars on right in distance, on left steamers and ships in distance. PROVIDENCE BANK Providence, R. I.	ONE Female seated, holding roll of goods.
Full length figure of female standing in large ornamental 2 which reaches from bottom to top of bill.	Vig. State arms, with female seated on left holding liberty pole and cap; ship in distance; cogwheel and [illegible] on right. PROVIDENCE BANK Providence, R. I. State Arms.	TWO 2 TWO
Large ornamental figure 2 with female seated within, [illegible] behind her.	PROVIDENCE BANK Providence, R. I. Vig. same as second description of ones.	2 Female seated on bale of goods, holding figure 2 in right hand; cornucopia in left; building and water in distance.
III 3 III	Vig. Female and state arms. PROVIDENCE BANK Providence, R. I. 3	Full length figure of female in ornamental fig. 3.
3 Female seated on bale of goods with figure 3 in right hand; cornucopia in left; building and water in distance.	PROVIDENCE BANK Providence, R. I. Vig. same as second description of ones.	THREE Lighthouse and rocks seen through large ornamental 3; female seated reclining on rocks in front of 3.
5 Female with horn of plenty. FIVE	Vig. Ornamental figure 5, supported by female on right; cupid and sickle; cupid in centre of five; female on left with sword and balances; cupid with cornucopia. 5 Title of Bank. State Arms.	FIVE Female erect with sword and balances. FIVE
FIVE Large ornamental V; female seen through V; females on right and left; factory in distance. 5	PROVIDENCE BANK Providence, R. I. Vig. Female seated on bale of goods holding state arms; bridge and train of cars in distance; on left steamer and ship in distance.	FIVE Shield surmounted by two cupids; in centre of shield figure 5 and V.

10 Indian female with bow in hand, quiver on back. TEN	Vig. Cupid holding $10 gold piece; chest, money bag and keg on right; on left horn of plenty, barrels, &c. PROVIDENCE B'K, Providence, R. I. State Arms.	TEN Female erect with helmet on head, spear in hand; left arm resting on shield, which rests on column. TEN
10	PROVIDENCE BANK Providence, R. I. Vig. same as five above, with words "ten dollars" on right and left of vignette. 10	10
X X Female seated on rock writing; child with wreath at feet.	PROVIDENCE B'K, Providence, R. I. Words ten dollars on word ten and fig. 10.	10 State Arms.
Female seated resting on shield, key in left hand, cornucopia in right. 20 Spread eagle.	XX Vig. Female with XX right arm resting on stone column, in left hand bunch of wheat; on left packages of goods, sloop, and rocks in distance on right. Title of Bank. Spread eagle.	Female seated, pole and cap, ship in distance on left. 20 Spread eagle.
TWENTY Female resting on pillar with torch in hand; left resting on mortar.	PROVIDENCE B'K, Providence, R. I. Words twenty dollars on words twenty and figure 20.	20 Female head.
FIFTY	Vig. State arms surmounted by wreath; female on right with spear and shield, helmet on head; bridge and cars in distance; female on left with pole and cap, bales of goods. PROVIDENCE BANK Providence, R. I.	50 State arms; Indian with bow on left; female on right. 50
ONE HUNDRED	Vig. Same as fifty. PROVIDENCE BANK Providence, R. I.	100 Same as Fifty 100
D Medallion head with figures 500 running across.	Vig. Female holding keys, &c., in right hand, with cherubs, all floating in clouds, over guarding a city. PROVIDENCE BANK Providence, R. I 500	500 Med. head with figures 500 running across. 500
1000	Vig. Same as 500s. PROVIDENCE BANK Providence, R. I. 1000	Large letter M with one thousand running across. Med. head with figures 1000 running across.
ONE 1	Farmer sowing grain and man and horses harrowing. 1 RAIL ROAD BANK, Cumberland, R. I.	1 Ship. ONE

Left	Centre	Right
TWO 2	Spread eagle on a bale, grain, &c., cars and man plowin distance. 2 RAIL ROAD BANK, Cumberland, R. I.	2 TWO Salicrat and sheep.
THREE 3	Wharf scene with Sailor, bales being shipping, store-houses, &c. 3 RAIL ROAD BANK, Cumberland, R. I.	3 THREE Train of cars
Large V and word FIVE.	Wharf scene with female sitting among agricultural implements and merchandise holding sickle and rake. Large V and figure with bow and arrow, RAIL ROAD BANK, Woonsocket, R. I.	5 Portrait of Washington.
10 X 10	(First Plate.) Oxen, man, &c. 10 RAIL ROAD BANK, Cumberland, R. I.	TEN Female with cornucopia in left hand.
X	(Second Plate.) Signing the declaration of independence X RAIL ROAD BANK, Woonsocket, R. I.	10 Train of cars building with steeple.
20 Female seated with book on lap	XX Eagle. XX RAIL ROAD BANK, Cumberland, R. I.	20 Ship.
FIFTY Female holding flowers in one hand and a wreath in the other. FIFTY	50 Man and horse. 50 RAIL ROAD BANK, Cumberland, R. I.	FIFTY Female with a Barometer in one hand and flowers in the other. FIFTY
ONE HUNDRED and figures 100. Portrait of Harrison.	Wharf scene with men putting barrels into a large covered wagon, shipping, &c., in distance. RAIL ROAD BANK, Cumberland, R. I.	ONE HUNDRED and figures 100. Male Portrait.
Water and trees and an Indian in a canoe. 500	500 RAIL ROAD BANK, Woonsocket, R. I.	500 [illegible]
1 Blacksmith with sledge.	Man watering three horses from trough by side of wall, goat, kid and sheep; cattle, trees and house in distance. RICHMOND BANK, Alton, R. I. Stockholders, etc.	1 Jenny Lind.

Left	Centre	Right
2 Female erect and another kneeling.	Shield containing a sheaf and agricultural implements; two females on right; cars, &c., on left. RICHMOND BANK, Alton, R. I. Stockholders, &c.	2 Two cherubs soaring, with distaff and sheaf.
3 Anvil, hammer, anvil, etc.	RICHMOND BANK, Alton, R. I. Spread eagle on State Arms, horse either side; steamer on right; factories and cars on left. Stockholders, etc.	3 Two men erect, female seated; factories, etc.
5 5 in red. Rolling machine.	Three females, one in centre with wings; one on right has quadrant; the other cornucopia. RICHMOND BANK, Alton, R. I. V in red.	5 5 in red. Stockholders etc.
10 Clay.	Title of Bank. Scene in an iron mill—five men at work. X, Stockholders, etc., on right of vig.	10 Female feeding fowls.
Female child in ornamental die.	1 Ships and sea scene. R. I. UNION BANK, Newport, R. I. Clasping hands.	1
Wharf scene.	2 Portrait of Gen. Green. R. I. UNION BANK, Newport, R. I. Clasped hands.	2
Indian with bow and arrow, horse on right and dog on left	5 Vig. Winged female cupid and anchor. R. I. UNION BANK, Newport, R. I. Clasped hands.	5
10 X 10	(Old Plate.) Vig. Man with oxen 10 R. I. UNION BANK, Newport, R. I.	TEN Female figure with cornucopia of fruits and flowers.
TEN	Vulcan seated, anvil, sleigh, &c.; train of cars and buildings in distance. X R. I. UNION BANK, Newport, R. I.	10 Farmer with sheaf on his knee.
20 Female.	XX Eagle. XX R. I. UNION BANK, Newport, R. I.	20 Ship sailing.

Left	Centre	Right
FIFTY Female with wreath. FIFTY	50 Man and Horse. 50 R. I. UNION BANK, Newport, R. I.	FIFTY Full length female, Globe, Rule, &c. FIFTY
Words one hundred and figures 100 Male portrait.	Vig. Market scene, shipping on left. R. I. UNION BANK, Newport, R. I.	Words one hundred, and figures 100 Male portrait.
Portrait of female. Spread eagle. Portrait of Indian female.	1 Portrait of female with trident in left hand; quadrant, anchor, bale, &c., on right; antique vase, painter's pallet, &c. on left 1 ROGER WILLIAMS BANK, Providence, R. I.	Portrait of female with cornucopia. Spread eagle on limb. Portrait of Indian with bow and arrows.
THE WILLIAM	ROGER 'S BANK, Spread eagle. Providence, R. I.	1 Female with flowers.
2 Words Two Dollars on red die.	Title of Bank. Three females in clouds; one crowning bust.	2 Words Two Dollars on red die.
Portrait of two females. Male portrait Portrait of farmer with sickle.	2 Vig. Portrait of female with left arm resting on pail, scythe, rake, and pitcher on right; sieve, sheaf of grain, &c. on left. 2 Title of Bank.	Portrait of three females Portrait of Washington. Portrait of young girl seated.
Male portrait.	5 Vig. Female reclining, with right hand upon anchor, overlooking sea on which is dimly seen a ship. 5 Title of Bank. Spread eagle.	State die.
Three females erect, supporting shield.	Vig. Shepherd boy reclining watching sheep; village in distance. 5 Title of Bank. 5 5 Spread eagle.	FIVE Female erect with sickle in right hand.
Male portrait.	10 Vig. Neptune seated with trident. 10 Title of Bank.	Spread eagle upon limb of a tree.
Female seated holding up fig. 10. 10	Title of Bank. Vig. Mercury seated upon clouds; bag in outstretched left hand.	Female seated holding up figure 10. 10

Left end	Centre	Right end
20	Vig. State arms, on right of which is farmer seated on sheaf of grain, with sickle in hand; in distance behind him man on horse and man driving swine; on left of vig. female seated; steamer in distance. Title of Bank. Female seated.	20 Portrait of female.
50 Female seated in shell with trident; ship on either side.	Title of Bank. Indian.	50 Sailor standing erect; ship on either side.
100 Two ships under sail one after the other, schooner in distance.	Vig. Female portrait. Title of Bank.	100 Indian seated on rock, gun in right hand.
D Medallion head.	Vig. Female seated holding roll of goods and atlas with left hand; bale, barrels, cogwheels and church in extreme distance on right; steamboat and factories on left. Title of Bank.	500 Medallion head.
Female erect holding sickle in her right hand. 1000	Large steamship under sail at sea, three sailing vessels on right; two left. Title of Bank.	Female representing Justice. 1000
1 Minerva with shield, spear, sprig and laurel.	View of Pawtucket falls. SLATER BANK, N. Providence, R. I. State Arms.	1 Male portrait.
TWO Female holding figure 2.	View of Pawtucket falls. SLATER BANK, N. Providence, R. I. State arms.	2 Male portrait.
V	View of Pawtucket falls. Male portrait. SLATER BANK, N. Providence, R. I. State arms.	5 Female with roll of cloth.
10 Male portrait.	SLATER BANK, N. Providence, R. I. View of Pawtucket falls. State arms.	10 X
50 Cupid. Mechanic.	SLATER BANK, N. Providence, R. I. Lovers at the well. State Arms.	50 Cupid. Portrait of Slater.

Left end	Centre	Right end
Letter C. Portrait of Slater.	Liberty and Eagle. SLATER BANK, N. Providence, R. I. State Arms.	100 Female Manufacturer.
500 Portrait.	Fame, viz., Female blowing trumpet. SLATER BANK, N. Providence, R. I. State Arms.	500 Mechanic.
ONE Washington. 1	Milkmaid seated, cows, &c. 1 SMITHFIELD EXCHANGE BANK, Greenville, R. I.	1 Portrait of elderly female. ONE
2 State arms. TWO	Stone cutters at work, &c. 2 SMITHFIELD EXCHANGE BANK, Greenville, R. I.	TWO Franklin. Med. head and word two.
5 State arms. FIVE	Portrait of Gen. Taylor. Large figure 5 and word five at top. Female portrait. SMITHFIELD EXCHANGE BANK, Greenville, R. I.	5 Med. head. 5
X	Signing Declaration of Independence. X SMITHFIELD EXCHANGE BANK, Greenville, R. I.	10 Train of cars, man with wheelbarrow.
20 Female with book on lap.	XX Eagle. XX SMITHFIELD EXCHANGE BANK, Greenville, R. I.	20 Ship.
FIFTY Female erect FIFTY	50 Man and horse. 50 SMITHFIELD EXCHANGE BANK, Greenville, R. I.	FIFTY Female erect FIFTY
Figures 100 and words one hundred across. Portrait of Harrison.	Wharf scene, &c. SMITHFIELD EXCHANGE BANK, Greenville, R. I.	Same as on left. Male portrait.
ONE	Sea view with shipping, &c. 1 SMITHFIELD UNION BANK, Woonsocket, R. I.	ONE Female Indian with bow & arrow. ONE

Left end	Centre	Right end
2 TWO 2	Vessels, &c. 2 Title of Bank.	TWO Female drawing water. TWO
THREE	Female with hat in right hand and sheaf in left, farmer resting, with man behind him with grain in his arms. 3 Title of Bank.	THREE Steamship. TH 3REE
FIVE	Female lifting drapery from a shield on which is figure 5. V Title of Bank.	5 Vessel.
Large V and word FIVE.	Wharf scene with female sitting among agricultural implements and merchandise holding sickle and rake. Large V and figure with bow and arrow. Title of Bank.	5 Portrait of Washington.
Vulcan with anvil, hammer, &c. TEN	X Title of Bank.	10 Female with sickle and grain.
20 Female sitting; right hand resting on book; open book on lap.	XX Eagle. XX Title of Bank.	20 Ship.
FIFTY Female erect with wreath of flowers in right hand, and flowers in left. FIFTY	50 Man and horse. 50 Title of Bank.	FIFTY Female erect holding cornucopia in left hand, [illegible] in right. FIFTY
Figures 100 and words one hundred. Head of Harrison.	Wagon with horses and goods; ship at a distance. Title of Bank.	Figures 100 and words one hundred. Head and bust of [illegible].
1 Ship. 1	Indian female seated, with left arm pointing; a deer, trees &c. in distance. SOWAMSET BANK, Warren, R. I. Vessel.	1 Indian reclining supporting figure 1.
TWO Train of cars. Steamship. TWO	Wild horses. SOWAMSET BANK, Warren, R. I.	2 Human figure holding ear of corn and figure 2.

Left	Center	Right
Vessels, &c. THREE	Indians trading with white men. SOWAMSET BANK, Warren, R. I. Loading hay.	3 Indian princess with bow and arrow.
V	Large view of steamship, ships, &c. SOWAMSET BANK, Warren, R. I.	FI5VE Figure 5, represented by female, eagle, portrait of Washington. FIVE
Sailor boy in act of rowing. 10	Female soaring in air with eagle. SOWAMSET BANK, Warren, R. I. Vessel on stocks.	X Female portrait gazing intently.
50 Man with rake, fork, canteen, and dog.	SOWAMSET BANK, Warren, R. I. Train of cars, load of hay, men, &c.; city, mills, &c. in distance.	50 Two females, one with dinner horn; table, dishes, &c.; chickens, &c.
Female with scroll, pole, and cap; shield, pedestal, &c. 100	Scene—Whale fishing in Arctic regions. SOWAMSET BANK, Warren, R. I.	100 Sailor with left hand on capstan; bale, bales, ships' masts, &c.
1 1	STATE BANK, Providence, R. I. Vig. Female seated, resting upon state arms; ship and steamship on right; sailing vessels in distance on left. Dog, safe, and key.	1 View of house and trees.
2	Vig. Locomotive and cars. Female portrait. STATE BANK, Providence, R. I. State arms.	2 View of house and trees.
3 View of house and trees.	STATE BANK, Providence, R. I. Vig. Female resting upon State Arms, with steamship and ship on right; ships on left. Eagle.	3 Female portrait.
5 View of house and trees.	Vig. Female resting upon State Arms, with steamship and ship on right; ships on left. STATE BANK, Providence, R. I. Locomotive.	5 Portrait of Washington.
10 Three females upon a rock; one erect with hand upon anchor. TEN	10 Vig. Female resting upon State Arms, with steamship and ship on right; ships on left. STATE BANK, Providence, R. I.	10 View of house and trees.

Left	Center	Right
Three females on rock, anchor, etc. TEN	10 Female resting on State Arms; ship and steamship on right; ships on left. STATE BANK, Providence, R. I.	10 View of house and trees.
Sailor holding flag aloft, with anchor, bale of goods and female reclining.	20 Vig. Cupid, etc., female seated upon a safe, with vessel and locomotive on the right; sheaf of wheat and plow on left. STATE BANK, Providence, R. I. State Arms.	20 View of house and trees.
50 Female portrait.	STATE BANK, Providence, R. I. Vig. Female resting upon state arms; steamship on right; ship on left.	50 Female portrait.
View of house and trees. 100	Vig. Spread eagle, American shield, &c. STATE BANK, Providence, R. I. State Arms.	100 Female portrait.
500 Indian female with bow and arrow.	STATE BANK, Providence, R. I. Vig. Female seated; on her left, female seated, with sheaf of grain; god on her right, railroad in extreme distance; man with spade. Eagle.	500 500
M 1000	STATE BANK, Providence, R. I. Vig. Female seated upon bale; figure kneeling at her feet; cars crossing bridge; shield. Scene on right; ship and town on left. ONE THOUSAND	1000 1000
1	Female seated; train of cars on right; man on horseback, and canal scene on left. Group of male figures, in large 1. TRADERS' BANK, Newport, R. I.	1 Female and sheaf of wheat.
1 Cupid, flowers, &c. 1	1 Farmers' implements; city on right, and cars on left. TRADERS' BANK, Newport, R. I.	ONE Man erect, with axe in right hand, and sickle in left; sheaf, plow, &c. ONE
2	Vig. Farmers washing sheep; 4 men, 2 on right. TRADERS' BANK, Newport, R. I.	TWO Female sitting, holding wreath of flowers. TWO
2 TWO 2	Vig. Ships on sea. TRADERS' BANK, Newport, R. I.	TWO TWO

Left	Center	Right
3 Mech. hand. 3	3 Vig. Female sitting; building, safe, horn of plenty, &c. on right; man plowing with horses and sheaf of grain on left. TRADERS' BANK, Newport, R. I.	3 Female bathing.
THREE Beehive. THREE	Vig. Female sitting; in right hand sickle; in left rake; sheaf of grain and vessels on right; locomotive and building on left. THREE TRADERS' BANK, Newport, R. I.	Word Three and figure 3. Farmers gathering grain. Word Three, and figure 3.
FI V VE	Vig. Female sitting; sickle in right hand, holding rake in left; vessels, sheaf of grain, on right; building, &c., in background, on left. Large letter V in which is sitting an Indian female. TRADERS' BANK, Newport, R. I.	5 Portrait of Washington.
FIVE	Vig. Female kneeling, with arms extended. TRADERS' BANK, Newport, R. I.	5 Vessel.
X Indian with bow and arrow.	Vig. Scene on river; steamboat, vessels, &c. TRADERS' BANK, Newport, R. I.	10 Female, sheaf of grain; and in her right hand, hat.
10 X 10	Vig. Man and oxen. 10 TRADERS' BANK, Newport, R. I.	TEN Full length female.
20 Female sitting.	XX Eagle. XX TRADERS' BANK, Newport, R. I.	20 Ship, &c.
FIFTY Female erect with wreath of flowers in right hand, and flowers in left. FIFTY	50 Man and horse. 50 TRADERS' BANK, Newport, R. I.	FIFTY Female, globe, &c., standing; elbow resting on ornamental pillar FIFTY
Words one hundred, and figures 100. Male portrait.	Vig. Wharf scene; loading wagon; men, horses, shipping, &c. TRADERS' BANK, Newport, R. I.	Words one hundred, and figures 100. Male portrait.
1 Portrait of Female.	Female reclining supporting ornamental figure 1. 1 TRADERS' BANK, Providence, R. I. Fisher.	ONE Sailor erect gazing down upon female seated at his feet.

Left end	Centre	Right end
ONE Sea... upon wharf, ship, steamboat, &c. ONE	Three females one seated receiving wreath...; Griffin standing upon safe on left; schooner, &c., locomotive and train in distance on right TRADERS' BANK, Providence, R. I. Clasped hands.	ONE Female seated with staff and liberty cap, ship on left. ONE
TWO ...er erect ...beside sheaf of grain and ..., female with ... ...at his feet. 2	2 Female reclining upon State Arms, spread eagle upon right, bales &c., on left. TRADERS' BANK, Providence, R. I. Ox.	2 Sailor erect leaning upon binnacle spy glass in his left hand.
St. George fighting the dragon. 2	2 Neptune seated in his car, drawn by two sea horses, winged figure with cornucopia soaring above. TRADERS' BANK, Providence, R. I. Cupid on Horse.	2 Hercules contending with many headed dragon.
THREE Female, anchor, lighthouse, vessel, etc.	3 Vessel under full sail, lighthouse and steamer in distance. TRADERS' BANK, Providence, R. I.	3 Two children with fruit.
3 Drovers and cattle. 3	Indian chief, dog beside him. Vig. Two In... ... water fall in background, forest scene around. TRADERS' BANK, Providence, R. I. Large goblet.	3 Washington with his hand upon white horse
V Ship launching. V	5 Vig. Sheaf of grain and agricultural implements in foreground; locomotive and bridge in distance on left; waterfall and city on right. 5 TRADERS' BANK, Providence, R. I. Steamboat.	V Female seated among bales, &c. V
V Female portrait.	Sailor reclining; anchor, boat, etc.; steamship in distance. Title of Bank.	5 Eagle.
Ten Dollars. Vulcan seated beside anvil, figure beside and behind him. 10	X Vig. Mammoth ox standing looking to left of note. X TRADERS' BANK, Providence, R. I. Spread eagle.	TEN Drover and cattle. 10
XX Ship upon the stocks.	Vig. Scene upon a wharf, men loading dray, before which is two horses. TRADERS' BANK, Providence, R. I. Locomotive.	20 Indian erect extending hand to female seated on left. XX
FIFTY	Vig. Same as 20s. TRADERS' BANK, Providence, R. I. Cattle standing in water.	50 Scene in a shoemaker's shop, two men at work. 50

Left end	Centre	Right end
ONE HUNDRED	TRADERS' BANK, Providence, R. I. Vig. Female erect holding wreath and wand in right hand; bag in left; her right foot upon a small globe; C each side.	100 Samson overcoming the lion. 100
Female seated, holding scales in left hand; sword in right 1	Vig. Female reclining upon bale; ships on right; schooner on left. UNION BANK, Providence, R. I. State Arms.	1 Female seated, holding spy glass; ship on left.
TWO Female seated upon rocks; pail at her feet. TWO	Vig. Three females reclining; one on right, with sword and scales; one on left, with cornucopia; ships in distance on right. UNION BANK, Providence, R. I. State Arms.	2 Ship under sail. TWO
Three females upon rocks; one erect with ... hand upon Anchor stock.	Vig. Large ship sailing at sea, off light house, vessel in distance on left. UNION BANK, Providence, R. I. State Arms.	3 Portrait of Washington.
Female holding sheaf of grain in left arm. 5	Vig. Female seated upon plough, with left arm on sheaf with sickle; bunch of grain in right hand; cars crossing viaduct on right; bridge on left. UNION BANK, Providence, R. I. State Arms.	5 Steamboat.
X Portrait of Franklin. 10	Vig. Large steamship in foreground; sailing vessels on either side. UNION BANK, Providence, R. I. State Arms.	10 Female seated, resting left arm on scroll on pillar; pen in right hand
50 L 50	50 Female reclining upon basket with 50 upright; ship on stocks upon left, wood in distance on right. 50 UNION BANK, Providence, R. I.	L Rhode Island. L
100 C 100	100 State Arms in shield; harvest and factories in distance on right; bales, boat with two men in it, and ships on left 100 C C UNION BANK, Providence, R. I. 100	C Rhode Island. C
500 D 500	500 Ships upon water opposite a city, light house upon left. 500 UNION BANK, Providence, R. I. D D State Arms.	500 Rhode Island 500
1 Female with liberty cap; emblem of Liberty.	Vig. Cupid holding silver dollar; churches and steamboat in the distance. VILLAGE BANK, Smithfield, R. I.	1 Female figure, emblem of com. manufacturers.

Left end	Centre	Right end
2 Farmer with a cradle, seated on sheaves of grain.	Vig. Two silver dollars; two boys (nude); mountain and train of cars in background. VILLAGE BANK, Smithfield, R. I.	2 Female in round miniature.
THREE Standing female figure, with a spear and emblems of the arts.	Vig. Three silver dollars, and three Cupid's. VILLAGE BANK, Smithfield, R. I.	3 Bust of a sailor, with part of an oar in his hand.
5 Letter V., with 4 persons around it.	Vig. Five silver dollars, and five Cupid's. VILLAGE BANK, Smithfield, R. I.	5 Head of a female and a horse.
Standing female, with flowers and leaves in her hand. TEN	Vig. Railroad cars depot; shipping and wharf scene. VILLAGE BANK, Smithfield, R. I.	X Indian female in sitting posture.
20 Female seated, with a book.	XX Eagle. XX VILLAGE BANK, Smithfield, R. I.	20 Ships.
FIFTY Female standing, with wreaths and flowers. FIFTY	50 Man and horse. 50 VILLAGE BANK, Smithfield, R. I.	FIFTY Female standing. FIFTY
Figures 100, and words ONE HUNDRED across Portrait.	Shipping, baggage, wagon, &c. VILLAGE BANK, Smithfield, R. I.	Figures 100, and words ONE HUNDRED across Portrait
ONE Cattle. 1	(Old Plate.) 1 WAKEFIELD BANK, 1 Wakefield, R. I. Indian in a canoe. Bird feeding her 4 young in a nest.	1 ONE ONE ONE ONE 1
ONE	(New Plate.) Schooner, large Sloop, steamboat, and ship. 1 WAKEFIELD BANK, Wakefield, R. I.	ONE Female Indian with bow and arrow. ONE
ONE on fig. 1 ONE ONE on 1.	Two females with cornucopia; anvil between them; factory in distance WAKEFIELD BK., Wakefield, R. I. ONE ONE	1 Portrait of a female.

2 TWO 2
[New Plate.]
Ships and schooner. 2
WAKEFIELD BANK, Wakefield, R. I.
TWO Female drawing water at a spring with pail and rope. TWO

TWO Men ropeing; furnace, factory and canallocks in background. TWO
[Old Plate.]
Portrait of Washington. 2
WAKEFIELD BANK, Wakefield, R. I.
TWO Ship at sea. 2

2 Shearing sheep.
WAKEFIELD BANK, Wakefield, R. I.
Two females seated; house and steamship in distance
TWO DOLLARS
2 Washing sheep.

Rail road engine and cars. 3 Schooner and ship in the distance.
[Old Plate.]
3 Dairywoman churning. 3
WAKEFIELD BANK, Wakefield, R. I.
THREE Cattle. 3

THREE
Girl with hammer in right hand and sheaf of grain in left; on left man reaping. 3
WAKEFIELD BANK, Wakefield, R. I.
THREE Steamboat. Word THREE and figure 3.

5 Mechanic with, vise, anvil and tools; female figure and emblems of commerce. V
[Old Plate.]
WAKEFIELD BANK, Wakefield, R. I.
Archimedes lifting the world.
FIVE
5 Female sitting with cattle on her right and sheaf on her left. FIVE

Word FIVE and large letter V.
[New Plate.]
Female sitting, emblems of manufactures, commerce, and agriculture; factory and locomotive on left. V
WAKEFIELD BANK, Wakefield, R. I.
5 Portrait of Washington.

Indian with a drawn bow and arrow. 10
[Old Plate.]
X Jupiter with his car and horses. X
WAKEFIELD BANK, Wakefield, R. I.
Female with a sheaf of wheat.
10 Farmer with his scythe in his field. TEN

X
[New Plate.]
Signing the declaration of Independence. X
WAKEFIELD BANK, Wakefield, R. I.
TEN
10 Rail road cars.

20 Farmer plowing with pair of horses. 20
20 Milkmaids with pails, the milkmen, some standing and others sitting. 20
WAKEFIELD BANK, Wakefield, R. I.
Small ship. XX

50 Female Portrait. 50
Woodman with axe, and hunter with gun, seated on either side of a frame on which is a bull, on right in distance ships' masts and sails. 50
WAKEFIELD BANK, Wakefield, R. I.

100 Man sitting.
[New Plate.]
Eagle on branch of tree; cars, canal boats, &c., in background.
WAKEFIELD BANK, Wakefield, R. I.
C ONE HUNDRED 100 C
100 Female sitting.

100 Female figure reclining with a cap of liberty in right hand. 100
C Ships, &c. C
WAKEFIELD BANK, Wakefield, R. I.
100 100
100 Justice with scales. 100

ONE Goddess of liberty erect, shield beside her.
WARREN BANK, Warren, R. I.
Indian reclining upon shield, bow and arrows in hand; eagle soaring on left.
ONE ONE
1 Female portrait.

2
WARREN BANK, Warren, R. I.
Goddess of liberty seated, holding wreath over spread eagle on shield on right; pole, cap and portrait of Washington in right hand. TWO
2 Ornamental fountain.

3 Mercury in air, with caduceus and bag of coin. THREE
WARREN BANK, Warren, R. I.
Vig. Goddess of liberty with wreath and scales; spread eagle upon shield.
3 Female seated with cornucopia, &c. THREE

5 5
WARREN BANK, Warren, R. I.
Vig. Ship building, ship on stocks, &c., vessels at wharf.
FIVE Cars FIVE
5 Cupid astride of dragon.

FIVE
Female holding drapery over shield on which is a 5. V
WARREN BANK, Warren, R. I.
5 Ship.

10
Vig. Haying scene; loading hay in distance, farmers reclining in foreground.
WARREN BANK, Warren, R. I.
TEN Wheels, etc. TEN
X Sea horses. TEN

20 Female figure seated.
XX Eagle. XX
Title of Bank.
20 Ship with sails partly furled.

XX inverted
Justice on safe.
WARREN BANK,
Male portrait; 20 and word Twenty on red die on left; 20 and word Dollars on red die on right.
Warren, R. I.
20 Female churning.

FIFTY Girl with sheaf.
Title of Bank.
Male portrait. Fifty and 50 on red die on left; Dollars, and 50 on red die on right.
FIFTY Female with pole, cap, scroll, etc.

FIFTY Female erect with wreath. FIFTY
50 Man and horse. 50
WAR REN BANK, Warren, R. I.
FIFTY Female erect FIFTY.

100 Farmer with rake, fork, keg, jug, etc.
Title of Bank.
Male portrait. C and One Hundred on red die on left; C and Dollars on red die on right.
100 Portrait of female.

ONE
1 Vig. Portrait of Washington; bales, locomotive and ships on right; scene on wharf, men and dray and steamboat on left. 1
WASHINGTON B'K, Westerly, R. I.
Arm and hammer.
Med. head. ONE

TWO
2 Vig. Same as ones. 2
WASHINGTON B'K, Westerly, R. I.
Arm and hammer.
Med. head. TWO

THREE Female seated, eagle on her lap, grain in right hand. 3
3 Vig. Portrait of Washington, locomotive, bales, barrels, and sloop. 3
WASHINGTON B'K, Westerly, R. I.
Spread eagle.
THREE Female seated with grain and sickle. 3

FIVE
5 Vig. Same as threes. 5
WASHINGTON B'K, Westerly, R. I.
Spread eagle.
FIVE Female erect, hand upon shield, with balances. V

X Goddess of liberty, hand upon state arms, pole and cap. 10
10 Vig. Same as 5s. 10
WASHINGTON B'K, Westerly, R. I.
Cupid upon deer.
Female erect, scroll in right hand. X

TWENTY
XX Vig. Same as 5s. XX
WASHINGTON B'K, Westerly, R. I.
Spread eagle.
20 Mercury soaring in air. 20

FIFTY	L Vig. Same as 5s. L WASHINGTON B'K, Westerly, R. I. Female seated, with sickle, &c.	50 Portrait of Franklin. 50
ONE HUNDRED	C Vig. Same as 5s. C WASHINGTON B'K, Westerly, R. I. Ship under sail.	100 Justice with sword and scales. 100
1 Farmer, dog, horse, pigeons, etc.	WASHINGTON CO. BANK, Carolina Mills, R. I. Washington	1 Female feeding fowls.
2 Two mechanics at work on frame of wheel.	Man seated; two horses; male portrait on each side of vig. Title of Bank.	2 Washington.
3 Farmers at lunch.	Title of Bank. Female portrait.	3 Blacksmiths at work.
5 Soldiers erecting breast work.	Title of Bank. Soldier, shield with head on it; female, two Indians etc.	5 Female; cow, heifer, ducks, etc.
10 Female seated with pole, cap and shield; buildings in distance.	Indians apparently frightened at white men; men in distance on right. Title of Bank.	10
50 Blacksmith's apprentice.	Cattle WASHINGTON CO. BANK, Carolina Mills, R. I.	50 Train of cars.
1 Male portrait.	WESTMINSTER B'K, Providence, R. I. Vig. Country scene; one man seated on left, one standing on right.	1 Beehive.
2 Male portrait.	WESTMINSTER B'K, Providence, R. I. 2 Vig. Two females seated; town in distance on right. 2	2 Female portrait.

5 Male portrait.	Vig. View of city of Providence; cars leaving railway station; water in background. WESTMINSTER B'K, Providence, R. I.	5 Male portrait.
TEN Large steamship, vessels on either side.	Vig. Two male portraits. WESTMINSTER B'K, Providence, R. I.	10 Brig sailing.
20	Vig. Farming scene; farmer on horse drinking out of trough; two figures on right; sheep on left. Female portrait. WESTMINSTER B'K, Providence, R. I.	20 Male portrait.
50 Male portrait.	WESTMINSTER B'K, Providence, R. I. Male portrait. Vig. Female seated holding spy-glass; ship in distance on left. Male portrait.	50 Female portrait.
100	WESTMINSTER B'K, Providence R. I. Vig. A number of horses running in a field.	100 Male portrait.
FIVE HUNDRED	WESTMINSTER B'K, Providence, R. I. Vig. Eagle surmounting a globe; Indian seated with rifle on left; female seated with sickle and grain on right. Male portrait.	500 Male and female seated in foreground; two figures in background, one with a sickle, the other sharpening scythe.
RHODE Female erect with basket upon arm. ISLAND.	Vig. Indian paddling in a canoe. WEYBOSSET BANK, Providence, R. I. State arms.	1 ONE
1 Female portrait.	WEYBOSSET BANK, Providence, R. I. Vig. Meeting of the pilgrims with the Indians. Head of Indian.	1 Male portrait.
2 TWO	WEYBOSSET BANK, Providence, R. I. Vig. Sailor seated upon bale, holding flag in right hand; ships on either side. Spread eagle.	TWO State arms.
2 Female portrait.	WEYBOSSET BANK, Providence, R. I. Vig. Elliott preaching to the Indians.	2 Male portrait.

RHODE ISLAND.	Vig. Female seated [illegible] with right hand. WEYBOSSET BANK, Providence, R. I. Spread eagle.	Star with 5 upon it. Star with 5 upon it.
5 Female erect beside State arms.	Scene upon the prairie; Indians hunting buffalos. WEYBOSSET BANK, Providence, R. I.	5 Male portrait.
5 Female figure with shield, pole, and liberty cap.	Portrait of Washington. Vig. Ship under full sail. Portrait of Madison. WEYBOSSET BANK, Providence, R. I. State arms.	5 Female seated resting arm upon scroll upon pillar.
Spread eagle upon rock overlooking the sea. TEN	10 10 WEYBOSSET BANK, Providence, R. I. Vig. Cornucopia, wheel with wings on it, barrel, &c.; ship in distance on left.	Washington full length.
X Portrait of Harrison. 10	Female portrait. Vig. Dog and safe; bag of coin. Female portrait. WEYBOSSET BANK, Providence, R. I. Spread eagle	10 Portrait of Henry Clay. X
FIFTY	50 Vig. Female standing erect resting left hand on shield; anchor on right; ship on left. WEYBOSSET BANK, Providence, R. I. L	50 State arms. 50
Spread eagle upon rock. 100	100 WEYBOSSET BANK, Providence, R. I. Vig. Female reclining on state arms.	100 Male portrait. 100
500	Vig. Female reclining upon bales; ships on right; vessel on left. Portrait of Millard Fillmore. WEYBOSSET BANK, Providence, R. I. Female Indian head.	500
1 Female seated, foot on anvil, holding sledge in right hand.	Vig. Indian seated upon rocks, rifle in right hand; steamboat upon water and city in distance on right. WHAT CHEER B'K, Providence, R. I. Sheaf and plough.	1 Female portrait.
2 Female holding tablet upon pillar with left arm, pen in her right hand.	Vig. Three horses running loose in a field; farm house on left in distance. WHAT CHEER B'K, Providence, R. I. Spread eagle.	2 Female portrait.

R. ISLAND.

Female portrait. 5 — Vig. State arms, surmounted by [illegible]; female with sword and scales on right, female with cap and staff on left; ship in distance to right; steamboat on left. Title of Bank. Steamboat. — 5 Indian seated with gun in right hand.

10 Portrait of D. Webster. — Vig. Cattle, one lying down, two standing in water; sheep on left. WHAT CHEER B'K, Providence, R. I. Indian head. — 10 Anchor, bales, ship, &c.

FIFTY Female in clouds holding a torch in left hand, shield in right. — Vig. Three females floating upon water; eagle in centre with wings extended. WHAT CHEER B'K, Providence, R. I. — 50 Portrait of H. Clay.

100 Henry Clay seated with dog by side him. — Vig. Female seated between two pillars, eagle and shield at her feet; in distance on right [illegible] bridge, town and ships on left in distance. WHAT CHEER B'K, Providence, R. I. — 100 Female seated holding [illegible]; ship on left.

1 Blacksmith's boy at forge. — View of Falls, village, factories, etc. WOONSOCKET FALLS BANK, Woonsocket R. I. — 1 Portrait of female.

ONE 1 — Agricultural scene; farmer sowing, another in the distance harrowing. 1 WOONSOCKET BK, Cumberland, R. I. — 1 Ship. ONE

2 Henry Clay. — WOONSOCKET FALLS BANK, R. I. View of the falls; road and village in distance. — 2 Female portrait.

TWO 2 — Spread eagle, boat, [illegible], bales, machinery, &c. 2 WOONSOCKET B'K, Cumberland, R. I. — 2 TWO Schooner rigged boat.

THREE 3 — Female about to hand, reclining against bales; in the distance are vessels, warehouses, drays, barrels, &c. 3 WOONSOCKET B'K, Cumberland, R. I. — 3 THREE Train of cars.

5 Two males and female. — WOONSOCKET FALLS BANK, Woonsocket, R I. View of Village and Falls. — 5

CONN.

Eagle resting on United States shield and an anchor. FIVE — A large V, with female figure and shield. WOONSOCKET B'K, Cumberland, R. I. — 5 Female figure and basket.

10 Girl. — WOONSOCKET FALLS BANK, R. I. View of the falls; road and village in distance. — 10 Female feeding birds.

Male figure seated on machinery; cars at distance. TEN — X WOONSOCKET B'K, Cumberland, R. I. — 10 Male figure with sheaf in hand.

20 Female figure seated. — XX Eagle. XX WOONSOCKET B'K, Cumberland, R. I. — 20 Ship with sails partly furled.

Female. 20 — View of Village and Falls. WOONSOCKET FALLS BANK, Woonsocket, R. I. — 20 Washington.

50 — View of Village and Falls. Female. WOONSOCKET FALLS BANK, Woonsocket, R. I. — 50 Portrait of boy.

FIFTY Female figure standing, globe in her right hand, flowers at her right. FIFTY — 50 Man and horse. 50 WOONSOCKET B'K, Cumberland, R. I. FIFTY DOLLARS — FIFTY Female figure with wreath of flowers in right hand. FIFTY

Figures 100 and words one hundred. Head of Harrison. — Wagon with horses and goods; ship at a distance. WOONSOCKET B'K, Cumberland, R. I. — Figures 100 and words one hundred. Head and bust of male.

100 — WOONSOCKET FALLS BANK, Woonsocket, R. I. View of Village and Falls. State Arms. — 100 Female with sheaf of wheat.

ONE across figure 1. Sailor with spyglass looking to seaward; steamer in distance. — 1 Female, with arm resting on bundle of grain, pointing to left. Aetna in distance; ship, &c., on left of her. 1 THE AETNA BANK, Hartford, Conn. — ONE across figure 1. ONE ONE across figure 1.

CONN.

TWO Vessels. TWO — 2 Vig. Same as ones. AETNA BANK, Hartford, Conn. — 2 City Arms; deer, water, trees, etc. TWO

3 Two girls carrying grain. — AETNA BANK, Hartford, Conn. 3 Vig. Same as ones. 3 — 3 Agricultural implements and products. THREE across fig. 3.

FIVE — AETNA BANK, Hartford, Conn. V and words Five Dollars. Vig. same as ones. 5 — 5 CONNECTICUT FIVE

10 inverted. Train of cars. 10 inverted. — Vig. Same as ones with [illegible] V each side. AETNA BANK, Hartford, Conn. — 10 City Arms, deer, water, trees, etc.

FIFTY Female with [illegible] of [illegible] sickle. — 50 Vessel under sail, lighthouse, vessels, etc. AETNA BANK, Hartford, Conn. — 50 Portrait of female.

100 Shield and motto. — Title of Bank. 100 C 100 — 100 Female portrait.

Female portrait. 1 — Angel blowing a trumpet; eagle, globe, flag, &c. ANSONIA BANK, Ansonia, Conn. Sheaf, plow, &c. — 1 Male portrait.

Statue of Liberty. 2 — Eagle, shield, &c. ANSONIA BANK, Ansonia, Conn. Beehive. — 2 Male portrait.

3 Farmer seated, with scythe; man loading hay; bridge in distance. ANSONIA BANK, Ansonia, Conn. — 3 Female with tablet, cog wheel, &c.

5 Male portrait. — Five men working in foundry. ANSONIA BANK, Ansonia, Conn. — 5 Male portrait.

Left	Center	Right
10	Cars, steamboat, vessels, &c. ANSONIA BANK, Ansonia Conn	10 Indian reclining
Male head. 20	ANSONIA BANK, Ansonia, Conn. Female, steamship, vessels, &c.	20 Female.
Female with liberty cap, flag, &c.; U. S. Capitol. 50	50 ANSONIA BANK, Ansonia, Conn.	50 Indian squaw
100 Female with sickle, &c.	Male head. ANSONIA BANK, Ansonia, Conn.	100 Females, ships, tools, factory, cars, &c.
1 Female seated with mechanical tools, &c.; building on right.	B'K OF COMMERCE, New London, Ct. Vig. Ship carpenter at work; view of city. Ship on stocks.	1 Boy's Head
2 Female portrait.	Vig. View of ocean, upon which is a large ship and other vessels. B'K OF COMMERCE, New London, Ct. Locomotive and tender.	2 Two Cupids and 2.
3 Cooper at his work.	Vig. Girl seated, by her side basket of corn; also view of village and river B'K OF COMMERCE, New London, Ct.	3 View of church.
5	Train of cars; another train crossing bridge in distance. BK OF COMMERCE, New London, Conn. Eagle.	5 Female.
10 Cooper at work.	Vig. Whaling scene. BK OF COMMERCE, New London, Conn.	10 Female seated, ship on left.
[illegible] on right end of ocean, 50	B'K OF COMMERCE, New London, Ct Vig. Female seated in ornamental die, vases, &c. on left, bale of goods, anchor, wand, quadrant, &c. on right	50 Sailor, in left hand quadrant, right hand resting on capstan; ship on right; steamship on left

Left	Center	Right
[illegible] seated, globe at her right, upon which is an eagle, with American flag [illegible] 100	$ Female portrait. B'K OF COMMERCE, New London, Ct. Steamboat.	100 Anchor, bales, etc.
Deer 1	Masons at work. 1 ONE B'K OF HARTFORD COUNTY, Hartford. Ct. Female, anchor, &c.	1
ONE Spread eagle and flag. ONE	Bk of HARTFORD Co. Hartford, Conn. Words "One Dollar" across ONE on die.	1 Female portrait
2 2 Statue of female. 2 2	Bk of HARTFORD Co. Hartford, Conn. Words "Two Dollars" across Two on die.	2 Waterfalls, Indians, etc
Two cherubs TWO	Interior of a machine shop; mechanics at work. Ornamental Die with word TWO and fig. 2. B'K OF HARTFORD COUNTY, Hartford, Ct. Locomotive and Cars.	2
3 View of Rail Road Depot and Cars passing through	Three Male Figures. Two females on right. B'K OF HARTFORD COUNTY, Hartford Ct Eagle.	3
FIVE	Cars passing through a tunnel. Female portrait. B'K OF HARTFORD CO., Hartford. Ct. Female bathing	5
X	Female 10 B'K OF HARTFORD CO., Hartford, Ct. Two females seated, one looking up to move, dog on right, cattle on left. TEN	
X X	B'K OF HARTFORD CO., Hartford, Ct. 20 Vig. U. S. Capitol. TWENTY	20
50 THE Die work.	View of New York harbor with steamship and ship. BK. OF HARTFORD Hartford, Ct.	50 COUNTY Die work.

Left	Center	Right
100 THE C	Spread eagle; ship, steamship and steamboat in distance. BK. OF HARTFORD Hartford, Ct.	100 COUNTY $100
1 Female, arm resting on pillar; farm house and cattle on right.	State die. Vig. Harvest scene. BANK OF LITCHFIELD CO., New Milford, Ct. Dog & safe. ONE Goose.	1
Two and figure 2. View of cattle, telegraph and rail road.	Title of Bank. Vig. Farmers loading grain. State die.	2
3 Female, quadrant and anchor, eagle on shield.	Vig. Man plowing with horses and cattle. State die. Title of Bank. THREE	3
5	Train of cars. State die. Title of Bank. FIVE	5
X	Title of Bank. TEN State die.	10 State arms; two females and factories in distance.
XX 20	Title of Bank. Vig. Three females; one with harp and two engraving on tablet.	20 State die.
XX 20 on two strips of lathe work.	BK. OF LITCHFIELD COUNTY. New Milford, Conn. Three females seated with pen, tablet, book, harp, etc.	20 State Arms
1 Head of male. ONE	BANK OF NEW ENGLAND, East Haddam, Conn. View Goodspeed's landing	ONE Female. ONE
2 Male portrait	BANK OF NEW ENGLAND, East Haddam, Conn. View Goodspeed's landing.	TWO 2

Left	Center	Right
3	BANK OF NEW ENG-LAND. East Haddam, Conn. Steamboat Granite State. THREE	3 3
5	BANK OF NEW ENG-LAND, East Haddam, Conn. Ship building. Female	FIVE 5
X	View of Goodspeed's Landing. Male portrait on right. BANK OF NEW ENG-LAND, East Haddam, Conn. TEN	10
20	View of Goodspeed's Landing. BANK OF NEW ENG-LAND, East Haddam, Conn.	20 Head of D. Webster.
1 Female with sewing ma-chine	BK. OF NORWALK, Norwalk, Conn. Blacksmith's shop. Male portrait	1
TWO Scene in a blacksmith shop	Milkmaid seated, cows, &c. B'K OF NORWALK. Norwalk, Conn.	2 Male portrait
3	Sailors on shore; one looking through telescope; ships, men, etc., in distance. Male portrait BK. OF NORWALK. Norwalk, Conn.	3 Sheep
5 Blacksmith shop.	Male portrait Two females, shield, &c; ships, houses, etc., in distance. BK. OF NORWALK. Norwalk, Conn.	5 5
	B'K OF NORWALK. TEN Female stand-ing beside pillar. Steamship and vessels.	10 Male portrait
Male portrait 20	B'K OF NORWALK. Indian. Female seated beside eagle shield, &c. Sailor.	20 20
50 Male portrait	BK. OF NORWALK, Norwalk, Conn. Male and female harves-ters resting; cow, calf, etc.	50 Female portrait.
ONE Farmer at work.	Vig. View of the city of Bridgeport. BRIDGEPORT B'K, Bridgeport, Ct. Beehive.	1 Female portrait.
TWO Female hold-ing American flag.	Vig. Same as Ones. BRIDGEPORT B'K, Bridgeport, Ct. Eagle.	2 Female artist
Two females. THREE.	THREE on 3 Female reclining, globe, chart, &c. THREE on 3 BRIDGEPORT B'K. Bridgeport, Conn. Eagle	3 Dog and safe
3 Female Indian.	Vig. Female reclining on bale; goods, ships on right and left. BRIDGEPORT B'K, Bridgeport, Ct. Locomotive and tender.	3 Portrait of Daniel Webster.
5 Portrait of Clay 5	BRIDGEPORT B'K, Bridgeport, Ct. Vig. Same as ones. Female head.	5 Male portrait 5
TEN Washington on horse-back.	BRIDGEPORT B'K. Bridgeport, Ct. Female portrait. Vig. Large spread eagle. Female portrait. Steamship.	10 View of church.
20 Locomotive and cars. XX	Med. head on which is twenty. Vig. Whaling scene. Med. head on which is twenty. BRIDGEPORT B'K. Bridgeport, Ct. Steamboat.	20 Sculptor. XX
50 Female seated.	BRIDGEPORT BK., Bridgeport, Ct. Vig. View of the City of Bridgeport. FIFTY.	50 Figure sit-ting in niz.
100 Portrait. 100	Female seat-ed, mechan-ical tools, &c. Med. head on which is fig. 100. BRIDGEPORT B'K, Bridgeport, Ct. Locomotive and tender.	100 City of Bridgeport. 100
1 Boiler lean-ing on cap-stan.	BRIDGEPORT CITY BANK, Conn. ON1E DOLL1AR Vig. Portrait of Washington.	1 Female
2 Female	Vig. View of Ocean on which is two large ships; steamship between other vessels in distance. BRIDGEPORT CITY BANK, Conn.	2 Portrait of Calhoun.
5 Female seated at sewing ma-chine.	BRIDGEPORT CITY BANK. Catching horses; three boys, one on the ground, one by horse's side, and one hat in hand; some have green 5 on either side. Bridgeport, Conn.	5 Daniel Webster
Large manu-factory. 10	1 Female portrait. 0 BRIDGEPORT CITY BANK, Bridgeport, Conn.	10 Female with sewing ma-chine.
Two horses; farmer feed-ing hogs. 10	Female portrait. BRIDGEPORT CITY BANK, Conn.	10 Female portrait.
XX Female with wheat.	BRIDGEPORT CITY BANK, Conn. Large ornamental die with figure 20 engraved, also the words twenty dollars running across it.	Ornamental die with twenty at top also fig-ure 20.
Female with vase, flowers 50	BRIDGEPORT CITY BANK, Conn. Ornamental die on which is figure 50 and the word Fifty Dollars across it.	50 Female, ea-gle, shield.
Four cupids supporting figure 1. ONE	Vig. Horses; ones on the left. CENTRAL BANK, Middletown, Ct.	1 Female.
Eagle and shield. 2	CENTRAL BANK, Middletown, Ct. Vig. Train of cars.	2 Male portrait
3 Female and basket of flowers.	Vig. Farmer seated; farming scene and bridge on right; buildings on left. CENTRAL BANK, Middletown, Ct.	3 Female ar-tist; anvil and hammer on left.

Left	Centre	Right
4 FOUR 4	CENTRAL BANK Middletown, Ct. Vig. Female with triton riding on sea in shell; on either side ship.	4 FOUR 4
Three females on a rock; anchor, spyglass, &c. FIVE	Large ship; vessel on right; steamship on left. CENTRAL BANK, Middletown, Ct.	5 Male portrait
Washington. X	Females seated; eagle at top of globe, flag across eagles neck. CENTRAL BANK, Middletown, Ct.	TEN Female, sword and balances.
Indian with gun looking over precipice. 25	Female seated on bale of goods; steamship on right; mechanical implements, Depot and cars on left. CENTRAL BANK. Middletown, Ct. Female Head.	25 Washington on horseback
Female with grain. 50	Ship Carpenters at work. CENTRAL BANK, Middletown, Ct.	50 Portrait of Franklin.
Figure 1 and word ONE. 1	CHARTER OAK B'K. Hartford Ct 1 Soldiers under a large oak tree. 1 ONE	1 Figure 1 and word ONE. ONE
2 TWO 2	CHARTER OAK B'K. Hartford, Ct 2 Vig. Same as Ones. 2	2 Locomotive and Train Cars.
Soldiers under a large oak tree. 3	CHARTER OAK B'K. Hartford, Ct. THREE in ornamental Die Title.	3 THREE 3
FIVE Soldiers under a large oak tree.	CHARTER OAK B'K. Hartford, Ct. FIVE in Ornamental Die.	5 5
X Same as Fives.	CHARTER OAK B'K, Hartford, Ct. Ornamental Die in which is figure 10, letter X, and word TEN. X each side.	10 X

Left	Centre	Right
1 Male Portrait	CITIZENS' BANK, Waterbury, Ct. Male Portrait, train of cars on right; factories on left.	1 Male Portrait
2 Female.	CITIZENS' BANK, Waterbury, Ct. Portrait of Aaron Benedict; cars on right; factories on left.	2 Female, olive branch in left hand.
3 Drove of cattle, load of hay.	CITIZENS BANK, Waterbury, Conn. Interior of a Blacksmith shop.	3 Farmer carrying corn.
5 Bee Hive	CITIZENS' BANK, Waterbury, Ct. Portrait of J. M. L. Scovil; cars on right; factories on left. 5 on each side.	5 Bale of goods, machinery, &c.
10 Farming scene—male and female with child seated; man standing against tree.	CITIZENS BANK, Waterbury, Conn. X	10 Blacksmith standing beside anvil.
20 Cupid and cornucopia.	CITIZENS' BANK, Waterbury, Conn. Female feeding fowls. 20 Farmer, horse &c. [illegible]	20 Cupid and shield.
C Henry Clay and his dog.	CITIZENS BANK, Waterbury, Conn. Landing of the pilgrims.	100 Female portrait
ONE ONE ONE	Two horses alarmed at lightning; CITY BANK OF HARTFORD, Conn.	1 Boy, two horses and plough.
ONE Railroad bridge, cars and canal. ONE	Vig. View of Public building in Hartford. CITY BANK. Hartford, Ct.	1 ONE Female seated, eagle and shield on right.
2 Man dressing leather.	Mowing scene. Title of Bank.	2 Men gathering corn

Left	Centre	Right
TWO Two men, farming implements on their shoulders, dog at their side.	Vig. Same as ones. Med. head TWO across. CITY BANK, Hartford, Ct.	2 Female in figure 2 with sword and balances. TWO
THREE Two females and city in distance.	CITY BANK, Hartford, Ct. Vig. Shield, group of Indians on left; group of females on right, globe, &c. Eagle	3 Female.
3 State Arms.	Tree on shield; Indian one side, sailor on the other. Title of Bank.	3 Deer.
5 Female, sheaf of wheat and sickle.	Female seated; deer on a shield; sheep on right. CITY BANK, Hartford, Ct. Dog's head.	5 Female seated, locomotive, factory and cars on left. FIVE
10	Female with pole and cap, shield on right. Vig. Farmers loading grain. CITY BANK, Hartford, Ct.	10 Female, Indian and squaw.
20 Cattle. TWENTY	Vig. Female reclining on rock; canal locks, rail road and city in distance. CITY BANK, Hartford, Ct.	20 Med. head XX
50 Med. head FIFTY	Med. head. 50 on it. Vig. Man on either side of a shield, ship above it. CITY BANK, Hartford, Ct.	50 Two female Indians, one with sickle and grain the other with bow & arrow
Female sitting on a drum. C	Vig. Eagle on either side of shield; [illegible] at top; [illegible] on [illegible] and factory on left. CITY BANK, Hartford, Ct.	100 Med. head 100
1 Male portrait. 1	Vig. Public park in New Haven. 1 1 CITY BANK, New Haven, Ct. 1 Eagle. 1	1 Female Indian. 1
TWO	2 Vig. Same as ones. CITY BANK, New Haven, Ct. Farming implements.	2 Portrait of General Taylor.

THREE	3 Vig. Same as ones. 3 CITY BANK, New Haven, Ct. Locomotive and tender.	3 Three females supporting figure 3.
5 Shield, &c. FIVE	Large steamship; towboats in foreground; vessels, city, &c., in distance. CITY BANK OF NEW HAVEN. Eagle.	5 Male portrait FIVE
X Webster. 10	Four cupids, letter X, medallion head of Franklin and Washington blended together. CITY BANK OF NEW HAVEN. Bee-hive	10 Fillmore. 10
10 X	(Old Plate.) Vig. Same as ones. CITY BANK, New Haven, Ct. Females head.	10 X
20 Portrait of H. Clay. XX	Vig. Same as Ones. CITY BANK, New Haven, Ct. Indian.	20 Portrait of Gen. Taylor. XX
50 Female. 50	Vig. Same as Ones. CITY BANK, New Haven, Ct. Female Indian.	50 Medallion Head, the word Fifty engraved at top.
100 Portrait of Washington.	CITY BANK, New Haven, Ct. Vig. Same as Ones.	100 Male Portrait
ONE Farmer, female, boy, girl, dog, chickens, &c.	CLINTON BANK, Clinton, Conn. Train of cars; sloop, hills, trees, etc.	1 Female with sword, book, and scales.
Connecticut Female erect with hand on shield.	2 Farmer plowing with oxen; milkmaid, etc. CLINTON BANK, Clinton, Conn.	2 Female seated with sickle and sheaf.
3 THREE	CLINTON BANK, Clinton, Conn. Yacht race; males, females, etc., on beach.	3 Sailor

FIVE	5 Female and boy; girl and dog; man entering gate with rake. CLINTON BANK, Clinton, Conn.	5 DeWitt Clinton.
TEN TEN	Farmer gathering grain; on right man reaping; on left man on horse talking to farmer. CLINTON BANK, Clinton, Conn.	10 Portrait of boy.
1 Washingt'n	CONNECTICUT B'K Bridgeport, Conn. 1 Female seated with coffee bags, bbls., kegs, vessels, etc. 1	1 State Arms.
Portrait of of Washington Female, sickle and grain. Male portrait.	CONNECTICUT B'K. Bridgeport, Conn. 1 Vig. Female supporting figure 1. 1	1 Female with arms extended.
2	(First Plate.) View of wharf, steamboat, large ship and other vessels. CONNECTICUT B'K. Bridgeport, Conn. State arms.	2 Male portrait.
TWO Female seated on globe holding liberty pole and blowing trumpet.	(Second Plate.) Vig. Two females seated; factories on the right, ship on left; cog wheel, anvil and vise between them. 2 CONNECTICUT B'K. Bridgeport, Ct.	TWO Two females. Eagle at top of a shield. TWO
Two children.	Wharf scene—unloading boats; men, horses, etc. CONNECTICUT B'K Bridgeport, Conn.	2 Boy's portrait
Anchor, bales, bbls., etc. 3	Three on 3 Man buying paper of newsboy; hhds. etc CONNECTICUT B'K Bridgeport, Conn.	3 Indian female.
3	Locomotive and cars. Large figure 3 CONNECTICUT B'K. Bridgeport, Ct. State arms.	3 Female.
5 Washington on his horse.	Three females, ship in distance. CONNECTICUT B'K, Bridgeport, Conn. Shield, etc.	5 Liberty.

5 Farmer at work. 5	CONNECTICUT B'K. Bridgeport, Ct. Vig. Female with grain on ornamental 5.	5 Female Portrait. FIVE
Two females supporting letter X.	X Vig. view of ship yard; ship carpenter at work. X CONNECTICUT B'K. Bridgeport, Ct.	10 Female portrait. TEN
Washington and his horse. 20	Vig. Group of three females; ship on right. CONNECTICUT B'K. Bridgeport, Ct. State arms.	20 Female and shield, liberty pole and cap.
Female with sword and ballances. FIFTY	CONNECTICUT B'K. Bridgeport, Ct. Female seated, before her is winged figure holding wand; on right is Neptune in his car drawn by sea serpents. State arms.	50 50
Two females, farming implements on left, ship on right.	CONNECTICUT B'K, Bridgeport, Ct. Eagle holding shield on which is figures 100.	Three cupids 100
[illegible] head Portrait of Washington	Vig. Man on horse, drove of sheep, mill on left. Fig. 1 on shield. CONN. RIVER BANKING CO. Hartford, Ct. Eagle.	ONE Full length female. ONE
2 Portrait of Washington. 2	Vig. Head of Franklin in ornamental disc, on either side a female; steamboat and ships on right; farming scene on left. Title of Bank	2 Female seated in fig. 2, railroad cars and factory on left.
3 Portrait of Franklin 3	Vig. View of ocean, steamship and other vessels. Title of Bank Barrels, bales and goods.	THREE Female erect with spear in right hand THREE
5 5	Portrait of Gen. Taylor, with title of bank above and below it. Two females floating in air	5
TEN	Portrait of Washington, with title of bank above and below it. Indian group looking over precipice; view of city and river below. Locomotive and tender.	Letter X on American shield.

Left end	Centre	Right end
L L	50 Vig. Female seated with wand, right hand resting on shield; steamboat on left; anchor on right. 50 Title of Bank	L L
C C	100 100 Vig. Three females, two seated, one standing holding spear in her hand. Title of Bank	C C
1 Female with hands upraised holding sickle. ONE	[First Plate.] Male portrait. [illegible] at work. DANBURY BANK, Danbury, Conn. Farming implements.	1 Female and basket of flowers.
ONE Large monument.	[Second Plate.] DANBULY BANK, Danbury. Conn. Three figures, Farmer, Mechanic and Sailor representing industry.	1 Male portrait.
Man resting on oars. 2	[First Plate.] DANBURY BANK, Danbury, Conn. 2 2 Male portrait.	TWO Large monument.
2 Female with arms extended. 2	[Second Plate.] Vig. Farmers at lunch; Horse on right. DANBURY BANK, Danbury, Conn. Horse.	2 Farmer gathering corn.
3 Three cupids in figure 3.	Vig. Drove of cattle and sheep; mill in background; vessel in distance. DANBURY BANK, Danbury, Conn. Farming tools.	3 Female in figure 3.
5 Female.	[First Plate.] Vig. Female seated, liberty pole across her lap, eagle and shield on right. DANBURY BANK, Danbury, Conn. Bank building.	5 Mal. head.
Male portrait FIVE [illegible]	[Second Plate.] DANNURY BANK, Danbury, Conn. U. S. Capitol. 5 Female.	5 5
10 Portrait of Washington.	[illegible] DANBURY BANK, Danbury, Conn. Bank building.	10 Female.

Left end	Centre	Right end
20 Female seated with sw'rd and balances 20	20 Vig. Three females with wand, sickle and grain; ship and steamer on shield on right; cars on left. DANBURY BANK, Danbury, Conn. Eagle.	20
50 Med. head.	DANBURY BANK, Danbury, Conn. Female blowing trumpet; globe and eagle on right; flags on left.	50 Med. head.
ONE ONE Washington.	Word and figure 1. Map of Conn. on which is seen words New Haven, Hartford, Norwich, Deep River, and L. I. Sound; globe and ship on left, factory on right. 1 DEEP RIVER BANK, Deep River, Ct.	ONE
Head. TWO Head.	2 Same as ones. 2 DEEP RIVER BANK, Deep River, Ct. 2	TWO
Three heads or portraits on this end.	3 Same as ones. 3 DEEP RIVER BANK, Deep River, Ct. 3	THREE
Same as 3s.	5 Same as ones 5 DEEP RIVER BANK, Deep River, Ct. 5	Head FIVE Head.
TEN Map same as on ones. TEN	10 Eagle 10 DEEP RIVER BANK, Deep River, Ct. 10	TEN Female figure of Liberty. TEN
XX Elephant. TWENTY	Map—same as ones. 20 DEEP RIVER BANK, Deep River, Ct. 20	Figure of Justice. TWENTY
1 Female Indian with bow and arrows.	Female blowing trumpet; eagle on right; flags on left. EAST HADDAM B'K, East Haddam, Ct. Farming implements.	1 Female artist at work.
ONE Blacksmith with sledge.	1 Female seated; ship on left; lighthouse, etc., on right. EAST HADDAM BK, East Haddam, Conn.	1 Cars passing over and out the under arch.

Left end	Centre	Right end
TWO Female and child, flag, liberty pole and cap.	Vig. Female with horn of plenty at her feet, flags, bale, shield, eagle at top of globe; steamship on right; cars and factory on left. EAST HADDAM B'K, East Haddam, Ct. Cogwheels, &c.	2 Ship. TWO
2 Buchanan.	EAST HADDAM BK, East Haddam, Conn. Two females on either side of anvil; buildings on right.	2 Female portrait.
3 Female with sword and balances.	Portrait of Washington. Male portrait. Vig. Female seated among merchandise; vessels on right. EAST HADDAM B'K East Haddam. Ct. Beehive.	3 Female, sickle and grain. THREE
THREE Female feeding owls.	3 Inside of factory; females weaving. EAST HADDAM BK, East Haddam, Conn.	3 THREE Farmer shearing sheep.
5 Female. 5	Vig. Large spread eagle. EAST HADDAM B'K, East Haddam, Ct. Steamboat	5 Female with sword and balances; shield, safe, eagle, &c.
V Ship' head.	EAST HADDAM BK. East Haddam, Conn. View of ship yard; men at work, etc. V V	5 Sailor boy, shield, barrels, etc.
X Washington. 10	EAST HADDAM B'K, East Haddam, Ct. 10 Vig. Female seated; factories and cars on left. Steamship & merchandise.	X Male portrait. 10
XX Male portrait. XX	XX XX Vig. Female seated; ship on right. EAST HADDAM B'K, East Haddam, Ct. Vessels, &c.	20 Washington. 20
Female with some branches on head, load of hay and village in distance. ONE	ELM CITY BANK. New Haven. Conn. Portrait of Washington.	1 Boy with rabbits.
2 Female with chickens.	ELM CITY BANK, New Haven, Ct.	2 Three men by side of a small boat, partly finished; ship on stocks.

Left	Centre	Right
3 Three females with liberty pole and cap, &c.	Three male figures, blacksmith, sailor and farmer; interior of blacksmith shop; horse, anvil and man. ELM CITY BANK, New Haven, Ct.	3 3
5 Eagle on shield.	View of steamboat Elm City; vessels in distance. ELM CITY BANK, New Haven, Ct. Sailing vessels.	5 Female.
10 Mower drinking from jug; scythe, fence and field.	Two sailors, one standing, the other seated on box; wharf scene; steamship in distance. ELM CITY BANK, New Haven, Ct.	10 Portrait of female.
20 Portrait of Columbus.	Large ship, steamships; ships in distance. ELM CITY BANK New Haven, Ct.	20 Boy with globe and compass.
Three females representing liberty, justice, and agriculture; field &c.	ELM CITY BANK, New Haven, Ct. L 50 L	50 Portrait of Franklin.
100	ELM CITY BANK New Haven, Ct. Mechanics and farmer; horse, trees, &c. Indian in distance in lower left corner of note. Cow right.	100 Female Indian, left hand on rock.
ONE Medal. Head ONE	[First Plate.] EXCHANGE BANK, Hartford, Ct. Two females, view of river, steamboat and sail vessel on left, locomotive and cars on right; medal. head with word ONE on either side.	ONE Full Length Female. ONE
ONE Small male fig., anvil and hammer 1	[Second Plate.] Rail Road Depot, cars passing through. EXCHANGE BANK, Hartford, Ct. Barrels, &c.	ONE DOLLAR
TWO Indian reclining on shield. TWO	[First Plate.] Med. Head, with word TWO across. Med. Head, with word TWO across. A female on either side of a shield. EXCHANGE BANK, Hartford, Ct	Medallion Head with word TWO across.
Full length female, right hand resting on shield. TWO	[Second Plate.] 2 Locomotive and Cars. EXCHANGE BANK, Hartford, Ct	2 Female with pole and cap on right. Eagle standing on shield.

Left	Centre	Right
THREE Locomotive and cars. THREE	Female seated with pole and cap, before her two youthful artists; shipping on left; cars on right. EXCHANGE BANK, Hartford, Ct.	3 Two farmers carrying implements on their shoulders, farm house on right.
Female with starry drapery holding pole and cap, eagle and American shield on right.	5 View of public buildings in Hartford. EXCHANGE BANK, Hartford, Ct. Locomotive and tender.	5
Full length female with spear. TEN	X Vig. Three females, eagle, &c.; bridge, locomotive and cars on right; ship on left. EXCHANGE BANK, Hartford, Ct. Steamship.	X Female with pole and cap resting on shield.
20 View of city, bridge, rail road and cars.	EXCHANGE BANK, Hartford, Ct. Vig. Three female figures; sickle, anchor and quadrant. XX	20 Large ship, view of city and shipping.
50 Man under large tree; church on right; building on left. FIFTY	EXCHANGE BANK. Hartford, Ct. Vig. River scene; view of city in distance. Eagle.	FIFTY 50
100 Sculptor.	Vig. Group of female figures, eagle between them, waterfalls in background. EXCHANGE BANK, Hartford, Ct. Head of female.	100 Spread eagle, shield, &c. 100
ONE Washington. ONE	Vig. Banking house. FAIRFIELD CO. BK. Norwalk, Ct.	Figure 1 on shield.
ONE Male portrait	FAIRFIELD CO. BK. Norwalk, Conn. View of buildings, etc.—general street view.	1 1
TWO Male portrait. TWO	2 Milkmaid seated with cattle. FAIRFIELD CO. BK. Norwalk, Ct.	2
TWO Blacksmith	Female with two calves; ox, canal scene, dogs, etc., in distance on left. Title of Bank.	2 Male portrait

Left	Centre	Right
THREE Female. THREE	View of sea, on which is two ships; Light house on right. FAIRFIELD CO. BK. Norwalk, Ct.	3
THREE Male portrait	Large fig. 3 on which is Title of Bank, words "Three Dollars," etc.	3 Female rising in clouds with quadrant.
Female with sword and balances. FIVE	Vig. Steamship and other vessels. FAIRFIELD CO. BK. Norwalk, Ct.	5
Female with shield, liberty pole and cap.	10 Female with cornucopia. FAIRFIELD CO. BK. Norwalk, Ct.	10
TWENTY Female Indian with bow & arrow	Vig. Train of cars; wharf, steamboat and depot in the background. FAIRFIELD CO. BK. Norwalk, Ct.	XX Female between 2 & 0.
50 Male portrait FIFTY	Drove of cattle. FAIRFIELD CO BK. Norwalk, Ct.	50 Male portrait
Med. head and figure 100.	Two horses alarmed at two Indian men. FAIRFIELD CO BK. Norwalk, Ct	Same as the other end.
ONE ONE	FARMERS' BANK, Bridgeport, Conn. Female portrait on large die; words "one dollar." Two females tending looms.	1 ONE
Four Cupid's holding figure 1 1	Vig. Mechanic seated; by his side mechanical tools; farmers at work, on left. FARMER'S BANK, Bridgeport, Ct. Locomotive and tender.	1 Male portrait.
2 Washington	FARMERS' BANK, Bridgeport, Conn. Milkmaid and boy.	2 Female with rose.

2
Female; sheaf of wheat.
Vig. Female seated; on right, farmers at work; and locomotive and cars in distance.
FARMER'S BANK,
Bridgeport, Ct.
Steamship.
2
Male portrait.

3
Male portrait.
Vig. Horses and hogs; one horse drinking out of trough; female on left, feeding hogs; farm houses in background.
FARMER'S BANK,
Bridgeport, Ct.
Locomotive and tender.
3
Female with wreath of flowers.

FIVE
FARMERS' BANK,
Bridgeport, Conn.
Vigs. in lower right and left corners. Blacksmiths' shop, men shoeing horse, etc.; farmer, wife and boy at lunch &c.
5

5
Male portrait.
Mechanic and large letter V; also, mechanical tools.
FARMER'S BANK,
Bridgeport, Ct.
Eagle.
5
Female with sword and balances.

X
Female portrait.
10
Three females seated; ship on right.
FARMER'S BANK,
Bridgeport, Ct.
Sheaf of wheat, plow, &c.
10
Male portrait.

Female with compass.
20
Vig. Group of figures, supporting figure 20.
FARMER'S BANK,
Bridgeport, Ct.
Dog's head.
20
Male portrait.

Male portrait.
50
Vig. Female Indian seated; steamship on right; cage, shield, eagle, safe, locomotive and cars, on left.
FARMER'S BANK,
Bridgeport, Ct.
Locomotive and tender.
50
Female holding American flag.

100
Portrait of Washington.
100
FARMERS' BANK,
Bridgeport, Ct.
Vig. Sailor standing erect holding American flag.
100
Male portrait.
100

1
Milkmaid and cattle.
FAR. & MECH. BK.,
Hartford, Conn.
Vig. Blacksmith, arm and hammer.
1
Spread eagle.

Full length female, with pole and cap.
1 Vig. Milkmaid seated, with cattle.
FAR. & MECH. BK.,
Hartford, Ct.
ONE
Cupid, anvil and hammer.
ONE

2
Mechanic and anvil; mechanical tools; bridge, locomotive and cars on right.
FAR. & MECH. BK.
Hartford, Ct.
Vig. Two in ornamental die.
Portrait of Washington.
2
Farmer; view of farm on left.

Full length female with grain and sickle.
Shield; Indian on right; female with sickle on left.
FAR. & MECH. B'K.,
Hartford, Conn.
2
Female with sheaf and sickle.

3
Ship under full sail.
Farmer and blacksmith on either side of shield; cows on right; view of farm on left.
FAR. & MECH. B'K.,
Hartford, Conn.
3
Female

Female seated, with pole and cap; shield with figure 2 on left.
Eagle with wings extended.
FAR. & MECH. BK.
Hartford, Ct.
Two females, one reclining, the other soaring in air between them, is figure 2.

5
Sculptor or engraver.
V
Med. head, five across V; Med. head, five across. Interior of a blacksmith's shop.
FAR. & MECH. BK.,
Hartford, Ct.
V
Cattle.
5

10
Farmer seated; by his side sickle, rake, etc.
X
Female clasping book; mechanical implements; steam boat in distance. Med head and ten on either side.
FAR. & MECH. B'K.,
Hartford, Conn.
X
10 on med. head.
10

TWENTY
20 Group of 3 male figures.
FARMERS AND MECHANICS BANK,
Hartford, Ct.
20
Two females, one with sickle and grain.

Full length female with wand in her left hand, shield in right, on which is engraved medal head.
Family group, woman seated, by her side a little boy, now coming towards him with rake on his shoulder in front of him is a little girl, by her side is dog in attitude of barking. Figures 50 at left of vig.
Title of Bank
Barrels, bales, &c.
50

100
Mechanical implements.
100
Bank Building.
FAR. AND MEC. BK.,
Hartford, Ct.,
Horse.
100

1
ONE
Female portrait.
HARTFORD BANK,
Hartford, Ct.
Vig. Two females and eagle; portrait of Washington, ship on left.
1
Portrait of Jenny Lind.

1
Med. head.
1
Med. head; one across. Signing the Declaration of Independence. Med. head; one across.
HARTFORD BANK,
Hartford, Conn.
Female and anchor.
1
Med. head
1

2
Med. head.
2
Med. head; two across. View of river, steamboat and ship; city on right. Med. head; two across.
HARTFORD BANK,
Hartford, Ct.
Dog's head.
2
Med. head.
2

TWO
Female portrait.
TWO
2 Vig. Sailor reclining; nautical implements, &c., view of sea and three vessels.
HARTFORD BANK,
Hartford, Ct.
2
Female seated in fig. 2; factory and locomotive on left.
TWO

THREE
Two females seated, above them sailor and mechanic; view of city and mountains in distance.
HARTFORD BANK,
Hartford, Ct.
Vig. Anchor, anvil, and sheaves.
3
Male
Two females, cattle, dog, &c.

Female, liberty pole, and cap.
Figure 4
4 Vig. Ships storming a fort. 4
HARTFORD BANK,
Hartford, Ct.
Dog, safe, and key.
Female with sword
Figure 4

5
Squaw and papoose.
View of the Deaf and Dumb Asylum.
HARTFORD BANK,
Hartford, Conn.
5
Male head.

FIVE
Med. head; five across. Vig. Sailor erect, with flag; view of harbor scene and shipping. Med. head; five across.
HARTFORD BANK,
Hartford, Ct.
Eagle.
5
5 on med. head.
5

TEN
Med. head, and fig. 10 on it. Vig. Railroad and train of cars. Med. head, and fig. 10 on it.
HARTFORD BANK,
Hartford, Ct.
Mechanics, arm and anvil.
TEN
Steamboat and row boat.
TEN

10
Male portrait.
Steamboat "Granite State;" hills and raft.
HARTFORD BANK,
Hartford, Conn.
10
Female.

XX
XX
20 Vig. Female seated, with figure 20 on right; vessel on left. 20
HARTFORD BANK,
Hartford, Ct.
20
20

Left	Centre	Right
XX Female with cornucopia.	HARTFORD BANK, Hartford, Conn. Vig. Same as fives.	20 Male portrait
L L	50 Vig. Female seated; view of canal in distance. 50 HARTFORD BANK, Hartford, Ct.	L L
Female with flowers. 50	Title of Bank. Shield on which is a figure; eagle at top, horse on either side; bridge and city in distance on right; building on left.	50 Indian.
C C	HARTFORD BANK, Hartford, Ct. 100 Vig. Female seated on rock; wood scene. 100	C C
100	View of U. S. Capitol. C HARTFORD BANK, Hartford, Conn.	100 Liberty surrounded by stars.
ONE ONE	Three females binding hats; hatter on left pressing hats. HATTERS' BANK, Bethel, Ct.	ONE Milkmaid pail on her head, farmhouse on right, cattle on left.
TWO Female binding hats.	Two horse team, boy on the horse, man attaching team to plow. HATTERS' BANK, Bethel, Ct.	2 Mechanics and mechanical implements; sledge on her back.
2 Indian head 2	HATTERS' BANK, Bethel, Conn. Scene in stable—two horses and colt.	2 Female binding hats.
3 Portrait of Washington.	Two females, Cornucopia between them; one seated with pole and cap; view of river and vessel, bridge, locomotive and cars on right. HATTERS' BANK, Bethel, Ct.	3 Man pressing hats.
5 5	HATTERS' BANK, Bethel, Conn. Female portrait with train of cars and view of river on right; steamboat, factories and mast on left	5 5

Left	Centre	Right
FIVE and fig. 5. FIVE FIVE	Train of cars; telegraph and bridge. HATTERS' BANK, Bethel, Ct.	FIVE Man pressing hats.
TEN TEN X	Large spread eagle on globe; flags with the names of different States on either side. HATTERS' BANK, Bethel, Ct.	X Portrait of Webster.
20 Two men with guns.	XX Portrait of Washington. XX Horses on right, cattle on left. HATTERS' BANK, Bethel, Ct. X X	20 Two soldiers, one seated with gun and pipe, the other standing holding gun.
50 Eagle and figures 50.	Drove of cattle and sheep. HATTERS' BANK, Bethel, Ct.	50 Male portrait
1 Figure of Mercury with bag of money.	HOME BANK, Meriden, Conn. Drover and farmer bargaining for ox.	1 Female figure.
2 Wheelwright and apprentice.	Female figure of manufactures. HOME BANK, Meriden, Conn.	2 Genius of America.
3 Indian looking over rock.	HOME BANK, Meriden, Conn. Arm and hand with hammer.	3 Female feeding chickens
5 Justice with scales.	HOME BANK, Meriden, Conn. Apotheosis of Washington.	5 Beehive.
10 Female holding up counter. TEN	HOME BANK, Meriden, Conn. Train of cars. Female head.	10 Female figure.
Word twenty and three dies above on which is Title and figs. 20. Machinist at work; vice, etc.	Spread eagle on shield. HOME BANK, Meriden, Conn.	20 Beehive.

Left	Centre	Right
Female portrait 50	Man plowing with two horses. HOME BANK, Meriden, Conn.	50 Horse's head.
100 Washingt'n	ONE HUNDRED DOLLARS ONE HUNDRED Title of Bank ONE HUNDRED	100 Webster.
1 State die.	(First plate.) HULBURT BANK, West Winsted, Ct. 1 Large ornamented Die, with One Dollar, running across it. 1	1 Male portrait
Wild horses ONE	[Second Plate.] Girl HULBURT BANK, West Winsted, Ct.	1 Male portrait
TWO	HULBURT BANK, West Winsted, Ct. 2 Vig. Female in circular die; Harvest farm, house scene, &c. on right; cattle on left, man blowing trumpet, calling farmers to lunch. 2	TWO Cow.
3 Male portrait	Vig. Shield and Indian on right, with tomahawk; Female on left, with wand; steamboat, vessel, and city in distance, on left. HULBURT BANK, West Winsted, Ct. Female bathing.	3 Male portrait
Drove of cattle. V	State die. HULBURT BANK, West Winsted, Ct. Cows.	5 Spread eagle Ox.
X Male portrait	HULBURT BANK, West Winsted, Ct. Vig. Group of Indians; view of city and cars crossing bridge, and also cars passing through tunnel. TEN	10 State die.
20 Man on horseback.	HURLBUT BANK, West Winsted, Conn. Female holding pole and cap in left hand, and frame with 20 on it in right.	XX Soldier with musket.
ONE View of town ONE	Male Portrait Vig. Puddling in an iron mill Male Portrait IRON BANK, Falls Village, Conn. Locomotive and cars.	ONE Mechanic's arm. ONE

2 — TWO — Locomotive and cars. | 2 Vig. View of falls, and town. 2 — IRON BANK. Falls Village, Conn. — Cog wheel. | 2 — Female, sword, and balances.

3 — Farmer with scythe. | Two milkmaids seated; one milking cow, and one with pail on her lap; farm house on right; wagon on left. — IRON BANK. Falls Village, Conn. — Bee hive. | 3 — Mechanic at work.

5 — Man at work in iron foundry. | View of Falls and village. — IRON BANK, Falls Village, Conn. — Building and trees. | 5 — Male portrait.

5 — Man forging iron. | Two men tending furnaces. — IRON BANK. Falls Village, Conn. | 5 — Franklin.

5 — Mechanic at work. | Puddling in an iron mill. — IRON BANK, Falls Village. Conn. — Building and trees. | 5 — Portrait of Franklin.

10 — Portrait of Washington. | Vig. Puddling in an iron mill. Male portrait. Male portrait. — IRON BANK. Falls Village, Conn. — Steamboat. | 10 — Male portrait.

Male Portrait. — 20 | View of Falls Village. — IRON BANK, Falls Village, Ct. — Beehive. | 20 — View of factories, etc.

1 — Portrait of Gen. Taylor. — ONE | Man on horseback; dog, flock of sheep, grist mill, &c. — JEWETT CITY B'K. Jewett City. Conn. — Chartered June, 1, 1831 | 1 — Cars. — ONE

ONE 1 — Female with scales, eagle and portrait of Washington — ONE | Female seated holding eagle with olive leaf; horn of plenty at her feet; ships in distance. — JEWETT CITY B'K. Jewett City. Conn. — Sheaf, plow, rake, &c. | 1 — Female resting on an altar; ship in distance.

TWO — Female, scales, eagle, rod, portrait of Washington, &c. — TWO | 2 Female, anchor, and bale, cars in distance on right; on left spinning wheel, factory, &c. 2 — JEWETT CITY B'K. Jewett City, Conn. — House, cattle, plow, trees, &c. | Female reclining on anchor.

2 — Portrait of Washington. — TWO | Signing the Declaration of Independence. — JEWETT CITY B'K, Jewett City, Conn. — Spread Eagle. | 2 — Portrait of Martha Washington. — TWO

Female, scales, eagle, horn of plenty, casks &c. | 3 Two females and one male; horn of plenty, cars, ship, safe, &c. — JEWETT CITY B'K, Jewett City, Conn. — Agricultural Implements. | 3

5 — Female, scales, eagle, horn of plenty, casks &c. — FIVE | Two females, horn of plenty, goods, shipping, steamboat, &c. — JEWETT CITY B'K. Jewett City, Conn. — Dog, safe, &c. | 5 — Female, scales, &c. — FIVE

5 — Female with scales and rod; eagle and portrait of Washington. — FIVE | Figure 5; two females, Cupid with scales, eagle &c. surrounding the figure. — JEWETT CITY B'K. Jewett City, Conn. | 5 — Two Heads. — 5

XX — Three children seated. | JEWETT CITY B'K, Jewett City, Conn. — View of manufacturing village. — TWENTY | 20 — Washington on horseback

Female erect resting right arm on an altar; ship in distance. — FIFTY | 50 State arms; on left female erect with horn of plenty at her feet; on right female erect with key in right hand, and "charter 1831" on left. 50 — Title of Bank. — Female seated on rock. | FIFTY V

1 — Washington. — ONE | State of Connecticut. — View of river and town. — MANUFACTURERS BANK, Birmingham. — ONE — Locomotive. | 1 — Ship. — ONE

2 — Male portrait. — TWO | View of town and river. — MANUFACTURERS BANK, Birmingham. — TWO — Mechanic's arm & tools. | 2 — Train of cars, village in back ground. — TWO

THREE 3 THREE — Male portrait. — THREE | State of Connecticut. — View of town and river. — MANUFACTURERS BANK. Birmingham. — THREE — Steamboat. | 3 — Agriculture female, grain, and sickle. — THREE

5 — Female. — FIVE | State of Connecticut. — Man plowing, with horse and oxen. — MANUFACTURERS BANK, Birmingham, — FIVE — Spread Eagle. | 5 — Blacksmith at work. — FIVE

10 — Female and cornucopia. — TEN | Connecticut. Liberty, Justice, and Truth, on either side of shield; eagle on top of shield. — MANUFACTURERS BANK. Birmingham. — X TEN X | 10 — Mechanic's arm, anvil, hammer, &c. — TEN

TWENTY | State of Connecticut. Indian and female on either side of shield. — MANUFACTURERS BANK. Birmingham. — TWENTY. | 20 — Mechanic seated, factories on left.

50 — Three dogs barking at birds. | State of Connecticut. — Three female figures; Agriculture, Liberty, and Art. — MANUFACTURERS BANK. Birmingham. | 50 — Female reaping.

C — Little girl and dog. | State of Connecticut. — Wild horses. — MANUFACTURERS BANK. Birmingham. — C 100 C | 100 — Machinery female at work

1 — Portrait of Franklin. — 1 | 1 Vig. Female seated; ships on right. 1 — MECHANICS' BANK. New Haven. Ct. — Banking house. | 1 — Portrait of Washington. — 1

2 — 2 | Vig. same as ones. — MECHANICS' BANK. New Haven, Ct — Banking house. | 2 — Mechanics and mechanical implements.

3 — Female with tiller. — 3 | 3 Vig. Female seated on bale of goods, vessel on either side. — MECHANICS' BANK, New Haven, Ct. — Banking house. | 3 — Female — 3

5 — Mechanic's arm. — V | MECHANICS BANK, New Haven, Conn. — Female seated; eagle on globe, flag across his back, &c. — Bank building. | 5 — Ship. — 5

5 — Mechanic's arm — V | MECHANICS BANK. Group of five Am. Presidents in letter V; two flags and eagle at top. — New Haven, Conn. | 5 — Ship. — V

10 — Female Indian. — 10 | Sailor seated holding flag; ship on left. — MECHANICS' BANK, New Haven, Ct — Mechanic's Arm. | X — Female seated with sword and balance; safe and shield.

20 — Three females overlooking precipice, one holding sword and balance. — 20
MECHANICS' BANK, New Haven, Ct.
20 — Banking House. — Female.

Artist at work, building on right. — 50 — Male figure, the word Franklin engraved on pillar.
MECHANICS' BANK, New Haven, Ct.
50 — Male Portrait — State Arms.

Female Erect with sword and balance. — State Arms. 100 100 — Female feeding an eagle.
MECHANICS' BANK, New Haven, Ct.
100 — Portrait of Washington. — 100

Figure 1, and one running across. — MERCANTILE BK., Hartford, Ct. — 1
Vig. Female seated; sals, sheep &c.
Female portrait. — Sailor seated; spy glass in left hand.

TWO DOLLARS — MERCANTILE BK., Hartford, Ct. — 2
2 — View of ocean; steamship and other vessels.
2

3 — Vig. shield and figure 3; eagle at top of shield; on other side a horse, steamboat on right; canal, bridge, cars and locomotive on left. 3 — THREE
Female portrait. — MERCANTILE BK., Hartford, Ct.

5 — Three females seated, with cornucopia, sickle, and quadrant. — 5
FIVE — MERCANTILE BK., Hartford, Ct. — Sailor.

10 — Indian head, 10 and X. — TEN
X — Two female Indians; one seated with sickle and grain; the other with bow and arrow.
10 — MERCANTILE BK., Hartford, Ct.

XX — MERCANTILE B'K. Hartford, Ct. — 20
Sailor at wheel.
Female gathering wheat. — Female with flowers in her apron.

Female with cornucopia. — MERCANTILE B'K. Hartford, Ct. — 50
Male Portrait.
FIFTY
50 — Ship.

Figures 100 and $ mark. — MERCANTILE BK. Hartford, Ct. — 100
Large die with figures 100, and words one hundred dollars.
Large red letter C. — Large red letter C.

Full length female with pole and cap, starry drapery across her shoulder. — 1 Floating female with cornucopia. — 1
MERCHANTS' BANK. New Haven, Ct. — Female.

TWO — View of Ocean steamship and other Vessels. — 2
Female floating in air.
MERCHANT BANK. New Haven, Ct.
TWO — Female Bathing. — Female feeding an Eagle.

3 — Vig. Three females with quadrant, liberty pole and cap, grain, &c. — 3
Two male figures.
MERCHANTS' B'K. New Haven, Ct.
THREE — Shells — Male portrait.

View of public square in New Haven. 5 — FIVE
Sailor and mechanic, sailor with flag, mechanic seated, anchor at his feet.
5 — MERCHANTS' B'K. New Haven, Ct.
Barrels, bales, goods, &c.

TEN — Vig. Public square in New Haven. — 10
Train of cars.
MERCHANTS' B'K. New Haven, Ct.
TEN — Female bathing. — Sailor.

20 — Vig. Three females; building in background. — 20
MERCHANTS' B'K. New Haven, Ct.
XX — Eagle. — XX

Land Fifty — MERCHANT'S B'K. New Haven, Ct. — 50
Floating female.
Vig. Group of Indians overlooking precipice; view of city below.
Female. — Female standing.

C — MERCHANTS' B'K. New Haven, Ct. — 100
Vig. Sailor reclining, quadrant in left hand, coil of rope, capstan, &c. on right; river, ships, &c. on left.
Ship — Eagle — Male portrait.

ONE — 1 Vig. Female with wand in right hand; ship on left. 1 — 1
Female and balance, state arms, eagle, &c. — Female seated with pole and cap; ship on left.
MERCHANTS' B'K. Norwich, Ct.
ONE — 1

Female erect with spear in left hand, right hand resting on shield, on which is figure 2. — 2 Vig. Female seated; state arms, anvil and cogwheel on right; ship on left. 2 — Female head with wreath.
2
MERCHANTS' B'K. Norwich, Ct.
TWO — Female head.

3 — MERCHANTS' BK., Norwich, Conn. — THREE DOLLARS
Agricultural machine. — Whaling scene. Three on 3 on left; Ducats on 3 on right.
3

FIVE — [First Plate.] — Female soaring in air with wand in right hand.
Portrait of Washington. — 5 Vig. Whaling scene. 5
FIVE — MERCHANTS' B'K. Norwich, Ct. — 5

5 — [Second Plate.] — 5
Vig. Locomotive and train of cars.
Male portrait — Sailor seated with spy glass, steamboat on left.
FIVE — MERCHANTS' B'K. Norwich, Ct.

TEN — [First Plate.] — Female erect with spear; state arms on right.
Portrait of Washington. — 10 Vig. Whaling scene. 10
TEN — MERCHANTS' B'K. Norwich, Ct. — 10

10 — [Second Plate.] — 10
Vig. Whaling scene. — Male portrait.
Male portrait. — MERCHANTS' B'K. Norwich, Ct. — X

20 — XX Two men, cattle &c., in circular die. XX — 20
Ship. — Machinery.
20 — MERCHANT BANK, Norwich, Conn. — 20

Two winged figures and urn. — L Vig. Man seated with horn of plenty, safe, Liberty pole and scales on right; ship, bales of goods, &c. on left. L — 50
Launching a ship.
Portrait of General Harrison. — MERCHANTS' B'K. Norwich, Ct. — 50
Sail vessel.

A collection of vessels. — C Vig. Female seated, eagle on her lap; ships on left. C — 100
Shearing sheep.
MERCHANTS' B'K. Norwich, Ct. — 100
Steamboat.

1 — Female holding flowers. Large 1 40 left. — 1
MER. & MANUFA'RS BANK Hartf'rd, Conn.
Goat and kids.

Left end	Centre	Right end
Sailor with bundle; steamer. TWO	Large 2 with Title of Bank to the right.	2 Dog's head.
FIVE [illegible] Sailor seated on bales; female, vessel and steamer above him. Green 5 and word Five.	MERCHANTS' AND Green tinted V and machinery MANUFACT'S B'K., Hartford, Conn.	5 Female gazing at stars.
X State Arms sailor, bale, etc.	MERCHANTS' 10 AND Two females seated, wolf, boat, globe, etc.; steamship, etc., on left; buildings, monument, &c., on right MANUFACT'S B'K. Hartford, Conn.	10 Two children with fruit and butterfly.
20 Connecticut Female seated on safe with sword and scales.	THE MERCHANTS' Female either side of anvil; one on left has cornucopia of flowers; factories, etc.; in distance on right. AND MANUFACTUR'S BK	20 Hartford, City Arms—deer, tree, water, &c.
FIFTY DOLLARS	MER. & MAN. BANK, Hartford, Conn. 50 50 Male portrait.	FIFTY DOLLARS
100 Female on rock gazing at ocean on which is steamer, etc.	Title of Bank. Green C. Male portrait.	100 C
1 ONE Portrait of John Hancock.	MERIDEN BANK. Meriden, Conn. Farmer ploughing with oxen and horse. Elephant.	1 Train of cars.
ONE Portrait of Lafayette. ONE	Blacksmith seated, anvil, &c.; factories in distance. MERIDEN BANK, Meriden, Conn. Locomotive.	1 Two Indians, one holding spear.
TWO Portrait of Franklin.	Group of persons separated by a shield; child with hand on globe, &c. MERIDEN BANK. Meriden, Conn. Blacksmith's arms, anvil, &c.	2 Female portrait.
3 Village showing factories, &c. THREE	Train of cars MERIDEN BANK, Meriden, Conn. Horse.	3 Blacksmith with hammer resting on anvil, &c.
5 Washington. 5	Female holding sickle and sheaf of grain; village in the distance. MERIDEN BANK, Meriden, Conn. Arm, anvil, &c.	5 Goddess of Liberty.
Goddess of Liberty.	10 Female, sickle, sheaf of grain; village in distance. MERIDEN BANK, Meriden, Conn. Eagle.	TEN Youth hammering on anvil. 10
20 XX 20	20 Female 20 seated on bales, leaning against rock, sheaf of grain at her feet; vessels in the distance. MERIDEN BANK Meriden, Conn.	TWENTY
50 Female leaning on rock, &c.; Steamboat in distance. 50	50 MERIDEN BANK Meriden, Conn.	FIFTY
C Washington. C	100 100 Man pouring water; bales, &c.; vessel in distance. MERIDEN BANK Meriden, Conn.	ONE HUNDRED
1 Male portrait ONE	Stone Quarry; view of city and cars crossing bridge. MIDDLESEX CO B'K Middletown, Ct. Machinery.	1 Female.
Female, liberty pole and shield; starry drapery across her shoulder	TWO Male portrait with female each side; steamboat and vessel on right; farmers at work on left. 2 2 MIDDLESEX CO. B'K, Middletown, Conn. Mechanics arm.	TWO Two Indians with spear and arrows. TWO
3 Portrait of Franklin. 3	Signing the Declaration of Independence. Spread Eagle on shield. MIDDLESEX CO B'K, Middletown. Ct. 3 3 Goods, &c.	Fig. 3 on American shield. Female pole and cap eagle at top of shield.
5 Washington. 5	Milkmaid seated with cattle. 5 MIDDLESEX CO. B'K, Middletown, Ct. Female Bathing.	FIVE Female. FIVE
10 Vessel, train cars crossing bridge. TEN	Two Horses and train cars. 10 MIDDLESEX CO. B'K, Middletown. Ct Steamship.	TEN Large ship. TEN
20 20	20 20 Vig. Female giving eagle drink. MIDDLESEX CO. B'K, Middletown, Ct. A	TWENTY
50 50	50 50 Vig. Spread eagle. MIDDLESEX CO B'K. Middletown, Ct.	FIFTY
ONE	1 Dog and safe. 1 MIDDLETOWN B'K. Middletown, Ct. Ship.	ONE
TWO	Three milkmaids and two cows; vessels and cottage. MIDDLETOWN B'K, Middletown, Ct. Cogwheel and cylinder.	TWO
THREE	3 Three females seated, one with Mercury's wand, and leaning on shield. 3 MIDDLETOWN B'K. Middletown Ct. State arms.	THREE
5 FIVE 5	5 Female resting on anchor and bale of goods; schooner and steamboat on right; city and shipping on left. 5 MIDDLETOWN B'K. Middletown, Ct. Agricultural implements.	5 Portrait of H. Clay. V
10 TEN 10	10 Female, agricultural products and implements around her; on left canal, boat and lock; on right cars and bridge. 10 MIDDLETOWN B'K. Middletown, Ct. Locomotive.	10 Washington. 10
TWENTY	20 Two winged figures and two cupids upholding large 20. MIDDLETOWN B'K, Middletown. Ct. Steamship.	20 TWENTY 20
50 FIFTY 50	50 Female seated upholding large 50; safe, casks, cornucopia, &c.; two ships on left. MIDDLETOWN B'K, Middletown, Ct. Spread eagle.	FIFTY
100 HUNDRED 100	C Sailor with spyglass, compass leaning against bales, bale in rear; ship and steamer on left. MIDDLETOWN B'K, Middletown, Ct. Horse.	ONE HUNDRED

ONE Ship. ONE	MYSTIC BANK, Mystic, Conn. 1 1 Vig. Indian in canoe going over rapids. Locomotive and tender.	Male figure erect. ONE
2 Female, sickle and grain; figure 2 on left. TWO	2 Vig. female seated with wand; ship on left; State Arms on right 2 MYSTIC BANK, Mystic, Conn. State Arms.	Female warrior with spear; right hand resting on shield on which is figure 2. TWO
THREE Female and mechanical tools. 3	3 Beehive. 3 Vig. Indian and native American on either side of a shield, eagle at top of shield; ship on right. MYSTIC BANK, Mystic, Conn. Female grain and sickle.	3
5 Female with rake. 5	V Vig. Female with balances representing Industry. 5 MYSTIC BANK, Mystic, Conn.	FIVE
10 Launching a ship. 10	X Vig. Female with grain, leaning on pillar vessel on right. X MYSTIC BANK, Mistic, Conn. Canal lock, &c.	10
TWENTY	MYSTIC BANK, Mystic, Conn. Vig. Archimedes raising the world. XX	Indian with bow & arrow. 20
1 Portrait of Washington.	View of ship-yard. MYSTIC RIVER B'K, Conn.	1 Groton. Girl's head.
2 Groton.	MYSTIC RIVER B'K, Conn. Female feeding swine, three horses drinking, and man.	2 Portrait of Cass.
3 Groton. Portrait of Clay.	MYSTIC RIVER B'K, Conn. Ships, &c.; city in distance.	3 Portrait
Female portrait 5	MYSTIC RIVER B'K, Conn. Ships.	5 Groton. Portrait of Webster.

Female, sheaf of wheat. X	10 10 MYSTIC RIVER B'K, Conn. Portrait of Fillmore.	Female with sheaf of wheat. X
20	Whaling scene. Indian Queen. MYSTIC RIVER B'K, Conn.	20 Cooper and barrel.
50	MYSTIC RIVER B'K, Conn. Female reclining on a bale of goods, city and ship in distance. Eagle.	50 Groton. Female head.
C	Female reclining on a bale; portrait of Franklin on right, ships in distance. MYSTIC RIVER B'K, Conn. Dog and Safe.	100
Dog's head. 1	NEW BRITAIN B'K New Britain, Conn. Blacksmith's shop—man at vise; anvil, hammer, etc. 1	1 Beehive.
2 Barn-yard, fowls, etc.	Farm horse; farmers resting; man playing with child, horse, dog, fowls, etc. NEW BRITAIN B'K New Britain, Conn.	2 Man, girl, machinery, etc.
3	Mill; boy on horse, men, child, dog, fowls, etc.; horse crossing bridge on right 3 NEW BRITAIN B'K New Britain, Conn.	3 Female holding flowers
5	Cars crossing bridge; cattle in stream drinking; trees, fence, etc. Male portrait NEW BRITAIN B'K New Britain, Conn.	5 Head of horse.
Female with pole and cap leaning on column, flowers at her feet.	X Spread eagle and shield. NEW BRITAIN B'K New Britain, Conn.	Ten inverted. 10
1 First Sabbath.	[First Plate.] Female seated; ship on right. Female. NEW HAVEN B'K, New Haven, Ct. Bee hive.	1 Sailor at work.

1 First Sabbath.	[Second Plate.] Vig. Council of Indians. NEW HAVEN B'K, New Haven, Ct.	1 Beehive.
ONE First Sabbath.	Wharf scene—horses, boxes, bbls., carts, ship, steamship and other vessels. Female. NEW HAVEN B'K, New Haven, Conn. Bee hive.	ONE 1
Female and sheaf of wheat. 2	Vig. Two females seated; cars and canal scene on right; ships on left. NEW HAVEN BK., New Haven, Ct. Beehive.	2 First Sabbath.
Female as twined in fig. 2. Female.	Two females and shield; steamship in distance. NEW HAVEN BANK New Haven, Conn. Bee-hive.	2 First sabbath.
3 First Sabbath.	Vig. large ship. NEW HAVEN BK., New Haven, Ct.	3 Female Indian.
3 Female head. First sabbath.	NEW HAVEN BANK New Haven, Conn. Mechanic, sailor and farmer with implements. Beehive.	THREE 3
5 Female seated on globe; scythe, holding sickle and grain. FIVE	[First Plate.] Cupid Cupid and grain. Female reclining on bale of goods; ship on either side. NEW HAVEN BK., New Haven, Ct. Beehive.	5 First Sabbath.
Drover selling cattle. Beehive.	[Second Plate.] Female portrait. NEW HAVEN BK., New Haven, Ct.	5 First Sabbath.
FIVE Large figure crossing bridge; two Indians and water falls. FIVE	Two males and a female representing Agriculture, Commerce, &c.; steamboat, train of cars and city in distance. NEW HAVEN BANK New Haven, Ct. Beehive.	Letter V, and three females. The first Sabbath preaching.
10 Female artist at work.	[First Plate.] Vig. Female and mechanic representing trade and industry; ship on right, bridge, locomotive and cars on left. NEW HAVEN BK., New Haven, Ct. Beehive.	10 First Sabbath.

Left	Centre	Right
Beehive. 10	[Second Plate.] NEW HAVEN BK. New Haven, Ct. Vig. Three figures; blacksmith shoeing horse. Ship.	10 First Sabbath.
Female portrait. Large X, word Ten in centre. Female, cow, &c.	Vessels at sea. NEW HAVEN BANK. New Haven, Conn. Bee-hive.	10 First Sabbath
First Sabbath. 20	Vig. City, depot, and cars. NEW HAVEN BK., New Haven, Ct. Beehive.	20 Female.
First Sabbath. XX	Female resting on shield; steamer, ship, cars, bridge, &c., in distance. NEW HAVEN BANK. Bee-hive.	20 Female.
FIFTY Female erect holding flag and spear.	NEW HAVEN B'K. New Haven, Ct. Vig. Female and child; steamboat on right; vessels on left. 50 50 Beehive.	50 First Sabbath.
100 First Sabbath.	NEW HAVEN B'K. New Haven, Ct. Female and Indian on either side of globe, eagle at top; female holding grain, Indian gun, letter C between them. Beehive.	100 Mechanic and tools, sledge on his shoulder.
Fig. 1 on American shield. River, steamboat, view and city in distance.	N. H. CO. BANK. New Haven, Ct. View of sea, ship and other vessels. 1 1 Dog, Safe and Key.	ONE Female erect with spear.
TWO Sailor leaning on Capstain, spy-glass in hand. TWO	N. H. CO. BANK. New Haven, Ct. View of River; two ships, steamboat and smaller vessels. 2 2 Dog, Safe and Key.	Medal Head and figure 2. Ship.
3 Female grain and sickle. THREE	N. H. CO. BANK. New Haven, Ct. Farming scene, man on horse. 3 3 Dog, Safe and Key.	THREE Milkmaid.
5 Mechanic at work.	N. H. CO. BANK. New Haven, Ct. Large spread Eagle on limb of tree, ships on right, steamboats and vessels on left. 5 Dog, key, safe 5	5 Female Portrait.

Left	Centre	Right
X Bulls Head TEN	[First Plate. N. H. CO. BANK, New Haven, Ct. Cattle, Man Plowing with oxen and horses; men at work. Dog, key and safe.	Medal Head and fig. 10. Male Portrait.
10 Sailor seated; bale of goods, &c.	N. H. CO., BANK, New Haven, Ct. Vig. Female seated on chest; small child and dog on right; plough and sheaf of grain, shield, &c., on left. Eagle.	10 Portrait.
XX 20	N. H. CO., BANK, New Haven, Ct. Vig. State Arms; American group on right, Indian, squaw and papoose on left. Dog, safe and key.	XX 20
50 View of city and cars crossing bridge; head of boy on left.	N. H. CO., BANK, New Haven, Ct. Vig. Three females with sickle, quadrant, and cornucopia. Dog, safe and key.	50 View of river and ship; city in distance.
Group of figures; two females seated, spinning wheel by their side; sailor and mechanic above them; city in distance.	N. H. CO., BANK, New Haven, Ct. C The vig. extends on both ends and across lower margin of note. C Anchor and mechanics. implements; oxen	Three figures Two females seated; one with sickle; man standing with pitchfork in right hand dog on right.
Female erect with grain in right hand, and sickle in left. ONE	(1s and 2s are alike.) Med. head and fig. 1. Vig. View of sea upon which is two ships; light-house in distance on right. Med. head and fig. 1. NEW LONDON B'K. New London, Ct.	ONE DOLLAR
FIVE Female; eagle on right, anchor, Capstan, &c., on left. 5	5 Vig. Indian and native American seated between the arms of one of the States, upon which is standing an eagle; also ship on right. 5 NEW LONDON B'K. New London, Ct.	5 Beehive. 5
X CONNECTICUT X	10 Vig. View of harvest field and reaper sitting under a tree. 10 NEW LONDON B'K. New London, Ct.	10 10
XX XX	20 Vig. Farmer preparing for work; sail vessel on left. 20 NEW LONDON B'K. New London, Ct.	20 20
1	NORFOLK BANK, Norfolk, Conn. Drove of cattle, horses and sheep; trees, barn, house and boy in distance.	1 1 ONE

Left	Centre	Right
2	NORFOLK BANK, Norfolk, Conn. Drove of cattle, drover on horseback, boy to water; trees and farmhouse in distance.	2 2 TWO
3 Man dressing leather.	NORFOLK BANK, Norfolk, Conn. Two horses frightened at train of cars.	3 3 3
5, V & FIVE. Six men at work in an iron mill.	NORFOLK BANK, Norfolk, Conn.	5 5 5
5	State arms; eagle at top; two females, cars and trees on right; female and ship on left. NORFOLK BANK, Norfolk, Conn.	FIVE FIVE 5
TEN on X. TEN	Female with cornucopia. Female with wings. NORFOLK BANK, Norfolk, Conn.	10 Female with quadrant.
XX 20	NORFOLK BANK, Norfolk, Conn. State Arms with eagle at top and horse each side; cars, bridge and city in distance, on right and a building on left.	20
L FIFTY	NORFOLK BANK Norfolk, Conn. Portrait of Washington.	50 Male, two females, dog, cattle and sheaves.
ONE Female, shield, eagle, liberty pole and cap. ONE	1 Female seated; farming implements, &c.; bridge, locomotive and cars on right. 1 NORWICH BANK, Norwich, Ct. Barrels, Goods, &c.	ONE Female drawing water from a well steamboat on left.
Female. ONE Female.	View of Norwich Bank Building; female pole and cap on right; vessel on left. NORWICH BANK, Norwich, Ct. Eagle.	Female. ONE Female.
2 Two Cupids in Ornamental fig. 2.	Spread Eagle on limb of tree; vessels on right; steamboat on left NORWICH BANK, Norwich, Ct. Bank Building.	2 Two figures in Ornamental fig. 2.

TWO — Female seated in Ornamental fig. 2, sword in left hand, Balances in right.
NORWICH BANK, Norwich, Ct. Three females, between them the Arms of one of the States, eagle at top of shield. Eagle.
Fig. 2 on Anstalese shield. Female seated in Ornamental fig. 2, City on left.

CONNECTICUT.
Figure 4. Figure 4. Group of females seated. Grain, sheaf, &c.; one resting arm on chest, key in her right hand; eagle on left, building on right; vessels in distance. NORWICH BANK, Norwich, Ct.
Figure 4. Figure 4.

5
Five females supporting figure 5; vessels on right. NORWICH BANK, Norwich, Ct. Bank Building.
5

FIVE — Sailor with glass; anchor at his feet. FIVE
NORWICH BANK, Norwich, Conn. Three characters with flag, grain, rake, etc., on right; sheep on left, vessels in distance. Female bathing.
5 — Eagle on shield. FIVE

X CONNECTICUT X
X Vig. River, on which is sail-boat; also, man on horse. X NORWICH BANK, Norwich, Ct. Female, grain and sickle.
10 10

XX CONNECTICUT XX
20 Vig. Female seated, left hand extended; under it is engraved figure 20; vessel on left. 20 NORWICH BANK, Norwich, Ct. Steamboat.
20 20

CONNECTICUT.
L Vig. An ox. L NORWICH BANK, Norwich, Ct. Steamboat.
50 50

Washington and C.
Vig. Signing the "Declaration of Independence." NORWICH BANK, Norwich, Ct. Eagle.
100 Female.

D 500
NORWICH BANK, Norwich, Ct. Group of females on right; Indian, squaw and child on left; between them the Arms of one of the states.
500 Portrait of Daniel Webster.

1 1
OCEAN BANK, Stonington, Conn. 1 Locomotive and cars. Steamboat.
1 Female seated on building spy glass; ship on left.

Sailor seated upon bale of goods with American flag on left, anchor on right. TWO
Steam ship and other vessels. OCEAN BANK, Stonington, Conn. State Arms.
2 Female Portrait.

Group of three females supporting figure 3.
3 Ships. 3 OCEAN BANK, Stonington, Conn. Steam ship.
3 Sailor, spy glass, &c.; vessel on right.

5 Locomotive and cars. FIVE
OCEAN BANK, Stonington, Conn. V V Female seated resting upon State Arms of Connecticut, steam ship and ship on right, also vessels on left.
5 Female Portrait.

Sailor seated by his right foot is a coil of rope, flag on left, also hat raised aloft in left hand. TEN
Large spread eagle on American shield, &c. OCEAN BANK, Stonington, Conn. Locomotive and Tender.
10 Large ship.

Female reaching sheaf of grain on left and in right hand sickle. XX
20 OCEAN BANK, 20 Stonington, Conn. View of sea, large ship; light house on right in distance; sail vessel in distance on left.
Female sitting upon barrel with wand in left hand, ship on right. XX

Three females on a rocky cliff, glass, anchor, &c. 100
View of city of New York and Brooklyn with shipping. OCEAN BANK, Stonington, Conn. Eagle.
100 Female reclining on bale of goods, ships on right, also one on left.

ONE Mechanic &c.
1 Indian looking down upon city. PAHQUIOQUE BANK Danbury, Conn.
1 Female.

Female Indian, farm scene in distance. 2
PAHQUIOQUE BANK Danbury, Conn. 2 Vig. Two oxen; farm house on right. Indian's head.
2 Eagle.

Child and chickens. 3
PAHQUIOQUE B'K, Danbury, Ct. Drover and cattle.
3

5 FIVE Female
PAHQUIOQUE BANK Danbury, Conn. 5 Vig. Wild horses. 5
FIVE 5 FIVE Female Indian.

TEN — Three cupids, anvil, hammer, grain, globe, &c.
PAHQUIOQUE B'K, Danbury, Ct. Child with rabbits. TEN
10 Franklin.

XX — Word twenty and two XX.
PAHQUIOQUE B'K, Danbury, Conn. State Arms with female on either side. TWENTY
20 — Word dollars and two XX.

On this end is figure 50, $ mark, word fifty, and letter L.
PAHQUIOQUE B'K, Danbury, Conn. State Arms, horse on either side and eagle at top; on right train of cars and city; on left building.
On this end is figure 50, word dollars and letter L.

ONE — Two Indians seated. ONE
Vig. Female reclining on horn of plenty. Portrait of Washington. PAWCATUCK BANK, Pawcatuck, Ct. Bales and barrels.
1 — Two females, one erect, the other kneeling with grain.

TWO — Portrait of Zachary Taylor. TWO
Vig. State Arms; eagle surmounting it; two females on right, seated Goddess of Liberty on left. PAWCATUCK BANK, Pawcatuck, Ct. Weaving loom.
2 — Female with sickle and sheaf. 2

THREE — Female seated feeding eagle. THREE
Vig. State arms; female and three children on right; Indian squaw and papoose on left. PAWCATUCK BANK Pawcatuck, Ct.
3 — Farmer with rake, dog, &c.; barn background.

FOUR — Stonecutter at work.
Vig. Planing machine, man standing beside it. PAWCATUCK BANK Pawcatuck, Ct.
4 — Girl swinging; farmhouse in background.

FIVE 5 FIVE
Vig. Indian, squaw, and child on precipice overlooking city. Portrait of two females. PAWCATUCK BANK. Pawcatuck, Ct. Female swimming.
5 — Goddess of Liberty; eagle upon shield behind her.

10 — Locomotive crossing bridge, city in distance.
PAWCATUCK BANK, Pawcatuck, Ct. Vig. Three females representing Commerce, Agriculture, and Science. Hand and hammer.
10 — Ships sailing in front of city.

Female seated resting upon column, right hand upon shield. TWENTY
PAWCATUCK BANK, Pawcatuck, Ct. Vig. Blacksmith seated, anvil, &c., city in background, the left of vignette is 20 with words twenty dollars across it.
20 XX

Left	Centre	Right
50 Portrait of John Adams.	PAWCATUCK BANK, Pawcatuck, Ct. Vig. Winged female seated on clouds, female soaring on either side. Steamship.	50
ONE Farmers loading wagon.	PEQUONNOCK B'K, Bridgeport, Ct. ONE	ONE One male and two female Indians overlooking precipice; city in distance. ONE
2	PEQUONNOCK B'K, Bridgeport, Ct. Mechanics at work; view of shipyard. 2	2 Two female Indians; one seated, the other erect.
Portrait of P. T. Barnum. 3	PEQUONNOCK B'K, Bridgeport, Ct. Vig. Country seat of P. T. Barnum. 3 3	3 Portrait of Jenny Lind.
5 Portrait of Barnum.	Same as threes. PEQUONNOCK B'K, Bridgeport, Ct. V V	5 Portrait of Jenny Lind.
Female gathering wheat. X	PEQUONNOCK B'K, Bridgeport, Ct. Vig. Shield, on either side sailor and Indian; eagle at top of shield.	10 Female with flowers.
20 Two Indians, canoe, &c.	Vig. Harvest scene. PEQUONNOCK B'K, Bridgeport, Ct. XX	20 Two females seated, bales, shield, &c.
FIFTY Mechanic, sailor and 2 females; city on right.	PEQUONNOCK B'K, Bridgeport, Ct. Harvest scene, man erect, dog by his side, two females seated, one holding sickle; also oxen, grain, &c., Indian with bow and arrow, in shield on right.	50
100 Two Indians with bow and arrow.	Vig. Sailor seated amid nautical instruments; view of sea and ships on left. PEQUONNOCK B'K, Bridgeport, Ct.	100 C
1 Portrait of Washington. ONE	1 Vig. Female seated on barrel; cars on left. 1 PHENIX BANK, Hartford, Ct. Locomotive and cars.	Full length female. ONE

Left	Centre	Right
ONE Full length female, hand resting on shield.	[New Plate.] 1 1 ONE PHENIX BANK, Hartford, Ct. Safe.	ONE Blacksmith at work.
2 Portrait of Washington. TWO	Vig. Two females seated, one holding sickle; grain on left; ship on right. 2 PHENIX BANK, Hartford, Ct. Steam propeller.	TWO Sculptor at work. TWO
2 Male portrait.	PHENIX BANK, Hartford, Ct. TWO	2 Head of sailor.
3 Portrait of Gen. Taylor. THREE	Vig. Group of mechanics; ship building on left, vessels on right. PHENIX BANK, Hartford, Ct. Mechanic's arm and hand.	3 Female. THREE
Male portrait.	Group of figures drawing a chariot. 5 on left. 5 PHENIX BANK, Hartford, Ct. State Arms.	Female and sword. FIVE
5 V 5	PHENIX BANK, Hartford, Ct. Vig. Three females seated, one with sickle, the other with quadrant. FIVE	5 V 5
5 Five across V 5	PHENIX BANK, Hartford, Conn. View of a river and steamboat; town in distance.	FIVE 5 FIVE
10 Portrait of Washington. 10	Female seated, letter X on shield. Female seated with horn of plenty, letter X on shield. PHENIX BANK, Hartford, Ct. Female seated; view of ocean; ship on right, goods and ships on left.	10 Female with pole and cap. 10
10 X 10	PHENIX BANK, Hartford, Ct. Vig. Locomotive and train of cars.	10 X 10
TWENTY DOLLARS	Two females seated with grain and sickle; 20 on either side of vig., and also on each side of title. PHENIX BANK, Hartford, Conn. 20	CONNECTICUT

Left	Centre	Right
TWENTY DOLLARS	20 Vig. Two females seated, one with grain. 20 20 20 PHENIX BANK, Hartford, Ct. 20	CONNECTICUT
FIFTY DOLLARS	50 Vig. Female seated, with wand in right hand; river, vessels and houses on left; barrels, &c., on right. 50 50 50 PHENIX BANK, Hartford, Ct. L	CONNECTICUT
FIFTY DOLLARS	50 Female seated representing Commerce; boxes, bbls, etc. 50 50 Title of Bank. 50 L	CONNECTICUT
ONE HUNDRED	Female seated holding letter C; ship in distance—C and 100 on each side. 100 Title of Bank. 100 C	CONNECTICUT
ONE HUNDRED	100 Vig. Female seated overlooking sea, on which is ship. C 100 100 PHENIX BANK, Hartford, Ct. C	CONNECTICUT
1 Female seated on bale of goods, with arms extended. 1	View of City Hall, R. R. Depot and Train of Cars. QUINEBAUG BANK, Norwich, Ct. Cogwheel.	1 Main Mast Head.
2 Two Cupids in fig. 2.	Female Indian reclining, bow and arrows by her side; steamboat on left. QUINEBAUG BANK, Norwich, Ct. Locomotive and Tender.	2 Female seated, child by her side holding sickle.
3 Female sheaf of wheat and sickle.	Two females seated; locomotive and cars on right, buildings and vessels on left. QUINEBAUG BANK, Norwich, Ct. Cogwheel.	3 Three Graces in fig. 3.
5	Spread Eagle; grain, mechanical implements, &c., by his side; ships on right; sheep on left. QUINEBAUG BANK, Norwich, Ct. Female.	5
TEN Female, sword, and balances. TEN	10 Female soaring in air. QUINEBAUG BANK, Norwich, Ct. Eagle.	10

20 XX XX Representation of making the Globe, Indian. 20 QUINEBAUG BANK, Norwich, Ct. TWENTY	Vig. same as ones. 100 QUINNIPIACK B'K, New Haven, Ct. 100 Vessel.	2 SAUGATUCK BANK, Westport, Conn. TWO 2 2 Train of cars. State Die. Village scene.
50 QUINEBAUG BANK, Norwich, Ct. 50 Male Portrait Female, American shield, eagle, liberty pole and cap. 50 50	1 Two Ladies, girls weaving. 1 ONE ROCKVILLE BANK, Rockville, Conn. 1 Portrait of Webster. Female bathing.	3 View of Westport village. 3 SAUGATUCK BANK, Westport, Conn. Female. Portrait of Daniel Webster.
100 QUINEBAUG BANK, Norwich, Ct. 100 Female with grain, leaning. Male Portrait 100 ONE HUNDRED 100	2 Agricultural scene; cattle grazing. 2 ROCKVILLE BANK, Rockville, Conn. Man on horseback. Ducks. Male portrait.	V Interior of a Blacksmith shop, man shoeing horse. 5 SAUGATUCK BANK, Westport, Conn. Indian with bow and arrow. State Die.
1 QUINNIPIACK BK., New Haven, Ct. 1 Sailor, capstan, etc. Male portrait. Vig. Indian, squaw and pappoose in a canoe. ONE	Word three and figure 3. Agricultural scene; dairy maid with pail, cows, &c. THREE Indian girl in door of wigwam. ROCKVILLE BANK, Rockville, Conn. Three female figures with emblems of peace, &c. Dog.	TEN 10 Shoemaker shop, man at work and female binding shoes. 10 X SAUGATUCK BANK, Westport, Conn. Indian. Jackson.
Male portrait. QUINNIPIACK BK., New Haven, Ct. 2 2 Vig. Same as ones. Two Cupids in large 2.	FIVE ROCKVILLE BANK, Rockville, Conn. 5 5 Load of hay; boy sleeping on top; boy walking by side of oxen. 5 Ducks. Female head	Ship; other vessels and city in background. Female with sheaf and sickle. 50 SAUGATUCK BANK, Westport, Conn. 50 Henry Clay
Portrait of Webster, QUINNIPIACK BK. New Haven, Ct. 3 Beehive, etc. Three cupids in figure 3. Vig. Same as ones. THREE	X ROCKVILLE BANK. Rockville, Conn. 10 State Arms. Iron foundry Girl.	100 100 Ship; other vessels and lighthouse in distance. 100 Sailor and blacksmith, each with implements of profession. SAUGATUCK BANK, Westport, Conn. Sailor leaning on capstan with quadrant in hand.
5 Vig. Same as ones. 5 QUINNIPIACK B'K, New Haven, Conn. Anchor, bales, goods, etc. Female.	XX ROCKVILLE BANK, Rockville, Conn. 20 Figures 20, two XX's and words twenty dollars. Sheep shearing. Boy's head	ONE Eagle, ships, &c. 1 View of Essex and the Conn. River at Essex. SAYBROOK BANK, Essex, Ct. ONE ONE Bust of female. Female, ships, bales of goods, &c. 1
Vig. Same as ones. 10 Male portrait. 10 QUINNIPIACK B'K, New Haven, Ct. Male and female. TEN	1 SAUGATUCK BANK, Westport, Conn. ONE 1 Drove of sheep, boy on right. 1 Dogs head. State Die.	2 Train of cars, three females, ship, &c. 2 TWO Shipbuilding SAYBROOK BANK, Essex, Ct. View of Essex and Conn. River at Essex. 2 Agricultural implements, &c. TWO
20 QUINNIPIACK B'K, New Haven, Ct. 20 Vig. same as ones. Mechanic, anvil, and cogwheel. Female in a shell.	1 SAUGATUCK BANK, ONE Westport. 1 Drove of sheep, boy on right. 1 ONE Connecticut. Man mowing; man ploughing in distance.	THREE Female, bale, hhd., ship, &c. 3 SAYBROOK BANK, Essex, Ct. Beehive. THREE
50 QUINNIPIACK B'K. New Haven, Ct. 50 Ship. Vig. same as ones. Female and mechanical implements	2 SAUGATUCK BANK, Westport, Conn. TWO 2 Boy asleep on load of hay drawn by two oxen; boy walking with pitchfork in hand. 2 Train of cars. Village scene.	Female, bale of goods, shipping, &c. 5 5 SAYBROOK BANK, Essex, Ct. 5 Steamboat. Female with pallet, &c.

Left end	Centre	Right end
10 Indian, liberty cap, shield, &c.	Man, woman, bales, train of cars, anvil, nautical instruments, shipping, &c. X SAYBROOK BANK. Essex, Ct. Fish.	10 Female bust.
20 Washington on horseback	Two females, bale, train of cars, steamboat, state arms, and horn of plenty. SAYBROOK BANK. Essex, Ct. Elephant.	20 Female resting on bale, shipping, &c.
1 Female.	SHETUCKET BANK, Norwich, Ct. Vig. Three figures, bird, wounded, and child.	1 Sailor.
2 Female and flowers.	Vig. Milkmaid seated with cattle; farmhouse and trees in background. SHETUCKET BANK, Norwich, Ct.	2 State do.
3 Load of hay, drover, and cattle; view of street, buildings, &c. in distance.	Title of Bank Vig. Farmers resting from work. Eagle.	3 Female
Female reclining, sailor holding dagger-hole guard, anchor, &c. by his side. FIVE	Vig. View of ocean, steamship and other vessels. SHETUCKET BANK. Norwich, Ct.	5 Child.
10 Mason at work; building on left.	Vig. Horses, farm house and cottages. SHETUCKET BANK, Norwich, Ct.	10 State do.
50 Cass.	SHETUCKET BANK, Norwich, Conn. Signing the Declaration of Independence.	50 Webster.
C C	United States Capitol. SHETUCKET BANK, Norwich, Conn.	100 Female hea.
1 Washington	State Arms; eagle at top; two females on right; one on left with pole and cap. SOUTHPORT BANK, Southport, Conn.	1 Martha Washington

Left end	Centre	Right end
Two and figure 2. Large ship and shipping in distance.	Vig. Three male figures; view of city on right. SOUTHPORT BANK. Southport, Ct.	2 Female Indian and child.
THREE THREE	Train of cars. Vig. Group of Indians, looking down upon a city. SOUTHPORT BANK. Southport, Ct.	3 Two farmers and dog; two men and farm-house in background.
5 Head-quarters of Gen. Washington at Newburgh FIVE	Vig. Female reclining on chest; State Arms on right. 5 5 SOUTHPORT BANK, Southport, Ct.	5 Portrait of Jenny Lind.
10	Vig. View of ocean; steamship and other vessels. X SOUTHPORT BANK, Southport, Ct. Eagle.	10 X, 10, Ten.
Female with shield, liberty pole, and cap.	50 Vig. Female seated with grain; cars crossing bridge on right; farming implements and canal scene on left. SOUTHPORT BANK, Southport, Ct.	50 Mechanic and mechanical tools, sailor holding flag.
C View of cars crossing bridge; city in distance; load of hay on left.	Title of Bank. Vig. Three females holding quadrant, sickle, and compass, cornucopia between them. 100	100 View of river and ship; city in distance.
1 Washington.	STAFFORD BANK, Stafford Springs, Conn. Two females beside [illegible]	1 Female head.
1 Washington.	STAFFORD BANK, Stafford Springs, Ct. Man talking to a stone cutter, masons at work in background. Female.	1 Fig. 1 and word ONE.
1 Child and rabbits.	Drovers and cattle. STAFFORD BANK, Stafford Springs, Ct.	1 Locomotive.
Farmer with scythe, village in distance. TWO	STAFFORD BANK, Stafford Springs, Ct. Boy with horses.	2 Child holding hen and chicken.

Left end	Centre	Right end
3 Female.	STAFFORD BANK. Stafford Springs, Ct. 3 Three Cupids anvil, hammer, grain, globe, compass and square. 3	3 Portrait of Franklin.
Female with grain on her head; harvesting in the background.	Dog chasing deer. 5 STAFFORD B'K. Stafford Springs, Conn. FIVE	5 FIVE
Farm yard scene. 5	STAFFORD BANK, Stafford Springs, Ct. FIVE Female.	5 Female.
5 FIVE	5 STAFFORD B'K, 5 Stafford Springs, Ct. Female on either side of portrait of Webster representing Commerce and Agriculture.	5 FIVE
TEN Farmer sickle and grain. 10	STAFFORD BANK. Stafford Springs, Ct. Spread eagle on shield, cornucopia on left; view of ocean and ships. X X	10 Man and horse. X
Three females representing Liberty, Justice and Agriculture.	STAFFORD BANK, Stafford, Conn. TWENTY DOLLARS 20 20	20 Indian seated.
50 Farmer in act of drinking from mug.	STAFFORD BANK, Stafford, Conn. FIFTY DOLLARS FIFTY Lathe do.	50 Two females; ship on ocean
Female and shield, liberty pole and cap; starry drapery across her lap.	1 Vig. Bank building carriage, &c.; lady and gentleman on horseback. STAMFORD BANK. Stamford, Ct. Goods, &c.	1 Female.
TWO Female. TWO	Vig. Group of figures on either side of shield. STAMFORD BANK, Stamford, Ct. Females head.	2 Female, sheaf of wheat and sickle. 2
THREE Portrait of Washington. THREE	Female portrait. Female portrait. Vig. River on which is row boat; train of cars crossing bridge. STAMFORD BANK, Stamford, Ct. Eagle.	3 Female. THREE

Left	Centre	Right
5 Female portrait.	Steamer, ship, yachts, etc. STAMFORD BANK, Stamford, Conn.	5 Webster.
5 Female. FIVE	Vig. Three females with cornucopia, wand, sword and balances, overlooking precipice. STAMFORD BANK, Stamford, Ct. Farming implements.	5 Female Indian liberty pole and shield.
TEN Male, female and child	Sailor seated on anchor, two others erect; ship in distance. STAMFORD BANK, Stamford, Conn. CONNECTICUT	10 Clay.
10 Male portrait.	Vig. Female Indian seated, horn of plenty at her side, flags, safe, shield, &c.; eagle on globe; train of cars on left; steamboat on right. STAMFORD BANK, Stamford, Ct. Eagle.	10 Female.
20 Female portrait	Cattle, sheep, stream. STAMFORD BANK, Stamford, Conn.	20 Fillmore.
XX Washington. XX	Female seated, elbow on State Arms; steamship and vessel on right; farming implements on left. 20 on either side of vig. Title of Bank. Horse's head.	20 Cattle and sheep. 20
50 Male portrait	Depot, steamboat landing, wharf, buildings and shipping. Title of Bank.	50 Female portrait.
50 Two females with cakes 50	L Vig. Indian female reclining; sailor pointing to ship in distance. L STAMFORD BANK, Stamford, Ct. Eagle.	50 Male portrait. 50
100 Female portrait.	Launch of the Adriatic, river, ship-yard, city, etc. Title of Bank.	100 Male portrait.
ONE Blacksmith seated on a boiler. ONE	Vig. Man ploughing with two horses, river and steamboat on left. STATE BANK, Hartford, Ct. State arms.	1 Female seated, factories in background.

Left	Centre	Right
1 Female resting on ornamental pillar, mechanical tools, &c. around her.	Vig. View of Trinity College, Hartford. STATE BANK, Hartford, Ct.	1 Female and sheaf of grain.
TWO Female Indian with bow and arrows, liberty pole and cap; hands resting on shield.	Vig. Same as second plate of ones. STATE BANK, Hartford Ct. State Arms	2 Female with basket of flowers.
TWO Female seated on chest holding sword and balance. Locomotive and Tender.	2 Female and sailor seated, female with sickle and grain, sailor holding Quadrant. STATE BANK, Hartford, Ct. State Arms	2 Farmer and Basket of Corn.
THREE Female seated; American shield, &c.	Same as 2d Plate of Ones. STATE BANK, Hartford, Ct.	3 State Arms. THREE
3 Female, anvil and hammer.	Two females, one holding sword and scales, the other reclining with pole and cap; Eagle and State Arms on left; ship in distance. STATE BANK, Hartford, Ct. Horn of Plenty, bales, &c.	3 Male figure holding cornucopia.
5	Female on either side of State Arms, Locomotive and cars on left; steamship on left. Female Portrait. STATE BANK, Hartford, Ct. Sail Vessel.	5 Female in ornamental figure 5.
5 Sailor seated on bales of goods; Quadrant in right hand. FIVE	State Arms; female on right, flags on left. STATE BANK, Hartford, Ct. Horn of Plenty, Bales &c.	5 Female seated; mechanic tools, &c. FIVE
10 Sailor resting on bale of goods, hat in right hand, Quadrant in left; ship on right.	Female resting her left arm on bale of goods, wand in right hand; vessel on left. Locomotive and cars on right. STATE BANK, Hartford, Ct. State Arms.	10 Female seated with sickle and grain.
TWENTY Female resting her arm on barrel, wand in right hand; vessel on right. XX	20 View of Park and Public Building. 20 STATE BANK Hartford, Ct. State Arms.	TWENTY Blacksmith's anvil and hammer. XX
50 Female seated, factories in back ground.	Locomotive and Train of cars. 50 STATE BANK, Hartford, Ct. State Arms.	FIFTY Female, sword and balances. 50

Left	Centre	Right
100 Female seated with anvil and hammer 100	Vig. Large spread eagle on American shield. STATE BANK, Hartford, Ct. State arms.	100 Male figure holding cornucopia. 100
ONE 1 ONE	1 Fort, ships, &c. 1 STONINGTON B'K, Stonington, Ct Figure 1 and word One.	Small figure 1. Small figure 1.
Male portrait ONE	Sailor seated with nautical implements; vessels in distance. STONINGTON BK, Stonington, Conn.	1 Vessels.
TWO	Whaling scene. Male portrait. Title of Bank.	2 Sailor at helm.
TWO 2 TWO	2 Catching seals; ships in distance on left. 2 STONINGTON B'K, Stonington, Ct. 2	2 2
3 CONNECTICUT 3	[First Plate.] 3 Whaling scene, ship on right; men in small boat on left. 3 STONINGTON B'K, Stonington Ct. 3	3 THREE 3
Figures, anvil, sledge &c. 3	[Second Plate.] 3 Locomotive and Train Cars 3 STONINGTON B'K, Stonington, Ct. Steam Boat.	Female reclining, wand in right hand, key in left; building on right. Sail vessel. 3
3 Male portrait.	Steamboat "Plymouth Rock," and other vessels. Title of Bank.	3 Sailor with glass.
4 Female with Liberty pole and cap, also State Arms on right. 4	4 View of Ocean with large ship; ship in distance on right; sail vessel in extreme distance on left. 4 STONINGTON B'K. Stonington, Ct.	FOUR Vessel. FOUR
Chariot in which is seated a female. American shield, &c. to right, and Liberty pole and cap, ornamental figure of Neptune and car.	[New Plate.] STONINGTON B'K, Stonington, Ct. 5 Large ornamental letter V in which is a female, Eagle, Liberty Pole and cap on left; Globe at her feet.	5

5 Male Portrait 5 — (Old Plate.) 5 Chariot drawn by Sea horses in which is seated a female. 5 STONINGTON B'K, Stonington, Ct. Locomotive and cars. — FIVE DOLLARS

10 Sheaf of Wheat. 10 — (Old Plate.) STONINGTON B'K, Stonington, Ct. Neptune and chariot drawn by sea horses. Locomotive and cars. — TEN

10 — [New Plate.] Whaling scene. STONINGTON B'K, Stonington, Ct X — 10

20 Portrait of Washington. 20 — STONINGTON B'K. XX Chariot in which is seated a female holding key in left hand drawn by lions. XX Locomotive and cars. — TWENTY

50 — 50 STONINGTON B'K, 50 View of ocean upon which is a large ship, also vessel in distance on right; and vessel in extreme distance on left. — FIFTY

ONE Female supporting figure 1 ONE — [First Plate.] 1 Vig. Female seated, mechanical tools on right; farming implements on left. THAMES BANK. Norwich, Ct. Female head. — 1 Female head

1 Man resting on rails; the horses in background. — [Second Plate.] Vig. Drove of cattle; two men on horseback; one man sitting by a tree; public house on left. THAMES BANK, Norwich, Ct. Man and horse. — 1 Man on horse

Farmer in act of drinking from jug. ONE — THAMES BANK, Norwich, Conn. Circular die enclosing female head—"One" over it—"Dollar" beneath. — 1 Goddess of Liberty.

2 — Vig. Female overlooking sea, on which is some ships; anchor at her side light house on right, fig. 2 on right. THAMES BANK Norwich, Ct. Female Indian. — TWO View of ocean, steamship and ships, female in ornamental figure 2. TWO

TWO Gleaner with sheaf and sickle. — THAMES BANK, Norwich, Conn Henry Clay. — 2 State Arms.

3 Three females soaring in clouds — THAMES BANK, Norwich, Conn. Milkmaid erect holding stool in left hand; shading her eyes with right; boy beside; cows, etc. — 3 Eagle on shield.

THREE Three cupids in large figure 3. THREE — 3 Vig. Two females on either side of a shield, one with liberty pole and cap, and one with globe, steamboat on right; bridge, locomotive, and train of cars on left. 3 THAMES BANK, Norwich, Ct. Indian, bow, and arrows. — THREE Three figures in large figure 3. THREE

5 Female Indian seated with tomahawk. FIVE — 5 Vig. Five cupids in ornamental figure 5 5 THAMES BANK, Norwich, Ct. Female head. — 5 Female seated in letter V with a cup in right hand; bale of goods on right. FIVE

5 Male portrait — Vig. Two figures, sailor and farmer; farmer with sickle, grain, &c.; sailor with spyglass, capstan, and anchor at the feet; sheep on left. THAMES BANK, Norwich, Ct — 5 Female Indian.

V Female. V — Ship. Vig. Female seated emptying water out of pitcher; liberty pole and cap on left. FIVE THAMES BANK, Norwich, Ct. Cupid. Mech's arm — Five dollars running across three circular dies.

X Male head. X — Vig. View of Greenwich Falls in Connecticut. Med. head. Bee hive. THAMES BANK. Norwich, Ct. Machinery. — X TEN X

10 Portrait of D. Webster. — Vig. View of ocean in storm and boat putting off. THAMES BANK, Norwich, Ct. — 10 Two females; one seated with spyglass and one standing.

XX Male portrait XX — Vig. Three females seated; tackle, farming implements, &c. THAMES BANK, Norwich, Ct. TWENTY — 20 Male portrait 20

FIFTY Franklin FIFTY — FIFTY DOLLARS 50 Two children. 50 THAMES BANK, Norwich, Conn — 50 State Arms.

100 Male portrait 100 — 100 Vig. Female on either side of a shield holding balance and spear, eagle at top of shield; ships on right; bridge on left. 100 on right. THAMES BANK, Norwich, Ct. C — 100 Group of cupids in circular die. 100

1 Round die. 1 — 1 Female seated on the ground; eagle and shield; ship in distance. 1 THOMPSON BANK, Thompson, Conn. — ONE Female figure. ONE

TWO Female holding an eagle. TWO — THOMPSON BANK. Thompson, Conn. 2 2 Female with sickle and sheaf of wheat, also cows. Bird — 2 Female holding scales. TWO

THREE Female with anchor; merchandise. 3 — 3 Female feeding an eagle from a cup. 3 THOMPSON BANK, Thompson, Conn. — THREE Female, sickle, and sheaf of wheat. 3

FIVE — 5 Female and wheel. V THOMPSON BANK, Thompson, Conn. Ferns. — FIVE

10 — 10 Two female figures and eagle; ship and canal in background. 10 THOMPSON BANK, Thompson, Conn. — X Female. 10

TWENTY — 20 Female and lion; steamboat in distance XX THOMPSON BANK, Thompson, Conn. Cupid astride deer. — 20 Female. XX

50 Female and anchor; steamboat in distance. 50 — FIFTY DOLLARS 50 THOMPSON BANK, Thompson, Conn. — FIFTY

C Portrait of Washington. C — 100 Neptune, merchandise; ship in distance. 100 THOMPSON BANK. Thompson, Conn. — ONE HUNDRED

ONE Female supporting a figure 1. ONE — 1 Female seated on a bale; factories in background. 1 TOLLAND CO. BANK. Tolland, Conn. — ONE Portrait of Washington. ONE

TWO A cooper at work. TWO — 2 Harvest scene. 2 Title of Bank. — TWO Female with grain, and shield with sickle. TWO

THREE Female figure and cherubs in fig. 3 THREE	3 Farmer boy, with cradle and sheaf of wheat; house in background. 3 Title of Bank. Female head.	THREE Interior of a blacksmith shop. THREE
5 Female supporting the above figure. V	Five female figures and figure 5. Title of Bank. Machinery.	5 Farmer boy
10 Female with sickle and sheaf.	Two females; factories in background. Title of Bank.	10 Indian girl.
50 Female figure.	Male and female Title of Bank.	50 Cupid in a sail boat. 50
100 Vulcan the blacksmith seated.	Spread eagle standing upon a tree; railroad and canal in background. Title of Bank.	100 Female with rake.
1 Female head ONE	TRADESMENS' B'K, New Haven, Conn. Battle scene. ONE ONE	1 View of Bank building.
2 Cows and dairy maids.	TRADESMENS' B'K, New Haven, Conn. Blacksmith and anvil; farmer, horse and dog.	2 Sailor, and shipping.
3 Landing of R. Williams.	TRADESMENS' B'K, New Haven, Conn. THREE 3 DOLLARS 3	3 Female and bale of goods; factories in the distance
5	Railroad, steamboat and wharf scene. TRADESMENS' B'K, New Haven, Conn.	5 View of Bank building.
10 Cattle field	Farmers resting at noon; two horses attached to plough, feeding. TRADESMENS' B'K, New Haven, Conn.	10 View of Bank building.

20 TWENTY	TRADESMENS' BK. Three blacksmiths with forge and implements. New Haven, Conn.	20 DOLLARS
Indian with gun overlooking precipice. 1	UNCAS BANK, Norwich, Ct. Vig. Cotton factories and two females at work.	1 State die.
Indian erect with bow, arrow, and tomahawk. TWO	Vig. Three females and cupid bathing. UNCAS BANK, Norwich, Ct. Horse.	2 State die.
3	Vig. Indian with gun overlooking river. State die. UNCAS BANK, Norwich, Ct. Steamboat.	THREE Full length female
5	Vig. Three cattle in water, one reposing; sheep on left. State die. UNCAS BANK, Norwich, Ct.	5 Female Indian. FIVE
Three females on rock; anvil, scale, &c., between them. TEN	Vig. Spread eagle on American shield. UNCAS BANK, Norwich, Ct. Indian head.	10 State die.
50 Female with chickens.	UNCAS BANK, Norwich, Conn. Indian seated resting his head on right hand.	50 Child and rabbits.
100 C	UNCAS BANK, Norwich, Conn. State Arms, female on either side.	100 C
ONE Small boy, anvil and hammer. ONE	Vig. Whaling scene. UNION BANK, New London, Conn. Arm, hammer and anvil.	ONE
TWO Female, shield, Liberty pole, cap and eagle TWO	Vig. Milkmaid, seated with cattle. UNION BANK, New London, Conn. Steamboat.	TWO

THREE Same as Twos. THREE	Vig. Milkmaid; one cow standing, and one reposing in front of her. UNION BANK, New London, Conn.	THREE
FIVE Large ship. FIVE	Vig. Farmer's loading hay. UNION BANK, New London, Conn. Machinery.	FIVE
TEN Male portrait. TEN	Vig. View of river, upon which is large ship, steamboat and other vessels. UNION BANK, New London, Ct.	TEN
20 Male portrait. TWENTY	Vig. Stone cutter's at work. UNION BANK, New London, Ct.	20
50 Male portrait. FIFTY	Vig. Ship carpenter; ship building on left; ships and view of city on right. UNION BANK, New London, Ct.	50
100 Portrait of Washington. 100	Vig. Group of three male figures. UNION BANK, New London, Ct.	100
1 Two females, one with sword and balances, one with shield and spear.	Vig. Female on either side of State arms. WATERBURY BANK Waterbury, Ct. Goods, cog-wheels, &c.	1 Two females erect, with wand, sickle, and grain.
2 Female.	Vig. Female and eagle, liberty pole and cap, shield, horn of plenty, &c. WATERBURY BANK Waterbury, Ct. Farming implements.	2 Male portrait
3 Mechanic and anvil.	Title of Bank Vig. Female seated, one foot resting on globe, left hand resting on shield, which stands upright on a gate, arm around eagle's neck, right hand holding pole and cap, cornucopia at her feet; farming scene on left; factories and cars on right. Cornucopia bale, etc.	3 Mechanic at work.
5 Three figures —females gathering flowers.	Vig. Female and spread eagle; steamship in distance on right; miniature portrait of Washington; factories, bridge, and cars on left. WATERBURY BANK Waterbury, Ct. State arms.	5 Female with wand and sickle; man in full armour and a.

Left end	Centre	Right end
10 Female, sword, and balances.	Female seated between figures 10, key in left hand; cornucopia, safe, bridge, railroad cars on left; goats on right. Title of Bank. Dog's head, and collar marked Fidelity.	10 Female, hand resting on capstan, &c.
20 Female 20	Female seated between flowers 20, rake in right hand. WATERBURY BANK Waterbury, Ct. Imp. and products.	20 Female 20
100 Portrait of Washington.	Vig. Female seated, bridge, locomotive, and cars on right; canal scene on left. WATERBURY BANK Waterbury, Ct. Bale of goods, cogwheel, &c.	100 Female.
1 Grecian monument. 1	1 Vig. Whaling scene. 1 WHALING BANK, New London, Ct. Ship, barrel, anchor, &c.	1 Female seated, anchor in right hand key in left. 1
TWO Hunter, gun in right hand dog at his feet. TWO	2 Vig. same as ones. 2 WHALING BANK. New London, Ct. Steamboat.	TWO Female, sheaf of wheat, sickle, plow, rake, &c. TWO
THREE	3 Vig. same as ones. 3 WHALING BANK. New London, Ct. Blacksmith's arm and hammer.	3 Female; on right state arms, on which is eagle standing, on left scales, barrels, &c. 3
FIVE 5	WHALING BANK. New London, Ct. Vig. same as ones. Three circular dies with words five dollars running across. Indian in canoe.	5 Female giving eagle drink. V
TEN Female seated, eagle on her lap, in right hand sprig of flowers. 10	TEN Vig. same as TEN ones. WHALING BANK. New London, Ct. Cupid seated on reindeer.	TEN Female resting on stone pillar, upon which is engraved letter X. X
20	XX Female seated giving eagle drink. 20 WHALING BANK. New London, Ct. Ship.	TWENTY
FIFTY	WHALING BANK. New London Ct. L Vig. same as ones. L Indian and canoe.	50 Female seated, sheaf of wheat on right, on left scroll on which is engraved figure 50. 50

Left end	Centre	Right end
100	Vig. same as ones. 100 WHALING BANK, New London, Ct. Indian and canoe.	100 Male portrait 100
1 Indian female figure.	Agricultural scene. WINDHAM BANK, Windham, Conn.	1 Froggs.
2 Head of Washington. 2	WINDHAM BANK. Windham, Conn. Large figure 2, Indian male with gun on left, white female with sheaf of wheat on right.	2 Froggs.
3 Med. head. THREE	Manufacturing scene; state arms, cotton, and wheat. Female head. WINDHAM BANK, Windham, Conn.	3 Froggs.
5 Train of cars FIVE	WINDHAM BANK. Windham, Conn. Large V, with female figure and wheat inside, and female head on either side.	5 Froggs.
X TEN 10	WINDHAM BANK, Windham, Conn. Two females, state arms, steamboat, railroad. X	10 Froggs.
ONE Mechanic erect, with arms folded; buildings in distance.	Two cows with no horns; one standing, the other laying down; mill on right. WINDHAM CO., BK., Brooklyn, Conn. Agricultural implements.	1 Female Portrait.
Little girl, with sheaf of grain on head; harvesting scene in distance. 2	Farmer, sailor, and 2 blacksmith, apparently talking; horse and man on right. WINDHAM CO., BK., Brooklyn, Conn.	2 Female with pole and cap, word Liberty, at her feet; building and train of cars on left.
3 Male portrait.	Loading hay; two horses and four men; house in distance. WINDHAM CO., BK., Brooklyn, Conn.	3 THREE 3
FIVE 5 FIVE Head of Washington.	Title of Bank Two men; one with no hat, horse and buildings in background.	5 FIVE

Left end	Centre	Right end
10 Two females. TEN	View of the Capitol at Washington. WINDHAM CO., BK., Brooklyn, Conn.	10 Female portrait.
20 Ind. Head. 20	Train of cars, hills, &c.; a train of cars, city and bridge in distance. WINDHAM CO., BK. Brooklyn, Conn. Two men; one with spade.	20 Female with flowers.
50 Female seated, with helmet and shield.	Male and female seated. WINDHAM CO., BK., Brooklyn, Conn. 50	50 Cupid in a sail-boat. 50
100 Male figure sitting.	Large eagle on a tree; with canal and boats, and railroad with cars, in background. WINDHAM CO., BK., Brooklyn, Conn. C C 100	100 Female figure with rake, sitting; load of hay in the distance.
1 Female, and [illegible] ONE	(First Plate.) Mechanic and tools; factories, bridge and railroad cars on left. WINSTED BANK, Winsted, Ct. Female Bathing.	1 Two females sickle and grain.
1 Portrait of Webster. 1	(Second Plate.) Train cars, City in distance. WINSTED BANK. Winsted, Ct. Machinery.	Figure 1 on American shield. Male Portrait ONE
2 Portrait of Gen. Taylor. TWO	Two men, one on horse, the other trying to get horse off track, cars coming towards them. WINSTED BANK, Winsted, Ct. Mechanic's arm, &c.	2 Female, wheat and sickle. 2
THREE Female, shield, Liberty pole and cap. THREE	Vig. Male figures; view of city on right. WINSTED BANK, Winsted, Ct. Dog, safe, and key.	Figure 3 and word three on either side. Female. THREE
FIVE 5 FIVE	(First Plate.) Group of Indians. Female overlooking [illegible]. Anchor, signs, view of &c. city below. WINSTED BANK. Winsted, Ct. Loading Hay.	5 Female seated with pole and cap, eagle and shield on right.
5 Female. FIVE	(Second Plate.) Two females seated with liberty pole and cap, scroll, &c., river steamboat and vessels on left. WINSTED BANK, Winsted, Ct. Machine.	5 Dairymaid. FIVE

Left end	Centre	Right end
Med. head, and figure 10. View of city, bridge, and train of cars passing over it; head of bay on left.	WINSTED BANK, Winsted, Ct. Vig. Three females holding compass; sickle and quadrant. Farming implements.	Med. head, and figure 10. River and ship; city in distance on left.
20 / 20	WINSTED BANK, Winsted, Ct. Vig. Group of figures on either side of a shield; farm house in distance on right. Locomotive and tender.	20 / 20
1 / Male portrait	Vig. Steamship under way, vessels in distance. AM. EX. BANK, New York. Locomotive.	1 / Compt's die.
Male portrait / 2	Vig. A farmer buying cattle of drover; cattle on right, sheep on left. AM. EX BANK, New York. Steamboat.	2 / Compt's die.
3 / Male portrait	AM. EX BANK. New York. Vig. Drove of horses, fences, trees, etc., in background. Eagle.	3 / Compt's die.
5 / Eagle.	AM. EX. BANK, N. Y. City. Five Dollars; FIVE and figure 5 on green die.	5 / Compt's die.
5 / Female, safe, eagle, scales, etc. / FIVE	V 5 and three females; shipping, cars, etc., in distance. V / AMERICAN EX. BK, New York City. Eagle.	5 / Med. head. / FIVE
10 / Same as fives / TEN	Female on either side of shield; shipping, city, canal scene, etc. AMERICAN EX. BK New York City. Eagle.	10 / Two females, eagle, cornucopia and motto "Excelsior." / TEN
TWENTY / Same as fives / TWENTY	20 Female seated; scientific apparatus; in distance steamship. 20 / AMERICAN EX. BK, New York City. Eagle.	Die. / XX / Die.
FIFTY / Female seated; steamboat. / 50	Two Indians and white man. FIFTY on med. head on each side. AMERICAN EX. BK, New York City. Capitol.	FIFTY / Female seated; screw-press buildings in distance. / 50

Left end	Centre	Right end
HUNDRED / Female / 100	100 on med. head. Female on either side shield, eagle at top; cars, shipping, etc. 100 on med. head. AMERICAN EX. BK, New York City. Capitol.	ONE HUNDRED
500 / Same as fives / 500	500 Ceres; steam-vessel in distance. AMERICAN EX. BK, New York City. Eagle.	500
1000 / Same as fives / 1000	Steamship and other vessels; houses, etc. Figs. 1000 on each side. AMERICAN EX. BK, New York City.	ONE THOUSAND
1 / Male portrait	Spread eagle; ship on either side. ATLANTIC BANK, New York City.	1 / Compt's die
2 / Compt's die.	Steamship and other vessels. ATLANTIC BANK, New York City.	2 / Male portrait
Large steamship and other vessels / THREE	Male portrait ATLANTIC BANK, New York City.	3 / Compt's die.
5 / Compt's die	Three females and Cupid in water. ATLANTIC BANK, New York City. Fire Engine.	5 / Henry Clay.
10 / Anchor, bales, &c	Steamship and other vessels. ATLANTIC BANK, New York City. Secured, etc.	10 / Compt's die.
20 / Portrait of Webster.	ATLANTIC BANK, New York City. Sailor erect; vessels in distance.	20 / Compt's die
50 / Male portrait	ATLANTIC BANK, New York City. Female with pole, cap, eagle, &c.	50 / Compt's die

Left end	Centre	Right end
C / Male portrait	Vessels, view of city, &c. ATLANTIC BANK, New York City.	100 / Compt's die.
5 / Large white V on red ground work / Compt's die.	FIVE Goddess of Liberty, eagle, shield, &c. FIVE / BANK OF AMERICA, New York City.	5 / Large white 5 on red ground work
5 / Compt's die. / 5	5 Two females and two spread eagles. 5 / B'K. OF AMERICA, New York City.	5 / FIVE / 5
X / Red end with white X across the end. / Compt's die.	TEN Goddess of Liberty, eagle, shield, &c. TEN / BANK OF AMERICA New York City.	10 / White X across red end.
X / Compt's die. / X	Vig. Same as fives. 10 / B'K. OF AMERICA, New York City.	TEN
Compt's die.	B'K OF AMERICA, New York City. Vig. Spread eagle; stars on left; vessels on right. XX	20
50 / Compt's die.	B'K OF AMERICA, New York City. Eagle.	50
100 / Compt's die. / 100	B'K. OF AMERICA, New York City. Eagle.	100
500 / Compt's die. / 500	500 Spread eagle. / B'K. OF AMERICA, New York City.	
Female portrait. / Compt's die. / Female portrait.	1000 Eagle. 1000 / B'K. OF AMERICA, New York City.	

Left	Centre	Right
One and fig. 1 across. Female seated with eagle, shield, etc.	BANK OF THE COMMONWEALTH, New York City. Large die on which is words "one dollar" and Compt's die.	One and fig. 1 across. Sailor at wheel.
Large die and word two repeated.	Man plowing. BANK OF THE COMMONWEALTH, New York City. Compt's die.	Same as on left.
Bank of the Die with fig. 3, and word three.	Large die with female portrait, words three dollars, and Compt's die at bottom.	Commonw'h. Same as on left.
Figure 5, and words of same.	Milkmaids and cows; in distance on right, rural scene; on left house. BANK OF THE COMMONWEALTH, New York City. Compt's die.	Figure 5 full length of the note; view of city at top, and wharf scene and shipping at bottom.
TEN 10	The arms of each State of the Union in miniature cuts, completely surrounding the whole note. BANK OF THE COMMONWEALTH, New York City. Compt's die.	TEN 10
Compt's die. Sailor leaning on capstan.	Steamship, sail vessels, view of city, etc. BANK OF THE COMMONWEALTH, New York City.	50 Blacksmith, anvil, forge, etc.
100 Male portrait	BANK OF THE COMMONWEALTH, New York City. View of New York harbor and city life scenery generally. Compt's die.	100 Male portrait
500 500	Compt's die. BANK OF THE COMMONWEALTH. N. Y. City.	500 500
1 Compt's die.	Horse. Eagle. B'K OF NEW YORK, N. Y. City. 1 Female with tablets; child at her feet. 1	1 ONE on 1.
1 Compt's die	Bee hive surrounded by flowers. Large red fig. 1 across face of bill. BK. OF NEW YORK, New York City. Eagle.	1 1

Left	Centre	Right
2 Compt's die.	Bee hive surrounded by flowers. Red fig. 2 across face of bill. BK. OF NEW YORK, New York City. Female head.	2
2 Compt's die.	Title of Bank. TWO on 2. Female with sword and shield. TWO on 2.	2 TWO on 2.
Compt's die. 3	Bee hive surrounded by flowers. Red figure 3 across face of bill. BK. OF NEW YORK, New York City. Head of Indian.	3
Compt's die. 3	Female with quadrant, scroll, compass and globe. Title of Bank. Three Green dies with fig. 3 on each.	THREE on 3. 3
Female portrait. 5	View of N. Y. harbor, shipping, etc. Word Five in red letters across face of bill. BK. OF NEW YORK, New York City.	5 Compt's die.
Sailor with flag; female reclining at his feet, anchor, bale, etc.	10 Shipping. Word Ten in red letters across face of bill. BK. OF NEW YORK, New York City.	10 Compt's die
20 Compt's die. 20	Male portrait. Eagle on rock; shipping. Word Twenty in red letters across face of bill. BK. OF NEW YORK, New York City.	20
50 Compt's die. 50	Winged female seated on flags; globe, eagle, etc. Word Fifty in red letters across face of bill. BK. OF NEW YORK, New York City. Secured, etc.	50
C Compt's die.	Female seated on bales, pointing with wand to shipping in distance; lighthouse on left of note. BK. OF NEW YORK, New York City. Secured, etc.	100 Male portrait
Shipping. 300	Compt's die. BK. OF NEW YORK, New York City.	300 Portrait of J. Q. Adams.

Left	Centre	Right
400 Male portrait	Spread eagle on rock; shipping. BK. OF NEW YORK, New York City.	400 Compt's die.
500 Med. head of Washington	Two females seated on either side of a frame, surmounted by an eagle, on which is a view of a city, and word "Excelsior" shipping in distance. BK. OF NEW YORK, New York City.	500 Compt's die.
ONE THOUSAND	View of New York harbor, with shipping, city, &c. BK. OF NEW YORK, New York City.	1000 Compt's die.
ONE Compt's die. ONE	1 Neptune and female in a shell, drawn by two horses on the sea. 1 BANK OF THE NEW YORK DRY DOCK CO. New York City. Ship.	ONE
2 Compt's die 2	2 Female with safe and key, bird perched on safe, female in background. 2 Title of Bank. Ship.	TWO Female with sheaf in her hand. TWO
3 Compt's die. 3	3 Goddess of Liberty with pole and cap, flag around her, leaning on a shield; money flowing from the base of the shield. 3 Title of Bank. Ship.	THREE Female with sheaf. 3
5 Compt's die. 5	5 Neptune in a sea car drawn by two horses, placing his arms towards a wing of female. 5 Title of Bank. Ship.	FIVE Franklin. 5
10 Compt's die. 10	X Vig. Same as fives. X Title of Bank running around the vig. Ship.	Female with pole leaning on an anchor. 10
20 Compt's die 20	XX Vig. Same as fives, with title running around it. XX Red figures 20. Ship.	Female with scroll in her hand. 20
50 Compt's die.	Female seated with sheaf and sickle; steamboat in distance. 50 Title of Bank.	Sailor with coil of rope on his shoulder looking at females sitting with head raised.

100 Compt's die.	Female seated with pole, cap and key, eagle, sale etc. Title of Bank.	100 Female, horn of plenty, etc.
1 Compt's die. ONE	Spread eagle; steamer and buildings in distance. BK. OF NORTH AM., New York City. Sheaf, plow, etc.	1 Female with ear of corn and fig. 1.
Compt's die. Indian princess.	2 Vig. Same as ones. BK. OF NORTH AM., New York City. City Arms.	TWO Two females. TWO
THREE Compt's die. THREE	3 Vig. Same as ones. BK. OF NORTH AM., New York City. Cog-wheel, etc.	3 Two males bearing aloft a female.
Compt's die. Indian with bow, arrow and belt.	5 Vig. Same as ones. BK. OF NORTH AM., New York City. Steamboat.	FIVE Squaw and papoose.
Compt's die. 10 Steamship.	Vig. Same as ones. 10 BK. OF NORTH AM., New York City. Arms.	TEN Helmeted female with spear and shield. TEN
Compt's die. 10 Steamer.	TEN Washington. X BK. OF NORTH AM., New York City. Arms.	TEN Helmeted female with spear and shield. TEN
20 Female seated with spear and shield.	Compt's die. Vig. Same as ones. BK. OF NORTH AM., New York City. Machinery.	XX Female with vase of flowers, etc.
50 Female with flag and helmet; buildings in distance. FIFTY	Compt's die. Vig. Same as ones. BK. OF NORTH AM., New York City Steamship.	50 Female with spear and shield.
100 Helmeted female with spear and globe.	Compt's die. Vig. Same as ones. BK. OF NORTH AM., New York City. Merchandise.	100 Female seated.

500 Compt's die. 500	Vig. Same as ones. BK. OF NORTH AM., New York City. Safe.	500 Female with flag, and three cupids in clouds.
1000 Female, eagle, wreath, shield, etc.	Compt's die. Vig. Same as ones. BK. OF NORTH AM., New York City. Arms.	1000
Sailor with spy glass 3	BK of the REPUBLIC, New York City. 3 Ship under full sail; steamboat on left. 3 Compt's die.	3 Female with eagle and shield.
5 Compt's die.	BK of the REPUBLIC, New York City. V View of shipping. V Female and anchor.	5 Sailor with flag in left hand, and hat in right.
10 Compt's die.	Shipping and view of city on right in distance. BK of the REPUBLIC, New York City. Building.	10 Eagle on a shield.
20 Compt's die.	View of steamship and other vessels. BK of the REPUBLIC, New York City. Dog, key and safe.	20 Agricultural implements.
FIFTY Compt's die. 50	Eagle on limb of tree; cars and canal scene in distance. BK of the REPUBLIC, New York City. Shield.	50 Female leaning on a column; two females in background.
100 Compt's die. 100	Two females and bust of Washington on shield in centre; shipping, etc. 100 BK of the REPUBLIC, New York City. Shield.	Merchandise. Female portrait. Train of cars.
Steamboat, schooner, buildings, men, etc. ONE Compt's die.	1 Two females, shield, surmounted by an eagle; cars; shipping, etc. 1 BK OF THE STATE OF NEW YORK, New York City.	Spanish dollar.
II Compt's die. TWO	Vig. Same as ones. 2 Title of Bank.	Two spanish dollars lapped.

Two spanish dollars and one American lapped.	3 Vig. Same as ones. Title of Bank.	III Compt's die. THREE
5 Compt's die. 5	5 Two females; steamboat and sail vessels in distance. 5 BK. OF THE STATE, New York City. Eagle and shield.	FIVE Female representing Justice. FIVE
10 Compt's die. 10	X Vig. Same as fives. X BK. OF THE STATE, New York City. Canal Lock.	10 Cupid. X
20 Compt's die 20	20 Vig. Same as fives. 20 BK. OF THE STATE, New York City. Eagle on view of rising sun.	XX Justice. TWENTY
50 Compt's die. 50	L Vig. Same as fives. L BK. OF THE STATE, New York City. Eagle, &c.	50 Steamboat and sail vessels. 50
100 Compt's die. 100	C Vig. Same as fives. C BK. OF THE STATE, New York City. Eagle, &c.	100 Sail Vessel. 100
500	500 Vig. Same as fives. BK. OF THE STATE, New York City. Eagle, sunrise, etc.	Die. Compt's die. Die.
1000	Vig. Same as fives. 1000 BK. OF THE STATE, New York City. Eagle, sunrise, etc.	Die. Compt's die. Die.
ONE Building, street, &c. Compt's die.	1 Spread eagle; steamer, ships, etc. BROADWAY BANK, New York City. Implements.	ONE Female and fig. 1.
TWO Building, street, etc. Compt's die.	2 Female, shield, eagle, portrait of Washington; cars, vessels and buildings in distance. BROADWAY BANK, New York City. Arm.	2 Female seated, building, etc.

Left	Centre	Right
THREE Building, signed, etc. Compt's die.	3 Two females seated, ship between; on left steamboat and ship; on right in distance, cars, schooner, etc. BROADWAY BANK, New York City. Sheaf, plow, &c.	3 Mechanic in frame; cars in distance.
FIVE 5 Compt's die.	Two females seated on either side of shield, surmounted by an eagle; miniature view of sunrise and river; on right, cars; on left steamboat. BROADWAY BANK, New York City. Cog-wheels, etc.	5 Figure of Justice in clouds.
Compt's die. Female seated with spear and head on shield.	10 Female reclining on merchandise; on left, cars, canal scene; on right ships and city. BROADWAY BANK, New York City. Safe.	10
Two females representing Liberty and Justice. Compt's die.	20 Female seated with sheaf; cars and canal scene in distance. BROADWAY BANK, New York City. Bales, bbls., bales, etc	20 Female seated between 2 and 0.
50 Compt's die. FIFTY	Female with pole, cap and shield. 50 BROADWAY BANK, New York City. State Arms	FIFTY Winged female seated.
100 Compt's die. 100	Vessels and view of city. BROADWAY BANK, New York City. Steamship.	100 Female erect with right hand on capstan.
1 with ONE running across it. Telegraph, railroad, etc.	BULL'S HEAD BANK, New York City. Vig. Bull's head with title of Bank running around it. 1, one running across it. 1, one running across it.	1 with ONE running across it. Compt's die.
2 Compt's die.	Vig. Same as Ones. BULL'S HEAD BANK New York City. 2 with Two running across it. 2 with word dollars running across it.	2 TWO 2
3 Compt's die. THREE	Vig. Same as ones. BULL'S HEAD BANK New York City. 3 3	3 THREE 3
5 Compt's Die.	Bull. BULL'S HEAD BANK New York City. Man buying newspaper of boy, birds, etc.	5 Bull's head. FIVE

Left	Centre	Right
5 Compt's die.	BULL'S HEAD BANK New York City. Vig. Houses and tree.	5 Bull's head. FIVE
10 Bull's head. 10	Vig. Agricultural scene; oxen in foreground. BULL'S HEAD BANK New York City.	10 with TEN running across it. Compt's die.
XX Compt's die.	BULL'S HEAD BANK New York City. Vig. Mill, drove of sheep and men on horseback in foreground.	20 Bull's head. 20
50 Bull's head.	BULL'S HEAD BANK New York City. Vig. Two horses. State Arms.	50
ONE HUNDRED Bull's head. Compt's die.	ONE HUNDRED DOLLARS. BULL'S HEAD BANK New York City.	100
1 Compt's die 1	BUTCHERS & DROVERS' BANK, New York City. 1 Drovers and cattle in a friend. 1	ONE DOLLAR
2 Compt's die 2	2 Vig. Same as 1s. 2 Title of Bank.	2 Female 2
3 Compt's die 3	3 Vig. Same as ones. 3 Title of Bank.	3 Female bathing 3
5 Compt's die. 5	5 Two females with ornamental figure 5; two cupids on either side. 5 BUTCHERS' AND DROVERS' BANK. New York City. Wheat, plough, spade.	5 Cattle, 5
5 Compt's die. 5	5 Cattle and sheep. 5 Title of Bank. Die.	5 Four females 5

Left	Centre	Right
10 Compt's die. 10	Cattle and sheep lying on the ground. 10 Title of Bank	TEN
20 Compt's die. 20	20 Vig. Same as tens. 20 Title of Bank Ship.	TWENTY Female bust TWENTY
50 Compt's die. 50	50 Female with sheaf; cars and factory in distance. 50 Title of Bank. Ship.	50 FIFTY Drovers and cattle. DOLLARS 50
100 Compt's die 100	C Two females leaning on a view of drovers and cattle. C Title of Bank. Ship.	Female erect with sheaf and sickle. 100
ONE Compt's die. ONE	1 Firemen, fire engine, buildings, etc. CHATHAM BANK, New York City. Male portrait	1 Secured, &c. ONE
2 Compt's die. TWO	Female seated surrounded by mechanical implements. CHATHAM BANK, New York City. Male portrait	2 Secured, &c TWO
Sailor seated on Compt's die; vessel below	3 Female seated on left of City Arms. 3 CHATHAM BANK, New York City. Male portrait	Ship. 3
Sailor erect, leaning on bale. Compt's die.	5 Steamship and other vessels. CHATHAM BANK, New York City. Male portrait	Large 5; cars, bridge, mill, Indians, etc 5
10 Compt's die. 10	Female seated on left of shield, sheafs of grain; cars and bridge in distance. CHATHAM BANK, New York City. Male portrait	10 City Arms. 10
Female seated on Compt's die. TWENTY	20 Sailor and female seated; steamer on left in distance; on right farming scene. CHATHAM BANK, New York City. Male portrait	20 Secured, etc Female seated.

50 Compt's die. 50
Two females on right of shield, eagle and vessel on left.
CHATHAM BANK, New York City.
Male portrait
50 Steamboat FIFTY

100 Compt's die.
Spread eagle.
CHATHAM BANK, New York City.
Male portrait
100 Female with sledge.

500 Compt's die.
Portrait of Washington, with flags and cannon on each side.
CHATHAM BANK, New York City.
Male portrait
500 City Arms. 500

Large figure of Mercury with bag of coin and wand. 1000
Portrait of Washington.
CHATHAM BANK, New York City.
Compt's die.
Female with sickle and sheaf. 1000

1 Compt's die
CHEMICAL BANK.
Female figure standing across shield and anchor, torch in hand.
One 1 Dollar 1
City of New York
1 Dog on safe.

ONE Two sailors and females.
Compt's die. Vig. Forest scene; dogs in pursuit of game.
CHEMICAL BANK, New York City.
1

2 Compt's die. TWO
CHEMICAL BANK, New York City.
Vig. Same as last.
2 Two females; one kneeling.

TWO Compt's die. TWO
Two females and sheaf; ship in the distance. Medallion head and 2 on either side.
CHEMICAL BANK, New York City.
Female bust. Male portrait. Female bust.

Female with pole and cap.
5 Female reclining with cornucopia.
CHEMICAL BANK, New York City.
5 Compt's die.

5 Red figure 5.
CHEMICAL BANK, New York City.
Female. Word five and fig. 5. Female.
Compt's die.
5 Red fig. 5.

TEN Compt's die TEN
X Spread eagle
CHEMICAL BANK, New York City.
X Female with shield, eagle, pole and cap.

TEN
X on 10 Female seated with torch, eagle, portrait of Washington, &c. X on 10
CHEMICAL BANK, New York City.
Chemists laboratory.
X Compt's die. X

TWENTY
XX on 20 Eagle and shield. XX on 20
CHEMICAL BANK, New York City.
Chemical laboratory.
XX Compt's die XX

TWENTY Compt's die.
20 Two females, shield, cars, etc.; ship in distance.
CHEMICAL BANK, New York City.
TWENTY Washington

Compt's die, fig. 50 on either side. Female seated with fig. 50.
CHEMICAL BANK, New York City.
Secured, &c.
50

100
Female with shield. C
CHEMICAL BANK, New York City.
100 Compt's die 100

D
Compt's die.
500
CHEMICAL BANK, New York City.
Three females; building in background.
500

M
CHEMICAL BANK, New York City.
Figures 1000 and words one thousand across.
Compt's die.
1000

1 Compt's die. ONE
Drover and cattle.
CITIZENS BANK, New York City.
City Arms.
1 Female portrait ONE

TWO Compt's die. TWO
Farmer with basket of corn; farmers gathering corn; cars in distance.
CITIZENS BANK, New York City.
Bbls., boxes, etc.
2 Two females

3 Compt's die
Farmer reclining on sheafs, with pitcher, dog, basket, &c.
CITIZENS BANK, New York City.
Cog wheel, box, &c.
3 Med. Head. THREE

5 Compt's die. V
Blacksmith reclining on anvil, hammer in his hand; factory, cars, &c. in distance.
CITIZENS BANK, New York City.
Cog wheel, bales, &c.
5 Med. head and word five. FIVE

10 Compt's die.
Sailor with glass in hand, reclining on bales, etc.; shipping in distance.
CITIZENS BANK, New York City.
City Arms.
10 Med. head. TEN

20 Compt's die. XX
Washington. Female with cap, shield, grain, etc. Franklin.
CITIZENS BANK, New York City.
Female
20 Female between 2 and 0.

50 Med. head.
Compt's die. Female with globe, chart, quadrant, book, ink stand, pen, &c.; cars, shipping, factory, etc., in distance.
CITIZENS BANK, New York City.
Anchor, bale, &c.
50 Two females.

100 Med. head. 100
Compt's die. Female with eagle, shield, safe, ship, harrow, sheaf, etc.
CITIZENS BANK, New York City.
Dog, key and safe.
100 Female with fruit hanging on anchor

Compt's die. ONE Male portrait
1 Indian princess, fig. 1, shield, water fall and rainbow. 1
CONTINENTAL BK., New York City.
City Arms.
ONE Female erect; ship in distance.

Compt's die. TWO Male portrait
2 Female seated on either side of a fig. 2. 2
CONTINENTAL BK., New York City.
City Arms.
TWO Spread eagle Male portrait

Compt's die. 3 Male portrait
Three females and fig. 3; buildings in distance. 3
CONTINENTAL BK., New York City.
View of sunrise.
Male portrait THREE Male portrait

Male portrait 5 Male portrait
Compt's die. Five females and fig. 5; shipping, cars and buildings in distance. 5
CONTINENTAL BK., New York City.
Eagle.
Male portrait Male portrait Male portrait

10 Continental officer.	Compt's die. Signing Declaration of Independence. CONTINENTAL BK., New York City.	10 Female with pole, cap, shield and Declaration of Independence.
TWENTY Two females representing Liberty and Justice.	Compt's die. Male portrait 20 CONTINENTAL BK., New York City.	Winged female erect; female seated with pole, cap, eagle and cornucopia.
FIFTY Male portrait Compt's die.	50 Steamer at sea. CONTINENTAL BK., New York City. Shield.	50 Sailor with quadrant, globe, etc.
100 Compt's die. 100	Female on either side of a shield, surmounted by an eagle; steamboat, vessels, cars and buildings in distance. CONTINENTAL BK., New York City. Cornucopia and anvil.	100 Male portrait 100
Female erect; an eagle in act of drinking from urn. 500	500 Compt's die. CONTINENTAL BK., New York City.	500 Male portrait
1000 Washington and other military officers. Compt's die.	Vig. The Globe. CONTINENTAL BK., New York City.	1000 Head of Washington.
1 Compt's die.	CORN EX. BANK, New York City. Two male figures; sheafs; house and ship in distance ONE	1 ONE
2	CORN EX. BANK, New York City. Vig. Same as ones. Compt's die.	2 2
3	Vig. Same as ones. CORN EX. BANK, New York City. THREE	THREE Compt's die 3
FIVE Compt's die.	CORN EX. BANK, New York City. Female with pole, cap, eagle, etc.	5

10 TEN	CORN EX. BANK, New York City Vig. Same as fives.	10 Compt's die.
Compt's die. 50	Male portrait CORN EX. BANK, New York City.	50 Four females representing Agriculture, Merchandise etc.
Compt's die. C	CORN EX. BANK, New York City. Vig. Four females, representing Agriculture, Merchandise, etc.	100 Male portrait
1 Compt's die. 1	Farmer and child at lunch; boy playing with dog, &c EAST RIVER BANK, New York City.	ONE Some have portrait of girl; others Sailor at capstan on this end.
1 Compt's die. 1	View of buildings in course of erection; laborers, horse, truck, &c. EAST RIVER BANK, New York City.	ONE Sailor leaning on capstan with quadrant in hand.
TWO Female sewing on a cap.	Train of cars passing a railroad station; ladies on platform. EAST RIVER BANK, New York City.	2 Compt's die. TWO
3 Female portrait.	EAST RIVER BANK, New York City. Faust, Gutenburg and Schoeffer, chests, wheels, books, etc.	3 III Compt's die.
5 FIVE	View of ship yard, three ships on ways; factory in left; men at work, &c. EAST RIVER BANK, New York City.	V Compt's die. V
5 FIVE	Two females reclining; factory on right; sheep and cattle on left. EAST RIVER BANK New York City.	V Compt's die. V
TEN Dogs head.	Compt's die. Two blacksmiths in shop; one shoeing horse, the other blowing forge. EAST RIVER BANK, New York City.	X

20 Sailor with spy glass, quadrant and compass.	Compt's die. Steamboat, wharf, etc. EAST RIVER BANK, New York City.	XX
50 Compt's die.	Steamship. Portrait of Franklin. EAST RIVER BANK, New York City.	50 Female portrait. L
C	Sailor seated on ground with quadrant, telescope, compass, &c., houses, hills, shipping in distance. Compt's die. EAST RIVER BANK, New York City.	100 Arm and hammer.
Steamboat.	1 1 FULTON BANK, New York City. Bust of Fulton, mechanic seated on right; cars and steamship in distance.	ONE One Dollar Sailor erect; vessel in distance. One Dollar ONE
Steamboat.	2 Vig. Same as ones. FULTON BANK, New York City.	2 Female with sheaf and sickle. TWO
Compt's die. Male portrait THREE	Bust of Fulton; mechanic seated on right; cars and steamship in distance. FULTON BANK. New York City.	3 Steamboat.
Steamboat.	5 Vig. Same as ones. FULTON BANK, New York City. Eagle.	5 Female with trident. 5
Steamboat.	10 Vig. Same as ones. FULTON BANK, New York City.	X Boy in corn field.
Steamboat	50 Vig. Same as ones. FULTON BANK, New York City. Female and ship.	50
Steamboat.	100 Title of Bank. Vig. Same as ones. Sheaf and plow.	100

Left	Centre	Right
ONE Compt's die ONE	1 Winged female with sword and scales, holding fig. 1. 1 GREENWICH BANK, New York City.	ONE Female with flowers. ONE
2 Compt's die.	Ship carpenter at work, with axe lying beside him; ship in background. GREENWICH BANK, New York City.	2 Two Cupids holding an ornamental figure 2.
3 Compt's die.	Three females, representing Agriculture, Manufactures and Commerce. GREENWICH BANK, New York City.	THREE Three Cupids supporting a fig. 3. THREE
FIVE Full length female figure	Compt's die. Figure of Justice. FIVE GREENWICH BANK, New York City. Steamboat.	FIVE DOLLARS
10 Washington. 10	Compt's die. Eagle on City Arms. TEN GREENWICH BANK, New York City.	X Male portrait X
20 Compt's die. 20	20 Figure of Justice with sword and scales on left; on right Goddess of Liberty with pole and cap; between them an eagle surmounting figure on which is a view of America. Title of Bank running around them. 20	20 Ship. 20
50 Compt's die. 50	50 Female representing Commerce, resting her arm on a frame with an anchor on it; ship on the left. 50 GREENWICH BANK, New York City. Eagle.	50 Male portrait 50
100 Compt's die. 100	100 Female seated on the base of a column pointing to a sloop in the distance; sheaf and rake. 100 GREENWICH BANK, New York City. Steamboat.	Male portrait 100 Male portrait
ONE Female seated with fig. 1	Compt's die. View of street, buildings, pedestrians, etc. GROCERS BANK, New York City.	1
TWO Female seated on bbl.	Compt's die. Female on either side of a fig. 2 GROCERS BANK, New York City. Bales and barrels.	2 Male portrait

Left	Centre	Right
3 Mechanic, sailor, farmer and fig. 3 THREE	Compt's die. Female reclining on merchandise; ships, cars, canal scene in distance. GROCERS BANK, New York City.	3
FIVE Three males, two on either side and letter V	Compt's die. Sailor seated with telescope; vessels in distance. GROCERS BANK, New York City.	5 Five females and fig. 5
Compt's die Sailor erect, capstan, masts, etc.	10 Female on either side of ship; cars, vessels, etc., in distance. GROCERS BANK, New York City. Safe.	TEN 10
20 Mercury between 2 & 0.	Compt's die. Female between 2 and 0. GROCERS BANK, New York City. City Arms.	XX Ship and other vessels
50 Compt's die. 50	Ships and other vessels; city in distance. GROCERS BANK, New York City. Machinery, etc.	50 Male portrait FIFTY
Merchandise Compt's die. Cars.	100 Three females seated. GROCERS BANK, New York City. Bbls., bales, etc.	100 Male portrait
1 Compt's die.	Ship and other vessels. 1 HANOVER BANK, New York City. Bbls. and bales.	ONE Female head Horses with wings.
Compt's die. Indian princess erect.	2 Female seated with pole, cap, fig. 2, and eagle. HANOVER BANK, New York City. Sailor reclining.	2 Female portrait. TWO
3 Compt's die. THREE	Winged female and cupid in act of raising drapery from shield on which is an eagle. HANOVER BANK, New York City. City Arms.	3 Female seated.
5 Compt's die.	Female with shield, pole and cap. Washington. HANOVER BANK, New York City. Safe.	5 Sailor erect, leaning on capstan.

Left	Centre	Right
Female seated; vessel & steamer in distance. Compt's die.	10 Female, shield and eagle soaring in clouds. HANOVER BANK, New York City. Boxes, bbls., &c.	10 Franklin. TEN
20 Mercury seated between a 2 and 0.	Compt's die. Two females, bust and shield between them; ship in distance. HANOVER BANK, New York City. Bbls., bales, etc.	20 Jefferson.
50 City Arms. 50	Compt's die. Female reclining on a view of river; cars, steamer, &c., in distance. HANOVER BANK, New York City. Dragon and key.	50 Female, horn of plenty, etc. FIFTY
100 Female with pole, cap and shield.	Compt's die. Female and cupid on either side of a view of sunrise. HANOVER BANK, New York City. Sailor reclining.	100 Ship and other vessels.
ONE	Head of Washington. Ornamental figure 1. IMPORTERS' & TRADERS BANK, New York City. Compt's die. Secured, &c.	ONE
2 TWO	Title of Bank. Sailor and sailor boy. Compt's die. Secured, etc.	2 TWO
5 FIVE	Female seated; shield and eagle. Title of Bank. FIVE DOLLARS	5 Compt's die FIVE
X TEN	Two females, one erect, the other kneeling. NEW YORK TEN DOLLARS Title of Bank.	10 Compt's die
50 Female soaring in clouds with cornucopia of flowers.	Title of Bank. Large 50 in red dies. Compt's die.	50 Female soaring in clouds.
100 New York	Title of Bank. Large figures 100 in red die; on right sailor seated, and ship in distance; on left mower on the ground with scythe, trees, etc. Compt's die.	100

Left end	Centre	Right end
1 Steamship. Compt's die.	1 Head of Irving. 1 IRVING BANK, New York City	1 Steamboat. ONE
Ship. Compt's die.	2 Head of Irving. 2 IRVING BANK, New York City.	Female with sheaf. TWO
Compt's die. Dolphin. THREE	3 Indian reclining, and another approaching IRVING BANK, New York City.	3 Male portrait 3
Compt's die.	Old man seated with gun. 5 Male portrait IRVING BANK, New York City.	5 Milkmaid seated.
10 Compt's die. 10	View of a cottage covered with vines. 10 IRVING BANK, New York City.	Ten Dollars. Female with sword. Male portrait
Cupid on a dolphin, holding aloft Compt's die. TWENTY	20 Two females on right of shield; eagle and vessel on left. IRVING BANK, New York City. Steamship.	20 Male portrait TWENTY
Female. Compt's die.	50 Eagle and shield. IRVING BANK, New York City.	50
Compt's die.	Eagle, shield, &c. IRVING BANK, New York City.	100 Male portrait 100
1 Compt's die. 1	Female on horse catching buffalo; hunting buffaloes in distance. ONE LEATHER MANUFACTURERS' BANK, New York City. Shield.	Cupid and grindstone. ONE
2 Compt's die. 2	2 TWO Title of Bank. Shield.	Same as vig. of ones. 2

Left end	Centre	Right end
3 Compt's die. 3	3 Cupid and grindstone. 3 Title of Bank. 3	Goat's head. THREE Goat's head.
5 Compt's die. 5	V Vig. Same as ones. 5 Title of Bank. 5	FIVE Female, vessel, cow, sheep, etc. V
10 Compt's die. 10	Cupid and grindstone. X Title of Bank. Steamboat.	Same as vig. of ones. 10
20 Compt's die. 20	20 Vig. Same as ones. TWENTY Title of Bank.	SAFETY Cupid and grindstone FUND 20
50 Compt's die. 50	50 Title of Bank. 50 Cupid and grindstone.	FIFTY
100 Compt's die. 100	100 Vig. Same as ones. Title of Bank.	100
500 Compt's die. 500	Female with eagle; ships in distance. Title of Bank.	Statue of Washington 500
Die Compt's die. Die.	1000 Cupid and grindstone. 1000 Title of Bank.	1000 Full length Female with anchor.
1 Compt's die. 1	1 Male figure and Indian on either side of a shield, on which is a view of N. Y. harbor; female raising drapery from shield MANHATTAN CO., New York City. Man reclining.	ONE Indian erect
2 Compt's die. 2	Vig. Same as ones. 2 MANHATTAN CO., New York City. Man reclining.	TWO Indian with bow.

Left end	Centre	Right end
3 Compt's die. 3	Vig. Same as ones. 3 MANHATTAN CO., New York City. Man reclining.	THREE Indian with bow.
FIVE Compt's die. 5	V Title of Bank. Vig. Same as ones.	5 Head of Indian.
TEN Head of Indian.	Compt's die. MANHATTAN CO., New York City. Vig. Same as ones.	TEN X 10
TWENTY 20	Vig. Female reclining with jar of water; Indian in canoe, trees, etc. in distance. Compt's die. MANHATTAN CO., New York City. Man reclining.	Indian in act of drawing arrow.
FIFTY Compt's die. Head of Indian.	MANHATTAN CO., New York City. 50 Vig. Same as the. 50 Man reclining.	FIFTY
100 Compt's die. 100	MANHATTAN CO., New York City. C Vig. Same as twenties. Man reclining.	100 Head of Indian 100
500 Compt's die D	Vig. Same as twenties. MANHATTAN CO., New York City. Man reclining.	500 500
1000 Head of Indian.	Compt's die. Vig. Same as twenties. MANHATTAN CO., New York City.	1000 Letter M and words "One thousand" around it.
Female, man with horses and gleaning machine. Compt's die.	MAN. & MERCH. BK. N. Y. City. Female seated with mechanical implements; buildings, etc.	1 Anchor, bales, etc.
2 Compt's die. TWO	Title of Bank. Sailor on beach; steamer, ships, etc., in distance.	2 Female portrait TWO

N. Y. CITY.	N. Y. CITY.	N. Y. CITY.
FIVE Female with sewing machine. FIVE Title of Bank. Sailor and Indian either side of shield, surmounted by eagle. Red tinted 5 either side. 5 Compt's die. 5	L Ship under full sail. Compt's die. MARINE BANK, New York City. 50 Male portrait	Compt's die on a large fig. 1. ONE Two mechanics, etc.; cars and ship in distance. ONE MECHANICS' BANKING ASSOCIATION, New York City. Steamship. Washington on a large figure 1.
Sailor, quadrant, capstan vessels, etc. 10 Title Eagle. Female seated with bale, cloth, etc.; pedestrians, buildings, falls, etc. in distance. Red X either side. X Compt's die.	100 Ship wreck scene. MARINE BANK, New York City. Compt's die. C Male portrait	TWO Compt's die Carpenter at his bench. Figure 2 with portrait of Washington and word two. Title of Bank. Stone cutter seated. 2
L Female seated; buildings FIFTY Title of Bank. Shipping and dock scene in general. Compt's die. 50 Two sailors and female seated.	1 Female with flowers. Drovers and cattle; cars, bridge, buildings, &c., in distance. MARKET BANK, New York City. Dog, key and safe. 1 Compt's die.	Two females; figure 3 between them. 3 Indian princess, surrounded by flags, drums, cannon, etc. Title of Bank. Arm. 3
C 100 Female seated with wheels, bales, etc.; buildings and steamer in distance. Title of Bank. Female portrait. Compt's die. 100 Female with spinning wheel, buildings.	TWO Male and female seated, anvil, &c. 2 Steamship and other vessels. MARKET BANK, New York City. Eagle. 2 Compt's die	5 Female, rake, etc. FIVE V Three females and a fig. 5; cars, shipping, etc., in distance. V Title of Bank. Arm. 5 Med. Head. FIVE
ONE Male portrait Compt's die. Steamship. MARINE BANK, New York City. 1 1	Three females, anchor, etc. THREE 3 Milkmaid and cattle; houses and trees in distance. 3 MARKET BANK, New York City. Steamboat. 3 Compt's die	10 Same as fives TEN Two females on either side of a shield; cars, buildings, canal, shipping, &c., in distance Title of Bank. Arm. 10 Two females, eagle, etc. TEN
TWO Indian on his knees with gun. 2 MARINE BANK, New York City. Compt's die. Red figure 2 Ship under full sail.	5 Female portrait. Female reclining on bale of merchandise; ships in distance. MARKET BANK, New York City. Female seated, buildings and fig. 5; ship in distance. Compt's die.	TWENTY Same as fives TWENTY 20 Female seated at table, scientific apparatus on her right; steamer in distance. 20 Title of Bank. Arm. Die. XX Die
3 View of a ship wreck, mariners, etc. Compt's die. MARINE BANK, New York City. 3 Male portrait	10 Female bust. Train of cars; in distance two other trains; water scene, houses, trees, etc. MARKET BANK, New York City. 10 Compt's die	FIFTY Female seated, steamboat on right 50 Two Indians, and white man with gun. Medallion head and word fifty on either side of vig. Title of Bank. Arm. FIFTY Female seated; house in distance. 50
FIVE Mechanic seated and sailor with flag and quadrant Compt's die Male portrait MARINE BANK, New York City. 5 V	Henry Clay seated; dog by his side. 20 Spread eagle. MARKET BANK, New York City. 20 Compt's die	HUNDRED Figure of Justice. 100 Two females on either side of a shield, surmounted by an eagle; shipping in distance. Med. head and figs. 100 on either side of vig. Title of Bank Arm ONE HUNDRED
Sailor seated with nautical implements, &c.; shipping in distance. X X Compt's die MARINE BANK, New York City. TEN Male portrait	50 Cattle and sheep. Female portrait. MARKET BANK, New York City. 50 Compt's die	500 Same as fives 500 500 Train of cars; steamboat and other vessels in distance. Title of Bank. Arm. 500
20 Male portrait Female reclining on bales of goods. MARINE BANK, New York City. XX XX Compt's die. 20	100 Sailor with flag, bbl. anchor, bale and quadrant Three females in clouds; ships on right. MARKET BANK, New York City. 100 Compt's die	1000 Same as fives 1000 1000 Steamship, row-boat, other vessels and view of city. Title of Bank. Arm. ONE THOUSAND

Left end	Centre	Right end
Arm. ONE	1 Male and female mounted in foreground; ship, cars and bridge in distance. 1 MECHANICS' BANK, New York City. Horse.	Female. Compt's die. Female.
TWO Cooper at work. TWO	2 Vig. Same as ones. 2 MECHANICS' BANK, New York City. Locomotive.	Washington. Compt's die. Male portrait.
3 Compt's die. 3	3 Archimedes raising the world. MECHANICS' BANK, New York City. Arm.	3
5 Compt's die. 5	5 Vig. Same as three. MECHANICS' BANK, New York City. Arm.	V
Figure of Blacksmith. TEN	MECHANICS BANK. 10 Eagle on rock. 10 TEN DOLLARS. City of New York.	10 Compt's die.
10 Compt's die.	MECHANICS' BANK, New York City. Mechanic with hammer and anvil; buildings in distance. Red figs. 10 on either side.	10
Figure of Justice with sword and scales. 20	20 Compt's die 20 MECHANICS BANK. TWENTY DOLLARS on XX City of New York.	Figure of blacksmith. 20
Medallion head and word twenty. Compt's die.	20 Vig. Same as threes. MECHANICS' BANK, New York City. Arm.	20
50 50	MECHANICS' BANK, New York City. Arm and hammer.	Compt's die. 50
100 Compt's die.	MECHANICS' BANK, New York City. Arm and hammer.	100 100

Left end	Centre	Right end
500	MECHANICS' BANK, New York City. 500 Female reclining. FIVE HUNDRED	Arm and hammer.
1000	1000 Vig. Same as threes. MECHANICS' BANK, New York City. ONE THOUSAND.	Arm and hammer.
1 Compt's die. 1	ONE Blacksmith with hammer and anvil, female with bag of money and barrels; shipping in background. ONE MECHANICS' & TRADERS' BANK, New York City.	1 Clock. 1
2 Compt's die 2	2 Vig. Same as ones. Title of Bank.	2 2
3 Compt's die. 3	Vig. Same as ones. 3 Title of Bank.	3 Clock. 3
Vulcan with anvil and hammer and two females. V	5 Five Dollars. Figure of Justice with scales; shipping in distance. MECHANICS' & TRADERS' BANK, New York City. Ship.	5 Compt's die. 5
5 Compt's die. 5	5 5 Title of Bank. Vig. Same as ones.	FIVE Female leaning on an urn. 5
10 Compt's die. 10	Blacksmith with hammer and anvil. 10 Title of Bank.	Female with liberty cap, leaning on cornucopia. X
20 Compt's die 20	Male and female figure with frame between them enclosing three cupids. Title of Bank.	20 Mercury reclining on a bale. 20
50 Compt's die. 50	50 Two Cupids with globe and chart. 50 Title of Bank.	50 FIFTY 50

Left end	Centre	Right end
100 Compt's die. 100	100 Title of Bank.	Male and female; male with sickle.
ONE Female holding fig. 1, leaning on bale of merchandise.	Cupid. Compt's die. 1 MERCANTILE B'K., New York City.	ONE Female holding fig with emblematic figures around her.
TWO Indian female holding spear and bow	2 Compt's die. Cupid and fig. 2. MERCANTILE B'K., New York City.	TWO Female with fruit and flowers.
THREE Female with wheat in hand.	Cupid and fig. 3. Compt's die. Cupid and fig. 3. MERCANTILE B'K., New York City.	THREE Same as 2s.
FIVE	5 Female reclining with shield, anchor, and the word "Hope"; cars and building in distance. Compt's die. MERCANTILE B'K., New York City. Mechanic with hammer.	5 V 5
10 Mechanic with hammer. 10	X Emblematic group of females in clouds; one with keys. Compt's die. MERCANTILE B'K., New York City.	TEN
50	Female with eagle, shield, portrait of Washington, etc. Compt's die. MERCANTILE B'K., New York City.	50 Human figure with spear and shield.
100 Figure of Justice.	Compt's die. Female with pole, cap and eagle; latter on shield. MERCANTILE B'K., New York City.	100
Male portrait. Compt's die.	(Have Lymch's Protection.) ONE 1 MERCHANTS' BANK N. Y. City,	1 Title across large fig. 1.
Compt's die with word Two above and below and fig. 2 on right.	Male portrait. 2 2 Title across large 2.	2

Left end	Centre	Right end
Compt's die. 3	Title of Bank. Child's head	3
5	V BANK, Child's portrait MERCHANT'S	5 Compt's die.
5 Compt's die. 5	5 Mercury seated with cornucopia and wand; sale, lion, etc; cars, canal scene, vessels, etc., in distance. 5 MERCHANTS' BANK New York City. Bank building.	Male portra Female erect building in distance.
10 Compt's die. 10	X Vig. Same as fives. X MERCHANTS' BANK New York City. Bank building.	Die 10 Die
20 Compt's die. 20	20 Vig. Same as fives. 20 MERCHANTS' BANK New York City. Die.	Sea monsters Vessels Sea monsters
50 Compt's die. 50	50 Vig. Same as fives. 50 MERCHANTS' BANK New York City. Die.	Sea monsters Same as fives Sea monsters
100 Compt's die. 100	C Vig. Same as fives. C MERCHANTS' BANK New York City. Bank building.	100 Boy's head 100
Die Compt's die. Die.	Figs. 500, with Cupids on each figure. MERCHANTS' BANK New York City Bank building.	Same as vig of fives. 500
1 Compt's die. ONE	MER. EX. BANK, New York City. Female seated with cornucopia and wand; bble., quadrant, etc; in distance vessels, buildings, cars, canal, &c.	1 Ship and other vessel
TWO	MER. EX. BANK, New York City. Vig. Same as ones. Compt's die.	2 Female seated; building in distance.

Left end	Centre	Right end
Compt's die. THREE	MER. EX. BANK, New York City. Vig. Same as ones.	3 Mercury with wand, bag of coin and cornucopia.
FIVE	Vig. Same as ones. Compt's die. MER. EX. BANK, New York City.	5 Sailor leaning on capstan; masts in background.
10	Steamship and other vessels. Compt's die. MER. EX. BANK, New York City.	10 Female with flag, and 3 cupids.
Compt's die. Mercury seated between 2 and 0.	Spread eagle; steamship and other vessels in distance. MER. EX. BANK, New York City.	20 Female seated between 2 and 0.
50 Female with spear and twig and shield.	Compt's die. Female crowning eagle with wreath, right hand on portrait of Washington, in distance, vessels, cars, buildings, etc. MER. EX. BANK, New York City.	50 Ship and other vessels.
Compt's die. 100	Female, eagle, safe, balances, etc., cars, buildings, and vessels. MER. EX. BANK, New York City.	100 Female seated; building in distance.
1 Compt's die.	METROPOLITAN BK New York City. Words "one dollar" over portrait of Washington in large die.	1 Die
2 Compt's die.	METROPOLITAN BK New York City Words "two dollars" over a male portrait in large die.	2 Die
3 Compt's die.	METROPOLITAN BK New York City. Words "three dollars" over a male portrait in large die.	3 3
5 Compt's die.	METROPOLITAN BK New York City. Vig. Three females representing the Arts and Sciences; building in distance.	5 FIVE

Left end	Centre	Right end
Compt's die. 10	METROPOLITAN BK New York City. Vig. Three females in clouds.	10 X
Compt's die. Figures of Justice, globe, etc.	50 View of a building. 50 METROPOLITAN BK New York City	FIFTY DOLLARS
100 Female seated with pole and cap; flowers, etc.	Compt's Die. Female reclining on a part of City Arms; vessels in distance 100 METROPOLITAN BK New York City.	ONE HUNDRED
500 Female erect and flowers.	500 Vig. Female reclining with pole, cap, eagle, drapery, &c.; vessels in distance. METROPOLITAN BK New York City. View of sunrise.	500 Compt's die
1000 Female with spear and shield; owl, globe, &c.	Compt's die. Female reclining with scroll, globe, etc.; ship and steamer in distance. METROPOLITAN BK New York City. View of sunrise.	1000
1 Franklin.	Faust, Guttenburg and Schoeffer, chests, wheels, books, etc. NASSAU BANK, New York City.	ONE Compt's die 1
2 Compt's die. TWO	Steamer at sea. NASSAU BANK, New York City.	TWO Female portrait with grain. 2
3 Compt's die. 3	Five persons representing Agriculture, Manufactures and Commerce. NASSAU BANK, New York City	THREE Full length female figure with sickle and cornucopia; sheaf by her side.
5 Stone cutter at work.	Compt's die. View of the N. Y. Crystal Palace. NASSAU BANK, New York City.	FIVE V
TEN Compt's die	View of the Battery, Castle Garden and Governor's Island, New York city. NASSAU BANK, New York City.	X X

20 Compt's dis.	Vig. Same as tens. NASSAU BANK, New York City.	XX
L	Female reclining on a bale of merchandise; steamship and yacht in distance. NASSAU BANK, New York City.	50 Compt's dis.
100 One hundred Compt's dis.	Hunter with dog and gun warming himself by a fire, enclosed in a large ornamental letter C. NASSAU BANK, New York City.	C Dollars
1 Compt's dis. 1	1 Male portrait. 1 NATIONAL BANK, New York City.	Statue of Washington.
2 Compt's dis. 2	2 Male portrait. 2 NATIONAL BANK, New York City.	Statue of Washington.
3 Compt's dis. 3	THREE Male portrait. THREE NATIONAL BANK, New York City.	3 Eagle. 3
Statue of Washington. FIVE	5 Compt's dis. Male portrait NATIONAL BANK, New York City.	5 Female feeding an eagle.
10 Compt's dis. 10	TEN TEN NATIONAL BANK, New York City. Vig. Female feeding an eagle.	Ten Dollars Statue of Washington.
20 Compt's dis. 20	Female feeding an eagle. 20 NATIONAL BANK, New York City.	Statue of Washington.
50 Compt's dis. 50	50 50 NATIONAL BANK, New York City.	Female feeding an eagle. Eagle.

100 Female feeding an eagle. Eagle.	100 Compt's dis. 100 NATIONAL BANK, New York City.	Statue of Washington.
Female feeding an eagle. Compt's dis.	1000 1000 NATIONAL BANK, New York City.	1000 Statue of Washington.
ONE ONE Compt's dis.	Large vessel; ship and steamship on left. NEW-YORK COUNTY BANK, New-York City, N. Y. Female bathing.	1 Portrait of boy.
2 Compt's dis. 2	Coat of Arms of the City of New-York. Title of Bank.	2 Portrait of a boy.
V Soldier with a musket.	State Arms. Title of Bank. Ducks.	5 Compt's dis. 5
10 Men shearing sheep.	Farmers at work loading hay. Title of Bank.	10 Compt's dis.
20 XX	Indian in a canoe. Title of Bank. Compt's dis.	20 Clay.
1 Female reclining [illegible], globe, pole, cap, etc.	N. Y. EX. BANK, New York City. Vig. Female seated, with pole and cap; Compt's dis. on her left.	1 Female seated with balance.
TWO Male seated; female seated.	N. Y. EX. BANK, New York City. 2 2 Compt's dis.	TWO Male seated; female seated.
3 Female reclining on a view of cars, mountains, &c.	N. Y. EX. BANK, New York City. Compt's dis.	3 Female seated in oval frame.

5 Compt's dis. FIVE	N. Y. EX. BANK, New York City. Females and Cupids surrounding figure 5.	5 Male bust. FIVE
TEN Compt's dis. TEN	N. Y. EX. BANK, New York City. Steamship and other vessels.	10 Washington.
20 Compt's dis. TWENTY	N. Y. EX. BANK, New York City. Train of cars; buildings, etc.	20 Female portrait.
50 Compt's dis. FIFTY	N. Y. EX. BANK, New York City. Drover and cattle.	50 Female portrait.
100 Compt's dis. 100	N. Y. EX. BANK, New York City. Female, harbor, city, etc.	100 Head of little girl.
ONE Compt's dis. ONE	ONE Hendrick Hudson landing in 1609; ship, etc. ONE NORTH RIVER BK., New York City. Medallion Head.	Male portrait 1 Male portrait
TWO Compt's dis. TWO	2 Female, shield, Indian, etc. 2 NORTH RIVER BK., New York City. Ship.	Washington Male portrait
THREE Compt's dis. THREE	3 Neptune, ship, etc. 3 NORTH RIVER BK., New York City.	Washington. Jefferson. Madison.
FIVE Compt's dis. FIVE	5 Vig. Same as ones. 5 NORTH RIVER BK., New York City.	FIVE FIVE
TEN Compt's dis. TEN	10 State Arms, cars and ship in distance. 10 NORTH RIVER BK., New York City.	X Ship. X

TWENTY Compt's die. TWENTY	20 Female seated, sheaf, cattle, etc. 20 NORTH RIVER BK., New York City.	TWENTY
FIFTY Female 50	50 Two females; cars and vessels in distance. 50 NORTH RIVER BK., New York City. Steamboat.	50 Female portrait. 50
Washington. Sailor and blacksmith.	Compt's die. Two females, eagle, shield, etc. NORTH RIVER BK., New York City.	50 Male portrait.
C	Steamship. Compt's die. NORTH RIVER BK. New York City.	100 Male portrait.
Hundred. Female Justice. 100	100 Two females, eagle and shield. 100 NORTH RIVER BK., New York City.	100 Med. Head. 100
1 ONE Compt's die.	1 Neptune, steamship, and other vessels. OCEAN BANK, New York City.	Ship. ONE
II Man and female in row-boat.	OCEAN BANK, New York City. Vig. Same as ones.	II Compt's die. Sailor seated.
III 3 Female seated.	OCEAN BANK, New York City. Vig. Same as ones.	Die. 3 Die.
5 Sailor at wheel.	Ship loading; dray, boxes; sailor with glass; steamer and other vessels in distance. OCEAN BANK, New York City.	5 Compt's die. 5
5 Compt's die. Word five and figure 5 across.	Vig. Neptune, steamship, &c. OCEAN BANK, New York City.	FIVE Female erect on a rock; lighthouse, etc. FIVE

Sailor and letter X. Compt's die.	OCEAN BANK, New York City. Vig. Same as ones. Ship.	10 10
20 Compt's die. TWENTY	OCEAN BANK, New York City. Vig. Same as ones. Ship.	20 Dolphin. TWENTY
50 Compt's die. 50	Vig. Same as ones. OCEAN BANK, New York City.	View of the bank building. FIFTY
C Compt's die.	Vig. Same as ones. OCEAN BANK, New York City.	Indian. 100
1 Compt's die.	ORIENTAL BANK, New York City. Wood cutter seated, gold dollar on right; house, wagon, trees, etc in distance. Bird.	ONE Oriental female reclining, playing with a bird, a fan in her right hand; fountain in background.
2 Same as on right of 1s.	ORIENTAL BANK, New York City. Compt's die. Farmer and milkmaid seated; two gold dollars; house cattle and trees in distance. Bird.	2
3 Compt's die. THREE	ORIENTAL BANK, New York City. Farmer, sailor and mechanic; three gold dollars on the ground. Bird.	3 Same as ones.
5 Two Elephants. Compt's die.	Indian female, hunter with gun, five gold dollars and three cupids. ORIENTAL BANK, New York City. Bird.	5 Same as ones.
10 Machinists at work; ship and factory. Compt's die.	ORIENTAL BANK, New York City. Machinist resting against piece of machinery with tools in his hand. Bird.	TEN Same as ones.
XX Female portrait. Compt's die.	ORIENTAL BANK, New York City. View of ship yard, with two vessels on ways. Bird.	20 Same as ones.

50 Compt's die. FIFTY	Architect lying against fallen column with plans before him, compass in his hand; in the background, piece of architecture, two men; man with truck and horses. ORIENTAL BANK, New York City. Bird.	50 Same as ones.
100 Compt's die. Female swimming with arm around neck of swan.	Female reclining against box, bale and bbl.; shipping in distance. ORIENTAL BANK, New York City. Bird.	100 Same as ones.
1 Compt's die. Dolphin.	Female reclining holding a fig. 1; cars and steamboat in distance. PACIFIC BANK, New York City. City Arms.	1 Steamship. ONE
Figure 2 supported by two mythological figures. Steamship.	Compt's die. Train of cars. PACIFIC BANK, New York City. City Arms.	2 Two dolphins.
THREE 3 Compt's die.	Ship under full sail; vessels in distance. PACIFIC BANK, New York City. City Arms.	Shell. 3 Steamship and dolphin.
5 FIVE Compt's die.	Sailor reclining with spy-glass in his hand; shipping in distance. PACIFIC BANK, New York City. City Arms.	FIVE Steamship. 5 Shipping and wharf.
TEN Compt's die. TEN	10 Two females, one crowning bust of Washington with wreath; bales, sheaf, etc. PACIFIC BANK, New York City. City Arms.	TEN Boy holding a shell, his foot on a dolphin. TEN
XX Compt's die. 20	Female reclining, right arm on a view of steamboat, &c.; cornucopia, safe, etc.; cars and steamship in distance. PACIFIC BANK, New York City. City Arms.	20 Vessel. TWENTY
50 Two dolphins. Compt's die.	Female with globe, quadrant, chest, book, pen and ink; shipping and factory in distance. 50 PACIFIC BANK, New York City. Steamship.	Bale of goods. City Arms. Train of cars.
100 Compt's die. Two ornamental male and female figures.	Female with eagle, shield, safe, &c; agricultural implements in background. 100 PACIFIC BANK, New York City. City Arms.	Ship. Shell. 100

Sailor by side of shield, bbls. &c. Compt's die.	PARK BANK. New York City. Word one and figure 1. Red silver dollar. Word one and figure 1. View of Park Fountain, and the City Hall.	Indian on cliff. ONE
TWO Compt's die. Spread eagle and shield.	PARK BANK. New York City. Red silver dollar. Red silver dollar. View of Park, City Hall, Hall of Records, etc.	2 Portrait of girl.
Compt's die. Mexican lassoing wild cattle.	PARK BANK, New York City. 3 Three gold dollars. 3 Steamships and ships at sea.	3 Drove of cattle, sheep, hogs, &c.; house in distance.
5 Sailor and Indian seated by side of shield; eagle at top.	PARK BANK, New York City. Five cherubs and five silver dollars. 5	5 Compt's die. FIVE
10 Portrait of girl.	PARK BANK, New York City. Female seated with nine cherubs, shield, cornucopia and ten gold dollars; locomotive and steamboat in distance.	TEN Sailor, bales, barrels. Compt's die.
TWENTY Full length female with sword and scales.	PARK BANK, New York City. Three females representing agriculture, commerce and manufactures; ship in distance. Compt's die.	XX Sailor and Indian seated by shield.
FIFTY Full length female with spear and shield.	PARK BANK. New York City. Female and eagle in clouds, surrounded by American flag. Compt's die.	50 Portrait of Washington.
100 Male portrait.	PARK BANK, New York City. View of the New York City Hall. Compt's die.	100 Steamship.
500 Male portrait.	PARK BANK, New York City. Sailor and Indian by side of shield, two females by side of State Arms; shipping in distance. Compt's die.	500 D
1000 Sailor crest, flag, &c.	PARK BANK, New York City. Steamship at sea in storm. Compt's die.	M

ONE Compt's die. Word one and fig. 1.	Train of cars passing under a bridge. PEOPLE'S BANK. New York City.	1 Portrait of Taylor.
TWO Compt's die. TWO	View of the bank building with sign on top. PEOPLES BANK, New York City.	2 Male portrait.
3 Compt's die. THREE	Mechanic seated on machinery with hammer on his shoulder; men and factory in distance. Title of Bank running around the vignette.	3 Male portrait.
FI V VE Compt's die. FI V VE	One of the Peoples Line of steamers, with flag on it and words "Peoples Line" back on the right. PEOPLES BANK, New York City.	FIVE Portrait of Franklin.
TEN Compt's die. 10	Female and Goddess of Liberty seated; ship on left; cars, chest, &c., on right. Title of Bank running around vignette.	X Head of Washington.
20 Compt's die.	Female representing Commerce, resting right arm on a bale of goods; shipping on the right. PEOPLES BANK, New York City. Eagle.	20 Male portrait.
50 Compt's die.	Spread eagle, his feet on an olive branch and Am. shield. Title of Bank running over the shield. Horse.	50 Male portrait.
100 Male portrait.	Large steamship with shipping on right and left. Title of Bank running over the vignette.	100 Compt's die.
1 Compt's die. 1	1 Spread eagle. 1 PHENIX BANK, New York City.	1
2 Compt's die. 2	2 Spread eagle. 2 PHENIX BANK, New York City.	2

3 Compt's die. 3	3 Spread eagle. 3 PHENIX BANK, New York City.	3
5	Spread eagle. PHENIX BANK, New York City.	5 Compt's die. 5
10 Compt's die. 10	Spread eagle. PHENIX BANK, New York City.	10
20 Compt's die. 20	XX PHENIX BANK, New York City.	Spread eagle.
50 Spread eagle.	Compt's die. 50 PHENIX BANK, New York City.	50
100	C Spread eagle. C PHENIX BANK, New York City.	100 Compt's die. 100
Compt's die.	500 Spread eagle. PHENIX BANK, New York City.	D
1000 Compt's die.	Spread eagle. PHENIX BANK, New York City.	M
Goddess of Liberty. Compt's die.	1 Female seated with frame on which is agricultural implements, &c.; shipping in distance. SEVENTH WARD BK. New York City. Vessels.	1 Steamer. ONE
2 Compt's die. TWO	Female seated with mechanical implements; on right in distance cars and bridge; on left ship building. SEVENTH WARD BK. New York City. Steamship.	2 Man-of-war. TWO

3 Compt's die. THREE | Male and female in sea car drawn by horses; male and female on left of car; steamship and steamboat in distance. SEVENTH WARD BK New York City. Steamship. | 3 Ship building. THREE

5 5 | Title of Bank. 5 Female seated receiving horn of gold from Mercury; eagle on right of female. Eagle. | 5 Compt's die. 5

10 Jefferson. 10 | Launch of a vessel. Title of Bank. Launch of a vessel. Vig. Same as fives. | 10 Compt's die 10

20 Female with book, torch, eagle and portrait. XX | XX Vig. Same as fives. XX SEVENTH WARD BK New York City. | 20 Compt's die. 20

50 Compt's die. 50 | 50 Vig. Same as fives. 50 SEVENTH WARD BK New York City. | New York Safety Fund. Same as on left of 20s 50

100 Compt's die. 100 | Washington. Title of Bank. Male portrait. Vig. Same as fives. | 100 Launch of a vessel. 100

FIVE HUNDRED | Compt's die. Vig. Same as fives. SEVENTH WARD BK New York City. | 500 Launch of a vessel.

Compt's die. Launch of a vessel. | Vig. Same as fives. SEVENTH WARD BK New York City. 1000 | 1000 Launch of a vessel.

1 Female Portrait. | Men on horses catching wild cattle with lasso. SHOE & LEATH. BK. New York City. Spread Eagle. | 1 Compt's die.

Compt's die 2 | SHOE & LEATH. BK. New York City. Vig. Same as ones. Steamboat. | 2 Female Portrait.

Man carrying leather. Compt's die. | 3 Vig. Same as ones. SHOE & LEATH. BK. New York City. Steamship. | 3 Female portrait.

5 FIVE Two female children. | SHOE & LEATH. BK. New York City. Men on horses lassooing wild cattle. 5 5 | 5 Compt's die

X 10 | Men on horses lassooing wild cattle. Female portrait. SHOE & LEATH BK. New York City. Bee hive. | 10 Compt's die

Figure of Mercury holding bag of coin. 20 | Same as ones. SHOE & LEATH BK. New York City 20 | 20 Compt's die

50 Male head. | SHOE & LEATH. BK. New York City. Vig. Same as ones. | 50 Compt's die.

Male head. ONE 100 | SHOE & LEATH. BK New York City. HUNDRED Vig. Same as ones | 100 Compt's die

ONE Male portrait Compt's die. | 1 View of the St. Nicholas Hotel. 1 ST. NICHOLAS B'K. New York City. Game Cock. | ONE Santa Claus filling the stockings. ONE

TWO Male portrait Compt's die. | 2 Santa Claus riding over tops of houses. 2 ST. NICHOLAS B'K., New York City. Game Cock | Merchandise City Arms. Merchandise

THREE Male portrait Compt's die. | View of the St. Nicholas Hotel. 3 on left. ST. NICHOLAS B'K., New York City. Cock | 3 Santa Claus filling the stockings.

Compt's die. | Santa Claus in sleigh drawn by reindeers. ST. NICHOLAS B'K., New York City. Eagle. | 5 Male portrait.

10 Compt's die. | Santa Claus with sleigh and reindeer. ST. NICHOLAS B'K., New York City. Bee hive. | 10 Bank building.

20 Children asleep in bed; Santa Claus entering from chimney. | ST. NICHOLAS B'K., New York City. Compt's die. | 20 Male portrait

50 Compt's die | ST. NICHOLAS B'K., New York City. Children asleep in bed; Santa Claus entering from chimney. | 50 Male portrait

Compt's die. | U. S. Capitol; pedestrians, horses, carriages, etc. ST. NICHOLAS B'K., New York City. Gamecock. | 100 Male portrait

1 Farmer with bundle under his arm, dog, horse, etc. | TRADESMEN'S B'K., New York City. Blacksmith shoeing horse; man seated on log; man in background. | 1 Compt's die

2 Blacksmith's boy at forge. | Portrait of boy. 2 Portrait of girl. TRADESMEN'S B'K., New York City. | 2 Compt's die.

3 Two men at work on frame of cart. | Compt's die. Sailor seated on anchor smoking pipe, and apparently conversing with two others; ship in distance. TRADESMEN'S B'K., New York City. | 3 Portrait of little girl.

5 Compt's die. | Sailor reclining against bale of goods, supporting flag; vessels and light-house in distance. TRADESMEN'S B'K., New York City. | Figure 5, and large letter V, on this end.

X Compt's die. | Stone cutter seated with mallet, chisel, etc. TRADESMEN'S B'K., New York City. | Figs. 10, and large letter X on this end.

TEN Female with infant; child at her feet. | X Sailor and two farmers; ship in distance. TRADESME"S' B'K. N. Y. City. | 10 Compt's die.

N. Y. CITY.

Left end	Centre	Right end
TWENTY Compt's die.	Eagle and figs. 20 on shield. Bull's head, horses, shipping, etc. TRADESMEN'S B'K., New York City.	TWENTY
Indian female, shield and eagle; steamer in distance. XX	Compt's die. Title of Bank.	20 Cooper at work.
FIFTY Female with sword and shield. FIFTY	Compt's die. Man buying paper from boy, bales, barrels, etc. Title of Bank.	50 Female.
Compt's die. 50	50 Vig. Same as twenties. TRADESMEN'S B'K., New York City.	FIFTY
C 100	Title of Bank. Compt's die. Sailor and Indian on either side of shield; eagle at top.	100 Female seated on bale with sword and cornucopia at her feet.
ONE HUNDRED	100 Vig. Same as 20s. 100 TRADESMEN'S B'K., New York City.	Med. head Compt's die. Med. head
5 Compt's die. 5	V Female reclining, vase of flowers, eagle, etc. V UNION BANK, New York City. Secured, etc.	FIVE Figure 5 and a female. FIVE
10 Compt's die. 10	10 Vig. Same as fives. UNION BANK, New York City. Secured, etc.	10 Female seated. TEN
20 Female seated. TWENTY	Compt's die. 20 Vig. Same as ones. UNION BANK, New York City. Secured, etc.	20 Female seated. TWENTY
50 Compt's die. 50	50 Vig. Same as fives. 50 UNION BANK, New York City. Secured, etc.	50 Female in oval frame. 50

N. Y. STATE.

Left end	Centre	Right end
C Compt's die. C	100 Vig. Same as fives. UNION BANK, New York City. Secured, etc.	100
Die work. Compt's die. Die work	D Female seated feeding an eagle; clouds, etc. D UNION BANK, New York City. Secured, &c.	500
Die work Compt's die. Die work	M Female seated with pole and cap; on her right shield with the words "Manufacturers and Commerce," over it, cornucopia at her feet, steamboat and cars in distance. M Title of Bank. Secured, etc.	1000
ONE on med. head. ONE Compt's die.	Spread eagle on shield in clouds. ADDISON BANK, Addison, N. Y. One Dollar One Dollar	1 Female.
TWO TWO TWO 2 Compt's die. TWO	Rafting scene—man in boat with two birds; females, female and child on raft; another raft in distance. ADDISON BANK, Addison, N. Y. Two Dollars Two Dollars	2 TWO on med. head. TWO TWO TWO
F I V V E Portrait of Martha Washington	ADDISON BANK, Addison, N. Y. Three females with sickle, quadrant, cornucopia and compass. Five Dollars Five Dollars	5 Compt's die. FIVE
10 on med. head. Male portrait	ADDISON BANK, Addison, N. Y. Portrait of Washington; female, train of cars, scythe and grain on right; female, anchor, barrels, men and ship on left. Ten Dollars Ten Dollars	10 Compt's die.
Compt's die. Head.	Indian, globe, ship, female, eagle, &c. ALBANY CITY BK., Albany, N. Y.	1
1 Compt's die. 1	ALBANY CITY B'K. Albany, N. Y. 1 1 Vig. Artisan with two females. City Hall	ONE
Compt's die. Portrait of female.	Vig. Indian and female with American eagle on the world over capitol. ALBANY CITY B'K. Albany, N. Y.	2

N. Y. STATE.

Left end	Centre	Right end
2 Compt's die. 2	2 Male, two females, anvil, sledge, etc. 2 ALBANY CITY BK., Albany, N. Y. Horses.	TWO
Male, female, anvil, etc. 3	Building. 3 ALBANY CITY BK., Albany, N. Y.	3 Compt's die. 3
3 Compt's die.	Vig. Female pointing to shipping in distance. ALBANY CITY B'K. Albany, N. Y.	3
5 Compt's die. 5	5 5 Vig. Same as ones. ALBANY CITY B'K. Albany, N. Y.	Capitol. 5 Dwelling with trees.
10 Compt's die. 10	ALBANY CITY B'K. Albany, N. Y. X X Vig. Same as ones.	X in wreath. Capitol. 10
20 Compt's die 20	20 XX ALBANY CITY BK., Albany, N. Y.	Male, two females, anvil and sledge. 20
20 Compt's die. 20	20 20 ALBANY CITY B'K. Albany, N. Y. Vig. Female with wheel; cars in distance. Capitol.	20 Medallion head. 20
50 Compt's die. 50	House in die; words Fifty Dollars around it, 50 on right. ALBANY CITY BK., Albany, N. Y.	Same as 20s. 50
ONE HUNDRED.	Male, females, anvil, etc. 100 Building. Title of Bank.	100 C
1 Male portrait	Vig. Three artisans, shipping in distance. 1 ALBANY EXCHANGE BANK, Albany, N. Y. Female portrait	ONE Compt's die. Female portrait.

2 | Male portrait. — ALBANY EXCHANGE BANK, Albany, N. Y. Female seated representing commerce, &c. On right is Compt's die, and word 2 on large 2 — 2 | Female portrait.

5 | Compt's die. | FIVE — V Vig. Female seated in figure 5, females on either side V. ALBANY EXCHANGE BANK, Albany, N. Y. Building. — 5 | Medallion head. | FIVE

10 | Compt's die. | TEN — Vig. Shield with female on either side, eagle, shipping and buildings in distance. ALBANY EXCHANGE BANK, Albany, N. Y. Building. — 10 | State Arms. | TEN

FIFTY | Female with pole and cap. | 50 — Two Indians and boy in vessels on left in distance and on right a wood. On each side of vig. is a medallion head and word "Fifty" on it. ALBANY EX. BANK, Albany, N. Y. Building. — FIFTY | Female reclining with ornamental implements. | 50

HUNDRED | Justice. | 100 — Two females reclining, eagle, &c.; vessels on left and bridge on right. Figs. 100 on med. head, on each side of vig. Title of Bank. Building. — ONE HUNDRED

1 | Compt's die. | 1 — 1 Shipping. 1 ATLANTIC BANK, Brooklyn, N. Y. Shield with anchor on it. — Full length female on a large figure 1.

2 | Compt's die. | 2 — 2 Shipping. 2 ATLANTIC BANK, Brooklyn, N. Y. Shield with anchor on it. — Liberty with cap, pole and cornucopia, standing in a large ornamental fig. 2.

3 | Compt's die. | 3 — 3 Vig. Same as 1s. 3 ATLANTIC BANK, Brooklyn, N. Y. Shield with anchor on it. — Female with flowers standing in a large ornamental fig. 3.

5 | Compt's die. | 5 — 5 Neptune riding in a sea shell on the sea drawn by two horses, female by his side. 5 ATLANTIC BANK, Brooklyn, N. Y. Sea shell. — FIVE | Ships. | FIVE

10 | Compt's die. | 10 — X Vig. Same as fives. X ATLANTIC BANK, Brooklyn, N. Y. Sea shell. — TEN | Shipping. | TEN

20 | Compt's die. | 20 — XX Vig. Same as 5s. XX ATLANTIC BANK, Brooklyn, N. Y. Sea shell. — 20 | Shipping. | XX

50 | Compt's die. | 50 — ATLANTIC BANK, Brooklyn, N. Y. Vig. Same as 5s. Letter L in med. die work. — 50 | 50

Compt's die. | 100 — 100 Vig. Same as fives. ATLANTIC BANK, Brooklyn, N. Y. Sea shell. — 100 | 100

Compt's die. | 500 — 500 Vig. Same as fives. ATLANTIC BANK, Brooklyn, N. Y. — 500

1000 — Vig. Same as fives. 1000 ATLANTIC BANK, Brooklyn, N. Y. — Compt's die. | 1000

ONE | Full length female. — Compt's die. Rainbow and falls; female seated, with one hand on figure 1; U.S. shield, &c. AUBURN CITY BANK, Auburn, N. Y. Emblems of commerce and agriculture. — 1 | Female portrait.

TWO | Female holding liberty pole and cap; eagle feeding, horn of plenty. — Compt's die. Vig. Two females, figure 2 between them liberty pole, cap and balance. AUBURN CITY BANK, Auburn, N. Y. Female seated. — 2 | Female portrait.

3 | Female portrait. | Compt's die. — Vig. 3 on bale; female with distaff on left; two females on right. 3 AUBURN CITY BK., Auburn, N. Y. — THREE | Female crest with shield, cap, etc.

5 | Compt's die. | FIVE — Vig. Ornamental 5 in centre; five females, sword, balances, &c.; horn of plenty, locomotive and building, in background; shipping in distance. AUBURN CITY BANK, Auburn, N. Y. — 5 | Washington.

TEN | Full length Indian, with bow, arrows and spear. — Compt's die. Vig. Female reclining, eagle at her back, globe and liberty cap; shipping in distance. AUBURN CITY BANK, Auburn, N. Y. — 10 | Male portrait. | TEN

20 | Compt's die. | TWENTY — Female seated with rake between 2 and 0. AUBURN CITY BK., Auburn, N. Y. Shield. — 20 | Franklin. | TWENTY

Female with battle ax. | Compt's die — AUBURN CITY B'K. Auburn, N. Y. 50 — FIFTY | Female and anchor.

ONE | Male portrait. | Compt's die. — AUBURN EX. B'K. Auburn, N. Y. Red figure 1. Red silver dollar. Red figure 1. Train of cars; load of hay drawn by four horses; men, cows, etc., city and bridges in distance. — ONE on 1. | Two females, one at table, the other with horn in hand.

TWO | Compt's die. | Two females seated by side of shield. — Spread eagle. AUBURN EX. B'K. Auburn, N. Y. Red silver dollar. Red silver dollar. TWO — 2 | Male portrait.

Compt's die. | THREE | Male portrait. — 3 Cattle, sheep, two men, horses and dog; house in distance. AUBURN EX. B'K. Auburn, N. Y. — 3 | Man feeding pigs.

FIVE | Full length figure of Justice. — 5 Five cherubs and five silver dollars. AUBURN EX. B'K. Auburn, N. Y. Shield, bales and navy. — 5 | Compt's die. | FIVE

X | Male portrait. — AUBURN EX. B'K. Auburn, N. Y. 10 Train of cars; steamboat and hills in distance. — Indian looking over cliff. | Compt's die.

20 | Indian and deer on ground; hills and water in distance. | TWENTY — AUBURN EX. B'K. Auburn, N. Y. Eagle and shield; on either side is word twenty and figures 20. Compt's die. — XX | Female Indian reclining; deer in distance.

seated, &c. | ONE — 1 Female with child. BALLSTON SPA B'K. Ballston, N. Y. House. — ONE | Female seated.

TWO | Compt's die. | TWO — 2 Female reaper seated. 2 BALLSTON SPA B'K. Ballston, N. Y. Public building. — Artisan.

5 — Compt's die. — FIVE | V Female seated in figure 5; female on both sides. V — BALLSTON SPA B'K. Ballston, N. Y. — Building. | 5 — Medallion head. — FIVE

10 — Compt's die. — TEN | Shield, with female on either side. — BALLSTON SPA B'K. Ballston, N. Y. — Building. | 10 — State Arms. — TEN

TWENTY — Compt's die. — TWENTY | 20 Vig. Female seated with 20 chemical apparatus, pointing to shipping in distance. — BALLSTON SPA B'K. Ballston, N. Y. — Building. | XX

Secured by pledge, &c. — ONE | 1 Vig. Female Die. with sweet child, cornucopia, anchor, agricultural implements, &c; ship in distance. — BANK OF ALBION, Albion, N. Y. — Dog's head. | ONE — Female seated, cars and vessel in distance.

TWO — Compt's die. — TWO | 2 Vig. Female 2 seated; agricultural implements, factory on left; canal boat and cars on right; steamboat in distance. — BANK OF ALBION, Albion, N. Y. — Female reclining. | Mechanic seated, tools, horn of plenty, &c. surrounded with corn.

Secured by pledge, &c. — Male and female, figure 3 in centre. — Compt's die. | 3 Vig. Female portrait in frame, surrounded by flags, drum, cannon, &c. — BANK OF ALBION, Albion, N. Y. — Female reclining. | 3

5 — Compt's die. — FIVE | Vig. Group of persons, centre female holding grain in one hand, key in the other, seated in chariot; boxes at her feet; vessel and steamship in the distance — BANK OF ALBION, Albion, N. Y. — Female. | 5 — Female pointing towards cars in the distance; man cradling. — FIVE

X — Washington. — 10 | Vig. Signing Declaration of Independence. Compt's die — BANK OF ALBION, Albion, N. Y. — Mechanics arm, hammer, anvil, &c. | X — Martha Washington. — 10

1 — Compt's die | BK OF AMSTERDAM Amsterdam, N. Y. — 1 Female, smoking urn, flowers, etc. 1 | 1 — Male portrait

2 — Compt's die. | BK OF AMSTERDAM Amsterdam, N. Y. — Two on 2 Old man, child and bust of Washington Two on 2 — TWO | 2 — Male portrait.

5 — Male portrait | BK OF AMSTERDAM Amsterdam, N. Y. — Corn grinding scene—three men, dog, etc. | 5 — Compt's die — Five on 5

10 — Female, cotton, measure, etc | BK OF AMSTERDAM Amsterdam, N. Y. — TEN Male portrait TEN | 10 — Compt's die

Secured, &c. — ONE | 1 Female with child. — BANK OF ATTICA, Buffalo, N. Y. | ONE — Female seated.

TWO — Compt's die. — TWO | 2 Vig. Female reaper. 2 — BANK OF ATTICA, Buffalo, N. Y. — Drover and oxen. | Corn — Artisan in circular die. — Corn

Secured, etc. — Figure 3, female on either side. — III | 3 Vig. Portrait of female in oval die, with flags on either side. — BANK OF ATTICA, Buffalo, N. Y. — Oxen and trees. | 3

5 — Compt's die. — FIVE | Vig. Vig. Group of females; plough, wheel, hay, &c. &c. &c. — BANK OF ATTICA, Buffalo, N. Y. — Oxen and trees. | 5 — Female with shield, reaper in distance. — FIVE

TEN — Public building, street, omnibus and people. — Compt's die. | 10 Farmer ploughing, with two horses. — BANK OF ATTICA, Buffalo, N. Y. | 10 — Oxen and pigs.

TWENTY — Reaper sharpening scythe — Compt's die. | 20 Vig. Agricultural scene. — BANK OF ATTICA, Buffalo, N. Y. | 20 — Female seated, holding 20; right hand, 6 in left.

1 — ONE — Compt's die. | ONE ONE ONE ONE ONE — Female, right arm resting on a fence; mill and a mill in distance. — BANK OF AUBURN, Auburn, N. Y. — ONE ONE ONE ONE ONE | 1 — Female and fig. 1, with one on it. — 1

1 — ONE — Compt's die. | Vig. Country scene; female figure, farm house and water mill in back ground. — BANK OF AUBURN, Auburn, N. Y. | 1 — Female figure. — 1

2 — Compt's die. — 2 | Vig. Female seated with cap and liberty pole. — BANK OF AUBURN, Auburn, N. Y. | 2 — Female figure. — 2

Compt's die. — Med head — 3 | THREE THREE — Shield, eagle at top; on right two females with scales, cars in distance; on left, Liberty, ship in distance. — BANK OF AUBURN, Auburn, N. Y. — The word Three five times. | 3 — Female with flowers. — 3

5 — Compt's die. — 5 | Vig. Medallion head, supported on left by female figure of art and science, and on right by female figure of commerce. — BANK OF AUBURN, Auburn, N. Y. | 5 — Medallion head. — 5

Compt's die. | Vig. Eagle on rock, shipping, &c, on left. 10 — BANK OF AUBURN, Auburn, N. Y. | TEN

ONE and 1 — Male portrait | BANK OF BATH, Bath, N. Y. — Vig. Blacksmith shop; smiths shoeing horse; one dollar. | 1 — Compt's die — ONE

2 — TWO — Male portrait | Vig. Drover, cattle and sheep, cars in distance. — 2 2 — BANK OF BATH, Bath, N. Y. — TWO TWO | TWO and 2 — TWO — Compt's die.

5 — Male portrait | Vig. Harvest scene. — 5 5 — BANK OF BATH, Bath, N. Y. — FIVE FIVE | 5 — F I V V E — Compt's die

TEN | Compt's Die. Drover on horse back with boy in water, and drove of cattle, trees, farmhouse, &c., in distance. — BANK OF BATH. Bath, N. Y. — Bath. | 10 — Male portrait

TWENTY | Female Portrait. Goddess of Liberty reclining with pole and cap in right hand, eagle on left. — BANK OF BATH, Bath, N. Y. — Compt's Die. | 20 — Male portrait

ONE — Fillmore. | Compt's die. — Vig. Female seated holding figure one, card in distance. — BANK OF BINGHAMPTON, Binghampton, N. Y. | Female standing in large figure 1.

N. Y. STATE.	N. Y. STATE.	N. Y. STATE.
2 Female seated with spear and shield. BANK OF BING-HAMPTON, Binghampton, N. Y. Spread eagle on limb of tree; train of cars, packet boats, &c. Figure 2 on either side of vignette. Compt's die. 2 Female seated with scales and sword; safe on left.	1 Portrait of Washington. ONE Vig. Locomotive and cars. BANK OF CAYUGA LAKE, Painted Post, N. Y. 1 Compt's die	5 Compt's die. FIVE Vig. Oxen. BANK OF CHEMUNG Elmira, N. Y. Deer. 5 Fillmore.
3 Female portrait. Compt's die. Vig. Farmers at dinner. BANK OF BING-HAMPTON, Binghampton, N. Y 3 Artisan in figure 3, arm on either side. THREE	TWO Farmers loading grain. TWO Medallion head, with TWO on it. Compt's die. Medallion head, with TWO on it. BANK OF CAYUGA LAKE, Painted Post, N. Y. TWO Female seated in large figure 2	Male portrait. Compt's die. Vig. Female seated by safe; pictures; ships to the right. BANK OF CHEMUNG Elmira, N. Y. 10 Locomotive.
FIVE FIVE Compt's die. 5 Locomotive and cars. BANK OF BING-HAMPTON, Binghampton, N. Y Safe. FIVE Large figure 5 and five females.	5 Male portrait Medallion head. Vig. Signing the declaration of independence. BANK OF CAYUGA LAKE, Painted Post, N. Y. FIVE Compt's die.	Female standing erect holding a shield. TWENTY State arms. Vig. Capitol building. BANK OF CHEMUNG Elmira, N. Y. 20 Medallion head.
Compt's die. Male portrait. TEN 10 Vig. 3 females. BANK OF BING-HAMPTON, Binghampton, N. Y. American Shield. 10 Goddess of Liberty in wreath, with busts of Washington and Franklin.	ONE B'K OF CAZENOVIA. Cazenovia, N. Y. Large one in red die. Compt's die. 1 ONE 1	Full length male portrait. ONE 1 Vig. Canal boat and locks. Compt's die. BK. OF CHENANGO, Norwich. Canal locks. ONE Female, sheaf of wheat and sickle. 1
TWENTY Justice erect and Goddess of War seated. 20 Indian princess with shield. BANK OF BING-HAMPTON, N. Y. Shield, etc. 20 Female	TWO DOLLARS B'K OF CAZENOVIA, Cazenovia, N. Y. Large Two in red die. Compt's die. 2 TWO 2	2 Canal boats and locks. 2 Vig. Cupid inscribing on rocks. BK. OF CHENANGO, Norwich. Canal locks. Full length figure with shield and spear. TWO
FIFTY Indian female erect with bow and arrows. Compt's die. Female portrait. 50 BANK OF BING-HAMPTON, Binghampton, N. Y Horn of plenty and anvil. Winged female erect; female seated at her feet, also an eagle.	FIVE BK. OF CAZENOVIA, Cazenovia, N. Y. Large five in red die. 5 Compt's die. FI V VE	3 Female. THREE Vig. Female with arm resting on wheel. BK. OF CHENANGO, Norwich. Canal locks. Full length male figure. THREE
ONE Compt's die. ONE Vig. Indian and squaw in canoe. BANK OF CANANDAGUIA, Canandaguia. Fowls. 1 Male portrait.	TEN Washington BK OF CAZENOVIA, Cazenovia, N. Y. TEN in large red die. 10 TEN Compt's die	5 Compt's die. 5 5 Vig. Female seated. 5 BK. OF CHENANGO, Norwich. Female seated, holding an eagle; three vessels on left in distance. V
TWO Compt's die. Vig. Wild horses. BANK OF CANANDAGUIA, Canandaguia. T W O Dog. 2 Male portrait.	Die. 20 Die. BK OF CAZENOVIA, Cazenovia, N. Y. TWENTY in large red die. 20 Franklin.	10 Compt's die. 10 Vig. Allen surveying plain, cars and village in distance. 10 each side. BK. OF CHENANGO, Norwich. Cupid riding deer. Full length female. X
V Railroad; train of cars. BANK OF CANANDAGUIA, Canandaguia. Compt's die Vig. Female seated, arm resting on bale of goods; steamboat on left; vessel on right. 5 FIVE	1 Compt's die. ONE Vig. Men loading hay. BANK OF CHEMUNG Elmira, N. Y. Wheelbarrow 1 Bridge and canal boat. ONE	Full length female. 20 Vig. Two female figures soaring in the air. BK. OF CHENANGO, Norwich. Canal locks. Full length male figure. 20
TEN Female in field of grain. Vig. Train of cars passing under bridge; Telegraph, &c. BANK OF CANANDAGUIA, Canandaguia. Dog. X Compt's die	TWO Compt's die. TWO Vig. Female seated in figure 2. BANK OF CHEMUNG Elmira, N. Y. Load of hay. 2 Female with wheat. 2	FIFTY Vig. Cupid inscribing on rock. BK. OF CHENANGO, Norwich. Canal locks. FIFTY

1 Compt's die.	Female reclining with bale, bbl., spinning wheel, etc. BANK OF COHOES, Cohoes, N. Y.	1 Two males erect; female seated; buildings.
Cupid and 2 Compt's die. TWO	Title of Bank. Two females at work on looms.	2 2
Compt's die. 3	Two females seated on bale; factory in distance. Title of Bank.	3 Girl's head.
Cupid and 5. Male portrait.	Title of Bank. Eagle. Female seated by bale; factory and falls in distance.	5 Compt's die. 5
10 Two Indians on cliff; city in distance.	Two females seated by anvil; factory in distance. Title of Bank. 10 TEN TEN	10 Compt's die.
20 Female with sword and shield. TWENTY	Compt's die. Spread eagle. BANK OF COHOES, Cohoes, N. Y.	20 Female portrait.
1 Compt's die.	Vig. Female seated, with mirror, &c.; cars on right, steamer and ship on left. B'K OF COMMERCE, Carmel, N. Y.	ONE Reaper clasping figure 1
1 Compt's die	Wild horses. B'K OF COMMERCE, Carmel, N. Y. ONE on 1.	1 Female.
2 Compt's die. 2	B'K OF COMMERCE, Carmel, N. Y. 2 Horses, load of hay, men and barn; load of hay in distance. 2	2 TWO
2 Compt's die.	Vig. Crystal Palace, N. Y. B'K OF COMMERCE, Carmel, N. Y. 2	Female seated, in large figure 2. TWO

3 Compt's die.	Vig. Artisans; vessel cars and factory in distance. B'K OF COMMERCE, Carmel, N. Y. 3	111 Fig. 3 and Female seated on rocks.
FIVE Goddess of Liberty.	B'K OF COMMERCE, Carmel, N. Y. Large V with FIVE running across it. Vig. Locomotive and cars, oxen and water in foreground.	5 Compt's die.
10 Male portrait	Cattle in pasture; one drinking. B'K OF COMMERCE, Carmel, N. Y. TEN and ten dollars across	10 TEN Compt's die.
20 Male portrait	Cattle and sheep; water in distance. B'K OF COMMERCE, Carmel, N. Y. Compt's die, X on TWENTY on left and X on DOLLARS on right.	20 XX
1 Portrait of Daniel Webster. Compt's die.	BANK OF COOPERSTOWN. Vig. Woodchopper, gold dollar; farm house and waggon in distance. Shield, etc.	1 Goddess of liberty supporting figure one.
2 Portrait of Franklin. Compt's die.	BANK OF COOPERSTOWN. Vig. Farmer, milk maid, two gold dollars, and cattle. Farm house in distance. Dog.	2 Indian with bow, spear, and arrows.
3 Portrait. Compt's die.	BANK OF COOPERSTOWN. 3 Vig. Farmer, mechanic and sailor, seated, holding implements; three gold dollars lapped. Goddess of liberty.	THREE Full length female.
FIVE Washington. Compt's die.	BANK OF COOPERSTOWN. Vig. Five figures and five gold dollars lapped. Safe.	5 Female holding balance; small figure 5; safe; and soldier in armor. FIVE
10 Compt's die. TEN	BANK OF COOPERSTOWN. Vig. Two females seated, hogshead and bale of goods; farmer plowing; cars and steamship in the distance. Safe.	10 Female Indian holding ear of corn and small X
1 Compt's die ONE	Vig. male ploughing. BANK OF COXSACKIE. Coxsackie, N. Y.	1 Indian seated with gun in hand.

Female holding figure 2. Compt's die.	Vig. Horse running from locomotive in distance. BANK OF COXSACKIE, Coxsackie, N. Y.	2 Female milking cow.
3 Portrait of Female. 3	BANK OF COXSACKIE. Coxsackie, N. Y. Vig. Female seated on safe, with dog and child.	3 Compt's die.
5 Compt's die.	B'K OF COXSACKIE, Coxsackie, N. Y. Female seated with anchor; city and shipping in background.	5 Portrait of Washington
State Arms. 10	Male portrait. BANK OF COXSACKIE, Coxsackie, N. Y.	10 Compt's die.
1 Compt's die. ONE	Vig. Man and two boys washing sheep, and dog. fig. 1 on left. BK. OF DANSVILLE. ONE DOLLAR. Banking house.	NEW YORK on fig. 1
2 Die. TWO	Vig. Agricultural scene, family group; horses and men in the distance. BK. OF DANSVILLE. TWO DOLLARS. Banking house.	2 Two female figures.
3 Die. THREE	Vig. Three figures, two male, one female, and a dog. BK. OF DANSVILLE. THREE DOLLARS. Banking house.	3 Three men, one crouching or holding up figure 3.
5 Compt's die. FIVE	V Females and fig. 5. V BK OF DANSVILLE, Dansville, N. Y. Eagle.	5 Med head FIVE
10 Compt's die. TEN	Female either side of shield; vessels, etc., in distance. BK OF DANSVILLE, Dansville, N. Y. Grain, etc	10 Arms. TEN
20 Compt's die.	Vig. Dairy scene, with maid in midst of cows, in sitting posture, with pail. BK. OF DANSVILLE. Machine	20 Banking house.

50 Compt's die.	Vig. Indian sitting, bow in left hand, and viewing agricultural scene. ... resting on hand, ... on woods BK. OF DANSVILLE. Eagle	50 Portrait of Gov. Hunt.
Female seated, holding spear and branch; and large figure 1. Compt's die.	Female portrait; cupids on either side. BANK OF FAYETTE-VILLE, Fayetteville, N. Y.	... Vig. Female bearing; ... in one hand, branch in the other; eagle; steamship and vessels. 1
Female holding figure 2. Compt's die.	Male portrait; cupids on either side. BANK OF FAYETTE-VILLE, Fayetteville, N. Y. Vig. Two females; mechanic reclining against safe; implements, cars, steamship, &c.	2 TWO
Female holding figure 3. Compt's die. THREE	Franklin; cupids on either side. BANK OF FAYETTE-VILLE, Fayetteville, N. Y. Vig. Boy plowing; Farm house, steamboat.	III 3
FIVE Girl. 5	Compt's die. Cupids on either side. BANK OF FAYETTE-VILLE Fayetteville, N. Y. FIVE	FIVE Flower girl with basket of flowers. 5
X with letters TEN running across it. Female, liberty pole, cap, &c.	BANK OF FAYETTE-VILLE, Fayetteville, N. Y. Vig. Farmer, sailor, and mechanic; implements, &c. Two vessels, cars, &c, in back ground.	10 Farm house and boat. Compt's die.
20 Indian woman, bow and spear.	BANK OF FAYETTE-VILLE, Fayetteville, N. Y. Compt's die, Vig. Train cars, village; female holding book and pen.	20
ONE Large figure 1 with portrait of Washington.	Vig. Train of cars; village in distance on left, steamboat on right. BANK OF FISHKILL, Fishkill Village, N. Y. Secured, &c.	1 Compt's die
2 Farmer ploughing. Female portrait.	BANK OF FISHKILL, Fishkill Village, N.Y. Secured, &c.	2 Compt's die.
THREE Compt's die.	Vig. Horses drinking, pigs on right. 3 BANK OF FISHKILL, Fishkill Village, N. Y. Secured, &c.	3 Washington on horseback.

5 Compt's die. 5	Large ... Vig. Arithmetical ... figure 5, with word five on it. BANK OF FISHKILL, Fishkill Village, N. Y. Secured, &c.	5 Portrait of Washington
Female with sheaf. Compt's Die.	X Milkmaid seated; one milking cow; sail vessels, cows, etc. BANK OF FISHKILL, Fishkill Village, N.Y. Secured, etc.	10 Steamboat.
20 Female Indian.	BANK OF FISHKILL, Fishkill Village, N.Y. X Vig. Eagle. X	20 Compt's die. Secured, &c.
1 Compt's die.	Vig. Locomotive and train of cars; canal boat and village in distance. BANK OF FORT EDWARD, Fort Edward, N. Y.	1 Male portrait
2 Compt's die. TWO	Vig. Female with liberty pole and cap, shield, balloon, cannon and drum. BANK OF FORT EDWARD, Fort Edward, N. Y.	2 Male portrait
3 Compt's die. 3	Vig. Reaper, cattle and sheep; man on horseback watering his horse. BANK OF FORT EDWARD, Fort Edward, N. Y.	3 Male portrait 3
FIVE Compt's die. FIVE	5 Vig. Two females, one reclining; liberty pole and cap, balance, sword, shield and eagle; ship in distance. BANK OF FORT EDWARD, Fort Edward, N. Y.	5 Franklin.
Compt's die. Female, liberty pole in one hand, the other resting on X.	Male portrait. 10 BANK OF FORT EDWARD, Fort Edward, N. Y.	TEN Two Indians, female kneeling between them. 10
Compt's die. Two Indians and female. TWENTY	Male portrait. 20 BANK OF FORT EDWARD, Fort Edward, N. Y.	Vig. Canal boat, and cars crossing bridge, horse
1 Compt's die. 1	Vig. Two females ONE with sword ONE balances, & spear; eagle mounted over a figure 1. BANK OF GENESEE, Batavia, N. Y.	1 Portrait of Washington ONE

2 Compt's die. 2	2 BANK OF GENESEE, Batavia, N. Y. Two dollars on die work.	Vig. Two females on either side figure 2; liberty cap, bee hive, and flowers. TWO
3 Compt's die. 3	3 Vig. Neptune in his car; female on left; ship in distance on right; canal on left. 3 BANK OF GENESEE Batavia, N. Y. Die	Full length Male portrait. THREE
5 Compt's die. 5	5 Vig. Three females; agricultural implements; sheaf of wheat, bee hive, &c. 5 BANK OF GENESEE, Batavia, N. Y. Die,	5 Male Portrait 5
10 Compt's die. 10	TEN TEN Vig. Agricultural implements, sheaf wheat, trees. BANK OF GENESEE, Batavia, N. Y.	10 Male portrait 10
Compt's die. Female head	1 Human Washington figure floating in air. BANK OF GENEVA, Geneva, N. Y. ONE	1 Female figure, holding 1.
1 Compt's die.	Vig. Female seated, sickle grain, reapers at work. Portrait of Washington BANK OF GENEVA Geneva, N. Y.	1 Female, ship in distance. ONE
2 Compt's die.	Vig. Angel blowing trumpet. Male portrait. BANK OF GENEVA, Geneva, N. Y.	2 Two cupids seated on large figure 2
5 Compt's die. 5	Female seated on plow holding sheaf and sickle. 5 BANK OF GENEVA, Geneva, N. Y.	Female holding sheaf. 5
Portrait of male. Compt's die.	5 Vig. Man standing with flag and sword, others kneeling around. BANK OF GENEVA, Geneva, N. Y.	5 Male portrait V
X Compt's die. 10	Vig. Harvest scene. BANK OF GENEVA, Geneva, N. Y. Locomotive.	10 Goddess of Liberty.

Left	Centre	Right
Mechanic at bench. Compt's die.	BANK OF HAVANA, Havana, N. Y. 1 Male portrait. 1	1 Female seated; houses in distance.
2 Compt's die. 2	Male portrait. Vig. Female kneeling, with pail; cattle lying down, &c. BANK OF HAVANA, Havana, N. Y.	2 Male portrait
Compt's die. Male portrait.	5 Portrait of Washington. 5 BANK OF HAVANA, Havana, N. Y. Canal boat.	FIVE Female standing; canal lock in the distance.
1 ONE Compt's die.	Cattle and sheep. BANK OF KENT, Ludingtonville, N. Y.	1 Men gathering corn.
2 Compt's die. 2	Woodcutters at work. BANK OF KENT, Ludingtonville, N. Y	2 Men gathering corn.
Female seated by side of portrait of boy. V	Men harvesting. BANK OF KENT, Ludingtonville, N. Y	5 Compt's die 5
1 Figure of Knickerbocker on his travels. Compt's die.	Vig. Sheep washing; man with shell, dog, &c.; team ploughing in the distance. Fig. 1 with letter one running across it. BANK OF KINDERHOOK. ONE	The word New York is printed on a large figure 1
TWO Justice with scales and sword; eagle, safe, key, &c. TWO	2 2 Vig. Female holding dove in right hand, and extending sceptre with left hand; sheaf of wheat, horn of plenty. In the distance a mill and stream, canal, train of cars, &c. BANK OF KINDERHOOK. Anchor between sigs.	Ears of corn. Blacksmith with his implements.
5 Justice with scales and sword; eagle, safe, key, &c. FIVE	Vig. Group of four figures, two lions, chariot, plough and rake, horn of plenty; ships in distance. BANK OF KINDERHOOK. Anchor between sigs.	5 Minerva with head of Medusa on a shield; reapers in the distance. FIVE
10 Justice with scales and sword; eagle, safe, key, &c. TEN	Vig. Shield bearing coat of arms of the several States, female on either side; rake, plough, sickle, barrels, steamboat, factory, train of cars, and city in the distance. BANK OF KINDERHOOK. Anchor between sigs.	10 State Arms TEN

Left	Centre	Right
TWENTY Compt's die Man whetting scythe.	20 Cattle, sheep, two men, horse and Dog. BANK OF KINDERHOOK. Kinderhook, N. Y. Bee hive.	Twenty across the bill on either side of 20
ONE Webster. ONE	1 Two milkmaids, one erect, the other seated. 1 BANK OF LANSINGBURGH, Lansingburgh, N. Y. Horse's head.	Franklin. Compt's die. Male portrait
TWO Male portrait TWO	2 Three reapers at work in field. 2 BANK OF LANSINGBURGH, Lansingburgh, N. Y.	Female head. Compt's die Male portrait
FIVE V A female sitting on the point of the 5. 5	BANK OF LANSINGBURGH. 5 Vig. Two men on horseback, driving cattle and sheep; dog; barn in the distance, a small sloop. 5	Head of Washington. State Arms. Chief Justice Marshall.
10 on med. head. Washington	Compt's die. Eagle; light house, vessels, man ploughing, etc., in distance. BANK OF LANSINGBURGH, Lansingburgh, N. Y. TEN	10 on med. head. Martha Washington.
20 State Arms. 20	BANK OF LANSINGBURGH. 20 Vig. Two children; one astride a fish, surmounted with an eagle; one lying down; a steamboat in the distance. 20	20 Figure of Justice with scales; American eagle; head of Washington. 20
50 State Arms. 50	BANK OF LANSINGBURGH. 50 Vig. Three females sitting; sheaf of wheat, sickle, plough handle; hay stack in rear. 50	50 Cattle and two men. 50
Henry Clay Compt's die.	1 Boy on horse driving sheep; cows, colt, &c. BANK OF LIMA, Lima, N. Y.	1 Cattle passing under and cars over arch.
TWO Compt's die. TWO	BANK OF LIMA, Lima, N. Y. Anvil; female on either side; cornucopia; factory in rear.	2 Webster.
5 Male portrait	Engine entering depot; one leaving; two trains in distance. BANK OF LIMA, Lima, N. Y.	5 Compt's die. FIVE

Left	Centre	Right
10 Female and little girl seated; man drinking out of a jug.	Men reaping. Portrait of Washington. BANK OF LIMA, Lima, N. Y.	10 Compt's die.
ONE Female, sickle, etc. ONE	Bird on branch of tree. B'K OF LOWVILLE, Lowville, N. Y.	Female enclosed in large ornamental fig. 1.
Secured by pledge, &c. ONE	1 Vig. Female with child; ship in distance. B'K OF LOWVILLE, Lowville, N. Y. Dog's head.	ONE Female seated; cars in distance.
TWO Compt's die. TWO	2 Vig. Female reaper 2 B'K OF LOWVILLE, Lowville, N. Y. Dog's head.	Artisan pouring gold out of horn.
Large figure 3 with female on either side.	3 Vig. Female portrait, with female on either side. B'K OF LOWVILLE, Lowville, N. Y. Dog's head.	3
5 Compt's die. FIVE	V Vig. Female in figure 5; female on either side. V B'K OF LOWVILLE, Lowville, N. Y. Dog's head.	5 Boat FIVE
10 Compt's die. TEN	Vig. Wreath with female on either side; shipping, cars and buildings in distance. B'K OF LOWVILLE, Lowville, N. Y. Dog's head	10 State Arms. TEN
Vig. Boat, load of hay, canal boat, &c. 25	B'K OF LOWVILLE, Lowville, N. Y. Male portrait. Cornucopia, bales, &c.	25 Compt's die. 25
ONE Compt's die. ONE	1 Vig. Man on horseback watering his horse; drover and cattle. BANK OF MALONE, Malone, N. Y.	1 Franklin.
2 Compt's die TWO	Saw mill, horses and wagon; yoke of oxen; men at work, &c. BANK OF MALONE, Malone, N. Y.	2 Train of cars. TWO

5 — Compt's die. — V | Train of cars. BANK OF MALONE, Malone, N. Y. | Large ornamental 5; waterfall, cars, Indians, &c.

10 — Compt's die. — 10 | Vig. Female seated; globe and cars behind her; wheat, &c., on right. BANK OF MALONE, Malone, N. Y. | 10 — Franklin. — 10

20 — Compt's die. — TWENTY | BANK OF MALONE, Malone, N. Y. Vig. Cattle and sheep; farm house in distance. | 20 — Male Portrait. — TWENTY

1 — ONE — Compt's die. | Blacksmith shoeing horse; old man by side of horse; man at anvil. BK OF NEWARK, Newark, N. Y. | 1 — Female portrait.

1 — ONE — Compt's die. | View of harbor of New York, with steamship Pacific and ship. BANK OF NEWARK, ONE. Female bathing. | 1 — Wayne co. Cattle, telegraph and railroad.

TWO — Two Indian chiefs with bows. | Railroad trains coming out of a tunnel; two ladies standing looking on. BANK OF NEWARK. TWO | 2 — Compt's die. — TWO

TWO TWO TWO — 2 — Compt's die. — 2 | Old man seated under tree with boy and dog; sheep in distance. Title of Bank. | 2 — Female with dove. — TWO TWO TWO

5 — Female feeding fowls. | Three females and bust of Washington. Title of Bank. Five Dollars Five Dollars | 5 — Compt's die — FIVE

Compt's die. — Five, V, &. | Three female figures seated, with shield in centre and eagle perched on it. BANK OF NEWARK. Locomotive. | 5 — Squaw and child seated.

TEN | Vig. Mechanic, sailor, and farmer making offerings to Goddess of Liberty, with eagle seated above the Goddess. BANK OF NEWARK. | 10 — Railroad with locomotive.

X — City. | Female and two cattle; canal scene, cars, town, etc., in distance. Title of Bank. | 10 — Compt's die.

TWENTY — Eagle on shield, female with quadrant seated. — TWENTY | BANK OF NEWARK. Vig. Ploughman and horses, with houses in distance. | 20

Compt's die. — 1 | Vig. Train of cars, &c. BK OF NEWBURGH Newburgh, N. Y. Large figure 1 running lengthwise of the note. | ONE — 1

2 — Compt's die. — 2 | 2 Vig. Female seated, sickle in hand. Wheat & cattle on either side. 2 BK OF NEWBURGH Newburgh, N. Y. Steamboat. | TWO — Cupid engraving. — TWO

Compt's die. — 3 | BK OF NEWBURGH, Newburgh, N. Y. Figure of Justice. | THREE — 3

3 — Compt's die. — 3 | 3 Vig. Blacksmith at work, two females. 3 BK OF NEWBURGH Newburgh, N. Y. Steamboat. | THREE — Full length male figure. — THREE

5 — Compt's die. — 5 | 5 Vig. Female leaning on a wheel, monument behind her. 5 BK OF NEWBURGH Newburgh, N. Y. Steamboat. | V — Female seated, one arm around a column, the other extended. — V

Compt's die. — 10 | BK OF NEWBURGH Newburgh, N. Y. X Vig. Two females seated, cask and bales in rear; canal boat in distance. |

Compt's die. — XX | Vig. Mechanic seated holding a sledge hammer on his shoulder, cars on right, &c. BK OF NEWBURGH Newburgh, N. Y. | 20

FIFTY | 50 BK OF NEWBURGH Newburgh, N. Y. Title of bank on each side of vignette. Vig. Female seated holding balances, anchor and small sail vessel. Compt's stamp on back of note. |

HUNDRED | 100 BK OF NEWBURGH Newburgh, N. Y. Title of bank on each side of vignette. Vig. Female seated holding balances, sickle, wheat and small vessel. Compt's stamp on back of note. | 100

1 — Agricultural implements and products. — Compt's die. | Mowing and harvesting scene; load of hay in distance. BK OF NEWPORT, Newport, N. Y. | ONE — Female portrait.

TWO — Compt's die. — TWO | Milkmaid seated; farmer reclining on ground; two gold dollars; cattle on left; farm houses on right. Title of Bank. | 2 — Cars.

Compt's die. — Cow. — Three on 3. | Farmer, sailor and mechanic; three gold dollars, &c. Title of Bank. | 3 — Ox passing over and cattle passing under arch.

5 — City. | Female seated either side of anvil. Title of Bank. | 5 — Compt's die. — 5

Full length statue on background. | 10 Cattle in stream; boy and child on bank. BK. OF NEWPORT, Newport, N. Y. | 10 — Compt's die.

XX — Youthful portrait with cap. | Compt's die. Boy on horse, colt, sheep, cattle, etc. Title of Bank. | 20 — Cooper at work on barrels.

Farmer with scythe. — Compt's die. | 1 Indian and ornamental fig. 1. BANK OF NORWICH. Norwich, N. Y. | Word one and figure 1. Male portrait. ONE

TWO — Compt's die. — TWO | Female on either side of fig. 2. TWO BANK OF NORWICH, Norwich, N. Y. | 2 — Male portrait.

Compt's die. — Male portrait. | Three females and ornamental fig. 3; factory in distance. Fig. 3 on left. BANK OF NORWICH. Norwich, N. Y. | Word three and fig. 3. Mechanic, sailor and farmer in fig. 3.

5 Male portrait FIVE	Five females, and fig. 5, shipping, and factories in distance. BANK OF NORWICH Norwich, N. Y. Loading hay.	5 Compt's die FIVE

Male portrait TEN	Nine cherubs and ten gold dollars; female with cornucopia, shield, &c. BANK OF NORWICH Norwich, N. Y.	10 Agricultural implements. Compt's die.

TWENTY DOLLARS	BK. OF NORWICH, Norwich, N. Y. Female seated on either side of male portrait; sword, spear, bales, steamboat, cars, etc.	20

FIFTY	Boy on horse back; cows, sheep, etc. FIFTY, Compt's die. Title of Bank.	50 Male portrait

Female seated by side of fig. 1. Compt's die.	Indian, squaw and child in canoe; wigwams, trees, etc. in distance. BANK OF OLD SARATOGA, Schuylerville, N. Y. Soldier and cannon.	1 Female seated and fig. 1

2 Compt's die. 2	Indians on horse back viewing train of cars. Title of Bank. Sentinel and cannon.	2 Female and figure 2.

5 Male portrait	Female in clouds with shield, pole, cap and eagle. Title of Bank. Sentinel and cannon.	5 Compt's die. 5

TEN Spread eagle. 10	Surrender of Burgoyne. 10 BANK OF OLD SARATOGA, Schuylerville, N. Y. Soldier and cannon.	Justice. Compt's die.

Two horses, man, dog, plow, etc. XX	Compt's die female each side. BANK OF OLD SARATOGA, Schuylerville, N. Y. Soldier and cannon.	20 Blacksmith with anvil.

Medallion head. Compt's die. Medallion head.	1 Vig. Dairy maid with cows. 1 B'K OF ORANGE CO. Goshen, N. Y. Dog's head.	ONE Female portrait. ONE

Female portrait. Compt's die. Female portrait.	2 Vig. Farmer with drove of cattle. B'K OF ORANGE CO. Goshen, N. Y. Eagle.	TWO Locomotive and cars. TWO

Female portrait. Compt's die. Female portrait.	5 Vig. Locomotive and cars. B'K OF ORANGE CO. Goshen, N. Y.	FIVE Male portrait FIVE

FIVE	5 Girl milking cow. V BK. OF ORANGE CO., Goshen, N. Y. Agricultural tools.	Compt's die.

FIVE Two girls with sheaf.	5 Boy, horses, colt, cows and sheep. BK. OF ORANGE CO., Goshen, N. Y.	5 Compt's die FIVE

TEN Man sharpening scythe	X Milkmaid seated with hat on lap; dog, cows, etc Title of Bank. Man plowing.	10 Compt's die.

TEN	10 Female churning. X B'K OF ORANGE CO. Goshen, N. Y. Agricultural implements.	10 Compt's die.

TWENTY	20 Female churning. 20 B'K OF ORANGE CO. Goshen, N. Y. Farming tools	Compt's die.

20 Cattle, telegraph, arch, cars, etc.	Milkmaid milking cow, etc. Title of Bank. Compt's die.	20 Man shearing sheep.

1 Compt's Die.	BK of ORANGET'WN Orangeburg, N.Y. 1 Female with basket of flowers 1	1 Two children.

Two on 2 Compt's Die. TWO	BK of ORANGET'WN Orangeburg, N.Y. 2 Female seated by wheel with flowers and sickle 2	2 Female seated with basket of fruit

Female with tablets on which is words "Five Dollars," child at her feet. FIVE	5 Two mermaids in water; vessels and ocean scene BK of ORANGET'WN Orangeburg, N.Y.	5 Compt's Die. 5

1 surrounded by small 1's. Compt's die.	BANK OF OTEGO, Otego, N. Y. One Dollar on large 1 — Portrait of Winfield Scott — One Dollar on large 1.	1 surrounded by words one. Female embracing child.

2 Compt's die. TWO	BANK OF OTEGO, Otego, N. Y. Two Dollars on 2 — Two Dollars on 2 Farmer seated on fence, holding scythe.	2 surrounded by small 2's and two. Female head.

5 in centre, with small 5's above and below it.	Dog's head. 5 Three children, with book open on table in an oval. BANK OF OTEGO. Otego, N. Y. FIVE DOLLARS.	5 Compt's die. 5

ONE Compt's die. Male portrait.	Vig. Portrait with females on either side, farmers at work; ship and steamboat in distance. BANK OF OWEGO. Wheelbarrow, &c.	ONE Female with sickle and grain. ONE

TWO Compt's die. Portrait of Taylor.	Vig. Three females surrounding frame, on which is perched an eagle; ship and cars in distance. BANK OF OWEGO. Locomotive.	TWO Two Indians. TWO

5 Compt's die. 5	5 Vig. Female holding an eagle; horn of plenty at her feet; ships in distance. 5 BANK OF OWEGO. Raft.	V Female, eagle, &c. V

TEN	X Female holding an eagle; horn of plenty; ships in distance. X BANK OF OWEGO, Owego, N. Y. Spread Eagle.	10 Compt's die. 10

TWENTY	20 Female holding an eagle; horn of plenty at her feet; ships in distance. 20 BANK OF OWEGO. Ark.	TWENTY. Compt's die. XX

FIFTY	L L BANK OF OWEGO, Vig. Female seated on rock, with eagle in left hand, horn of plenty at her feet. Canal boat.	50 Cattle. 50

Left	Centre	Right
ONE HUNDRED	10) 100 BANK OF OWEGO. Female seated on rock with eagle in left hand; horn of plenty at her feet. Ark.	ONE HUNDRED
1 Compt's die. ONE	1 Three cows and two females. 1 BK OF PAWLING, Pawling, N. Y.	1 Franklin. 1
2 Wm. Penn 2	Vig. Spread eagle. Compt's die BK OF PAWLING	2 Spotted heifer. 2
5 Compt's die. Washington. 5	Compt's die. BANK OF PAWLING Vig. Wagon and oxen, two men loading hay, four men and scythes, and female with child. Spread eagle, etc.	5 FIVE
X Compt's die. 10	Vig. Drove of cattle and sheep; driver on horse with arms and whip extended. B'NK OF PAWLING.	10 Goddess with liberty pole and cap and small eagle.
20	Compt's die. Vig. Drove of cattle and sheep; driver on horse with arms and whip extended. B'NK OF PAWLING.	20 Female in an oval circle, dark ground.
FIFTY Female with sickle and sheaf of wheat on back. Compt's die.	Vig. Two females, one holding liberty pole and cap, horse's head and neck between them. B'NK OF PAWLING.	50 Female in circle, with Duchess on over.
100 Compts. die 100	BANK OF PAWLING Goddess, American eagle and flag.	100 on head. Man with scythe.
ONE Male portrait.	Vig. Canal and boats hills on either side BANK OF PORT JERVIS. Port Jervis, N. Y.	1 Compt's die. 1
TWO Male portrait.	Vig. Men at work loading hay, horse and ox for the team. BANK OF PORT JERVIS. Port Jervis, N. Y.	2 Compt's die. TWO

Left	Centre	Right
Compt's die. Male portrait	Cattle and sheep. BK of PORT JERVIS, Port Jervis, N. Y.	3 Sailor
V Male portrait.	Vig. Train of cars, bridge and telegraph poles. BANK OF PORT JERVIS, Port Jervis, N. Y.	5 Compt's die.
X Compt's die.	Vig. Female reclining on bale of goods, barrels and ships, in distance on right, steamship on left. BANK OF PORT JERVIS, Port Jervis, N. Y.	TEN Male portrait.
10 Compt's die.	Two females reclining; spinning wheel, sickle, etc.; cattle and factories in distance. BK of PORT JERVIS, Port Jervis, N. Y.	10 Penn.
20 Female kneeling with sheaf and sickle.	Compt's die. Sailor on globe, shield, goods and flags. Title of Bank.	20; old issues has XX
Female with sickle and flag.	50 Interior of blacksmith shop; four men and boy. Title of Bank. 50 Compt's die 50	50 Female portrait
1 Female seated; eagle, sword, balances, &c.	Vig. Milk maids, cows, &c. Farm house in distance. BANK OF POUGHKEEPSIE Poughkeepsie, N. Y. Building.	1 Compt's die.
2 Compt's die. 2	Small port. of Jefferson. Small port. of Washington. Vig. Female seated on plough holding sickle and grain; steamboat and cars in distance. BANK OF POUGHKEEPSIE Poughkeepsie, N. Y. Building.	TWO Female Indian, liberty cap and pole. TWO
3 Female holding shaft with flag, ship in background.	3 Vig. Female leaning upon anchor, shipping and harbor in distance. 3 BANK OF POUGHKEEPSIE Poughkeepsie, N. Y. Building.	Female with wheat in her arms Compt's die.
Compt's die. 5	Vig. Spread eagle. BANK OF POUGHKEEPSIE Poughkeepsie, N. Y. Building.	5 Washington on horseback.

Left	Centre	Right
10 Compt's die. 10	Vig. Large X in centre. Portrait on either side, the whole surrounded by scroll work, within which is seated cupids. BANK OF POUGHKEEPSIE Poughkeepsie, N. Y. Building.	10 Washington.
50 Steamboats shipping and harbor. 50	50 Compt's die. Vig. Harvest field in background; work man and woman in foreground, dog at their feet. BANK OF POUGHKEEPSIE Poughkeepsie N. Y. Dog, key and safe.	50 Indian in canoe.
Artist seated 100	BANK OF POUGHKEEPSIE Poughkeepsie, N. Y. 100 Compt's die. Vig. Cupid in clouds. Dog, key, and safe.	Artist. 100
1 [illegible] Cass. 1	Vig. Female looking at shipping in distance. B'K OF RHINEBECK, Rhinebeck, N. Y.	1 Compt's die
Vig. Farmers [illegible] haying making [illegible] background 2	Portrait of Franklin. B'K OF RHINEBECK, Rhinebeck, N. Y.	2 Compt's die
3 Male portrait	Vig. Farmer with two horses; locomotive and cars in background. B'K OF RHINEBECK, Rhinebeck, N. Y.	3 Compt's die.
Portrait of Henry Clay. 5	B'K OF RHINEBECK, Rhinebeck, N. Y. 5 Vig. Farmer with oxen and sheep. 5	5 Compt's die
10 Female seated, right hand on pail; cattle and trees on left.	X Farmer with children right shoulder, female holding its hand X BK OF RHINEBECK, Rhinebeck, N. Y.	10 Compt's die
ONE Man wearing, holding horn of plenty and wheat, vessel in distance. Compt's die	Vig. Winged female, kneeling in front of large case, sword and balances. BANK OF ROME, Rome, N. Y. Indian.	1
TWO Compt's die. TWO	2 Vig. Farm house, milk maids, cows, Barn, &c. 2 BANK OF ROME, Rome, N. Y. Indian's bust.	TWO Two cupids, surrounded by large ornamental figure 2. TWO

Left	Centre	Right
THREE Compt's die. THREE	3 Vig. Spread eagle on bow; canal boat, locks and train of cars. 3 BANK OF ROME, Rome, N. Y. Horse.	3 Three females standing.
5 Compt's die 5	5 Vig. Five figures surrounding ornamental figure 5, vessel in distance. BANK OF ROME, Rome, N. Y. V	5 Female holding aloft figure 5. 5
20 TWENTY 20	20 20 BANK OF ROME, Rome, N. Y. Vig. Two females holding State Arms between; liberty pole and cap, sword and balances.	Round building, with flag flying; view of ... [illegible]
ONE Child's head.	State Arms. View of Rondout. BANK OF RONDOUT.	1
Blacksmith and anvil. TWO	2 State Arms. BANK OF RONDOUT. The letters TWO, with the words Two Dollars running across.	TWO Two female heads.
Farmer and milkmaid. 3	3 State Arms. and THREE BANK OF RONDOUT. The letters THREE, with the words Three Dollars running across.	Head of Washington.
Two females supporting a figure 5 with three Cupids around them.	State Arms. BANK OF RONDOUT. The letters FIVE, with the word Five Dollars running across.	5 Portrait.
Two females supporting a shield, on which is a small view of Rondout. 10	State Arms. BANK OF RONDOUT. TEN DOLLARS.	10 Portrait.
10 10	Female reclining on cornucopia; vessel in distance. Compt's die. BANK OF RONDOUT, Rondout, N. Y.	.10 Male portrait.
Two females with sickle and goods; mechanics, design, anvil and sails. Compt's die.	BANK OF SALEM. O N E Vig. Train of cars; cattle drinking; steamship and vessel in distance. Gold dollar.	1 Farmer in cornfield, supporting ornamental figure 1.

Left	Centre	Right
2 Compt's die.	Vig. Female reclining on bale of goods, with liberty cap, &c.; cars, steamship and vessel in distance. BANK OF SALEM. T W O Two gold dollars.	2 Farmer in cornfield with basket of corn.
5 Indians, locomotive and cars. Compt's die.	Vig. Drover on horseback; cattle and sheep. BANK OF SALEM. Five gold dollars.	5 Milkmaid seated; farm house in distance.
Compt's die. Female seated; horn of plenty and liberty cap, village in distance.	Vig. Three figures, mechanic, farmer and sailor, implements, &c.; steamship and vessel in distance. BANK OF SALEM.	10 Female seated with balances and sword; locomotive in distance.
TWENTY Goddess of Liberty.	TWENTY DOLLARS. Compt's die. BANK OF SALEM.	Female soaring in the air with garland of flowers in either hand; train of cars and houses in distance. 20
50 Female with sword in one hand, shield and branch in other.	BANK OF SALEM. FIFTY DOLLARS. Railroad depot. Compt's die.	50 Three figures, farmer, mechanic and sailor supporting die 50, with implements.
1 Compt's die. 1	BANK OF SALINA. 1 Female standing. Indian sitting. 1 Shield. 1 1	1 Eagle. 1
2 Compt's die. 2	BANK OF SALINA. Eagle on a rock. Female filling goblet from a pitcher. Indian in a canoe between dies	TWO Archimedes with lever and globe. TWO
3 Compt's die. 3	BANK OF SALINA. 3 Man lying and vase. Pump-house & millworks. 3	THREE Portrait. 3
5 Compt's die. 5	BANK OF SALINA. FIVE Vig. Lady in chariot drawn by three lions; boy in uplifted hand. FIVE on right. Lion's head.	5 Portrait. 5
10 Compt's die. 10	Title under vig. 10 Vig. Female resting one arm on shield; male riding in car and looking suspiciously at female. 10 Cupid on a deer.	TEN Female & X

Left	Centre	Right
TWENTY	BANK OF SALINA. 20 Vig. Woman with helm on a pedestal; lion by her side. 20	20 Compt's die. 20
50 Man sitting. 50	BANK OF SALINA. Face. Eagle. Face.	50 Compt's die. 50
Female. Compt's die.	1 Female with key and safe. Spread eagle B'K OF SARATOGA SPRINGS, Saratoga, N. Y. Secured by pledge of public stock.	1 Male portrait.
Two men holding ... in their arms Compt's die.	2 Vig. Mirror, with farmer at milk, dairymaid on right. B'K OF SARATOGA SPRINGS, Saratoga, N. Y.	2 Locomotive and cars.
Female seated, in figure 5, Cupids Compt's die.	Vig. Portrait of female. B'K OF SARATOGA SPRINGS, Saratoga, N. Y.	5 Two females, one holding figure 5.
TEN Building. Compt's die.	1 Female. 0 B'K OF SARATOGA SPRINGS, Saratoga, N. Y.	10 Female standing.
20 Building and street. TWENTY	2 Female. 0 B'K OF SARATOGA SPRINGS, Saratoga, N. Y.	20 Female holding 2 in right and 0 in left hand.
FIFTY Indian princess.	Compt's die. Female on either side of shield and bust; ship in distance. BANK OF SARATOGA SPRINGS. Saratoga Springs, N. Y.	50 Female bust.
Compt's die. Country road with oxen, load of hay, &c.	Vig. Locomotive and cars crossing bridge, canal boats, &c. BANK OF SENECA FALLS, N. Y. Fire Engine.	1 Portrait of female.
2 Compt's die.	Ocean steamer. Portrait of Washington. BANK OF SENECA FALLS, N. Y. Eagle.	2 Female.

5 Compt's die. | Vig. Locomotive and cars. BANK OF SENECA FALLS, N. Y. Wrand and pollars. | 5 Portrait of female.

10 Compt's die. | BANK OF SENECA FALLS, Seneca Falls, N. Y. Drovers, horses, &c. ; peers on left. X X | 10 Blacksmith with sledge &c., beside forge and anvil.

20 Steamship. | BANK OF SENECA FALLS, Seneca Falls, N. Y. Niagara Falls ; female, shield, &c. 20 20 | 20 Compt's die TWENTY

ONE Female with sickle in right hand, grain in left hand. ONE | BANK OF SILVER CREEK. 1 Vig. Eagle sitting on fallen tree. 1 The word one in large ornamental letter across the bottom of the note. | Statue of female, in reclining right hand, and a sceptre in upraised left hand ; dox on rock, encircled by scroll work.

TWO Female sitting; in right hand Liberty cap ; in left, a shield, &c., ox reclining on bank side. TWO | Title of Bank under vig. 2 Vig. Female sitting, right arm resting on knee; sickle in right hand, sceptre in upraised left hand; plough and sheaf of wheat behind her. 2 Medallion head. | Mechanic sitting at bench ; hammer in right hand ; left hand resting on horn of plenty ; wares at his feet, &c. Scroll work.

Female sitting on left side ; right arm resting on figure 3, holding Liberty Cap. III | Title of Bank under vig. 3 Vig. Female encircled by the arms of several States ; female on the right, sitting, and one on the left with sickle in left hand ; railroad cars, &c. behind. Medallion head. | 3 Fucrated in scroll work.

5 Female sitting, holding scales in left hand and Liberty Cap in right ; eagle on bank safe, &c. FIVE | Title of Bank under vig. V Vig. Large figure 5 ; female sitting in circular part ; female and commercial scene on her left ; female and agricultural implements on her right ; railroad cars, &c. V | 5 Medallion head. FIVE

10 State Arms. Two females sitting, one with Liberty Cap in hand. 10 | BANK OF SILVER CREEK. 10 Vig. Two human figures in sitting posture, one with sceptre in right hand, cornucopia in left ; the other right arm resting on a shield, in the centre of which is the letter X. Grain in background. | 10 Statue of female, with upraised right hand staff or wand.

20 Compt's die. XX | Railroad cars, mill ; Female seated ; sheaf of wheat by her side ; sceptre in upraised left hand ; sickle in right. BANK OF SILVER CREEK Silver Creek, N. Y. | 20 Spread eagle

ONE Female portrait. ONE | 1 Vig. Eagle on branch. 1 BANK OF SYRACUSE Syracuse, N. Y. Cupid and ONE running across. | Full length female, on large 1

TWO Compt's die. TWO | 2 Vig. Female seated ; canal and cars on right ; plow, wheat on left. 2 BANK OF SYRACUSE Syracuse, N. Y. Canal locks. | Mechanic ; frame surmounted by vase.

Two females, ornamental figure 3. III | 3 Vig. Three females ; centre one in frame. BANK OF SYRACUSE Syracuse, N. Y. Locks. | 3

5 Compt's die. FIVE | V Vig. Three females ; centre one seated with, in large figure 5. V BANK OF SYRACUSE Syracuse, N. Y. Locks. | 5 Medallion head. FIVE

10 Compt's die. TEN | Vig. Two females holding sickle and balances ; steamship, barrels, &c., on right ; cows, implements of agriculture, &c., on left. BANK OF SYRACUSE Syracuse, N. Y. Locks. | 10 Liberty and Justice. TEN

TWENTY Compt's die. TWENTY | 20 Vig. Female seated ; globe, chemical instruments, steamship. 20 BANK OF SYRACUSE Syracuse, N. Y. Locks. | Die. XX Die.

Compt's die. Female, Minerva and shield. | 25 Vig. Man seated, mechanic's tools and steam manufactory. BANK OF SYRACUSE Syracuse, N. Y. | 25 Iron safe. 25

ONE HUNDRED | Vig. Female seated leaning on cask and bales ; ship in distance on one side ; canal boat on the other. BANK OF SYRACUSE Syracuse, N. Y. | 100 Compts' die.

1 Compt's die. | Train of cars, trees, houses, chimney, sloop, hills, &c. BANK OF TIOGA, Owego, N. Y. Secured &c. | 1 Webster.

2 Compt's die. TWO | Portrait of Daniel Webster ; female, cornucopia, scythe and cars on right ; female, distaff, bale, men, anchor and steamship on left. BANK OF TIOGA, Owego, N. Y. Secured &c. | 2 Cattle, telegraph and railroad.

FIVE 5 FIVE | Portrait of Henry Clay ; milkmaid and cows on right ; two females and sheaf on left. BANK OF TIOGA, Owego, N. Y. Secured &c. | 5 Compt's die V

5 Cattle, men, horses and wagons. | Leather dressers at work. BANK OF TIOGA, Owego, N. Y. | 5 Compt's die V

10 Two horses, boy and plough | Title of Bank Milkmaid milking cow ; child, man, cattle, fence, etc. | 10 Compt's die

1 Word one below and a fig. 1. Compt's die. | BANK OF TROY, Troy, N. Y. Liberty surrounded by stars in red die with words one dollar at top. | 1 Same as on left. Die.

2 Compt's die. TWO | BANK OF TROY, Troy, N. Y. Red 2 across. Male portrait in red die work with the words two dollars at top. | 2 Red 2 across Die.

Compt's die. Red 3 across. 3 | BANK OF TROY, Troy, N. Y. Washington in red die work, with words three dollars at top. | 3 Red 3 across 3

5 FIVE in red. FIVE | BANK OF TROY, Troy, N. Y. Three shepherds forming a 5 ; shepherd, rake, sheep ; ship in distance. | FIVE in red. 5 Compt's die. FIVE

TEN Female, shield, sword and cap | BANK OF TROY, Troy, N. Y. Man oiling machinery. X | 10 Compt's die

1 ONE Compt's die. | Puddling in an iron mill. BANK OF ULSTER, Saugerties, N. Y. | 1 City.

Portrait of Jackson. TWO State Arms. | BANK OF ULSTER, Saugerties. Vig. Local view of an iron mill and stream of water. | 2 Woman in a shell, with trident in right hand.

3 Supported by three female figures. | BANK OF ULSTER, Saugerties. THREE DOLLARS. Vig. Female figure in a reclining position with bales of goods, &c. ; a ship to the right in the distance. | 3 State Arms

5 — Compt's die. — FIVE
Th [illegible] Bank under vig.
Vig. Ridge and Falls; woman in sitting posture, holding a bundle of sticks, left arm resting on a shield.
5 — Portrait of female.

Three female figures representing Faith, Hope, and Charity. — TEN
BANK OF ULSTER, Saugerties.
TEN DOLLARS
Vig. Woman reclining on a bale of goods; two ships to the right and one to the left.
10 — State Arms.

1 — ONE — Compt's die.
Indian family seated.
BANK OF UTICA, Utica, N. Y.
Canal Locks.
1 — Male portrait

1 — Drover and cattle. — ONE
Vig. Female, &c.
BANK OF UTICA, Utica, N. Y.
Dog's Head.
1 — Compt's die — ONE

2 — Female with grain on head, and under her arm.
Female 2 Female
B'K OF UTICA, Utica, N. Y.
II
2 — Compt's die. — TWO

TWO — Compt's die. — TWO
Farmers mowing; men and haying on right.
BANK OF UTICA, Utica, N. Y.
Two horses.
2 — Female with dog; square seated.

3 — Franklin. — THREE
Vig. Farmer pulling corn.
BANK OF UTICA, Utica, N. Y.
3
3 — Compt's die. — THREE

Compt's die. — 3
BANK OF UTICA, Utica, N. Y.
Three females, seated representing agriculture, Commerce and arts.
Cow and Calf.
3 on Three — Female portrait.

5 — Male portrait
Female seated leaning on cornucopia and pointing to ship on right.
BANK OF UTICA, Utica, N. Y.
Anvil, sledge &c.
5 — Compt's die. — FIVE

5 — FIVE — 5
5 Compt's die.
Vig. Artisan painting.
BANK OF UTICA, Utica, N. Y.
5
FIVE DOLLARS

TEN DOLLARS
10 Vig. Indian standing. Compt's die.
BANK OF UTICA, Utica, N. Y.
X
10 — TEN — 10

10 — Train of cars — 10
X Indian with drawn bow. X
B'K OF UTICA, Utica, N. Y.
X
TEN — Ten one dollar pieces or a column — TEN

10 — Two females carrying grain.
Nine cherubs making an offering to female seated beside Cornucopia; ten Gold dollars.
BANK OF UTICA, Utica, N. Y.
Grain.
10 — Farming implements and products — Compt's die

20 — XX
Farmer seated beside cradle; basket of fruit and grain. Compt's die.
BANK OF UTICA, Utica, N. Y.
Beehive.
20 — Drove of cattle and hogs

20 — Indian — 20
Train of cars; village in distance.
B'K OF UTICA, Utica, N. Y.
XX
20 — Female with scales and sword; lion and key. — 20

ONE — Compt's die.
1 Vig. Farmer ploughing.
BANK OF VERNON, Vernon Village, N. Y.
Secured, &c.
1 — Female seated. — ONE

2 — Compt's die. — TWO
Vig. Dairymaid seated, cattle in distance. 2
BANK OF VERNON, Vernon Village, N. Y.
TWO — Reaper with bundle of wheat.

THREE — Female seated. — Compt's die — THREE
3 Vig. female with wheat. 3
BANK OF VERNON, Vernon Village, N. Y.
Wheat, &c.
Secured, &c. — Portrait of Female. — THREE

5 — Compt's die. — FIVE
FIVE Vig. Same as 3. FIVE
BANK OF VERNON, Vernon Village, N. Y.
Dog.
5 — Female with shield, reaper in back ground. — FIVE

10 — Compt's die. — TEN
Vig. Mirror, with female on either side, shipping, &c. in distance.
BANK OF VERNON, Vernon Village, N. Y.
Dog.
10 — State Arms. — TEN

Compt's die. — Reaper sharpening sythe.
Vig. Farmer ploughing, two horses.
BANK OF VERNON, Vernon Village, N. Y.
Secured, &c.
50 — Female with rake.

Compt's die. — Cattle.
Washing sheep; house in distance.
BANK OF VERNON, Vernon, N. Y.
100 — Female churning.

Secured &c. — ONE
1 Female and child; ship in distance. Die.
BANK OF WATERTOWN, Washington, N. Y.
Anvil and hammer.
ONE — Female seated.

TWO — Compt's die. — TWO
2 Female reaper. 2
BANK OF WATERTOWN, Washington, N. Y.
Wheat &c.
Artisan with horn of plenty.

Secured &c. — Figure 3, female on either side, — III
3 Female. Portrait of female. Female.
BANK OF WATERTOWN, Washington, N. Y.
Wheat &c.
3

5 — Compt's die. — FIVE
V Females with large figure 5. V
BANK OF WATERTOWN, Washington, N. Y.
FIVE
Wheat, etc.
5 — Hd. Head. — FIVE

10 — Compt's die. — TEN
Vig. Mirror with female on either side; ships and shipping in distance.
BANK OF WATERTOWN, Washington, N. Y.
Wheat &c.
10 — State arms. — TEN

1 — Washington
Signing Declaration of Independence. Compt's die.
BK of WATERVILLE Waterville, N. Y.
1 — Female.

TWO — Compt's die. — TWO
2 Female with sickle, grain, plow, etc. 2
BK of WATERVILLE Waterville, N. Y.
Eagle.
Ears of corn. — Male figure with hammer. — Ears of corn.

5 — Compt's die. — 5
V Three females with fig. 5 in centre. V
BK of WATERVILLE Waterville, N. Y.
Eagle.
5 — Med. head. — FIVE

10
Two females representing Agriculture and Commerce.
10
Compt's dis.
BANK OF WATERVILLE. Waterville, N.Y.
State Arms.
TEN
TEN
Eagle and X.

20
BK of WATERVILLE Waterville, N.Y.
20 on med. head.
Compt's dis.
Cattle, cows, &c.
TWENTY
20 Dog and safe. 20
Fillmore.

50
BK of WATERVILLE Waterville, N.Y.
50
Indian, squaw and papoose; sheaf; female instructing children.
50
50
Compt's dis.

1
Vig. Lady reclining on bale of goods, with arm resting on large wheel; hammer and other tools lying about; in the distance, steam vessel to the right, railroad cars and building to the left.
1
Plank road, load of hay drawn by horses, group of cattle, two on horseback and standing, buildings, trees, &c.
BK. OF WEST TROY.
O N E
Compt's dis.

2
Vig. Two females resting; weaving machine in the background to the right.
2
Sailor standing, compass in left hand, and bale of goods, hogshead, &c.; steamboat and vessel in the distance.
BK. OF WEST TROY.
T W O
Fire engine between sigs.
Compt's. dis.

Vig. Two steamboats; three ships in the distance; dock and men.
5
Portrait of D. Webster.
BK. OF WEST TROY.
F I V E
5
Compt's. dis.
Fire engine between sigs.

10
BK. OF WEST TROY.
10
Portrait of Gen. Wool.
Vig. Man with flag and large cannon.
X X
Compt's. dis.

Female sharpening scythe.
1 Vig. Female reaper seated.
ONE
B'K OF WESTFIELD Westfield, N. Y.
Compt's dis.
Ship.

Compt's dis.
2 Vig. [illegible] ploughing.
2
B'K OF WESTFIELD Westfield, N. Y.
Pigs.
Female, churning.

Compt's dis.
5 Vig. Washing sheep.
5
B'K OF WESTFIELD Westfield, N. Y.
Artisan.
Female stacking hay by figure 5.

TEN
X Boy on horse; cattle, &c.
10
BK OF WESTFIELD, Westfield, N. Y.
Blacksmith with sledge, beside anvil.
Compt's dis.

1
1 Vig. Boy with [illegible] on [illegible] eagle, female with liberty cap and pole. 1
1
Compt's dis.
Clock; Child on each side.
B'K OF WHITEHALL Whitehall, N. Y.
1
1

1
1 Cattle, children and trees. 1
1
BK OF WHITEHALL, Whitehall, N. Y.
Compt's dis.
ONE
Portrait of female.

TWO
Title of Bank.
2
Compt's dis.
Boy on horseback with another horse by trough, female, etc.
TWO
TWO
Female portrait.

2
2 Vig. Mechanic at work, tools, &c. anchor; two females, ship in distance. 2
2
Compt's dis.
Ship on stocks.
B'K OF WHITEHALL Whitehall, N. Y.
2
Steamboat.
2

Compt's dis.
Title and word THREE on large green dis.
3
Female portrait.
Chickens.

3
3 Vig. Shield surmounted with eagle, female on either side; balloons, ship, &c. 3
3
Compt's dis.
Male portrait
B'K OF WHITEHALL Whitehall, N. Y.
Locomotive.
3
3

(Old Plate.)
FIVE
5 Vig. Three females seated; agricultural implements, &c.
5
Cattle and sheep [illegible]
B'K OF WHITEHALL Whitehall, N. Y.
Steamboat.
5

5
Vig. Female, [illegible], plow, sickle, wheat, &c. canal boat, cars, &c.
5
Compt's dis.
B'K OF WHITEHALL Whitehall, N. Y.
Sailor leaning against capstan, glass in hand.
FIVE
Anchor, horn of plenty, &c.

(Old Plate.)
X
X Vig. Two females with liberty cap, pole, balances, &c.; shield surmounted with eagle in centre.
10
Full length male portrait.
TEN 10 TEN
B'K OF WHITEHALL Whitehall, N. Y.
Steamboat.
10

10
Vig. Female, key in one hand, liberty pole in other; balances on safe; spread eagle, ships, and cars in distance.
10
Compt's dis.
B'K OF WHITEHALL Whitehall, N. Y.
TEN
Female churning.
Locomotive and cars.

20
Compt's dis.
Vig. Female holding liberty pole, seated between figures 2 and 0.
20
Farmer sharpening scythe.
B'K OF WHITEHALL Whitehall, N. Y.
Female raking hay.

50
50 Washington on horseback. 50
FIFTY DOLLARS
Head of McDonough.
BK OF WHITEHALL Whitehall, N. Y.
50

1
Vig. Farmers at lunch; loading hay in distance.
1
Compt's dis.
BANK OF WHITESTOWN, Whitestown, N. Y.
Goddess of liberty.

TWO
2 Vig. Female seated with sickle, wheat, &c. 2
Compt's dis.
BANK OF WHITESTOWN, Whitestown, N. Y.
African with horn of plenty
TWO
Trees &c.

Washington and horse.
Vig. Cows, sheep &c.
FIVE
BANK OF WHITESTOWN, Whitestown, N. Y.
Female with wheat.
Compt's dis.
5

10
Vig. Mirror with female on either side; shipping and cars in distance.
10
Compt's dis.
BANK OF WHITESTOWN Whitestown, N. Y.
State arms.
TEN
Trees, &c.
TEN

TWENTY
20 Female seated; scientific apparatus; steamship in distance. 20
Compt's dis.
XX
BANK OF WHITESTOWN, Whitestown, N. Y.
TWENTY
Cattle, trees, etc.

1
Female portrait.
Vig. Female and figure 1.
1
BK OF YONKERS, Yonkers, N. Y.
Orange dis.
Secured, &c.
Bee hive.

2
Vig. Three females and a child in water, the females are holding up the child.
2
BK OF YONKERS, Yonkers, N. Y.
Female portrait.
Secured, &c.
Compt's dis.

Left	Centre	Right
Compt's die. Female portrait.	BK OF YONKERS, Yonkers, N. Y. 5 Vig. A view of Yonkers; train of cars, sloops, etc. Secured, etc.	5 5
10 Compt's die. TEN	Vig. View of Yonkers, train of cars, sloops &c. BK OF YONKERS Yonkers, N. Y. Secured, &c.	10 Female Portrait.
Compt's die. 20	BK OF YONKERS Yonkers, N. Y. Vig. Cattle, three of which are standing up and one laying down three sheep on left. Secured, &c.	20 Child's Portrait.
ONE State Arms ONE	Vig. Milkmaid sitting with pail, cattle, &c. 1 BLACK RIVER B' Watertown, N. Y.	1 Boy and anvil. ONE
TWO Compt's die TWO	Two females; one with sickle; sheaf; ship in distance. 2 on med. head. BLACK RIVER BK., Watertown, N. Y.	Female. Portrait. Female.
Female with Liberty Cap. State Arms.	BLACK RIVER BK. Watertown. Vig. Female with cornucopia on right, female with shield, on which is inscribed the figure 3 to the left, an eagle soaring, with figure 3 under eagle.	3
FIVE Female with sickle and grain. FIVE	5 Man plowing with two horses. BLACK RIVER BK., Watertown, N. Y.	5 Compt's die
Liberty area	5 Female in clouds with cornucopia. BLACK RIVER B'K, Watertown, N. Y.	5 Compt's die
TEN Compt's die. TEN	X Two females; cars, vessels, etc. BLACK RIVER BK., Watertown, N. Y.	10 Boy and anvil. X
20 Forest, and cars crossing bridge.	BLACK RIVER BK Watertown Vig. Three females representing Hope, Industry, and Charity Compt's die.	20 City, shipping, &c.
FIFTY Female with Liberty Cap and shield.	BLACK RIVER BK. Watertown. State Arms. Angel and female on right receiving a ball, and one on left, extending hand to angel.	50
1 ONE Compt's die.	Drove of cattle; man on horseback, boy in water; trees, house, fence, etc. BRIGG'S BANK OF Clyde, N. Y. Safe.	1 Portrait of female.
2 Compt's die. TWO	Horse and oxen before load of hay; three men and a boy, trees, etc. Train of cars BRIGG'S BANK OF Clyde, N. Y.	2 Canal scene village in distance.
5 Two men and dog; man and boy behind them; trees and house in distance.	Man plowing with two horses; trees and farmhouse in distance. BRIGG'S BANK OF Clyde, N. Y.	5 Compt's die FI 5 VE
TEN Male, female, two boys, lamb, etc.	Two oxen before hay cart, men loading hay; three men at work in distance. On left of vig. letter X. BRIGG'S BANK OF Clyde, N. Y.	Word ten, figs. 10, and letter X. Compt's die
1 Compt's die 1	1 Three small male figures with compass, charts, globe, &c.; shipping on right. 1 BROOKLYN BANK. Brooklyn, N. Y. Secured by pledge of public stock	Female seated. ONE
2 Compt's die 2	Two Doll's Two Doll's 2 Female on either side of a shield, on which is a fig. 2. 2 BROOKLYN BANK. Brooklyn, N. Y. Secured by pledge of public stock.	Head laughing. TWO Head laughing.
3 Compt's die 3	3 Female seated with sickle, sheaf and plough; cattle lying on ground. 3 BROOKLYN BANK, Brooklyn, N. Y. Secured by pledge of public stock.	Female with sickle. THREE
5 Compt's die 5	5 Archimedes raising the world 5 BROOKLYN BANK. Brooklyn, N. Y. Secured by pledge of public stock.	FIVE Winged female beside urn; with trumpet. V
10 Compt's die 10	Archimedes raising the world. 10 BROOKLYN BANK, Brooklyn, N. Y. Secured by pledge of public stock.	Horse. TEN
20 Compt's die 20	Horse with Title of Bank around him. Archimedes raising the world. Secured by pledge of public stock.	20 XX
50 Compt's die 50	BROOKLYN BANK. Brooklyn, N. Y. FIFTY DOLLARS. 50 (Secured by pledge of public stock.	Horse. FIFTY
100 Compt's die 100	Archimedes 100 raising the world; Title of bank running around the vignette. 100 Secured by pledge of public stock.	Female with sword and scales; eagle with portrait of Washington on breast.
ONE Compt's die. Female head.	Vig. Harvest scene; Lunch time. 1 BROOME CO. B'K. Binghampton, N. Y.	1 Female 1
2 Compt's die. 2	Vig. Spread eagle on branch, cars, &c. 2 BROOME CO. B'K. Binghampton, N. Y.	2 Female, sickle, &c. TWO
5 Compt's die. FIVE	Farming scene; farmer seated with scythe, load of hay in background. Fig. 5 on right and left. BROOME CO. BANK, Binghampton, N. Y.	5 Female seated. FIVE
5 Compt's die. FIVE	BROOME CO. BANK, Binghampton, N. Y. Vig. Farmer about to sharpen his scythe, canal and cars in distance.	Figure 5 with Cupid on left. Franklin.
10 Compt's die. 10	Vig. Harvest scene, female seated with infant. BROOME CO. BANK, Binghampton, N. Y.	10 Female, sheaf, &c.
1 Compt's die 1	Vig. Sailing with shipping in distance. BUFFALO CITY B'K. Buffalo, N. Y.	1 ONE Canal boat under bridge
2 Compt's die.	Vig. Indian female overlooking City in distance BUFFALO CITY B'K. Buffalo, N. Y.	2 Sailor seated

FIVE Vig. Three artisans, one holding wheel to goddess of Liberty on throne, with eagle.	Compt's die. BUFFALO CITY B'K. Buffalo, N. Y.	5 5
X Bridge.	BUFFALO CITY B'K. Buffalo, N. Y. Vig. Three females seated. Compt's die	10 Shipping
Head of Major Burnett. ONE Compt's die.	Vig. Dairy maid in sitting posture; one cow reposing in front of her, and one standing; farm-house, trees and flocks in background. BURNET BANK, Syracuse. Eagle.	1 Indian princess holding staff with Liberty Cap on it; hand resting on shield.
TWO Compt's die. Head of Major Burnett.	State Arms. BURNEL BANK, Syracuse. Sheep, plough, rake, &c.	TWO Goddess of Justice; balance on left hand fore-finger; sword in right hand.
FIVE Male portrait. 5	Cow and calf in stream; cattle and house in distance. Female portrait. BURNET BANK, Syracuse, N. Y.	5 Compt's die. 5
5 FIVE Compt's die.	BURNET BANK, Syracuse. 5 Vig. Goddess of Liberty; staff and Liberty Cap across her lap; starry drapery; shield on her left; United States Capitol on her left and rear. 5	5 Head of Major Burnett.
10 Soldiers seated; one with drum.	Male portrait. Male portrait. BURNET BANK, Syracuse, N. Y.	10 TEN Compt's die
ONE Man seated	CAMBRIDGE VALLEY BANK, North White Creek, New-York. Interior of a blacksmiths' shop; mechanic and tools.	1 State arms.
Word two and $ mark Female drawing water from a well; steamboat on left.	Title of Bank. Horse on either side of a shield; eagle at top; cars crossing bridge and view of city on right; building on left.	2 State Arms
5 State Arms.	Title of Bank below vig. Drovers and cattle; view, farm-house.	5 Two females with bow, grain and distaff

X State Arms.	Portrait of Washington; milk maid with pail and cattle on right; two females representing agriculture on left. Title of Bank.	10 Portrait of Jenny Lind.
XX Male portrait	State Arms. Liberty and eagle. Title of Bank.	20 Male portrait
1	CANAJOHARIE BK., Canajoharie, N. Y. Compt's die. The vig. extends the whole width and ends of the note. Vig. Hop scene, gathering hops; two horses attached to wagon; numerous male and female figures at work; trees, &c.	1
2 Portrait of Calhoun.	CANAJOHARIE BK., Canajoharie, N. Y. Vig. Same as ones, only a different view with farm houses, &c.	2 Compt's die.
3 Shearing sheep.	CANAJOHARIE BK., Canajoharie, N. Y. Compt's die. 3	3 Two men gathering corn.
5 Compt's die.	CANAJOHARIE BK., Canajoharie, N. Y. Five farmers at work, gathering hay; two oxen before hay wagon.	5 Clay.
X Two females, one charming; cars in distance on left.	CANAJOHARIE BK., Canajoharie, N. Y. X Portrait of a girl. X	10 Compt's die.
ONE ONE Compt's die.	Indian behind rock watching deer; trees, etc. CANASTOTA BANK, Canastota, N. Y. Female bathing.	1 Girl.
2 Compt's die 2	Shield with Indian on right and female on left; ship, city, steamboat, wigwams, trees, &c., in distance. CANASTOTA BANK, Canastota, N. Y. Dog.	2 Two soldiers.
5 Two Indians on cliff viewing city.	Men at work harvesting; two oxen before cart. CANASTOTA BANK, Canastota, N. Y.	5 Compt's die. 5

TEN Two males on cliff.	X Load of hay drawn by two horses; female and child on top; blacksmith's shop and men at work; dog, girl and boy. CANASTOTA BANK, Canastota, N. Y.	10 TEN Compt's die
XX	Males and females gathering hops. CANASTOTA BANK, Canastota, N. Y. Compt's die. Twenty Dollars	20 Two horses before wagon; two men and dog; men in distance.
1 Compt's die. 1	ONE Vig. Female, shield and eagle, wheel and anvil on right; ships in distance on the left. ONE CATSKILL BANK, Catskill, N. Y. Steamboat.	Steamboat. 1 Steamboat.
2 Compt's die. 2	2 Vig. Ship and small boat, and hills in background. 2 CATSKILL BANK. Catskill, N. Y. Steamboat.	TWO DOLLARS.
THREE Sheaf of grain. THREE	CATSKILL BANK, Catskill, N. Y. 3 Vig. Large ship, female seated in representation of commerce. 3 Ferry boat.	THREE Figure of Liberty erect supporting vase of flowers.
5 Compt's die 5	V Vig. Female and eagle, female holds a goblet. V CATSKILL BANK, Catskill, N. Y. Eagle.	FIVE
10 Compt's die. 10	Vig. Female with bucket, sheep on right, and cattle on left. X CATSKILL BANK, Catskill, N. Y.	Female reclining, and word TEN. 10
FIFTY	50 Vig. A Female seated working a spinning wheel. 50 CATSKILL BANK, Catskill, N. Y.	FIFTY DOLLARS.
ONE HUNDRED	Mule and medallion wreath. 100 Vig. A female seated large eagle and figures 100. CATSKILL BANK, Catskill, N. Y.	ONE HUNDRED
ONE Compt's die	1 Vig. Portrait of Washington. 1 CAYUGA Co. BANK, Auburn, N. Y. ONE Child seated. ONE DOLLAR. DOLLAR.	ONE Figure standing.

TWO Compt's die.	2 Vig. Male portrait; shipping and cars in background. CAYUGA Co. BANK, Auburn, N. Y. Man's head.	Bee hive. TWO Figure standing.
Compt's die. THREE	3 Vig. Portrait of Andrew Jackson, female on either side. CAYUGA Co. BANK, Auburn, N. Y. Eagle.	3 Indian in canoe. THREE
5 Compt's die. 5	Public building. Vig. Fig. are standing. Wheat, &c. CAYUGA Co. BANK, Auburn, N. Y. FIVE	FIVE 5 FIVE
Compt's die. Man with scythe.	CAYUGA CO. BANK, Auburn, N. Y. Female with sheaf of wheat seated in large letter V.	5 Cattle and hogs.
Compt's die. Blacksmith.	CAYUGA CO. BANK, Auburn, N. Y. Large ornamental X enclosing figures of justice and liberty.	10 Figure of Justice.
10 Compt's die. 10	Locomotive and cars. Vig. Figures are standing. Canal scene. CAYUGA Co. BANK, Auburn, N. Y. Indian in canoe.	TEN X TEN
XX Compt's die. 20	20 Female feeding Eagle. 20 CAYUGA CO. BANK, Auburn, N. Y. Eagle.	XX Justice. 20
50 Compt's die. 50	L Portrait of Washington. L CAYUGA Co. BANK, Auburn, N. Y. Sampson and lion.	Female with eagle. 50
1 Compt's die. ONE	CENTRAL BANK, Brooklyn, N. Y. Farmer and farm scene; boy with horse and sleigh.	1 Male portrait.
2 2	Santa Claus drawn by reindeer. Compt's die. CENTRAL BANK, Brooklyn, N. Y.	TWO Male portrait.

3 3	CENTRAL BANK, Brooklyn, N. Y. Female reclining on bale of goods; sail vessel on right, and steamboat on left.	3 Compt's die.
5 Compt's die. V	CENTRAL BANK, Brooklyn, N. Y. View of the Brooklyn City Hall.	5 Male portrait.
TEN Compt's die. X	CENTRAL BANK, Brooklyn, N. Y. X Ship under sail. X	TEN Male portrait.
50 Compt's die. L	Goddess of Liberty and female representing Agriculture. CENTRAL BANK, Brooklyn, N. Y.	50 Male portrait.
100	CENTRAL BANK, Brooklyn, N. Y. Compt's die. Male portrait.	C Three men at work.
Medallion head. Compt's die. Medallion head.	One on medallion head. Vig. Farmer with oxen and sloop. One on medallion head. CENTRAL BANK, Cherry Valley, N. Y. Loading hay.	1 Female with rake. 1
Med. head Compt's die Med. head	2 on medallion head. Vig. Female seated in figure 2; two farmers in background. 2 on medallion head. CENTRAL BANK, Cherry Valley, N. Y. Dog's head.	TWO Female seated in figure 2 with balance and sword. TWO
Med. head. Compt's die. Med. head.	CENTRAL BANK, Cherry Valley, N. Y. THREE on Med. head. Two females with liberty pole and cap. THREE on Med. head. Wheat, &c.	Female erect. 3
FIVE Compt's die. FIVE	5 Vig. Large figure 5, females on either side. 5 CENTRAL BANK, Cherry Valley, N. Y. Female with anchor.	FIVE Female. FIVE
X Compt's die. 10	Medallion head, with TEN on it. Female holding 1 in right, and 0 in left. CENTRAL BANK, Cherry Valley, N. Y.	X Portrait of female. 10

20 Compt's die. 20	Female looking towards sea. 0 Female with sickle & sheep. CENTRAL BANK, Cherry Valley, N. Y.	20 Medallion head. 20
ONE Miniature view of female seated.	Vig. Indians, geese, shrubbery, &c. Compt's die. CENTRAL BANK, Troy, N. Y.	1 ONE Male portrait.
TWO Male portrait.	Title under vig. Vig. Locomotive, train of cars and depot; locomotive crossing bridge in the distance. Compt's die.	TWO 2
3 Compt's die.	Vig. Santa Claus riding in a car drawn by reindeers. CENTRAL BANK	3 Portrait of female
FIVE Male portrait. 5	Compt's die. Vig. Man on horseback; cattle and sheep. CENTRAL BANK.	V Head and shoulders of dog.
TEN Compt's die. X	CENTRAL BANK, Troy. Vig. Spread eagle.	TEN Male portrait.
20 XX 20	CENTRAL BANK, Troy. Vig. Miniature view of female reclining on bale of goods. Compt's die.	TWENTY Group of three females representing Agriculture, Commerce, &c.
ONE Stonecutter at work. ONE	Compt's die. Blacksmith shoeing horse; mule; locomotive in distance. CENTRAL CITY BK., Syracuse, N. Y.	1 Blacksmith; anvil, hammer. ONE
Compt's die. Two cherubs. Female portrait.	2 Farming scene—farmers at lunch; haying in background. CENTRAL CITY BK., Syracuse, N. Y. Agricultural Implements.	2 Flower girl.
Compt's die. Two sea nymphs. Steamship.	5 Three females representing Agriculture, Commerce and arts. CENTRAL CITY BK., Syracuse, N. Y.	5 Five figures around large V.

FIVE Spread Eagle and shield. Compt's die.	Female crowning an Eagle with left hand, holding Portrait of Washington; with buildings on left; ships on right. CENTRAL CITY BK. Syracuse, N. Y. Agricultural implements	5 Five females around fig. 5.

10 Compt's die. TEN	Man looking at chart; two stonecutters, etc.; men, horses and cart in distance. Title of Bank.	10 Female head. TEN

Female seated with anchor. Compt's die.	20 View of N. Y. bay, vessels, &c. Title of Bank.	TWENTY Sailor hoisting flag.

1 Compt's die. 1	1 Vig. Man seated by die with 1 and 11, an engine on top, with motto—" Internal Improvements." 1 CHAUTAUQUE Co. BANK. Jamestown, N Y.	1 Oxen. 1

2 Compt's die. 2	2 Vig. Oxen in small die. 2 CHAUTAUQUE Co. BANK Jamestown, N. Y.	2 Vessel ready to launch. 2

3 Compt's die. 3	3 Vig. Oxen in small die. 3 CHAUTAUQUE Co. BANK Jamestown, N. Y.	3 Male portrait. 3

5 Compt's die. 5	CHAUTAUQUE Co. BANK Jamestown, N. Y. Vig. Indian unstringing bow	FIVE Female Portrait. V

10 Compt's die. 10	Vig. Farmer mowing CHAUTAUQUE Co. BANK Jamestown, N. Y.	Oxen. Female Portrait. 10

Compt's die. Steamer.	1 Vig. Locomotive and cars. CHEMUNG CANAL BANK, Elmira, N. Y. Farmer, plow, etc.	Figure 1 with "ONE" running across it. Female leaning on figure 1.

Female in Oval. Compt's die.	2 Vig. Dairy maid, cash, &c. CHEMUNG CANAL BANK, Elmira, N. Y. Dogs head.	2 Child with cash, &c. TWO

3 Compt's die. 3	3 Cattle. 3 CHEMUNG CANAL BANK, Elmira, N. Y. Indian in canoe.	3 Canal locks. 3

Compt's die. Portrait of female.	3 Vig. Farmer with oxen and sheep. CHEMUNG CANAL BANK, Elmira, N. Y. Wheat and flowers.	3 Two females standing.

5 Compt's die. 5	5 5 Title of Bank. Two females, eagle, shield, cars, shipping, etc. Canal locks,	FIVE Male portrait 5

FIVE FIVE Compt's die.	5 Vig. Two females with the bust of Washington, and American shield. CHEMUNG CANAL BANK, Elmira, N. Y. Locomotive and cars.	FIVE Female seated in a large figure 5. FIVE

10 Eagle. Compt's die.	(New Plate) Vig. Female seated, with shipping in the distance. CHEMUNG CANAL BANK, Elmira, N. Y. Wheat &c.	Bale of goods &c. 10 Train of cars

10 Male portrait. 10	X Vig. Compt's die. X CHEMUNG CANAL BANK, Elmira, N. Y. Head of horse	Female holding the word "TEN." 10

20 Male seated, between figures 2 and 0	Compt's die. Female seated; bridge, train of cars, steamer, city, &c. CHEMUNG CANAL BANK, Elmira, N. Y. Cog wheels, &c.	20 Female between a 2 and 0. TWENTY

Female seated with pole and cap. 50	50 Title of Bank. 50 Compt's die, Boy astride a deer.	Female portrait. 50

100 Male figure destroying serpents 100	100 Compt's die 100 Title of Bank. Canal locks.	100 Neptune in car; female floating in air. 100

Two tables with female and shoulders. Compt's die.	1 Vig. Female seated holding figure 1. CHESTER BANK, Chester, N. Y.	1 Female standing.

2 Compt's die. TWO	Vig. Mirror with male on right, female on left. CHESTER BANK. Chester, N. Y.	2 Locomotive and cars.

5 Compt's die. FIVE	Vig. Female with liberty pole, seated by American eagle with figure 5. CHESTER BANK, Chester, N. Y.	5 Figure of Justice standing.

10	Female seated between 1 and 0, with cornucopia and key. Compt's die. CHESTER BANK, Chester, N. Y. Secured &c.	10 Man, cattle, and sheep.

Vig. Female holding 2 in right, and 0 in left hand. 20	Compt's die. CHESTER BANK. Chester, N Y	20 Female portrait.

1 Female with Liberty cap in left hand.	CHITTENANGO BK. Vig. Comptroller's die, landscape in the background; wood chopper with left foot and axe on stump; one dollar leaning against another stump; wagon, horse, &c. Sheaf of wheat, plough, shovel, rake, and &c.	ONE Two females, one with rake, the other turning hay with a fork.

1 ONE Compt's die	CHITTENANGO B'K. Chittenango, N. Y Female seated by side of silver dollar; red figure 1 on either side. Gold dollar.	1 Female seated with shield and sword.

2 Compt's die. 2	Female, cherub and two silver dollars CHITTENANGO B'K. Chittenango, N. Y. Rising Sun.	TWO Large figure 2 and female

2 Portrait of female. TWO	Title under vig. Vig. Compt's die; cows lying and standing; milkmaid sitting, pail on right arm; farmer with rake lying down, hat in left hand; two gold dollars before him. Dog, his name, "Wave," on collar.	2 Two females.

Compt's die. 3	Indian, squaw and papoose in canoe; wigwam and hills in distance. CHITTENANGO B'K. Chittenango, N. Y. Bales and cornucopia.	3 Female with figure 3.

5 FIVE Compt's die.	Title under vig. Vig. Indian reclining on left; hunter on right, sitting, gun in right hand resting on ground, and pointing left hand at heap of seven five gold dollars at feet. Smith reclining on anvil bot. sign.	FIVE Figure 5 embellished so as to show an eagle, beehive, woman, placing head of Washington. FIVE

Left end	Centre	Right end
Female with balances; sheaf of wheat, etc. Compt's die.	10 Harvest scene; farmers mowing; loading wagon, etc. CHITTENANGO BK., Chittenango, N. Y. Female reclining.	10 Squaw and papoose.
XX Indian with lance and bow in right hand.	CHITTENANGO BK. Vig. Comptroller's die: Indian reclining on a shield, bow and arrow in right hand; eagle flying above him; water on his right and left; on his right deer and canoe in water; on his left three deers, one lying down and two standing. Safe.	20 Portrait of D'l Webster. TWENTY
50 Portrait of Franklin Pierce. Compt's. die.	CHITTENANGO BK. Vig. Commercial scene; vessels and houses in background; in foreground female sitting; cornucopia in right hand, sceptre in left, and sheaf of wheat on her right; cornucopia of coin on left; also, barrels, boxes, &c. Steamboat.	Angel or Cupid holding shield with 50 on it. Female standing.
ONE State Arms. ONE	Portrait and flag. Female in sitting posture, staff in left hand. 1 A CITIZENS' BANK, Fulton.	ONE Female in standing position, left hand resting on ledge of rock; right arm raised; monument in view. ONE
TWO Roman figure seated, left foot slightly elevated, right arm extended. State Arms.	2 Vig. Female resting, flag, &c. CITIZENS' BANK, Fulton. Sail vessel.	Large 2, word TWO twice, and portrait.
Fig. 5, cars, bridge, Indians, water, etc. Compt's die.	5 Washington 5 CITIZENS' BANK, Fulton, N. Y. Spread, etc.	Female seated with sheaf. 5
5	Vig. Female in sitting position, left arm reclining upon shield; motto of U. S. inscribed; eagle, &c. Figure 5 with representations of cupid. B CITIZENS' BANK, Fulton.	FIVE State Arms. FIVE
State Arms. Horseman. X Women with mirror; boy in skiff.	10 Vig. Two human figures—male and female; female holding sickle and sheaf of wheat; house and farm scene to the right in the distance; vessel under sail to the left. CITIZENS' BANK, Fulton.	10 Portrait. 10
20	Vig. Female reclining, holding in right hand a sledge hammer; in left, a pair of compasses; vessel under sail in the distance; four men working with horse on right in the distance. State Arms with Cupid on either side. CITIZENS' BANK, Fulton.	TWENTY Portrait of female. 20
Neptune and fig. 1. Compt's die. ONE	View of Atlantic Basin, Brooklyn. CITY BANK OF BROOKLYN, Brooklyn, N. Y. Female with scales and money.	1 Female resting on a large fig. 1; shield by her side.

Left end	Centre	Right end
TWO Compt's die. TWO	2 Female with sickle and grain. Title of Bank. Female with scales.	2 Female raking hay.
Ship under sail. Compt's die.	3 Train of cars. Title of Bank. Female with scales and money.	3 Ship on the stocks. THREE
Merchandise and anchor. Compt's die. Train of cars.	FIVE Female and eagle on either side of a shield with fig. 5 on it. Title of Bank. Same as threes.	5 Female with fig. 5 on a safe; warrior with shield and spear in background.
TEN View of the ship houses at the Navy Yard; ships. TEN	Compt's die. Female seated between 1 and 0. Title of Bank. Same as threes.	10 Two females, one with spear and shield, the other with sword and scales.
20 View of the City Hall. TWENTY	Compt's die. Female seated between 2 and 0. Title of Bank. Same as threes.	20 Female seated between, and holding 2 and 0.
Neptune with tridents. Compt's die.	50 Female on right of shield covering bust of Washington with wreath; Goddess of Liberty and sheaf, on the left bale, bales and ship on right. Title of Bank. Same as threes.	50 Portrait of a child.
100 Compt's die. 100	Female seated on either side of view of ship and water, surmounted by an eagle; bale of goods, cars, steamboat, &c. Title of Bank. Same as threes.	100 Female Portrait.
ONE Compt's die. ONE	Sailor and female seated, sheaf, quadrant, etc.; in distance, ship and house. 1 CITY BANK, Oswego, N. Y. Spread &c.	ONE Female seated; factory in distance. ONE
1 Compt's die.	Vig. Woodman kneeling, &c. Gold dollar. CITY BANK, Oswego, N. Y. State Arms.	1 Public building. ONE
TWO Compt's die. TWO	2 Vig. Ship in dis. 2 CITY BANK, Oswego, N. Y.	Sailor. 2

Left end	Centre	Right end
FIVE 5 Compt's die.	Five human figures and five gold dollars. 5 CITY BANK, Oswego, N. Y. Implements.	FIVE Female feeding eagle.
Large figure 5, cars crossing bridge; Indians. Compt's die.	Vig. Female seated on bales; cars and shipping in distance. CITY BANK, Oswego, N. Y.	5 FIVE 5
TEN Sailor seated. Compt's die.	10 Amer. eagle. CITY BANK, Oswego, N. Y.	TEN Female seated. 10
20 Compt's die.	Vig. Two females with mirror, eagle, &c. CITY BANK, Oswego, N. Y.	20 Portrait of Washington.
1 Compt's die.	1 Cow, calf and sheep. 1 CITY BANK OF POUGHKEEPSIE, N. Y.	1 Dog and safe.
TWO Compt's die. TWO	Title of Bank. 2 Ox. 2	TWO on 2. Female portrait. TWO
Compt's die. 3	CITY BANK of Poughkeepsie, N. Y. Large red 3; on right boy and sheep; on left, female, gleaning scene, etc.	3 3
5 Fowl.	Title of Bank. Female portrait. 5	5 Compt's die. FIVE
10 Two females.	Eagle—Ten Dollars above; red X each side. CITY BANK of Poughkeepsie, N. Y.	10 Compt's die.
20 Full length figure of female. 20	Compt's die. CITY BANK, Poughkeepsie, N. Y. 20 Female portrait. 20	20

Left	Centre	Right
1 Compt's die.	Female reclining, eagle behind; train of cars, bridge and city in distance. 1 CLINTON BANK, Buffalo, N. Y. Horse.	Statue of DeWitt Clinton.
2 Compt's die. TWO	Portrait of Clinton; city, steamboat, bridge and cars on right; farm scene on left. CLINTON BANK, Buffalo, N. Y. 2 2	2 Two cherubs soaring with distaff and sheaf.
Compt's die. 3	CLINTON BANK, Buffalo, N. Y. Three females reclining, representing Liberty, Agriculture and Manufactures. 3 3	THREE Justice erect and a female seated.
V Fillmore. FIVE	CLINTON BANK, Buffalo, N. Y. Truth reclining on safe looking at shield on which is ship on stocks and rising sun; sheep and sheaf on right. 5 5	5 Compt's die. V across five.
X Justice seated.	Shield on which is word Hope and anchor; cars crossing bridge and factories on right; ship, steamboat and city on left. Webster. CLINTON BANK, Buffalo, N. Y. TEN	10 Compt's die
1 On die with words one and small 1s. Compt's die	COLUMBIA BANK, Chatham Four Corners, N. Y. Portrait of Washington. ONE DOLLAR	1 On die with words one and small 1s. Female representing agriculture.
2 Compt's die. 2	COLUMBIA BANK, Chatham Four Corners, N. Y. Portraits of Andrew Jackson, and Winfield Scott. TWO DOLLARS.	2 Bust of Female holding flowers.
Compt's die 3 On die with words THREE and small 3s.	Portrait of Webster, Franklin, and Clay. COLUMBIA BANK, Chatham Four Corners, N. Y. THREE DOLLARS	3 On die with words THREE and small 3s
Figure of liberty erect, wreath in right hand shield beside her. FIVE	Eagle clutching arrows, shield, and olive branch. COLUMBIA BANK, Chatham Four Corners, N. Y. FIVE DOLLARS.	5 Compt's die. 5
Female bust 10 On die with ten.	COLUMBIA BANK, Chatham Four Corners, N. Y. Three children with book on table, in oval. TEN DOLLARS. X	10 On die with ten. Compt's die

Left	Centre	Right
20 On die with small 20's	View of train of cars crossing bridge, canal, boats, men, horses, &c. COLUMBIA BANK, Chatham Four Corners, N. Y. TWENTY DOLLARS. Compt's die.	20 On die with small 20's
Farmer ploughing with two horses, farm house in back ground. 50 On die with small fifty's.	Compt's die COLUMBIA BANK. Chatham Four Corners, N. Y. FIFTY DOLLARS.	50 On die with small FIFTY'S. Female bust.
Female holding child grain, &c. 100 On die with small 100's.	Figure of justice, with sword and scales, surrounded by clouds. Compt's die. COLUMBIA BANK, Chatham Four Corners, N. Y. ONE HUNDRED DOLLARS.	100 On die with small 100's.
1 Compt's die. 1	1 Vig. Three females seated, sheaf of wheat, and quadrant on right, trees in distance on left, ship in distance. 1 COMMERCIAL BANK Albany, N. Y. 1 Secured, &c. 1	ONE Male portrait. ONE
2 Compt's die. 2	TWO on Med head. Vig. Female looking over a rock, cars, steamboat and canal on right. COMMERCIAL BANK Albany, N. Y. 2 Secured, &c. 2	TWO Franklin. TWO
3 Compt's die. 3	3 on Med. head. 3 on Med. head. Vig. Two females and shield, one on right holds a sickle. COMMERCIAL BANK Albany, N. Y. 3 Secured &c. 3	THREE Portrait of Jackson. THREE
5 Portrait of Washington. V	Med. head and word five. Compt's die. Vig. Three females seated, sheaf of wheat, and quadrant, on right trees in distance on left ship in distance. COMMERCIAL BANK Albany, N. Y.	5 Male portrait V
10 Male portrait 10	Med. head and word Ten. Compt's die. Vig. Three females seated sheaf of wheat, and quadrant on right trees in distance on left ship in distance. COMMERCIAL BANK Albany, N. Y.	10 Portrait of Washington. 10
20 Male portrait 20	20 Vig. Two females reclining, ships in distance on right, and shield on left. Compt's die. COMMERCIAL BK Albany, N. Y. Secured, etc.	20 Portrait of Washington 20
50 Portrait 50	Vig. Three females seated, representing agriculture and commerce, Medallion head and figure 50 on left of Vig. State Arms on right. COMMERCIAL BK Albany, N. Y.	50 Male portrait 50

Left	Centre	Right
100 Portrait of Washington. 100	100 Vig. Three females seated, sheaf of wheat on right, and quadrant and ship on left in distance. Compt's die. COMMERCIAL BK. Albany, N. Y. Secured, etc.	100 Male portrait 100
ONE Compt's die. ONE	COMMERCIAL BK. Clyde, N. Y. 1 Vig. Female seated, ship in distance. 1	On 1
II Compt's die. II	2 Vig. Female seated on bale, &c. 2 COMMERCIAL BK, Clyde, N. Y.	Female seated holding two. TWO
5 Compt's die. 5	5 Vig. Neptune seated with eagle, ship and cars in distance. 5 COMMERCIAL BK. Clyde, N. Y. Vessels.	Eagle. FIVE
Ten dollars. Mechanic, sailor and farmer making offering to Goddess of Liberty; implements, &c.	Compt's die. COMMERCIAL B'K. OF CLYDE, N. Y.	10 Female
TWENTY Two males and two females with tablets and anvil; city in distance	COMMERCIAL B'K, OF CLYDE, N. Y. 20 Compt's die.	20 Male two females, dog and cattle.
Compt's die. Mechanic; safe and anvil; two females, steamship in distance.	1 Female in clouds over city, distributing flowers; view of rising sun. COMMERCIAL BANK Glenn Falls, N. Y. Secured, &c.	ONE Washington. ONE
Compt's die. Figure 2 with sailor and female.	Two female figures, Justice and Liberty, village on right, cars on left; eagle mounted between the two. COMMERCIAL BANK Glenn Falls, N. Y. Secured, &c.	TWO Figure 2 and female.
Compt's die. 3	Goddess of Liberty on globe; eagle and shield. COMMERCIAL BANK Glenn Falls, N. Y. Secured, &c.	THREE 3 Lighthouse and female seated.
Compt's die. Square; Indian in canoe; wigwam in distance	V and letters FIVE Spread eagle and shield V and letters FIVE COMMERCIAL BANK Glenn Falls, N. Y.	5 Female seated with book and pen.

Left	Centre	Right
[illegible] pt's die. Large X and sea scene.	COMMERCIAL BANK Glenn Falls, N. Y. Female blowing trumpet; steamboat and ship on right; village, load of hay and trees on left.	X and letters TEN Mechanic seated on a boiler. TEN

Left	Centre	Right
1 Washington. 1	1 Compt's die. Vig. Female leaning on rock, looking down on steamboat, &c. COMMERCIAL B'K. Rochester, N. Y. Plow, &c.	1 Female with liberty pole, U. S. shield, &c.

Left	Centre	Right
TWO Compt's die. TWO	2 Vig. Female with wings, sword, sickle, &c. 2 cars on right, agricultural implements, &c, on left. COMMERCIAL B'K. Rochester, N. Y.	Mechanic seated; cornucopia; implements &c. surrounded with corn.

Left	Centre	Right
3 Male portrait 3	Vig. Female, bales, &c.; cars and ship in distance. 3 COMMERCIAL B'K. Rochester, N. Y. Eagle.	Compt's die. 3 Female seated.

Left	Centre	Right
FIVE Female holding cap, eagle, ship, and U. S. flag Compt's die.	Vig. Shield with 5 in centre; Indians on left; female teaching children on right. COMMERCIAL B'K. Rochester, N. Y. Female.	5 Male portrait

Left	Centre	Right
TEN Female portrait. Compt's die.	COMMERCIAL B'K. Rochester, N. Y. Vig. Three females, cornucopia, anchor, &c. Propeller	10 Male portrait TEN

Left	Centre	Right
20 Compt's die.	XX Vig. Three females, shield and eagle mounted in centre; cars on right, ship on left. COMMERCIAL BK. Rochester, N. Y.	Full length female standing on globe with word TWENTY on it.

Left	Centre	Right
50 Compt's die. 50	Vig. Two females; bales and bbls behind them; ship in the distance. 50 COMMERCIAL BK. Rochester, N. Y.	FIFTY Sailor leaning on a capstan, telescope in his hand, anchor behind him FIFTY

Left	Centre	Right
Three females, one [illegible] chor. 100	COMMERCIAL BK. Rochester, N. Y. Vig. Steamship and vessels.	100 Compt's die.

Left	Centre	Right
ONE Female and fig. 1. Compt's die.	COMMERCIAL B'K. Saratoga Springs. N. Y. ONE DOLLAR. ONE	1 Male reclining; sheep, dog, &c. cars crossing bridge 1

Left	Centre	Right
2 Compt's die. TWO	Female seated with distaff, ships and cars in distance. Title of Bank Eagle.	TWO Man sharpening scythe; fig. 2 at his back.

Left	Centre	Right
5 Eagle. FIVE	Title of Bank. Female in clouds with eagle, pole, cap, shield and drapery. Rising sun.	Word five and letter V. Compt's die 5

Left	Centre	Right
Letter X and word Ten. Sailor. TEN	Title of Bank. Two males and a female; train of cars, steamboat and city in distance. Eagle.	TEN Female and letter X. Compt's die.

Left	Centre	Right
20 Washington TWENTY	Title of Bank. Female portrait. Female crowned blowing trumpet; ship, steamboat and city in distance. Compt's die. Tree.	XX Sailor, wheel scene. TWENTY

Left	Centre	Right
1 Compt's die	Large spread eagle on shield. COMMERCIAL B'K. Troy, N. Y. ONE DOLLAR.	1 Female portrait.

Left	Centre	Right
1 Female with wheat. 1	COMMERCIAL B'K. Troy, N. Y. 1 Female with pail on head, cows, &c. 1	1 Compt's die.

Left	Centre	Right
1 Compt's die	Spread eagle, clutching shield, arrows, and olive branch. COMMERCIAL B'K OF TROY, Troy, N. Y. ONE DOLLAR.	1 Female Portrait.

Left	Centre	Right
TWO Compt's die TWO	Man with two horses; boats in the right. COMMERCIAL B'K. Troy, N. Y. TWO DOLLARS.	2 Girl's head.

Left	Centre	Right
2 Compt's die. TWO	Male portrait. Female seated on bales steamer in distance. COMMERCIAL B'K. Troy, N. Y.	2 2

Left	Centre	Right
TWO surrounded by 2's. Compt's die. TWO surrounded by 2's.	Man exercising two horses; house, hills, &c. in background. COMMERCIAL B'K OF TROY, Troy, N. Y. TWO DOLLARS.	2 surrounded by 2's. Head of girl.

Left	Centre	Right
TWO Compt's die. TWO	2 Female seated with wheat, &c. 2 COMMERCIAL B'K, Troy, N. Y. Washington.	Artisan with gold.

Left	Centre	Right
Compt's die 3	COMMERCIAL B'K. Troy, N. Y. Three children in circular die reading from book. THREE DOLLARS.	3 Horse's head.

Left	Centre	Right
Compt's die 3 surrounded by 3's.	COMMERCIAL B'K OF TROY. Troy, N. Y. Three children with book open on table, in oval. THREE DOLLARS.	3 surrounded by small 3's. Horse's head

Left	Centre	Right
3 Vig. 3 figures with printing press, &c. Faust, Gutenburg and Schoeffer.	COMMERCIAL B'K. Troy, N. Y. Compt's die.	3 Male portrait 3

Left	Centre	Right
5 Compt's die. FIVE	Five females with hose, keys, &c. COMMERCIAL B'K. Troy, N. Y. Coach.	5 Female with shield. FIVE

Left	Centre	Right
5 Farmer with corn.	COMMERCIAL B'K. Troy, N. Y. Laborers working; one yanking a pipe, another wheeling a barrow. 5 5	5 Compt's die. FIVE

Left	Centre	Right
10 Blacksmith at work.	Scene at depot, cars, steamboats, drays, etc. COMMERCIAL BK of Troy, N. Y.	X Compt's die.

Left	Centre	Right
10 Female, eagle, keg, and sails. TEN	View of all the State Arms of the Union; two females on either side; steamship on left; on right men mowing, factories, etc. COMMERCIAL B'K. Troy, N. Y. Portrait.	10 Two females, eagle shield, cornucopia, &c. TEN

Left	Centre	Right
20 Male portrait	Three men shipping, &c.; ship on stocks on left, and steamboat, ship, and city on right. COMMERCIAL B'K. Troy, N. Y. Building small boat.	20 Compt's die

Left	Centre	Right
50 [illegible] portrait	Two wild horses alarmed at train of cars, trees, etc. COMMERCIAL B'K. Troy, N. Y. Female and anchor.	50 Compt's die

100 Deer. | Indians spearing buffaloes. COMMERCIAL BK., Troy, N. Y. Compt's Die. | 100 Dog and game.

ONE Compt's die. | Farmer ploughing. COMMERCIAL B'K, Whitehall, N. Y. | ONE Female.

2 Compt's die TWO | Sailor. Por. Female trait of reaper. Washington. COMMERCIAL B'K, Whitehall, N. Y. | 2 Compt's die TWO

Compt's die. 3 Arm's arms. | Steamboat leaving wharf. COMMERCIAL B'K, Whitehall, N. Y. Schooner. | 3 Cupid. THREE

Female with sword. Compt's die. | 5 Vig. Female seated with artisans tools, steamer in distance. COMMERCIAL B'K, Whitehall, N. Y. | 5 Male with basket of corn.

Compt's die. Sailor with implements. TEN | Oxen, horse; house in distance. COMMERCIAL BK of Whitehall, N. Y. | 10 Female seated. TEN

Compt's die. Sailor with quadrant; ship in distance. | Spread eagle on shield; cars and house in distance. 50 COMMERCIAL BK of Whitehall, N. Y. | Female seated on bale. 50

1 Compt's die. | CROTON RIVER B'K. Southeast N. Y. ONE DOLLAR | 1 Female seated by side of silver dollar; bales, sacks and house.

2 Compt's die. 2 | Horse, cows and fence; bridge and train of cars in distance. CROTON RIVER B'K. Southeast, N. Y. Dog's head. | TWO 2 Male portrait.

Cattle and sheep, boy on horse, trees, &c. V | FIVE Eagle. CROTON RIVER B'K. Southeast, N. Y. Locomotive and tender. | 5 Compt's die 5

10 Boy with pigeons. | Cows, sheep, fence, house, &c. CROTON RIVER B'K. Southeast, N. Y. Dog's head. | 10 Eagle and shield. Compt's die.

Male and female by side of wall; fence, etc.; load of hay going in barn. 20 | Compt's die. TWENTY DOLLARS. CROTON RIVER B'K. Southeast, N. Y. Cow's head. | 20 Milkmaid with pail.

100 | Man, woman, child, cows, chickens, fence, houses, etc. Compt's die. CROTON RIVER BK. South East, N. Y. Horse. | 100 Letter C, female bust, sheaf, etc.

1 Compt's die. | CUBA BANK, Cuba, N. Y. Ornamental die work, on which is "One Dollar" in circular form, with portrait of girl at bottom; portrait of Washington on right; woodman felling a tree on left. Cottage. | 1 Portrait of female.

2 Compt's die. 2 | Train of cars approaching depot; passengers about to get aboard; train of cars crossing bridge in distance. CUBA BANK, Cuba, N. Y. 2 | Ornamental die work, on which is "Two Dollars" in circular form; portrait at bottom. TWO

V Locomotive and cars coming down hill; cabin, trees and hills in distance. | Three men rolling log; two more on right, one of which is felling tree; and still another on left standing by side of team; trees, &c. CUBA BANK, Cuba, N. Y. Woodman felling tree. | 5 Compt's die in square form. 5

Portrait of female. X | 10 Two oxen before hay-cart; boy by side, with pitchfork on his shoulder; another boy laying on top of cart. CUBA BANK, Cuba, N. Y. Ducks and young ones. | TEN Indian hee. Compt's die.

Two females, one churning; the other turning out cheese; hen and chickens; cows in distance; stand, &c. | Compt's die. Female with pail; hand resting on hen roost; two cows, one laying down; hens and rooster; shed, &c.; two oxen on right, with sheep in distance. CUBA BANK, Cuba, N. Y. | 20 XX

1 Surrounded by ornamental die work. | 1 Compt's die. 1 CUYLER'S BANK, Palmyra. | 1 Female with anchor and wreath.

2 Surrounded by ornamental die work. | 2 Compt's die. 2 CUYLER'S BANK, Palmyra. | 2 Man with sheaf of wheat.

5 Surrounded by ornamental die work. | 5 Compt's die 5 CUYLER'S BANK, Palmyra. | 5 Portrait of Lady Washington.

10 Ornamental die work. | X Compt's die. X CUYLER'S BANK, Palmyra. | 10 Portrait of Washington

ONE Woman with a sickle in her hand. ONE | DELAWARE BANK. Vig. An eagle resting on a broken tree-top. | 1 Enclosing full length female with distaff in one hand and wand in the other.

TWO Compt's die. TWO | 2 Female with sickle and wand; sheaves, mill, canal, railroad, etc. 2 DELAWARE BANK, Delhi, N. Y. TWO Agricultural scene. | Ears of corn. Man surrounded by devices. Ears of corn.

THREE Liberty leaning on one side, and Justice sitting on the other. 1 1 1 | DELAWARE BANK. Vig. Female Indian in frame of State arms; on each side figures representing Agriculture and Commerce. Cows and sheep. | 3

5 Compt's die. FIVE | DELAWARE BANK. Vig. Female figures representing Agriculture and Commerce, on each side of a length, in which a woman is seated; railroad, canals, &c. in the background. V each side. Agricultural scene. | 5 Medallion head. FIVE

10 Compt's die. TEN | DELAWARE BANK. Vig. Figures Agriculture and Commerce on each side of a shield; ships, railroad, canals, &c. in the distance. Agricultural scene. | 10 Medallion work. TEN

TWENTY Compt's die. TWENTY | Title of Bank under vig. Vig. Female seated at a table, on which is a map, quadrant, compasses, &c.; Adams's express near her, and globe behind. Steamship in the distance. XX each side. Agricultural scene. | Die work. XX Die work.

ONE as fig. 1. Three woodmen, cultivated team of oxen and driver in distance. | DEPOSIT BANK. 1 | 1 Compt's die.

2 Compt's die. | DEPOSIT BANK. Vig. Drove of cattle and sheep, drover on horseback; train of cars in distance. 2 on either side. | 2 Male portrait.

5 | Compt's. die.
Vig. Train of cars; houses in background; small sail-boat on right.
DEPOSIT BANK.
5 | Drove of cattle, drover, dog, telegraph wires, &c.

10 on ised head. | Compts. die.
Male portrait; on right two females; on left three females in sleeping; train of cars in distance on right.
DEPOSIT BANK,
Deposit, N. Y.
10 | Two Indians.

XX | Male Portrait.
Compts. die. Three females.
DEPOSIT BANK,
Deposit, N. Y.
Female bathing
20

ONE | Eagle, shield, &c. | Compt's die.
DOVER PLAINS B'K,
Dover Plains, N. Y.
Farmer mowing with cradle; binding grain on left.
1 | Deer in water.

2 | Compt's die. | 2
Engine and tender entering depot; train of cars leaving it.
DOVER PLAINS B'K.
2 | Two children playing with flowers.

5 | Farmer with scythe.
V Drover on horse; drove of cattle, sheep, &c. V
DOVER PLAINS B'K
5 | Compt's die. | 5

X | Cattle passing under, and cars passing over bridge.
Farmer ploughing with team of horses.
DOVER PLAINS B'K.
10 | Compt's die. | TEN

20
DOVER PLAINS B'K.
Drover on horse; drove of cattle, sheep, &c. Compt's die.
20 | Milkmaid churning.

1 | Compt's die.
Vig. Three horses prancing; farm houses in distance.
ELMIRA BANK.
1 | Female portrait.

2 | Compt's die.
Vig. Three females bathing; cupid in centre.
ELMIRA BANK.
2 | Female portrait.

3 | Compt's die.
ELMIRA BANK.
Vig. Male and female with little child.
3 | Female portrait.

5 | Compt's die.
Vig. Raft, two men poling; female seated with child in arms.
ELMIRA BANK.
5 | Female portrait.

Compt's die.
Vig. Two trains of railroad cars; water and small vessel on the left; mountains in the distance. X
ELMIRA BANK.
10 | Portrait of Daniel Webster.

Male portrait | 20
Vig. Train of cars, canal boat passing thro' lock; farmers at work.
ELMIRA BANK.
20 | Compt's die.

ONE | Indian head. | ONE
1 Vig female ornamented with wheat 1
ESSEX CO., BANK.
Keeseville, N. Y.
Eagle.
1 | Compts die | 1

2 | 2
TWO 2
Female 2 Indian
ESSEX CO., BANK
Keeseville. N. Y.
Mechanics' arm.
2 | Compts die | 2

3 | 3 | 3
3 Vig. female seated by furnace with pestle and mortar. 3
ESSEX CO., BANK
Keeseville, N. Y.
Steamboat.
3 | Compts die | 3

5 | Compt's die. | 5
5 Female seated; Eagle. 5
ESSEX CO., BANK
Keeseville, N. Y.
cupid riding a deer.
FIVE

10 | Compts die. | 10
10 Vig. 10
Eagle Goddess of liberty mechanics' arm and justice.
ESSEX CO., BANK
Keeseville. N. Y.
TEN

TWENTY
20 Vig. Archimedes raising the world with lever resting on mountain. 20
ESSEX CO., BANK
Keeseville, N. Y.
Artisan at work.
TWENTY

FIFTY
Male figure seated with left hand resting on wheel, anvil, hammer, etc., ship in distance, 50 either side.
ESSEX CO. BANK.
Keeseville, N. Y.
FIFTY

1 | Compt's. die.
EXCHANGE BANK,
Lockport, N. Y.
Large die with male portrait and words one dollar in part circle across the top; red figure 1 on either side.
1 | 1

ONE | Female bust with sickle. | ONE
1 Vig. Eagle. 1
EXCHANGE BANK,
Lockport
ONE in large ornamental letters.
Large ornamental figure one; full length female figure.

2 | Compt's die. | 2
EXCHANGE BANK,
Lockport, N. Y.
Large die with male portrait and words two dollars across it in part circle; red figure 2 on either side.
2 | TWO | 2

TWO | Compt's die. | TWO
2 Vig. Female seated; farming implements; grain; factory on left, canal boat on left. 2
EXCHANGE BANK.
Lockport
Eagle and safe.
Mechanic; die surrounded with stars.

Compt's die. | 3
EXCHANGE BANK,
Lockport. N. Y.
Large die with portrait of Washington, and words three dollars in part circle at top; red figure 3 on either side.
Word dollars and figure 3. | 3

Compt's die. | 111
3 Vig. Female portrait surrounded by statearms; two females on either side. 3
EXCHANGE BANK,
Lockport
Eagle and safe.
3

5 | Compt's die | 5
V 5
Vig. Two figures, one holding key; the other cornucopia; winged messenger standing upon a safe.
EXCHANGE BANK,
Lockport.
FIVE | Full length female with balances and sword. | FIVE

10 | Compt's die. | 10
Vig. Male figure soaring in clouds with cornucopia in arms. 10
EXCHANGE BANK,
Lockport.
X | Eagle perched upon a shield. | TEN

1 | Compt's die. | 1
State arms.
FALL KILL BANK,
Poughkeepsie, N. Y.
1 | View of falls

Left	Centre	Right
Justice. Compt's die.	2 Drover watering his horse. FALL KILL BANK. Poughkeepsie, N. Y.	2 Falls.
3 Compt's die.	3 Boiler maker seated on boiler. FALL KILL BANK. Poughkeepsie, N. Y.	3 Falls.
Falls. 5	Two female figures emblematic of manufactures. FALL KILL BANK, Poughkeepsie, N. Y.	5 Compt's die.
TEN Female TEN	FALL KILL BANK. Poughkeepsie, N. Y. 10 Falls. 10	Liberty and large X. Compt's die.
Falls. 20	FALL KILL BANK. Poughkeepsie, N. Y. 20 Washington. Compt's die.	TWENTY Liberty, eclence, globe, &c.
50 Falls.	Female portrait. Compt's die. FALL KILL BANK. Poughkeepsie, N. Y.	FIFTY Railroad. FIFTY
C 100	FALL KILL BANK. Poughkeepsie, N. Y. View of falls, American and Indian female on either side. Steamship.	Compt's die. 100
ONE	FARMERS' BANK, Amsterdam. 1 Vig. Female and child standing; female with rod and scroll, and child with horn of plenty; small anchor, cogwheel, ship in the distance. Man on horseback, whip in hand.	ONE Female in sitting posture.
TWO Female with balance. Eagle. TWO	Title under vig. 2 Vig. Female with sickle in right hand; with sheaf of wheat, &c. Two cattle, two trees, plough, sheaf of wheat.	Two ears of corn. Man sitting in undress with horn of plenty. Two ears of corn.
5 Female with scales; eagle, key, safe, &c. FIVE	Title under vig. V Vig. Three females in sitting posture; implements of agriculture, steamship, railroad cars, &c. V Two cattle, two trees, plough, sheaf of wheat.	5 Med. head. FIVE

Left	Centre	Right
10 Female with scales; key, safe, &c. TEN	Title of Bank under vig. Vig. Two females, one on each side of a circle, one holding a sickle; implements of agriculture, steamship, casks, &c. Two cattle, two trees, plough, sheaf of wheat.	10 Two females, eagle, Liberty staff, cap, &c. TEN
FIFTY Female with distaff and shield; med head on shield and resting on pedestal.	FARMERS' BANK. Amsterdam, N. Y. Men mowing, gathering and loading wagon with wheat. Compt's Die.	Strong medal lion head. Female.
100 Man seated; scythe hanging on tree.	FARMER'S BANK. Amsterdam, N. Y. State Arms, with female and cows on right; two females and sheaf on left; horn of plenty at bottom.	100 Portrait of Washington.
1 ONE Compt's die.	Drove of cattle, four drovers on horseback; town in distance. FARMERS' BANK OF ATTICA, N. Y.	1 Female.
2 Compt's die. 2	Mechanic, sailor and farmer; man and horse in distance. FARMERS' BANK OF ATTICA, N. Y.	2 Female with bundle on her head.
5 Farmer drinking.	FARMERS' BANK OF ATTICA, N. Y. 5 Male portrait 5	5 Compt's die. 5
Secured &c. ONE	1 Vig. Female with child, sheaf of wheat on right; ship in distance on left. One mental die. FARMERS BANK Hudson, N. Y. Man, dog and birds.	ONE Female seated.
TWO Compt's die. TWO	2 Vig. Female seated with sickle and grain factory on left, and canal boat, locomotive and cars on right in distance. 2 FARMERS BANK, Hudson, N. Y. Cattle.	Man seated with mechanical implements.
5 Compt's die. FIVE	Vig. Group of females, holding globe, dragon and bags. Steamship, and ship on right. FARMERS BANK Hudson, N. Y. cattle.	5 Female seated, resting on shield, man mowing in distance. FIVE
10 Compt's die. TEN	Vig. Two females seated resting on shield, steamship on right locomotive, factory, cars on left in distance. FARMERS BANK Hudson, N. Y. cattle.	10 State arms TEN

Left	Centre	Right
20 Male portrait.	Compt's die. Vig. Ox, wagon and farmers loading grain. FARMERS BANK Hudson, N. Y.	TWENTY Full length female. TWENTY
ONE Compt's die.	FARMERS' BANK OF LANSINGBURGH, N. Y. Vig. Train of cars, bridge, canal boat; village in background, rural scenery, &c.	ONE Female and large figure 1.
TWO TWO	Vig. Drove of cattle, 2 men, one on horseback, and horse drinking from trough at a pump. Compt's die. FARMERS' BANK OF LANSINGBURGH, N. Y. 2	TWO Large figure 2, and a female with pail behind her.
Vig. Indian, temple, mechanic, ship and steamer on left; buildings, viaduct, &c., on right. Three females and a large ornamental V.	Compt's die. FARMERS' BANK OF LANSINGBURGH, N. Y. 5	FIVE Large figure 5, two Indians viaduct, train of cars, water fall, and rural scenery.
Sailor, mechanic and farmer holding aloft a wreath on which is figures 10.	FARMERS' BANK OF LANSINGBURGH, N. Y. Vig. Two horses and a plow, man engaged in fastening the traces to plough, horse on right; steamboat on left.	Large X with ten across; milk maid with pail, cow, viaduct, train of cars &c. Compt's die.
1 Compt's die. 1	1 Vig. Male and female erect, female hang wreath in left hand, on left a sheaf of wheat, on right an anvil. 1 FARMERS' BANK, Troy, N. Y. Female reclining with sheaf of wheat.	Female erect with staff, shield and eagle. ONE
2 Compt's die. 2	2 Vig. Two females, shield and figure 2, one on left holds shield, one on right a sickle, on right a sheaf of wheat, on left a ship in distance. 2 FARMERS' BANK, Troy, N. Y. 2	Female erect with staff, shield and eagle on left. 2
3 Compt's die. 3	3 Man erect with mantel around him, a plough on right, shield, cap and spear on left. 3 FARMERS' BANK, Troy, N. Y. Female reclining	Female erect with staff, shield and eagle on left. 3
5 Compt's die. 5	FIVE Vig. Man erect and calf on left [illegible] FIVE FARMERS' BANK, Troy, N. Y. Secured &c.	5 Large vase Horse.
X Farmers at work. 10	TEN Vig. Dog lying down; large safe and house in distance. TEN FARMERS' BANK, Troy, N. Y.	10 Compt's die. X

20 Compt's die. 20	Vig. Man on horseback; cattle, &c. Female portrait. FARMERS' BANK, Troy, N. Y. Farmers at work.	20 Cars and man with wheelbarrow. 20

L Compt's die. 50	Vig. Man on horseback; cattle, sheep, &c. FARMERS' BANK, Troy N. Y. Dog, safe and key.	FIFTY Female standing holding scales.

Compt's die.	Female seated, flowers, &c.; factories and man plowing in distance. FARMERS' BANK OF WASHINGTON CO. Fort Edward, N. Y.	1 Female shading her eyes with her hand.

2 Compt's die. 2	Female at [illegible], boy, girl, dog, horses, &c. FARMER'S B'K OF WASHINGTON CO. TWO DOLLARS. Fort Edward, N. Y. Monument.	2 TWO

2 Compt's die. 2	Farmer seated, girl and horses on right; boy and dog on left. Title of Bank. Tomb of Jane McCrea.	2 TWO

Compt's die 3	Female reclining on grain, [illegible] on right. 3 FARMER'S B'K OF WASHINGTON CO. THREE DOLLARS.	3 Dog and safe.

5 Portrait of a boy	Female seated on grain; house, cattle, loading hay, etc., in distance. Title of Bank.	5 Compt's die. FIVE

X Female seated with sword; word TEN on shield.	Two horses before load of hay; man on one of the horses, woman and child on top of hay; boy with rake, and girl with flowers; dog; blacksmith with sledge and interior of shop with men at work. Title of Bank.	10 Building, pedestrians, etc. Compt's die

20 XX 20	Female with pole and cap on right of shield; female with sickle on left. Compt's die below. FARMERS' BANK of Washington Co., N.Y.	20 Man with musket.

50 Female seated [illegible]	Title of Bank. Compt's die.	50 Farmer carrying corn stalks.

Compt's die. Road scene; horses and cattle; load of hay, etc.	1 Female with ears of corn; vessels and city in distance. FARMERS' & CITIZENS' BK OF LONG ISLAND, Williamsburg, N. Y. Agricultural implements.	1 Train of cars, Engine, etc. in distance.

2 Compt's die TWO	Shipwright at work; vessels, men, etc. Title of Bank. Steamship.	2 Female seated with lob[s]ters.

3	Horses drinking from trough, man seated; female feeding hogs, buildings, etc. Compt's die. Title of Bank. Eagle.	3 Female with shield, etc.

Three females, one above the other. FIVE	Title of Bank. Female with trident seated in a shell; vessels in distance.	5 Compt's die

10 Female portrait.	Steamship and other vessels. Title of Bank. Eagle.	10 Compt's die

Female seated with sword, etc. TWENTY	Title of Bank. Milkmaid seated, cows; house in distance. Steamboat.	20 Compt's die

Sailor erect, flag; female reclining. FIFTY	Title of Bank. Female with pole, cap and shield; buildings in distance.	50 Compt's die

Mercury with wand and bag of coin. 100	Title of Bank. Indian, shield, eagle, female and letter C.	100 Compt's die

ONE Female portrait. ONE	1 Vig. Eagle on branch of tree. 1 FARMER'S & DROVER'S BANK, Somers, N Y. View of Croton dam between signatures.	Female in standing position, figure 1 full width of note.

TWO Compt's die TWO	2 Vig. Female seated; agricultural implements, factory on left; canal boat and cars on right; steamboat in distance. 2 FARMER'S & DROVER'S BANK. Somers, N. Y. Men and cattle.	Mechanic seated, tools, horn of plenty, &c.; surrounded with [illegible]

3 Compt's die III	3 Vig. Female portrait in frame, surrounded by [illegible], cattle, &c. FARMER'S & DROVER'S BANK. Somers, N. Y. Men and cattle.	3

5 Female seated, balances, eagle, key, safe, &c. FIVE	V Vig. Three females seated; surrounded by ornamental figure 5. V FARMER'S & DROVER'S BANK, Somers, N. Y. Men and cattle.	5 Medallion head. FIVE

10 Female adjusting scales, eagle, key, safe, &c. TEN	Vig. Two females representing agriculture, &c., spread eagle in main case, farming implements, locomotive and cars, houses &c. on left; steamship, barrels, &c. on right. FARMER'S & DROVER'S BANK. Somers, N. Y. Men and cattle.	10 Two females, liberty cap mounted, eagle, vase of flowers, &c. TEN

TWENTY Same as title. TWENTY	20 Vig. Female in sitting posture, globe by her side, steamship in the distance. 20 FARMER'S & DROVER'S BANK. Somers, N. Y. Men and cattle.	XX

1 Compt's die. 1	1 Eagle. 1 FARMERS AND MANUFACTURERS BK Poughkeepsie, N. Y. Head of horse.	ONE Portrait 1

2 Compt's die. 2	Title under vig. Male Portrait. Portrait of Washington. Arm	2 Farmer with cradle. TWO

3 Compt's die. 3	3 Ship and other familiar vessels. FARMER'S AND MAN. BANK. Poughkeepsie. Barrels, &c.	THREE Portrait. 3

5 Compt's die. 5	Title under vig. 5 Vig. Two human figures, male erect; female reclining. 5	FIVE 5 FIVE

Male and female, male erect, female reclining. 10	10 Compt's die. FARMERS' AND MANUFACT'RS BK. Poughkeepsie.	TEN 10 TEN

TWENTY	XX Compt's die. XX FARMERS' AND MANUFACT'RS' BK Poughkeepsie.	Male and female reclining, the one resting the other erect. XX

Male and female; male standing, female reclining. 50	FIFTY FARMERS' AND MANUFACT'ERS BK. Poughkeepsie. Eagle between signatures.	Compt's dis. 50
Male and female; the one reclining, the other erect. 100	ONE HUNDRED FARMERS' AND MANUFACT'RS' BK. Poughkeepsie. Eagle between signatures.	Compt's dis. 100
Secured by pledge of &c. ONE	1 Vig. Female with sword, child, cornucopia, anchor, agricultural implements, &c., ship in distance. FARMERS & MECHANICS' BANK OF GENESEE, Buffalo, N. Y.	ONE Female seated, cows, and vessel in distance.
TWO Compt's dis. TWO	2 Vig. Female seated, agricultural implements, factory, canal boat and cars; steamboat in distance. 2 FARMERS' AND MECHANICS' BANK OF GENESEE, Buffalo, N. Y.	Mechanic seated, tools, horn of plenty, &c. surrounded with corn.
5 Compt's dis. FIVE	V FI 5 VE V Vig. Three females, centre one seated in large figure 5; factories, cars, and agricultural implements on the left, vessels and articles of commerce on the right, wheat, &c. FARMERS' & MECHANICS' BANK OF GENESEE, Buffalo, N. Y.	5 Medallion head. FIVE
10 Two Indians.	Portrait of Franklin surrounded by five females. FAR. & MECH. B'K. OF GENESEE, Buffalo, N. Y.	10 Compt's dis.
Yatch, men, various male and female figures. XX	Compt's dis. Title of Bank.	20 Female seated; cars and factories in distance. TWENTY
ONE Compt's dis. ONE	1 Vig. Female and child, ship in distance. Oval dis. FARMERS AND MECHANICS' BANK, Rochester, N. Y. Anvil, etc	ONE Female seated, cars in distance.
TWO Compt's dis. TWO	2 Vig. Female reaper seated. 2 FARMERS' AND MECHANICS' BANK, Rochester, N. Y. Farmer gathering corn.	Artisan with horn of plenty.
Female on either side of figure 3. III	3 Vig. Portrait of female in wreath, with flags, drum, &c. FARMERS' & MECHANICS' BANK, Rochester, N. Y. Farmer gathering corn.	3

5 Compt's dis. FIVE	Vig. Female with lions, boy, &c. Title of Bank. Farmer gathering corn.	5 Portrait of female. FIVE
10 Compt's dis. TEN	Vig. Wreath with female on either side, cars, shipping, &c., in the distance. Title of Bank. Arm.	10 State Arms. TEN
TEN Female feeding fowls.	X Man, horse, dog, cattle and sheep. FAR. & MECH. BK., Rochester, N. Y.	10 Male portrait
TWENTY Compt's dis. TWENTY	20 Vig. Female with chemical apparatus, pointing to steamer in distance. 20 Title of Bank. Arm.	XX
1 Compt's dis.	FLOUR CITY B'K. Rochester, N. Y. Farming scene.	1 Man and barrels
TWO Compt's dis. TWO	Two cherubs; two silver dollars; train of cars and cattle in background. FLOUR CITY BANK. Rochester, N. Y.	2 Male portrait
5 Male portrait.	FLOUR CITY BANK. Rochester, N. Y. Two flour barrels, sheaf of wheat; men in distance.	5 Compt's dis. FIVE
X Two figures carrying sheaves.	Male portrait in frame; winged female on left; cherub on right. FLOUR CITY BANK. Rochester, N. Y.	TEN Compt's dis.
20 20	Compt's dis. Milkmaid seated; cows on left; dog and pail on right. FLOUR CITY BANK. Rochester, N. Y.	TWENTY Mechanic; barrels, bale, ship in distance. TWENTY
1 Female with spear, figure one at her feet.	Compt's dis. Vig. Milkmaid seated, and cattle. FORT PLAIN BANK, Fort Plain, N. Y. Dog.	ONE on fig. 1 Female portrait. ONE

TWO Compt's dis. TWO	2 Vig. Female, sheaf of wheat, plow, canal, railroad cars &c. 2 FORT PLAIN BANK, Fort Plain, N. Y. Round building, &c.	Mechanical tools, and horn of plenty surrounded with corn.
Compt's dis.	3 Vig. Three females; one in frame. FORT PLAIN BANK, Fort Plain, N. Y. Round building.	3
5 Compt's dis. FIVE	Vig. Group of females; centre one in car; lions at her feet; key in one hand; globe in other. FORT PLAIN BANK, Fort Plain, N. Y. Round building.	5 Female seated; canal at feet; man cradling. FIVE
10 Compt's dis. TEN	Vig. Two females, cars and houses on left; steamship, barrels and bales on right. FORT PLAIN BANK, Fort Plain, N. Y. Round building.	10 Two females in round frame. TEN
Man seated, holding 0 and bag of coin. Compt's dis. TWENTY	FORT PLAIN BANK, Fort Plain, N. Y. Vig. Steamboats; cars; female seated, holding balances, key, safe, steamship, coin, &c.	20 Female portrait.
50 Compt's dis. FIFTY	FORT PLAIN BANK, Fort Plain, N. Y. Farmers at lunch, loading hay, &c.	50 Full length female Indian.
100 Spread eagle Compt's dis.	FORT PLAIN BANK, Fort Plain, N. Y. Cattle and sheep; drover on horse back.	100 Full length female (liberty) pole and cap.
Compt's dis. Water scene, bridge, boat, etc.	1 Indian seated; agricultural scene. FORT STANWIX BK Rome, N. Y.	ONE Female with grain and sickle. ONE
Med. head and TWO. Compt's dis.	Man plowing with two horses. FORT STANWIX BK Rome, N. Y. Locomotive.	2 Female head. TWO
Portrait of Wm. Penn. Compt's dis.	FIVE on med. head. Signing the Declaration of Independence. FORT STANWIX BK Rome, N. Y.	5 FIVE on med. head. 5

TEN on med. head. Compt's die. | Goddess of Justice, Liberty and Truth. FORT STANWIX BK Rome, N. Y. | X TEN on med. head, 10

TWENTY on med. head. Indian family contemplating the progress of civilization. | FORT STANWIX BK, Rome, N. Y. Two females. | 20 on med. head. Compt's die.

L on med. head. Compt's die. | FORT STANWIX BK, Rome, N. Y. Scene in the battle of New Orleans. | 50 on med. head. Male portrait

1 Compt's die. ONE | Vig. Cupid rolling gold piece; locomotive in distance. FRANKFORT BANK Frankfort, N. Y. Dog. | 1 Female seated with shield and figure 1.

2 Compt's die. TWO | Vig. Two children tossing, with gold pieces for shields, one standing; locomotive in distance. FRANKFORT BANK, Frankfort, N. Y. | 2 Female seated with figure 2.

3 Compt's die. THREE | Vig. Three children with three gold pieces. FRANKFORT BANK, Frankfort, N. Y. Loading hay. | 3 Large figure 3 with three men, one in centre, and one on either side.

5 Compt's die. FIVE | Vig. Five children with 5 gold pieces. FRANKFORT BANK, Frankfort, N. Y. Oxen. | 5 Female seated with sembl and figure 5.

10 Compt's die. TEN | Vig. Sailor, Indian, and two females with eagle, liberty pole and cap, bust, &c. FRANKFORT BANK, Frankfort, N. Y. Bee hive. | 10 Female portrait.

20 Compt's die. TWENTY | Vig. Oxen, sheep, farmers, &c. FRANKFORT BANK, Frankfort, N. Y. Two horses. | 20 Female portrait.

1 ONE Compt's die. | Female and fig. 1; cars and steamboat in distance. ONE FREDONIA BANK, Fredonia, N. Y. | Indian on cliff. ONE

TWO Compt's die. TWO | Farmer and wife seated; two gold dollars; cows, horses, etc. 2 FREDONIA BANK, Fredonia, N. Y. | TWO Two females erect. TWO

Compt's die. THREE Mechanic, sailor, farmer and figure 3. | 3 Three females representing Agriculture, Commerce and Manufactures; ship in distance. FREDONIA BANK, Fredonia, N. Y. | 3 Female.

5 Female. | Five females, fig. 5 in centre; shipping, factory, locomotive and tender in distance. 5 FREDONIA BANK, Fredonia, N. Y. | 5 Compt's die. 5

TEN Blacksmith, anvil, hammer, forge, etc. TEN | FREDONIA BANK, Fredonia, N. Y. 10 Nine cherubs making offering to female seated with cornucopia and ten gold dollars. | 10 TEN Compt's die

XX Portrait of girl with curls. | Female representing Agriculture; ship in distance. 20 FREDONIA BANK, Fredonia, N. Y. Compt's die. | TWENTY Female erect with spear and shield. TWENTY

1 Compt's die. | Female milking cow; cornfield, man, boy, trees, house, etc. FRONTIER BANK. Potsdam, N. Y. Locomotive. | 1 Female with sewing machine.

Female with hammer and anvil. Compt's die. | 1 Portrait of Washington. FRONTIER BANK Potsdam, N. Y. | 1 Female seated with sheaf of wheat.

Child standing. Compt's die. | 2 Male portrait. FRONTIER BANK Potsdam, N. Y. | 2 Female portrait.

2 Compt's die. TWO | Eagle. Children, cows, sheep, etc. Title of Bank. | 2 Two children

Compt's die. 3 | Men, horse, dogs, logs, trees, &c. Title of Bank. | 3 Two children

Large figure 5 with Indian at the bottom. Compt's die. | 5 Male portrait. 5 FRONTIER BANK Potsdam, N. Y. | Sailor standing. 5

5 Female in 5. | View of a street. Title of Bank. FIVE V on FIVE. FIVE | 5 Compt's die. 5

Large X, figure 10, sailor looking through a telescope and a sailor in a boat. Compt's die. | 10 Male portrait 10 FRONTIER BANK Potsdam, N. Y. | TEN Ship at sea. TEN

10 Hatter at work. | Old man on horse; boy on rail fence; colt, sheep, etc.; house in distance. Male portrait. Title of Bank. 10 | 10 X Compt's die

Mechanic at work. Compt's die. | FULTON CO. BANK Gloversville, N. Y. 1 Vig. Male portrait. 1 | 1 Deer. ONE

2 Deer. | Compt's die. Vig. Mechanics at work. FULTON CO. BANK, Gloversville, N. Y. Bale of goods. | 2 Female seated.

5 Female seated. | FULTON CO. BANK Gloversville, N. Y. Compt's die. Vig. Mechanics at work. Bales of goods. | 5 Portrait of George Washington.

TEN Geo. Washington. Compt's die. | Vig. Large eagle resting on liberty cap. X FULTON CO. BANK, Gloversville, N. Y. Bales of goods. | 10 Mechanic at work. TEN

ONE Compt's die. ONE | 1 Vig. Goddess of Industry, shield, bale of goods, anchor, plow, &c. ship in distance. GENESEE CO. BK. Leroy. | ONE Female seated; cattle, cars, &c.

TWO Compt's die. TWO | 2 Vig. Female seated, sickle in hand, plow and grain house, farm and canal boat in distance. 2 GENESEE CO. BK Leroy. Trees and cattle. | Mechanic seated; hammer and cornucopia in his hands; surrounded by corn.

Left end	Centre	Right end
3 Franklin. 3	Compt's. die. Vig. Farmer plowing. GENESEE CO. BK. Leroy.	3 Female with sickle. sit. grain in each hand. 3
5 Compt's die. FIVE	V Vig. Three V female figures; middle one surrounded by ornamental figure 5; stage-house in distance, on right; cars on left. GENESEE CO. BK. Leroy. Trees and cattle.	5 Medallion head. FIVE
X Male portrait. TEN	Compt's die. Goddess of liberty. Vig. Signing declaration of Independence. GENESEE CO. BK. Leroy.	X Male portrait. TEN
Female holding figure 1. Compt's die.	Vig. Female seated, with basket of grain; river and vessels in distance. GENESEE RIVER BANK, Mount Morris, N. Y. Sheaf of wheat and agricultural implements.	1 Female holding a shield and pole.
2 Portrait of female.	Vig. Locomotive and cars going over bridge; canal boats and hay makers. GENESEE RIVER BANK, Mount Morris, N. Y.	Compt's die. 2
Compt's die. 5	Vig. Cattle and sheep, some standing and some lying down. GENESEE RIVER BANK, Mount Morris, N. Y.	5 Indian reclining.
10 Compt's die.	GENESEE RIVER BANK, Mount Morris, N. Y.	10 Man felling a tree, own children seated on ground.
20 Compt's die.	Vig. Indian seated, gun in right hand; city in distance, and steamship. GENESEE RIVER BANK, Mount Morris, N. Y.	20 Female with tablet, resting on column.
Female with vase. Compt's die.	1 Vig. Female seated with oxen. GENESEE VALLEY BANK. Geneseo, N. Y. Safe.	1 Cows, and pigs.
2 Compt's die. TWO	Vig. Farmer seated with jug, basket, dog, &c. GENESEE VALLEY BANK Geneseo' N. Y. Wheat.	2 Two Females standing

Left end	Centre	Right end
5 Spread eagle Compt's die.	Vig. Oxen and sheep. GENESEE VALLEY BANK, Geneseo, N. Y. Ox.	5 Female leaning on figure 5.
Indian. Compt's die.	10 Vig. Farmers at dinner; loading hay, &c. GENESEE VALLEY BANK, Geneseo, N. Y. State Arms.	10 Male portrait
20 Compt's die. XX	Two females, shield, buildings, etc. GENESSEE VALLEY BANK, Geneseo, N. Y. Sheaf.	20 Male portrait TWENTY
1 Compt's die. ONE	Female portrait in centre; angel on left, cupid on right. GEORGE WASHINGTON BANK, Corning, N. Y. Wheat, plow, anvil &c.	1 Washington
2 Compt's die. TWO	Vig. Washington. GEORGE WASHINGTON BANK, Corning, N. Y. TWO Shield.	2 Lady Washington.
5 Male portrait	V Vig. Indian seated beside slain deer. GEORGE WASHINGTON BANK. Corning, N. Y. Female portrait.	5 Compt's die.
TEN Full length Washington.	X Vig. Sailor, Indian, Justice and liberty. GEORGE WASHINGTON BANK, Corning, N. Y. Dogs head.	10 Compt's die
1 Female with sheaf of wheat on her shoulder.	Vig. Milk maids—one milking cow; farm house on right, vessel on left. GLENN'S FALLS BK. Glenn's Falls, N.Y. Bee-hive.	1 Compt's die
2 Hunter, dog and gun.	Vig. Female seated; eagle at her feet; bags of coin and pickaxe on her right; vessels in distance on left; cars on right end. GLENN'S FALLS BK. Glenn's Falls, N.Y. Agricultural implements.	2 Compt's die.
3 Man, woman, and child.	Vig. 3 females,—one holding sword and balances; ship on right. GLENN'S FALLS BK. Glenn's Falls, N.Y. Eagle.	3 Compt's die

Left end	Centre	Right end
Female with liberty cap; large building in background. 5	GLENN'S FALLS BK. Glenn's Falls, N.Y. Male Portrait. 5 5 Indian.	5 Compt's die.
10 Indian, gun and waterfall	Vig. Spread eagle. GLENN'S FALLS BK. Glenn's Falls, N.Y.	10 Compt's die
1 Female seated. 1	Compt's die. 1 Female seated on sheaf of wheat; cars on right and steamboat on left. GOSHEN BANK Goshen, N Y	1 Female erect.
2 Compt's die. TWO	Vig. Farming scene; on right cow loading hay. GOSHEN BANK Goshen, N. Y. Sheaf of wheat plough &c.	2 Female seated, basket on each side.
FIVE Compt's die. FIVE	Vig. Drove of cattle and man on horse. GOSHEN BANK Goshen, N. Y. Female.	5 5, and group of females
TEN Compt's die. X	10 Vig. Train of cars, house and steam boat on left. GOSHEN BANK Goshen, N. Y. Ox.	10 Female erect shield on left.
20 Eagle, shield &c. Compt's die.	XX Vig. Female seated, sale, sheaf of wheat, farming implements and cars on right, steamship on left GOSHEN BANK Goshen, N.Y. Man shearing a sheep.	20 2 Female seated. 0
ONE Two large buildings; shade trees, cattle, &c. ONE	Compt's die. Vig. Wood chopper seated on fallen log; house and waggon in back ground; gold dollar on left. HAMILTON BANK, Hamilton, N. Y. Dog.	1 Female erect holding figure one.
2 Two large buildings; shade trees, cattle &c. TWO	Compt's die. Vig. Man and woman; rake and pail; two gold dollars; cattle and farm house. HAMILTON BANK. Hamilton, N. Y. Mechanic.	2 Female raking
FIVE Female portrait. Compt's die.	Vig. Five human figures; five gold dollars lapped. HAMILTON BANK, Hamilton, N. Y. Farming tools	5 Ornamental & surmounted by five human figures

10 — Vig. Female reclining upon a sheaf; locomotive on left, female and cattle on right. — 10
Compt's die. — HAMILTON BANK. Hamilton, N. Y. — Female portrait.
TEN — Anvil and horn of plenty. — TEN

1 — HAMPDEN BANK, Northcastle, N.Y. — 1
ONE Male portrait ONE — Female erect with flag and shield, Indian figure at her feet.
Compt's die — One Dollar.

1 — HAMPDEN BANK. — 1
Farming implements, etc.
Compt's die — North Castle, N. Y. — Daniel Webster.

2 — Zouaves charging. — 2
Compt's die — HAMPDEN BANK, North Castle, N. Y.
TWO — Henry Clay.

TWO — Man, two horses, pig, ducks, etc., at pump; cattle and barn in distance. — 2
Compt's die — HAMPDEN BANK. Northcastle, N.Y.
Two on 2 — Beehive.

5 FIVE 5 — HAMPDEN BANK. Soldier with gun & flag. 5 surrounded by oval device, which ... name of bank and ... North Castle, N. Y. FIVE DOLLARS. — 5 Compt's die 5

5 — Train of cars; steamboat, man, horses, canal boat, etc. — 5
Head of Liberty surrounded by stars. — HAMPDEN BANK. Northcastle, N.Y. — Compt's die
5

1 — HERKIMER Co. B'K. Little Falls, N. Y. — Female seated with wheat.
Compt's die. — 1 Portrait of child with wheat and sickle. 1
1 — 1

2 — HERKIMER Co. B'K. Little Falls, N. Y. — Female standing by large figure 2.
Compt's die. — 2 Vig. Female seated with sheaf of wheat. 2
2

3 — 3 Title of Bank. Vig. Eagle on branch of tree; train of cars. 3 — THREE
Compt's die. — Portrait of child.
3 — TH 3 REE — THREE

5 — HERKIMER Co. B'K. Little Falls, N.Y. — FIVE
Compt's die. — 5 Vig. Oxen, sheep, &c. 5 — Female seated in large figure 5.
5 — 5 — FIVE

10 — TEN TEN HERKIMER Co. B'K. Little Falls, N. Y. — TEN
Compt's die. — State arms.
10 — Vig. Female seated with eagle, &c. — X

100 — HERKIMER Co. B'K. Little Falls, N. Y. — 100
Goddess of liberty with eagle; Union is strength; E Pluribus Unum. — Male portrait. Male portrait. — Female churning.
100 — Vig. Man killing snakes with club.

Man's portrait. — 1 H. G. HOTCHKISS & Co's BANK, Lyons, N.Y. — 1
Boy on horse, colt, female, etc., at trough.
Compt's die — Child's head.

Compt's die — Title of Bank. — 3
3 Man, two horses, pig, etc. at pump; cattle, barn, etc. in background.
Male portrait. — THREE

1 — HIGHLAND BANK, Newburgh. 1 1 — 1
Compt's die. — Vig. Entrance to the Highlands from Newburgh Bay; steamboat under way, with ship at dock in foreground; mountains in distance, with schooner under way in left of vig. — Head of Geo. Jas. Clinton.
1 — ONE DOLLAR. — ONE

2 — HIGHLAND BANK, Newburgh. — 2
Compt's die. — Portrait of Washington. Head of Clinton.
2 — Vig. Same as above. TWO DOLLARS. 2 — A man gathering corn.

3 — HIGHLAND BANK, Newburgh. — 3
Compt's die. — 3 Head of Clinton.
3 — Vig. Same as above. THREE DOLLARS. — 3

5 — 5 5 Vig. Same as above. — Head of Lafayette.
Compt's die. — HIGHLAND BANK, Newburgh.
5 — FIVE. Head of Washington. — Washington on horseback.

10 — 10 10 Vig. Washington's head quarters at Newburgh. — TEN Same as the vig. of 1s, 2s, and 5s, except the schooner, which is not seen.
Compt's die. — HIGHLAND BANK, Newburgh.
10 — TEN DOLLARS. X — TEN

20 — 20 Vig. Washington's head quarters at Newburgh. — XX
Compt's die. — HIGHLAND BANK, Newburgh. — Head of Jas. Clinton.
20 — TWENTY DOLLARS. Head of Washington. — 20

50 — Vig. Washington's head quarters. — 50
Compt's die. — HIGHLAND BANK, Newburgh. — Head of De Witt Clinton.
50 — FIFTY DOLLARS. — 50

100 — Vig. Washington's head quarters. — 100
Compt's die. — HIGHLAND BANK, Newburgh. — Head of De Witt Clinton.
100 — ONE HUNDRED DOLLARS. — C

1 — Steam mill, carts, boat, etc. — 1
H. J. MINER & Co's BANK, Dunkirk, N. Y.
Compt's die. — Female with flowers.

2 — Locomotive and depot. — 2
Compt's die. — Title of Bank.
2 — Girl.

V — Steamboats and vessels. — 5
Title of Bank. — Compt's die.
Woman with sheaf. — Secured, etc.

TEN — River and wharf scene—barge and steamboat with tow. — 10
Secured, etc.
Title of Bank.
Mechanic with sledge. — Compt's die.

1 — H. J. MESSINGER'S BANK, Marathon, N. Y. — 1
Milkmaid, cows, etc., house and trees in distance.
Compt's die. — Male portrait.

2 — Title of Bank. — 2
Compt's die. — Horses alarmed at lightning; cows in distance.
TWO — Male portrait.

5 — Drove of cattle and sheep; man bargaining. — 5
Title of Bank.
5 — Horse — Compt's die.

10 Man plowing with two horses; boy leading horses | Title of Bank. 10 | 10 Compt's die.

1 Compt's die. 1 | 1 Vig. Farmers at work in field; bee hive, plough, rake &c. 1 HUDSON RIVER B'K, Hudson, N. Y. Steamboat. | ONE

2 Compt's die. 2 | 2 Vig. Two children seated, in centre sheaf of wheat, on right ships in distance, on left steamboat. 2 HUDSON RIVER B'K, Hudson, N. Y. Steamboat. | TWO

3 Compt's die. 3 | Two children seated, sheaf of wheat in centre, on right a ship, on left a steamboat. 3 HUDSON RIVER B'K, Hudson, N. Y. Steamboat. | THREE

5 Compt's die. 5 | 5 Male and female reclining, monument &c. 5 HUDSON RIVER B'K, Hudson, N. Y. Portrait of Washington. | FIVE

10 Compt's die. 10 | 10 Vig. large ship under sail, small boat and whale on left in distance, vessels in distance on right. 10 HUDSON RIVER B'K, Hudson, N. Y. Male portrait. | TEN

20 TWENTY 20 | Vig. Male portrait with female on the right and male on left. HUDSON RIVER B'K Hudson, N. Y. | 20 20

L Female standing erect. L | 50 Vig. Three females, liberty pole and cap, beehive on left. 50 HUDSON RIVER B'K Hudson, N. Y. | 50 Portrait of Washington 50

[illegible] and eagle. Compt's die. | 1 Vig. White men trading with Indians. HUGUENOT BANK New Platz, N. Y. Shield. | 1 Buck staff and torch ONE

TWO Buck staff and torch. Compt's die. | 2 Vig. White men trading with Indians. HUGUENOT BANK New Platz, N. Y. Dog. | 2 Two female standing erect.

Compt's die. Buck staff and torch. FIVE | Vig. Group of children white man with gun on right, and Indian on left cars on right in distance. HUGUENOT BANK New Platz, N. Y. | 5 Group of females with senior shield &c. large figure 5.

10 Compt's die. X | Vig. Females and males on right, horses and load of hay. HUGUENOT BANK New Platz, N. Y. Sheaf of wheat plough &c. | 10 Buck torch and staff. TEN

XX Portrait of Washington. Compt's die. | Vig. Female seated, goods and bales on right, cars and vessels on left. HUGUENOT BANK New Platz, N. Y. Female seated. | 20 Buck torch and staff. TWENTY

ONE Compt's die. | figure 1 on shield. Female milking cows. HUNGERFORD'S BK Adams, N. Y. | 1 Female with yoke. 1

Figure 2 on shield. Male portrait. | Compt's die. Loading hay. HUNGERFORD'S B'K Adams, N. Y. Female portrait. | 2

3 Compt's die. | HUNGERFORD'S BK Adams, N. Y. 3 Vig female with shield, steamer in distance 3 | 3 on medallion head. female portrait.

5 Compt's die. | Vig. horses, colt, trees, &c. HUNGERFORD'S BK Adams, N. Y. | 5 Canal boat and bridge. 5

TEN male portrait. | Compt's die. Vi. drove of sheep man on horse; mill in background. HUNGERFORD'S BK Adams, N. Y. Wheat, plough, &c. | X on shield.

20 Male portrait | Compt's die. Men loading hay; cows, etc. HUNGERFORDS' BK, Adams, N. Y. | TWENTY Full length figure in Roman costume TWENTY

1 Compt's die | Vig. Dairy maid, cows, &c. 1 ILLION BANK, Illion, N. Y. Dog. | ONE Artisan.

Indian standing. Compt's die. | 2 Mirror, female with pail on right; man with rake on left. ILLION BANK, Illion, N. Y. Dog. | 2 Two females.

3 Medallion head. | Compt's die. Vig. Three females seated. ILLION BANK, Illion, N. Y. Dog. | 3 Figure 3 and three men. THREE

Compt's die. Large V and females, sailor and two men. | 5 Female with mirror, liberty pole and cap, motto Agriculture and Commerce. ILLION BANK, Illion, N. Y. | FIVE Figure 5 and five females.

10 Eagle. Compt's die. | Female seated with scales, and sword; ship, house, trees, sun and cupid. X ILLION BANK, Illion, N. Y. Dog's head. | Dec. 10 Buffalo.

20 Compt's die. TWENTY | Drover on horseback; drove of cattle and sheep. ILION BANK, Ilion, N. Y. | 20 Female with rake; female in distance.

Goddess of Liberty. Compt's die. | 1 Vig. Male portrait; female with trumpet and wreath of flowers on left; Cupid on right. 1 INTERNATIONAL BANK, Buffalo. Shield. | 1 Female, Falls, rainbow and figure 1.

2 Male portrait. | Compt's die. Vig. 4 figures, sailor, Indian, Goddess of Liberty and Justice head in centre. INTERNATIONAL BANK Buffalo. Mechanic reclining on anvil. | 2 Male Portrait.

3 Male Portrait THREE | Compt's die. Vig. Two men and horse, dog, cattle and sheep. INTERNATIONAL BANK. Buffalo. Two horses. | 3 Male portrait THREE

FIVE Male portrait. Compt's die. | 5 Vig R R depot, locomotive, drayman loading goods harbor and ships INTERNATIONAL BANK Buffalo. Canal locks. | Five human figures surrounding ornamental figure 5. FIVE

10 Portrait of male. | Compt's die. 10 Vig Female seated bale of goods, shipping &c., lighthouse and canal boat. INTERNATIONAL BANK Buffalo. Farmers loading hay. | Two female figures one erect, the other seated, liberty cap and eagle.

20 / Suspension bridge, two steamboats and falls. / TWENTY
Compt's die. Vig. Female figure seated, three cupids riding sea animal. INTERNATIONAL BANK Buffalo. Goddess of liberty.
20 / Portrait of Male

Compt's die. / Male portrait
50 INTERNATIONAL BANK Buffalo. Vig. Steamship on left ship on right, ship and steamer in distance.
50 / Male portrait

1 / Compt's die.
Vig. Santa Claus in sleigh drawn by reindeer. IRON BANK, Plattsburgh, N. Y.
ONE / Smith with hammer on his shoulder

TWO / Compt's die.
IRON BANK, Plattsburgh, N. Y. Large red 2. Vig. Female seated on bale; steamboat in distance.
2 / 2

3 / Mechanic and sailor.
3 Compt's die. IRON BANK. Plattsburgh, N. Y. Large red 3 length wise of note.
3 / Dog's head

5 / V
Vig. Indian hunting deer. Compt's die. IRON BANK. Plattsburgh, N. Y.
5 / Female seated in harvest field.

TEN / Compt's die.
IRON BANK. Plattsburgh, N. Y. Vig. Steamboat and vessel; train of cars, light house &c. in distance.
X

Female with sheaf of wheat and sickle in her hand. / ONE
JAMESTOWN BANK, Jamestown, N. Y. Vig. Farmer, sailor, and mechanic; city, locomotive and ship in distance.
1 / Compt's die / ONE

2 / Compt's die.
JAMESTOWN BANK, Jamestown, N. Y. Vig. Two females seated; steamboat, factory, cars, canal, &c., in the distance.
TWO / Female seated in large figure 2

FIVE / Franklin Pierce. / FIVE
Compt's die. Vig. Farmer and Indian seated on either side of frame; Indian hunts on left, cars and canal on right. JAMESTOWN BANK, Jamestown, N. Y.
V

ONE / Male portrait / Compt's die.
JEFFERSON CO. BK Watertown, N. Y. Vig. Locomotive and cars.
1

3 / Compt's die. / 3
3 Female with an Eagle and shield 3 JEFFERSON CO. BK Watertown, N. Y. American eagle.
Female portrait.

Compt's die. / large figure 3 and three cupids.
Farmer seated with sickle loading hay in distance. JEFFERSON CO., BK Watertown, N. Y. Secured, etc.
3 / Female portrait.

5 / Compt's die.
Shipping, steamer &c. JEFFERSON CO., BK Watertown, N. Y. Engine
5 / Female with wheat.

10 / Compt's die. / 10
X Two females with safe boy horn of plenty &c X JEFFERSON CO., BK. Watertown, N. Y. Locomotive and cars.
TEN / Farmer ploughing / 10

Female with cornucopia. / X
JEFFERSON CO. BK, Watertown, N. Y. Figs. 10, words Ten Dollars on three red dies. Horse.
10 / Compt's die.

XX / Female gathering wheat.
JEFFERSON CO. BK, Watertown, N. Y. Figs. 20 and words Twenty Dollars on three red dies. Compt's die.
20 / Female with flowers.

ONE / Compt's die
Chasing buffaloes. J. N. HUNGERFORD'S BANK. Corning, N. Y.
ONE / Daniel Webster.

ONE / State of N. Y. / Compt's die.
Hunters killing buffaloes. J. N. HUNGERFORD'S BANK. Corning, N. Y.
ONE / Webutor

2 / Compt's die. / TWO
Man and boy plowing with two horses. Title of Bank.
2 / Child's head.

Compt's die. / 3
Dogs pursuing deer. Title of Bank.
3 / Girl's head.

Five inverted / Sailor seated with female, ships, etc. above him.
Rafting scene on river; steamboat, etc. Title of Bank.
5 / Compt's die. / Cornucopia, bale, etc.

Male portrait / Compt's die.
1 Milkmaid, cattle, sheep, &c. 1 J. T. RAPLEE'S BK Penn Yan, N. Y. ONE
1 / Female portrait.

2 / Compt's die. / 2
J. T. RAPLEE'S BK, Penn Yan, N. Y. 2 Two young girls holding flowers. 2
2 / Male portrait

Two Indians overlooking water fall; deer. / Fig. 5, with five on each side.
Indian camp. V Webster V J. T. RAPLEE'S BK, Penn Yan, N. Y. Farmer seated on plow
5 / Compt's die. / 5

10 / Male portrait / TEN
X Male, two horses, canal boat, cars, steamboat, mountains, etc., in distance. X J. T. RAPLEE'S BK., Penn Yan, N. Y.
10 / Compt's die.

20 / Two girls, vase on left.
Title of Bank. 20 Females at column, steamer, etc. 20 XX Compt's die. XX
20 / Male portrait

1 / Compt's die. / ONE
Vig. Am. eagle, E Pluribus Unum; shipping &c. JUDSON BANK, Ogdensburgh, N. Y.
1 / Female portrait.

2 / Locomotive.
JUDSON BANK, Ogdensburgh, N. Y. Vig. Indians feeding horse.
Compt's die. / 2

Locomotive and cars. / FIVE
JUDSON BANK, Ogdensburgh, N. Y.
5 / Compt's die. / FIVE

ONE 1 Vig. female seated on sofa, [illegible] child; ship in distance on right, plough on left. 1
Female reclining.
KINGSTON BANK Kingston, N. Y.
Compt's die.
Park.

Compt's die. Female on either side of a shield on which is a ship, plow, etc.; vessels and city in distance. 2
Farmer seated with scythe.
KINGSTON BANK, Kingston, N. Y.
Carpenter at his work bench.
Building, &c.

THREE Vig. Three females seated on a shield, ship on right, sheaf of wheat and oars, on left. Compt's die. 3
Steamboat.
3 KINGSTON BANK Kingston, N. Y.
3 A park. 3

FIVE DOLLARS 5 Vig. State arms ship on right, oars on left. 5 V
KINGSTON BANK Kingston, N. Y.
Compt's die.
Hands joined together. V

TEN X Vig. Female; sheaf of wheat and plough, and cattle on left. X 10
Cupid, grind stone &c.
KINGSTON BANK Kingston, N. Y.
Female and wheel.
10 Steamboat. 10

---

1 LAKE ONTARIO BK. Oswego, N. Y. ONE
Female representing Agriculture, sailor and blacksmith with implements; ship city and cars in distance.
Compt's die.
Male portrait
Anchor on shield.

---

2 Vessels at sea. TWO
Compt's die.
LAKE ONTARIO BK, Oswego, N. Y.
2
Male portrait
Anchor on shield.

Scene on wharf; various vessels in distance; men at work on dock; horse cart, etc.
Male portrait
5 on Five.
Compt's die.
V LAKE ONTARIO BK, Oswego, N. Y. 5
Anchor on shield.

---

1 Drivers, cattle, and sheep. 1
View of drovers men and cattle, load of hay, [illegible] in distance.
LAKE SHORE B'K, Dunkirk, N. Y.
State Arms

---

2 LAKE SHORE B'K, Dunkirk, N. Y. 2
Sailor leaning on cap stan.
Catching wild horse.
State Arms

Compt's die. 3 Male portrait. 3 3
Indians hunting buffaloes.
LAKE SHORE BANK, Dunkirk, N. Y.
Man cutting tree, two children, oxen, etc

---

5 Landing of the pilgrims. 5
Female artist and implements.
LAKE SHORE B'K, Dunkirk, N. Y.
State Arms

---

10 Title of Bank. 10
Sailor on ship with quadrant.
Anchor, bales, bbls., etc.
Compt's die.

ONE Drove of sheep, dog, &c.; man on horseback, mill and trees in distance. 1
LEONARDSVILLE BANK, Leonardsville, N. Y.
Compt's die.
Cattle, telegraph and railroad.
Agricultural Implements.

---

2 Horses, cattle and sheep; boy, trees, fence and house in distance. TWO
Compt's die.
Title of Bank.
TWO Dog, key and safe.
Male, female, boy, girl, dog, hen and chickens.

Compt's die. Two females and a male at work making shoes. 3
Title of Bank.
3 THREE
Pig pen, pigs and chickens.
Fish.

FIVE Title of Bank. 5
Blacksmith, hammer and anvil; factories in distance.
Man tending large machinery.
Compt's die.
5 Arm. 5
V across die.

X Title of Bank. 10
Indian on shield; eagle at top; horse each side; steamboat in distance on right; cars, factory and canal boat on left.
Liberty seated with pole, cap, shield and eagle.
Compt's die.
TEN TEN

XX Title of Bank. 20
Spread eagle on half of the globe.
Farmer, tree and scythe.
20 Compt's die. 20
Sailor seated with telescope.

---

1 LINCOLN BANK. 1
ONE Portrait of Abraham Lincoln. DOLLAR
Clinton, N. Y.
Compt's die

---

2 LINCOLN BANK. 2
Portrait of Abraham Lincoln.
Compt's die
Clinton, N. Y.
TWO DOLLARS

Compt's die Portrait of Abraham Lincoln. LINCOLN BANK. 3
THREE DOLLARS.
3 Clinton, N. Y.

Vig. Female seated, leaning on rock, canal boats, steamboat, &c., village in distance. Compt's die. 1
1 LOCKPORT CITY B'K Lockport, N.Y.
Canal boat and bridge.

TWO Vig. Anchor with Hope, [illegible] in scroll, [illegible] on right; steamboat and harbor on left. 2
Compt's die
TWO LOCKPORT CITY B'K Lockport, N.Y.
Drove cattle [illegible]

---

3 Vig. Ship and schooner under full sail; steamboats and cars in distance 3
Train cars.
Compt's die
3 LOCKPORT CITY B'K Lockport, N.Y.
THREE

FIVE LOCKPORT CITY B'K Lockport, N.Y.
V with letters Five running across it.
Indian with bow and tomahawk.
Compt's die.
Vig. vessels, steamboat and harbor.
Large 5 across note.

X LOCKPORT CITY B'K Lockport, N.Y. 10
View of the Suspension Bridge.
Squaw.
Compt's die

---

20 LOCKPORT CITY B'K Lockport, N.Y. 20
Cattle; stream of water, trees, etc.
XX XX

L LOCKPORT CITY B'K Lockport, N.Y. 50
View of the Crystal Palace; pedestrians, horses, carriages, etc
Compt's die

Soldier on a galloping horse. ONE
Washington
LONG ISLAND B'K, Brooklyn, N. Y.
Compt's die.
Female resting on a rock.
Deer

Left end	Centre	Right end
2 Compt's die. 2	TWO Same vig. as ones. Title running around the vig. 2 Fish.	TWO
3 Compt's die 3	3 Vig. Same as ones. LONG ISLAND B'K, Brooklyn, N. Y. Chicken.	THREE
5 Compt's die 5	Male figure seated on rock in clouds; buildings in background. 5 LONG ISLAND B'K, Brooklyn, N. Y. Deer.	FIVE
X Compt's die. X	10 Title of Bank. Vig. Same as fives. Fish.	TEN
50 Compt's die.	Indian standing beside block of stone, in his right hand a sword; in background an ox with plow. 50 LONG ISLAND B'K, Brooklyn, N. Y. Deer.	Die Work. Franklin. Die Work.
100 Compt's die.	100 Vig. Same as ditto, with the Title running around it. 100	Med. head. Washington. Med. head.
ONE Female with sickle and grain. ONE	1 Eagle on limb of tree. 1 LYONS BANK, Lyons, N. Y.	Female seated in large fig. 1.
TWO Female seated with safe, scales, eagle, etc. TWO	2 Female seated with sickle and wand; factory and canal in distance. 2 Title of Bank. Farmer cradling.	Vulcan seated with implements; horn of corn above and below him.
5 Indian, safe, eagle, scales, etc. FIVE	V Three females and fig. 5 cars, ships, farm scene, etc., in distance. V Title of Bank. Farmer cradling.	5 Med. head. FIVE
1 Female with pen and tablets.	Sailor steering ship. MANUFACTURERS' BANK of Brooklyn, N. Y.	1 Compt's die

Left end	Centre	Right end
Indian on cliff. 2	Title of Bank. Mechanic with hammer, anvil, cog-wheel, etc.	2 Compt's die.
THREE View of wharves, vessels, etc. THREE	Milkmaid and cows; houses in distance. Title of Bank.	3 Compt's die.
5 Female portrait	Title of Bank. Mechanic erect in a letter V; anvil, hammer, cog wheel, etc.; buildings, &c., in distance.	5 Compt's die.
10	Spread eagle; buildings, street, etc. Female portrait. Title of Bank.	10 Compt's die.
20 Arm and hammer. 20	Title of Bank. Figures 20, winged female on either side, two cupids between 2 and 0.	20 TWENTY Compt's die
50 50	Three female and winged cupid floating in water. Compt's die. Title of Bank.	50 Female with compass, &c.
100 Female reclining with sheaf and sickle.	Cattle and stream of water. Title of Bank.	100 Compt's die
Female and figure 1. Compt's die.	Mechanics at work in an iron mill; large wheel in distance. 1 MANUFACTURERS' BANK, Troy, N. Y. Secured, &c.	ONE Female seated. ONE
TWO Compt's die. 2	Vig. Train of cars; steamboat on right, trees and rocks on left. MANUFACTURERS' BANK, Troy, N. Y. Secured, &c.	TWO Sailor seated on bollard. TWO
Compt's die Canal and dolphin. THREE	Vig. Sailor seated holding a quadrant; female with sheaf of wheat and sickle, on right sheaf of wheat and men at work in distance, on left steamship in distance. MANUFACTURERS' BANK, Troy, N. Y. Secured, &c.	THREE Female portrait. 3

Left end	Centre	Right end
FIVE Male portrait. Compt's die.	Vig. Locomotive, mill and houses, large house in distance on a hill on left, on right houses in distance. MANUFACTURERS' BANK, Troy, N. Y. Secured, &c.	Blacksmith at work FIVE
TEN Liberty by X Compt's die.	MANUFACTURERS' BANK, Troy, N. Y. Large steamboat leaving wharf. Secured &c.	Man with scythe. 10
20 Compt's die.	Two females seated; factory in distance. MANUFACTURERS' BANK, Troy, N. Y. Secured, etc.	20 Female seated on bale
1 ONE	MAN. & TRADERS' BANK, Buffalo, N. Y. Compt's die. Blacksmith, anvil and hammer; city in distance.	1
2 TWO	Title of Bank. Compt's die. Ship yard; men at work and ship on stocks.	TWO Figure 2, in top curve of figure 2.
3 THREE	Compt's die. Bull's head on shield; on left female binding sheaf; on right man dressing leather. Title of Bank.	THREE Large figure 3, in top curve of fig. 3.
5 FIVE	Title of Bank. Three cherubs with lever, &c., breaking stone. 5	5 Compt's die. FIVE
X TEN	Title of Bank. Five cherubs with globe, anvil hammer, &c. X	Word ten, letter X and figure 10. Compt's die.
ONE Ship in full sail.	Compt's die. 1 Vig. Houses and shipping, sailor in foreground. MARINE BANK, Buffalo, N. Y.	ONE Ship in full sail.
2 Compt's die.	TWO TWO Shipping and marine view. MARINE BANK, Buffalo, N. Y.	2 Sailor holding flag

5 Compt's die. FIVE FIVE Marine view. MARINE BANK, Buffalo, N. Y. 5 Canal boat passing under a bridge.

X Compt's die. X Whaling scene. X MARINE BANK, Buffalo, N. Y. 10 Ship in full sail.

1 ONE Farmer seated with scythe. Sailor seated. On demand, and one dollar in red die. MARINE BANK, Oswego, N. Y. Compt's die. 1

TWO TWO Compt's die. 2 2 MARINE BANK, Oswego, N. Y. Female with wheat. 2 Female with flowers. TWO DOLLARS

Compt's die. THREE 3 Ships and other vessels; city in distance. 3 MARINE BANK, Oswego, N. Y. THREE

5 Compt's die. FIVE View of N. Y. Harbor, with a steamer and ship. MARINE BANK, Oswego, N. Y. 5 FIVE

10 Sailor by capstan. Three horses drinking from trough; sheep, &c.; farm scene in general. MARINE BANK, Oswego, N. Y. X Ship on stocks. Compt's die.

XX Two sailors and female in a boat. TWE Compt's die. NTY MARINE BANK, Oswego, N. Y. 20

1 Compt's die. ONE Vig. Farmers at work; cars in distance. MARKET BANK, Troy, N. Y. 1 Female, sheaf of wheat and sickle.

Compt's die. 2 Vig. Two farmers and man on horse, sheaf of wheat on right, and trees on left. MARKET BANK, Troy, N. Y. 2 Female portrait.

Compt's die. 5 Vig. Man on horse, cattle and sheep, horses and waggons on right. MARKET BANK, Troy, N. Y. 5 Group of soldiers with shield and spear.

X Cattle head. X MARKET BANK, Troy, N. Y. Three females, two seated and one in centre erect, one on right is drawing, on left playing a harp; house in background. 10 Compt's die. X

50 Drove of cattle. MARKET BANK, Troy, N. Y. Two females on either side of Washington; on right, steamboat and ship; on left, sheaf and men mowing. 50 Compt's die.

1 Compt's die. Blacksmith shoeing horse. MECHANICS' BANK, Brooklyn, N. Y. 1 Squaw and papoose.

2 Compt's die. Stone cutters at work. Title of Bank. Female portrait. 2 Franklin.

3 Compt's die. Carpenter at work; tools lying on the bench. Head of Washington. MECHANICS' BANK, Brooklyn, N. Y. 3 Mechanics' arm, with hammer, anvil, and cog wheel.

5 Compt's die. MECHANICS' BANK, Brooklyn, N. Y. Three Cupids with props and levers trying to raise a large stone. 5 Locomotive and tender.

10 Compt's die. Masons working on scaffold, building a house, man coming up a ladder with hod. MECHANICS' BANK, Brooklyn, N. Y. 10 Jenny Lind.

50 Compt's die. Two females reclining inside a kind of shell, with bee hive between them; female on left has sword and scales. MECHANICS' BANK, Brooklyn, N. Y. 50 Blacksmith resting on hammer and anvil; female in background.

100 Compt's die. 100 View of the Brooklyn City Hall. 100 MECHANICS' BANK, Brooklyn, N. Y. C Female seated with shield beside her.

Compt's die. ONE 1 Man seated on a boiler, with sledge in right hand. 1 MECHANICS' BANK, Syracuse, N. Y. Man bearing a hide. ONE

II Compt's die. Female seated; boiler, anvil, etc.; ship in distance. MECHANICS' BANK, Syracuse, N. Y. II Blacksmith with forge and anvil.

3 Compt's die. 111 MECHANICS' BK. Syracuse. Vig. Two females sitting; factory, canal, cars, steamboat, &c., in the distance. 3 Indian viewing a ship.

5 Compt's die. 5 MECHANICS' BANK, Syracuse, N. Y. Two Indians one with gun and the other lying down. Secured, etc. FIVE 5 Cars. Waterfall. FIVE

X Sailor, light house, etc. Compt's die. Locomotive and cars. MECHANICS' BANK, Syracuse, N. Y. 10 Female and anvil. 10

Female with sword in right hand. Compt's die. TWENTY MECHANICS' BK. Syracuse. Vig. Female sitting; two sheafs of wheat, scroll, and globe; car in distance. 20 Canal view.

Three males supporting 50. Girl's head. MECHANICS' BANK, Syracuse, N. Y. Cupids and 50. L Compt's die.

100 Liberty seated. Girl's head. MECHANICS' BANK, Syracuse, N. Y. Compt's die. 100 Stone cutter.

1 Compt's die. 1 1 Vig. Female, grain, farmers' and mechanics' tools, &c. 1 MECHANICS' AND FARMERS' BANK, Albany. ONE Head of Washington. ONE

2 Compt's die. 2 2 Title of Bank. II Vig. Same as ones. 2 Washington 2

Left end	Centre	Right end
3 Compt's die. 3	3 Title of Bank. 3 Vig. Same as ones.	3 Washington 3
5 Compt's die	MECH. & FAR. BK., Albany, N. Y. Blacksmith seated by anvil, forge, factories, vessels, etc. FIVE	5 Agriculture.
5 Compt's. die.	Title of Bank under vig. FIVE DOLLARS Vig. Female, scale, grain, farmers' and mechanics' tools, &c. 5 on right	FIVE A female standing, a guard, and resting her right hand upon a shield, upon which is a 5.
X Compt's. die.	MECHANICS' AND FARMERS' BANK. Albany. Vig. Female, scale, grain, farmers' and mechanics' tools, &c.	X TEN
50 Male and female seated.	MECH. & FARMERS B'K. Albany, N. Y. FIFTY DOLLARS. Compt's die.	50 Male portrait.
50 FIFTY 50	MECHANICS' AND FARMERS' BANK, Albany. Vig. Mechanic seated. FIFTY DOLLARS 50	
C Male portrait. 100	MECH & FARMERS BK. Albany, N. Y. One Hundred Dollars. Compt's die.	100 Male and female seated
ONE HUNDRED	MECHANICS' AND FARMERS' BANK, Albany. Vig. Mechanic seated, ONE HUNDRED 100	
Male Portrait ONE Compt's die.	MERCANTILE BANK Plattsburgh, N. Y. Vig. Two Indians in the forest—one reclining on the ground, the other in the back ground.	1 Male figure sleeping, ornamental figure 1.
Compt's die. Male Portrait	MERCANTILE BANK Plattsburgh, N. Y. Vig. Steamer coming into the dock. Small vessel on left.	TWO Large 2. Man sharpening scythe.

Left end	Centre	Right end
Male Portrait Compt's die.	MERCANTILE BANK Plattsburgh, N. Y. Vig. Mechanics at work, machinery, &c.	THREE Large 3. Female seated. Man in small boat.
5 Male Portrait	MERCANTILE BANK Plattsburgh, N. Y. Vig. Train of cars. Cattle drinking.	Large 5. Indians, and train of cars. Compt's die.
1 Eeod of Be-Witt Clinton.	MERCHANTS' BK. Albany. Vig. Scene on the Erie Canal; railroad with train of cars crossing a bridge over the canal; farmers loading hay on the left.	1 State Arms.
2 Head of Washington.	Vig. Female figure representing Agriculture in the foreground; Hudson River in the distance. MERCHANTS' BK. Albany.	2 State Arms.
Head of female. 3	Vig. Three female figures supporting the figure of Cupid. MERCHANTS' BK. Albany.	3 State Arms.
5 Head of John Hancock.	Vig. Railroad scene on the Susquehanna River; train of cars in the foreground; bridge over the river in the distance. MERCHANTS' BK. Albany.	5 State Arms.
X 10	Vig. Very fine view of one of the Collins' line of steamers at sea, under both sails and steam. Head of John Jay MERCHANTS' BK. Albany.	10 State Arms.
20 Female figure. TWENTY	MERCHANTS' BK. Albany. Vig. Goddess of Liberty; eagle to the left of the figure.	20 State Arms.
ONE State Arms. ONE	MERCHANTS' BK. Lancaster. Title under vig. Vig. Spread eagle, cask, bale, shield, &c.; village, dam, cars, &c. in background	1 Female reading book, guard chain on her neck, chin resting on hand, in circle. ONE
TWO State Arms. TWO	MERCHANTS' BK. Lancaster. 2 Vig. Female and spread eagle, in clouds; one hand holds horn of plenty and the other over eagle's neck, shield in eagle's talons.	2 Half nude female sitting, eagle overreaching her. TWO

Left end	Centre	Right end
5 State Arms. FIVE	MERCHANTS' BK. Lancaster. Vig. An old gentleman, two young men, and one lad, washing sheep; trees, dog, and water factories in the background.	5 Female standing with wreath in right hand and leaning other arm on large figure 5, with Liberty Cap.
10 State Arms. TEN	MERCHANTS' BK. Lancaster. Vig. An old man sitting nearly naked, sledge in right hand, skin on the left; shield with letter X on it; anvil, anchor, &c. Water, steamship, vessel, dock, &c. in the background	10 Female standing, right hand on capstan and left hand hold of her dress.
ONE Compt's die ONE	1 Female; shield in left [illegible]; ship in distance. MERCHANTS B'K in Poughaapsie, N. Y.	1 ONE
TWO Compt's. die.	2 Title under vig. Vig. Female sitting, globe on her left, and pen in her right hand; ship in the distance.	2 Female head.
3 Compt's die THREE	3 Female seated with pole, twig and shield; steamboat and sheep in distance. MERCHANTS' BANK Poughkeepsie, N. Y.	3 Female head THREE
V 5	Title of Bank under vig. Vig. Female holding stalk of corn in right hand and sickle in left; grain and ripe fruits at her feet, left of the centre. Canal and railroad in the distance. No numerals at the left.	5 Compt's die 5 Wm. Penn. FIVE
10 Female head. TEN	Compt's die. 10 Eagle, &c. MERCHANTS B'K in Foughkeepsie. N. Y.	X 10
Female with sword and shield. TEN	X Two children, cows, sheep, etc. MERCHANTS' B'K in Poughkeepsie. N. Y.	10 Compt's die.
20 Female erect.	Compt's die. 20 Male figure sitting; hammer in hand, &c. MERCHANT'S BK in Poughkeepsie. N. Y.	20
50 Compt's die 50	Infant figure holding shield with figs. 50; cask and cornucopia on the left; money chest and dollars on the right. MERCHANTS B'K in Poughkeepsie. N. Y.	50

100 Comp't's die 100	Goddess of Liberty, eagle and shield, with letter C in centre of it. MERCHANTS' B'K in Poughkeepsie, N. Y.	100
1 Comp't's die. 1	Man plowing with two horses. MERCHANTS' BANK Syracuse, N. Y.	1 Haymakers
2 Comp't's die.	Three females, setting sun; ship in distance. MERCHANTS' BANK Syracuse, N. Y.	2 Female portrait. TWO
5 Comp't's die	Female reclining; ship, sheaf, plough, sheep, etc. MERCHANTS' BANK Syracuse, N. Y.	5 Female portrait.
Ship. Comp't's die.	10 Female reclining on cornucopia. MERCHANTS' BANK Syracuse, N. Y. Still hunt.	X Female portrait.
20	MERCHANTS' BK. Syracuse. Vig. Three females, cornucopia, anchor, cars crossing bridge, trees, water, &c.; State arms, ship, city in distance.	20 Ocean ship.
ONE Female. Comp't's die	MERCHANTS' BANK OF WESTFIELD N.Y. Vig. Female seated, leaning on a shield, ship and steamboat in the distance on the left.	1 Portrait of Daniel Webster.
Female. Comp't's die.	Vig. Locomotive and train of cars. MERCHANTS' BANK OF WESTFIELD, N.Y.	II 2 TWO
5 Comp't's die FIVE	Vig. Cattle and sheep. MERCHANTS' BANK OF WESTFIELD, N.Y.	5 Portrait of Washington
Comp't's die ONE	1 Vig. Female, one hand extended over child's head, agricultural implements, anchor &c.; sail vessel in distance. Die. MERCHANTS' AND FARMERS' BANK, Ithica, N. Y. Building.	ONE Female seated, liberty pole and cap.

TWO Comp't's die TWO	2 Vig. Female seated, wand in left hand extended, sickle, wheat &c.; houses and railroad in distance. 2 MERCHANTS AND FARMERS' BANK. Ithica, N. Y. Steamboat.	Mechanic seated, horn of plenty &c.
5 Comp't's die FIVE	V Vig. Female seated within large 5, female on either side; implements of agriculture, carts, bales, steamboat &c. V MERCHANTS' AND FARMERS' BANK. Ithica, N. Y. Die.	5 Medallion head. FIVE
10 Comp't's die. TEN	Vig. Two females, shield between them, sickle, balances, implements of agriculture, barrels, bales, shipping, manufactories &c. MERCHANTS' AND FARMERS' BANK. Ithica, N. Y Steamboat.	10 Two females, horn of plenty, liberty pole, cap &c. TEN
ONE Comp't's die.	MER. & MECHANICS' BANK, Troy, N. Y. Male portrait; sailor on right; farmer on left.	1 Man carrying leather.
One on 1 Med. head 1	Female seated; sheaf, vessels, etc. 1 on med. head on each side. MERCHANTS' AND MECHANICS' BANK. Troy, N. Y.	ONE Comp't's die ONE
2 Comp't's die.	Title of Bank. Three men seated; shipping, &c. in distance. TWO DOLLARS	2
TWO Justice. TWO	Blacksmiths at work; one at anvil and one at bellows. 2 on med head on either side. Title of Bank.	TWO Comp't's die TWO
Comp't's die. 3	Title of Bank Indian princess with shield etc.; steamer in background.	3 Male portrait
3 Washington 3	Title of Bank under vig. 3 Vig. Female sitting on bale of goods; in background, on left, vessels, &c.; in background, on right, cars, &c. 3	THREE State Arms.
5 State Arms.	Title of Bank under vig. 5 Medallion head. Medallion head. 5 Vig. Signing Declaration of Independence. Steamboat.	5 He 5 ad. 5

TEN Comp't's die. TEN	Water scene, vessels, steamboats, etc. Ten on med. head either side. Title of Bank. Eagle	X TEN and med. head. 10
L Franklin FIFTY	50 Female seated by shield; male figure in a car drawn by sea monsters. 50 MER. & MECH. B'K. Troy, N. Y. Die.	Full length male figure
100 Washington. 100	MER. & MECH. B'K. Troy, N. Y. 100 100 Vig. Same as Fifties.	100 Three cherubs. 100
1 Comp't's die.	MIDDLETOWN B'K. Middletown, N. Y. Male and female hatters at work.	1 Boy's head.
Secured by pledge, &c. ONE	1 Vig. Female with sword, shield, cornucopia, anchor, agricultural implements, &c., ship in distance. Die. MIDDLETOWN B'K. OF ORANGE CO. Middletown, N. Y. Girl milking.	ONE Female seated, cars and vessel in distance.
TWO Comp't's die. TWO	2 Vig. Female seated; agricultural implements; factory on left; canal boat and cars on right; steamboat in distance. 2 Title of Bank. Female milking.	Mechanic seated, tools, horn of plenty, surrounded by ears of corn.
2 Comp't's die. TWO	Title of Bank. Boy and horses; cars in distance.	2 Girl's head.
5 Two children.	Cows, milkmaid, man, ladder, tree, dog, etc. Title of Bank. 5 FIVE 5	5 Comp't's die. Female portrait.
5 Comp't's die. FIVE	Vig. Group of persons, centre female holding a globe in one hand, key in the other seated in chariot; lions at her feet; vessel and steamship in the distance. Title of Bank. Female milking.	Female pointing toward cars in the distance, foot cradling. FIVE
10 Comp't's die. TEN	Vig. [illegible] seated, sickle, between and sickle between them; mill, agricultural implements, cars, steamboat, barrels, &c. MIDDLETOWN BK. OF ORANGE CO. Middletown, N. Y. Female milking.	10 State die. TEN

Male portrait 10	MIDDLETOWN BANK, Middletown, N. Y. Farmer, sailor and mechanic.	10 Compt's die.
Two females and two cupids with fig. 20. 20	Compt's die. Title of Bank. TWENTY	20 Male portrait
TWENTY Compt's die. TWENTY	20 Vig. Female seated, left hand extended towards steam-boat, chemical apparatus, table and writing implements, globe, &c. 20 Title of Bank. Female milking	XX
FIFTY Female with sheaf and sickle.	Compt's die. Man reclining; sheep, etc. Title of Bank.	50 Two children
100 Apotheosis of Art.	Title of Bank. Compt's die. Fig 100 and words ONE HUNDRED.	100 Two children
1 Compt's die. 1	1 Vig. Indian seated in canoe going through rapids. 1 MOHAWK BANK, Schenectady, N. Y. Locomotive and cars.	1 Female seated. 1
2 Compt's die. 2	MOHAWK BANK. Schenectady, N. Y. 2 Vig. Indian seated in canoe going through rapids. 2	TWO TWO
3 Compt's die.	MOHAWK BANK. Schenectady, N. Y. 3 Vig. Indian seated in canoe going through rapids. 3 Secured, &c.	THREE Female, sheaf of wheat, sickle &c. 3
5 Compt's die. 5	5 Indian seated in canoe going over rapids. 5 MOHAWK BANK, Schenectady, N. Y.	FIVE Male portrait 5
5 Female portrait.	MOHAWK BANK. Schenectady, N. Y. Indian in canoe going over rapids. Canal lock	5 Compt's die. FIVE

5 Female portrait.	MOHAWK BANK, Schenectady, N. Y. 5 Indian seated in canoe going through rapids. 5 Canal lock.	FIVE Compt's die. 5
10 Compt's die. 10	Title of Bank Vig. Indian seated in canoe going through rapids. X	10 Male portrait. 10
TEN Male portrait	MOHAWK BANK, Schenectady, N. Y. Indian in canoe going over rapids. Loading hay.	10 Female portrait. Compt's die.
Farmer ploughing with two horses, 50 Compt's die.	L Indian seated in canoe going through rapids. MOWHAWK BANK. Schenectady, N. Y. Cars.	FIFTY Old soldier reading 50
1 Secured, &c. Compt's die	Three Indians; train of cars, hill, &c., in distance. 1 MOHAWK RIVER BANK, Fonda, N. Y.	ONE and 1 Male portrait.
2 Compt's die. 2	Title of Bank. Three Indians; suspension bridge, etc. TWO Train of cars.	2 Male portrait
Compt's die. Building. 3	Three Indians; THREE cars, hills, etc., in distance. Title of Bank.	3 Male portrait
5 Male portrait	Title of Bank. Three Indians; cars, hills, etc. Secured &c.	5 Compt's die. FIVE
10 Three Indians seated, etc.	Title of Bank. Large X across the title. TEN Male portrait. DOLLARS TEN	10 Building. Compt's die.
ONE Female seated, holding figure ONE	1 Compt's die. Cupid. MOHAWK VALLEY BANK, Mohawk, N. Y.	ONE Indian with bow and spear.

Indian drawing bow. Compt's die.	2 Vig. Farmers harvesting; two seated at lunch; female holding rake, and pouring drink. 2 MOHAWK VALLEY BANK, Mohawk, N. Y.	Female portrait surrounded by cars.
Indian drawing bow. Compt's die.	3 Vig. Female portrait in frame, surmounted with eagle; antelopes, on either side. Vessel in distance. MOHAWK VALLEY BANK, Mohawk, N. Y.	3
Indian drawing bow. Compt's die.	5 Vig. Deer and Indians in canoe hunting them. MOHAWK VALLEY BANK, Mohawk, N. Y.	FIVE Full length male figure.
Indian drawing bow. Compt's die.	10 10 Two females seated; shield between them; sickle and hammer; barrels and steamship on right; train of cars and houses on left. MOHAWK VALLEY BANK, Mohawk, N. Y.	Eagle and deer. Secured, etc. Deer.
50 Compt's die. 50	50 Vig. Farmer plowing MOHAWK VALLEY BANK, Mohawk, N. Y.	50 Female portrait.
100 Compt's die. 100	Vig. Indian seated, canoe on right, deer on left, letter C. 100 MOHAWK VALLEY BANK, Mohawk, N. Y.	Reaper with sheaf of wheat and sickle. 100
1 Compt's die.	Men moulding in iron mill. MONROE CO. BANK, Rochester, N. Y. ONE	1 Factory.
TWO Compt's die. 2	Male portrait Anchor on shield; shipping, city and cars in distance. MONROE CO. BANK, Rochester, N. Y. TWO	2 View of cattle, telegraph, railroad, etc.
Compt's die. 3	Female seated by chest, shield with ship on stocks, sheep, sheaf, &c. MONROE CO. BANK, Rochester, N. Y. THREE	3 View of canal
5 Male portrait	Milkmaid seated with pail by side of shield on which is cars; sheaf, on right; cable on left. MONROE CO. BANK, Rochester, N. Y. FIVE	5 Compt's die. FIVE

X Man dressing leather.	Male portrait with female, cars, sheaf, etc. on right; female, boxes, bale, cars and steamer on left. MONROE CO. BANK, Rochester, N. Y.	10 Compt's die.
XX Bricklayers at work.	Male portrait; Justice, bridge and cars on right; manufactories on left. MONROE CO. BANK, Rochester, N. Y. Compt's die.	20 Female sewing shoes.
1 Compt's die. 1	Vig. Female seated with bucket and dog at her feet, cattle on either side. 1 MONTGOMERY CO. BANK Johnstown, N. Y. Farming implements.	Large house. 1 Church.
1 Compt's die.	Man and woman watering horses at trough. MONTGOMERY CO. BANK. Johnstown, N. Y.	1 Milkmaid, cow, calf and ducks.
2 Compt's die 2	Man and boy plowing with two horses. Title of Bank.	2 Fowls.
3 Compt's die	Vig. Farmers washing sheep. 3 MONTGOMERY CO. BANK Johnstown, N. Y. 3 Sheafs of wheat and rake. 3	Large house.
5 Compt's die.	Vig. Farmers ploughing, large V with boy running across. MONTGOMERY CO. BANK Johnstown, N. Y. 5 Large house. 5	5 Church.
V Clay.	Cattle, sheep, etc. Title of Bank.	5 Compt's die. V
X Washington.	Man and three horses at well; goats, kids, sheep, houses, etc. Title of Bank.	10 Compt's die.
10 Compt's die.	Vig. Farmers at work. 10 MONTGOMERY CO BANK Johnstown, N. Y. X	House. X Church.

50 Female seated with eagle. 50	MONTGOMERY CO. BANK Johnstown, N. Y. L Vi. Female seated and large eagle. L	50 Female, shield and anchor. 50
100 Male sculptor on his knees. 100	C Vig. Female and two males; wheel, locks, cars and houses in distance. C MONTGOMERY CO BANK, Johnstown, N. Y.	Female seated and large eagle. 100
ONE Compt's die.	MUTUAL BANK, Troy, N. Y Vig. Artisans at work	1 Male portrait.
2 Female portrait.	Compt's die. Vig. Artisans at work. MUTUAL BANK. Troy, N. Y.	2 TWO
Vig. Artisans at work. 3	3 Compt's die. MUTUAL BANK. Troy, N. Y.	3 Male portrait.
V Male portrait.	MUTUAL BANK. Troy, N. Y Compt's die. 5	5 Vig. Old man seated talking to children.
TEN Male portrait.	10 Vig. Old man seated talking to children. 10 MUTUAL BANK, Troy, N. Y TEN	X Compt's die.
XX Compt's die.	Old man seated talking to children. XX MUTUAL BANK, Troy, N. Y. XX	20 Male portrait.
ONE Compt's die.	View of Fulton Ferry, City Railroad Station, etc.; New York in distance. NASSAU BANK, of Brooklyn, N. Y.	ONE Boy and rabbits.
2 Compt's die. TWO	Two Cupids and two silver dollars; cattle, locomotive, etc., in distance. Title of Bank.	2 Female portrait.

Compt's die. 3	Launching the Adriatic. Title of Bank.	3 Franklin.
V Female.	Sailor reclining on beach; steamer and vessels in distance. Title of Bank.	5 Compt's die.
10 Girl's portrait.	Spread eagle. Title of Bank.	10 Compt's die.
20 Steamboat; Governor's Island in distance.	Title of Bank. Three females seated with compass, sickle, etc. Compt's die.	20 Ship.
50 Washington.	Title of Bank. Female reclining with shield, flag, etc.; ship in distance. Compt's die.	50 Female seated and figs. 50.
100	Spread eagle; steamer, building, etc.; in distance. Compt's die. Title of Bank.	100 Sailor and captain.
1 Compt's die. 1	Vig. Large steamboat. NEW YORK & ERIE BANK, Buffalo, N. Y.	1 Portrait of Franklin.
2 Compt's die. TWO	Vig. Female with sheaf of wheat and sickle; farm house, viaduct with train of cars passing over it in the distance. NEW YORK & ERIE BANK, Buffalo, N. Y.	2 Locomotive.
5 Compt's die. FIVE	Vig. Locomotive and train of cars passing under a bridge. NEW YORK & ERIE BANK, Buffalo, N. Y.	V Portrait of Washington.
Vig. Cattle and sheep, some lying down. TEN	Compt's die. NEW YORK & ERIE BANK, Buffalo, N. Y.	X Portrait of Webster.

20 — Portrait of Gen. Taylor. | Vig. Spread eagle, holding the American flag in its talons. NEW YORK & ERIE BANK, Buffalo, N. Y. | 20 — Compt's die.

---

1 — Compt's die. — 1 | NEW YORK STATE BANK Albany, N. Y. 1 Vig. State arms. 1 Male portrait. | ONE

---

2 — Compt's die — 2 | 2 NEW YORK STATE BANK. Albany, N. Y. Vig. Two females and eagle; female on left holding scales, on right ship in distance. Male portrait. | 2 — 2

---

3 — Compt's die. — 3 | 3 Vig. State arms 3 NEW YORK STATE BANK Albany, N. Y. Male portrait | THREE

Die Work — Compt's die — Die work | 5 Vig. State arms. 5 NEW YORK STATE BANK Albany N. Y. Secured &c. | Die Work — 5 — Die Work

---

Med. work — Compt's die. — Med. work | 10 Vig. State arms. 10 NEW YORK STATE BANK Albany, N. Y. Secured, &c. | Medallion work.

---

20 — Compt's die. — 20 | Female on either side of shield on which is [illegible] &c. 20 on right and left. N. Y. STATE BANK, Albany, N. Y. Secured &c. | XX — Canal scene, buildings, etc. — 20

---

50 — State Arms — 50 | 50 Vig. Two Females with scales &c. on right a ship in distance. 50 N. Y. STATE BANK Albany, N. Y. Secured, etc. | FIFTY

---

100 — Compt's die — 100 | 100 N. Y. STATE BANK, Albany N. Y. State Arms Male head. | 100

---

1 — ONE | Henry Clay. NIAGARA CO. B'K. Lockport, N. Y. Compt's die. | ONE

TWO 2 | NIAGARA CO. B'K. Lockport, N. Y. 2 Compt's die. Male Portrait. | 2 TWO

THREE | Compt's die. NIAGARA CO. B'K Lockport, N. Y. Stone cutters at work. | 3

FIVE | Male portrait. 5 NIAGARA CO. B'K. Lockport, N. Y. Female, sheaf, plow, &c; in distance, cars, bridge, canal lock, boat, &c. | 5 — Compt's die — FIVE

X — TEN | NIAGARA CO. B'K Lockport, N. Y. Mechanic with anvil and hammer; city in distance. X | 10 — Compt's die.

TWENTY | NIAGARA CO. BK. Lockport, N. Y. Two cherubs in clouds. Red die with figure 20 and words twenty dollars. Compt's die | 20 — Sheep.

ONE — Compt's die. — ONE | ONEIDA BANK, Utica. Vig. [illegible] scene, cows, milk maid and pail. | ONE — Canal boat and sloop. — ONE

TWO — Compt's die. — TWO | 2 [illegible] ONEIDA BANK, Utica, N. Y. | II — Canal boat and sloop.

---

3 — [illegible] die. — 3 | 3 Three females and an [illegible] guarded by a [illegible] ONEIDA BANK, Utica, N. Y. | III — Train of cars

---

5 — Compt's die. | 5 Title of Bank. 5 Female, Cupids and a figure 5. | FIVE — Female portrait — 5

---

10 — Compt's die. — 10 | X Train of cars; building with cupola. X ONEIDA BANK, Utica, N. Y. Canal Locks | 10 — Female. — 10

---

20 — Portrait of a female. — 20 | ONEIDA BANK, Utica. XX XX Vig. Reapers with sickles and sheaf of wheat. | 20 — 20

---

100 — Factory, ship, cars, etc. — 100 | ONEIDA BANK. Utica, N. Y. Male figure seated in clouds with staff, lightning, eagle and shield, C each side. | 100 — Cherub with basket of flowers. — 100

1, with letters one running across. — Vig. Cattle, man plowing | ONEIDA CENTRAL BANK, Rome, N. Y. Compt's die. | 1 — Henry Clay.

---

2 — Compt's die — 2 | ONEIDA CENTRAL BANK, Rome, N. Y. Vig. Blacksmith shop; smith shoeing horse. | 2 — 2

FIVE — Man and woman; two boys and sheep. | Vig. Two females with sword and balances; beehive, &c. ONEIDA CENTRAL BANK, Rome, N. Y. | 5 — Compt's die. — 5

TEN — Compt's die. — 10 | X Vig. Group of ten figures; ten gold dollars; steamboat in distance. ONEIDA CENTRAL BANK, Rome, N. Y. | 10 — X

---

20 — Female portrait. — Compt's die. | Vig. Female sitting; three cupids sporting on water. ONEIDA CENTRAL BANK, Rome, N. Y. | XX — 20

---

1 — With two small images on either side. — Compt's die. — ONE | ONEIDA CO. BANK. Vig. Three small figures with scythe, anvil and capstan; ship and railroad cars in the distance. Gold dollar between [illegible] | 1 — Man clasping ornamental figure 1.

---

2 — Compt's die. — TWO | ONEIDA CO. BANK. Vig. Two females with man reclining on anvil and axle, steamship and railroad cars in the distance | Large figure 2, with man wheeling sextile. — TWO

V — With word five running across. — Compt's die. — 5 | ONEIDA CO. BANK. Vig. Shield, Indian and farmer on either side; canoe, Indian lands, and railroad cars in the distance. Dog between [illegible] | FIVE — Portrait of a female.

Left	Centre	Right
10 Compt's die.	ONEIDA CO. BANK. Vig. Drover with cattle and sheep.	10 Female reclining with pen and book.
Female pointing frame, on which is mechanic, anvil and hammer; locomotive, steamship and vessel in the distance. 20	Comptroller's die. ONEIDA CO. BANK	Shepherd reclining, with dog and flock around him; cars in distance. 20 TWENTY
ONE Squaw. State Arms.	ONEIDA VALLEY BK 1 Vig. Female, eagle, safe, key, &c. Sheaf of wheat, plough, &c.	1 Female resting on figure 1, and holding ear of corn.
Indian with bow and arrows, &c. Compt's die.	ONEIDA VALLEY BK 2 Vig. Female, eagle, Cap of Liberty. Title to the right. State Arms.	2 Two females with spear, sword and scales. TWO
Indian with bow and arrows in right hand and a compass left in left.	ONEIDA VALLEY BK 3 Vig. Female, shield; staff with Cap of Liberty. Steamboat and railroad in the distance. Dog and safe.	3 Female, sword and scales.
5 Med. head FIVE	Compt's die. Shield surmounted by an eagle; man on right; female with sword and scales on left. ONEIDA VALLEY BK Oneida, N. Y. Compt's die.	5 Female with flowers and anchor.
Compt's die Female bust.	Vig. Goddess lifting drapery from an eagle. X ONEIDA VALLEY BK Safe.	Harvest scene. TEN
Compt's die Female and Neptune drawing sea horse. Ship.	20 Baropial coat of arms. ONEIDA VALLEY BK Female in sitting posture.	20
Male head.	ONONDAGA BANK Syracuse, N. Y. Vig. Cattle standing in water.	1 Compt's die
Compt's die. Plank road, cattle, &c.	Vig. Indian on rock and city in distance. ONONDAGA BANK Syracuse, N. Y. Beehive.	2 Male head.

Left	Centre	Right
3	Vig. Blacksmith shoeing horse, &c. ONONDAGA BANK Syracuse, N. Y.	3 Sea nymph in shell
Compt's die. Indian looking over a rock.	ONONDAGA BANK Syracuse, N. Y. Vig. Drover selling oxen to Farmer.	5
10 Compt's die.	ONONDAGA BANK Syracuse, N. Y. Three sea nymphs supporting Cupid in water.	10 Female head
Boy's head. Compt's die.	Vig. Horses running, prominent feature, three horses. ONONDAGA BANK Syracuse, N. Y.	50 Female head
Female head.	Vig. Capitol at Washington. ONONDAGA BANK Syracuse, N. Y.	100 Male head.
1 Compt's die.	Man and boy plowing with two horses. ORLEANS CO. B'K, Albion, N. Y.	1 Female feeding fowls.
2 Compt's die. TWO	Milkmaid milking cow; one reclining; man, ladder, dog, houses, etc. Title of Bank.	2 Girl's head.
Compt's die. 3	Man drinking, two horses, plow, boy, etc. Title of Bank	3 Male portrait
Male portrait 5	Black and white horse alarmed at lightning; cattle in distance. Title of Bank	5 Compt's die. 5
10 Girl's head.	Farmer grinding scythe; negro turning; man mowing, house and barn in distance. Title of Bank.	10 Compt's die. TEN

Left	Centre	Right
ONE Compt's die. 1	Vig. Female resting on a bale, on right females, cattle &c, on left locomotive. OSWEGATCHIE B'K Ogdensburgh, N. Y. Blacksmith.	1 Female Portrait.
2	Vig. Water scene, female and children. Compt's die. OSWEGATCHIE B'K Ogdensburgh, N. Y.	2 Female Portrait.
FIVE Compt's die. V	Vig. Female seated on right, bales of goods, steamship and ship, and on left vessels &c. in distance. OSWEGATCHIE B'K Ogdensburgh, N. Y.	5 Male Portrait.
TEN Compt's die. 10	10 Vig. Train of cars leaving depot; people. OSWEGATCHIE B'K Ogdensburgh, N. Y.	10 Male portrait. TEN
XX Compt's die. 20	Vig. Large eagle on which a female is reclining with an American flag around her. OSWEGATCHIE B'K Ogdensburgh, N. Y. Men loading hay.	20 Male portrait.
Female in clouds, small figure 1 to left. Compt's die.	OSWEGO RIVER BK. Fulton, N. Y. Indian seated by fig. 1, trees, water fall, hills, &c. in distance	1 Male portrait
TWO Compt's die. TWO	OSWEGO RIVER BK. Fulton, N. Y. Figure 2, with female on either side. Canal Lock.	2 Male portrait
5 Male portrait	OSWEGO RIVER B'K. Fulton, N. Y. Female reclining; 5 in front of her; ships in distance. 5	5 Compt's die 5
X Two girls with sheafs of grain.	Men harvesting; man seated on sheafs; farm house. OSWEGO RIVER BK. Fulton, N. Y. Beehive.	10 Male portrait Compt's die.
XX Male portrait TWENTY	Indian reclining, deer on ground at his back, stream of water, hills, &c. in distance. OSWEGO RIVER BK. Fulton, N. Y. Compt's die.	TWENTY Female erect with shield and spear. TWENTY

Left end	Centre	Right end
1 Compt's. die. 1	Vig. Three females seated, agricultural implements, beehive, sheaf of wheat, &c. 1 OTSEGO COUNTY B'K Cooperstown, N. Y. Eagle.	ONE DOLLAR
2 Compt's. die. 2	Female with scroll in each hand, on which is two dollars. 2 OTSEGO COUNTY B'K Cooperstown, N. Y.	Door in frame surmounted with eagle female on either side, with sword spear and balances. 2
3 Compt's die. 3	3 Vig. Man seated within large figure 3; spread, gun, battle axe, &c. 3 OTSEGO COUNTY B'K Cooperstown, N. Y.	3 Female with sword and balances; portrait of Washington. 3
FIVE FIVE FIVE	5 Vig. Pillar on which is the word Otsego and V, male and female on either side; implements of war, science and arts. Compt's die. OTSEGO COUNTY B'K Cooperstown, N. Y. Fish.	FIVE FIVE FIVE
X Male portrait. 10	10 Vig. Circular die on which is X surmounted with scroll on which is Otsego; male and female on either side implements of war, science and arts. Compt's die. OTSEGO COUNTY B'K Cooperstown, N. Y. Fish.	X TEN 10 TEN X
1 Compt's die	Sailor and Indian on either side of shield; ship on left. PALISADE BANK. ONE DOLLAR. Yonkers, N. Y.	1 Female and child.
2 Compt's die 2	PALISADE BANK. Canal, boat, road, cars crossing bridge, etc. TWO DOLLARS. Yonkers, N. Y.	2 Artisan leaning against machinery.
Compt's die. 3	PALISADE BANK. Three children in circular frame reading from book. THREE DOLLARS. Yonkers, N. Y.	3 Bee hives
1 Compt's die.	PERRIN BANK, Rochester, N. Y. Indians hunting buffaloes. ONE ONE	1 1
2 Compt's die. 2	Title of Bank. The word two running down and repeated six times; on left conflict between dog and bear, man with uplifted axe; on right, mower at work, house in distance. TWO TWO	2 2

Left end	Centre	Right end
5 Male portrait	Train of cars; two men at work, hills and large body of water in distance. PERRIN BANK, Rochester, N. Y. FIVE FIVE	5 Compt's die 5
1 Compt's die.	Indian seated with fig. 1 1 1 P. R. WESTFALL'S BANK, Lyons, N. Y.	ONE
2 Compt's die. 2	Liberty and Justice seated with fig. 2. Male portrait. Title of Bank.	2 2
5 Justice seated on fig 5.	5 Boy, cattle and trees. Title of Bank.	5 Compt's die. 5
10 Female portrait.	Nine cherubs, female, shield and ten gold dollars Title of Bank.	10 Compt's die.
1 with letters one running across it. Female portrait.	PULASKI BANK, Pulaski, N. Y. 1 1 One dollar in part circle Male portrait.	1 Compt's die Large figure 1 and one dollar.
2 Compt's. die. 2	Vig. Two women over wash tub; mechanic at work, machinery, &c. PULASKI BANK, Pulaski, N. Y. 2 2	2 2, with letters TWO running across. 2
3 Compt's die. THREE	PULASKI BANK, Pulaski, N. Y. Vig. Three men, one holding pole. 3 3	3 THREE 3
5 Compt's die.	PULASKI BANK, Pulaski, N. Y. Vig. Two horses; eagle mounted; figure 5 in centre; steam boat on right, cars, &c, on left. 5 5	5 5, with letters F I V E running across it. 5
X Compt's die. TEN	Vig. Woman reclining on altar; male portrait, horn of plenty, sheep, &c. PULASKI BANK, Pulaski, N. Y. X X	10 X 10

Left end	Centre	Right end
1 Train of cars, boys, telegraph wires, Washington's head quarters, &c.	QUASSIACK BANK, Newburgh, N. Y. Bust in oval. Compt's die.	1 Scene on a plank road, carriage, man on horseback, sheep, omnibus, load of hay, &c.
2 Same as on ones.	QUASSIACK BANK, Newburgh, N. Y. Bust in oval, Compt's die.	TWO Same as on ones.
5 Train of cars, boys, telegraph wires, Washington's head quarters, &c.	QUASSIACK BANK, Newburgh, N. Y. Bust in oval. Compt's die.	5 Man and merchandise on wharf, steamboat, barges, vessels, &c.
V Same as on 1s and 2s.	QUASSIACK BANK, Newburgh, N. Y. Bust in oval, Compt's die.	V Man and merchandise on wharf, steamboat, barges, vessels, &c.
X Vig. Indian with gun, behind a ledge of rocks, watching deer.	QUASSIACK BANK, Newburgh, N. Y. Compt's die.	TEN Bust in oval
XX Vig. Same as tens.	QUASSIACK BANK, Newburgh, N. Y. Compt's die.	20 Bust in oval
FIFTY DOLLARS. Two Continental soldiers, one sitting with rope in hand—the other standing and reclining on his gun.	Compt's die. Vig. Indians in a canoe, rocks, trees, and mountains. QUASSIACK BANK, Newburgh, N. Y.	50 Little girl sitting at a table, with left hand over left eye to protect it from the light.
100 Man and boy with guns.	Compt's die. Vig. Buildings, viaduct, locomotive and train of cars on right; Indians and wigwams on left. QUASSIACK BANK, Newburgh, N. Y.	100 C
1 Male portrait.	Compt's die. Vig. Milk maid seated, cattle, &c. RANDALL BANK, Cortland, N. Y.	ONE Female, sword and balances.
2 Male portrait	Vig. Three females, sword, balances, horn of plenty, &c.; vessels on right. Compt's die. RANDALL BANK, Cortland, N. Y.	2 Full length female.

5 — Male portrait — FIVE
Vig. Train of cars; group of persons; some seated; most prominent one holding gun; hat in hand extended. Compt's die.
RANDALL BANK, Cortland, N. Y.
5 — Female portrait.

Female seated, holding frame, on which is map; shipping; locomotive, steamship and vessel in distance. 1
Vig. Male portrait in frame, cupids on either side.
RENSSALAER COUNTY BANK, Lansingburgh, N. Y.
Gold dollar.
1 — Compt's die — ONE

2 — Compt's die. — TWO
RENSSALAER COUNTY BANK, Lansingburgh, N. Y
Vig. Two females holding liberty cap sword and balances; two gold dollar and eagle mounted between them; ocean on left, village on right.
2 — Portrait of Washington.

3 — Squaw seated holding bow and spear; two Indians in canoe, and wigwams in distance.
III Compt's die. III
RENSSELEAR COUNTY BANK, Lansingburgh, N. Y.
Three gold dollars. Male Portrait. Three gold dollars.
3 — Female seated, holding pen and book; cars, &c., in distance.

FIVE — Compt's die. — 5
Male portrait in frame, Cupid on either side.
RENSSELAER COUNTY BANK, Lansingburg, N. Y.
Five gold dollars lapped.
Vig. Boy seated, basket and dog beside him; flock of sheep, cars in distance. 5 FIVE

Compt's die. Light house, large X small 10 on it, two sailors, one in boat, the other standing with glass in hand.
RENSSELAER COUNTY BANK, Lansingburgh, N. Y.
Vig. Drover on horseback; drove cattle and sheep.
TEN — Male portrait. — 10

20 — Compt's die.
RENSSELEAR COUNTY BANK, Lansingburgh, N. Y.
Vig. Two females reclining, with liberty cap, sword and balances; sun rise, eagle and vessel in distance.
20 — Male portrait.

Male figure resting on horn of plenty. FIFTY
RENSSELAER COUNTY BANK, Lansingburgh, N. Y.
50 Male portrait 50
Compt's die.
Female soaring in the clouds, right arm extended over title of Bank; sickle in one hand, sheaf of wheat in the other. FIFTY

Male portrait — 100
RENSSELEAR COUNTY BANK, Lansingburgh, N. Y.
Vig. Mechanic reclining on anvil and safe, rule in one hand, hammer in the other, square, tongs, &c., beside him; two females: steamship on right, cars on left.
100 — Compt's die

Figure 1 with ink running across it. — Washington.
Vig. Female seated, farmers loading hay in background.
ROCHESTER BANK, Rochester, N. Y.
1 — Compt's die

2 — Goddess of liberty.
Vig. Dog and safe. Compt's die.
ROCHESTER BANK, Rochester, N. Y.
2 — Female seated.

3 — Compt's die.
Vig. Female seated on safe, with dog and child. Portrait of female.
ROCHESTER BANK, Rochester, N. Y.
THREE — Female reaper.

5 — Compt's die. — 5
Washington Jefferson
Vig. Female with sheaf of wheat.
ROCHESTER BANK, Rochester, N. Y.
5 — Locomotive. — 5

X — Compt's die.
Vig. Male portrait, with female on each side.
ROCHESTER BANK, Rochester, N. Y.
Eagle.
TEN — Male portrait — TEN

20 — Compt's die.
Vig. Male portrait, with female on left, with liberty pole; two females on right.
ROCHESTER BANK, Rochester, N. Y.
Locomotive.
20 — Portrait of Fillmore.

1 — Compt's die. — ONE
Vig. Female seated, clasping large figure one. 1
ROCHESTER CITY BANK, Rochester, N. Y.
ONE — Full length squaw, holding bow and spear.

2 — Compt's die. — TWO
Vig. Mechanic seated, with tools around him; cars and steam factory in distance.
ROCHESTER CITY BANK, Rochester, N. Y.
2 — Two females with sword, balances, &c.

3 — Compt's die — THREE
Vig. Farmer; team of horses and plow; steam boat in distance.
ROCHESTER CITY BANK, Rochester, N. Y.
3 — Female seated.

5 — Compt's die. — FIVE
Vig. Female reclining on bale of goods; shipping in distance on right; canal locks and boat on left; cars, &c.
ROCHESTER CITY BANK, Rochester, N. Y.
5 — Male portrait.

10 — Compt's die. — TEN
Vig. Female seated, holding horn of plenty, &c.; steam ship and shipping on right; canal boat, town on left.
ROCHESTER CITY BANK, Rochester, N. Y.
10 — Male portrait

Compt's die. — Man seated, holding a [illegible] and bag of coin. — 20
20 Washington.
ROCHESTER CITY BANK, Rochester, N. Y.
Columns.
XX — Female portrait.

50 — Compt's die. — 50
Vig. Eagle on limb of tree, railroad cars, canal boats, &c.
ROCHESTER CITY BANK, Rochester, N. Y.
Columns.
50 — Male portrait — FIFTY

Compt's die. — Female seated.
ROCHESTER CITY BANK, Rochester, N. Y.
100 Vig. Female holding liberty cap and pole; spread eagles, C between them.
Columns.
100 — Benjamin Franklin.

Female, wheel, and urn. — State Register's seal.
1 Child's head. 1
ROCHESTER EXCHANGE B'K, Rochester, N. Y.
1 on ONE. — Justice resting on pillar.

2 on TWO. — State Register's seal. — 2 on TWO.
ROCHESTER EXCHANGE B'K, Rochester, N. Y.
2 Old man, child, bust of Washington on table. 2
2 — Canal, horses, boats, &c.

ROCHESTER — Two females. — FIVE
V Merchant, bales, boxes, barrels &c. Boy with newspapers.
EXCHANGE BANK, Rochester, N. Y.
5 — State Register's seal. — FIVE

Cars, canal horses, men, boats, &c — 10
ROCHESTER 10
EXCHANGE BANK, Rochester, N. Y.
10 — State Register's seal.

20 — Dog on safe.
ROCHESTER
XX State Register's seal. XX
EXCHANGE BANK, Rochester, N. Y.
20 — Female resting on pillar, torch in hand, &c.

1 — Compt's die.
ROCKLAND CO. B'K, Nyack, N. Y.
Green die with ONE on it.
1
1 — Eagle.

Two on 2 — Compt's die — Two on 2
Steamboat "Armenia."
ROCKLAND CO. B'K Nyack, N. Y.
2 TWO 2
Two on 2 — Female head.

Compt's die 3 | ROCKLAND CO. B'K Nyack, N. Y. Steamboat "Armenia." 3 THREE 3 | 3 Female head.

FIVE Washington. | 5 Female, cows, sheep, etc. Title of Bank. FI 5 VE | 5 Compt's die. 5

10 Machinist at work. | Title of Bank. X Female pouring water in trough; sheep drinking. X | 10 Train of cars. Compt's die.

1 1 | ROME EXCHANGE BANK. Vig. Locomotive with train of cars. 1 | ONE Female with sheaf, and mechanic. Compt's die.

2 Compt's die. | Vig. Watering horses. 2 ROME EXCHANGE BANK. | 2 Female gleaner.

5 Compt's die. | Milking scene 5 5 ROME EXCHANGE BANK. | FIVE Female with scales and sword.

10 Compt's die. | Vig. Falls of Niagara in the distance; female figure in foreground. X ROME EXCHANGE BANK. | 10 Head of Washington.

20 Compt's die. | ROME EXCHANGE BANK. XX Reaping scene. | 20 Female head.

A female seated, resting her elbow on the head of a barrel. 1 | State Arms. Vig. Load of salt barrels drawn by two horses; man on top of load. SALT SPRINGS BK. Syracuse. | ONE Portrait. 1

2 Cupid sitting on a large ball. TWO | State Arms. Vig. Indians boiling salt, and white man sitting on a log learning the trade. Scene near the shore of a lake, canoe close by. SALT SPRINGS BK. Syracuse. | 2 Portrait.

A large figure 5 in the background, an arched bridge over a river, and in front two Indians and guns. | State Arms. Vig. Large coat of arms of this State, which is a little inclined to right of the centre of the bill. SALT SPRINGS BK. Syracuse. | FI 5 VE Portrait. FIVE

TEN Portrait. TEN | State Arms. 10 10 SALT SPRINGS BK. Syracuse. | Man boiling salt, &c. 10

TWENTY Portrait. 20 | State Arms. 20 20 SALT SPRINGS BK. Syracuse. | TWENTY Salt-house. 20

ONE DOLLAR | SARATOGA CO. BK. Vig. Oxen, plough, man, &c. 1 ONE 1 Female sitting, shield. | 1 Compt's die. 1

2 Compt's die 2 | 2 Harvest scene; reaper; farming utensils and beehive. 2 SARATOGA CO. BK., Waterford, N. Y. TWO | TWO DOLLARS

3 Compt's die. 3 | Vig. Sheaf, two youths, steamboat, vessels, &c. SARATOGA CO. BK. Portrait. | THREE

5 Compt's die. FIVE | SARATOGA CO. BK. Portrait. Vig. Eagle drinking; female with pitcher; urns. Fire engine. | 5 Figure of Justice.

10 Compt's die. 10 | 10 Cattle, sheep, &c. 10 SARATOGA COUNTY BANK, Waterford, N. Y. Cornucopia, &c. | X Med head. X

10 Compt's die. | SARATOGA CO. BK. Portrait. Vig. Head of Washington, female with liberty cap and wreath in hand; eagle and shield. Fire engine. | 10

50 Compt's die. 50 | SARATOGA CO. BK. Vig. Two females. 50 Small die. | 50 Likeness. 50

1 Compt's die. | SAUGERTIES BANK, Saugerties, N. Y. Scene in a stone quarry. | 1 Female portrait.

2 Compt's die. 2 | Two cows; female milking cow; cornfield, house, man and dog in distance. Title of Bank. | 2 Female portrait.

Two men plowing with two horses. FIVE | Milkmaid; cows in distance. Title of Bank. | 5 Compt's die. FIVE

Large X, female each side. | 10 Scene in a rolling mill. XX Title of Bank. | 10 Train of cars. Compt's die.

Female | Eagle. Female, column, steamer, etc. Compt's die. | 20 20

1 Compt's die. 1 | 1 Vig. Indian drawing his bow. 1 SCHENECTADY B'K Schenectady, N. Y. | ONE Houses &c. ONE

Compt's die. 2 | 2 Vig. train of cars. 2 SCHENECTADY B'K Schenectady, N. Y. Canal locks. | Indian drawing his bow 2

5 Compt's die. 5 | Vig. Indian drawing his bow. 5 SCHENECTADY B'K Schenectady, N. Y. | FIVE Indian drawing his bow

X Compt's die. 10 | Vig. Indian drawing his bow. X SCHENECTADY B'K Schenectady, N. Y. Canal locks. | Houses &c. 10 Train of cars.

20 Female with torch, eagle and medallion head of Washington. 20 | SCHENECTADY B'K Schenectady, N. Y. XX XX Vig. Indian with bow and arrow. | 20 Female with torch, eagle and medallion head of Washington. 20

Left	Centre	Right
50 Buildings 50	Vig. Female with urn, and medallion head of Washington. L L SCHENECTADY B'K Schenectady, N. Y. Eagle.	Indian with bow and arrow. 50
100	Vig. Indian with bow and arrow. 100 SCHENECTADY B'K Schenectady, N. Y. Eagle.	N. Y. Safety Fund. Female with torch, eagle and medallion head of Washington. 100
Female seated, wheat and balances. Compt's die.	1 Vig. Farmers sitting at lunch; female children and dog; team of horses. SCHOHARIE CO. BK. Schoharie, N.Y. 1	ONE Female holding rake.
Indian with bow and arrows. Compt's die.	2 Vig. Gathering corn; church and cars in back ground. SCHOHARIE CO. BK. Schoharie, N.Y. Building.	2 Female portrait. TWO
FIVE FIVE Compt's die.	Vig. Cattle, &c. SCHOHARIE CO. BK. Schoharie, N.Y. Building.	5 5, Two figures around a tel balances, &c.
Vig. Spread Eagle,—Eagle on either side. TEN	Male Portrait SCHOHARIE CO. BK. Schoharie, N.Y. Dog.	X Compt's die.
1 Compt's die. ONE	Mechanic seated with sledge and e, &c.; cars and factories in distance. SENECA CO. BANK, Waterloo, N. Y. Female bathing.	1 Justice.
1 Compt's die. 1	One Dollar One twice. 1 Spread eagle. 1 SENECA CO. BANK, Waterloo, N. Y. Steamboat. One Dollar four times.	1 Franklin. ONE
1 Two females sitting, with eagle and balances between. 1	SENECA CO. BANK. Vig. Locomotive and train of cars. Machine.	Shield with large figure 1 on it. Medallion head. ONE
2 Two females sitting, eagle and balances between. TWO	Vig. Farmer ploughing with team of horses 2 SENECA CO BANK	Female with Liberty Cap.

Left	Centre	Right
2 Compt's die. 2	Two Dollars. Two Dollars. 2 Female either side of fig. 2 on shield; words "speed the plow" at bottom; vessel in distance. 2 Title of Bank. Canal scene. Two Dollars. Two Dollars.	Male figure erect. TWO
3 Two females sitting; eagle and balances between. 3	SENECA CO. BANK. 3 Female reclining on monument; bunch of grain in hand; vessel in distance 3 Canoe.	3 3
3 Compt's die. 3	Title of Bank. 3 Female erect beside monument; sheep, hills, etc., in background. 3 Indian in canoe.	3 Lafayette 3
5 Two females sitting, eagle and balances between.	Sheaf of wheat, sickle, basket and child. Child in sail vessel, an angel above. SENECA CO. BANK.	5 Medallion head.
5 Compt's die. 5	5 Female, sheaf, cattle and plow. 5 SENECA CO. BANK. Waterloo, N. Y. Female.	Upright figure. FIVE
10 Two females sitting, &c. 10	10 Vig. Man reclining; left arm on vessel containing fluid, which is running out. SENECA CO. BANK. Eagle.	10
20 Two females sitting, &c. 20	SENECA CO. BANK. XX Indian full length. XX	Gentleman with hat and cane in hand.
FIFTY	SENECA CO. BANK. 50 Indian full length. Two females sitting, eagle and balances.	FIFTY
Indian.	100 C Two females sitting, eagle, balances, &c. SENECA CO. BANK.	C 100
One on 1 Compt's die.	SETAUKET BANK. Setauket, N. Y. Female pouring water into trough, from which sheep are drinking	1 Sailor, anchor, steamer, &c.

Left	Centre	Right
Two on 2 Compt's die Two on 2	Title of Bank. Sailor, farmer, boy, dog, capstan, anchor, boats, etc.	2 Female at work with sewing machine.
5 Ship carpenter.	Title of Bank. Boy and girl; boy cutting stick; girl reclining; cattle.	5 Compt's die 5
Farmer erect in field leaning on scythe; small village in distance. Compt's die.	Farmers loading cart with grain; two horses in front. SMITH'S BANK OF PERRY, N. Y. Secured, &c.	1 ONE
2 Compt's die. 2	Barn-yard scene—female seated on stool another erect; fowls, cows, haystacks, &c. SMITH'S BANK OF PERRY, N. Y. Secured, &c.	2 Boy and rabbits.
5 Little girl and fowls.	SMITH'S BANK OF PERRY N. Y. 5 Male portrait. 5 Secured, &c.	Large 5 and word five on either side. Compt's die. FIVE
10 Male portrait	X Female portrait. X SMITH'S BANK OF PERRY, N. Y. Secured &c.	10 Compt's die.
ONE Compt's die.	SPRAKER BANK, Montgomery Co., N.Y. 1 Vig. Man and boy at work; horse and sled. 1	1 Portrait of Gen. Cass.
2 Indian; small vessel in distance. TWO	SPRAKER BANK, Montgomery Co., N.Y. 2 2 Compt's die.	2 Waterfall; hunter on his knees drinking.
3 Compt's die.	Vig. Two females; cars on right, vessels on left. SPRAKER BANK, Montgomery Co., N.Y. Large red 3 lengthwise.	THREE Portrait of Webster.
Hunter warming himself at fire; dog and gun.	V Compt's die. SPRAKER BANK, Montgomery Co., N.Y. Large figure 5 lengthwise of note.	5 Male portrait.

TEN Male Portrait.	Vig. Spread eagle with U. S. flag in talons. SPRAKER BANK. Montgomery Co., N. Y.	X Compt's die. TEN
1 Female leaning on pedestal with tablet in hand.	Vig. Milk maid and cows; farm house in distance. STATE BANK, Troy. Grain and farming implements.	1 Compt's die.
Portrait of female. TWO 2	Vig. Iron works with forges and workmen. STATE BANK Troy. Steamboat.	2 Compt's die.
3 Team at work	Vig. Cattle standing in water. Sheep grazing. STATE BANK Troy. Eagle.	3 Compt's die.
5 Female sitting on anvil; mechanical tools, &c.	Vig. Shield, female on either side with liberty cap and balances, ship and steamboat in distance. STATE BANK Troy. Farming implements.	5 Compt's die.
Female with sickle. 10	10 Vig. Female 10 reclining on bale of goods, barrels, &c., houses and ship in distance. STATE BANK Troy. Eagle.	Female sitting on bale of goods. Compt's die.
50 FIFTY 50	STATE BANK. OF TROY, N. Y. Female portrait; on right female, column, steamer; on left, female, cow, calf, etc. Compt's die.	50 DOLLARS 50
ONE Compt's die ONE	Vig. Farmer and Indian on either side of a shield. STATE OF NEW YORK BANK, Kingston, N. Y. Gold dollar.	1 Man dressing leather.
Compt's die 2	State Arms. STATE OF NEW YORK BANK, Kingston, N. Y. Schooner.	2 Stone cutter at work.
3 Portrait of Dewitt Clinton.	STATE OF NEW YORK BANK, Kingston, N. Y. Vig. Railroad, women, ploughman, ship and steamboat in the distance.	3 Compt's die

V Compt's die.	Vig. Kingston Academy, with wagon loaded with flagstone, between, and driver. STATE OF NEW-YORK BANK, Kingston, N. Y. Clasped hands.	FIVE 5 Shakspeare.
Figure 10 with cupids on either side. View of Washington Irving's residence.	STATE OF NEW YORK BANK, Kingston, N. Y.	[illegible] Compt's die.
50 Washington.	STATE OF NEW YORK BANK, Kingston, N. Y. Indian reclining with dead deer. Compt's die.	50 Ceres.
ONE Girl leaning on bundle of grain. Compt's die.	Farm scene. 1 ONE on 1 STEUBEN COUNTY BANK. ONE ONE 1 ONE DOLLAR Bath, N. Y.	ONE Full length figure of General Steuben. ONE
ONE Compt's die. ONE	1 Vig. Female, eagle, shield, liberty cap and pole, cornucopia &c. 1 STEUBEN CO. BANK. Bath, N. Y. Cornucopia, anchor &c.	Full length portrait of an officer. ONE
TWO on 2 Compt's die TWO on 2	2 Female reclining; quadrant, globe, map, books, &c. STEUBEN COUNTY BANK. Two Dollars. Bath, N. Y.	Full length figure of General Steuben. New York.
TWO Compt's die. TWO	2 Vig. Female seated on bale, train of cars, sheaf, grain &c.; factory in distance. 2 STEUBEN CO. BANK. Bath, N. Y. Agricultural implements	Same as one's. TWO
3 Compt's die. 3	3 Vig. Farmer at lunch. 3 STEUBEN CO. BANK, Bath, N. Y. Agricultural implements	Same as one's. THREE
V Full length figure of General Steuben.	STEUBEN COUNTY BANK. FIVE on 5 Male portrait DOLLARS on 5 Five Dollars	5 Compt's die 5
V Compt's die. V	5 Vig. Large ornamental 5, female on either side, cupids &c. 5 STEUBEN CO. BANK, Bath, N. Y. Dog and safe.	Same as one's. FIVE

10 Male portrait.	STEUBEN COUNTY BANK. TEN DOLLARS Full length figure of General Steuben. TEN DOLLARS	10 Compt's die
10 Compt's die. 10	Vig. Female portrait in frame, surrounded by banners, drum, cannon &c. 10 STEUBEN CO. BANK, Bath, N. Y. Agricultural implements and wheat.	Same as one's. TEN
Full length figure of General Steuben. XX	20 Compt's die 20 STEUBEN COUNTY BANK. Twenty Dollars TWENTY.	XX Male portrait
20 Compt's die. 20	20 Vig. Spread eagle on bale and sheaf, cask, anchor, falls and train of cars in distance. 20 STEUBEN CO. BANK, Bath, N. Y. Agricultural implements and wheat.	Same as one's. TWENTY
50 Female seated on keg and shield. 50	STEUBEN CO. BANK, Bath, N. Y. Vig. Horse. 50	Full length portrait of a military officer.
Red 1. Compt's die.	Man and boy plowing with two horses. Female portrait. STISSING BANK, Pine Plains, N. Y.	Red 1. Indian with gun.
2 Compt's die. TWO	Title of Bank. Portrait of boy. Males, horse, colt, cart, etc., in corn field.	Red 2. Indian [illegible]
Red 5. Female seated in fig. 5.	Girl's portrait. Man with bag, horse, colt, falls, etc.; boys on bridge. Title of Bank.	Red 5. Compt's die. FIVE
Red X. Two females either side of X with cupid under side.	Cow and calf in stream; sheep, house, etc., in distance. Title of Bank. TEN	10 Compt's die.
* 20, XX and County.	Two winged females, figure 20 and two cupids. Girl's portrait. Title of Bank. Compt's TWENTY die. DOLLARS	Red 20. Fowls.

50 Boy's head.	STISSING BANK, Pine Plains, N. Y. Red die with 50 on it. Compt's die.	50 Two children
Goddess of Liberty. Compt's die.	1 Whaling scene; two ships, whale and whale boat. SUFFOLK CO. BANK Sag Harbor, N. Y.	ONE Bust of female. ONE
TWO Compt's die. TWO	Vig. Two females, box, barrel, sheaf of wheat; on left female with sickle 2 in hand, and ship in distance. SUFFOLK CO. BANK Sag Harbor, N. Y.	2 Medallion head of female. 2
3 Compt's die.	Large figure 3 with Eagle. Female on right and female in clouds on left. SUFFOLK CO. BANK Sag Harbor, N. Y.	
FIVE Compt's die.	Ship under sail. 5 Vig. Three females sitting; box; compass and sheaf of wheat; the female on left is pointing to ship. SUFFOLK Co. BANK Sag Harbor, N. Y.	FIVE Medallion head. FIVE
10 Compt's die.	Vig. Steamboat; ship under full sail leaving port, ship in distance. 10 SUFFOLK Co. BANK Sag Harbor, N. Y.	Full length female.
TWENTY Compt's die.	20 Female, sitting; ship in distance at left of female. Eagle and shield. SUFFOLK Co. BANK Sag Harbor, N. Y.	20
Figure 1 with word one running across. Train of cars.	Vig. Indian seated with bow; hut, plow, sheaf of wheat, &c. on left. SUSQUEHANNA VALLEY BANK, Binghampton, N. Y.	Same as on left. Compt's die.
Female with flowers; birds flying on left. 2	Compt's die. Vig. Shield with word Excelsior, on right of which is a female, three children, globe, &c.; on left Indian, squaw and child. Title of Bank.	2
5 Indian head.	Title of Bank. Compt's die. Vig. Two females seated on right of a shield, on which is agricultural implements; on right public building, on left train of cars.	Figure 5, a V, and word Five. Female with arm resting on pail.

Head of Webster. 10	Vig. Female seated with sickle, sheaf of wheat, plow &c., train of cars and canal lock in distance. Bridge, canal boat, horse, village and spire in the distance. Title of Bank.	Figure 10, a letter X and word Ten. Compt's die.
BROOME COUNTY Goddess of liberty, eagle, shield, liberty pole and cap.	TWENTY DOLLARS Compt's die. Three females, one with wings, represented as soaring, the others in the act of receiving gift from her. Title of Bank.	20 STATE OF N. Y.
Compt's die. Load of hay, &c. ONE	Vig. Female resting on sheaf of wheat, and on left a farming scene. fig. 1 on left. SYRACUSE CITY B'K Syracuse, N. Y. Dog's head.	ONE Female standing erect, and fig. 1.
Compt's die. Indian standing erect.	2 Vig. Indians and white men holding a council. SYRACUSE CITY B'K Syracuse, N. Y. Deer.	2 Indian female and pappoose. TWO
Female seated on rock. Compt's die.	5 Vig. Water scene water gods &c. SYRACUSE CITY B'K Syracuse, N. Y. Train of cars.	5 Female standing erect.
Compt's die. Indian with bow and spear in right hand.	TEN Vig. Deer and water scene. SYRACUSE CITY B'K Syracuse, N. Y. A Buffalo.	10 Female standing holding an ear of corn. X
1 Compt's die. 1	1 Vig. Male and female, most prominent figures group in rear, also train of cars. TANNERS BANK Catskill, N. Y. Cars.	1 Cattle. 1
2 Compt's die. 2	Vig. same as ones. 2 TANNERS BANK Catskill, N. Y.	TWO
FIVE	5 Vig. same as ones and twos 5 TANNERS BANK Catskill, N. Y. Steamboat.	5 Compt's die. 5
10 Female, liberty pole and cap. 10	Vig. frame with vessel surmounted with eagle, female on either side, cars on right, shipping on left. 10 TANNERS BANK Catskill, N. Y. Steamboat.	10 Compt's die. 10

1 Compt's die. Female portrait.	Female with spear, bales on left; quadrant, urn, pallet, etc., on right. TOMPKINS CO. BK Ithaca, N. Y.	ONE Female 1 ONE
2 Compt's die 2	Vig. Female reclining liberty cap and safe. TOMPKINS CO. B'K Ithica, N. Y.	TWO Large figure 2 and female standing. TWO
Female sitting on shield 5	Vig. Large figure 5, with five at top, female at each side. TOMPKINS CO., B'K Ithica, N. Y.	5 Compt's die
10 Female in air with vase in left hand; ships in distance. TEN	Female portrait X Female portrait TOMPKINS, CO., B'K Ithica, N. Y. Bee Hive.	10 Compt's die
20 Medallion head. 20	20 on med. head. Vig. Female, shield and sheaf of wheat; ship in distance. 20 on med. head. TOMPKINS CO. BK. Ithica, N. Y. B	20 Medallion head. 20
100 Medallion head and figures, 100. C	Medallion head and fig. 100 Vig. Eagle standing on a log; on the left a steamboat. Medallion head and fig. 100. TOMPKINS CO. B'K Ithica, N. Y. Letter A.	100 Medallion head and figure, 100. C
1 Compt's die.	Female pouring water in to trough from which sheep are drinking. TRADERS' BANK, Rochester, N. Y.	1 Two children
2 Compt's die. TWO	Indian female, eagle, shield, ship, steamer in distance. Title of Bank.	2 Six figure 2s on small die.
FIVE Female with pen and tablets; child at her feet.	Man buying paper of newsboy; hogsheads, cars, steamer, etc. Title of Bank.	5 Compt's die. 5
10 Man and dog; farm and mill on right.	Female seated pointing to factory, pedestrians, train, etc. Title of Bank.	10 Compt's die.

1 Compt's die. 1 | 1 Vig. Two females one seated and other erect holding a sheaf of wheat figure 1, in centre, on right plough, rake &c. 1 TROY CITY BANK Troy, N. Y. Steamboat. | 1 Male portrait. ONE

2 Compt's die. 2 | TROY CITY BANK Troy, N. Y. 2 Vig. Female standing erect and Indian seated holding a gun in left hand Vessel. | TWO 2

3 Compt's die. 3 | 3 Vig. Large steamboat under way. 3 TROY CITY BANK Troy, N. Y. Female reclining. | THREE Female standing erect with scales in right hand. 3

5 Compt's die 5 | V Vig. Female seated holding scales in left hand, on right ships barrels and male at work. V TROY CITY BANK Troy, N. Y. Steamboat. | 5 Female seated with grain in left hand V

5 Portrait of Washington. | Large letter V with female seated within. 5 TROY CITY B'K Troy, N. Y. | Compt's die. Female

5 Male portrait. | Vig. Large eagle resting on tree; falls in back-ground. TROY CITY BANK Troy, N. Y. Horse | Compt's die. 5

X Male portrait. 10 | X Vig. Female seated with key in left hand X TROY CITY BANK Troy, N. Y. Steamboat. | TEN Two females one on right holding a sheaf of wheat on left a rake. 10

10 Male portrait. | Vig. Large eagle and shield on right a vessel under sail, on left a vessel. TROY CITY BANK Troy, N. Y. Farm implements. | Compt's die TEN X

TWENTY Female with trumpet and staff. 20 | Vig. Two female and two children supporting the figures 20. TROY CITY BANK. Troy, N. Y. Eagle. | 20 Female. Compt's die.

50 Female with wand, reclining 50 | TROY CITY BANK, Troy, N. Y. L Spread eagle on rock. L FIFTY DOLLARS. Steamboat. | 50 Female holding scales seated 50

100 Female seated, with eagle and olive branch. 100 | Female seated, pouring liquid into urn, eagle on left. 100 100 TROY CITY BANK. Troy, N. Y. ONE HUNDRED DOLLARS. Steamboat. | 100 Female seated, with grain and sickle 100

1 Compt's die. 1 | 1 Vig. Two females hands clasped, harvest field on left, cars on right in distance. 1 ULSTER COUNTY BK Kingston, N. Y. Female reclining. | 1 Horse. 1

2 Compt's die. 2 | ULSTER COUNTY BK Kingston, N. Y. Vig. Three children with hammer, lever, and wedge, mill stone across &c. steamboat in distance. 2 Steamboat. | TWO Male Portrait TWO

3 Compt's die. 3 | Vig. Female in skiff. 3 ULSTER COUNTY BK Kingston, N. Y. Steamboat. | Man seated within large ornamental figure 3. 3

5 Compt's die. 5 | 5 Vig. Female in square frame with balance; on left ship in full sail on right. ULSTER COUNTY BK Kingston, N. Y. Engine. | FIVE

10 Compt's die. 10 | ULSTER COUNTY BK Kingston, N. Y. 10 Vig. Female in square frame with spear, implements of agriculture, grain, beehive, horn of plenty on each side. Male portrait. | 10

20 Compt's die. 20 | 20 Female on either side of shield on which is 20; ship in distance. ULSTER CO. BANK. Kingston, N. Y. Do. | TWENTY

50 Compt's die. 50 | 50 Vig. Knight on horseback. 50 ULSTER COUNTY BK Kingston, N. Y. | New York Safety Fund

1 ONE Compt's Die. | Vig. Wild Horses. UNADILLA BANK, Unadilla, N. Y. | 1 Child and rabbits.

ONE Compt's die. ONE | 1 Vig. Female in the air and figure 1. 1 UNADILLA BANK. Unadilla, N. Y. Secured, &c. | 1 Female seated, resting on shield 1

2 | Drover and Cattle. Compt's Die. UNADILLA BANK. Unadilla, N. Y. | 2 Female Portrait.

TWO Compt's die. TWO | 2 Vig. Two females seated, on right plough and sheaf of wheat, on left ships in distance. 2 UNADILLA BANK. Unadilla, N. Y. Secured, &c. | 2 Man with an axe in right hand, [illegible] &c. in distance.

5 | Two men; one a stone cutting; masons at work in background. UNADILLA BANK, Unadilla, N. Y. | 5 FIVE Compt's Die.

5 Compt's die. 5 | 5 Vig. Female seated, in right hand a sickle, sheafs of wheat and house on right, on left cars. 5 UNADILLA BANK. Unadilla, N. Y. | 5 Female portrait in left hand a sickle. V

Female gathering wheat. 10 | UNADILLA BANK, Unadilla, N. Y. Words ten dollars and figure 10. | TEN Female with cornucopia. Compt's die.

20 Two females with sheaf &c. | UNADILLA BANK, Unadilla, N. Y. TWENTY DOLLARS. Compt's die. | XX Milkmaid with tub.

ONE 1 Compt's die. | Vig. Building, load of hay, &c. UNION BANK, Albany, N. Y. Canal boat | ONE 1 Male portrait.

TWO 2 Compt's die. | Vig. Buildings, street, &c. UNION BANK, Albany, N. Y. Drover. | 2 Male portrait.

FIVE 5 Compt's die. | Vig. Male portrait, with locomotive on left factory on right UNION BANK, Albany, N. Y. Secured, etc | FIVE 5 Portrait of Washington.

TEN Male portrait. 10 | UNION BANK, Albany, N. Y. X Vig. Cupid with wheat. X | Large X with the word "ten" running across it and 10. Compt's die. 10

TWENTY Male portrait. 20	20 Vig. Female with shield, American eagle, &c. UNION BANK, Albany, N. Y. Secured, etc.	XX Compt's die. XX
Compt's die. Figure 1 and the words one dollar.	One Vig. Female sitting with pail on her lap, cows, &c. UNION BANK Kinderhook, N. Y.	1 Bust of female with sheaf of grain; man [illegible]
2 2	Vig. Female reclining, factories in an oval frame, sheep, grain, &c. Compt's die. UNION BANK, Kinderhook, N. Y.	2 Two females one standing and the other kneeling.
3 Compt's die	UNION BANK, Kinderhook, N. Y. 3 3 Vig. Eagle on branch of a tree, cars, &c., in the distance.	The word "Three" with the figure 3 running across. Female walking with pail.
5 Compt's die.	UNION BANK, Kinderhook, N. Y. V Vig. Three females sitting, the middle one a little above the others, one with a quadrant, another with a pair of compasses and the middle one with sickle. V	5 Man driving cattle; trees, bridge, telegraph poles, &c.
Female standing and resting on her left elbow. TEN	UNION BANK Kinderhook, N. Y. Compt's die. Three females seated, one of whom is reclining, and a pair of compasses in her hand.	10
XX Man talking to a boy who is sitting on the ground.	UNION BANK Kinderhook, N. Y. Compt's die.	20 Mechanic sitting with hammer in right hand; factories &c.
1 Compt's die	Canal boat nearing lock, cars passing over bridge, etc. UNION BANK, Medina, N. Y.	1 Female portrait.
2 Compt's die 2	Man with two horses; canal, farmhouse, &c. in distance. UNION BANK. Medina, N. Y.	2 Male portrait.
5 FIVE 5	Statue of the Goddess of Liberty; wreath, shield, etc. UNION BK. Five Dollars & green X extending nearly across bill.	5 Compt's die 5

ONE Compt's die. 1	Vig. Boy ploughing, steamboat on left; Farm house on right. UNION BANK Monticello, N. Y.	1 Man dressing leather.
2 Compt's die. TWO	Vig. Cattle and sheep, farm house in distance. UNION BANK Monticello, N. Y.	2 Blacksmith at work.
3 Compt's die.	Vig. Saw-mill and men at work. UNION BANK OF MONTICELLO, N. Y. Secured, &c.	3 Female with sheaf of wheat.
Large ornamental 5 car, &c. Compt's die.	Vig. Sailor and female seated. UNION BANK Monticello, N. Y.	5 Man carrying basket of corn.
X Compt's die. X	Vig. Two females, sword balances &c. eagle on left. UNION BANK Monticello, N. Y.	10 Cars. 10
20 Compt's die. 20	20 Vig. Public buildings &c. man on horseback and one on foot. UNION BANK Monticello, N. Y.	Female with sword and balances. Locomotive. TWENTY
Female standing resting on shield. Compt's die.	1 Vig. Female seated shield &c. figure 1, and falls on left. UNION BANK OF ROCHESTER, N. Y.	1 Eagle and shield. ONE
2 Male and female figures and steamship	Compt's die. Vig. figure 2 on die, each side a female and the one on right holding scales, and one on left a spear. UNION BANK OF ROCHESTER.	2 Two females standing erect.
5 Group of males and females, and large V.	Compt's die. Vig. figure 5, five females one in centre holding scales, on right large house and locomotive, steam ship and vessels. UNION BANK OF ROCHESTER, N. Y.	5 Portrait of Washington. FIVE
10 Compt's die. 10	Vig. Two females liberty cap and eagle in centre, on right cars and steamship [illegible] on left a man ploughing; ship and mill in distance. UNION BANK OF ROCHESTER N. Y. Wheels and bale of goods	10 Male portrait. TEN

20 Compt's die. XX	Vig. Female with spear in centre, fort vessels and steamboat in distance, on right cupid. UNION BANK OF ROCHESTER, N. Y. Sheaf of wheat rake plough and shovel.	20 Female eagle and money.
FIFTY Female standing erect with looking glass in right hand.	Vig. Female reclining, large eagle and globe; on left steamships and ship in distance. UNION BANK OF ROCHESTER, N. Y. Shield.	50 Compt's die.
100 Female resting on anchor.	UNION BANK OF ROCHESTER, N. Y. Vig. Two females seated, eagle and shield in centre; cars and steamboat in distance. Shield.	100 Compt's die.
Merchandise Compt's die. Train of cars	1 Female with horn of plenty; bundle of sheafs at her feet. UNION BANK, Troy, N. Y. Wheels, bale, etc.	One on 1. Female with fig. 1.
ONE Compt's die.	UNION BANK OF TROY, N. Y. View of large building, street, etc.	1 ONE 1
2 Compt's die. 2	Title of Bank. Vig. Same as above ones.	2 Male portrait.
Female standing. Compt's die.	Vig. Farmer with basket of corn. 2 on left. UNION BANK, Troy. Barrels and boxes between signatures.	2 Drove of cattle. TWO
THREE Female surrounded by circle with names of the different States inscribed thereon. Compt's die	Vig. Locomotive and cars; depot in distance. fig. 3 on left UNION BANK, Troy. Steamboat between signatures	THREE Figure three with blacksmith, sailor and farmer. THREE
5 FIVE Compt's die.	Vig. Figures of females, one holding wreath over head of Washington. UNION BANK, Troy. Wheels, bale, etc.	FIVE 5 surrounded by [illegible].
10 Two male and female figures, lower extremities like a fish. Steamer	Compt's die. Vig. Eagle on branch; canal lock on right, and railroad cars on left. UNION BANK, Troy. Sailor.	TEN 10 Sea horses.

XX — Male portrait. — Compt's die. | Vig. Two females on either side of shield; eagle perched on top in centre; liegehead and isle on left, cars and steamship on right. UNION BANK. Troy. Safe. | 20 — Vessel in circular die. — TWENTY

1 | Vig. Indian and sailor seated on either side of frame, surmounted by an eagle. Compt's die. UNION BANK, Watertown, N. Y. | 1 — Female reaper.

2 | Vig. Three mechanics on right, bridge, factory, &c. in the distance. Compt's die. UNION BANK, Watertown, N. Y. | 2 — Locomotive and tender.

5 | Vig. Three females, two seated, and the other reclining. Compt's die. UNION BANK, Watertown, N. Y. | 5 — Two females, one with arm resting on shield.

Compt's die. — 10 | UNION BANK, Watertown, N. Y. Vig. Man, woman, girl, boy and dog, rural scenery, &c. | TEN — Sailor in the act of hoisting a flag.

20 — Compt's die. | UNION BANK, Watertown, N. Y. Vig. Spread eagle, seated on the globe. | 20 — 20

1 — Compt's die. | UTICA CITY BANK. Vig. Head of Martha Washington. | 1 — Head of a girl.

Compt's die. — Mowers sharpening scythe. | Vig. Liberty and Ceres; shield with crest of the head of a horse; iron chest, vessels, &c.; horn of plenty, sheaf of wheat, &c. UTICA CITY BANK. | TWO — Blacksmith at a forge.

Compt's die. — Head of Franklin on dark ground. | Vig. Indian and woodman; shield. UTICA CITY BANK. Secured, &c. | 5 — Girl with a hay rake. — V

Compt's die. — Head of Washington on dark ground. | UTICA CITY BANK. Vig. Two half length female figures. | 10 — Female with ear of corn in right hand and figure X on left.

Compt's die. — 20 | Female with the wand of Mercury; factory, viaduct, cars, steam vessels, etc. UTICA CITY BANK, Utica, N. Y. XX XX Secured, etc. | 20 — State of New York. — Female seated between 2 and 0.

1 — Compt's die. | Cars and view of Mathews Hunt & Co.'s Warehouse. WALLKILL BANK, Middletown, N. Y. ONE | 1 — Female Portrait.

2 — Compt's die. — TWO | Cattle in water, trees etc. Title of Bank. TWO | TWO — Female feeding fowls.

5 — Lady Washington. — FIVE | View of cars and saw manufactory. Title of Bank. FIVE | FIVE — Compt's die. — FIVE

10 — Building. | Bull's head on shield; man dressing leather on right; female sewing shoes on left. Title of Bank. TEN | 10 — Compt's die

XX — Female with dove. | Compt's die with female and children on right; squaw and papoose on left. Title of Bank. TWENTY | 20 — Male portrait.

Secured by pledge &c. — ONE | 1 Vig. Female and child; on left an anchor and vessel in distance. Die. WASHINGTON CO. BANK Greenwich, Y. N. Portrait of Washington. | ONE — Female seated.

TWO — Female seated with scales. — TWO | 2 Vig. Female seated holding sickle, on right bridge &c.; left sheaf of wheat and mill in distance. 2 WASHINGTON CO BANK Greenwich, N. Y. Man at work. | Female seated.

Secured &c. — THREE — Two females, one on left holding scales. — Compt's die. | 3 Vig. Two Females and in centre a female portrait, on left cars in distance. WASHINGTON CO. BANK, Greenwich, N. Y. Man at work. | 3

5 — Female holding scales, eagle safe and key — FIVE | V Three females and in centre figure 5, on right barrels, and steamship in distance, on left a plough, sickle and cars in distance. V WASHINGTON CO. BANK, Greenwich, N. Y. Man at work. | 5 — Medallion head. — FIVE

10 — Female with scales, eagle, safe and key. — TEN | Vig. Two females, in centre a shield with scales at top, on right barrels and steamship in distance, on left houses and cars in distance. WASHINGTON CO. BANK, Greenwich, N. Y. Man at work. | 10 — State arms. — TEN

TWENTY — Female with scales, eagle, safe &c. — TWENTY | 20 Vig. Female seated, steamship on right and globe on left. 20 WASHINGTON CO. BANK Greenwich, N. Y. Man at work. | XX

Medallion head and ONE — Compt's die. | Vig. Three blacksmiths at work. WATERTOWN B'K AND LOAN CO. Watertown, N. Y. Female in water. | 1 — Medallion head. — ONE

TWO — Compt's die. — Vessels and cars. | Three females reclining, two on left and one on right, eagle and shield in centre; ships on left in distance, bridge and cars on right. WATERTOWN B'K AND LOAN CO., Watertown, N. Y. Female in water. | 2 — Train of cars. — TWO

FIVE — Compt's die. — Male portrait. | Vig. Train of cars; in the background large rocks and a man on right, houses and hills in distance. WATERTOWN B'K AND LOAN CO., Watertown, N. Y. Female in water. | 5 — Female portrait. — 5

TEN — Compt's die. — Portrait of Washington. | Vig. Signing of the Declaration of Independence. WATERTOWN B'K AND LOAN CO., Watertown, N. Y. Eagle. | 10 — Male portrait. — TEN

Compt's die. — 25 | Vig. Mechanic seated, hammer in hand, anvil; factories and cars in distance. WATERTOWN B'K AND LOAN CO., Watertown, N. Y. Deer | 25 — Two females, one blindfolded holding balance, the other seated playing on harp.

50 — Compt's die | Three females representing Liberty, Commerce and Agriculture. WATERTOWN B'K AND LOAN CO., Watertown, N. Y. Safe. | FIFTY — Female giving eagle drink. — L

1 — Compt's die. | WAVERLY BANK, Waverly, N. Y. Large Die. | 1 — ONE

2 — Compt's die. — 2 | WAVERLY BANK, Waverly, N. Y. Die. Die. 2 DOLLARS | 2 — American shield.

Die. V FIVE
Die. Die. Die.
WAVERLY BANK,
Waverly, N. Y.
Female.
Die. Compt's die. 5

TEN
X WAVERLY BANK,
Waverly, N. Y.
Male portrait
10 Compt's die.

TWENTY
XX
WAVERLY BANK,
Waverly, N. Y.
Male portrait
TWENTY 20

Male portrait. Compt's die.
WEEDSPORT BANK,
Weedsport, N. Y.
1 Vig. Five boys sporting in wheat. 1
ONE Large build'g. One with figure 1 across.

TWO
Female erect with right hand resting on Compt's die.
WEEDSPORT BANK,
Weedsport, N. Y.
Male portrait with female on either side; buildings on right in distance.
Canal Locks.
2 Portrait of Washington.

FIVE 5 Compt's die.
Vig. Frame surmounted by an eagle, on either side is a female.
WEEDSPORT BANK,
Weedsport, N. Y.
Canal boat.
5 Male portrait

Male portrait X
WEEDSPORT BANK,
Weedsport, N. Y.
Female, eagle and shield.
10 Compt's die.

1 ONE
WESTCHESTER CO. BANK.
under vig.
Vig. Goddess of Liberty seated; ship in the distance. State Arms.
Sloop.
ONE Capture of Andre. ONE

Capture of Andre. 2
2 Compt's die.
WESTCHESTER CO. BANK,
Peekskill, N. Y.
Steamboat.
TWO Female and shield. TWO

3 State Arms 3
WESTCHESTER CO. BANK.
3 Capture of Andre. 3
THREE
3 THREE

5 State Arms. 5
WESTCHESTER CO. BANK.
Capture of Andre.
Women.
FIVE Sheaves of wheat. FIVE

10 State Arms. 10
X TEN
WESTCHESTER CO. BANK.
Capture of Andre.
Barrels, ships, &c.
TEN Gold Dollars. TEN

20 State Arms. 20
XX XX
WESTCHESTER CO. BANK.
Barrels, ships, &c.
Capture of Andre. 20

Capture of Andre. 50
WESTCHESTER CO. BANK.
50
50 State Arms. 50

100 State Arms. 100
WESTCHESTER CO. BANK.
Capture of Andre.
Portrait of Lieut. Gov. Van Cortlandt.
100

1 Load of hay, drove of cattle, &c.
Vig. Cr[illegible], three sheep reclining.
WEST WIN FIELD,
West Win field, N. Y.
1 Compt's die.

2
Drove of cattle and sheep. Compt's die.
WEST WIN FIELD,
West Win field, N. Y.
Locomotive.
2 Female.

5
WEST WINFIELD BANK,
West Winfield, N. Y.
Locomotive and train of cars crossing bridge; mountains in distance.
5 Compt's die.

Compt's die. Sailor, bbl. bale of cotton &c.
Steamship.
WEST WIN FIELD BANK,
West Win field, N. Y.
10 Blacksmith [illegible] forge, [illegible] anchor, &c.

Compt's die. Portrait of Jackson.
Vig. Capitol at Washington.
WEST WIN FIELD BANK,
West Win field, N. Y.
20 Portrait of Webster.

ONE Compt's die. ONE
1 Vig. Indians hunting buffalos. 1
WHITE'S BANK OF BUFFALO, N. Y.
Secured, &c.
1 Female 1

TWO Compt's die. TWO
2 Vig. Female reclining, shield, &c. in centre; on right [illegible] of ships, on left steamboat. 2
WHITE'S BANK OF BUFFALO, N. Y.
Secured, &c.
2

5 Compt's die. 5
5 Vig. Steamboat and vessels. 5
WHITE'S BANK OF BUFFALO, N. Y.
Secured, &c.
FIVE 5 Female, etc. FIVE

TEN Male and female figures. Compt's die.
Vig. Female holding a vase, steamship on right, sheaf, canal, cows and mills on left.
WHITE'S BANK OF BUFFALO, N. Y.
Safe.
10 Sailor and Indian, in centre a shield. X

1 Sailor with flag; anchor, bbl., quadrant and bale. ONE
Ship building; view of city in distance.
WILLIAMSBURG CITY BANK,
Williamsburg, N. Y.
Sloop.
1 Compt's die

Female portrait. TWO 2
Female seated, eagle etc.; in distance cars, city, vessels, &c.
Title of Bank.
Eagle.
2 Compt's die.

Indian on cliff. 3
Female seated with shield; falls in the distance.
Title of Bank.
Bee hive.
3 Compt's die.

Female seated holding a figure 5. FIVE
Vessels and view of city.
Title of Bank.
Head of Indian.
Female seated holding a 5; masts in background. Compt's die.

10 Female with flowers in her apron.
Female reclining on bales; vessels in distance.
Title of Bank.
Locomotive and tender.
10 Compt's die.

50 Drovers and cattle, load of hay, &c.; and mountain in distance.
Farmers at rest and nooning; loading hay in distance.
Title of Bank.
Yacht [illegible].
50 Compt's die.

N. Y. STATE.

Spread eagle. 100	Compt's die. Title of bank. Dog, key and safe.	100
One on 1. Compt's die	WM. WILLIAMS' BK of Hastings, N. Y. 1 Female either side of shield surmounted by eagle. 1	1 Female reclining with basket of fruit.
Two on 2 Compt's die Two on 2	WM. WILLIAMS' BK of Hastings, N. Y. 2 Man buying newspaper of boy; birds, etc. 2	2 Indian female.
ONE Female portrait. ONE	1 Vig. Eagle on a branch. 1 WOOSTER SHERMAN'S BANK, Watertown, N. Y. Male portrait	Female standing by large figure one.
TWO Compt's die. TWO	2 Female seated with wheat &c. 2 WOOSTER SHERMAN'S BANK, Watertown, N. Y.	Artisan with horn of plenty.
Figure 3 with female on either side. I I I	3 Female portrait, female on either side. WOOSTER SHERMAN'S BANK, Watertown, N. Y.	3
5 Compt's die. FIVE	V Female seated in large figure 5, female on either side. V WOOSTER SHERMAN'S BANK, Watertown, N. Y. Male portrait.	5 Medallion head. FIVE
ONE	Male portrait. Farming scene. WORTHINGTON BK. Cooperstown, N. Y.	1 State arms.
TWO DOLLARS	State arms. Man plowing with oxen; little girl on right with pail and jug. WORTHINGTON BK Cooperstown, N. Y.	2 Male portrait
3 THREE	Compt's die. Five females and a male gathering grapes WORTHINGTON BK. Cooperstown, N. Y. Male portrait	3

N. JERSEY.

FIVE	State arms. Farming scene; men at work. WORTHINGTON BK. Cooperstown, N. Y.	5 Male portrait
X TEN	Male portrait Hunter shooting a deer; dog, trees and stream. WORTHINGTON BK. Cooperstown, N. Y.	10 Compt's die
1 ONE State Arms	Vig. Two horse team; boy on one horse; man attaching team to plough. WYOMING CO. BK.	ONE Head of Franklin.
2 State Arms.	Vig. Train of railroad cars passing under bridge; also, through posts, stage coach crossing a bridge. WYOMING CO. BK.	TWO Head of Washington TWO
3 State Arms.	Vig. Blacksmith shop; smith shoeing horse, and another at the bellows. WYOMING CO. BK.	3 Head of Webster.
V 5 V State Arms.	Vig. Liberty with a sheaf of wheat in right hand, sickle in left; men cradling grain; farm house in distance; train of cars crossing a viaduct. WYOMING CO. B'K.	FIVE Head of Seward.
TEN State Arms.	Vig. Portage Bridge, and train of cars passing over. WYOMING CO. B'K.	10 X Indian bow and arrows slung at his side.
ONE	1 Blacksmith shoeing horse, man looking on, another by anvil. BK OF JERSEY CITY Jersey City, N. J.	1 Compt's die.
2 TWO	Female portrait. Ship under sail. Compt's die. Two on 2. Title of Bank.	2 TWO
3 THREE	THREE Eagle in shield; female seated with anchor and quadrant. 3 Title of bank on right of vignette.	3 Compt's die

N. JERSEY.

5 FIVE	V BK OF JERSEY CITY Jersey City, N. J. Locomotive and cars. 5	5 Compt's die. FIVE
X TEN	BK OF JERSEY CITY Jersey City, N. J. Female with cornucopia. American shield; female instructing children on right, Indian, squaw and papoose, on left. TEN TEN	10 Compt's die.
XX Female with wheat.	BK OF JERSEY CITY Jersey City, N. J. XX Compt's die. XX	20 Female with flowers in her apron.
50 Ship.	BK OF JERSEY CITY Jersey City, N. J. Red letter L on a shield; sailor, ship in distance on right; farmer with scythe on left.	50 Compt's die.
100	Steamboat, hills and raft. BK OF JERSEY CITY Jersey City, N. J.	100 C Compt's die.
ONE on 1. State Arms.	BK OF NEW JERSEY New Brunswick, N. J. Portrait of Columbus and words one dollar.	ONE on 1. Shipping, bridge and cars.
Female Portrait with figure 2 and word TWO twice over on top border.	BK of NEW JERSEY, New Brunswick, N. J. State Arms.	Female Portrait with figure 2 and word TWO twice over on top border.
Female with pen and tablets; child at her feet. THREE.	3 Female reclining with chart, dividers, quadrant, globe, &c. BANK OF NEW JERSEY, New Brunswick, N. J.	3 Boy.
Heavy ornamental engraving with figure 3 the middle and word THREE round the top.	BK. of NEW JERSEY, New Brunswick, N. J. State Arms enclosed in a heavy ornamental border with words THREE DOLLARS round the top.	Heavy ornamental engraving with figure 3 the middle and word THREE round the top.
5 Female Bust with sickle and wheat.	A large ornamental V with the word FIVE across it. BK. of NEW JERSEY, New Brunswick, N. J Anvil, &c.	Word FIVE letter V and figure 5. State Arms.

Same as on right. Female Portrait.
A large ornamental X with word TEN across it. BK. of NEW JERSEY New Brunswick, N. J. Figure of Commerce, Shipping, &c.
Word TEN letter X and figures 10. State Arms.

XX Female bust with sickle and wheat.
A large ornamental xx with word TWENTY across it. BK. of NEW JERSEY New Brunswick, N. J.
20 State Arms.

50 State Arms.
BK. of NEW JERSEY. A large ornamental letter L with female figure around and word FIFTY across it. New Brunswick, N. J.
50

100 State Arms.
A kneeling Female figure with sickle and sheaf of wheat, farm houses and mowers on right; railroad cars on left; the whole surrounded by a large ornamental letter C. BK. of NEW JERSEY New Brunswick, N. J.
100 C

1 State Arms. ONE
Female seated on a log with a pail, train of cars, sheaf of wheat &c. 1 BELVIDERE BANK, Belvidere, N. J.
ONE Female erect ONE

TWO Female with scales sword and figure 2. TWO
BELVIDERE BANK, Belvidere, N. J. Farmer at work loading wheat, one holds horse.
2 State Arms

THREE Female erect with liberty pole and cap. 3
Drove of sheep; Man on horse, dog; mill on left in distance. Hoe right. BELVIDERE BANK, Belvidere, N. J.
Female erect THREE

Male portrait Portrait of Washington. Male portrait
5 Two horses, farmers wagon, cattle, horses, trees, &c. hills in background. 5 BELVIDERE BANK, Belvidere, N. J. State Arms.
Portrait of Franklin. Male portrait Male portrait

Horse head. Male Figure standing in front of fig. X
10 Female seated on rock with spear; arm around eagles neck; men in boat in distance. 10 BELVIDERE BANK, Belvidere N. J.
Flowers. Female, Bust of Washington on pedestal with eagle and shield at bottom. 10

Female head. Male erect.
20 Three females, two seated, one erect. 20 BELVIDERE BANK, Belvidere, N. J.
TWENTY

Female erect with cornucopia. 50
50 Three females seated on bales &c, one nude looking toward vessels; on right sheafs of grain; farm houses, mills, &c., on left. 50 Title of Bank. State Arms.
Female erect with sheaf of grain and sickle. 50

1 Male with sledge.
BEVERLY BANK, Beverly N. J. General Harvest scene.
1 Indian princess.

1 Female, sword and shield.
Spread eagle on shield, factories, &c. THE BEVERLY B'K, Beverly, N. J.
1 Washington

2 Franklin
BEVERLY BANK, Beverly, N. J. Two children in circle.
2 Male and female with sheaf.

Two on 2 Continental soldier.
Two horses, brook, cows, &c. THE BEVERLY B'K, Beverly, N. J.
2 Franklin.

3 Female head.
BEVERLY BANK, Beverly, N. J. Indian squaw and child; plow, sheaf, etc.
3 Girl's head.

3 Gen. Smith
Cars, canal, three horses and men. THE BEVERLY B'K, Beverly, N. J.
3 Two children

1 ONE State Arms.
Locomotive and train of cars turning a curve. BORDENTOWN BANKING CO., Bordentown, N. J.
1 Male portrait

TWO 2 State Arms. TWO
Two horses, one man riding and one leading other horse crossing railroad track; locomotive and two cars in the distance. 2 Title of Bank.
TWO Male portrait 2

5 State Arms. FIVE
A female sitting on a log with a basket in her lap; two sheafs; locomotive and cars. Title of Bank
5 Head of Washington

10 Male portrait
Title of Bank. Two Indian figures and child. State Arms. Female, three children and globe. Locomotive.
TEN Milkmaid. TEN

50 Male portrait
Title of Bank. Female sitting arm resting on money chest. State Arms. Sheaf and two sheep. Locomotive.
50 50

100 Male portrait
Title of Bank. Female fig. and horn of plenty. State Arms. Female handing $100 bill to other fig.
C Locomotive and cars.

Male portrait 1
BURLINGTON BK., Burlington, N. J. 1 Milkmaid with stool in left hand, leaning on cow; cows, sheep, &c. 1
1 Child and rabbits.

Male portrait 1
BURLINGTON BK., Burlington, N. J. Steamboat John Stevens, and view of town.
1 Child and rabbits.

2 Farmer with scythe; church spire in the distance.
BURLINGTON BK., Burlington, N. J. Farming scene; farmers at work.
2 Head of William Penn.

3 Farmer drinking.
BURLINGTON BK., Burlington, N. J. Three females, liberty, commerce and manufacture.
3 Portrait of Henry Clay.

5 Male portrait
BURLINGTON BK., Burlington, N. J. Steamboat John Stevens, and view of town in distance. Locomotive and cars.
5 Male portrait

Male portrait X
BURLINGTON BK., Burlington, N. J. Canal scene, and cars crossing bridge; house on left.
Male portrait 10

20 Male portrait 20
Spread eagle on shield; ship on left. 20 BURLINGTON BK., Burlington, N. J.
Female with cornucopia. TWENTY

Left	Centre	Right
FIFTY Male portrait L	BURLINGTON BK., Burlington, N. J. Factories and train of cars.	50 Male portrait
Girl with grain on head; farming scene in the distance. 100	BURLINGTON BK., Burlington, N. J. C State Arms of N. J.; factories on left.	100 Portrait of Washington.
ONE Indian. 1	Harvest scene. 1 BURLINGTON COUNTY BANK, Medford, N. J.	ONE Two females, one with sickle and grain.
TWO Cattle. TWO	2 Liberty in large figure 2. 2 BURLINGTON COUNTY BANK, Medford, N. J.	2 Milkmaid.
THREE Man seated on rock. State arms.	3 Vig. Female representing agriculture; cars crossing bridge on right. 3 BURLINGTON COUNTY BANK, Medford, N. J.	THREE Female drawing water from a well; steamboat in distance.
5 Letter V on medal. head. FIVE	5 Vig. Cattle and teaming; view of town; bridge and coach in background. 5 BURLINGTON COUNTY BANK, Medford, N. J.	5 Letter V on medal head. FIVE
5 Male portrait	BURLINGTON CO. BK Medford, N. J. Drover and farmer bargaining for bull; negro, boy, dog, horse, sheep, barn, etc.	5 Male portrait
10 Male portrait	Title of Bank. Female, calves, canal scene, cars, etc.	10 Male portrait
10 Franklin. 10	10 Three female figures representing Agriculture, Science and Art. 10 BURLINGTON CO. BANK, Medford, N. J.	X Franklin. X
20 Male portrait XX	20 Interior of a manufactory, men at work, houses in foreground. 20 BURLINGTON CO. BANK, Medford, N. J.	20 Male portrait XX

Left	Centre	Right
50 Male portrait 50	50 William Penn, treating with the Indians. 50 BURLINGTON CO. BANK. Medford, N. J.	50 Male portrait 50
100 Washington. 100	100 Signing the Declaration of Independence 100 BURLINGTON CO. BANK, Medford, N. J.	100 Male portrait 100
1 State arms. ONE	CENTRAL BANK, Hightstown, N. J. Train of cars passing under bridge.	ONE Male portrait.
2 Man, peach basket trees, &c.	State arms. Train of cars passing under bridge. CENTRAL BANK, Hightstown, N. J.	TWO TWO
3 Portrait.	State arms. Men, oxen, load of hay, &c. CENTRAL BANK, Hightstown, N. J.	3 3
FIVE State arms. FIVE	Train of cars passing under bridge CENTRAL BANK, Hightstown, N. J.	V Man, peach basket trees, &c.
TEN State arms.	CENTRAL BANK, Hightstown, N. J. Railroad scenery.	X Male portrait.
20 State arms.	Male portrait, on either side of which is a female, ship, sheaf of wheat, &c., on left; on right train of cars. CENTRAL BANK, Hightstown, N. J.	20 XX
50	CENTRAL BANK, Hightstown, N. J. Market house, shipping, &c. State arms.	L Male portrait.
C 100	Male portrait on either side of which is a female; ship, sheaf of wheat, &c., on left; on right, train of cars. CENTRAL BANK, Hightstown, N. J.	C State Arms.

Left	Centre	Right
1 Two Indians on a cliff viewing city.	Various vessels. CITY BANK of Perth Amboy, N. J. Female bathing.	1 State Arms. ONE
TWO	Female reclining on bales; Girl. steamboat in distance. Title of Bank. Dog.	2 Train of cars. 2
5 Factory.	State Arms. Title of Bank. Ducks.	V Male portrait
ONE Female feeding fowls.	State Arms. CLINTON BANK of NEW JERSEY, Clinton, N. J.	1 Male portrait
2 Head of Franklin.	Farmer watering horses at a well; buildings, sheep, goats, &c. Title of Bank.	2 Washington
THREE 3	Three men, farmer, mechanic and tradesman. Title of Bank.	3 Female head
FIVE 5 Female with sickle, grain, &c.	Title of Bank. Blacksmith standing; anvil and tools.	5 Girl's head
TEN Female with flowers	Title of Bank. Head of Clinton.	10 Boy's head
TWENTY Female seated; eagle, &c.	Title of Bank. House, flag, etc.	20 Female with horn of plenty, grapes, &c.
Liberty, female, shield, carry ferry, and liberty pole.	Spread eagle. 1 Indian seated viewing the improvements of the white man. CUMBERLAND BK. Bridgeton, N. J. Female bathing.	ONE Milkmaid. ONE

Left	Centre	Right
ONE	1 on med. head. Eagle on a shield. 1 on med. head. CUMBERLAND BK., Bridgton, N. J.	1 ONE on med. head. 1
THREE Justice. 3	Female seated, eagle, rock, shield, etc.; ships in distance. 3 on med. head on either side of vig. CUMBERLAND BK., Bridgton, N. J.	THREE Ship. THREE
Liberty. THREE	Spread eagle. Harvest scene; men at work in distance. Figure 3, and word three on either side. CUMBERLAND B'K. Bridgeton, N. J.	Two females, one with sickle and grain.
5 Med. head. FIVE	V Spread eagle on a rock. V CUMBERLAND B'K. Bridgeton, N. J.	FIVE Med. head. 5
5 Male bust.	Man feeding cows with cornstalks; sheep, heifer, etc. Red V either side. CUMBERLAND B'K. Bridgeton, N. J.	5 Female with flowers.
Cupid with sheaf. TEN	Title of Bank. 10 Boy's head. 10	Cupid with cornucopia. TEN
10 Cupid and farming implements. 10	Med. head. State Arms of N. J. Med. head. CUMBERLAND B'K. Bridgeton, N. J.	X Cupid. X
20 Female soaring in air.	Female seated; safe, flags; eagle at top of shield; ship on right. CUMBERLAND B'K. Bridgeton, N. J. Horse.	20 Man sowing
Liberty and shield.	50 Eagle on limbs of tree. CUMBERLAND B'K. Bridgeton, N. J. Farming implements.	Female representation of Fame, Globe, and figures 50.
100 Indian on horse.	CUMBERLAND BK. Bridgeton, N. J. Washington.	100 Sailor boy.

Left	Centre	Right
1 Boy's head.	Carpenter at bench. ESSEX Co. BANK, Newark, N. J.	1 Girls' portrait
2 Girl's portrait	2 Farmers at rest, one seated, one leaning against fence. 2 Title of Bank	2 Fowls.
THREE 3 Anchor, bales, &c.	Title of Bank. Mechanic, tradesman and sailor.	THREE 3 Girls' head
V on a Two children	Title of Bank. Men & boiler shop.	5 Man dressing leather.
10 Head of sailor. TEN	Title of Bank. Four females—one reading.	10 Blacksmith.
L Clay.	Three female figures—liberty, protection, etc. Title of Bank.	50 Milkmaid and cows
C Sailor.	Title of Bank. Four female figures representing the Union.	100 Webster.
1 ONE Portrait of Franklin.	Man on horse, dog and drove of sheep, mill in distance. FARMERS BANK OF N. JERSEY, Mt. Holly.	1 Portrait of Washington. ONE
3 Portrait of Washington. THREE	Two horses (one white and the other black), and a train of cars. FARMERS BANK OF N. JERSEY, Mt. Holly.	3 Portrait of Franklin.
FIVE DOLLARS	5 Cow and Calf. 5 FARMERS BANK OF N. JERSEY, Mt. Holly, Eagle	FIVE DOLLARS

Left	Centre	Right
Female reclining on sheaf. 5	FARMERS BANK OF NEW JERSEY Mount Holly. V 5 Hens. 5	5 Male portrait
10 X	Title of Bank. Farmer watering horses; pigs, cattle, &c. TEN Sheep. X	10 Male portrait
TEN	10 Drove of cattle and sheep; man on horseback. 10 FARMERS BANK OF N. JERSEY. Mt. Holly. Deer	TEN
FIFTY	Female with a sheaf of wheat in her hands. FARMERS BANK OF N. JERSEY, Mt. Holly.	17 miles from Phila.
ONE HUNDRED	A Group of three females. FARMERS BANK OF N. JERSEY, Mt. Holly.	17 miles from Phila.
1 ONE	Agricultural scene; man, boy, horses, plow etc. FARMERS' BANK of WANTAGE, Deckertown, N. J.	Milkmaid, pail on head, cows, etc. ONE
2 2	Shield, three plows and horse's head, female seated on each side. 2 Title of Bank.	TWO Female erect with staff and cap of Liberty.
3 3	Man with hammer leaning on anvil; locomotive, foundry, etc. THREE Title of Bank.	Female erect with sickle, sheaf of grain, etc.
5 FIVE	5 Floating female with horn of plenty; ships, etc. V Title of Bank.	Indian with bow and arrow.
TEN Small Indian with bow and arrow.	X Shield, three plows, and horse head, female sitting either side. Title of Bank	10 10

Left	Centre	Right
20 Male portrait	Floating female with horn of plenty; ships, etc. Title of Bank.	XX
1 Men at work in mine.	Two females seated; cows in distance. FAR. & MECHANICS' BANK, Camden, N. J. Bee-hive	1 Three blacksmiths.
1 Coal diggers in a circular frame.	Two females seated with sickle, wheel, &c.; factory on right; cattle on left. FARMERS' & MECH. BANK, Camden, N. J.	1 Blacksmith at work.
2 Justice.	Farmer, blacksmith, girl with rake; boy, etc. Title of Bank. Female bathing.	2 Wm. Penn.
3 Factory.	Scene in an iron foundry. Title of Bank. Ducks	3 Female with grain, etc.
V Girl.	FARMERS' AND MECHANICS' BANK, Camden, N. J. Load of hay; woman and boy on top; two horses, man on one; dog, boy and girl; blacksmith shop and man at work. Dog.	5 FIVE 5
X TEN X	Title of Bank. Blacksmith shop, four men at work; boy, &c.; man plowing, house and trees in distance. Dog.	10 Female portrait.
XX Two male figures, sailor and blacksmith on board ship.	Title of Bank. Figure of liberty, right arm resting on shield, on which is portrait of Washington; drapery with stars on it, over the portrait. Dog.	20 Boy carrying bundle of corn stalks, boy and horse behind him.
50 Female with sheaf and sickle.	Title of Bank. State Arms with female on either side; ship and cars in distance. Dog.	50 Shipwright seated; woman with bundle of chips; ship on stocks.
Portrait of Washington. ONE C HUNDRED	Title of Bank. Boy reclining on load of hay, drawn by two oxen; boy with form side of oxen. Dog.	C 100 C

Left	Centre	Right
Die. 500 Die.	Title of Bank Female seated with sheaf and sickle; houses, trees and men mowing on right; train of cars crossing bridge on left. Dog.	500 Blacksmith shop; man at forge, anvil, &c.
ONE Milkmaid. ONE	[Old Plate.] 1 Long ornamental figure 1 enclosing a full length Female figure. FARMERS and MECHANICS BANK Rahway, N. J.	View of Town. 1 ONE
ONE Figure of Liberty leaning on an ornamental figure 1, with word ONE in center.	[New Plate.] 1 Long ornamental figure 1 enclosing a full length female figure. FARMERS and MECHANICS BANK, Rahway, N. J.	Banking House. 1
Milkmaid and cows. 2	[Old Plate.] Ornamental figure 1 enclosing a full length female figure. FARMERS and MECHANICS BANK, Rahway, N. J.	2 Female Head.
TWO Female Portrait. TWO	[New Plate.] 2 Ornamental figure 2 enclosing a full length female figure. FARMERS and MECHANICS BANK, Rahway, N. J.	Banking House. 2
THREE Female Portrait. THREE	3 Ornamental figure 3 enclosing a full length figure, the word THREE at top and small figure 3 at bottom. FARMERS and MECHANICS BANK, Rahway, N. J.	Banking House. 3
Banking House. 5	Ornamental figure 5 enclosing a full length figure of Washington. FARMERS and MECHANICS BANK, Rahway, N. J.	FIVE 5 Male and female supporting a small ornamental 5.
Oval Die. Female. Oval Die.	10 Two females supporting a shield. FARMERS and MECHANICS BANK, Rahway, N. J. Railroad cars.	TEN Female resting on pillar and shield. TEN
20 Female Portrait. 20	20 Male figure resting on bank with torch in hand; eagle &c. FARMERS and MECHANICS BANK, Rahway, N. J. A	20 Female Portrait. 20
50 Farmer with axe and sickle. 50	50 Country scene, locomotive, plough sheaf of wheat &c. 50 FARMERS and MECHANICS BANK. Rahway, N. J.	50 Female figure; plow, sheaf of wheat. 50

Left	Centre	Right
C Indian Female C	100 Mail figure, leaning on an easy plow, cattle, &c. 100 FARMERS and MECHANICS BANK, Rahway, N. J. Ship,	Figure of Justice 100
500 Female Portrait. 500	500 Two females supporting shield; shipping on left and building on right. FARMERS and MECHANICS BANK, Rahway, N. J. Head of Female.	500 Woman churning; country scene in distance.
ONE Female erect with sword and scales. ONE	1 Agricultural scene, plowing, oxen, &c. 1 FAR. & MER. BANK. Middletown P't. N. J. 1	1 Washington. ONE
1 Farmer carrying sheafs of grain. ONE	Title of Bank Horse running away; boys endeavoring to stop him.	1 Female portrait.
Red end with white 2. 2 Anchor, bales, &c.	FAR. and MER. BK, Middletown Pt, N. J. Two Dollars on large ornamental die. Eagle and Shield.	2 Female with flowers. Red end with white 2.
Unicorn. Eagle on shield. 2	2 Mercury. 2 Title of Bank.	TWO Washington 2
2 Female portrait.	Drover buying cattle. FAR. & MER. BANK, Middletown P't, N. J.	2 Male and female seated TWO
3 Drove of cattle, wagon &c.; scene upon road.	FAR. & MER. BANK, Middletown P't, N. J. Country scene—man on horse which is drinking from trough; female, sheep, &c.	3 Portrait of a little girl.
3 Plough, sales, &c. 3	3 Female seated upon bale; ships in background; water, &c. 3 FAR. & MER. BANK, Middletown P't. N. J.	3 Flowers. 3
FIVE Female with sword and scales, 5	5 State arms of N. J.; female on either side. 5 FAR. & MER. BANK, Middletown P't, N. J. V	FIVE Female leaning on ornamental figure 5.

Spread eagle on rock overlooking sea. TEN
10 10 FAR. & MER. BANK, Middletown P't, N. J. Plough, rake, &c. X
Goddess of Liberty seated. TEN

TWENTY
20 20 FAR. & MER. BANK, Middletown P't, N. J. Female seated on bale, water before her; anchor, &c.
XX Unicorn. XX

Female erect between ornamental 5 and 0. FIFTY
50 Female reclining 50 on state arms. FAR. & MER. BANK, Middletown P't, N. J.
Female erect with cornucopia. FIFTY

100 Female erect feeding eagle from cup.
Female reclining on shield. FAR. & MER. BANK, Middletown P't, N. J.
Same as 50's.

ONE Head of girl.
State Arms. Female seated resting on shield, on which is fig. 1. FREEHOLD BANKING CO. Freehold, N. J.
1 Male portrait.

Female seated by portrait of boy. 2
2 Two oxen before hay cart, boy asleep on top, another boy walking by side. Title of Bank.
2 Girl.

3
Two horses before hay cart; on top, woman and child; man on one of the horses; boy, girl, blacksmith shop, &c. Male portrait. Title of Bank.
Word three and figure 3. Webster.

5
Title of Bank. The vig. extends across the whole lower part of the note, and is men shearing sheep on left and men gathering corn right.
5

10 Train of cars.
Title of Bank. Female in clouds with eagle and sword.
10 Male portrait.

XX Female with sickle and sheaf.
Title of Bank. Shield with female on either side; train of cars and ship in distance.
20 Male portrait.

50 Male portrait.
Title of Bank. State Arms.
50 FIFTY 50

Shield, bust of female, soldier and war implements and female. C
Male portrait. Title of Bank. Letter C with words one above and hundred below.
Ide. Ide.

1 Blacksmith boy at forge. ONE
GLOUCESTER CO. BK. Woodbury, N. J. Vig. female on either side of a shield surmounted by horse's head; steamer and cars in distance.
1 ONE Female milking cow; little girl and another cow.

3 Horse running away, boys trying to stop him, horse, mill and house in distance.
GLOUCESTER CO. BK. Woodbury, N. J. Female on either side of a shield, surmounted by head of horse.
3 Head of a little girl.

5 Farmer seated with scythe in hand; village cars, factory, building, &c. in distance.
GLOUCESTER CO. BK. Woodbury, N. J.
5 Male portrait.

10
Cows standing in water; one reclining on bank; sheep on left. Small head of a girl. GLOUCESTER CO. BK. Woodbury, N. J.
10 Female portrait.

20 Farmer, horse, dog, and pigeons.
GLOUCESTER CO. BK. Woodbury, N.J. Blacksmith shoeing a horse; man seated on log looking on; man in distance.
20 Female portrait.

Full length male figure with scroll. FIFTY
Drovers and drove of cattle; in distance village, train of cars, building, &c. GLOUCESTER CO. BK. Woodbury, N.J. Bee-hive.
50 Currier at work.

100 Male portrait. 100
GLOUCESTER CO. BK. Woodbury, N. J. Signing the Declaration of Independence.
100 Portrait of Washington. 100

Farm scene; female at table blowing horn; three men in distance.
1 State Arms. HACK'TTSTOWN B'K, Hacketstown, N. dog.
1 ONE

TWO Head of girl.
Title of Bank. An ox and a sheep standing, three cows and two sheep lying down.
2 Female head.

3 Ox.
Two oxen before hay cart, boy asleep on top and another walking by the side of oxen. Title of Bank.
3 State Arms. 3

FIVE Locomotive and train of cars; trees, house, &c.
Female and Indian on either side of Portrait of Jackson; tents and trees on right; ships and city on left. Title of Bank.
5 Girl.

TEN X
Farm scene; men at work mowing, raking and loading wagon; two oxen before wagon. Title of Bank.
10 Boy.

XX Child.
Two cows, one standing the other lying down; milkmaid, chickens, sows and sheep; on right in distance trees, shed, &c. Title of Bank.
20 Female head.

50 Portrait of Washington.
Two boys one on horse driving sheep the other holding gate open. Title of Bank.
50 Henry Clay.

Male portrait ONE
HOBOKEN CITY BK, Hoboken, N. J. Treas. die on fig. 1. Fig. 1; farmers at lunch; boy playing with dog, &c.
1

TWO Boy.
Treas. die and 2. Team of oxen; load of hay, two boys and fig. 2. HOBOKEN CITY BK. Hoboken, N. J. Dog.

Male portrait. Treas. die.
Indian, squaw and papoose in canoe. Large white 3 across the vig. HOBOKEN CITY BK. Hoboken, N. J.
Three across 3. THREE Three dogs.

FIVE Train of cars. Coal heaver standing with pick; large white V across.
Men heaving coal. View of a yacht sailing. HOBOKEN CITY BK. Hoboken, N. J. Portrait of Buchanan. 5
5 Treas. die.

TEN / Train of cars with large white X across. — Treas. die. Shipbuilding; two carpenters in the foreground. 10 in white across. HOBOKEN CITY BK, Hoboken, N. J. — 10 / Girl with horn.

50 / Male portrait. — Female nursing child; boy and dog; reapers in background. Letter L across vignette. Treas. die. HOBOKEN CITY BK, Hoboken, N. J. — 50 / Female portrait.

1 / Compt's die / 1 — Jersey City ferry landing; ferry boat "Arcassin" coming in the slip. HUDSON CO. BANK, Jersey City, N. J. Steamship. — 1 / Blacksmith with anvil and hammer.

2 / Compt's die. — Farmer with two horses and a plough. HUDSON CO. BANK, Jersey City, N. J. Implements of war. — 2 / Man with basket of corn.

3 / Compt's die. / 3 — Locomotive and cars; factory on left. HUDSON CO. BANK, Jersey City, N. J. Schooner. — THREE / Steamer. / 3

3 / State Arms. / 3 — Seller farmer and blacksmith; factories, vessels, etc., in distance. HUDSON CO. BANK, Jersey City, N. J. — THREE / Steamship. / 3

State Arms. / FIVE — 5 Two females, child, cornucopia, &c. Title of Bank. Beehive. — 5 / Washington. / FIVE

State Arms. / FIVE — 5 Same as cuts. HUDSON CO. BANK, Jersey City, N. J. Sea monster. — 5 / Locomotive. / 5

X, 10; two sailors, boat, telescope and light house, &c. / Compt's die. — 10 View of a large building, &c. HUDSON CO. BANK, Jersey City, N. J. Shells. — 10 / Mechanic seated on a boiler; cars in distance.

X, 10, two sailors, telescope, light-house, etc. / Compt's die. — 10 View of a large building, etc. Title of Bank. — 10 / Female with cornucopia.

Compt's die. / Female instructing children. — Steamship and sail-vessels; city in distance. HUDSON CO. BANK, Jersey City, N. J. Bales of goods. — 20 / Locomotive.

FIFTY / Two males and two females with tablets and quadrant; city in distance. — HUDSON CO. BANK, Jersey City, N. J. Compt's die. — FIFTY / Male, two females, dog and cattle.

Indian family on cliff contemplating the progress of civilization. — HUDSON CO. BANK, Jersey City, N. J. Compt's die. — 100 / Mechanic seated with hammer; factory in distance.

Large figure 1, which covers the whole end of the bill. / ONE — Female bathing. ONE. State Arms. HUNTERDON CO. BANK, Flemington, N. J. Locomotive — 1 / ONE / Female

2 / Train of cars / 2 — HUNTERDON CO. BANK, Flemington, N. J. Cheese press, two females and man at work. 2 2 — 2 / Bridge and drove of cattle. / 2

THREE / Loading hay; two men and a horse; barn, &c. — HUNTERDON CO. BANK, Flemington, N. J. Three Dollars. Head of dog. — 3 / Milkmaid

5 — Large V, word "Five;" man with sickle in hand, sheaf of wheat in and around it. HUNTERDON CO. BANK, Flemington, N. J. Quails. — Letter "V" and word "Five." / Female bust / FIVE

Figure 10, word TEN, and letter X / Bull's head. — View of State House. HUNTERDON CO. BANK. TEN DOLLARS. Flemington, N. J. — Figure 10 word TEN and letter X / Female.

Horses and cattle. / XX — Canal and vessels. HUNTERDON CO. BANK. TWENTY DOLLARS. Fish. — 20 / Female.

L inverted / Male portrait — Red 50 on die; on right old man, boy, dog, etc.; on left milkmaid seated; Steamboat in background. HUNTERDON CO BK, Flemington, N. J. — L inverted / Female portrait with a bucket &c.

100 / Female portrait — Four females; one erect, reading. C C HUNTERDON CO. BANK One Hundred Dollars. — [illegible]

Word one and figure 1 across. / State Arms. — View of large building; horses and carriage in street. IRON BANK Morristown N. J. One Dollar One Dollar — 1 / Train of cars going under bridge; load of hay passing over bridge.

2 / State Arms. — Men at work in iron mill. IRON BANK, — 2 / Two men and dog in foreground, man and boy in background.

3 / State Arms — IRON BANK, N. J. View of New York Crystal Palace. Three dols Three dols — Word three and figure 3 / View of cattle, telegraph and railroad

FIVE — IRON BANK, 5 View of part of the globe with eagle on top. — 5 / State Arms

FIVE — 5 IRON BANK, Morristown, N. J. V Eagle on half of the globe. — 5 / State Arms

TEN / Bank building. — Working in an iron foundry; IRON BANK, N. J. — 10 / Compt's die / TEN

20 / Foundries. — IRON BANK, Morristown, N. J. View in rolling mill; men and machinery. — 20 / State Arms

50 / Foundries. — Title of Bank. Same vig. as 20s. — 50 / State Arms

1 / ONE — LAMBERTVILLE BK Lambertville, N. J. Sheep shearing scene. Female head Treas. die. — 1 / ONE

2 — TWO — Title of Bank. Treas. die. Railroad scene—train of cars, mountains, river, etc. — 2 — Female head. — TWO DOLLARS

THREE 3 — Girl with a dove. — Title of Bank. Treas. Die. Pigs, hen, chickens, etc. — 3 — THREE

5 — Treas. die. — 5 — Title of Bank. Interior of iron mill—men at work. FIVE — 5 — Indian boy paddling canoe.

10 — Treas. die. — 10 — Title of Bank. Mining scene—two men digging coal in mine. TEN — X — Female seated; two males behind her.

20 — 20 — Rafting scene—man, woman and child on raft; skiff, raft in distance. Treas. die. Title of Bank. 20 — 20 — Male portrait.

ONE — Mechanic seated. — ONE — 1 Ferry wharf; view of river and vessels. MECHANICS' BANK, Burlington, N. J. — 1 — Male portrait. — ONE

TWO — Mechanic and anvil. — TWO — 2 Female in frame, farming implements on either side. 2 MECHANICS' BANK, Burlington, N. J. — TWO — Portrait of Franklin. — TWO

THREE — Female in fig. 3. — THREE — 3 Harvest scene; girl, boy and dog, farmers at work in distance. 3 MECHANICS' BANK, Burlington, N. J. — THREE — Male portrait. — THREE

Spread eagle. — 5 Vig. Five Cupids and fig. 5. 5 MECHANICS' BANK, Burlington, N. J. — Portrait of Washington.

10 — View of river, steamboats &c. — 10 — 10 Female between two safes, cars on right. MECHANICS' BANK, Burlington, N. J. TEN — TEN — Male portrait. — TEN

20 — Ship. — 20 — 20 Cupid holding wand, dog, safe and key. 20 MECHANIC'S BANK, Burlington, N. J. — 20 — Male portrait. — 20

50 — Male portrait. — 50 — View of river, steamboat and row boat; also village. MECHANIC'S BANK, Burlington, N. J. — 50 — Train Cars. — 50

Indian with bow and arrow. — 100 — 100 Locomotive and train of cars. 100 MECHANICS' BANK, Burlington, N. J. — Washington and his horse. — 100

1 — Female with sheaf. — Mechanic seated on anvil, &c.; train of cars, buildings, hills, &c., in distance. MECHANICS' BANK, Newark, N. J. Arm. — 1 — ONE

ONE — Male seated supporting the world with a lever. — 1 — 1 on med. head. Female seated with book in hand; anvil, sledge, &c.; in distance on left ship. 1 on med. head. MECHANICS' BANK, Newark, N. J. — ONE — Male figure seated with tablets. — 1

TWO — Male supporting the world. — 2 — MECHANICS' BANK, Newark, N. J. 2 on med. head. Female seated with child in her arms; basket, sheafs of wheat; farmers mowing in background. 2 on med. head. Arm. — TWO — Female seated with book. — 2

2 — Two farmers with rakes; two in distance and house. — Three males apparently in conversation; view of city in distance on right. MECHANICS' BANK, Newark, N. J. Arm. — TWO 2

THREE — Male supporting the world, &c. — 3 — 3 Three females seated; trees on right; ship in distance on left. 3 MECHANICS' BANK, Newark, N. J. Arm. — Full length female with sickle. — 3

3 — Portrait of Jenny Lind. — Frame surmounted by an eagle; two females on right and female on left; ship, train of cars crossing bridge, in distance. MECHANICS' BANK, Newark, N. J. Arm. — THREE 3

5 — Blacksmith at work. — V — Med. head and fig. 5. Train of cars, man leaning on fence. Med. head and fig. 5. MECHANICS' BANK, Newark, N. J. Arm. — V — Sailor with hat in hand mast in distance. — 5

X — Canal scene; buildings in distance. — X — Med. head and letter X. Man seated on log with left hand on single head, letter trees, &c. Med. head and letter X. MECHANICS' BANK, Newark, N. J. Arm. — 10 — Brig. — 10

20 — Sheaf. — 20 — 20 Female seated with sword, in left hand scales; lion on right, steamboat on left. 20 MECHANICS' BANK, Newark, N. J. Arm. — 20 — Ship. — 20

50 — Beehive. — 50 — 50 Female seated arm resting on shield, on which is anchor; ship on left. 50 MECHANICS' BANK, Newark, N. J. Arm. — 50 — Eagle. — 50

100 — Plough, &c. — 100 — 100 Shield on which is figures 100, on either side of which female; reaping scene and steamboat in distance. 100 MECHANICS' BANK, Newark, N. J. Arm. — ONE HUNDRED

500 — Female erect supporting shield on which is med. head. — Med. head and figs. 500. Female reclining and looking up; steamboat on right; building on left. Med. head and figs. 500. MECHANICS' BANK, Newark, N. J. Arm. — 500 — Female erect with sword. — 500

1000 — Two med. heads and figures 1000. — M — 1000 Female seated on bale of goods, right arm resting on shield. 1000 MECHANICS' BANK, Newark, N. J. Arm. — Same as on left end.

ONE — Male portrait. — 1 — 1 Horse and two horsemen in the distance. 1 MECH. & MAN. BK. Trenton, N. J. Train of cars. — ONE — Drovers and cattle. — 1

2 — Washington. — 2 — 2 Horse terrified by a train of cars; buildings in the distance. 2 MECH. & MAN. BK. Trenton, N. J. — 2 — Medallion. — Liberty seated, ... distance.

3 — Male portrait. — 3 — 3 Two men ... farm house in distance. 3 MECH. & MAN. BK. Trenton, N. J. Canal lock. — 3 — Female reclining on a cog wheel, with ship in distance. — 3

FIVE — Shield with Liberty on right, and eagle on left; and motto "E Pluribus Unum." — 5 — [Old Plate.] 5 Eagle and shield, Justice on left, Liberty on right; train of cars and bridge in distance. Title of Bank. Docks, shipping, &c. — FIVE — Female feeding an eagle.

FIVE Male Portrait. 5	Same as above. 5 Title of Bank. Cattle, &c.	Precisely the same as above.
Indian springing a bow; landscape in distance. 10	10 Mechanic with anvil, &c.; two females, offering the one fruit; the other, money; shipping in distance. Title of Bank. Head of a horse.	X Franklin. 10
Female feeding an eagle; stars of America around. 20	XX State Arms. XX Title of Bank. Eagle feeding its young.	20 Three figures typifying home and plenty; hive, wheat, water mill, &c., in distance. 20
FIFTY 50 Mechanic, anvil, &c.	L Beehive, flowers, &c. L Title of Bank.	Same as on left of twenty. 50
Same as tens. 100	100 Benjamin Franklin seated. 100 Title of Bank.	Full length statue of Washington. 100
ONE Compt's die. ONE	Masons at work building a house. MECHANICS' AND TRADERS' BANK, Jersey City, N. J. ONE	1 Blacksmith with sledge.
Blacksmith shoeing a horse. 2	Compt's die. Title of Bank. TWO	2 Sailor with telescope.
THREE	Title of Bank. Carpenter at work. THREE	3 Compt's die
FIVE Mechanic, sailor and farmer looking offering to winged female.	Compt's die. Title of Bank.	5 5
X Compt's die.	Title of Bank. Locomotive and cars. TEN.	10 TEN

L Compt's die. Die Work.	Title of Bank. Portrait of Washington. Figures 50, letter L and words every each side. L L	L 50 Die Work.
100 Compt's die.	ONE HUNDRED surrounded by ornamental die work. Title of Bank.	100 C 100
1 Female with sheaf and sickle	MILLVILLE BANK, Millville, N. J. Scene in a glass blowing establishment. Dog.	1 Factory, &c
2	Scene in a factory; girls working at looms. Female portrait. Title of Bank. Ducks.	2 Mechanic.
3 Portrait of Boy.	Title of Bank. Female seated with infant child offering birds nest.	3 State Arms. 3
5 Female portrait.	Same as ones. Title of Bank.	5 Three Blacksmiths at work.
10 Reaper girl holding sheaf and basket.	Title of Bank. Two men conversing; one reclining on anvil; the other has his right arm around boy beside him.	10 Female portrait.
XX Farmer binding bundle of grain.	Scene in a ship yard. Title of Bank. XX	20 Justice.
1 Female seated with cornucopia.	Pigs and fowls. Chickens in pen. MT. HOLLY BANK, Mt. Holly, N.J One on red die.	1 Treas. Die.
TWO DOLLARS 2 Three cherubs.	State Arms; cars and factory in distance. MT. HOLLY BANK, Mt. Holly, N. J. Two on red die.	2 Treas. die.

5 Henry Clay.	MT. HOLLY BANK, Mt. Holly, N. J. View of large building and street. 5 5	5 Treas. die.
10 Treas. die.	Man watering three horses from trough by side of well; goat, kid, sheep, trees and house. MT. HOLLY BANK. Mt. Holly, N. J.	X Male portrait
20 Treas. die.	Three men at work with two horses and patent mowing machine; house in distance. MT. HOLLY BANK. Mt. Holly, N. J.	20 Female seated.
50 Female with flowers.	MOUNT HOLLY BK, Mount Holly N. J. Drover on horse; boy and drove of cattle; farm house etc., in distance.	50 State Arms.
Children. ONE	NEWARK BANKING COMPANY, Newark, N. J. Milkmaid under tree, boy painting.	1 Male portrait
ONE DOLLAR	1 Squaw contemplating progress of civilization; railroad and canal boat in distance; city in extreme distance. NEWARK BANKING COMPANY Newark, N. J. Eagle.	1 Portrait of Franklin.
2 Portrait of Washington. 2	2 Two females, sheaf of wheat and ships in distance. Title of Bank.	2 Female entwined in figure 2.
TWO	2 Ornamental figure 2, with two females entwined. Title of Bank. Implements of war.	Ornamental die. Portrait of Washington. Ornamental die.
2 Girl's head.	Scene at canal locks; train of cars crossing bridge and harvesting scene in distance. NEWARK BANKING COMPANY Newark, N. J.	2 Male portrait
3 Male portrait	3 Two females by loom. Title of Bank.	3 Blacksmith

Left end	Centre	Right end
3 Female with pole and cap; eagle and shield; ship in distance.	Title of Bank Steamer; train of cars.	Three females on ornamental figure 3; one representing liberty, justice, &c. THREE
3 Ornamental figure 3, with three females.	Title of Bank	Arms of the State of New Jersey; ship in distance.
5 Med. head, with V on it. 5	Title of Bank Female seated on bale of goods, with arm resting on shield.	5 Med. head, with V on it 5
5 Female with scales, seated on a barrel; cars in distance.	Goddess of Liberty resting on American shield. Ornamental figure, with two females and cherub. Title of Bank.	FIVE DOLLARS
5 Male portrait	Title of Bank. V Cattle and children. V	5 Female with spinning wheel.
5 Female with distaff, anchor and shield.	Arms of the State of New Jersey; ship in distance. Ornamental figure 5, with two females and cherub. Title of Bank.	Ornamental die. Portrait of Washington. Ornamental die.
10 Male portrait	Horse. Eagle. Female seated on grain; sheep, etc. Title of Bank. TEN	10 Male portrait
10 Med. head, with X on it. 10	Med. head. View of blacksmith shop; one at bellows and one at anvil; cars in distance. Med. head Title of Bank.	Med. head. TEN Med. head
20 Med. head, with Twenty on it. 20	Med. head, with two cherubs on left, and one on right. Title of Bank.	20 Med. head, with Twenty on it. 20
50 Canal boat. 50	State Arms; cars in distance. 50 NEWARK BANKING COMPANY Newark, N. J.	Justice full length. FIFTY

Left end	Centre	Right end
100 State Arms. 100	Spread eagle; cars on left; factory on right. 100 Title of Bank.	Full length female. 100
500 Female, eagle and shield.	Agricultural scene; cars on right. Title of Bank.	500 State Arms. 500
1 Portrait of female.	NEWARK CITY BK., Newark, N. J. Vig. Machinist and heavy turning lathe.	1 Female reaping.
2 Portrait of female.	NEWARK CITY BK., Newark, N. J. Vig. Stone cutters at work.	TWO Female, with small globe
3 Leather dresser.	NEWARK CITY BK., Newark, N. J. Three females reclining, representing liberty, agriculture and art.	3 Arm, hammer, and anvil.
V Fireman.	Two females, one seated; horn of plenty. NEWARK CITY BK., Newark, N. J.	5 Locomotive and tender.
10 Female resting.	NEWARK CITY BK., Newark, N. J. Three females representing music, poetry, and painting.	10
50 State Arms.	NEWARK CITY BK., Newark, N. J. L	FIFTY Male figure and two females seated; agricultural scene.
100 Two Indians.	State Arms Title of Bank. One hundred.	Two females, one seated, the other erect. 100
State Arms. Same as right end.	NEWARK CITY B'K, Newark, N. J. Female with tablets; shield at her feet. Small D either side and words Five Hundred below.	500 D and words Five Hundred Dollars on red die.

Left end	Centre	Right end
1 Girl	Two horses before hay cart; various male and female figures; blacksmith's shop. Large 1 in red on vig. ORANGE BANK Orange, N. J. ONE ONE	1 Head of a girl
2 on TWO Head of male	Title of Bank. Word TWO in red. TWO 2 TWO	2 Female reclining on bales; steamboat and schooner in distance.
Half length female figure.	3 Train of cars; water and hills in the distance. 3 ORANGE BANK, Orange, N. J.	
THREE on 3. Male portrait	Title of Bank. 3 Female seated with mechanical implements; cars, bridge and factory in distance. Red 3 on vig. 3 THREE	3 3
Farming scene and 5 horses. V	Large white V across note. Train cars. ORANGE BANK, Orange, N. J.	5 Male portrait
TEN Male portrait	ORANGE BANK, Orange, N. J. 10 Boy with kitchen; woman, child, dog, &c.; farmers in the rear. Large white X across vig 10	10 Male portrait
TEN Head. TEN	10 Female resting on a globe, with shield and eagle. 10 ORANGE BANK, Orange, N. J.	TEN DOLLARS
TWENTY Head. TWENTY	20 Figure of Justice, with a picture of Washington in her left hand; an eagle at her feet 20 ORANGE BANK, Orange, N. J.	TWENTY
50 Head. 50	50 State arms 50 ORANGE BANK, Orange, N. J.	50 Head. 50
Head. 100 Head.	100 Female in a chariot drawn by two horses and enveloped in clouds. 100 ORANGE BANK, Orange, N. J.	Head. 100 Head.

1 — Blacksmith shop, three men at work, and two more at work in background. — 1
PASSAIC CO. BANK. Paterson, N. J.
Compt'r die. — Male portrait.

2 — PASSAIC CO. BANK, Paterson, N. J. — 2
Large machinery, machinist standing, &c.
Compt's die. — Male portrait.

5 on med head. — Train of cars; large chimney, tram, houses, shop, &c., in background. — Five, V, 5.
PASSAIC CO. BANK, Paterson, N. J.
Treas. die. — Dog, key and safe. — Portrait of a female.

ONE — Train of cars coming through arch; two laborers. — 1
PHILLIPSB'RGH BK Phillipsburgh, N. J.
Puddling in an iron-mill.

2 TWO — Female feeding fowls. 2 Six men at work in an iron mill. — 2 TWO
PHILLIPSB'RGH BK Phillipsburgh, N. J.

3 — PHILLIPSB'RGH BK Phillipsburgh, N. J. — 3
Bull's head on a shield; man dressing leather on right and female sewing shoes on left.
Milkmaid with pail.

Female with flowers. — PHILLIPSB'RGH BK Phillipsburgh, N. J. — V
Bridge, two men on a raft; trees, houses and a mill in distance.
5 — 5 5 — Locomotive.

Female with cornucopia. — PHILLIPSB'RGH BK Phillipsburgh, N. J. — 10
Men at work in a glass manufactory, horse in distance.
10 — Blacksmith; anvil hammer and houses.

Indian family contemplating the progress of civilization. — Figure 20 with word Twenty, six times, around it on red die. — 20
PHILLIPSB'RGH BK Phillipsburgh, N. J.
20 — Mechanic and implements.

50 — Fig. 50 and words Fifty dollars on three red dies. — 50
PHILLIPSB'RGH BK Phillipsburgh, N. J.
Female with cornucopia. — Spread eagle — Female with quadrant.

ONE HUNDRED — Female greek — PHILLIPSB'RGH BK Phillipsburgh, N. J. — Helmeted female. — ONE HUNDRED
Fig. 100 and words One hundred dollars on three red dies.

1 — PRINCETON BANK, Princeton, N. J. — 1
Soldiers raising a breastwork. — State arms; in distance, on right, steamship; on left, train of cars. — Head of boy.

2 — Drover buying cattle. Picture of Buck. — 2
PRINCETON BANK, Princeton, N. J.
2 — Eagle — Head of a girl.

3 — Farm scene; milk-maid and two cows, one lying down. — 3
Female with veil. — PRINCETON BANK, Princeton, N. J. — Portrait of Washington.

V — PRINCETON BANK. Princetown, N. J. — 5
Woman with scales; eagle, &c. — 5 Death of Gen. Mercer. 5 — Portrait of Madison.
V — Eagle. — 5

10 — Portrait of female. Two females, one standing and the other seated; small ship in distance. 10 — X
Washington. — Madison.
10 — PRINCETON BANK. Princeton, N. J. — X
Pump, pony, and boy.

20 — Female portrait. State Arms. 20 — XX
Madison. — PRINCETON BANK, Princeton, N J. — Male portrait.
20 — Man and cow. — XX

50 — Female portrait. Female figure. 50 — 50
Male portrait. — PRINCETON BANK. Princeton, N J. — Male portrait.
50 — Pony and boy at a pump. — 50

100 — Female portrait. Female holding up to an eagle. 100 — 100
Male portrait. — PRINCETON BANK, Princeton, N. J. — Male portrait.
100 — Eagle. — 100

1 — Word one and figure 1. Female with child in arms, &c. Word one and figure 1. — 1
One in oval head. — SALEM BANKING CO. Salem, N. J. — One in oval head.
1 — 1

3 — 3 Shipping. 3 — 3
Mai. head. — SALEM BANKING CO., Salem, N. J. — Washington
3 — 3

5 — V Female reclining against iron chest; stag in distance, &c. V — 5
Female holding goblet to an eagle. — SALEM BANKING CO., Salem, N. J. — Two female figures.

Portrait of Franklin. — 10 Two female figures; 10 tree, sheep, &c. — Portrait of Washington.
SALEM BANKING CO., Salem, N. J. Eagle.

TWENTY — 20 Female erect, resting on anchor. 20 Female figure.
SALEM BANKING CO., Salem, N. J. Eagle. — Portrait of Franklin.

Portrait of Washington. — 50 Female; ocean scene. — 50
SALEM BANKING CO., Salem, N. J. Eagle. — Two females.

100 — Three females; eagle, cars, ship, &c. — C
State arms. — SALEM BANKING CO., Salem, N. J. — Portrait of Washington.
100 — Steamboat.

ONE — 1 Female on either side of Unicorn with horn of plenty, liberty pole and cap, cars and factories on the left. — Female with wreath of flowers.
Male portrait.
ONE — SOMERSET CO. B'K. Somerville, N. J. — ONE

2 — Head of Franklin. Farmer with pipe seated on plow, yoke of cattle on right, farm house on left.
Man Woman and dog. — SOMERSET CO. B'K. Somerville, N. J. Farm Implements. — 2

Indian with bow and arrow. — 3 Harvest scene farmers at lunch. — THREE
Female
THREE — SOMERSET CO. B'K. Somerville, N. J. — THREE

5 — SOMERSET CO. B'K. Somerville, N. J. — 5
Vig. Same as Ones. FIVE in circular Die. — Franklin.
Female. — Farming Implements. — 5

10 Washington. 10	Vig. Droves of cattle and sheep; man on horseback; public house on left. SOMERSET CO. B'K. Somerville, N. J. Farming implements.	10 Female with spear and balances; eagle and small portrait of Washington.
XX Female. XX	SOMERSET CO. B'K. Somerville, N. J. 20 Vig. Man plowing with two horses, also man with spade on his shoulder. Female.	20 Two farmers with cradle and grain.
50 Two females with wand and spyglass seated on merchandise	SOMERSET CO. B'K. Somerville, N. J. Vig. Two females seated, with cornucopia and wand; steamboat on right; anchor and vessel on left. 50	50 Male portrait.
Female erect with sword, cornucopia at her feet. HUNDRED	SOMERSET CO. B'K. Somerville, N. J. 100 Vig. Two females with flag overlooking the sea, on which is seen a ship in the distance; eagle on right. 100	
	STATE BANK, Camden, N. J. The 1's and 2's are nearly all withdrawn from circulation, and there has not been any issued for three years.	
3 Dog's head. 3	Female, boy, anvil, rake, plow, etc. STATE BANK, Camden, N. J	3 Dog's head 3
5 Male portrait V	Medal Head. Harvest scene. Medal Head. Reaper reclining. STATE BANK, Camden, N. J.	V Male portrait 5
10 Male portrait X	Medal Head. Liberty and shield, view of river, town, &c. Medal Head. STATE BANK, Camden, N. J.	X Male portrait 10
20 Harvest Scene. XX	Two Medal Heads. Female reclining with wand. Two Medal Heads. STATE BANK, Camden, N J.	XX Harvest Scene. 20
FIFTY	Man plowing. STATE BANK, Camden, N. J. Spread eagle.	50 State Arms. 50

100 Portrait of Franklin. 100	Vig. State Arms. STATE BANK, Camden, N. J. Spread eagle.	C 100 Hundred.
FIVE HUNDRED	500 Two females, Liberty and shield. Title of Bank. 500 D	500 500
ONE Portrait of Male. ONE	Medallion head. Shield with female figures on either side, the one holding liberty cap and pole, the other a cornucopia. Medallion head. STATE BANK, Elizabethtown, N. J.	ONE Portrait of Male. ONE
2 Medallion head. 2	Male Portrait. Shield with Female figures on either side, the one on right holding a sickle. Male Portrait. STATE BANK, Elizabethtown, N. J.	TWO
3 Medallion Head. 3	Male Portrait. Shipping, steamer, buildings in distance. Male Portrait. STATE BANK, Elizabethtown, N. J.	3 Medallion Head. 3
Circular Die. Female Portrait. Circular Die.	(Old Plate.) 5 Two females supporting an ornamental figure 5, and three boys representing Cupid, Mercury and Love. 5 STATE BANK, Elizabethtown, N. J.	Circular Die. Female Portrait. Circular Die.
5 Female Portrait.	(New Plate.) Neptune driving sea-horses in a shell car with Female seated thereon; mermaids &c. in the water; steamer in distance. STATE BANK, Elizabethtown, N. J. 5 and Cupid.	5 Portrait of Girl.
5 Portrait of girl.	Female, safe, shield, sheep, sheaf, etc. STATE BANK AT ELIZABETH, N. J. FIVE	5 on head. Male portrait.
10 Franklin. 10	Three females and bust of Washington. Title of Bank. TEN	TEN Portrait of girl. TEN
Circular Die. Female Portrait. Circular Die.	10 Two females supporting shield; 10 steamer on right and church on left. STATE BANK, Elizabethtown, N. J. 10	Oval Die. Female Portrait. Oval Die.

20 Shield and eagle with outstretched wings. 20	Female figure reclining; medallions representing Agriculture on right; railroad cars and shipping on left. STATE BANK, Elizabethtown, N. J. Mechanic and anvil.	20 Female Portrait
50 Female Portrait.	Female reclining with liberty cap and pole; eagle on right; globe on left, shipping in distance. STATE BANK, Elizabethtown, N. J. Sheaf of wheat and plow.	FIFTY Full length female figure leaning on anchor; ships in distance.
100 Portrait of Male. 100	Female reclining on bales and other articles of commerce; 100 ship on left and steamer on right in distance. STATE BANK, Elizabethtown, N. J. Dog.	Full length figure of Liberty. 100
500 Male Portrait	Shield supported by two females, the one on right holding liberty cap and pole, one on left ears of corn; steamship and railroad cars on right and factory on left. STATE BANK, Elizabethtown, N. J. Female.	500
1 ONE	Female reclining on horn of plenty; pole and cap, eagle and shield. STATE BANK, Newark, N. J. State Arms.	1 ONE
2 Goddess of liberty and Justice.	Two females seated; ship on left; train of cars and factory on right. STATE BANK, Newark N. J. Eagle.	2
3 Female and ornamental figure 3.	Three females seated; cars on left and ship on right. STATE BANK, Newark N. State Arms.	3
5 Ship; water in commotion.	View of banking house and church. STATE BANK, Newark, N. J. Eagle.	5 5
10 Female with cornucopia.	Vig. Same as 5's. STATE BANK, Newark, N. J. Head of Horse.	10 X
FIFTY Cooper at work. L	50 Female seated, agricultural scene on left; blacksmith shop on right. 50 STATE BANK, Newark, N. J. State Arms.	FIFTY Female seated. 50

Figure of Justice. 100 | C Female reclining on anchor; ship in distance. STATE BANK, Newark, N. J. State Arms. | ONE HUNDRED

500 Female seat on ship, &c., in distance. | State Arms; train of cars on left; Steamboat on right. STATE BANK, Newark, N. J. Agricultural Implements. | D

1 Female reclining. | State arms, with female on either side; buildings in distance. 1 STATE BANK, New Brunswick, N. J. | ONE Female bust. ONE

Word two in ornamental work. Female bust. TWO | 2 Same as ones. STATE BANK, New Brunswick, N. J. Train of cars. | 2

3 Female bust | Same as Ones. STATE BANK, New Brunswick, N. J. | 3 Female Indian. THREE

FIVE Cattle and farmers in a circle. 5 | Portrait of Washington. State Arms supported by two females, the one on left seated. Portrait of Franklin. STATE BANK, New Brunswick, N. J. Railroad cars. | FIVE Cattle and farmers in a circle. 5

TEN Venus in a sea shell, and ship in distance. 10 | 10 Same as Fives. 10 STATE BANK, New Brunswick, N. J. Schooner. | TEN Venus in a sea shell, and ship in distance. 10

20 State arms supported by two females, the one on left seated. 20 | 20 Male figure seated, with torch in left and scroll in right hand; eagle on left, with miniature of Washington round its neck. 20 STATE BANK, New Brunswick, N. J. Figure of Agriculture. | XX A shield supported by figures of agriculture on right, commerce on left, shipping &c., in distance. 20

50 Female Portrait. FIFTY. | State arms supported by two females seated; train of railroad cars, shipping, &c., in distance. STATE BANK, New Brunswick, N. J. | 50 A ship and shipping.

100 Stone cutter. | Same as Fifties. STATE BANK, New Brunswick, N. J. Figure of Agriculture. | 100 Blacksmith.

On this and the words five hundred dollars and portrait of Washington. | Same as Fifties. STATE BANK, New Brunswick, N. J. | 500 Female Portrait.

ONE State Arms. 1 | Female seated with pail on her lap; cows on left and right of her. 1 SUSSEX BANK, Newton, N. J. | Large fig. 1, whole length of note.

ONE | SUSSEX BANK, Newton, N. J. Men Loading Hay. | 1 ONE

TWO | Man seated; Girl and boy playing with dog; horses. SUSSEX BANK, Newton, N. J. | 2 Girl seated with hare in hand.

2 Washington. 2 | Two females with eagle in centre; anchor and ship on right, cornucopia on left. SUSSEX BANK, Newton, N. J. | 2 Female with pole and cap; figure 2.

THREE Female erect with cap of liberty. THREE | Portrait of Franklin, with female on either side; on right a sheaf of wheat, &c., on left steamboat, and ship. SUSSEX BANK, Newton, N. J. | 3 State Arms. 3

5 Female. 5 | 5 Two females one reclining on a sheaf with sickle in her left hand; the other on a shield containing a plow in its centre, her left hand on a cornucopia. 5 Title of Bank. Portrait of Washington. | FIVE

FIVE V FIVE V | Female seated with flowers around her; man plowing on left, buildings on right. SUSSEX BANK, Newton, N. J. Female bathing. | 5 V

TEN | 10 Two sheeps of war in an engagement. 10 SUSSEX BANK, Newton, N. J. Male Portrait with baton | SUSSEX BANK

TWENTY | 20 Female seated on sheaf of wheat, sickle in right hand; farming utensils on her left. XX Title of Bank. | SUSSEX BANK

50 Horses head. 50 | 50 Female seated with sickle in right hand; left hand resting on sheaf of wheat; and two cows at her right. 50 Title of Bank. Portrait of Jefferson. | FIFTY

100 Boys Head. | SUSSEX BANK, Newton, N. J. State Arms, female on either side. | 100 Female portrait.

1 Female portrait. | TRENTON BANKING COMPANY Trenton, N. J. Milkmaid erect; boy pointing. | 1 Female portrait.

ONE Medallion Head. ONE | Female figure seated supporting figure 1. Water; mill in distance. Female figure seated supporting figure 1. TRENTON BANKING COMPANY, Trenton, N. J. Stm. Engine and coal cars. | ONE Medallion Head. ONE

2 Female portrait. | Title of Bank. Female seated with agricultural implements and products. | 2 Sheep.

TWO A seated female with cornucopia, &c. TWO | Medallion head and 2. Dairy maid and cows; farm house in distance. TRENTON BANKING COMPANY. Trenton, N. J. | TWO Male portrait TWO

3 Three cherubs with bunches of grapes. 3 | 3 View of Old Trenton bridge. 3 TRENTON BANKING COMPANY, Trenton, N. J. Row Boat. | 3 Three cherubs with bunches of grapes. 3

3 Beehive | Title of Bank. Female seated with sheaf and sickle. | 3 Child's head

5 Boy and girl. | Horse, colt, man with bag on back, mill, wheel, boys on bridge, etc. Title of Bank. | 5 Male head.

5 Milk maid and pail. | TRENTON BANKING COMPANY, Trenton, N. J. View of Trenton State House. | 5 5 in ornamental engraving.

Left	Centre	Right
X Female portrait.	Title of Bank. Female seated, with right arm on rock; factories and man plowing in distance.	10 Children and butterfly.
Ornamental die. Male portrait. Ornamental Die.	10 Figures of Agriculture, Labor and science, with heads of cattle in distance. 10 TRENTON BANKING COMPANY, Trenton, N. J.	Ornamental Die. Male portrait. Ornamental Die.
20 Male portrait 20	State Arms of N. J., water-mill on left agriculture on right in distance. TRENTON BANKING COMPANY, Trenton, N. J	20 Male portrait 20
XX Female portrait.	Title of Bank. Female erect reading, two others seated listening.	20 Female portrait.
50 Male portrait 50	50 Shield with the words "liberty and prosperity" on base; figure of agriculture on left, and Minerva on right, holding a shield with the word FIFTY thereon. 50 TRENTON BANKING COMPANY, Trenton, N. J.	50 Male portrait 50
50 Squaw.	Girl's portrait. Title of Bank.	50 Female with pen and tablet.
100 Cattle, telegraph, railroad, etc.	Female seated pointing with right hand to ship. Title of Bank.	100 Portrait of girl.
10 0 Male portrait 100	Medallion Head. State Arms of N. J. Medallion Head. TRENTON BANKING COMPANY, Trenton, N. J.	100 Male portrait 100
1 Female portrait. ONE	UNION BANK, Dover, N. J. 1 Figure of America reclining on shield; goods on left, steamboat on right. 1	Full length female. ONE
2 2	UNION BANK OF DOVER, N. J State arms of N. Jersey TWO DOLLARS.	2 Train of cars.

Left	Centre	Right
Ornamental work. Med. head with word two thereon Ornamental work.	Small med. head and word 2. Coat of arms of N. J., supported by two female figures; bridges and cars on left in distance. Small med. head and word 2. UNION BANK, Dover, N. J.	TWO Figure of America. TWO
THREE Male portrait. THREE	Female figure apparently flying, typifying plenty; ships in distance. UNION BANK, Dover, N. J.	3 3
FIVE Male portrait. FIVE	UNION BANK, Dover, N. J. V State Arms supported by two females; cars in distance on left; steamship on right.	5 FIVE
TEN Female portrait. X	X Mechanic with hammer, anvil, &c. buildings and cars on right. UNION BANK, Dover, N. J.	X 10
20 Farmer and Plough. XX	XX Large vig. of cars, track, and telegraph wires. UNION BANK Dover, N. J.	20
Full length figure of Justice. 50	50 Female figure of science seated, balances, &c.; factory and water-mill in distance. 50 UNION BANK, Dover, N. J. State arms supported by two females.	Full length figure of Justice. 50
Hunter loading rifle, deer. ONE	Two oxen before cart; men loading it with hay; men, trees, and haystack in distance. UNION BANK. Frenchtown, N. J.	1 Registers die
2 Washington.	Female reclining; shield on which is ship in water; on right sheep and wheat; on left sheaf and bags of salt. UNION BANK, Frenchtown, N. J.	2 Registers die
Word Three and figure 3. Female feeding chickens.	Train of cars; trees, houses, sheep, etc, in distance. UNION BANK, Frenchtown, N. J.	3 Registers die
5 Registers die	UNION BANK, Frenchtown, N. J. Portrait of Washington; eagle at top; two females on right, one on left; cars and ship in distance.	5 Three dogs beside the trees.

Left	Centre	Right
Registers die X	UNION BANK, Frenchtown, N. J. Shield on which is cars; sheafs and fruit on right; milkmaid seated on left; in distance farmhouse, cows and trees.	TEN Female reclining, Indian female erect.
XX Dozen of cattle.	UNION BANK, Frenchtown, N. J. Portrait of Washington; female on either side; on right ship and steamboat in distance; on left sheaf and men mowing.	Figures 20, word twenty and two XX. Reg. die.
1 Female erect beside column; steamer, building, etc., in distance. ONE	UNION COUNTY BK, Plainfield, N. J Female reclining on ground beside scroll, shield, etc; view of falls in background.	1 Female feeding fowls.
2 Beehive.	Boy and horses at trough; female, ducks, etc.; horses in distance. 2 Title of Bank.	2 Female beside column; steamer, building, &c.
UNION THREE	COUNTY BANK Farmer, horse; wheelwright, man, ding cart, etc. Female beside column; steamer, building, etc.	3 Female head
5 Female beside column; steamer, building, etc. FIVE	FIVE DOLLARS. Man on horse at trough, man, boy, sheep; loading hay, etc. Title of Bank.	5 Girls head.
10 Female beside column; steamer, etc.	Title of Bank. Hunter, farmers, etc, viewing train of cars.	10 Female portrait.
20 Female beside column; steamer, building, etc.	Cattle, sheep, etc. Title of Bank.	20 Female with trident seated on shell.
Three females with anchor. FIVE	V Steamship and sail vessels. B'K. OF COMMERCE, Philadelphia, Pa.	5 Female seated with spy glass; ship in distance.
Do. 5 Do.	V Men loading truck with bales. V B'K OF COMMERCE, Philadelphia, Pa. 5 Indian head. 5	Do. 5 Do.

Left	Centre	Right
Old man, child and bust of Washington. 10	Title of Bank. 10 X Wheels.	10 Sailor.
TEN Sailor with flag and female at his feet; cornucopia, anchor bales, barrels, &c.	10 Shipping; storehouse on right; city on left. B'K. OF COMMERCE, Philadelphia, Pa.	10 Liberty with pole, cap and shield. TEN
Statue of Liberty with pole and cap.	20 Shipping. 20 B'K. OF COMMERCE, Philadelphia, Pa.	20 Artist seated with brush and canvass. 20
FIFTY	Med. head Fe- Med. head with male with 50 50 on it. seated on it. with eagle perched on shield on right, ship on left. B'K. OF COMMERCE, Philadelphia, Pa.	50 Cupid seated with pencil and paper 50
100 C 100	100 Female seated and giving eagle drink. 100 B'K. OF COMMERCE, Philadelphia, Pa.	100 C 100
500 Neptune with trident, seated in sea shell.	Female seated on bale of goods with wand in her right hand; shipping on left. B'K. OF COMMERCE, Philadelphia, Pa. Medallion head.	500 Ship under full sail.
POST Ship in a storm. NOTE	Neptune with trident seated in a shell on the sea. B'K. OF COMMERCE, Philadelphia, Pa.	POST Med. head. NOTE
1 Indian girl.	BANK OF GERMANTOWN, Philada phia. Pa. Red 1 across ONE. Sailors in boat attacked by white bear.	ONE across 1 Red 1 across ONE
2 Two children.	BANK OF GERMANTOWN Philadelphia Pa 2 Cows browsing on haystack. 2 TWO DOLLARS.	2 Gen. Scott.
5 Head of Wm. Penn. 5	Vig. Boy and man on horseback; drove of sheep and cattle; boy reclining at foot of tree; farmer, &c. in the distance. BANK OF GERMANTOWN, Philadelphia, Pa.	5 Head of Franklin. 5

Left	Centre	Right
Cupid and 5. Male portrait.	BANK OF GERMANTOWN, PA. Farmer gathering corn; horse, colt and wagon. V V	5 and Cupid. Male portrait.
10 Farmers at lunch.	Male portrait. Boy watering horses; girl standing beside, &c. BANK OF GERMANTOWN, PA.	10 Male portrait.
Female representing Agriculture with sickle in hand. TEN	10 Vig. Harvest scene, farmers reclined, female seated with child in arms, basket and pitcher by her side. BANK OF GERMANTOWN, Philadelphia, Pa.	10 Head of J. Q. Adams. TEN
10 Head of Washington. 10	Vig. Harvest scene; three men seated, taking lunch, hat and basket, house in the distance. BANK OF GERMANTOWN, Philadelphia, Pa. Agricultural implements.	10 Head of Penn. 10
20 Medallion head of female. 20	Vig. Man representing the mechanic arts; wheel, sledge hammer, compass and square; two men and house in the distance. BANK OF GERMANTOWN, Philadelphia, Pa.	20 Female seated, holding sheaf and sickle on right shoulder, left hand extended upwards. 20
50 Head of Marshall. 50	Vig. Female in sitting posture, holding a sheaf of grain in her right hand, reclining on a bale of cotton; tobacco stalk and hogshead, farm scene in the distance. BANK OF GERMANTOWN, Philadelphia, Pa.	50 Washington on horseback.
100 Head of Lafayette. 100	Vig. Dairy scene, female in sitting posture, and woman milking, little girl in sitting posture; calf and farm house in distance. BANK OF GERMANTOWN, Philadelphia, Pa.	100 Head of Gen. Taylor. 100
500	BANK OF GERMANTOWN, Philadelphia, Pa. Vig. Eagle on globe, with female holding stalk of grain in her right hand on right; and Indian with rifle on left. Five Hundred 500 Dols.	500
1 Phila. Male portrait.	BANK OF NORTH AMERICA. 1 Camp scene. Officers, one on horseback, cannon, tents, &c. 1 ONE	1 Public building.
5 Wood Fire and fig. 5. 5	BK. OF NORTH AM., Philadelphia, Pa. Portrait of Franklin. Indian female in the centre of a V; eagle, shield, pole and cap. Female portrait.	5 Locomotive. 5

Left	Centre	Right
10 Portrait of Wm. Penn. TEN	Female and Indian on either side of a frame enclosing ship, plough and sheafs; cattle and factory in background. BK OF NORTH AM., Philadelphia, Pa. Dog, key and safe.	10 Franklin. TEN
20 Male portrait. 20	Female seated on bale; shield, barrel, sheaf, &c. BK OF NORTH AM., Philadelphia, Pa.	20 Female with arms extended resting on anchor; shipping in background.
50 Lafayette. 50	Female reclining; on left eagle, shield, flags, etc.; on right, shipping. BK OF NORTH AM., Philadelphia, Pa. Sheaf, plow, &c.	50 Justice. 50
100 Washington 100	Eagle on a rock; shipping on either side. BK OF NORTH AM., Philadelphia. Dog, key and safe.	100 Liberty with pole and cap. 100
Ornamental work. Dog and safe. Ornamental work.	500 Ship with sails set 500 BK OF NORTH AM., Philadelphia, Pa. Spread eagle.	Ornamental work. Sailor with telescope. Ornamental work.
Ornamental work. Dog and safe. Ornamental work.	1000 Ship with sails set. 1000 BK OF NORTH AM., Philadelphia, Pa. Spread eagle.	Ornamental work Sailor with telescope. Ornamental work.
Med. head of Franklin. 1000	BANK OF NORTH AMERICA. Philadelphia, Pa. Vig. Female seated with eagle and globe. Letter M either side. ONE THOUSAND in red.	Med. head of Washington. 1000
5 Med. Head and word five. V	Eagle mounted on escutcheon, group of persons representing various pursuits—Agriculture, Commerce, Manufactures, Justice, Liberty, and so on, ship on right. B'K. OF NORTHERN LIBERTIES, Philadelphia, Pa.	V Med. head and word five 5
10 Washington X	Vig. Same as fives. B'K. OF NORTHERN LIBERTIES, Philadelphia, Pa.	X Med. head and word ten 10
20 Med. head. 20	Vig. Same as fives. B'K. OF NORTHERN LIBERTIES, Philadelphia, Pa.	20 Washington 20

FIFTY. Group of persons, Liberty, Justice, spear, horse, eagle, &c. FIFTY. | Med. head and 50 on it. State Arms. Med. head and 50 on it. B'K. OF NORTHERN LIBERTIES, Philadelphia, Pa. | 50 Washington 50

100 Washington 100 | Female with babe in arms; shipping and sheafs; life boat; steamboat in distance. Med. head and 100 on it, on either side of the vignette. Title of Bank. | 100 Same as on left of bill. 100

500 Med. head. 500 | Liberty and Justice on either side of shield, surmounted by eagle; ship and plow in canton; heads of two horses. 500 Title of Bank. State Arms | Escutcheon, mounted eagle and group of persons.

| 1000 Escutcheon, mounted eagle, Goddess of Liberty, Justice, female with horn of plenty, and other persons; ship on right and two horses on left. Vig. on left end of note. Title of Bank. | POST Child's head. NOTE

Tomb of Washingt'n 1 surrounded by words ONE. | Group of three children with book on table, in an "oval." BANK OF PENN TOWNSHIP, Philadelphia, Pa. ONE DOLLAR. | 1 surrounded by words ONE. Portrait of Washingt'n

Bust of Female. 2 surrounded by words TWO | Ocean view, ships, &c. BANK OF PENN TOWNSHIP, Philadelphia, Pa. TWO DOLLARS. | 2 surrounded by words TWO Portrait of Winfield Scott.

5 Bust of Penn FIVE | Agricultural scene; group of five persons. BANK OF PENN TOWNSHIP, Philadelphia, Pa. | 5 Washington on horseback

Goddess of Liberty. Wm. Penn. Goddess of Liberty. | 10 Female seated, sickle, cornucopia, farming implements, house, etc. 10 Title of Bank. | Spread eagle. Washington Spread eagle.

20 Franklin. 20 | Title of Bank. Portrait of Penn. Two females embracing each other; safe in foreground; ship in background; steamboat on left. | Washington 20

50 Locomotive and cars; Train of cars ascending hill. 50 | Portrait of Penn. Female seated on bale of goods; houses and spires in distance. Portrait of Washington. Title of Bank. | 50 Franklin. 50

100 Washington 100 | Title of Bank. Portrait of Penn. | Mill; small cottage in distance. 100

Die. FIVE HUNDRED Die. | Three females seated, cornucopias, &c. Figure on either side of vig. Title of Bank. Eagle. | Die. Head of Penn. Die.

Die. POST 1000 NOTE Die. | 1000 Washington and others on horseback; soldiers and cannon. 1000 Title of Bank. Spread eagle. | Die. Wm. Penn. Die.

1 1 1 | Philadelphia 1 City arms of Phila. Indian girl leaning on shield, in which is fig. 1. CITY BANK. | 1 1

2 2 | Two females either side of shield, in which is ship. Phila. Pa. 2 CITY BANK across TWO 2 TWO DOLLARS. | 2 Female with flag and shield; Indian girl seated.

5 Portrait of a boy 5 | CITY BANK, Philadelphia, Pa. Signing of the "Declaration of Independence." | 5 Portrait of a girl. 5

Female erect with vase of flowers. 10 | Two females seated on either side of a shield; in centre of shield, a ship; the female on the left holds a scroll. CITY BANK, Philadelphia, Pa. | X Sailor at the helm.

20 XX | CITY BANK, Philadelphia, Pa. Head of Washington on shield; right Indian seated, female with pole and cap; on left a Continental soldier. Portrait of Penn on right of vignette, and Franklin on left. | 20 XX

50 Large anchor, box, barrel and bale of goods | CITY BANK, Philadelphia, Pa. Portrait of Washington. State arms. | 50 Beehive and flower bushes.

100 | CITY BANK Philadelphia, Pa. Female reclining, and eagle; on left, train of cars crossing a bridge; view of a harbor and city in distance. 100. | 100

Female seated with sickle and portrait of Washington. 500 | Male portrait CITY BANK, Philadelphia, Pa. | Shield and letter D, bust of female at top; male on right, female at left. 500

M Shearing sheep. | 1000 Female reclining on shield, on which is a scroll and tree; drapery with stars over the shield. CITY BANK, Philadelphia, Pa. | 1000 M

1 Man loading paper barrels, ship, 1 | COMMERCIAL BK. Boy, bales, &c. Large green 1 on ONE. Sailors reefing sail. Philadelphia, Pa. | 1 Female head ONE

2 TWO 2 | COMMERCIAL BK, Philadelphia, Pa. Ship towed by tug. Female TWO 2 | 2 TWO

FIVE Sailor with flag. | Shipping; schooner on the right with figure 5 on the sail; on left small steamboat. COMMERCIAL BANK OF PENNSYLVANIA, Philadelphia, Pa. | 5 Locomotive. Landscape, etc.

10 Anchor and bale of goods | Sailor on deck of ship with quadrant; shipping in background. Title of Bank running over the vignette. | 10 Female Portrait.

Die Work. Washington Die Work. | 20 Two females representing Agriculture and Manufactures; between them shield with 20 on it; ships on left, and sheep on right. 20 Title of Bank. Spread eagle. | Die Work Lafayette Die Work.

Die Work. Franklin. Die Work. | 50 Female seated on anchor, right arm resting on shield with 50 on it; sheaf, ship, &c. 50 Title of Bank. | Die Work. Male portrait Die Work.

Die Work. Male portrait Die Work. | 100 Female seated, eagle beside; shipping in distance. 100 Title of Bank. Sword. | Die Work. Male portrait Die Work.

Figures 500 written with a pen. Med. head. Figures 500 written with a pen. | Med. head. Female reclining with sprig and wand; shipping in distance. Med. head. Title of Bank. | Same as on left.

Vig. 1000 written with a pen. Med. Head. Vig. 1000 written with a pen.
Med. head. Vig. Same as 500s. Med. head. Title of Bank.
Same as on left.

1 Horses, men, &c., in circular die.
Ships, steamers, &c. Philadelphia. COMMONWEALTH BANK. ONE DOLLAR.
1 Cars, canal boat &c. in circular die

Goddess of Liberty resting her arm upon pillar, on which is the word TWO.
2 Portrait of Gen. Scott. Two Dollars. COMMONWEALTH BANK, Philadelphia.
2

Die. 5 Die.
COMMONWEALTH BANK, Philadelphia. Pa. Male portrait. Figure 5 on word FIVE either side.
Die. 5 Die.

5 Farmer, dog, horse, bench, implements, bird flying, &c.
Girls' head. Man, horse, colt, bridge, two boys; hills in background. COMMONWEALTH BANK, Philadelphia, Pa. FIVE FIVE FIVE
5 Two sailors pulling rope, etc.

10 Mechanic and bench.
Title of Bank. Two females seated representing Agriculture and Commerce; factories and buildings on right; cows, shery and village in distance on left.
10 Sailor; ships, houses, etc., in background.

20 Female seated, dog beside her.
Three male figures erect beneath motto with "Faust, Guttenberg, and Schoeffer, upon it; printers' names on left; press, &c., on right. Title of Bank.
20 Wm. Penn.

50 Female shading her eyes with hand.
Title of Bank. Circular die containing outline map of Penn., N. Y., O., Va., Md., N. J., surmounted by bust of Washington; soldier on right; goddess of liberty, cannon, &c., on left.
50 Sailor seated.

100 Franklin.
Title of Bank. State Arms.
100 Scene in an iron mill.

ONE across 1 1
CONSOLIDATION BANK. View of ship yard and ship launch. Philadelphia. Pa.
ONE across 1 1

2 TWO on 2 TWO
CONSOLIDATION BK. Large public building. Philadelphia, Pa.
2 TWO on 2 TWO

5 Portrait of Wm. Penn.
CONSOLIDATION BANK, Phila., Penn. Steamer Quaker City under way, and view of Phila. Harbor. Portrait of Female Child.
5 Portrait of Governor Pollock.

10 Female on a platform working a mechanical instrument.
A Drove of cattle and drovers driving them to the water; house and trees in background and church in the extreme distance. CONSOLIDATION BANK, Phila., Penn. Portrait of a Female Child.
10 Sailor seated with spy glass.

20 Interior view of a blacksmith shop.
CONSOLIDATION BANK, Phila., Penn. Raft floating down a river, man in boat holding up two birds on the right, another raft in back ground, trees, hills, &c.
20 Workman dressing leather.

50 Cattle, telegraph poles and wires; cars and bridge in background.
CONSOLIDATION BANK, Phila., Penn. The Globe or the world, and an eagle surmounting it. Portrait of a boy.
'50 Woodman erect, hand resting on axe.

100 Female with liberty pole and cap, left hand resting on a shield, eagle sitting on the ground.
Title of Bank. C 100 Female erect holding sickle in right hand, and grain in left.
100 Sailor, blacksmith and anchor.

Female with flowers in her apron. D
CONSOLIDATION BK. Philadelphia. Pa. Ornamental portrait of Gen. Scott. D D Five Hundred Dollars.
500 Female feeding fowls.

1000 Man seated; scythe hanging on tree.
CONSOLIDATION BK. Philadelphia, Pa. Horses drinking from trough by a well; man, goat and kid, sheep, etc. house in background. One Thousand Dollars.
M Female portrait.

1 Female with sickle and sheaf of wheat.
CORN EXCHANGE BANK. Philadelphia, Pa. ONE across 1 Portrait of Gen. Scott. ONE across 1
1 Female resting on bank; basket of fruit at feet.

2 Male portrait.
CORN EXCHANGE BANK, Philadelphia, Pa. TWO across 2 Female stepping into pool of water. TWO across 2
TWO across 2 Dog on safe.

5 Portrait.
CORN EX. BANK, Philadelphia, Pa. Miller and farmer beside wagon, two horses, one drinking out of trough, mill in back ground. Farmer seated on plow.
5 Female head.

10 Female gleaner.
X Sailor, farmer and blacksmith. Title of Bank.
10 Male portrait.

TWENTY Male portrait.
CORN EX. BANK, 20 Philadelphia, Pa.
Corn husking scene. 20

50 50
Western steamers, etc. 50 Title of Bank.
FIFTY Milkmaid, erect, with stool; cows etc.

C 100
Marine view—ships sailing. C Title of Bank. 100
100 Two farmers gathering corn.

500
CORN EX. BANK, Philadelphia, Pa. Train of cars, cars, horses, steamboat, &c. 500
500

5 Sailor seated.
FAR. & MECH. B'K., Philadelphia, Pa. Blacksmith, farmer and horses; spire in distance.
5 Female seated; house in background.

X Female portrait. 10
Female seated between 1 and 0; agricultural scenery, house, &c. 10 on right. FAR. & MECH. B'K., Philadelphia, Pa. Arm, anvil and hammer.
X Female portrait. 10

10 Female with wheat.
Blacksmith shop, farmer, two horses, plow, rake, etc. FAR. & MECH. BK., Philadelphia, Pa.
10 Mechanic and lathe.

20 20
Title of Bank. Female with bundle of grain. Cogwheels, etc.
20 Farmer, two horses, plow, blacksmith, anvil, etc. TWENTY

20 — Farmer leaning against a tree; female seated. — 20
Two cupids, flag, vessel, &c., word Twenty and Medallion head each side.
FAR. & MECH. B'K., Philadelphia, Pa.
XX — Blacksmith at forge. — XX

50 — Female seated; house in distance. — FIFTY
Blacksmith, farmer, horses, farming utensils, &c., spire in distance.
FAR. & MECH. B'K., Philadelphia, Pa.
Bee-hive.
50 — Sailor seated, vessel, &c. — FIFTY

C — Vig. same as right of 20.
Mechanic and lathe.
Title of Bank
100
100 — C — 100

Female erect with shield and spear. — 100
FAR. & MECH. B'K., Philadelphia, Pa.
100 Female, harvest scene, vessel, houses, &c. 100
100 — Word hundred on Med head. — 100

FIVE HUNDRED
Female seated; anvil, screw, hammer, &c. Steamboat in distance.
FAR. & MECH. BANK. Phila. Pa.
Female erect, sheaf, plow and ship. — 500

ONE THOUSAND
FAR. & MECH. B'K., Philadelphia, Pa.
1000 Vulcan.
ONE THOUSAND

ONE
GIRARD BANK, Philadelphia, Pa. 1
Female seated on bales, water mill on right, canal lock on left.
ONE
ONE — Female with sickle and grain — ONE

5 — Female portrait.
GIRARD BANK, Philadelphia, Pa.
Goddess of Liberty and eagle.
5 — Female portrait.

10 — Male portrait. — X
10 Market scene; wagons, horses, pedestrians, &c. 10
GIRARD BANK, Philadelphia, Pa.
X — Male portrait. — 10

10 — Washington
GIRARD BANK, Philadelphia, Pa.
Portrait of Girard; plow and ship. Word Ten on either side.
10 — Male portrait.

20 — Head of Girard. — XX
20 Female reclining; anvil and hammer; cars in distance. 20
GIRARD BANK, Philadelphia, Pa.
XX — Head of Girard. — 20

L — Head of Girard. — 50
Two females seated on bale of goods; shipping, &c. Word Fifty on either side of vig.
GIRARD BANK, Philadelphia, Pa.
50 — Head of Girard. — L

100 HUNDRED 100
Female seated in chariot drawn by sea horses. Head of Girard on either side of vignette.
GIRARD BANK, Philadelphia, Pa.
100 HUNDRED 100

500 — Head of Girard. — 500
View of the Bank building. Figures 500 on either side of vig.
GIRARD BANK, Philadelphia, Pa.
500 — Head of Girard. — 500

1000 — Head of Girard. — 1000
Female seated representing Commerce, Manufactures and Arts; ship and engine in distance. Word Thousand on either side of vignette.
GIRARD BANK, Philadelphia, Pa.
1000 — Head of Girard. — 1000

ONE — Mechanic resting arm upon column on which is the word ONE, with bust on top.
KENSINGTON B'K. Philadelphia, Pa.
1 across ONE. Female with fan in hand. 1 across ONE.
ONE across 1 — Mechanic at work in ship yard.

2 — Female figure leaning against column.
2 across TWO. Wm. Penn surrounded by Indians, etc.
KENSINGTON B'K, Philadelphia, Pa.
2 — Female portrait.

5 — Female bust. — V
Vessels; ship building and houses in distance. Double med. head on either side of vig.
KENSINGTON B'K., Philadelphia, Pa.
V — Female portrait. — 5

10 — Female erect and vessel in distance. — X
Med. head. Rafts, boats, and other water craft; mountain scenery, houses, etc. Med. head.
KENSINGTON B'K., Philadelphia, Pa.
X — Female and spinning wheel. — 10

Die. — Columbus. — Die.
20 The Old Elm Tree; harbor or city in distance. 20
KENSINGTON B'K., Philadelphia, Pa.
Sword.
Die. — Wm. Penn. — Die.

20 — Indians contemplating the progress of civilization.
KENSINGTON B'K., Philadelphia, Pa.
Vig. Same as 20s above. Large red 20 in centre of bill.
XX XX
20 — Portrait of Wm. Penn.

Die Work. — Male portrait — Die Work.
50 Two females seated; cornucopia between; eagle and ship; ship in distance. 50
KENSINGTON B'K., Philadelphia, Pa.
Eagle.
Die Work. — Washington — Die Work.

50 — Franklin.
KENSINGTON B'K., Philadelphia, Pa.
Female seated in a letter L with machinery, etc.; cars on left; factory on right.
Female in water.
50 — Washington

Justice and head of Washington
100 Female seated on globe; cattle, harvest scene, horses, agricultural implements, &c. Title of Bank on either side of vig. 100
Male figure.
Die Work. — Lafayette. — Die Work.

C — 100 — C
KENSINGTON B'K., Philadelphia, Pa.
View of ship yard, three vessels on stocks. Large red C.
100 PENNSYLVANIA 100
100 — Female with sheaf and sickle.

500 — Interior of a rolling mill.
KENSINGTON B'K., Philadelphia, Pa.
Steamship at sea; large red letter D.
PENNSYLVANIA.
500 — Factory and creek.

ONE on 1 — Girl's head.
State Arms of Penn.
MAN. & MECH'NICS' BANK. Philadelphia, Pa.
1 — Figure of Justice.

2 — Two females with sickle and grain.
State Arms of Penn.
MAN. & MECH'NICS' BANK Philadelpaia, Pa.
2 — Girl's head

5 — Portrait of little girl.
MAN. & MECH. B'K Philadelphia, Pa.
Vig. Two horses; houses, shrubbery &c. in background.
5
5

10 — Female and cows; farm scene.
MAN. & MECH. B'K Philadelphia, Pa.
Large 10 and words ten dollars.
X
10 — Log-rolling, forest, yoke of oxen, &c.

20 | MAN. & MECH. B'K, Philadelphia, Pa. | 20
Canal scene, men unloading wood and coal from canal boats; man, horse and cart, &c., city in distance. The vig. extends across the whole lower part of note.

50 | MAN. & MECH. B'K, Philadelphia, Pa. | 50
City Arms, with female on either side; train of cars and sheaf on right; steamboat and barrel on left. The vig. extends across the whole lower part of note.

100 C | MAN. & MECH. B'K, Philadelphia, Pa. | 100 C
Trains of cars, bridge, factory, &c.; cars, hills and houses in distance.

500 Male portrait | MAN. & MECH. BK., Philadelphia, Pa. | 500
Five Hundred Dollars in ornamental die work.
Red letter D. The State House as it looked in 1776.

1000 M | MAN. & MECH. BK., Philadelphia, Pa. | 1000 M
Frame enclosing view of shipping.
M M

Steamboat building. 5 | 5 Portrait of a female; globe, &c. 5 | Washington and horse. 5
MECHANICS' BANK, Philadelphia, Pa.
Blacksmith's arm.

5 Sailor leaning on capstan | MECHANICS' BANK, Philadelphia, Pa. | 5 Female head.
Mechanic, letter V and mechanical implements; factories in distance; FIVE across V on left; on right DOLLARS across V.

TEN Female with cornucopia. TEN | 10 Blacksmith reclining on anvil; house in distance. 10 | Liberty. TEN
MECHANICS' BANK, Philadelphia, Pa.

20 XX | MECHANICS' BANK, Philadelphia, Pa. | 20 XX
Penn. Goddess of Liberty holding bust of Washington; soldier and two Indians looking at it. Franklin.

TWENTY Miniature view of female reclining on bags, bread, etc.; steamboats in distance | MECHANICS' BANK, Philadelphia, Pa. | 20
20 Spread eagle on trunk of fallen tree; cars on left; depot on right.
Mechanics' Arm.

50 | MECHANICS' BANK, Philadelphia, Pa. | 50 Vessels and harbor.
Train of cars crossing bridge; vessel at the farther end; house, wagon, horses, etc.
Goddess of Liberty.

50 Male portrait. Die. | Two females representing Agriculture and Commerce. | 50 Washington. Die.
MECHANICS' BANK, Philadelphia, Pa.
Mechanics' Arm.

100 Mechanics' arm. 100 | MECHANICS' BANK, Philadelphia, Pa. | ONE HUNDRED
Agricultural implements.

500 | MECHANICS' BANK, Philadelphia, Pa. | FIVE HUNDRED
500 View of the building formerly occupied by the Bank. 500

1000 | MECHANICS' BANK, Philadelphia, Pa. | ONE THOUSAND
1000 Vig. Same as 500s. 1000

Two females and Goddess of Liberty. 5 | PHILADELPHIA BK, Philadelphia, Pa. 5 | FIVE Female seated with bird, globe and spear.

5 Male portrait | Female either side of shield on which is ship; building, factories, cars, etc., in background. Red V below. | 5 Male portrait
PHILADELPHIA BK, Philadelphia, Pa.

10 Male portrait | Vig. Same as 5s. | 10 Clay.
Title of Bank.
Red X.

TEN Female portrait. TEN | Female seated on bale of goods; shipping and light-house. Figs. 10 on either side of vignette. | TEN Female portrait. TEN
PHILADELPHIA BK, Philadelphia, Pa.
Dog's head.

20 Wm. Penn. 20 | Female on either side of escutcheon; vessels and houses in distance. Portrait on either side of vignette. | 20 Franklin. 20
PHILADELPHIA BK, Philadelphia, Pa.
Spread eagle.

20 | PHILADELPHIA BANK, Philadelphia, Pa. | 20
TWENTY.
TWENTY Male Portrait. DOLLARS.

50 Franklin. 50 | PHILADELPHIA BK, Philadelphia, Pa. | 50 Wm. Penn. 50
Vig. Same as 20s.
Washington

Male Portrait. | 50 PHILADELPHIA BANK. Philadelphia, Pa. | 50
FIFTY Franklin. DOLLARS

100 Male portrait 100 | PHILADELPHIA BK, Philadelphia, Pa. | 100 Male portrait 100
Vig. Same as 20s.
Bee hive.

100 Male head. | Female either side of ship, on shield, buildings and vessels in distance. | 100 Male head
PHILADELPHIA BANK. Philadelphia, Pa.
Bee hive.

Med. head. Female erect | View of impending cliff; locomotive, omnibuses, forest trees, &c. Figures 500 on either side of vig. | Med. head. Three females.
PHILADELPHIA BK, Philadelphia, Pa.
Ship.

Female statue 1000 | PHILADELPHIA BK, Philadelphia, Pa. | Female erect with horn of plenty. 1000
Female seated and raising lid of chest; cars in distance. Figures 1000 on either side of vignette.
Male reclining.

Justice eagle and head of Washington | SOUTHWARK BANK, Philadelphia, Pa. | Die. Wm. Penn. Die.
5 Large fig. 5, two females, cupid and eagle. 5
Eagle.

5 Portrait | Spread eagle on a rock; ship and steamboat in distance. Large V and two figure 5s in red ink. | 5 Wm. Penn.
SOUTHWARK BANK, Philadelphia, Pa.

10 Indian on rock with bow and arrow. | Two females reclining; city, vessels and light-house in distance. | 10 Female with eagle and portrait of Washington. TEN
SOUTHWARK BANK, Philadelphia, Pa.

X on a med. head. Justice and head of Washington on breast of eagle.
SOUTHWARK BANK Philadelphia, Pa. Female representing the Arts, angel; sea horses and car and man thereto; Vessel on left.
TEN Indian with bow and arrow. TEN

20 Indian with bow and arrow.
SOUTHWARK BANK Philadelphia, Pa. Two females representing Agriculture and Commerce. 20
Justice and head of Washington on breast of eagle. Washington

Indian with bow and arrow. 50
SOUTHWARK BANK Philadelphia, Pa. Two females reclining; cars and vessels in distance. 50
Same as 20s. Female portrait.

Same as 50s. 100
SOUTHWARK BANK Philadelphia, Pa. Goddess of Liberty and eagle; vessels, etc. Figs 100 on either side of vig. Steamboat
Same as 50s. C

Indian with bow and arrow.
SOUTHWARK BANK Philadelphia, Pa. 500 Steamboat.

FIVE Blacksmith and female seated. 5
5 Female seated, supporting arm; vessels on right. 5 TRADESMEN'S B'K., Philadelphia, Pa. Steamship.
FIVE Blacksmith erect. FIVE

Female encircled by heavy folds of dress, left arm extended.
10 Goddess of Liberty and spread eagle. TRADESMEN'S B'K., Philadelphia, Pa. X
10 Franklin. TEN

TWENTY Bust of Penn TWENTY
20 Two females; one reclining on cornucopia, the other apparently elevated in the air. XX TRADESMEN'S B'K., Philadelphia, Pa.

50 Canal scene; bridge, houses and spire. FIFTY
Female with right arm leaning on hogshead; cars and vessel on left; house on right. Portrait of female on either side of the vignette. TRADESMEN'S B'K., Philadelphia, Pa.
50 Ship. FIFTY

100 Indian squaw and papoose. 100
C Group of three mechanics; vessel on right; man and horse on left. TRADESMEN'S B'K., Philadelphia, Pa.
100 Med. head. 100

500 Washington 500
Spread eagle; houses on right; cars on left. TRADESMEN'S B'K., Philadelphia, Pa. Female bathing.
Two females; one standing the other kneeling. 500

Die work. 1
UNION BANK. Philadelphia. ONE ONE 1 across ONE. Officer on horse receiving returns. 1 across ONE.
1 Die work.

TWO Soldier leaning on musket.
UNION 2 BANK. Philadelphia 2 2 2 across TWO. Female globe, shield, &c. 2 across TWO
TWO Sailor seated on gun

5 FIVE
UNION Eagle BANK. Female, column, steamer, buildings, etc. Red V. Female head. Philadelphia, Pa.
5 FIVE

Cupid with sheaf. X
Title of Bank. Female in clouds with shield, pole, cap, eagle, etc. Sailors hoisting. TEN.
10 Girl's portrait.

20 Sailor and farmer each side of shield on which is deer and tree
UNION Washington BK. TWENTY.
20 S. C. arms, Cupid, female, soldier, etc.

50 Female with sledge hammer; factories, etc.
Calhoun. Title. Webster. Female and Mercury; ships on right; canal and railroad scene on left.
50 Sailor boy; two sailors and man-of-war in distance.

100 UNION One Hundred
Med. head of Franklin. HUNDRED. Med. head of Washington. Penn's treaty with the Indians.
100 BANK One Hundred

500
Title. 500. Mechanic and boy repairing cart; farmer, horse, etc. Child's head. Red 500. Red D.
Goddess of Liberty.

1000 1000
Female head. Red M. Title of Bank. Female seated with shield, starry drapery, pole and cap across her lap; building in distance.
1000 Female holding glass; ship, water, etc.

5 FIVE
WESTERN BANK, Philadelphia, Pa. Indian, squaw and papoose; buildings, etc. FIVE
5 Female kneeling; buildings and spire.

5 Boy gathering corn. Med. head.
5 Farmers reposing beneath a tree and enjoying their dinner; basket, horses, etc. WESTERN BANK, Philadelphia, Pa. Agricultural Implements.
5 Female representing Agriculture; figure 5. 5

5 Farmer sharpening scythe.
WESTERN BANK, Philadelphia, Pa. Large V.
5 Mason at work on wall

FIVE 5 FIVE
Female erect with shield, etc. Eagle and shield WESTERN BANK, Philadelphia, Pa.
5 Female with flowers.

10
Deer grazing, trees, waterfall, etc. WESTERN BANK, Philadelphia, Pa.
10 Female portrait.

Two Indians, one erect the other kneeling; wigwams.
WESTERN BANK, Philadelphia, Pa. 10 Female representing agriculture; cars crossing bridge in distance. Mechanics arm.
Letter X and word Ten. Female reclining.

10 Indian warrior on horseback.
Title of Bank. Large X.
TEN Female erect with shield on which is med. head.

X Med. Head. X
10 Female with trumpet, globe and eagle. 10 WESTERN BANK, Philadelphia, Pa. Steamship.
X Med. head X

Female seated on bale. 20
WESTERN BANK, Philadelphia, Pa. Two females seated; ship, steamboat and small sail vessel on left; cars on right. Med. head & word Twenty on each side of vignette. Steamboat and sail vessel
20 Med. head. 20

Human figure reclining 50
WESTERN BANK, Philadelphia, Pa. Portrait of Washington. Instructor and pupil; house on right. Med. head; figs. 50 on it. Dog's head.
50 Med. head. 50

100 Med. head. 100	WESTERN BANK, Philadelphia, Pa. C Eagle; ship and other small sail vessel. C Steamboat and life-boat.	Female erect with horn of plenty. 100
500 Female representing Agriculture. 500	Indian seated; grain, agricultural implements, etc.; house seen amid the wood. WESTERN BANK, Philadelphia, Pa. Female bathing.	500 Liberty reclining.
1000 Med. head. 1000	Goddess of Liberty and two other females; eagle surmounted; ship and cars in distance. WESTERN BANK, Philadelphia, Pa. Spread eagle.	1000 Milkmaid erect.
1 Female with rake.	Western river scene—steamboats, raft, men, etc. ALLEGHANY BANK Pittsburgh, Pa.	1 One Dollar.
Farmer with scythe seated on fence. TWO	Man, boy and girl in factory; machinery, etc. ALLEGHANY BANK Pittsburgh, Pa.	2 Two Dollars.
Five on 5. Locomotive and tender.	Steamboat; city and steamboat in distance. ALLEGHANY BANK, Alleghany, Pa. FIVE	5 Female portrait.
X Female with dove.	Three cherubs with lever sledge, wedge and stone. ALLEGHANY BANK. Alleghany, Pa.	10 Head of bull.
20 Girls portrait	Two females and shield on which is farming implements; man and factory in distance. ALLEGHANY BANK, Alleghany, Pa.	20 Negro holding bull; sheep, fence etc.
50 Female portrait.	View of the wharf at Pittsburg with steamboats receiving and discharging freight. ALLEGHANY BANK, Alleghany, Pa.	50 Indian portrait.
100 Female with sickle and grain.	Mexican lassoing wild cattle. ALLEGHANY BANK Alleghany, Pa	C Portrait of boy.

1	Man, horses, pig, fowl, &c. at trough; cattle, barn, &c. 1 Female portrait ALLENTOWN B'K, Allentown, Pa.	One on 1. Spread eagle.
2 Clay.	2 Horse either side of shield surmounted by an eagle. 2 ALLENTOWN B'K, Allentown, Pa.	2 Female with sewing machine
5 Boy and rabbits.	Drovers and drove of cattle; city on right, in distance. ALLENTOWN BK., Allentown, Pa. Sheaf of wheat, rake &c.	5 Female portrait.
Female erect with sheaf of wheat on her head. 10	ALLENTOWN BK., Allentown, Pa. Farmer, sailor and blacksmith; farmer seated, and holds sickle and sheaf of wheat; anvil, horse and man on right; sheaf of wheat on left. X on left.	10 Male portrait
TWENTY Farmer reclining; female seated.	ALLENTOWN BANK Allentown, Pa. 20 XX	Female with fowl. 20
Female with cornucopia. FIFTY	50 Farmers loading wagon with hay; two horses &c. Title of Bank. L L	50 Female portrait.
100 inverted Blacksmith, anvil, and sledge.	Title of Bank. C Washington C 100 100	100 inverted Locomotive
Sailor with flag, female at his feet.	1 ANTHRACITE B'K, Tamaqua, Pa. Miners at work in mine.	1 Washington on horseback
Two on 2. Washington	2 ANTHRACITE BANK, 2 Tamaqua Pa. Milkmaid milking cow; one cow reclining, man, dog, &c. TWO 2 TWO	2 Drummer boy and soldiers
5 Three sheep; two laying down; one standing. 5	Train of cars, &c.; mining view, iron furnace, &c.; train of cars on left, in distance. ANTHRACITE BK., Tamoqua, Pa.	5 Portrait of Henry Clay

X Portrait of Gov. Pollock. TEN	10 Farmers at work, loading hay. ANTHRACITE BK., Tamoqua, Pa. Female bathing.	10 TEN 10
20 XX 20	ANTHRACITE BK., Tamoqua, Pa. Portrait of boy. Female reclining with sheaf of wheat and sickle; Farmers at work on right; train of cars and bridge on left.	20
Miners at work and a coal shaft; train of cars in back-ground. FIFTY	50 Portrait of Gov. Pollock. ANTHRACITE BK., Tamoqua, Pa.	50 L
100 ONE C HUNDRED. 100	Portrait of a girl. Woodman at work; yoke of oxen on left, in back-ground. ANTHRACITE BK., Tamoqua, Pa.	C Portrait of Webster.
V	Farmer seated; girl and team of horses on left; boy and dog, hay on his back on right. V BK OF BEAVER CO, New Brighton, Pa. Dog	5 Franklin.
Full length flying female; country scene, river, steamboat, locomotive, &c; in back-ground.	Title of Bank Two females seated representing Agriculture and Manufacture; factories on right; cows, &c., on left.	10
1 Eagle.	BK OF CATASAQUA, Catasaqua, Pa. ONE DOLLAR. Female portrait. ONE DOLLAR.	1 Man working at vice.
2 Soldier in battle.	BK OF CATASAQUA. Catasequa, Pa. 2 Farmers resting, female, child, &c. Eagle	2
V Male plowing	BK OF CATASAUQUA, Catasauqua, Penn. Depot, factory, etc. FIVE	5 Squaw and papoose.
10 Female feeding fowls.	Scene in barnyard—farmer and drover bargaining for ox. Title of Bank 10	10 Female with sheaf and sickle.

Left	Centre	Right
20 Train of cars.	Title of Bank. Female head.	20 Man at work in coal mines.
50 Hunter loading rifle.	Men at work in iron mill. Title of Bank. FIFTY	50 Scene on a canal.
100 Farmer and family.	Title of Bank. Letter U on large red die.	100 Squaw.
1 Benjamin Franklin seated in library.	B'K OF CHAMBERSBURG, Chambersburg, Pa. ONE on 1 1 1	1 Old man seated with child, pointing to bust of Washington.
2 Two females with sickle and grain.	Agricultural implements. BANK OF CHAMBERSBURG, Chambersburg, Pa. TWO DOLLARS on TWO	2 Female with wreath on her head.
Portrait of Washington. 5 Male portrait.	5 Vig. Two female reclining, farming implements, &c. 5 BANK OF CHAMBERSBURG, Pa.	Male portrait. 5 Male portrait.
X Medallion head and word "TEN" 10	Med. head TEN on it. Vig. Instructor and pupil; houses in distance on right. Med. head TEN on it. BANK OF CHAMBERSBURG, Pa.	Female representing Agriculture. X
10 Med. head of Washington.	Man with bag, horse, mill, etc.; boys on bridge. BK OF CHAMBERSBURG, Chambersburg, Pa.	10 Printer at his stand.
20 Bust of Penn XX	Med. head. Vig. Spread eagle. Med. head. BANK OF CHAMBERSBURG, Pa.	XX Bust of Washington 20
50 Med. head. 50	Vig. Female reclining on sofa; commerce and agriculture; tree, sheep on right. BANK OF CHAMBERSBURG, Pa.	50 Male portrait FIFTY

Left	Centre	Right
100 Male portrait 100	Vig. Wild horses. BANK OF CHAMBERSBURG, Pa.	Med. head and figures "100" on it. 100
Medallion portrait of late Cashier of the bank. 5	Vig. Female seated on ground, with right hand on a milking pail. Cows near, cottage and cattle in the distance. BANK OF CHESTER COUNTY, Westchester, Penn.	5 Male portrait.
10 Half length figure of a city lady, with basket of flowers in her hand. TEN	Vig. Farmer with scythe in hand seated on ground, dinner basket beside him; haymakers, aqueduct and warehouses in background. BANK OF CHESTER COUNTY, Westchester, Penn.	10 Country girl with sheaf of wheat on her shoulder. TEN
20 Drove of cattle, waggon load of hay, and travelers on a plank road.	Vig. Female seated on ground; basket of corn, melons, grapes, &c., at her side; bay, vessels, town and mountains in the distance. BANK OF CHESTER COUNTY, Westchester, Penn.	20 Locomotive. 20
50 Daniel Boone and dog.	Vig. Female seated on the ground left arm resting on shield; both hands holding a bundle of fasces; Niagara falls in distance. BANK OF CHESTER COUNTY, Westchester, Penn.	50 Indian seated gun in hand.
100 Portrait of lady.	Female figure seated in chair; eagle on shield at her feet, &c.; city, bay, and mountains in the distance. B'K OF CHESTER CO., Westchester, Pa.	100 Milkmaid, cattle, &c. 100
500 Medallion head of Washington. 500	Vig. Two men standing and one seated on a stone in the foreground; railroad viaduct, and city in the background, mountains in the distance. Medallion head. BANK OF CHESTER COUNTY, Westchester, Penn.	Full length figure in Roman toga. 500
Female head. 1000 Female head.	Vig. Locomotive and train of passenger cars, coming round a rocky bank; city and mountains in distance. BANK OF CHESTER COUNTY, Westchester, Penn.	1000 Medallion head of Washington. 1000
5 Male portrait	Bridge at Coatesville; iron works; mule team; hills in the background. BANK OF CHESTER VALLEY, Coatesville, Pa. FIVE	5 Male portrait
10 Female with sickle and sheaf; dog; houses in distance.	Title of Bank. Interior of a rolling mill. TEN	10 [illegible]

Left	Centre	Right
XX Three smiths at work at anvil.	Title of Bank. Female seated on sheaf with sickle; farm building and man loading hay in distance. XX Geese and goslings.	20 Female shading her eyes with her hands.
50 FIFTY 50	Title of Bank. Oxen before load of hay; driver with fork; man reclining on top of hay. FIFTY	50 Male portrait.
100 Buchanan.	Vig. Same as 5's. Title of Bank. 100	100 Clay.
1 surrounded by words one. Girl and child with sickle and grain.	[illegible] Women crossing bridge in distance. B'K OF CRAWFORD CO ONE DOLLAR, Meadville, Pa.	1 surrounded by words one. Basket of corn.
2 Man seated on fence with scythe.	B'K OF CRAWFORD CO. Meadville, Pa. [illegible] TWO DOLLARS.	2 Female, child [illegible]
5 Buchanan.	Man and boy plowing with horses; trees, dog and fence in distance. [illegible] on each side of Vig. BK. OF CRAWFORD COUNTY, Meadville, Pa. FIVE FIVE	Fig. 5 lettered. Female feeding fowls.
X 10	Farmer eating lunch; horses, hay, plow, etc. in background. Eagle. Child's head. Title of Bank. TEN TEN	X Male portrait.
20 Farming implements and products.	Coal mining scene; men resting; man hewing timber; cars, etc. Title of Bank. TWENTY	20 Male portrait.
50	Surveying scene. Head of Penn. Title of Bank. FIFTY	50 Two sailors with boat; sailor boy in front; man-of-war in distance.
100 Washington	Title of Bank. Two beavers knawing limbs of trees. 100	100 Farmer feeding pigs; head of horse over fence.

Left	Centre	Right
1 Female seated, with flowers, sinking arm, &c. 1	B'K OF DANVILLE, Danville, Pa. Words "One Dollar" across ONE. ONE	1 Farmer with scythe, &c. 1
One man, child bust on table. 2	2 Female reclining with scroll quadrant, globe, &c. 2 B'K OF DANVILLE, Danville, Pa.	Two on 2. Dog and safe.
5 FIVE 5	BANK OF DANVILLE, Pa. Vig. Large letter "V" and mechanic in standing position, anvil, cog wheel, &c., houses in back-ground. Bust of female on either side of vig.	FIVE Iron furnace FIVE
10 Female representing Justice.	Female portrait. Vig. Puddling in an iron Furnace. Female portrait. BANK OF DANVILLE, Pa. Dog's head.	X TEN 10
20 Washington on horse-back.	BANK OF DANVILLE, Pa. Female portrait. Vig. Spread eagle, Am. shield, olive leaves, &c. Female portrait. Implem'ts of manufacture.	20 Goddess of Liberty, Am. flag in one hand and Roman shield in the other.
50 Train of cars 50	BANK OF DANVILLE, Pa. Female portrait. Vig. [illegible], woman talking; vessel in distance. Wagon Team.	50 50
100 Female portrait. 100	Vig. View of Danville, furnaces, canal, river, &c. Female portrait. BANK OF DANVILLE, Pa. Agriculture Implements.	100 Goddess of Liberty in Indian costume, with shield, pole and Liberty cap. 100
5 Medallion head. V	Pat Lyon at forge Five on [illegible] head each side. BANK OF DELAWARE CO. Chester, Pa. Locomotive and cars.	5 Medallion head. V
10 Double Medallion head, and TEN X	View of sea with ships, &c. BANK OF DELAWARE CO. Chester, Pa.	X Double Medallion head, and TEN 10
10	Man and boy plowing with two horses. B'K OF DELAWARE COUNTY, Chester, Pa. Vessel and lighthouse.	10 Girl's head.

Left	Centre	Right
20 Medallion head. 20	(Old Plate.) [illegible] 20 Vig. Harvest field, farmer under tree, house in distance.	20 Medallion head. 20
20 Head of Wm. Penn.	(New Plate.) Vig. View of Upland, a manufacturing village. BANK OF DELAWARE CO. Chester, Pa.	20 Head of female.
Female with rake. FIFTY Female with rake.	Vig. Female reclining under sheaf of wheat. BANK OF DELAWARE CO. Chester, Pa.	Female with rake. FIFTY Female with rake.
100 Medallion head. 100	Vig. Female figures of Justice and Liberty with shield between them, also eagle and ships. FANK OF DELAWARE CO. Chester, Pa.	100 Medallion head. 100
500 Head of Wm. Penn D	Vig. Eagle to the right, factory to the left, locomotive and train of cars. BANK OF DELAWARE CO. Chester, Pa. Steamship.	500 Female head.
1 In centre of circular die with words one and small 1's in red, all over it.	BANK OF FAYETTE COUNTY Uniontown, Pa. Cattle passing through a gate. Female, child, poultry, &c. ONE DOLLAR	1 In centre of circular die with words one, and small 1, ornamented all over it.
2 In die with words two. Two Dollars 2 on ornamental die.	BANK OF FAYETTE COUNTY Uniontown, Pa. Foal. Circular [illegible] die, with words two and 2 [illegible] ornamental 2 [illegible] TWO DOLLARS.	2 In circular die with words two. Two Dollars ornamental die.
V Clay.	BK OF FAYETTE CO, Uniontown, Pa. Female seated with calves, canal and railroad scene on left.	5 Penn.
10 Jackson.	Title of Bank. Drovers and cattle in stream; country scene in general.	X Female head.
20 Washington.	Title of Bank. General reaping scene with "patent reaper;" city in distance.	20 Lafayette.

Left	Centre	Right
5 Female head. FIVE	Vig. American shield in centre containing figures of ship, plough, and sheaf of wheat. On left two Indians male and female with child; mountains in distance. On right female with three children, sheaf of wheat, trees and farm houses in distance. BK OF GETTYSBURG Gettysburg, Pa. Loading hay.	5 Female head FIVE
TEN head. X	Vig. Two females supporting shield, containing the arms of the different states, with a representation of an eagle. BK OF GETTYSBURG Gettysburg, Pa. Female bathing.	TEN head 10
20 Female holding cup, eagle in the act of drinking. XX	Vig. Washington surmounted by an eagle, on the left female seated having in right hand pole with liberty cap, on the right, two females, one reclining and the other kneeling behind her; ship on the left, and railroad bridge on right in distance. Title of bank. Agricultural implements.	XX Female head. 20
L 50 L	Vig. Three farmers harvesting in foreground; town and water on right in distance, trees and hay stacks on left. BK OF GETTYSBURG Gettysburg, Pa. Eagle.	Medallion head of female with 50 on it. 50
One on 1. Female with sickle and dog.	Man feeding pigs, horses, &c. Vig. 1 either side. B'K OF LAWRENCE COUNTY Newcastle, Pa.	One on 1. Dog & safe.
2 TWO	2 State arms. 2 B'K OF LAWRENCE COUNTY, Newcastle, Pa.	2 Female and sewing machine.
Cupid and ornamental work Mechanic with sledge.	5 Man and boy plowing with two horses. BK of LAWRENCE COUNTY, Newcastle, Pa.	5 Girl's portrait.
X Female TEN	10 Surveyors at work. Title of Bank.	10 Female feeding fowls.
1 Portrait of Gen. Scott.	Rafting scene. BANK OF MIDDLETOWN, Middletown, Pa. ONE DOLLAR.	1 Head of girl.
2 on red 2. 2	TWO DOLLARS. Female head. Female with sheaf and sickle. Female head. BANK OF MIDDLETOWN, Middletown, Pa.	2 on red 2. 2

5 Female Portrait. 5 — V Female on either side of shield; eagle at top. V BANK OF MIDDLETOWN, Middletown, Pa. — 5 Female with grain, &c. 5

5 Male portrait. V — Female seated with child; reapers and house in distance. 5 on med. head on either side of vig. BANK OF MIDDLETOWN, Middletown, Pa. — FIVE

5 Reaper seated. FIVE — 5 Spread eagle 5 BANK OF MIDDLETOWN, Middletown, Pa. — FIVE Female erect with shield and helmet. FIVE

5 Female head. 5 — V Two females, eagle, &c. V BANK OF MIDDLETOWN, Pa. — 5 Female head with grain, &c. 5

TEN — Shield on which is letter X—female bust at top; soldier and war implements on right; female on left, and head of female on right of vig. BK OF MIDDLETW'N Middletown, Pa. Ducks. — 10 10

10 Ten on Medallion 10 — 10 on medal. Vig. Two horses; shield in centre, surmounted with eagle, scroll with motto, Liberty and Independence. 10 on medal. BANK OF MIDDLETOWN, Pa. — TEN

Die. Male portrait — 20 Milkmaid and two cows; other cows in distance. Title of Bank. Dog. — 20 Female head.

20 Medallion head, twenty across it. 20 — 20 Vig. Female seated with sickle 20 grain, &c.; house, &c. in distance. BANK OF MIDDLETOWN, Pa. — XX Twenty on Medallion head. XX

50 Male portrait — Female in clouds with sword and eagle. Female with grain. Title of Bank. — 50 Male portrait

50 Artist seated at work. 50 — 50 Vig. Cupids at work at press, lever and sledge. 50 BANK OF MIDDLETOWN, Pa. — 50 50 across medallion head. 50

5 Male portrait. FIVE — Vig. View of Norristown and bridge. BANK OF MONTGOMERY CO., Pa. Vessel, trees, houses, &c. — 5 Male portrait. FIVE

10 Canal boat and scenery. X — Portrait of Washington. Goddess of Liberty reclining. Portrait of Rittenhouse. BANK OF MONTGOMERY CO., Pa. Train of cars. — 10 Male and female. X

TEN Male portrait — Male portrait. View of building, trees and part of street. Male portrait. BANK OF MONT. CO. Norristown, Pa. Dog. — 10 Male portrait

XX Male portrait — Men at work in iron mill. Bank building. Title of Bank. Dog's head. — 20 Male portrait

20 Male portrait. 20 on medal lion head. — Portrait of La Fayette. Vig. Signing the Declaration of Independence. Portrait of Washington. BANK OF MONTGOMERY CO., Pa. "B" — 20 Portrait of Rittenhouse. 20 on medal lion head.

100 Goddess of Liberty. — Vig. Cattle, sheep, &c.; steamboat in distance on right. BANK OF MONTGOMERY Co., Pa. — 100 Portrait of Washington.

TWO Female and Cupid. TWO — 2 Female either side of portrait of Wm. Penn. 2 BANK OF NORTHUMBERL'ND Northumberland, Pa. State arms. — TWO

5 Female head. — BANK OF NORTHUMBERLAND, Pa. Vig. Farmers loading hay, canal and boat, train of cars. — 5 Girls head.

Three female figures, anchor, &c. TEN — BANK OF NORTHUMBERLAND, Pa. Vig. Female seated, scythe, sickle and pitcher; train of cars in distance, grain and implements. — 10 Male head. TEN

20 Dog. 20 — Vig. Spread eagle on rock; ship on either side. BANK OF NORTHUMBERLAND, Pa. — Female with grain. 20

1 In die with small 1s. Child in chair holding kitten, poultry, &c. — Views of factory, railroad, canal, boats BANK OF PHOENIXVILLE Phoenixville, Pa. ONE DOLLAR on ONE Phoenix — 1 In die with small 1s. Bust of Female.

Portrait of Andrew Jackson. 2 In die with two's. — Herd of cattle, two drovers, one on horse; factory in distance. BANK OF PHOENIXVILLE, Phoenixville, Pa. TWO DOLLARS on TWO Phoenix. — 2 On die with TWO. Head of Newfoundland Dog

5 Male portrait — BANK OF PHOENIXVILLE, Phoenixville, Pa. Cars. Washington at Valley Forge. Eagle Phoenix. — 5 Female feeding fowls.

X Chy. TEN inverted — Man holding horse, sack on back; wheelwrights repairing cart. Title of Bank. Phoenix. — 10 Cars.

Cupid and 20. Penn. — BANK OF PHOENIXVILLE, Phoenixville, Pa. Train of cars; others in distance. 20 Phoenix. 20 — 20 and cupid Female portrait.

50 Farmer at lunch; horses, plow, etc. L — Title of Bank. Buchanan. FIFTY Phoenix FIFTY — 50 Man on gate, dozen horses, colt, sheep, dog, etc. L

100 Washington. — Title of Bank. State Arms—horse either side; steamer in distance. Phoenix. — 100 Franklin.

5 Female and sheaf of wheat, sickle in left hand, grain in right. FIVE — Vig. Three artisans with implements, ship yard factory and bridge in distance. BANK OF PITTSBURG, Pa. — 5 Train of cars. FIVE

X Locomotive and tender. TEN — Vig. Blacksmith is sitting, picture hammer in right hand; anvil train of cars crossing a bridge in distance, workshops; river and hills in distance. BANK OF PITTSBURG, Pa — 10 Head of Washington X

20 Head of Dewitt Clinton. 20 — 20 Vig. Blacksmith sitting with forge and anvil to right; cars crossing bridge in distance. 20 BANK OF PITTSBURG, Pa. — 20 Head of Jackson. 20

50 Medallion head 50
50 Vig. Female reclining with sickles of grain in left hand, shipping and farm house in distance. 50
BANK OF PITTSBURGH, Pa.
Die Figure of Justice. Die

Female with harp.
100 Vig. Female sitting on a bale; Mercury descending; shipping in distance. 100
BANK OF PITTSBURG, Pa.
Figure of Justice.

Artisan and sailor standing; two females sitting; spinning wheel and capstan to right; view of city in distance.
D Vig. Shield on which is a view of a city; Indian, squaw, and child on left; female teaching group of children on right.
BANK OF PITTSBURG, Pa.
500

1000 Two blacksmiths at work.
Vig. Group of three, farmer and two artisans, half length figures
BANK OF PITTSBURG, Pa.
1000 Female standing among grain; sickle in right hand 1000

1 On die with ones on it. Male Portrait.
B'K OF POTTSTOWN, Potts own, Pa.
State arms of Pa. Two horses rearing on shield with ship, plough and grain on it. Motto "Virtue, liberty, and independence."
ONE DOLLAR on die
1 On die with words one. Male Portrait.

2 On die with words two. Portrait of Abe Lincoln.
Agricultural group, man, female, children, horse, dog, swine, chickens, poultry, &c. One man lifting child.
B'K OF POTTSTOWN, Pottstown, Pa.
TWO DOLLARS on large ornamental die.
2 On die with words TWO. Portrait of General Scott.

Bust of female with basket of flowers. 3 On die with words THREE
Train of cars crossing stone bridge, cattle in stream below, boy with fishing rod, shrubbery, &c.
B'K OF POTTSTOWN, Pottstown, Pa.
THREE DOLLARS on die.
3 On die with words "THREE." Portrait of Wm. H. Seward.

5 5
BK OF POTTSTOWN, Pottstown, Pa.
Buchanan on left of title and female portrait on right.
V Farmer and boy plowing with two horses. V
5 5

Cupid, sheaf, etc. Female portrait.
10 Title of Bank 10
X Scene at grist mill; carrying out grain; horses; boys on bridge. X
10 10
Cupid, cornucopia, etc. Male portrait.

1 ONE
CITIZ'NS' B'NK, Pittsburgh, Pa.
1 Two females seated; anvil, hammer, &c. 1
1 ONE

Man oiling machinery TWO
CITIZENS' BANK, Pittsburgh, Pa.
Steamboat. 2 Cars.
2 TWO 2 TWO
2 Girl.

Hhds. bales, pig lead, ship, steamboat, &c. THREE
CITIZEN'S BANK, Pittsburgh, Pa.
Word "Three" across white 3 on red die.
Female, steamer in distance.
3 Word "Dollars" across white 3 on red die

5 Female head.
CITIZENS' BANK, Pittsburgh, Pa. Male portrait.
Scene in a grist mill; man leading horse with grain; boys fishing in brook.
5 Blacksmith with hammer in hand, standing beside anvil.

X Female.
Interior of an iron foundry. Female with flowers.
CITIZENS' BANK.
10 Female standing beside pillar.

Girl seated. TWENTY
CITIZENS' BANK.
Robert Morris. Coal heavers leaning against cart.
20

50 Battle scene, soldiers charging bayonet.
Female head. Blacksmith mending cart, farmer standing beside him with horse.
CITIZENS' BANK.
50 Thomas Jefferson

C Boy's head.
CITIZENS' BANK.
Farmer riding horse; boy on fence.
100 William Penn.

5
State Arms Raft scene on Western river
CLEARFIELD CO. BK Clearfield, Pa.
Bear.
5

State Arms. 10
Woodcutting scene in forest. X each side.
CLEARFIELD CO. BK Clearfield, Pa.
Die.
10 Female portrait.

ONE Wm. Penn. ONE
1 Male and female gleaning, harvest scene in general. 1
COLUMBIA BANK, Columbia, Pa.
Locomotive.
ONE Female clasping 1 ONE

2 Washingt'n. 2
2 Spread eagle, cars, bridge, &c. 2
COLUMBIA BANK, Columbia, Pa.
Indian head.
TWO Female, cupid, &c. TWO

V Female seated in letter V. 5
5 Five cupids encircling figure 5. 5
COLUMBIA BANK, Columbia, Pa.
Dog's head.
V Female seated in 5. 5

5 Washington V
COLUMBIA BANK, Columbia, Pa.
Vig. Female and cupid with wand seated, vessel in distance. 5 on medallion head.
5 Train of cars. V

10 Male portrait 10
COLUMBIA BANK, Columbia, Pa.
Vig. Wood chopper seated, dog and axe beside him.
X Medallion head with ten across it. X

20 Franklin 20
COLUMBIA BANK, Columbia, Pa.
Medallion head. Vig. Horse and train of cars. Medallion head.
Goddess of liberty 20

50 Wagon, horses, bales, standing on dock. 50
50 on medallion head. Vig. Fat. Leon in his shop. 50 on medallion head.
COLUMBIA BANK, Columbia, Pa.
50 Cattle; landscape in distance. 50

Medallion head. 100 Medallion head.
COLUMBIA BANK, Columbia, Pa.
Female figure seated on bale of merchandise, right arm resting on a shield, with plough in centre and ship above it. 100 on medallion head.
ONE HUNDRED
HUNDRED Female standing, her right hand over shield resting on a pedestal, head of man on shield. HUNDRED

5
DOWNINGTON B'K, Downington, Pa.
Cattle on bank and in stream. State arms
5
5 Female head

10
Scene at mill; two men, two horses, wagon, &c. State arms
DOWNINGTON B'K, Downington, Pa.
10 Male head.

ONE Drummer boy and soldiers.
DOYLESTOWN B'K, Doylestown, Pa.
1 Scene in grist mill, men at work. 1
1 Female head

2 2 2 — DOYLESTOWN B'K, Doylestown, Pa. Man, two horses, plough, boy, Scott, trees, &c. — 2 2 2

5 FIVE on Ingot. 5 — William Abogt Franklin Penn. V and lin. a female between the heavy part of the letter and the right part. DOYLESTOWN B'K. Doylestown, Penn. — 5 Man sharpening scythe. 5

10 Female and sellos. — Vig. Haymakers, agricultural scene. DOYLESTOWN B'K. Doylestown, Penn. State Arms. — 10 Female Indian sitt'g.

20 Blacksmith. 20 — Vig. Female sitting, haymakers; railroad in the distance. DOYLESTOWN B'K. Doylestown, Penn. Eagle. — 20 Portrait of Chief Justice Marshall.

50 Head of female. 50 — 50 Vig. Female, plough oxen, two children, anvil, &c. 50 DOYLESTOWN B'K. Doylestown, Penn. — 50 Head of female. 50

100 Drove of cattle. 100 — 100 Vig. View of Fairmount water works, female, two trains. 100 DOYLESTOWN B'K. Doylestown, Penn. — 100 Drove of cattle. 100

Man plowing with two horses. 1 — EASTON BANK, Pennsylvania. ONE DOLLAR. Chartered 1814. — 1 Female with flowers.

2 5 dies with name of b'k and word two. 2 — Figure of Atoart. EASTON BK. Pennsylvania. ex with wreath shield, &c. Chartered 1814. — 2 Horse's head.

5 Male portrait. — Scene at mill—horse, man, wheel; boys on bridge. EASTON BANK, Easton, Pa. Red 5. — 5 Male portrait.

5 Hunter with rifle. 5 — Medallion head, 5 on it. Vig. wood chopper, seated, dog and axe beside him, cabin in distance. Medallion head, 5 on it. EASTON BANK Easton, Pa. — 5 Male Portrait. 5

10 Girl's head. — EASTON BANK, Easton, Pa. Female with bowsalves; canal and railroad scene on left. 10 — 10 Female head.

10 Male portrait. 10 — Medallion head Vig. Indian head Medallion across it. seated across it. bow and arrow, canoe in distance. EASTON BANK Easton, Pa. — 10 Medallion head. 10

20 Washington. 20 — Child seated in stone reading, plow and wheat Vig. child seated, house in distance, Child artists tools in hand, &c. EASTON BANK Easton, Pa. Locomotive and cars. — 20 Male Portrait. 20

50 Male portrait. FIFTY — Vig. Female seated, agricultural implements wheat, &c. cars locks, &c., in distance. Female portrait. EASTON BANK Easton, Pa. — 50 Male portrait. FIFTY.

100 Head of male. 100 — Vig. Female seated, shield, sickle, &c. two Indians on right. Female portrait on right. EASTON BANK Easton, Pa. — 100 Head of male. 100

ONE Two Females. — 1 Cows and river. 1 EXCHANGE BANK, Pittsburgh, Pa. — One on 1

2 Man and girl at well, man drinking. — 2 Horse drinking at brook, boy on his back, dog, trees, &c. 2 EXCHANGE BANK OF PITTSBURGH, Pittsburgh, Pa. — 2 Female Portrait.

5 Male portrait. 5 — Vig. View of the city of Pittsburgh; spread eagle on the other side of the river. EXCHANGE BANK, Pittsburgh, Penn. State Arms. — 5 Portrait of Millard Fillmore. 5

5 Girl's head. — EXCHANGE BANK of Pittsburg, Pa. View of Pittsburg, river bridge, boats, etc. — 5 Female feeding fowls.

10 Female portrait. — Steamboat "Mail packet Pittsburgh," on wheel house. Title of Bank. — 10 Indian warrior on horse.

10 Figure of Wm. Penn standing. — Female portrait. Vig. View of the interior of a rolling mill, men at work. EXCHANGE BANK, Pittsburgh, Penn. Steamer. — 10 Male portrait. TEN

20 Portrait of Gen. Scott. TWENTY — Title of Bank. Vig. Train of cars. — 20 Female with sheaf. TWENTY

50 Male portrait. — State arms. EXCHANGE BANK, Pittsburgh, Penn. — Goddess with horn of plenty in the clouds over landscape. 50

100 Male portrait. 100 — Vig. Eagle standing on a shield. EXCHANGE BANK, Pittsburgh, Penn. — 100 Male portrait. 100

500 Female holding a medallion head on a pedestal, in left a staff with two serpents coiled around it. — Medallion head. Vig. A female sitting with a plank in her hand; steamboat in the distance. Medallion head. EXCHANGE BANK, Pittsburgh, Penn. — A figure in the act of pouring a liquid from a vessel. 500

Small medallion head. 1000 Small medallion head. — Infant figure. Vig. Eagle standing on a log; steamer in the distance. Infant figure. EXCHANGE BANK, Pittsburgh, Penn. — Small medallion head. 1000 Small medallion head.

1 ONE on Med. head. 1 — Female with pail, cows, &c., ONE on med. head, either side. FARMERS BANK OF BUCKS CO., Bristol, Pa. — 1 ONE on Med. head. 1

5 Wm. Penn. V — Farmer reclining against tree, woman seated holding child; harvest scene and house in distance. FIVE on med head either side. FARMERS' BANK of BUCKS CO., Pa. — V Washington. 5

10 Portrait of Washington. 10 — FARMERS' BANK OF BUCKS CO., Pa. 10 Vig. Same as two's. Medallion head. — X Head of Penn. X

20 Portrait of Penn. 20 — FARMERS' BANK OF BUCKS CO., Pa. Vig. View of bridge over canal; horses, teams, cattle, &c., canal on right of vig. — 20 Portrait of Washington. 20

Left	Centre	Right
FIFTY Farmer's loading a wagon with grain.	FARMERS BANK OF BUCKS CO., Pa. Large six with $0, and words FIFTY DOLLARS thereon.	50 Portrait of Washington.
100 Male reclining with sickle in hand. 100	FARMERS' BANK OF BUCKS CO., Pa. Vig. Female reclining on bale or chest; Escutcheon bearing the Arms of State. Farming implements.	C Portrait of Washington. 100
ONE Female stepping in pool of water.	1 Dog on safe. 1 Cattle, sheep, &c. Farm house in distance. FARMERS BANK OF LANCASTER, Pa. ONE DOLLAR.	1
2 TWO across	Horse either side of shield surmounted by eagle. Child's head. FARMERS BANK OF LANCASTER, Pa.	TWO
Figure of Justice. 5	Cattle in the water; one lying down; sheep in the distance. FARMERS B'K OF LANCASTER, Pa. Dog and safe.	FIVE Two females, one standing; sickle, wheel, &c. FIVE
FIVE Man on horseback talking with a farmer. FIVE	Vig. Farmers at lunch Female with basket seated, load of hay, and farm houses in distance. 5 FARMERS BANK OF LANCASTER, Pa. Dog, key, and Safe.	Pennsylvania. Two females one standing sickle, wheat &c. FIVE
10 Drove of cattle in circle. 10	Medallion head with ten across. Medallion head with ten across. Vig. Female seated, canal locks in front of her, wheat in rear. FARMERS BANK OF LANCASTER, Pa.	10 Boy with spade and basket of flowers, man spading, woman [illegible] ling. 10
X Female blowing dinner horn, table &c., farmers and load of hay.	[New Plate.] Vig. Farmers at work loading hay, horse and ox for the team on right hay stack & trees on left background. FARMERS BANK OF LANCASTER, Pa.	X TEN X
Female with portrait and sickle. XX	FARMERS' BANK OF LANCASTER, Pa. Man at lunch, girl, horses, dog, boy on his back, etc. State Arms.	20 Farmer sharpening scythe.
20 Female with rake, load of hay, &c. 20	Med. head with twenty across it. Med. head with twenty across it. Vig. Woodman seated, dog, and axe beside him. FARMERS BANK OF LANCASTER, Pa.	Same as left.

Left	Centre	Right
50 Man and dog. 50	Med. head with fifty across it. Med. head with fifty across it. Vig. Medallion head, cupids on either side, spinning wheels, &c. FARMERS BANK OF LANCASTER, Pa.	50 Man and dog. 50
Farmer sowing seed.	[New Plate.] L Large building, people, trees, &c. FARMERS' BANK OF LANCASTER, PA.	50 Portrait of boy
100 Washington.	FARMERS BANK OF LANCASTER, Pa. Vig. Harvest field farmers at work	100 Female, U. S. shield, eagle and liberty pole and cap.
ONE on 1 Girl, boy, and pitcher.	1 Cattle, boy and girl, trees, &c. 1 FARMERS' BANK, Reading, Pa.	1 Dog and safe.
2 2	FARMERS' BANK, Reading, Pa. Female with sword and shield. Gen. Scott.	2
FIVE Portrait of female, with sickle and sheaf. V	Vig. Britannia and sons. 5 FARMER'S BANK, Reading, Penn. Wagon load of hay.	5 Child in imitation of blacksmith. 5
TEN Two females around miniature; agriculture and commerce. TEN	X Vig. City Hall and scenery. FARMER'S BANK, Reading, Penn. X Farming implements. X	X Portrait of female. 10
2 Female reclining, shield, &c. 20	20 Vig. Farmer ploughing. FARMER'S BANK. Reading, Penn. Dog and safe.	20 medallion head. 20
50 Double medallion head. 50	Male Portrait. Male Portrait. Vig. large house, with cupola, spire, and smaller house in back ground. FARMER'S BANK, Reading, Penn.	50 Double medallion head. 50
L 50	[New Plate.] Cattle, and drovers driving them in the water; houses and trees in background; a church in extreme distance. FARMERS' BANK OF READING, PA. Locomotive.	50 Female erect with vase of flowers.

Left	Centre	Right
C Two female figures; one reclining.	[New Plate.] FARMERS' BANK OF READING, PA.	100 Male and female; two boys, dog and a hen.
100 Medallion Head, and figure 100 inscribed. 100	Head of Washington. Vig. Three horses. Head of Lafayette. FARMER'S BANK, Reading, Penn.	100 Medallion Head, and figure 100 inscribed. 100
ONE Male portrait. ONE	Men on horses, and dogs, pursuing fox. FARMERS' B'K OF SCHUYLKILL CO., Pottsville, Pa	1 Male head.
5 Male portrait FIVE	5 5 Vig. Two females, shield, mansion, cars, &c. in distance. FARMERS BANK OF SCHUYLKILL CO. Pottsville, Pa.	V and Five Male portrait FIVE
TEN Female. TEN	X Vig. Female in a sitting posture with a sickle and sheaf. X FARMERS BANK OF SCHUYLKILL CO. Pottsville, Pa. Locomotive.	10 Bridge, hand barns, horse, &c. in distance. TEN
20 Portrait of Wm. Penn.	Vig. Female sitting on a log with hands resting on a pail; cottage, steamboat, &c. FARMERS BANK OF SCHUYLKILL CO. Pottsville, Pa. Safe; dog with key in left paw.	20 Portrait of Benj. Franklin.
100 Male portrait	Man watering three horses at trough; sheep, &c.; houses and trees in distance. FARMER'S BK. OF SCHUYLKILL CO. Pottsville, Pa. 100	100 Male portrait
500 Portrait of Washington. 500	Vig. Female sitting on a plough, left hand with sickle resting on sheaf of wheat, right hand uplifted with stems of wheat. 500 FARMERS' BANK OF SCHUYLKILL CO. Pottsville, Pa.	500 Portrait of Marshall 500
ONE	Female reclining on sheaf of grain; hoe resting on arm mowing machine in background. FARMERS' & DROVERS' BANK. Waynesburgh, Pa. ONE DOLLAR on ONE and 1.	1 Girl reclining, with basket of flowers.
2 Two children, with bundles of grain.	2 2 Farmer, two horses drinking at trough, woman with pails, ducks, &c. FARMERS' & DROVERS' BANK. Waynesburgh, Pa. TWO DOLLARS.	2 Female feeding poultry.

5 Cattle. 5	(2d. Plate.) Medallion Vig. Medallion head. Further head leaning against a tree, female sitting along side of him; farmers reaping on right, also farm house. FARMERS & DROVERS BANK Waynesburg, Pa.	FIVE Cattle. FIVE
5 Portrait of Washington. FIVE	(3d. Plate.) Vig. Cattle; farmers reaping on right; and farmer ploughing with oxen and horse on left. FARMERS & DROVERS BANK. Waynesburg, Pa.	5 Female. FIVE
FIVE Female with sheaf of wheat and sickle.	(3d. Plate) Vig. Farmer and boy loading hay oxen and horse before cart. FARMERS & DROVERS BANK, Waynesburg, Pa.	5 Female portrait
10 Farmer and dog. 10	(Old Plate.) X on med. head Vig. Male and female male with pitchfork in right hand, farmers loading hay, &c. X on med. head. FARMERS & DROVERS BANK, Waynesburg, Pa.	X Farmer and dog. X
X Bull's head TEN	(New Plate.) Vig. Man on horseback, another holding pitchfork in hand and another tying up bundle of grain. X FARMERS & DROVERS BANK, Waynesburg, Pa.	Two females one with sickle and sheaf of wheat. TEN
10 Sheep.	FAR. & DROVERS' BANK, Waynesburg, Pa. Harvesting scene; man bearing sheaf on shoulder; boy on his knees apparently unhitching team of horses.	10 Female with dove.
20 Female with pitchfork. 20	(Old Plate.) Vig. Country wagon and four horses and drove of cattle crossing a stream of water; bridge, houses mail coach, wharf, &c in background. head. FARMERS & DROVERS BANK. Waynesburg, Pa.	20 Female with pitchfork. 20
XX Milkmaid. TWENTY	New Plate. Vig. Drover on horseback, dog and flock of sheep; mill in background on left. FARMERS & DROVERS BANK, Waynesburg, Pa.	20 Female seated.
20 Female portrait.	Title of Bank. Shield containing a portion of N. Y., Pa., and Va.; farmer seated on right, locomotive, etc.; female with lake seated on left.	20 Female portrait
1 One Dollar	FAR. & MECH. B'K. Easton, Pa. 1 in red. Portrait of Geo. Read. 1 in red.	1 One Dollar

2 Basket of corn.	Railroad, canal, road and farming scene in general. FAR. & MECH. B'K. Easton, Pa.	2 Clay.
5 surrounded by ornamental dies. FIVE DOLLARS Ornamental die.	FARMERS & MECHANICS BANK, Easton, Penn. Agricultural Implements. This bill has 5 repeated 87 times around border.	5 surrounded by ornamental dies. FIVE DOLLARS Ornamental die.
5 Small head. FIVE	Vig. Harvest scene four human figures, cradler sharpening his scythe. 5 FARMERS & MECHANICS BANK OF EASTON, Pa.	FIVE Mechanic, anvil, tools &c. FIVE
TEN Farmer with scythe	FARMERS & MECH. B'K. 10 in ornamental dies. 10 in ornamental dies. Easton, Pa. TEN DOLLARS This bill has X repeated 49 times around border.	TEN Blacksmith at work.
Full length female with shield, wand, &c. TEN	10 on medallion head. Vig. Public buildings. FARMERS AND MECHANICS BANK OF EASTON, Pa.	10 Male portrait
TWENTY Female figure, one arm resting on a pedestal, the other on shield.	20 on medallion head. Vig. Female seated, leaning against safe; sheep on right, church in centre, cornucopia, &c. FARMERS AND MECHANICS BANK OF EASTON, Pa.	XX 20
Goddess of Liberty; fifty on shield and eagle.	50 on medallion head. FARMERS AND MECHANICS BANK OF EASTON, Pa. Vig. Milkmaid seated on a log, farm house on left, steamboat on right.	50 50
100 on medallion head. Farmers going to work house in the distance.	FARMERS AND MECHANICS BANK OF EASTON, Pa. Vig. Mechanic seated, sledge in hand, showing factories and train of cars, &c. 100	Two females, one seated with sickle and bunch of grain. C
5 Head of Ben Franklin FIVE	FRANKLIN BANK, Washington, Pa. Vig. Men loading hay on waggon; oxen. Head of female.	5 Washington. FIVE
10 Franklin. TEN	Man on horse, sheep, dog and mill. Washington. FRANKLIN BANK, Washington, Pa. Eagle.	TEN Milkmaid TEN

20 Franklin XX	Harvest scene; man with fork, female with rake; men loading wagon with hay. 20 on med. head on either side. FRANKLIN BANK, Washington, Pa.	XX Washington 20
50 Fifty on medallion head. 50	Wash- Vig. Harvest ington. scene, reapers man standing by a tree, with arms folded, sickle in his hand, female sitting, child on her lap, baskets, &c. Franklin. FRANKLIN BANK, Washington Pa.	50 FIFTY on med head 50
1 Female writing on tablet, child at feet.	HARRISBURG B'K. Harrisburg, Pa. Large portrait of Gen. Scott.	1 Two females, flowers, &c.
2 Female, bee hive, and flowers.	HARRISBURG B'K. Harrisburg Pa. 2 Sailor seated on gun-carriage. Soldier resting on flags, fort in the distance. 2 2 2	2 Female leaning on pillar, with torch in hand, foot resting on mortar.
5 5 Boys head. V	HARRISBURG B'K. Harrisburg, Pa. Female figure erect. FIVE FIVE	5 5 Girl's head. V
FIVE Two male figures; two females seated; Indian, houses and city in distance. V	HARRISBURG BK. Harrisburg, Pa. 5 State House.	5 Male figure; two females sitting; yoke of oxen and dog.
10 Two females seated; vessel in distance. 10	Female seated with liberty cap and book in lap; houses on left. TEN on either side of vig. HARRISBURG B'K., Harrisburg, Pa.	X Same as left. X
Indian. 20	20 Vig. State House. HARRISBURG BK. Harrisburg, Pa. Eagle.	20 Washington. 20
50 Figure of Justice. 50	Female in stooping posture, men in boat, and State House on right, in distance 50 50 HARRISBURG B'K., Harrisburg, Pa.	L Figure of Justice. L
100 Cupid reading; plow, sheaf of wheat, &c. 100	Female seated, holding liberty cap; State House in distance on right 10 10 HARRISBURG B'K. Harrisburg, Pa.	100 Cupid reading, plow, sheaf of wheat, &c.

1 — Boy whittling under a tree, child tending cows and sheep. 1 — 1 Male Portrait. HONESDALE B'K, Honesdale, Pa. ONE DOLLAR. — ONE on 1. Dog watching safe.

2 — Male portrait. — HONESDALE BANK, Honesdale, Pa. 2 Interior of mine, men at work. 2 TWO 2 DOLLARS 2 — 2 Girl seated with fruit, &c.

V — Female sitting; arm resting on shield. V — 5 Vig. Three human figures; winged monster standing upon safe; cars in distance on right; vessel on left. 5 HONESDALE BANK, Honesdale, Pa. Dog. — V Female seated; book, portrait, eagle, &c. V

TEN — X Vig. Male and female seated; Jupiter in rear, anvil, hammer, &c. X HONESDALE BANK, Honesdale, Pa. — X

Female seated; ship on left; State Arms on right. XX — 20 Vig. Cupid soaring in clouds. XX HONESDALE BANK Honesdale, Pa. Eagle. — TWENTY

TWENTY — XX State Arms. HONESDALE BANK, Honesdale, Pa. — 20 Male portrait.

FIFTY Inverted. FIFTY — Mining scene. Title of Bank. — 50 Male portrait.

FIFTY — 50 L on circular die. HONESDALE BANK, Honesdale, Pa. Head of dog. — Vig. Female seated, arm resting on bale of goods; Jupiter and eagle with scroll in mouth. 50

100 Mining scene — C Indian seated with left arm resting on shield. Title of Bank. — 100 Male portrait.

Female Portrait. ONE on 1 — IRON CITY BANK, Pittsburgh, Pa. 1 Military men, horse, cannon balls, drum, &c 1 — ONE on 1 Blacksmith, sledge, anvil, &c

2 Female erect beside column, steamer in distance. — 2 Female reclining, with chart, compass, globe, &c. 2 IRON CITY BANK, Pittsburgh, Pa. — 2 Male Portrait.

5 Agricultural implements and products — Male portrait. Scene in a rolling mill, two men at work, etc. IRON CITY BANK, Pittsburgh, Pa. — 5 5

10 Female portrait. — View of Banking House. 10 Title of Bank. — Pennsylva'a Smith at forge. TEN

Male portrait 20 — Title of Bank. Wharf scene, railroad depot, steamboats, vessels, cars, men, horses, carts, etc. — 20 Portrait of girl.

50 — Launch of the Adriatic. Female portrait. Title of Bank. — 50 Fowls

100 C — Half length figures of the inventors of printing; press, &c. Male portrait. Title of Bank. One Hundred in red. — 100 Male portrait

Mechanic with sledge, anvil, &c. D — IRON CITY BANK, Pittsburgh, Pa. Raft scene, steamboat in distance. Eagle. — 500 Female portrait

Cupid and sheaf — IRON CITY BANK, Pittsburgh, Pa. Boiler makers at work in shop. Female portrait. — 1000 Cupid and cornucopia.

Farm yard, horses drinking, man, pump, hog, cows, &c ONE — 1 Female portrait. JERSEY SHORE B'K, Jersey Shore, Pa. — 1 Male portrait.

V on Five. Female reaper seated. — JERSEY SHORE BK, Jersey Shore, Pa. Scene on a raft, etc. — 5 Men at work in mine.

5 Female portrait. — JERSEY SHORE B'K. Jersey Shore, Pa. V Old man and child, bust of Washington on table V — 5 Male portrait.

X Male portrait — JERSEY SHORE BK, Jersey Shore, Pa. Female seated on a log beside shield with cars on it; sheafs of grain on right; farm house in distance on left — 10 Male portrait

XX Maleportrait — JERSEY SHORE BK, Jersey Shore, Pa. Bull's head on shield; men dressing leather on right; female sewing shoes on left. 20 — 20 Female portrait.

Portrait. — KITTANING BANK, Kittaning, Pa. Man plowing with two horses, boy, dog, &c. — 1 Two children

Five on 5. Female head — KITTANNING BK., Kittanning, Pa. Three females representing the Arts and Sciences; bust of Washington. FIVE — 5 Male portrait

10 Girl with dove — Title of Bank. Four females on globe; shield, flag and sword. — 10 Male portrait

LANCASTER CO. BANK. Lancaster, Pa. Female reaper seated with grain, straw hat and sickle beside her. 1 1 Continental soldiers, one on horse, one with paper, cannon, tents, &c — 1 surrounded by small 1's. One Dollar.

2 surrounded by small 2's and two. Eagle on rock. — Milkmaid with pail and stool, cows lying down, farmhouse in distance. LANCASTER CO. B'K, Lancaster, Pa. 2 2 — 2 surrounded by small 2's and two. Female with flowers.

FIVE Reaping scene. FIVE — 5 Vig. Farm scene, harvesters at lunch LANCASTER CO. BANK, Pa. Dog's head. — 5 V 5

Female and churn. 10 — Vig. Female representing a flax spinner. X LANCASTER CO. BANK, Pa. Dog's head. — Agricultural scene. TEN

Left end	Centre	Right end
XX Farmer gathering corn. 20	Med. head. 20 Med. head. LANCASTER CO. BK. Lancaster, Pa. Eagle.	Head of female surmounted by an eagle. XX Bust of a mechanic.
50 Medallion head. 50	Vig. Farmers cradling grain; houses in back ground. L LANCASTER CO. BK. Lancaster, Pa. Dogs head.	50 surrounded by the words fifty dollars. Farmer sowing grain, another harrowing.
100 Allegorical figure representing manufactures; water in distance. 100	Vig. landscape, load of hay drawn by oxen, man on horseback, mill, viaduct, train of cars &c in distance. LANCASTER CO. BANK. Pa. Dogs head.	100 Farmer ploughing.
ONE	1 Female seated on rock with eagle, shield, &c.; vessels, &c. 1 LEBANON BANK, Lebanon, Pa.	1 Med. head 1
2 Med. head. 2	2 Two females, one pointing to vessel on ocean. LEBANON BANK, Lebanon, Pa.	2 Med. head. 2
FIVE Female leaning on cane copse. FIVE	LEBANON BANK Lebanon, Pa. 5 Vig. female seated on barrel of merchandise, anchor, vessel, houses &c. V Childs head.	FIVE Justice seated and head of Washington.
10 TEN X	LEBANON BANK Lebanon, Pa. 10 Vig. Female seated; eagle at her feet; shipping in background. X Childs head.	TEN Same as fives.
TWENTY	LEBANON BANK, Lebanon, Pa. 20 Vig. Female seated representing agriculture and commerce. XX	20 Same as fives
50 Female with sword in right hand. FIFTY	50 Vig. Male and female agricultural scene. 50 LEBANON BANK. Lebanon, Pa. Babe.	50 Female standing with sword in left hand. FIFTY
100 Female seated on bale of goods; ship in distance. 100	100 Vig. Two females; one of whom, Goddess of liberty is seated on a stone on which the figures "1776," are inscribed. 100 LEBANON BANK Lebanon, Pa. Deer.	100 Female seated on bale of goods ship in distance. 100
Figure 1 surrounded by small 1s.	LEBANON VALLEY BANK, Lebanon, Pa. Cows and calf passing through gate; female and boy. ONE DOLLAR	Same as left end.
2	LEBANON VALLEY BANK. Lebanon, Pa. TWO DOLLARS Chickens 2 Ducks TWO DOLLARS	2
5 Clay.	LEBANON VALLEY BANK, Lebanon, Pa. Female seated; cow, sheep, etc Beehive.	5 Female seated with pole and cap.
TEN Justice.	Title of Bank. Three military men; one on horseback; flag in distance.	10 Eagle.
Twenty inverted. Man with sheaf. 20	Title of Bank. Spread eagle; town, etc., in distance.	20 Female head
50 Med. head. 50	Goddess of Liberty reclining against U. S. Arms; Indian on right; two females on left. Title of Bank.	50 Man with corn, basket, etc.
100 Blacksmith and anvil.	Title of Bank. C Horses at trough; railroad and canal scene; steamboat, etc.	100
1 Male portrait.	LEWISBURG BANK, Lewisburg, Pa. Two soldiers and drummer.	1 Male portrait
5 Male portrait	Two females seated; factories, &c., on right; cows, sheep, &c., on left. LEWISBURGH BK. Lewisburgh, Pa. Ducks.	5 Male portrait
10 Male portrait	Title of Bank. Blacksmith with hammer; farmer with scythe; girl with rake; child with fruit. Female bathing.	10 Male portrait
LEWIS 20	BURG BANK. Lewisburg, Pa. Boys attempting to catch running horse; dog, horses, etc. Male head	20 Man carrying corn stalks.
1 Soldier with flags, cannon, etc.	LOCKHAVEN BANK, Lockhaven, Pa. 1	One on 1 Gen. Scott.
2 Portrait of Henry Clay.	LOCKHAVEN B'K. Lockhaven, Pa. 2 Revolutionary scene, man firing on enemy, woman loading gun. 2	2 Portrait of Jackson.
5 Woodmen felling trees; oxen in back ground.	LOCKHAVEN BANK. Lockhaven, Pa. Female with sheaf of wheat.	Male portrait 5
Male portrait TEN TEN	LOCKHAVEN BANK, Lockhaven, Pa. DOLLARS Men at work with patent mowing and raking machine drawn by two horses.	10
XX 20	LOCKHAVEN BANK, Lockhaven, Pa. Shield with train of cars and rising sun; on right, sheafs and sheep; on left female seated with tub; house in distance.	20 Portrait of Washington
Male portrait 50	LOCKHAVEN BANK, Lockhaven, Pa. State Arms with horse on either side; cars, boats, factories, etc.	50
100 C	LOCKHAVEN BANK. Lockhaven, Pa. Female with small tub.	100 Eagle on branch of tree; cars, canal, factories, etc.
1 Male portrait. ONE	ONE DOLLAR. MAUCH CHUNK BK. Mauch Chunk, Pa. Two females	1 Female head. ONE
2 Girl & boy at well.	MAUCH CHUNK BK, Mauch Chunk. Pa. 2 Female reclining with torch, &c. 2 2 TWO DOLLARS.	2 Male portrait.

5 | Vig. Mining scene; loaded coal car, two miners [illegible] [illegible] in distance on left. | 5
Male portrait. | | Head of young girl with curls.
FIVE | MAUCH CHUNK BK. Mauch Chunk, Pa. Bear. | FIVE

10 | Head of young girl. Title of Bank. Vig. Lumbering scene; men felling trees; [illegible]; saw mills in distance. TEN DOLLARS.
Harvest scene; male and female seated; man in act of drinking from pitcher.

Man, horse, dog, &c. in field of grain; man with sheaves under right arm. | 20 Train of cars passing a group of people; some seated, consisting of huntsmen, hay makers, women, &c. 20 | Young girl erect with glass in her hand.
Title of Bank. Child's Head.

50 | Vig. Scene on canal; boat locking through; harvest scene and cars on viaduct in background. | 50
Scene upon road, drovers driving herd of cattle; Hay wagon, &c. in distance. | Title of Bank. | Locomotive and train of cars coming round curve; steamboat in distance.

C | 100 Vig. Cupid surrounded by three mermaids floating on water. | C
Woman with basket on left arm leading child. | MAUCH CHUNK BK. Mauch Chunk, Pa. Spread eagle. | Head of female.
100

1 | MECHANICS' BANK of Pittsburgh, Pa. | 1
Beehive. | Mechanic at work at vice, etc. | Female with flowers.

Mechanic and machinery. | Males, female, child, horse, dog, hogs, fowls, etc. | 2
2 | MECHANICS' BANK of Pittsburgh, Pa. | Female and child.

5 | MECH. BANK OF PITTSBURGH, PA. | 5
Two men at work on a locomotive boiler. | | Female portrait.

X | MECH. BANK OF PITTSBURGH, PA. | 10
Carpenter at work at bench, bench at his back. | Portrait of Washington. | Man in shirt sleeves erect, houses in background.

Word "Twenty" in part circle running up. | MECH. BANK OF PITTSBURGH, PA. | Three figures [illegible]; one on left is Mercury; the middle one holds pole and cap.
Blacksmith, anvil and sledge; building in distance. | 20 | 20

FIFTY | 50 Cattle, farmer and [illegible]; farmer holding sickle and sheaf of wheat; man and horse and anvil on right; sheaf on left. | 50
Female erect with sword. | MECH. BANK OF PITTSBURGH, PA. | Sky and [illegible].

Two men [illegible], in distance, two [illegible] at work. | C Mechanic, farmer, wheel, tree, horse, &c., in background, bridge and buildings.
100 | MECH. BANK OF PITTSBURGH, PA. | 100

Farmers binding wheat; yoke of oxen, horse, &c. | MECH. BANK OF PITTSBURGH, PA. 500 | 500
Female Indian erect.

Farmer standing with scythe, &c. | M Interior view of an iron mill, and men at work. | 1000
1000 | MECH. BANK OF PITTSBURGH, PA. | Female portrait.

1000 | Train of cars crossing bridge; in background another train and ship. | M
Farmer seated with scythe. | MECHANICS' BK. OF Pittsburg, Pa. | Female portrait.

5 | MECHANICSBURG BANK. Mechanicsburg, Pa. | 5
State Arms.
5 | Old man, child, and bust on table. | 5

10 | MECHANICSBURG BANK. Mechanicsburg, Pa. | 10
State arms. | TEN DOLLARS on X | Man at [illegible], two horses, pigs, cattle, &c.
10

1 | MER. & MAN. BANK of Pittsburgh, Pa. | 1
Female with tablets, child at her feet. | ONE One on 1 ONE | Male portrait.
ONE

Two females in [illegible]. | TWO DOLLARS across 2 | Male portrait.
TWO | MER. & MAN. B'K. Pittsburgh, Pa. Dog's head. | 2

THE MERCHANTS' & | PITTSBURGH, | 5
General wharf scene. | Indian head.
MANUFACTURERS BK. of Pittsburgh, Pa. | Sailors on ship hoisting.
5

5 | Vig. Group of three farmers and two artisans, half length figures. | FIVE
Canal boat passing under a bridge. | MERCHANTS AND MANUFACTURERS BANK. Pittsburgh, Pa. | Medallion head.
FIVE | Blacksmith's arm, hammer and anvil. | FIVE

View of city, bridge, canal, steamboat and river scene. | Child's head. | 10
X | MER. & MAN. B'K. Pittsburgh, Pa. TEN DOLLARS across 10 | X

10 | MERCHANTS AND MANUFACTURERS BANK. Pittsburg, Pa. | 10
Blacksmith with hammer in right hand resting on anvil. | Vig. Female figure, left hand resting on a vase, pitcher in right hand pouring water; [illegible] out of which an eagle is drinking. | Blacksmith with right hand resting on an anvil.
10 | | 10

20 | MERCHANTS AND MANUFACTURERS BANK. Pittsburg, Pa. | 20
Farmer cleaning scythe. Railroad bridge, locomotive and cars in background. | Vig. Three female figures. Right end figure of Justice with sword and scales. Centre figure with wand of Mercury in left hand; left end figure with basket of fruit. Liberty. | XX
| | 20

50 | Med. Vig. Female Med. head sitting on a head of Franklin; [illegible] shipping, [illegible] anvil and hammer at her feet; railroad bridge, locomotive and cars in the background. | 50
Female with hands on spinning wheel. | Title of bank. | Female with hands on spinning wheel.
50 | | 50

Scene in a rolling mill; men at work. | 50
50 | MERCHANTS' AND MANUFACTURERS' BANK of Pittsburg, Pa. Anvil. | Portrait of girl.

100 | Title of Bank. | 100
Scene in an iron foundry, men carrying metal, etc. | Letter C. | Man engaged in moulding.

100 | Medallion head. Vig. Mercury [illegible] with wand pointing to a steamboat, female with right arm resting on bale of goods, in the background Neptune drawn by horses. Medallion head. | 100
Steamboat. | Title of Bank. | Canal boat.
100 | | 100

500 | Vig. Locomotive and train of cars. | 500
Franklin. | MERCHANTS AND MANUFACTURERS BANK. Pittsburg, Pa. Ship. | Figure resting on shield; sextant and compass at her feet, in right hand a bow.
D

1000 | Vig. Blacksmith seated, left arm resting on an anvil; factories, shipping in the back ground; [illegible] on right. | 1000
Washington. | MERCHANTS AND MANUFACTURERS BANK. Pittsburg, Pa. | Female head and bust.
1000 | | M

Cupid. Words "Secured," &c., on red die. FIVE
MIFFLIN CO. BANK, Lewistown, Pa. V FIVE V Female and calves; canal and railroad scene on left.
5 Male Portrait

X 10
MIFFLIN CO. BANK, Lewistown, Pa. Scene at mill, two men, two horses, wagon, &c. Words "Secured," &c., on red die. Cars.
10 Male portrait

ONE Washingt'n ONE
1 Blacksmith at work 1 MINERS' BANK, Pottsville, Pa. Locomotive.
ONE Milkmaid seated ONE

TWO Female Cupid, &c. 2
2 Blacksmith shoeing horse; boy, dogs, man, &c. MINERS' BANK, Pottsville, Pa. Agricultural implements and products.
TWO Male portrait. 2

5 Washington. 5
Vig. Train of cars, village in the distance. MINERS BANK OF POTTSVILLE, Pa. Eagle.
5 Female. 5

10 Webster. TEN
Head of Randolph. Vi. Eagle on branch of tree; train of cars and canal and boats in the distance. MINERS BANK OF POTTSVILLE PA.
10 Fillmore. TEN

20 Female. 20
Columbus. Vig. Winged female blowing a trumpet, globe, eagle, flags &c. Washington. MINERS BANK OF POTTSVILLE, PA. Dogs Head.
20 Female 20

50 Female 50
Franklin. Vig. A. Fulton. female seated between 5 and 0, barrel, bales, &c. ship on left. MINERS BANK OF POTTSVILLE, PA. Eagle.
50 Female. 50

C Portrait of Washington.
Vig. Eagle on branch of tree; view of Niagara Falls, in the background. MINERS BANK OF POTTSVILLE, PA. Horse
100 Franklin.

Medallion head of Washington
MONONGAHELA B'K Brownsville, Pa. 5 Vig. Large V, with female and sheaf of wheat in centre of V. 5
Fame blowing a trumpet, and holding pole with liberty cap. 5

X Medallion head. X
10 Vig. Harvest scene, and farmers taking lunch. MONONGAHELA BK Brownsville, Pa.
Large X with persons supporting it on either side; sledge and anvil at bottom.

Female portrait.
20 Vig. Goddess of Liberty, with pole and cap, reclining against U. S. Coat of Arms. MONONGAHELA BK Brownsville, Pa.
20 Portrait of Washington

1 Officer with drum and sword.
MOUNT JOY BANK, Mount Joy, Pa. Female head. Men and two horses at pump; pig, cattle, &c.
1

2 Girl's head.
Boy and girl under a tree; cattle, sheep, &c. MOUNT JOY BANK, Mount Joy, Pa.
2 Female with basket of fruit

Female reclining on sheaf, binding sheaf. 5
Female portrait. MOUNT JOY BANK, Mount Joy, Pa. Turkey.
5 Man carrying corn stalks.

X Mt. JOY Bk Mt. Joy Pa. Female head. X
Milkmaid, cows, man, dog, &c TEN DOLLARS.
10 10

Cupid and 20 Boy's head.
MOUNT JOY BANK. Mount Joy, Pa. Corn gathering scene; men husking, &c.
20 and Cupid. Cars, telegraph, cattle, &c.

ONE across 1 Male portrait.
NORTHUMB'RLAND CO. BANK, Shamokin, Pa. 1 Indian maiden with corn, people, arm resting on shield. 1 Safe, eagle, flags, &c. ONE.
1

2 Male portrait.
NORTHUMB'RLAND CO. BANK, Shamokin. TWO across 2 Blacksmith at work, tools, &c. Pennsylvania.
2 Female portrait

5 Henry Clay
NORTHUMB'RLAND CO. BANK, Shamokin, Pa. Girl seated on sheaf of wheat; engine and cars on right. Pennsylv'a State arms on left.
5 Gen. Scott.

Female head. I
NORTH WEST'N BK Warren, Pa. Cars crossing bridge; cattle and boy in stream; man on horse, etc.
1 Basket of corn.

2 Beehives.
Deer in forest; waterfall, trees, etc. NORTH-WEST'N BK Warren, Pa.
2 Female portrait.

5 V
NO. WESTERN BK Warren, Pa. Ornamental fig. 5; female on each side; houses, etc., in distance.
5 FIVE

Portrait of Washington. 5 surrounded by words FIVE.
Herd of cattle, two drovers, one on horse; factory in distance. NO. WESTERN B'K Warren, Pa. FIVE DOLLARS. FIVE
5 surrounded by words FIVE. Bust of Female holding flowers.

X Female reaping.
NO. WESTERN BK. Warren, Pa. Red die with letter X, words "Ten Dollars" and figs. 10 on it.
10 Female with flowers in her apron.

1 Female seated with pail, cows, &c.
OCTORARA BANK, Oxford, Pa. Cows, mill, stream, &c.
One on 1 Female seated with basket of fruit.

Indians on cliff watching deer. 2
2 Boy's portrait. OCTORARO BANK, Oxford, Pa.
2 Boy's head.

5 Plowman and horses.
OCTORARO BANK, Female with two calves, tree; canal boat, cars, etc., in distance. Oxford, Pa. V V V V
V Female with dove.

10 Washington.
Four females—one erect. Title of Bank. TEN TEN
X Two girls.

20 Bull's head.
Title of Bank. Reaper man at work in field of wheat; town in distance. TWENTY
20 Rams head.

ONE Female at well ONE	PITTSTON BANK. Pittston, Penn. Man hunting Buffaloes.	ONE across figure 1. Female.
Eagle, shield etc. TWO across figure 2.	2 Female PITTSTON BANK. Pittston Penn.	2
Female soaring above buildings, river, cars, steamboat, etc.; on upper right country scene.	Coal train and mine. PITTSTON BANK, Pittston, Pa.	5 Indian.
10 Female seated and dog's head.	Title of Bank. Female seated among implements; cars on bridge and factories in distance.	10 Female with sheaf. 10
Men with pick; coal-pit and men shoving coal car.	Title of Bank. Men at work with wheel-barrows on dock, horse, cart, coal, etc.	10
Mechanic with sledge. 20	Moonlight scene on canal, men, horses, boat, hills, and distant city. Title of Bank.	20 Female portrait.
1 Die work	STROUDSBURG B'K, Stroudsburg, Pa. ONE Man DOLLAR and dog fighting with bear in woods ONE ONE	1 Die work
2 TWO 2	STROUDSBURG B'K. Stroudsburg, Pa Train of cars. TWO TWO	2 DOLLARS. 2
5 Franklin.	STROUDSBURG BK Stroudsburg, Pa. Men dressing leather. FIVE	5 Wm. Penn.
X Washington	Man watering three horses from trough by side of well; goat, kid, sheep, trees and house. Title of Bank.	10 Lady Washington.

20 View of cattle, telegraph and railroad.	Washington—female, scythe, sheaf, cars, etc., on right; female, anchor, men, boxes, barrels and steamer on left. Title of Bank.	XX Two cherubs with sheaf and distaff. XX
50 Locomotive.	Title of Bank. Rafting scene; man on raft. FIFTY	50 Male portrait
100 Farmer seated at lunch.	Horse on either side of shield; eagle at top; cars, factory and steamboat in distance. C Title of Bank.	ONE HUNDRED
1 Portrait of Washington.	Farmer seated, with boy, girl, and dog; two horses, &c. TIOGA COUNTY B'K, Tioga Pa. ONE DOLLAR.	1 Indian seated, with axe
2 TWO on 2 2	TIOGA COUNTY B'K, Tioga, Pa. Train of cars in an oval.	2 Portrait of Jefferson.
5 Female with hand on head	TIOGA COUNTY BK, Tioga. Pa. Men and children with load of hay; mechanic standing near anvil and column. V Ducks. V	5 Penn.
10 Male portrait	Title of Bank. Jolly raftsmen on Western river; steamboat on left. X X	10 Sailor
20 Franklin.	Title of Bank. Mining scene	20 Washington.
50 Buchanan.	Farmer at lunch; girl, boy, dog, horses, etc. Title of Bank.	50 Indian seated.
C 100 C	Locomotive. Title of Bank.	100 Male portrait.

FIVE Female seated with grain and sickle.	5 Washington on horseback with his staff around him. UNION BANK OF Reading, Pa.	5 Male portrait
10	Miller and farmer beside wagon; two horses, one drinking from trough; mill in background. Male portrait UNION BANK OF Reading, Pa.	X Female. Portrait
Farmer with pitcher, etc. 20	UNION BANK, Reading, Pa. Man cutting a stick; horse, cow, sheep and trees.	20 Female with flowers.
50	Two men and horses; factories in distance. 50 Title of Bank.	FIFTY Milkmaid; boy pointing.
100 Female with sword and scales.	C Two females and machinery. C Title of Bank.	Farmer seated with sickle; men reaping in distance.
Female with flag, shield, etc.	WEST BRANCH BK. Williamsport, Pa. Canal, railroad and farming scene.	One on 1. Man loading gun.
2 Female with sword and scales.	WEST BRANCH BK. Williamsport, Pa. 2 Man mowing in field; female seated. 2	2 2 Female feeding fowls.
5 Justice reclining.	Vig. View of a public building, miniature view of female on right of vig. WEST BRANCH BK. Williamsport, Pa. Dog and safe.	5 Sailor and shipping in background.
5 Washington 5	Farmers at lunch. Franklin. WEST BRANCH BK, Williamsport, Pa. Agricultural implements.	5 Canal and boats. 5
10 Medallion head. 10	Vig. Spread eagle poised on trunk of tree; locomotive and cars in background. 10 WEST BRANCH BK. Williamsport, Pa. Arms of Pa.	Portrait of Washington. TEN Portrait of Harrison.

PENN.

Left	Centre	Right
XX Miniature view of farm girl drawing pail of water from well.	Vig. Iron furnace, locomotive and farm, forest scenery in back ground, locomotive and cars on left of vig. in fore ground. WEST BRANCH BK. Williamsport, Pa. Indian paddling canoe.	20 Portrait of Lafayette. 20.
5 Franklin. V	(Old Plate.) 5 Vig. Female with sheaf of wheat, pole head with two men in distance. 5 WYOMING BANK, Wilkes Barre, Pa. State Arms.	5 Jackson. V
5 Head of Ben. Franklin. FIVE	(New Plate.) WYOMING BANK, Wilkes Barre, Pa. Agricultural implements.	Large V, a figure 5 and FIVE. Male portrait.
FIVE 5 5	FIVE DOLLARS Female portrait. 5 Statue of Liberty WYOMING BANK, Wilkesbarre, Pa.	Same as left.
Fig. 10 inverted. X	Railroad, bridge, canal, haying and country scenes. Title of Bank.	10 Female with flowers.
X Mars. X	(Old Plate.) Vig. Female with rake sitting on plough, and small figures walking at forge. 10 10 Title of Bank. State Arms.	Canal locks, boats passing through.
10 Two Indians in front of boat, one standing, the other on right knee.	(New Plate.) WYOMING BANK, Wilkes Barre, Pa. Girl bathing.	10 Male portrait. TEN
Canal, lock, and boats passing through.	20 Female on either side of a shield, surmounted by an eagle. 20 WYOMING BANK, Wilkesbarre, Pa. State Arms.	20 Washington. 20
50 Canal scene. 50	50 on medallion head. State Arms. 50 on medallion head. WYOMING BANK, Wilkes Barre, Pa.	Female with sickle and wheat. 50
100 Portrait of Washington. 100	100 on medallion head. Signing of Declaration of Independence. 100 on medallion head. WYOMING BANK, Wilkes Barre, Pa.	100 Portrait of Dewitt Clinton. 100

PENN.

Left	Centre	Right
1 Medallion head. 1	Mikmaid, cows, &c. ONE, on medallion head on either side. YORK BANK, York, Pa.	1 Medallion head. 1
TWO Female seated in fig. 2. TWO	2 Old man and youth with plow; mill in distance. 2 YORK BANK, York, Pa.	2 Medallion head. 2
5 Male portrait. FIVE	Vig. Public buildings, stage coach, fountain, shrubbery, &c. YORK BANK, York, Pa.	5 Male portrait. FIVE
10 Male portrait. TEN	Vig. Daguerreotype view of York. YORK BANK, York, Pa.	10 TEN & Male portrait.
1 YORK 1	COUNTY BANK, York, Pa. Signing Declaration of Independence. Scott. Eagle.	1 Indian princess.
2 Farmer seated under a tree.	YORK COUNTY B'K. York, Pa. Female with pitcher and rake; men loading cart, &c.	2 Female portrait.
5 Half length figure of girl.	Corn husking scene. YORK COUNTY BK. York, Pa.	5 Blacksmith at forge.
5 Farmer sitting, woman with rake and pitcher, dog behind her.	FIVE Vig. Boy plowing with two horses; boy by his side with shovel on his shoulder. YORK COUNTY B'K. York, Penn. Female with sickle.	5 Wm. Penn. 5
Farmer seated holding glass and scythe; woman with victuals.	Jefferson. Males and females and train of cars. Title of Bank.	X
Female with grain and sickle. 10	Vig. Two boys on horse back, driving cattle and sheep; boy sitting beside a tree, dog behind him. YORK COUNTY B'K. York, Penn. Farming utensils.	10 Portrait. 10

DELAWARE.

Left	Centre	Right
XX Portrait. XX	Vig. Blacksmith shop; one smith at work on anvil, another shoeing horse; man standing in door. YORK COUNTY B'K. York, Penn. Farming utensils.	20 Washington.
1 Female figure.	State arms; locomotive and ship in background. B'K OF DELAWARE, Wilmington, Del.	1 Ship.
Female seated. ONE	Scene at sea; lighthouse and vessels. 1 on medallion on either side. BK. OF DELAWARE, Wilmington, Del.	ONE DOLLAR
TWO Washington. TWO	Shipping scene, houses, etc.; 2 on medallion head on each side. BK OF DELAWARE, Wilmington, Del.	TWO DOLLARS
2 Half of the State Arms.	Spread eagle on a tree, ship and steamboat in background. B'K OF DELAWARE, Wilmington, Del.	2 Other half State Arms.
5 Dog, key and safe. V	State arms. B'K OF DELAWARE, Wilmington, Del. Chartered 1795.	5 FIVE V
X Two harvest men, with dog.	Female with sheaf of wheat, sickle, &c. B'K OF DELAWARE, Wilmington, Del.	10 Female. 10
TWENTY	B'K OF DELAWARE, Wilmington, Del. 2 Female figure, 0	20 Gen. Taylor. XX
FIFTY	Figure 50 and female head. Two ships and whale boat out. Figure 50 and female head. B'K OF DELAWARE, Wilmington, Del. Engine and cars.	FIFTY
100 Dog.	Female, in background, engine and cars; shot tower. B'K OF DELAWARE, Wilmington, Del. Railroad train.	100 Female holding anchor.

1 — Male portrait. | Man on horse; men harvesting in distance. BANK OF NEWARK, Newark, Del. Sheep. | 1 — Head of girl.

Male figure erect. TWO | 2 Blacksmith shoeing horse, drover seated on log; blacksmith in background. BANK OF NEWARK, Newark, Del. Cock. | 2 — Male portrait.

5 — Washington. | Milkmaid seated with pail, cows, &c.; farm house in distance. BANK OF NEWARK, Newark, Del. | 5 — Chelvens

10 — X | Drove of cattle, pigs, &c.; two men on horseback; train of cars, bridge and village in distance. BANK OF NEWARK, Newark, Del. Beehive. | 10 — X

Man gathering corn. TWENTY | 20 Head of girl. 20 BANK OF NEWARK, Newark, Del. | Mower sharpening scythe. TWENTY

Female haymaker with rake. 1 On die with words one. | BANK OF SEAFORD, Seaford, Del. Herd of cattle, two drovers, one on horse, factory in distance. ONE DOLLAR on ONE | 1 On die with words one. Beehives, bees, &c.

Female representing agriculture holding sheaf. 2 On die with words two and small 2's. | BANK OF SEAFORD, Seaford, Del. Man, two horses, mill, canal, &c. TWO DOLLARS on TWO | 2 On die with words two and 2's. Female embracing child.

V — Cow and calf, tree, &c. | Train of cars crossing bridge, canal, boatmen, horses, railroad, depot, &c. BANK OF SEAFORD, Seaford, Del. FIVE DOLLARS on FIVE | 5 — Female holding flowers.

10 — Bust of female. | Spread eagle clutching arrows, shield, and olive branch. BANK OF SEAFORD, Seaford, Del. Ten Dollars on TEN | 10 — Female beside plough, sheaf of grain, etc.

1 — One and head of female. 1 | Man reaping, child, dog, and agricultural implements in the foreground. 1 1 BANK OF SMYRNA, Smyrna, Del. Female. | 1 — One and head of female. 1

1 ONE 1 | Man watering horse from trough; sheep, goats, trees and house. B'K OF SMYRNA, Smyrna, Del. | 1 — Washington.

TWO DOLLARS | 2 Drover bargaining for ox; negro, boy, horse, cattle, dog, etc. BANK OF SMYRNA, Smyrna, Del. | 2 — Female feeding fowls.

TWO — Female seated in large figure 2. TWO | Female seated with child in her arms; shipping in the distance. 2 on med. head each side. BANK OF SMYRNA, Smyrna, Del. State arms. | TWO — Same as left. TWO

3 — Drove of cattle. 3 | Med. Three. Shipping—three men in small boat; town in distance. Med. Three. BANK OF SMYRNA, Smyrna, Del. | 3 — Head of Washington. 3

5 — Head of female. 5 | Med. Five. Country scene—male and female; four reapers in distance. Med. Five. BANK OF SMYRNA, Smyrna, Del. | 5 — Head of female. 5

5 — Female, male, boy, girl, dog and chickens. | Female driving cows home; train of cars and city in distance. B'K OF SMYRNA, Smyrna, Del. | V 5

10 — Female portrait. | Drover and drove of cattle; boy in water, trees, and house in distance. BANK OF SMYRNA, Smyrna, Del. | 10 X

10 — Female with rake in hand. 10 | Med. X. Woodsman seated on a log with his left hand on his dog's head. Med. X. BANK OF SMYRNA, Smyrna, Del. | 10 — Drove of cattle. 10

Head of Franklin. | 20 Female seated on a rock; left hand resting on a stalk of corn, right resting on a cornucopia. 20 BANK OF SMYRNA, Smyrna, Del. Double med. head. | Head of Washington.

Male at the work with statue in niche. | Med. 50. State arms, with female on either side, representing Agriculture and Commerce. Med. 50. BANK OF SMYRNA, Smyrna, Del. Male portrait. | Same as left.

100 — State arms with female on either side. 100 | Female portrait. Country scene; two men loading hay; pair of oxen to wagon. BANK OF SMYRNA, Smyrna, Del. Steamboat. | 100 — Ship under sail. 100

1 — Female portrait. ONE | Sailor reclining, coil of rope, anchor, windlass, boat, &c. Ships on left in distance. WILMINGTON AND BRANDYWINE B'K, Delaware. Wheelbarrow, &c. | 1 — Mechanic. ONE

2 TWO — Female seated on barrel, scales, &c. | Sailor and Indian, eagle, shield, &c.; Ship on right in distance, tents on left. WILMINGTON AND BRANDYWINE B'K, Delaware. Arm, anvil, &c. | 2

FIVE — Farmer reclining with sickle. FIVE | Three men erect, one holds a pole; village and water on right. WILMINGTON AND BRANDYWINE B'K, Delaware. Locomotive. | 5 — Female, sheaf of wheat, &c.

X — TEN on Med. Head. 10 | Man and boy seated; man is drawing; mill on right; Med. Head and word TEN on either side. WILMINGTON AND BRANDYWINE B'K, Delaware. | 10 — Man seated drawing. X

20 — Portrait of Washington. 20 | Two females seated, shield eagle, &c.; Med. Head and word TWENTY on either side. WILMINGTON AND BRANDYWINE B'K, Delaware. | 20 — Male portrait. 20

50 — Ship under weigh. 50 | Female seated, plow, barrel, bale of goods, &c.; portrait of Washington on left; portrait of Lafayette, vessels, &c., on right. WILMINGTON AND BRANDYWINE B'K, Delaware. Cupid. | 50 — Steamboat and small boat. 50

100 — Female seated, shield &c. 100 | Cars and People, Steamboat on left in distance. WILMINGTON AND BRANDYWINE B'K, Delaware. Ship. | 100 — Female seated, letter C, eagle, shield, &c. 100

1 — Machinist. | CITIZENS' BANK, Middletown, Del. 1 Man sharpening scythe on grindstone; negro turning; men at work in distance. 1 | 1 — Girl's head.

2 — 2 — Cupid. | 2 2 Title of Bank. Girl's head. Female portrait. 2 2 2 TWO TWO | 2 — 2 — Cupid.

Left	Centre	Right
3 THREE Head.	Title of Bank Two females reclining; factories in distance. Horse.	THREE Female with birds.
5 Female portrait.	Hunter and farmer with implements on either side of shield; vessels in distance. Title of Bank 5 Man and plow. 5	5 Male portrait.
10 Female portrait.	Girl with rake; child, farmer and blacksmith. CITIZENS BANK. X Middletown, Del. X 10	10 Male portrait.
20 Washington.	Group of male and female figures looking at train of cars. Title of Bank. 20 Wheels. 20	20 Girl's head.
1 Head of Wm. Penn. ONE	Female figure and hole; man loading hay wagon on right. DELAWARE CITY BANK. Del.	1 Locomotive, train of cars, and bridge. ONE
2 Head of J. Quincy Adams. TWO	Female figure with sickle and sheaf of wheat in left hand, and bunch of grain in right, plow in background DELAWARE CITY BANK, Del.	2 Steamboat. TWO
3 Head of Wm. Penn. 3	Three females in a sitting posture, the one on the left with sickle and sheaf of wheat. DELAWARE CITY BANK, Del.	Goddess of Liberty. THREE
5 Medal. Head Washington. 5	[Old Plate.] State Arms, ship in background. DELAWARE CITY BANK. Del. Bee Hive.	5 Canal Boat Train of cars in the distance. 5
5 Head of Female.	[New Plate.] DELAWARE CITY BANK. Del. State Arms; mill, &c., in background. Chicken.	5 Medal. Head J. M. Clayton.
TEN Man and women in a sitting posture; man with balance in right hand, women with sheaf of 10	Two female figures, one has her left hand on a cogwheel; ship-building in background. DELAWARE CITY BANK. Del. Bee Hive.	10 Medal. Head Washington. 10

Left	Centre	Right
20 Medal. Head Washington. 20	Man Plowing. DELAWARE CITY BANK. Del. Bee Hive.	TWENTY Washington on horseback TWENTY
Male portrait.	ONE Female seated and figure 1. 1 FARMERS BANK OF DELAWARE Three cupids reclining.	Female standing with sickle. ONE
1 Man dressing leather.	FARMERS' BANK OF THE STATE OF DELAWARE, Dover, Del. Three males and female, harvest scene; cars and house in distance.	1 Washing sheep; houses in distance
2 Woodcutter.	Title of Bank. Deer and tree on shield; on right, sailor, ship in distance; farmer with scythe on left. Locomotive.	2 Female erect and another kneeling.
Male portrait.	TWO Female with sickle, figure 2 and cupid. 2 FARMERS BANK OF DEL. Female seated and sheep.	Female standing with sickle. TWO
Male portrait.	3 Three females, eagle, figure 3, &c. 3 FARMERS BANK OF DEL. Male reclining.	Female erect with scales. THREE
Male portrait.	5 Drove of cattle, man on horse, &c. 5 FARMERS BANK OF DEL. Female erect.	Male portrait.
Portrait of Franklin.	10 Two females, [illegible] &c. 10 FARMERS BANK OF DEL. Double med. head.	Portrait of Wm. Penn.
Portrait of Washington.	20 Two females reclining; ship on right. Two cupids, beehive, and figs. 20. FARMERS BANK OF DEL.	Male portrait.
50 Sailor erect with American flag. 50	FARMERS BANK OF DEL. Four cupids with baskets, sheaf of wheat, sickle, &c.; house in background.	50 Med. head and figs. 50. 50

Left	Centre	Right
100 Med. head and word Hundred. 100	FARMERS BANK OF DEL. View of the landing of Columbus; boats on right; Indians on left in background.	Female erect with shield and pole. 100
Interior of blacksmith's shop, with men at work; cottage in distance. 1	MECHANICS' BANK. Wilmington, Del. Portrait of Washington. Fire Engine.	1 1
2 Two dollars. 2	MECHANICS' BANK, Wilmington, Del. Three blacksmith's at work with their tools; anchor and boiler; on the left of vig. portrait of female; on right portrait of male.	2 TWO 2
5 Female portrait.	MECHANICS' BANK, Wilmington, Del. Ship yard with vessels on the stocks, and men at work; city and sloop in distance. V Eagle. V	5 Female feeding chickens.
10 Blacksmith at forge.	Portrait of female. Sailor seated on an anchor smoking pipe, and conversing with two other men. MECHANICS' BANK, Wilmington, Del. Cock.	10 10
20 Sailor leaning on capstan; bale, etc.; ship in distance.	Five men at work at a pudding furnace. MECHANICS' BANK, Wilmington, Del.	20 Figure of Justice.
50 Farmers at dinner in field.	Train of cars, city in distance. MECHANICS' BANK, Wilmington, Del. Steamboat.	50 Female portrait.
100 C	MECHANICS' BANK, Wilmington, Del. Female seated; factories in the distance; on right of vig. male portrait, on left female portrait.	100 C
1 Milk maid and churn.	NEW CASTLE CO. BANK. Cantwell's Bridge, Del. Blacksmith's shop—two smiths shoeing horse, farmer with hand on horse's back; two men at anvil in background.	Female bathing ox ONE
2 Bridge and train of cars; yacht in foreground.	Farmer ploughing with two horses; farm house in distance. Title of Bank.	2 2

DELAWARE.

Left	Centre	Right
5	Title of Bank. Scene reaping—two men, negro and two horses; barn in distance. V	V 5
X TEN	10 Female between 1 and 0, with basket and plow at her feet; on right man plowing with two horses, farm house in distance; on left man plowing with two oxen. Title of Bank.	Female loosely dressed standing; shield. TEN
XX 20	Title of Bank. Female seated on log; train of cars; wheat; cattle and house in distance.	20 Sailor leaning on rail of ship.
Farmer feeding hogs, horses etc. 1	REAL ESTATE BANK OF DELAWARE. ONE	1 Penn.
2 Female with sheaf and sickle. Two on 2.	Title of Bank. Scene in iron foundry.	Female with flowers. 2 Dollars on 2 TWO
5	Man watering horses at trough; pigs, cattle, &c. Female portrait. Title of Bank. FIVE V FIVE	5 Jefferson.
10 TEN TEN	Title of Bank. Farmers nooning—four males, female and child. X each side.	10 TEN TEN
Steamboat. Female and and fig. 1. Cars.	1 Female Portrait, sheaf of wheat, &c. UNION BANK OF DELAWARE. Arm.	1
2 Farmer seated, dog; sheaf of wheat, &c.	UNION BANK OF DELAWARE.	Two females reclining; safe, &c.; steamboat on left. 2
5 Train of cars, house, &c.	UNION BANK OF DELAWARE.	Figure 5, and five cupids. 5

MARYLAND.

Left	Centre	Right
10 Bale of corn. X	X Farmers at work in corn-field. X UNION BANK OF DELAWARE. Steamboat.	10 Sheaf of wheat, &c. X
Ship. 20	20 View of harbor and village. 20 UNION BANK OF DELAWARE. Pump.	Farmer seated, dog, and pitchfork. 20
50 Male portrait 50	State Arms; steamship on right; cars and bridge on left. UNION BANK OF DELAWARE.	50 Male portrait 50
100 Female with pitcher and cake. 100	100 Spread eagle, shield &c. 100 UNION BANK OF DELAWARE. Female Portrait.	100 Portrait of Washington. 100
5 Med. head. V	Med. head with 5 on it. Sailor and farmer on either side of shield eagle at the top. Med. head, with 5 on it. BK OF BALTIMORE, Baltimore, Md.	5 Med. head. V
10 Med. head. 10	Med. head with Ten on it. Same as fives. Med. head with Ten on it. BK OF BALTIMORE, Baltimore, Md.	10 Med head. 10
20 Portrait of Z. Taylor. 20	BANK OF BALTIMORE, Baltimore, Md, Head of Indian female.	Same as vig. of fives. 20
50 Portrait of D. Webster. 50	Same as fives. BK OF BALTIMORE, Baltimore, Md.	50 Female with flag and shield.
100 Male portrait 100	Same as fives. 100 BK OF BALTIMORE, Baltimore, Md.	ONE HUNDRED
FIVE HUNDRED	500 Med. head. Same as fives. 500 Med. head. BK OF BALTIMORE, Baltimore, Md.	Female representing Agriculture. 500

MARYLAND.

Left	Centre	Right
Female erect with wand, shield, pillar and med head. 1000	1000 Three females seated with grain, sickle, quadrant, &c.; ship in distance. BK OF BALTIMORE, Baltimore, Md. ONE THOUSAND	ONE THOUSAND
5 Ship at sea.	Sailor seated and two standing; cannon, horse, barrels, &c., on left; and a ship on right. B'K OF COMMERCE, Baltimore, Md.	5 Squaw seated with cap, pole and shield.
FIVE Three females over figure 5.	B'K OF COMMERCE, Baltimore, Md.	5 Female head
10 Female head X	Harvest scene; four men, etc. B'K OF COMMERCE, Baltimore, Md.	X Sailor.
10 Male portrait	Large vessel; steamship and another vessel in the distance. Title of bank running around vignette.	10 Portrait of a girl.
20 Mechanic reclining on a boiler, cog-wheel; foundry in distance.	Large steamship; vessels in distance. B'K OF COMMERCE, Baltimore, Md. Female head.	20 Sailor seated, box, bales and barrels
Ship. 50	B'K OF COMMERCE, Baltimore, Md. 50 Portrait of Henry Clay. 50	FIFTY Female erect with sword and shield, fruit and flowers at her feet.
Blacksmith erect with hammer and anvil. 100	B'K OF COMMERCE, Baltimore, Md. C Portrait of Washington. C	100 Locomotive.
D Portrait of a girl.	B'K OF COMMERCE, Baltimore, Md. Three females representing Agriculture, Commerce and Manufactures.	500 Sailor with quadrant; steamship in distance.
View of a depot, buildings, factories, &c., canal, drays, steamboat, vessels, boxes, bales, &c. M	Male portrait B'K OF COMMERCE, Baltimore, Md.	1000 Vessel, houses, &c.

Indian with bow and arrow. FIVE	Fox chase. BANK OF WESTMINSTER, Md. Wagon.	5 Indian squaw.

10 10	Vig. Blacksmith shoeing a horse. 10 BANK OF WESTMINSTER, Md	Female with wreath of flowers.

20 20	20 Vig. Female sitting on a rock, bed of coin, mile stone, 23 miles to B. 20 BANK OF WESTMINSTER, Md	Female head.

50 50	50 Vig. Female with sickle in hand inclined on mile stone, marked 29 miles to B. 50 BANK OF WESTMINSTER, Md.	50

Female with sword. FIVE	5 Female with shield. 5 CECIL BANK, Port Deposit, Md. Raft and timber.	FIVE Female with horn of plenty. FIVE

TEN Justice. 10	10 Reapers. CECIL BANK, Port Deposit, Md. Raft and timber.	10 Female writing.

Full length figure of an Indian drawing bow. 20	Vig. Two females, steamboat on the right and vessel on left of them. CECIL BANK, Port Deposit, Md. Raft and timber.	20 Head of Washington. TWENTY

Farmer erect in act of drinking from mug. 50	CECIL BANK, Port Deposit, Md. Milkmaid erect holding stool in left hand; shading her eyes with right; boy beside; cows, etc.	50 Female head.

Farmer drinking. 50	Female erect with stool, etc. CECIL BANK, Port Deposit, Md.	50 Portrait of female.

100 Farmer with scythe; village, etc.	Milkmaid with stool, cows, sheep, etc. Title of Bank. Steamer.	100 Female with flowers.

1 1	CENTRAL B'K OF FREDE'K, Frederick, Md. Female with pen and tablet; child at her feet with wreath.	Old man with shield; bust of Washington. ONE DOLLAR on ONE. 1

5 head of female.	CENTRAL BK OF FREDERIC, Md. Vig. Female seated with pail, two cows, farm house and trees in the background.	5 head of Webster.

10 10	CENTRAL BK OF FREDERIC, Md. Vig. Female with sheaf of wheat in left hand, sickle in right; a cow and grain field in background. Medallions of Clay and Chief Justice Marshall on either side of vig.	10 10

20 Medallion portrait.	Vig. Three nymphs swimming, supporting a winged cupid. CENTRAL BANK OF FREDERIC, Md.	20 Milkmaid, child, two cows.

50 Medallion portrait of Pierce.	CENTRAL BANK OF FREDERICK, Md. Vig. Cattle, stream of water; three sheep in background.	50 Medallion portrait of Fillmore.

Am. shield surmounted by eagle. C	Vig. Medallion portrait of Washington. CENTRAL BANK OF FREDERICK, Md.	100

5 Train of cars; bridge with cars passing over. 5	V View of a harbor with shipping. V CHESAPEAKE B'K Baltimore, Md.	5 Washington 5

TEN Jackson. 10	CHESAPEAKE B'K., Baltimore, Md. 10 Female seated; Mercury approaching with cornucopia; spread eagle with scroll. 10 Eagle.	TEN Van Buren. 10

20 Jackson. 20	20 Indian and Sailor on either side of a shield surmounted by an eagle; schooner on right. 20 CHESAPEAKE B'K., Baltimore, Md. Ship.	20 Van Buren. 20

Female feeding an eagle. 50	Male portrait 50 Male portrait CHESAPEAKE B'K., Baltimore, Md. Schooner.	Indian with bow and arrow. 50

FIFTY Blacksmith.	50 Vessel; others in distance. CHESAPEAKE B'K, Baltimore, Md.	50 Female portrait.

Male portrait 100 Male portrait	Female with torch seated on a globe; on her left eagle with Washington on its breast. Figures 100 on each side of the vig. CHESAPEAKE B'K Baltimore, Md. Schooner.	Female with sea horses at her feet; cupid in the air. 100

100 Girl's head.	Title of Bank. C Sailor reclining; anchor, boat, etc.; steamer in distance.	100

V Female seated with rake in right hand; shield, etc. V	5 Wharf scene—bales, barrels, boxes, &c., steamboat, shipping, &c. 5 CITIZENS' BANK, Baltimore, Md. Clasped hands.	Female representing Agriculture, Vulcan with hammer and anvil; Mercury with a bag. V

V FIVE 5	5 5 CITIZENS' BANK OF Baltimore, Md FIVE on V. Female portrait. DOLLARS on V.	V FIVE 5

Same as on upper right of the 5's. 10	10 Same as 5ses. 10 CITIZENS' BANK, Baltimore, Md. Clasped hands.	10 Franklin seated with pen and book; book at his feet with motto on it. 10

Same as on right of 5s. 20	20 Ship at sea. 20 CITIZENS' BANK, Baltimore, Md. Clasped hands.	20 Female with scales; on right eagle on shield; bbls., bales, &c. 20

Same as on right of 5s. 50	50 Female seated; her left arm resting on a shield on which is a building. CITIZENS' BANK, Baltimore, Md.	L Female with torch; eagle with portrait of Washington on its breast.

C Same as on right of 10s.	Vig. Same as 50s. 100 CITIZENS' BANK, Baltimore, Md.	Same as on right of 5s. 100

Same as on right of 5s. 500	D 500 CITIZENS' BANK, Baltimore, Md. Clasped hand	500

Left	Centre	Right
1000	1000 M CITIZENS' BANK, Baltimore, Md. Clasped hands.	Same as on right of do. 1000
5 Schooner. 5	Cars. Two females; wagon and four horses on right; building on left. Cars. COMMERCIAL AND FARMERS' BANK, Baltimore, Md.	5 Female with rake and pitcher. 5
10 Ship. 10	X Sailor and farmer with hands clasped; landscape in distance. X Title of Bank.	10 Eagle on a shield. 10
10	Horse, cars and cattle running away from cars. COMMERCIAL AND FARMERS' BANK, Baltimore, Md. Female seated with horn of plenty; anchor, etc.	10 Male portrait
20 Schooner. 20	Med. head. Two females with shield between them with XX on it, and surmounted by an eagle. Med. head. Title of Bank.	20 Agricultural implements. 20
50 Ship. FIFTY	Med. head. Female seated with sickle; vessels on right; plow, bales, boxes, trees, etc., on left. Med. head. Title of Bank.	50 Statue of female with sheaf and sickle.
100 Female seated with cornucopia, cap, money, wand and book. 100	Med. head. Shipping; sheaf on right; plow on left. Med. head. Title of Bank.	100 Female seated with chart. 100
500 Med. head. 500	Female seated on a bale surrounded by boxes, bales, &c.; anchor and shipping. Title of Bank. Five Hundred Dollars	500 Justice.
1000 Female seated, bales, shipping, &c. 1000	Title of Bank. Three females representing Agriculture, Manufactures, and Commerce. ONE THOUSAND.	1000 Female seated with sickle. 1000
ONE Train of Cars. ONE	CUMBERLAND B'K. OF ALLEGHANY, Cumberland, Md. Head of female. 1 Head of child. on ONE ONE DOLLAR on ONE	1 ONE on 1

Left	Centre	Right
5 Female with horn of plenty. 5	A CUMBERLAND B'K. OF ALLEGHANY, Md. Vig. View of Cumberland with drover and cattle; road waggon in front; medallion head on each side.	FIVE Female with horn of plenty. FIVE
5 Indian seated. 5	B Vig. Same as above CUMBERLAND B'K OF ALLEGHANY, Md	5 Indian seated. 5
5 Drove of cattle 5	C Vig. Same as above CUMBERLAND B'K OF ALLEGHANY, Md.	FIVE Reaper lying down FIVE
10 Drove of Cattle 10	Medallion of Franklin. Medallion of Franklin CUMBERLAND B'K OF ALLEGHANY, Md Vig. Blacksmith sitting on his anvil.	10 Waggon unloading near a market women 10
20 Female with horn of plenty.	Vig. Female seated with a sheaf of wheat, bridge in background and medallions on either side CUMBERLAND B'K OF ALLEGHANY, Md	20 Same as on other end.
50 Female seated, sheaf of wheat in her lap. L	Vig. Reaper, male and female, seated on a rock in the woods. Medallion on either side. CUMBERLAND B'K. OF ALLEGHANY, Md	L Female seated, sheaf of wheat in her lap. 50
1 Farmer leaning on fence caressing dog.	EASTON BANK OF Maryland, Easton, Md. 1 Boy and child under tree, cows, etc. 1 ONE DOLLAR on ONE	1 ONE on 1
5 Indian girl kneeling, sickle in right hand, female standing behind with bow and arrow.	EASTON BANK OF MARYLAND. FIVE on lathe strip, large medallion V on face of note. Anvil.	5 FIVE 5
Large X on medallion shield. Hebe sitting on wheat, holding cup to eagle; ship in distance.	EASTON BANK OF MARYLAND. TEN on lathe strip; Large medallion X on face of note. Justice standing; barrels and ships behind.	10 X 10
20 Medallion head of Allston. XX	Vig. Representing Commerce, Agriculture, &c., with portrait of Franklin between. EASTON BANK OF MARYLAND.	TWENTY

Left	Centre	Right
50 Large ship, full sail; another ship in distance.	Shield draped with American flag, females with girl and globe on right, Indian squaw and child on left. EASTON BANK OF MARYLAND.	L 50 L
100 Farmers loading wagon with bundles of wheat, boy holding horse.	EASTON BANK OF MARYLAND. Spade, rake, sheaf of wheat, bee-hive and plow.	100 Portrait of Jenny Lind.
FIVE Two females with sickle, &c. FIVE	Drove of cattle and sheep; man sitting down on left. FARMERS' BANK OF MARYLAND.	FIVE 5 FIVE
Female crest shield, sword &c. TEN	10 Farmers at work in wheat field. 10 FARMERS' BANK OF MARYLAND.	TEN Female with sickle and sheaf of wheat. TEN
Female with caduceus, portrait of Washington, bale, anchor, ship masts seen in distance.	5 Vig. Two females one with helmet on her head, and the other a winged female with wand, ship on right. V FARMERS & MECHANICS BANK OF FREDERICK CO., Md.	FIVE
TEN Portrait of Washington. TEN	10 Vig. Female with sickle, cornucopia, &c., clouds back of female. 10 FARMERS AND MECHANICS BANK OF FREDERICK CO., Md	Male portrait.
Male portrait.	20 Vig. Drover and cattle, drover on horseback. 20 FARMERS AND MECHANICS BANK OF FREDERICK CO., Md	Male portrait.
Portrait of Lafayette.	50 Vig. Female, child, and another child stirring fire, yoke of oxen, plough, anvil, rake, &c. 50 FARMERS & MECHANICS BANK OF FREDERICK CO., Md.	Portrait of Washington.
Portrait of Washington.	100 Vig. Female seated on bales, barrels, sheaf of grain, cornucopia, rake, &c. two houses and a man in the distance on left. 100 FARMERS & MECHANICS BANK OF FREDERICK CO., Md.	Portrait of Jefferson.
5 Franklin. 5	Vig. Milkmaid seated. 5 FARMERS AND MECHANICS' BANK, of Carroll County, Westminster, Md. Horses and Wagon.	FIVE Female portrait. FIVE

FIVE	5 Female seated with boy leaning on her lap; man entering gate, and little girl running towards him; dog, fence, trees, etc. FARMERS' & MECHANIC'S BANK, Westminister, Md.	5 Male portrait.

TEN Women drawing water from a well.	Vig. Men on horse; farmer harvesting. FARMERS' AND MECHANICS' BANK, of Carroll County, Westminister, Md.	X Washington. TEN

20 Washington. TWENTY	FARMERS AND MECHANICS' BANK, of Carroll County, Westminister, Md. Vig. Cattle; farmer plowing in distance.	Medallion head with figure 20 on it. Male portrait.

50 Two male portraits. FIFTY	Vig. Farmer plowing. FARMERS' AND MECHANICS' BANK of Carroll County, Westminister, Md. Spread eagle.	50 Ship.

ONE HUNDRED 100 Milk maid with a pail.	FARMERS' AND MECHANICS' BANK OF CARROLL CO. Westminster, Md.	100 Female ONE HUNDRED

5 Washington	Man watering three horses at trough; house in background. Female portrait. FAR. & MECH. BK. OF KENT CO., Chestertown, Md. Beehive.	5 Cooper at work.

10 Female seated; X on a shield.	Man on horse; reaping scene etc., on right. FAR. & MECH BANK OF KENT CO. Chestertown, Md. Machinery.	10 Female portrait

20 Male portrait	Female seated leaning on a bale; vessels in distance. FAR. & MECH. BANK of Kent Co, Md.	20 Franklin.

Goddess of Liberty. FIFTY	Title of Bank. Female reclining in corn field; negro gathering corn.	50 FIFTY

100 Female with distaff and head.	Female seated holding ear of corn; man, boats and village in distance. Title of Bank.	100 Female portrait

5 Portrait of Girl. 5	FARMERS & MERCHANTS' BANK, Baltimore, Md. Vig.—Farming scene—farmer with sickle over his shoulder, female with grain under her arm; sailor with hands in his pocket; ship in distance on left. Five and 5. Five and 5.	5 5 5

Steamboat. 5	5 Female representing Agriculture. 5 FARMERS' & MERCHANTS' BANK, Baltimore, Md.	Steamboat. 5

TEN Shearing sheep. TEN	10 Female seated, stages, etc. 10 Title of Bank.	TEN Ship. TEN

10	Title of Bank. Vig. Same as fives. Letter X and words Ten Dollars. TEN	10 Milkmaid, cow, calf, ducks, &c.

20 Female; steamship and buildings in distance.	Title of Bank. TWENTY 20 Vig. same as fives.	20

20 Sheep. 20	20 Female spinning; houses, hay, box, etc. 20 Title of Bank.	20 Sail vessel. 20

FIFTY	Female representing Agriculture. Figs. 50 on left and 50 and L on the right of vig. Title of Bank.	Die. FIFTY DOLLARS Die

Cherub. Female portrait.	50 Surveying scene. Title of Bank. FIFTY DOLLARS	50 Anchor, bales, bbls., &c.

100	Female reclining on bales; ship, cornucopia, etc. Figs. 100 on either side. Title of Bank.	ONE HUNDRED

100 Man with corn stalks.	Sailor boy. Sailors; one looking through telescope, one seated on broken mast; one resting his face on hand; ships in distance on right; men seen in distance on left. Title of Bank. ONE HUNDRED	100 Female feeding fowls.

500	Farmer loading hay on ox team. Girls portrait Title of Bank. 500	500 Sailor boy; ship on right, sailors on left.

1000 Sailor leaning on capstan; ship in distance.	Farmer plowing; boy at horses head with branch; dog, basket, etc. Title of Bank. 1000	1000 Maryland Girl's portrait.

FIVE	5 Female representing Agriculture with sheaf and sickle; cattle on left. 5 FARMERS AND PLANTERS' BANK, Baltimore, Md. Schooner.	Statue of Washington. FIVE

TEN	X Two men cradling; houses in distance. X Title of Bank. Vessel.	Female with sheaf and sickle; reapers in distance. Drovers and cattle.

TWENTY	XX Female erect with bundle of grain, another seated with rake; shield with plow on it. XX Title of Bank. Schooner.	Manufacturing house in distance. Men ploughing with two horses.

FIFTY	50 Same as tens. 50 Title of Bank. Schooner.	Men ploughing with two horses. Men farming with two horses; in distance houses.

ONE HUNDRED	100 Same as fives. 100 Title of Bank. Schooner.	Man gathering corn. 100

500	500 Same as 20s. 500 Title of Bank. Schooner	Milkmaid churning in dairy.

1000	Two females soaring with wand, bag, grain and sickle; figures 1000 each side. Title of Bank. Schooner.	Female seated with scroll. 1000

1 ONE 1	Launching a vessel; city, steamboats, &c. FELLS POINT BANK, Baltimore Md. Printed in green tint.	1 Dog and safe.

Left	Centre	Right
5 Clay	FELLS POINT SAVINGS INSTITUTION of Baltimore, Md. Two sailors, one seated on merchandise, the other smoking a pipe, coil of rope, anchor, trumpet, bale, boxes, sails, etc.; steamship, schooner and brig in distance.	5 Washington
Female with flowers. TEN	10 Large steamship at sea; ship in the distance. Title of Bank	TEN
20 Jefferson.	Shield—two females on left—Indian on right. FELLS POINT SAVINGS INSTITUTION Baltimore, Md.	20 Female head
20 Ship under full sail.	Three men with plans on a table; ship yard scene, man and two horses; on right steamship. Title of Bank.	20 Female seated representing Commerce.
50	Marine view— East of ships sailing, etc. female Title of Bank.	50 Eagle on shield.
50 Webster.	Three vessels; lighthouse on right in distance. Title of Bank	FIFTY Sailor with telescope, leaning on capstan. FIFTY
100 Child with hen and and chickens in her arms.	View of the Capitol at Washington. Title of Bank.	100 Sailor with telescope seated on a bale, capstan, vessel, etc.
5 Franklin. FIVE	Shield with figure of Justice on it; on left Indian, squaw and papoose; on right female instructing children with globe. FRANKLIN BANK, Baltimore, Md. Head of female.	5 Milkmaid.
TEN Franklin. TEN	X Milkmaid seated; cattle, etc. FRANKLIN BANK, Baltimore, Md.	TEN
20 20 Ship. 20	Female with quadrant, chart, globe, compass, &c., fruit at her feet; man in the water. Franklin on either side of vig. FRANKLIN BANK, Baltimore, Md. Steamboat.	20 Ship. 20

Left	Centre	Right
XX 20	FRANKLIN BANK, Baltimore, Md. Portrait of Franklin; on right sailor, farmer on left.	20 20
50 50	Ship. Franklin. Ship. FRANKLIN BANK, Baltimore, Md. Man reclining.	50 50
50 Franklin.	FRANKLIN BANK, Baltimore, Md. Figure 50 and words Fifty Dollars on three large red dies.	50 Female feeding fowls.
100 Franklin. 100	Female representing Agriculture; farmers mowing in distance. Eagle on either side of vig. FRANKLIN BANK, Baltimore, Md. Dog, key and safe.	100 Franklin. 100
100 Female with flowers in apron.	FRANKLIN BANK, Baltimore, Md. Portrait of Franklin. ONE HUNDRED	100 Female seated; two men, cog wheel, buildings, etc.
Female seated representing Manufactures. 500	500 Franklin. 500 FRANKLIN BANK, Baltimore, Md. Justice.	Female seated with scroll; bridge and wagon in distance. 500
Three females grouped, one in centre has helmet; crate on the ground. 1000	1000 Franklin 1000 FRANKLIN BANK, Baltimore, Md. Justice.	Same as on left. 1000
5 Portrait of Washington. 5	Head of Clay. Vig. Female resting on anchor; harbor and shipping. Head of Cass. FREDERICK CO. BK. Frederick, Md. Bee-hive.	5 3 Females supporting globe. FIVE
10 Dog. 10	Train of cars. Large X with heads of ten of the Presidents. Farmers loading hay. FREDERICK CO. BK. Frederick, Md.	10 TEN 10
XX 20	Vig. Female with sword and balances; farmer ploughing, &c. FREDERICK CO. BK. Frederick, Md.	MARYLAND

Left	Centre	Right
Franklin. 5	50 50 Vig. Female on either side of 50; sheep; spinning wheel; ship in distance, &c. FREDERICK CO. BK. Frederick, Md. Female and sheep.	Washington.
Male head. Full length figure with spear and shield.	100 100 Vig. Female sitting on plough; child; agricultural implements; oxen, &c. FREDERICK CO. BK. Frederick, Md. Spread Eagle.	Washington.
Blacksmith.	FIVE'S FREDERICK TOWN SAVING INSTITUTION, Md. Vig. ploughman and two horses; laborer with shovel on his shoulder.	Carpenter sawing; another resting his right foot on the plank.
Portrait of Franklin.	TEN'S FREDERICK TOWN SAVING INSTITUTION, Md. Vig. harvest scene, harvesting wheat, &c.	Justice with scales.
20 Boy and rabbits.	Female, cows and sheep. FREDERICKTOWN SAV. INSTITUTION, Frederick, Md. Man seated on plow.	20 Female.
1 Ox, trees, &c.	Female, cows, trees, &c. 1 FROSTBURG BANK, Frostburg, Md.	1 Eagle.
Figure of Justice. FIVE	Train of cars, and two men; steamboat and hills in distance; figure 5 on left of vig. FROSTBURG BANK, Frostburg, Md. Mechanical Implements.	5 Die. 5
10 Two girls with sheaf of grain.	X Spread eagle. X Title of Bank. Two horses.	10 Indian on cliff.
Female. XX	Men harvesting; farm scene. Figs. 20 on either side of vig. Title of Bank.	Female. 20
5 5 on Die 5	5 Vig. Two female 5 soaring in the clouds, one with rake, sickle, spade and pitchfork. HAGERSTOWN B'K, Hagerstown, Md.	5 5 on Die. 5

Left end	Centre	Right end
X. Ten on medallion head. 10	10 on die. Boys bearing flowers on pole, another with sickle. 10 on die. HAGERSTOWN B'K. Hagerstown, Md.	Female with sickle and sheaf of wheat. X
20. Female with babe in her arms. 20	Medallion head. Vig. Two females, ships in distance on right. Medallion head. HAGERSTOWN B'K. Hagerstown, Md.	20. Man and cattle. 20
50. Portrait of Washington. 50	Medallion head. Vig. Boy in boat, with cupid staring over him; another boy in the act of digging. Medallion head. HAGERSTOWN B'K. Hagerstown, Md.	50. Female with rake and sheaf of wheat. 50
100. Female with sickle and sheaf of wheat. 100	100 on medal. Die head. Vig. Female with liberty pole and cap, eagle, and shield; vessels in distance on either side. 100 on medal. Die head. HAGERSTOWN BK. Hagerstown, Md.	100. Male with tablet. 100
ONE on 1. Two children.	HAGERSTOWN SAVINGS BANK. Hagerstown, Md. 1 Boy whistling under a tree; cattle, cows, sheep, &c. 1 ONE DOLLAR on ONE	1. Girl seated with flowers and fruit at her feet.
2. Man with pails. Farmhouse, &c. 2	Two horses drinking at trough. Female. Poultry, &c. Female head. HAGERSTOWN SAVINGS BANK. Hagerstown, Md. TWO DOLLARS on TWO	TWO. Man with armful of corn.
5. Two females on either side of bee hive in dark vignettes.	HAGERSTOWN SAVINGS BANK, Hagerstown, Md. Large V, on which is Five Dollars on lathe strip.	A V & FIVE. Part of Blacksmith.
X. Washington.	American shield; on right is female instructing children; on left is Indian, squaw and papoose. Title of Bank.	10. Female reaper.
20. XX	Title of Bank. Cows, man mowing and horse on right; man plowing on left. XX	20. Woodcutter.
5. Male portrait. FIVE	Male portrait; female on left with pole and cap; on right, two females reclining. HOWARD BANK, Baltimore, Md. Spread eagle.	FIVE. Milk maid and pail; house on the right.
10. Clay. 10	Female on either side of portrait of Washington; sheaf, farmers, etc. HOWARD BANK. Baltimore, Md. Locomotive.	X. Med. head and word Ten.
20. J. Q. Adams. TWENTY	Steamship, vessel, fort, etc.; city in distance. HOWARD BANK, Baltimore, Md. Anvil.	20. Portrait of a female.
50. Franklin.	Female seated; safe, money bags, etc.; on her right shield with view of Monument; sheep, grain, fruit, etc. HOWARD BANK, Baltimore, Md. Ship.	50. Interior of blacksmith's shop; smith resting.
100. Female leaning on a railing.	[illegible] harbor; on right, steamer with letter Con[illegible]; city in distance. HOWARD BANK, Baltimore, Md. Shells.	100. Jackson.
1. Medallion head. 1	ONE on Med. head. Three women; ships in distance, &c. ONE on Med. head. MARINE BANK, Baltimore, Md.	ONE. Man reclining; basket, rake, sheaf of wheat, &c. ONE
2. Medallion head. 2	Baltimore, Maryland. Female, eagle on shield, &c. MARINE BANK OF BALTIMORE. TWO DOLLARS.	2. Girl with sheaf of wheat. 2
2. Female head. 2	TWO on Med. head. Female seated on rock; eagle on right; ships in distance. TWO on Med. head. MARINE BANK. Baltimore, Md.	2. Female with rake. 2
5. Girl's portrait.	MARINE BANK, Baltimore, Md. Ships, &c.	5. Sailor raising sail.
Die Work. Male portrait. Die Work.	5 Ornamental figure band; two females with trident and figure 5; cupid, scales and eagle. 5 MARINE BANK. Baltimore, Md. Sword and scales.	Justice; part of column, shield, anchor, &c. FIVE
10. Sailor reclining on capstan.	MARINE BANK. Baltimore, Md. X Ship. Large eagle. Ship X	10. Female; bale, &c.; ship in distance.
10. Sailor with flag; bales, shipping, &c. 10	X on med. head. Neptune in a shell with trident; ship on right. X on med. head. MARINE BANK, Baltimore, Md.	X. Ship under full sail. X
Female portrait. TWENTY.	MARINE BANK, Baltimore, Md. 2 XX 0 Arctic explorers; boat, dogs, &c.	20
20. Med. head. 20	Med. head. Sailor with flag; warehouses, bales, boxes, shipping, dock, &c. Med. head. MARINE BANK. Baltimore, Md.	XX. Med. head. XX
50. Figure of Hope; vessels in distance.	MARINE BANK, Baltimore, Md. Female portrait. 50	50. Anchor with bales of goods.
50 Med. head. 50	50 Female seated with anchor; shipping in distance. 50 MARINE BANK, Baltimore, Md. Dog, and safe.	50. Med. Head with 50 on it. FIFTY
C. C	Ship building. MARINE B'K. Baltimore. Sailor with Am. flag, seated on bale, &c. C ONE HUNDRED.	100. Maryland. Eagle. 100
Med. head with 100 on it. Male portrait. Med. head with 100 on it.	Med. head with 100 on it. Female with wand representing Commerce seated on bales; shipping on left. Med. head with 100 on it. MARINE BANK, Baltimore, Md. Two cherubs in a boat.	Full length portrait of Lafayette.
FIVE. Blacksmith with implements. 5	5 Washington penning his farewell address. 5 MECHANICS' BANK, Baltimore, Md. Justice.	FIVE. Ship at sea. 5
Letter X between two females.	10 Ship carpenter at work; ship on way in background. MECHANICS' BANK, Baltimore, Md.	TEN. Ship under full sail. TEN
Ornamental scroll work. Stone cutter seated with tools. Ornamental scroll work.	20 Archimedes raising the world with lever; vessel on right, steamboat on left. MECHANICS' BANK, Baltimore, Md.	20. Female with sword and scales. 2

FIFTY
50 Steamboat on the water; man in a small boat in foreground; ship on the right in background. 50
MECHANICS' BANK,
Baltimore, Md.
FIFTY
50
Head of Indian.
50

50
FIFTY
Steamer, city, etc.
MECHANICS' BANK
OF BALTIMORE, Md.
50 Indian head. 50
50
FIFTY

Indian head.
100
Title of Bank.
Cars, factory, cow and dog.
C Wheels. C
100
100

100
Landscape, arched bridge in background.
100
Old fashioned train of cars; rocks, trees, &c.
MECHANICS' BANK,
Baltimore, Md.
100
Train of cars crossing an arched bridge.
100

500
Cut through a rock with rail track.
500
Male figure seated with pole; machinery; ship in distance on left.
Figs. 500 on either side.
MECHANICS' BANK,
Baltimore, Md.
Head of Indian.
View of a monument.

1000
Statue of Washington.
Female seated, her left arm resting on a large cog-wheel; on her left base and part of a column.
MECHANICS' BANK,
Baltimore, Md.
Spread eagle.
1000
Car track, rocks, trees, &c.
1000

V
Shipping, harbor, city in distance.
V
5 Female seated with key in her hand; Phoenix up on a safe; Mercury approaching with cornucopia of money; coin at side of female. 5
MERCHANTS' BANK
Baltimore, Md.
FIVE
Schooner.
FIVE

FIVE across and fig. 5 on it.
V Female reclining, anchor, bales, cornucopia, etc. 5
MERCHANTS' BANK
of Baltimore, Md.
C
FIVE DOLLARS across and V on it.

No.
Sailor barrel, shield, etc.
10 and X Same as 5s.
Title of Bank
10&X
Weighing cotton bales.

10
Female seated with wand, anchor, shield, beside her.
10
X Vig. Same as fives. X
MERCHANTS' BANK
Baltimore, Md.
10
Female seated with a torch; eagle with portrait of Washington on his breast.
10

TWENTY DOLLARS
20
Justice seated.
Same as 5s.
Title of Bank.
20

20
Female with scales; eagle on shield; table, bales, &c.
20
XX Vig. Same as fives. XX
MERCHANTS' BANK
Baltimore, Md.
20
Schooner.
20

FIFTY DOLLARS
50
50
Title of Bank.
Same as 5s.
50

50
Cupid on one knee looking at scroll with the words, Capital $2,000,000.
50
L Vig. Same as fives. L
MERCHANTS' BANK
Baltimore, Md.
50

100
Sailor outside and female with cornucopia.
Title of Bank.
Same as 5s.
C
100

100
C Vig. Same as fives. C
MERCHANTS' BANK
Baltimore, Md.
ONE HUNDRED
100

500
500 Vig. Same as fives. 500
MERCHANTS' BANK
Baltimore, Md.
FIVE HUNDRED
500

$500
Same as 5s.
Title of Bank.
D
500

ONE THOUSAND
1000
$1,000
Title of Bank.
M Same as 5s.
STATE OF MARYLAND

1000
1000 Vig. Same as fives. 1000
MERCHANTS' BANK
Baltimore, Md.
ONE THOUSAND
1000

5
Male portrait.
Five on 5.
PEOPLES' BANK,
Baltimore, Md.
Train of cars; canal scene, city, and general view of country in background.
5
Cupid with cornucopia.
FIVE on 5.

10
Vessels at sea. Female portrait.
Title of Bank.
Eagle.
10
TEN on large X; milkmaid, cow, etc.

20
Female seated with spear and shield.
Cattle; horse looking over fence.
Title of Bank.
Man and sheaf.
20
Blacksmith beside anvil.

50
Mechanic holding a lifter.
Sailor, female and blacksmith seated; city, bridge, vessels, etc., in distance.
Title of Bank.
Schooner.
50
Washington.

100
Franklin.
100 on Dollars.
Male and female at well, barn, load of hay, etc.
Title of Bank.
Eagle in clouds.
100
One Dollar.

5
Milkmaid with pail on her head, and stool in hand.
5
5 Male seated at a table, with pen and chart on it; column in back. 5
UNION BANK OF MARYLAND,
Baltimore, Md.
Cars.
5
Reaper with sickle.
5

10
Washington
10
Title of Bank.
Female on either side of a Male portrait in a frame.
Title of Bank.
Vessel.
10

20
Portrait of Washington with female seated on either side.
Title of Bank.
Steamship.
20
Male portrait.
20

50
Female seated with sword and sceptre.
Female seated with pen and chart; Mercury flying toward her with wand and bag of coin; Neptune with sea horses on right; ship on right.
Title of Bank.
50
50
Male portrait.
50

Die Work.
Male portrait.
Die Work.
100
Title of Bank.
Female holding scales, with shield beside her. Words one hundred on the left, and on right word dollars.
ONE HUNDRED

MARYLAND.	DIST. COL.	DIST. COL.
500 Med. head 500 | Spread eagle holding in his beak a shield with 500 on it. Title of Bank. | 500 Med. head 500	100 Sloop; city in distance. 100 | WESTERN BANK, Baltimore, Md. C Female seated; eagle on right, with medal in his beak; bbls., bales, boxes, etc. C 100 | 100 Female seated representing Art, carving a male bust. 100	X Female—Goddess of Liberty. X | 10 U. S. Capitol. 10 BANK OF THE METROPOLIS, Washington, D. C. | U Eagle. S
1000 Med. head 1000 | Three figures representing Agriculture, Manufactures and Commerce. Title of Bank. | 1000 Med. head 1000	500 | Cupid. 500 Cupid. WESTERN BANK, Baltimore, Md. Ship. | 500	The 20s are the same as 10s all through, with the exception of the denomination.
5 Spread eagle on shield. 5 | Vig. Female seated on a [illegible], plough, with [illegible] sickle, &c., reaping scene on her right hand; mill scene on her left. WASHINGTON CO. BANK, Williamsport, Md. | 5 Bust of Washington. 5	1 Abraham Lincoln. | Large spread eagle on shield. B'K OF COMMERCE, Georgetown, D. C. ONE DOLLAR. | 1 Female portrait.	L Goddess of Liberty. L | 50 U. S. Capitol. 50 BANK OF THE METROPOLIS, Washington, D. C. | U Eagle. S
TEN Justice with sword and scales, scroll with inscription under figure. TEN | 10 Bust of Washington surmounted by an eagle, female on either side. 10 WASHINGTON CO. BANK, Williamsport, Md. | TEN Female and dog.	Figure of Liberty leaning on column, on which is the word "TWO." | 2 in ornamental die. Portrait of General Scott. B'K OF COMMERCE, Georgetown, D. C. TWO DOLLARS. | 2 in ornamental die.	Letter C. Goddess of Liberty. Letter C. | 100 U. S. Capitol. 100 BANK OF THE METROPOLIS, Washington, D. C. | U Eagle. S
Two females with American flag furled beneath. | 20 Vig. Washington on horse with staff; artillery, camp, &c. in distance. 20 WASHINGTON CO. BANK, Williamsport, Md. Locomotive and cars. | Blacksmith and forge.	FIVE Female FIVE | B'K OF COMMERCE, Georgetown, D. C. Portrait of Washington, surmounted by spread eagle; female on either side; sickle, cornucopia and anchor. Female | 5 Liberty resting on coat of arms of U. S.; spread eagle.	FIVE Vig. head of Washington. FIVE | BK OF W'SHINGTON Washington, D. C. 5. Two female figures, one standing and one sitting, both leaning on figure 5. | Ship under sail. 5
FIFTY | 50 Vig. Female sitting at table, reading the "Farewell Address," large mill, water, &c. in the distance. 50 WASHINGTON CO. BANK, Williamsport Mass | Full length portrait of Washington in citizens dress.	X Cars crossing viaduct in the distance and a sloop in foreground. TEN | B'K OF COMMERCE, Georgetown, D. C. Same as 5's. | 10 Female	Female standing, in her right a sword and her left hand resting on a shield. | 10 Head of Washington surrounded by flags and trophies, quadrant, &c. 10 BK OF W'SHINGTON Washington, D. C. | X TEN 10
5 Med. head 5 | 5 Mercury seated with globe, wand, cornucopia, &c.; safe, desks, bales, etc. 5 WESTERN BANK, Baltimore, Md. Dog's head. | Washington in a large fig. 5.	20 Canal boat passing under a bridge. TWENTY | B'K OF COMMERCE, Georgetown, D. C. Same as 5's. | 20 Female.	XX Head of Washington. XX | 20 Two females one seated, and one kneeling; ship and steamboat in background. BK OF W'SHINGTON Washington, D. C. | 20 Female leaning on gate with pails.
Male and female [illegible], dog, etc. TEN | X Vig. Same as fives. X WESTERN BANK, Baltimore, Md. Dog's head. | Med. head. 10	50 Female figure. FIFTY | B'K OF COMMERCE, Georgetown, D. C. Same as 5's. Female and anchor. | 50 Shipping, city in the distance.	FIFTY Head of Washington. FIFTY | 50 Farmer seated on plough, lighting a pipe, cattle in the background. BK OF W'SHINGTON Washington, D. C. | 50 Female seated with pole and cap.
Winged head surrounded by flags, anchor, etc.; eagle at top. XX Head of Vulcan with hammer. | 20 Farmers mowing; female with rake, sheafs, etc. WESTERN BANK, Baltimore, Md. Dog's head. | 20	100 Female with sheaf of wheat. 100 | B'K OF COMMERCE, Georgetown, D. C. Same as 5's. Female and anchor. | 100 Large ship sails spread.	100 Female seated with cornucopia and wheat. HUNDRED | Head of Washington supported on right by sailor with anchor, and on left by figures representing agriculture and mechanics. BK OF W'SHINGTON Washington, D. C. | HUNDRED A representation of Washington monument.
50 Canal scene FIFTY | WESTERN BANK, Baltimore, Md. L Village with [illegible] boats, cattle, &c. L Sands. | 50 Female representing Commerce. FIFTY	V Female—Goddess of Liberty. V | 5 U. S. Capitol. 5 BANK OF THE METROPOLIS, Washington, D. C. | U Eagle. S	5 Portrait of Washington 5 | Farmer seated sharpening his scythe, summer farm scene on right, basket on left. FARMERS' & MECH. BANK, Georgetown, D. C. Eagle. | 5 Female seated. V

Left	Centre	Right
10 Portrait of Washington	Canal and boat. Female seated, holding basket, two others in background and one is milking; house in distance on right; two ships on left. Title of Bank.	10 Blacksmith at work.
20 Female erect with basket. 20	Portrait of Washington. Female shield, eagle horn of plenty, liberty pole and cap. Title of Bank. Plow, sheaf of grain, &c.	20 Two blacksmiths in shop. 20
50 Portrait of Washington. 50	Female in the air with a horn; globe and eagle, American colors on left. Ship on the blocks. Title of Bank. Wheel, &c.	50 Farmer standing, another in background plowing.
100 Mikrouli. 100	Washington. Male figure supporting the globe on lever. FAR. & MECH BK. of Georgetown, D. C.	100
Sailor boy, with a flag; sailor, &c. in background. FIVE	5 Female seated, resting her right elbow on the Coat-of-Arms of the U. S. PATRIOTIC BANK. Washington, D. C.	5 Female sitting.
10 Washington, leading by his horse	Vig. Same as Fives. PATRIOTIC BANK. Washington, D. C.	10 Female; eagle in her left hand, &c
Female with a sickle in her right hand. TWENTY	20 Vig. same as 5's. PATRIOTIC BANK. Washington, D. C.	20 Female figure, with U. S. flag in her right hand; also resting on the ground shield, &c., in her left.
50 Female holding scales; eagle under the scales. 50	Vig. Same as the 5's. 50 PATRIOTIC BANK. Washington, D. C.	Female figure. 50
100 Female figure sitting, holding wheel in her left hand; a parrot in her left.	Female figure sitting, resting her right elbow on the Coat of Arms of the U. S. PATRIOTIC BANK. Washington, D. C.	100 Figure of a man with scythe, &c.; buildings in background.
Female with sheaf of wheat. Figure 5 and words "FIVE" twice.	BK. OF BERKELEY. Martinsburgh, Va. 5 Three dogs hunting a stag.	5 Portrait of female. 5

Left	Centre	Right
Horse and oxen before a loaded wagon; three men.	10 Train of cars passing around a curve. BK. OF BERKELEY Martinsburgh, Va.	10
20 Med. head. 20	BK. OF BERKELEY Martinsburg. Va. Vig. Farm yard scene; two females, cows, fowls, &c.; on right, a house.	20 Female. Portrait.
1 ONE on 1	B'K OF CHARLEST'N. Charleston, Va. Boy whittling under a tree, child resting 1 cows, sheep, etc. 1 ONE DOLLAR on 1	1 Girl seated with fruit, flowers, etc.
5	Scene in Camp—soldiers, horses, cannon, tents, &c. Eagle BK OF CHARLESTON Charleston, Va	5 Jefferson.
Die. X Die.	BK OF CHARLESTON Charleston, Va. X Boy and milk maid with pail and stool. X	10 Female with fowl.
Female. TWENTY	20 Eagle and shield. BK OF CHARLESTON Charleston, Va. TWENTY	20 Female with sickle.
5 Negro, cow and calf.	B'K OF THE CITY OF PETERSBURG, Va. Female in large V. Five on 5 either side. V	5 Two children. 5
10 X	Title Scene on tobacco 10 Female with tablets; child at her feet X Eagle TEN	10 TEN 10
Two horses alarmed at lightning. 20	B'K OF THE CITY OF PETERSBURG, Va Washington 20 Dog's head	20 Indian female.
L Sailor and mechanic; vessel, etc.	Female with basket. L across Title and 50 below FIFTY Jefferson.	50 Warlike scene and implements

Left	Centre	Right
Female.	Cars 100 Steamer B'K OF THE CITY OF PETERSBURG, Va. 100 Child's head. 100	100 Cotton bud
FIVE Sailor and mechanic; U. S. flag, bales, &c.	V Ship in full sail BANK of COMMERCE Fredericksburg, Va.	5 State arms.
X TEN	BANK of COMMERCE Fredericksburg, Va. Female figure in sitting posture, with reaping hook in right hand, and sheaf of wheat on shoulder, with left hand over it. 10 10	X State arms.
XX XX	BANK of COMMERCE Fredericksburg, Va. Head of Washington and words twenty dollars on either side. 20 Spread eagle 20	20 State arms.
XX Female seated beside barrels; ship in distance.	BK OF COMMERCE, Fredericksburg, Va. Female, cows, chickens, &c.	20 Female
5 Washington.	BANK OF THE COMMONWEALTH, Richmond, Va. Two men; hhds. of tobacco, etc.	5 State Arms
10 Male portrait	Title of Bank. Head on shield surmounted by vessel; farmer on left; hunter, dog, etc., on right.	10 State Arms.
20 State Arms.	Title of Bank. Sailor and farmer either side of shield.	20 Jefferson.
50 Madison.	Title of Bank. L Negro woman holding child. L	50 State Arms.
100 Male portrait	Title of Bank. Female seated with sickle and sheaf.	100 State Arms.

Left end	Centre	Right end
5 Cars.	BANK OF DANVILLE Danville, Va. 5	5 Female, cow, calf, ducks, etc.
X TEN	Title of Bank. Female erect. Two men, with foot on tyrant's throat, buildings, etc.	10 Red head.
Female erect beside column; [illegible]. 20	Tobacco planter seated by [illegible]; men at work in field on left. Title of Bank.	20 Female portrait.
50 on red die. Female portrait.	Title of Bank. Two females, spinning wheel, etc.; buildings on right; cows, sheep, etc., on left.	50 on red die. Head of Liberty surrounded by stars.
Full length statue.	5 Horses, hay, and fowls at trough; houses in distance. BANK OF GILES, Pearisburg, Va.	5 Treas. die.
TEN Statue of Liberty.	Cupid. Ten Dol. Cupid. lars across red 10. Title of Bank.	10 Treas. die.
FIVE Female. 5	Portrait of female with cupids on either side. BANK OF HOWARDSVILLE, Howardsville, Va. Female.	5 [illegible] die. 5
7 Male portrait. SEVEN	Title of Bank. Negro harvesting tobacco—dog, [illegible], and trees in distance. Safe.	7 die. SEVEN
8 die. EIGHT	Male portrait with Cupid on either side. Title of Bank. Male.	8 Negro with basket of corn.
Canal, boat, [illegible], horses, men, road, load of hay, etc. 10	Title of Bank. Male portrait, with two cupids on either side. Locomotive and tender.	10 die. 10

Left end	Centre	Right end
5 Washington.	Treas. die. Female seated; ship in distance. BANK OF THE OLD DOMINION, Alexandria, Va.	FIVE Female with flag; squaw at her side.
FIVE	Female seated; quadrant, chest, bale, &c. around her; in distance, city, bridge, canal, boats, ships, steamers, &c. Treas. die. BK. OF THE OLD DOMINION, Alexandria, Va. Bale, bales, &c.	5 Washington. FIVE
10 Female seated, with spear and flag; shield.	Treas. die. Female reclining on bale; ships and town on right; on left, train of cars, canal boat, boats, &c. Title of Bank. Safe.	10
Treas. die. Two Mermaid's Steamship.	20 Train of cars; depot, steamboat, &c., in background. Title of Bank. Deer.	20 Male portrait. TWENTY
FIFTY Female with names of States on wreath, around her. 50	Treas. die. Female on either side of a shield, surmounted by an eagle; train of cars, steamship on right; on left buildings and man ploughing; &c. Title of Bank. Dog's head.	50 Female erect with spear and shield.
5 Treas. die.	5 Blacksmith; female on either side. 5 BANK OF PHILIPI, Philipi, Va. V, 5 and words Five dollars blended in one die.	5 Female feeding horse.
10 Treas. die.	Shield; farmer on left, Indian on right; cars, canal, city, wigwams, canoe, &c., in distance. BANK OF PHILIPI, Philipi, Va. X and TEN Dog.	TEN
20 Treas. die.	Cattle and sheep; houses in distance. BANK OF PHILIPI, Philipi, Va. Soldier and cannon.	20 Male portrait.
50 inverted. Treas. die.	BANK OF PHILIPI, Philipi, Va. Female on either side of a shield on which is eagle, cars, factory, steamship, etc. Horse.	50 inverted.
20 Cooper at work.	Three men loading truck with cotton bales. BANK OF RICHMOND, Richmond, Va. 20	20 Clay.

Left end	Centre	Right end
25 Sailor by capstan.	Two females seated with spinning wheel; factory in distance. Title of Bank. 25 Beehive.	25 Man gathering corn stalks.
50 Sailor and Mechanic with implements.	Clay. Man buying bale of hay, bales, &c. Title of Bank. L	50 Cooper at work.
100 Clay.	Title of Bank. Two farmers at work; Sailor pointing to ship in distance. HUNDRED Anvil.	100 State arms.
5 Male portrait.	Five females, fig. 5 and words "Five Dollars" blended together. BK OF ROANOKE, Salem, Va. Indian.	5 Treas. die.
10 Treas. die.	Title of Bank. 10 on X. Indian seated viewing the progress of civilization. Dog.	10
FIVE [illegible]	View of the Natural Bridge; Military Academy and College at Lexington. BK OF ROCKBRIDGE, Lexington, Va. Shield.	5 and FIVE. 5 5 and FIVE.
X 10 X	Vig. Same as fives. BK OF ROCKBRIDGE Lexington, Va. [illegible] and shield.	TEN
20 XX	Vig. Same as fives. BK OF ROCKBRIDGE Lexington, Va. Horse.	20 XX
50 Squaw seated.	Vig. Same as fives. BK OF ROCKBRIDGE Lexington, Va.	50 Female seated with [illegible] and tablets; [illegible], cars, buildings &c.
5 Load of grain, two [illegible] and one [illegible] in wagon.	Fox Chase. BK. OF ROCKINGHAM, Harrisonburg, Va.	5 Treas. die.

X Treas. Die.	Two females, one milking, the other feeding poultry. BK. OF ROCKINGHAM, Harrisonburg, Va.	10 Locomotive.
20 Portrait of Female.	Prairie on fire, six wild horses. BK. OF ROCKINGHAM, Harrisonburg Va.	20 Girl with sheaf of grain on her head.
Female. FIFTY.	50 Spread eagle on shield, ship in the distance. BK. OF ROCKINGHAM, Harrisonburg, Va.	50 Female Portrait.
5 Bridge, canal-boat, and village in distance.	Vig. Female seated on trunk of a tree with tub; steamboat on right; house, &c., on left. Treasurers' die. BANK OF SCOTTSVILLE, Scottsville, Va. Quails.	5 Portrait of Washington.
6 Female soaring in the clouds, and another seated.	Vig. Two females seated on right side of a frame, on which is agricultural implements; on right a large building; on left train of cars. Tres's die. BANK OF SCOTTSVILLE, Scottsville, Va.	6 Portrait of Henry Clay.
7 Male, female seated, and two boys and lamb; sheaf of grain.	Treas's die. Vig. Female seated, with pole and cap, and two cupids and easel; on right train of cars, on left ships, masts, &c. BANK OF SCOTTSVILLE, Scottsville, Va.	7 Male portrait.
9 Male portrait.	Vig. Harvest scene, farmers mowing; on right, in distance, houses, &c.; on left team loading hay, &c. BANK OF SCOTTSVILLE. Scottsville, Va.	9 Treasurer's die.
X Female portrait.	Man holding bull, sheep, boy holding horse, two men, dog, etc. BANK OF SCOTTSVILLE, Scottsville, Va,	10 State Arms.
Rooster loading rifle. XX	20 Female with pole, cap, eagle, etc. Title of Bank.	20 State Arms.
5 Male portrait 5	Female seated, bale of goods, &c.; farmers at work and team of oxen on right. BANK OF THE VALLEY, VA. Dog's head.	Female with sheaf of grain. 5

5 Female standing. 5	Med. head. Female anchor, figure 5, shield, &c. Med. head. BANK OF THE VALLEY, VA. Boy's head.	5 Female. 5
10 Med. head. 10	Three Cupids. TEN Three Cupids. BANK OF THE VALLEY, VA. Dog's head.	10 Med. head. 10
10 Portrait of Washington 10	Female seated; locomotive on right; cows on left. BANK OF THE VALLEY, VA. Locomotive.	10 Indian Queen seated.
20 Portrait of Millard Fillmore. 20	Two females, two Cupids and figure "Twenty." BANK OF THE VALLEY, VA. Indian Queen.	20
20 Med. head. 20	Female erect. Twenty Dollars. Female seated BANK OF THE VALLEY, VA. Boy's head.	20 Med. head. 20
50 Double Medallion head, and word Fifty. 50	Male and female; Female seated; male holds sickle and reclines against a tree; man at work in a field on right, and house in background. BANK OF THE VALLEY, VA.	50 Double Medallion head and word Fifty. 50
100 Med. head and figure 100. 100	Title of Bank. Female seated; shield, &c.	100 Med. head and figure 100. 100
V Med. Head. V	FIVE Female with a rake. FIVE BANK OF VIRGINIA.	5 Med. Head. 5
10 Med. Head. 10	TEN Three females seated. Ship on left in distance. TEN BANK OF VIRGINIA.	10 Med. Head 10
FIFTEEN Med. Head and figures 15. FIFTEEN	Med. Head Med. Head Man and boy seated; man is drawing; mill on right in distance. BANK OF VIRGINIA. Dog's Head.	FIFTEEN Med. Head and figures 15. FIFTEEN

20 Warrior standing, another on the ground. 20	Med. Head and figures 20. Med. Head and figures 20. Two females, one holds a scroll, the other liberty pole and cap. BANK OF VIRGINIA.	XX Med. Head and word TWENTY. XX
50 Med. Head. 50	FIFTY DOLLARS Female seated with liberty pole and cap. BANK OF VIRGINIA.	50 Med. Head. 50
ONE HUNDRED	Washington on a horse. ONE HUNDRED A G n. on a horse. BANK OF VIRGINIA.	ONE HUNDRED
State arms—Justice trampling upon the neck of a tyrant. 5	B'K OF WHEELING. Wheeling, Va. Vig. Large letter V and the word FIVE.	5 Medallion Head.
10 State arms—Justice trampling upon the neck of a tyrant.	B'K OF WHEELING. Wheeling, Va. Large letter X and words TEN DOLLARS. Female—Justice and Commerce.	10 Locomotive and cars. 10
Blacksmith leaning against anvil.	Three sheep under tree. 5 BANK OF WINCHESTER, Winchester, Va.	5 Portrait of Chief Justice Marshall. 5
10 Female with cornucopia.	Boy on horse driving cattle and sheep. BANK OF WINCHESTER. Winchester, Va.	10 Head of Female.
Female head. 20	BANK OF WINCHESTER Winchester, Va. Railroad and bridge. Female head.	20 Man leaning on box.
FIFTY Man leaning on sheaf of wheat. 50	Two females spinning under tree; Railroad and bridge in background. BANK OF WINCHESTER, Winchester, Va. Sheaf of wheat.	FIFTY Heads of a man and horse. 50
5 Drovers and droves of cattle.	Sample Die. Female seated; sheaf of rice, sickle plow, &c.; cars on right. CENTRAL BANK, Staunton, Va.	5 Urn. FIVE

Left end	Centre	Right end
Registers die. Male portrait.	Female seated, elbow resting on shield, view of falls, bridge and town. CENTRAL BANK, Staunton, Va.	6. Female and grain.
	Drove of sheep, man on horse, the horse drink- ing from trough; load hay in back- ground. Registers die. CENTRAL BANK, Staunton, Va.	7
Registers die. Beehive.	CENTRAL BANK, Staunton, Va.	8. Catching horse.
10. Farmer erect with scythe.	Man on horse and slaves at work in a field. Warrior erect and one on ground. CENTRAL BANK, Staunton, Va. Locomotive.	X. TEN. 10.
20. Female, scales and sword.	Warrior erect and one on right; houses on ground. McDonald seat- ed; corn in left in back- ground. CENTRAL BANK, Staunton, Va.	20. Train of cars.
50. Female portrait.	Title of Bank. Three females reclining; cars and canal on right. Warrior erect and one on ground.	50
50. Portrait of female.	CENTRAL BANK OF VIRGINIA, Staunton. 50 Rooster. L	Three fe- males in clouds; cars and canal in distance. 50
5. Sailor and blacksmith.	Farmers and a load of wheat. CORPORATION OF ALEXANDRIA.	5. Farmer with sheaf of wheat.
5. Sailor con- versing with mechanic on ship.	V Two oxen draw- ing load of grain; man on top; man with fork upon his shoulder or beside the oxen. V CORPORATION OF ALEXANDRIA.	5. Farmer with grain.
Two females erect with sheaf of wheat.	Drove of horses running across field. CORPORATION OF ALEXANDRIA.	6. Sailor lean- ing against windlass.
Farmer scat- tering grain from his right hand; man plough- ing in dis- tance. V on Seven.	Indian in canoe containing squaw and children. CORPORATION OF ALEXANDRIA.	7. Female seat- ed.
5. Portrait of Washington. V	Harbor scene, and city in background. EXCHANGE B'K OF VIRGINIA.	5. Male portrait. V
VI. 6.	6 Female with scales, sword, &c.; safe, &c. on right; globe, &c., on left. EXCHANGE B'K OF VIRGINIA. Eagle.	6. Cupid and dragon.
VII. 7.	7 Vig. Same as 6s. EXCHANGE B'K OF VIRGINIA. Eagle.	7. Cupid and dragon.
VIII	8 Vig. Same as 6s. EXCHANGE B'K OF VIRGINIA. Eagle.	8. VIII
IX	9 Vig. Same as 6s. EXCHANGE B'K OF VIRGINIA. Eagle.	9. IX
10. Cars, barrels, bales of goods, &c. X	Por- trait of Wash- ington. Warrior stand- ing with his left foot placed on another warrior laying on the ground, and who is apparently dead; cars on right; shipping on left; also steamboat. Male por- trait. Title of Bank.	10. Canal, sloop, houses, and shipping. X
15. Warrior erect, &c.	Por- trait of Wash- ington. Large ship under way; houses on left in distance. Male por- trait. EXCHANGE B'K OF VIRGINIA. Anchor and shield.	15. Mechanic, anvil, ham- mer, &c. 15
20. Warrior erect, &c.	Por- trait of Wash- ington. Indian seated with bow, &c.; ruins of a house in background. Male por- trait. EXCHANGE B'K OF VIRGINIA. Indian in a canoe.	20. Ship. XX
50. Two men, drove of cattle and sheep. 50	Por- trait of Wash- ington, &c. Two females seated, with key, horn of plenty, &c.; steam- boat on right; bbls. and shipping on left. Male por- trait. EXCHANGE B'K OF VIRGINIA.	50. Warrior erect, &c.
100. Male and female. 100	Same as 10s. EXCHANGE B'K OF VIRGINIA.	100. Man working in a corn field. 100
O N E. 1. 1	FAIRMONT B'K, Fairmont, Va. Women feeding hens, poultry, &c. Hunters making fire. Horse, dogs and game. ONE DOLLAR ONE. Train of cars.	1. 1
Female reclining on grain, straw hat beside her, mowing machine in distance. TWO 2	FAIRMONT B'K, Fairmont, Va. Sheep. Two females with grain. 2 TWO DOLLARS. TWO	2. Fowls. 2
V. Dog's head. V	Man on horseback, driving cow and sheep; boy hold- ing gate open; cattle, trees, &c. in distance; at right of vig. Treas's die. FAIRMONT BANK, Fairmont, Va.	5. Man loading wagon with hay.
X. Train of cars coming down grade, house in back- ground, two males in fore- ground.	Indian crouch- ing behind rock with gun, watch- ing two deers. Treas's die. FAIRMONT BANK, Fairmont, Va.	TEN. Dog's head.
5. Man with scythe.	Five cherubs and five sil- ver dollars. FARMERS' BANK of Fincastle, Va. Wheat.	5. Treas. die. FIVE
Treas. die. Mower seat- ed with scythe.	TEN Portrait of Washington. TEN Title of Bank.	10. Two females, one with flag and shield.
100. C	Black and white horse alarmed at lightning; cat- tle in distance. FARMERS' BANK OF FINCASTLE, Virginia.	100. Treas. die.
5. Med. head. 5	5 Eagle, shield, and ship on left in distance. 5 FARMERS' BANK OF VIRGINIA. V V	5. Med. head. 5
6. Man and dog. SIX	6 Woodman seated, and dog, axe, and hat on the ground. 6 FARMERS' BANK OF VIRGINIA.	Male erect. SIX

Female erect and figure 7. | 7 Female reclining on bale of goods; vessels on left. 7 | FARMERS' BANK OF VIRGINIA. | Female erect | 7

EIGHT | Female seated. | VIII | Large fig. 8. | Two females and one male; ship in background on right. | Large fig. 8. | FARMERS' BANK OF VIRGINIA. | EIGHT | Female, eagle shield, &c. | VIII

9 | Two cupids small. | Med. head. | Three cupids, two on left and one on right of figure 9; one on right holds sickle. | Med. head. | FARMERS' BANK OF VIRGINIA | 9 | Female seated.

Female erect, shield, eagle, liberty pole, and cap. | 10 Man on horse, drove of sheep, and dog; mill in distance. | FARMERS' BANK OF VIRGINIA | 10

Male portrait | 10 Female seated, sheaf of wheat, &c. TEN | FARMERS' BANK OF VIRGINIA | Portrait of Washington.

Med. head. | 10 | Med. head. | FARMERS BANK OF VIRGINIA | Female seated; grain, cornucopia, ship, etc. | TEN

20 | Portrait of Washington. | 20 | 20 Miniature view of a female; sickle, sheafs of wheat, &c. on right. 20 | FARMERS' BANK OF VIRGINIA. | XX XX | 20 | Med. head. | 20

Male portrait | 20 Female seated, &c. 20 | FARMERS' BANK OF VIRGINIA. | Portrait of Washington.

THIRTY | 30 Female reclining, bucket of water, &c. 30 | FARMERS' BANK OF VIRGINIA. | 30 | RICHMOND

50 | Med. head. | 50 | Male and female seated; ship in distance on left. | Title of Bank. | 50 | Med. head. | 50

Male portrait | 50 Female seated, sheaf of wheat, &c. 50 | FARMERS' BANK OF VIRGINIA. | 50 | Portrait of Washington

FIFTY | 50 Female seated, pole, and shield. 50 | FARMERS' BANK OF VIRGINIA. | 50 | RICHMOND

ONE HUNDRED | 100 Female, shield, plough, &c. 100 | FARMERS' BANK OF VIRGINIA. | RICHMOND

5 | Large fig. 5, two Indians, water fall, etc. | Steamboat, "Charleston & Cincinnati Packet," other steamboats at wharves. | MANUFACTURERS' BANK of Kanawha, Va. | Eagle. | 5 | Female with foot on tyrant's neck.

10 inverted. | Female with roll of cloth. | Title of Bank. | Train of cars; building in background on right. | Dog. | 10 inverted. | Same as above &c.

5 | Male portrait. | FIVE | MANUFACTURERS' AND FARMERS' BK. Wheeling, Va. | Vig. Interior of a glass work establishment; hands at work. | 5 | Female treading the neck of a tyrant. | 5

X | TEN | MANUFACTURERS' AND FARMERS' BK. Wheeling, Va. | Vig. Group of seven persons; three males and four females; commerce, agriculture, &c.; harbor and lighthouse in distance | 10 | State arms.

5 | Female, sheaf of wheat in left hand. | Three female figures, middle figure with map, book in left hand. | State Arms. | MERCHANTS BANK. Lynchburg, Va. | Merchandise | FIVE

6 | Tunnel, Rail road cars. | State Arms. | MERCHANTS BANK. Lynchburg, Va. | 6 | Blacksmith with hammer raised.

7 | 7 | Female figure, reclining on money chest; Deer in distance. | State Arms. | MERCHANTS BANK. Lynchburg, Va. | 7 | Bust of a Male.

EIGHT | Female figure, Eagle, &c. | State Arms. | Female figure; mechanics in shirt sleeves. | MERCHANTS BANK. Lynchburg, Va. | 8 | 8

9 | Rail road. | Female figure, train and buildings in distance. | State Arms. | MERCHANTS BANK. Lynchburg, Va. | 9 | Female, harness, &c.

10 | Three female figures; right in reclining posture. | State Arms. | MERCHANTS BANK. Lynchburg, Va. | Merchandise | X | Female, staff in left hand.

20 | 20 | XX | Treasurer. | Two men; one with tobacco in hand; hhds., &c. | MERCHANTS' BANK Lynchburg, Va. | 20

20 | 20 | XX | State Arms. | 3 vessels; steam boat in distance. | MERCHANTS BANK. Lynchburg, Va. | 20

50 | Female figure, grain in left hand. | State Arms. | Dock; vessel in distance. | MERCHANTS BANK. Lynchburg, Va. | 50 | Canal and bridge. | FIFTY

C | 100 | Sheafs of wheat; female, milking pail in lap on left; State Arms on right; rail road train &c., in distance. | MERCHANTS BANK. Lynchburg, Va. | C | Female, wheat in left hand. | 100

5 | 5 | MER & MEC. BANK of Wheeling, Va. | Man and three horses at well; goats, kids, etc. | 5 | Female head.

Cars on bridge; cattle, stream, etc. | Merchants' and Mechanics' B'k Wheeling, Va. | 5

V | Male portrait. | 5 | FIVE Vig. Large wagon and horses, steamboat, houses, &c. FIVE | MERCHANTS' AND MECHANICS' BANK Wheeling, Va. | 5 | Male portrait. | V

5 — Female seated with two calves; canal and railroad scene on left. — 5
Bull's head. — Title of Bank. — Female with flowers.

Red tinted V and 5 blended with sailor seated with glass, bales, bbls, etc.; ship in distance on left, and female with cog-wheel, bale, etc. on right, and Mer. and Mech. Bank above and below either vignette. — 5
5 — Dog's head. — Girl's portrait.

5 — Medallion head and figure 5. Medallion head and figure 5. — 5
Bust of Washington. — Vig. Harvest scene; bundles of grain; urchin sleeping. — Male portrait.
V — Title of Bank. — V

5 — Female portrait. Vig. Dog and safe. Female portrait. — 5
Male portrait. — Title of Bank — Male portrait.
5 — 5

Red TEN inverted. — Title of Bank. — TEN to right of fig. 10.
Cattle and sheep on bank; cow in stream.
Red TEN inverted. — Male portrait X — Jefferson.
Eagle.

Female, cows, sheep, ducks, etc. 10 TEN
Title of Bank.
X — Red TEN Red TEN — Hunter loading gun; game at his feet.

Red 10. — MERCHANTS' AND MECHANICS' BK., Wheeling, Va. — Red 10.
Sailor with quadrant; vessels. — TEN on red X. Washington. TEN on red X. — Wheelwright at work.

X — TEN Vig. Mechanic reclining on an anvil; house in background. TEN — 10
Portrait of Washington. — Title of Bank. — Male portrait.
10 — X

Washingt'n — Female portrait. — 10
MERCH & MECHS BK Wheeling, Va.
X — Basket of corn. — Cattle, tree, etc.

Female head. — Eagle and shield — 20
MERCH & MECHS BK Wheel ng, Va.
20 — Head of horse.

50 — Med. head. Vig. male figure in standing position. Med. head. — 50
Medallion head. — Title of Bank — Medallion head.
50 — 50

100 — Med. head. Vig. Harvest scene, houses and shrubbery in background. Med. head. — 100
Cattle shrubbery, &c. — Title of Bank. — Cattle.
100 — 100

5 — Vig. A building which was the residence of Thomas Jefferson. — Trea's die and letter V.
Male portrait. — MONTICELLO B'K, Charlottesville, Va. Dog's head. — Figure 5 and three cherubs, one holding flag which forms the top of the 5.

Female with flowers in her apron. — MONTICELLO BANK, Charlottesville, Va. — 6
View of tobacco plantation; two men, one holding tobacco leaves; both by side of hogsheads.
6 — Locomotive. — State Arms.

7 SEVEN — MONTICELLO BANK, Charlottesville, Va. — 7
Two horses running away from train of cars; trees, &c.
7 — State Arms.

8 — MONTICELLO BANK. Charlottesville, Va. — 8
Man seated; scythe on tree. — Three females, representing the Arts and Sciences; house and water in distance. — State Arms.

Female with cornucopia. — MONTICELLO BANK, Charlottesville, Va. — 9
Drover and drove of cattle; boy in water; farm house, trees, &c., in distance.
9 — State Arms.

Vig. Sampson. Trea's die, fives. — 10
MONTICELLO B'K, Charlottesville, Va.
Train of cars. — Spread eagle. — Male portrait.

20 — Trea's die. Sampson &c.
MONTICELLO B'K. Charlottesville, Va.
Milk maid; cows on right. — Horse. — Male portrait.

L FIFTY L — MONTICELLO BANK Charlottesville, Va. — 50
Female with sword and shield. L — Large building.

100 — Title of Bank. 100 100 C — 100
Large building. — Male portrait.

FIVE on med. head. — NORTH-WESTERN BANK, Wheeling, Va. — 5
Male portrait — View of Suspension bridge; steamboat and houses. — Male portrait

Med. head and word five — Indian and female reclining on either side escutcheon or arms of the State of Virginia. — 5
Locomotive and tender. — Title of Bank.
FIVE — Female bathing. — Med. head.

5 — NORTH WESTERN BANK of Virginia. — 5
Female, bale, bbls.; factories, vessels, etc., in distance. — Youthful portrait with cap. — Mechanic seated, wheel, hammer, etc.; two farmers, house, etc., in distance.

5 — Three females seated; ship in distance. 5 on med. head on either side of vig.
Washington. — NORTH-WESTERN BANK, Wheeling, Va. — FIVE
V

Male portrait — NORTH-WESTERN BANK, Wheeling, Va. — 5
FIVE — Suspension bridge.
Male portrait — Locomotive. — Med. head.

TEN — Title of Bank — 10
Male and female and two children, one holding a sheep, &c. — Large die containing the word ten, figures 10, and letter X. — Female with sickle.
10

X — Title of Bank. — 10
Female portrait. — Scene in blacksmith's shop. — Female with dove
10 — 10

X — NORTH WESTERN BANK OF VIRGINIA — 10
Female portrait. Female portrait. Three blacksmiths at work by anvil.
10 — 10

TEN — Title of Bank — 10
Male and female and two children, one holding a sheep. — Large die containing word ten, figures 10, and letter X. — Female with sickle in hand.
10

VIRGINIA.

X Med. head and word ten thereon. 10	Med. head and word Ten. Female reclining, representing Agriculture. Med. head and word Ten. Title of Bank.	Word Ten in ornamental Italics.
TEN Female erect holding sword and balance. 10	Med. head and word ten. Indian seated and gazing on vacancy. Med. head and word ten. Title of Bank.	TEN
20 Portrait of Washington. 20	Med. head. Instructor and pupil. Med. head. Title of Bank.	20 Med. head. 20
Med. head. 50 Med. head.	50 Group of three females representing Agriculture, Commerce, &c. 50 Title of Bank. Steamboat.	Med. head. 50 Med. head.
5 Portrait of Gen.	View of steamer, tug, vessels, man in row-boat, city, etc. RAPPAHANNOCK BANK, Tappahannock, Va. American Shield.	5 Treas. die.
10 Treas. die.	Title of Bank. Female reclining with quadrant, pole and cap, merchandise, etc.; ocean scene on left; buildings, etc. on right. Cornucopia, &c.	10 Letter X, Ten on it; milk-maid, cow, care, etc.
5 Male portrait	SOUTH WESTERN BK OF VIRGINIA. Female portrait. State Arms. Female portrait.	5 Male portrait
10 Male portrait	Two females seated, spinning wheel, sickle, etc.; cars, cattle, etc., in distance. State Arms. SOUTH WESTERN BK. OF VIRGINIA.	10 Male portrait
5 State Arms.	TRADERS' BANK, Richmond, Va. Words "Five Dollars, FIVE and figure 5, on green die. V V	5 Girl's head.
10 Washington.	Title of Bank. Negro with two horses; cotton plantation in distance. X Anvil. X	10 Boy's head.

N. CAROLINA.

TWENTY DOLLARS 20 Negro gathering cotton. Die.	Title of Bank. TWENTY on 20. Clay. TWENTY on 20. Eagle.	20 Female with spinning wheel. Die. TWENTY DOLLARS
50 Negroes gathering cotton.	Title of Bank. L Female seated on bale with sword and liberty cap; child at her feet; steamship and ship in distance. L	50 Female portrait.
State Arms.	100 Title of Bank. Girl's head in large C. 100	100 Old man, child and bust of Washington.
3 Female with grain and horn of plenty, seated. 3	BK OF CAPE FEAR. N. Carolina. Three males, one with model of boat and one with hammer with his hand resting on anvil; on left ship on stocks; on the right factories and bridge.	3 3
THREE	3 Female seated holding bonnet in left hand; basket on left. 3 Title of Bank.	Washington. Male portrait
THREE Farmer, dog, flock, &c. THREE	3 Men at work in a corn field. 3 Title of Bank. Ship.	Female.
Female erect Eagle. 3	3 Female; wheel and monument in background 3 Title of Bank. Two females.	3 Girls head. 3
4 Ship, brig, steamship and steamboats; city in distance.	Female seated on log with pail in her lap; shield with train of cars on it; sheafs of grain on right with cows and trees in distance; trees and farm house on left. Title of Bank.	4
Female seated with sickle and sheaf of grain. Locomotive	4 Man seated; ship-building in background. Title of Bank.	4 Cooper at work.
4	Female reclining; anchor, &c. ship on left. Large fig. 4. Title of Bank. Sheaf of grain, plow, &c.	FOUR Female erect shield, &c. FOUR

N. CAROLINA.

Female erect and eagle. Large fig. 4.	Large fig. 4. Man seated with crook; steamboat on left. Large fig. 4. Title of Bank. Two females.	Large fig. 4 Cupid. Large fig. 4
5 Male portrait	Title of Bank. Large V with FIVE in ornamental work across it.	5 Two females seated, bale, barrel and sheaf of grain.
Boy, girl, dog, &c. Female and basket.	5 Five cupids and large figure 5. Title of Bank.	Female and horn of plenty. Eagle. Indian.
Man seated drawing. 5	5 Female and cupid in a car, other cupids drawing it. 5 Title of Bank. Indian's head.	Female seated safe &c. 5
5 Male portrait	Shield containing ship; male seated on right, &c.; female seated with rake; steamboat, river, &c., on left. BK OF CAPE FEAR, Wilmington, N. C.	5 Sailor beside anchor; shipping in background.
Indian with bow and arrow. V	Double med. head. Female seated, ship on left in distance. Double med. head. Title of Bank. Two females.	5 Male portrait V
6 VI 6	Scene at sea, clipper ship, water in commotion, steamship and other vessels. Title of Bank.	6 6
SEVEN	Shield with Indian seated on right with axe; Indian tents with trees and fire in distance; Female, shield and cornucopia on left; steamboat and city in distance. Title of Bank.	7 VII 7
EIGHT	Train of cars coming under arch; with horses and carriage on top of arch; telegraph wires and poles, rocks, trees and fence, &c. Title of Bank.	8 8
NINE	Steamship, ship on left; water in commotion. Title of Bank.	9 IX

Left	Center	Right
X 10	Title of Bank. Two Females representing liberty and peace; train of cars on right; steamboat ship and small boat on left.	10 X
Man in corn field. TEN	10 Miniature view of female, anchor, &c. on right; vase, &c. on left. Title of Bank.	Masons at work. TEN
10 Male portrait	Title of Bank. Shield surrounded by eagle, containing cars, &c; sailor seated on right holding flag in his right hand; farmer with spade seated on left.	10 Male portrait
10 Female seated on a log.	Title of Bank. Male, female, and dog; sheaf of grain, &c.	10
TEN	10 Female seated; vase on right. X Title of Bank. Two females.	10 Med. head. X
20 Female, sheaf of wheat, cabin, &c. 20	Portrait of Washington. Two females reclining; wagon on right; steamboat and vessels on left. Title of Bank. Eagle.	20 Female with vase.
20 Portrait of female. 20	20 Female holding a goat by the horns. 20 Title of Bank. Bull's head.	20 Female erect. 20
Female drawing. 50	Female seated, figure liberty, horn of plenty, &c.; on left, two vessels in distance. Title of Bank. Locomotive.	50 Sailor with spy-glass.
50 Medallion head. 50	L Female reclining; ship in distance on right. L Title of Bank.	50 Female with a rake. 50
Female.	100 Male portrait, and a female seated on either side. 100 Title of Bank.	Female.

Left	Center	Right
100 Female figure. 100	Cupid and sheep. Female playing on harp. Cupid, bow and sheep. Title of Bank. Steamboat.	100 Med. head. 100
3 Head of Washington. THREE	Farmer plowing with two horses. BANK OF CHARLOTTE, N. C. Hornet's nest on the branch of a tree.	3 Man and head of a horse.
Tree over-hanging a wagon, loaded and drawn by two oxen and horses; hornets nest on tree.	4 Spread eagle. BANK OF CHARLOTTE, N. C.	4 Figure reclining with pole and cap; factories in distance.
Man leaning against an anvil, sledge by his side.	Mecklenburg Declaration inside of a shield. Train of cars. BANK OF CHARLOTTE, N. C. Same as 3s.	5 Med. with head of female. FIVE
	Man and boy plowing with two horses. Female portrait. BANK OF CHARLOTTE, Charlotte, N. C.	5 Female beside column, etc.
10 Female, cow, calf, etc.	Female head. Title of Bank. Three females and cupid floating in water.	10
TEN A female figure, full length, with a wreath and very light drapery, her thighs very plainly seen on examination.	Mechanic and farmer, horse's head and a tree with the Declaration of Mecklenburg; in distance foundry. BANK OF CHARLOTTE, N. C. Same as 5s.	10 Med. head of soldier. X
Male portrait. 20 Female portrait.	Blacksmith's shop; man shoeing horse, and a man at forge. BANK OF CHARLOTTE, N. C. Same as 5's.	Female portrait. 20 Male portrait.
Girl seated in chair. TWENTY	Surveyors at work. Title of Bank.	20 Farmer carrying corn stalks.
50 Farmer at lunch; two horses, plow, etc.	Male portrait. Title of Bank. FIFTY 50 FIFTY	50 Loaded cart with horse, express up.

Left	Center	Right
FIFTY Med. head, child with little dog, [illegible] FIFTY	BANK OF CHARLOTTE, N. C. Fox chase. Same as threes.	50 Female with grain on her head.
100 Female portrait. Hundred.	Man holding horse; man repairing cart, etc. Title of Bank.	100 Sailor boy. Hundred.
5	Large letter V and a female with a scroll. Two females, one seated, other seated. The one erect holds a scroll in right hand, and liberty pole and cap in left. B'K OF CLARENDON, Fayetteville, N. C.	5 5
6 6	Large raft floating down river, man in boat holding up two birds, another raft on the right. B'K OF CLARENDON, Fayetteville, N. C.	6 Sugar and female.
7 Farmer seated, scythe hanging on a tree.	Three females standing, one in center holds liberty pole and cap, one on right has a compass. B'K OF CLARENDON, Fayetteville, N. C.	7 SEVEN 7
8 8	Woodmen at work, one is seated, one is chopping down a tree and one chopping a tree on the ground. Man and oxen on right in background. B'K OF CLARENDON, Fayetteville, N. C.	8 8
9 Female with shield.	Southern scene—various male and female figures, horses, wagons, mules, &c. B'K OF CLARENDON, Fayetteville, N. C.	9 9
TEN Farmer reclining, female seated, two children, a sheep and sheaf of wheat.	Large letter X, word TEN and figures 10. Steamboat going up; hills in background. B'K OF CLARENDON, Fayetteville, N. C.	TEN
V Female gazing on ocean.	Scene on a steamers' wharf; men, horse, etc. Fig. 5 either side. B'K OF COMMERCE, Newbern, N. C.	5 Female portrait.
10 Female portrait.	BANK OF COMMERCE, Newbern, N. C. Female seated with sword, twig, eagle, shield; in distance cars, town, steamboat, vessel, etc.	10 Man carrying [illegible]

ONE Liberty and shield. 1 Floating female with cornucopia; view of ocean and ships. BANK OF FAYETTE-VILLE. Fayetteville, N. C. ONE	X X Negro, loaded cart and mules. THE BANK of North Carolina 10 TEN Male portrait. Negro and two horses; cotton scene in distance. X X	20 Male portrait. 20 Female seated, bale of goods, barrel, &c.; on right, men at work and train of cars. BK. OF THE STATE OF N. CAROLINA. 20 Med. head. 20
II Indian chief's head. Truck wagon and two-horse team; train of cars on left. BANK OF FAYETTE-VILLE, Fayetteville, N. C. TWO 2 2	20 Negroes gathering cotton. BANK OF NORTH CAROLINA Man with grain, horse and dog. Has Title either side with Washington on left and Male portrait on right. 20 20 20 Franklin at printers case.	50 Med. head. 50 Shield and two females; on right, saw mill and vessel; on left barrels and manufactory works. BK. OF THE STATE OF N. CAROLINA. FIFTY Gen. Washington on a horse. FIFTY
III 3 Western steamboat, cars, locomotive, etc. BANK of FAYETTE-VILLE, Fayetteville, N. C. 3 Male portrait.	L 50 FIFTY Six mules before wagon load of bales; negroes and plantation scene. L Title of Bank. Male portrait; female each side. 50 FIFTY	3 Female portrait. 3 Man, three horses at trough; female feeding hogs; houses etc. BANK OF WADES-BOROUGH, Wadesborough, N. C. Dog, boy and safe. 3 Two females. 3
FOUR Figure 4. BANK OF FAYETTE-VILLE, Fayetteville, N. C. Man hitching team to plow; man on horseback. 4 FOUR Indian. FOUR	THREE 3 Indian princess seated. 3 BANK of the STATE OF NORTH CAR-OLINA. THREE Three females, centre one kneeling. THREE	Female head 3 Child's head. BANK OF WADES-BOROUGH, Wadesborough, N. C. Horse, colt, and sheep; train of cars in distance. 3 3 Laborers at work, one with pipe.
V 5 Liberty, Agriculture, and Commerce, between them figure 5; cars on left. 5 BANK OF FAYETTE-VILLE, Fayetteville, N. C. FIVE Female, sickle, grain, and cornucopia.	Med. head. 4 Train of cars. Title of Bank. FOUR Female erect with sickle. FOUR	4 Two females. 4 Male portrait. Female with grain, plow, etc. BANK of WADES-BOROUGH, Wadesborough, N. C. 4 Female seated. FOUR
X Male portrait. 10 Two females; Liberty, Agriculture, and Commerce; ships on left. X BANK OF FAYETTE-VILLE, Fayetteville, N. C. 10 Washington. X	V Female seated, and bales. V. 5 5 Sailor and female seated and figure 5; vessel on left in distance. 5 BK. OF THE STATE OF N. CAROLINA. V Female seated and fig. 5 5	4 FOUR Title of Bank. Female with a cale and child. 4 4 Hunters on the Prairie—fighting fire—dog, horse, deer, etc. 4 Negress and child. FOUR
XX Cars, wharf, and city in distance. XX 20 Vig. same as 10s. BANK OF FAYETTE-VILLE. Fayetteville, N. C. 20 Male portrait.	5 Female and horn of plenty. 5 BK. OF THE STATE OF N. CAROLINA. Men in water.	FIVE Boy's head. FIVE Title of Bank. 5 Negro with cotton. 5 V V 5 Man surveying.
5 Negro picking cotton. BK. OF LEXINGTON. Lexington, N. C. 5 Two females seated; building in distance. 5 5 Cotton weighing scene.	X Med. head. X 10 Female, blowing a horn; globe and eagle, on left, American flag. 10 BK. OF THE STATE OF N. CAROLINA. Two females and large letter X; anvil and hammer. TEN	Soldier, cannon, and American flag. FIVE 5 Two females, bale of goods, &c., steamboat. B'K OF WADES-BOROUGH, N. C. House. 5 FIVE 5
10 Female with sickle. Patent reaping machine at work in field; city, etc. in distance. Title of Bank. 10 Female with sickle sheaf.	TEN Eagle, shield, &c. 10 Sheaf of wheat, &c. Sheaf of wheat, boat, man, horse, baskets, boxes, &c.; small boats in background. BK. OF THE STATE OF N. CAROLINA. Female seated. 10 Female. 10	10 Female reclining. BANK OF WADES-BOROUGH, N. C. Man on horse and slaves at work in a cotton field. 10 10 10 Female, shield, and American flag.
5 Two farmers, female and child. Male portrait. BANK OF NORTH CAROLINA Steamer, tug, vessels, city, etc. 5	Female and dog. 20 20 Men, mowing, sheep, etc. 20 Title of Bank. Female, ship, etc. Female and dog. 20	Sailor, female, anchor, bale of goods, American flag, &c. 20 Title of Bank. Large Spread Eagle, shield, &c. Beehive. 20

Left end	Centre	Right end
Farmer, sailor and blacksmith. 3	3 BANK OF WASHINGTON, North Carolina. Female swimming.	3 Portrait of Washington.
Portrait of Washington. 4	Shield; Indian, squaw and papoose on right of shield; mountain in distance; on left of shield female and three children studying globe; horses in distance. Title of Bank. Anvil.	FOUR Portrait of Mrs. Washington.
5 FIVE	BANK OF WASHINGTON, North Carolina. Three females with quadrant, anchor and sickle. Train of cars. Eagle.	5 Female. 5
TEN Female, hogshead, &c., train of cars in distance. 10	Head of Washington surmounted by an eagle; on left female, anchor and ship; on right female with horn of flowers. Title of Bank. Boxes and barrels.	X 10
20 Male portrait.	Indian seated, plow, &c.; in distance mountains and river. BANK OF WASHINGTON, North Carolina.	XX Indian female, female with sheaf and sickle.
Word fifty running up. Five female figures.	BANK OF WASHINGTON, North Carolina. FIFTY.	50 Bridge, telegraph wire and poles, cattle, trees, &c.
Small figure of Washington and figures 100. Three male figures, flag, windlass, anvil, &c.	BANK OF WASHINGTON, North Carolina. 100 100	100 Slave scene; Palmetto trees, cotton growing and in baskets.
5 FIVE	Yatching scene. B'K OF WILMINGTON, Wilmington, N. C. Boxes, bales, &c.	5 Ship sailing.
6 Horse. 6	Train of cars. B'K OF WILMINGTON. Wilmington, N. C. Schooner.	6 Eagle. 6
Two sailors and two figures on ship, city in distance.	Dairy maid and cows. 7 B'K OF WILMINGTON Wilmington, N. C.	7 7

Left end	Centre	Right end
8 Ship sailing.	Jackson between two girls; harvest scene on left; ship and steamboat on right. B'K OF WILMINGTON, Wilmington, N. C. Locomotive.	8 Sailor on ship.
9 Mechanics at work. 9	Female reclining; eagle on right; train of cars and bridge on left; city in distance. B'K OF WILMINGTON, Wilmington, N. C. Ship.	9 Water, trees, fruit.
X 10	B'K OF WILMINGTON, Wilmington, N. C. Yatch scene.	10 Girl.
Twenty and state arms. X X	Steamboat. B'K OF WILMINGTON, Wilmington, N. C. 20	TWENTY 20 XX
20 TWENTY	Steamboat. B'K OF WILMINGTON, Wilmington, N. C. XX Child's head. XX DOLLARS.	20 TWENTY
50 Die.	Large spread eagle; ships on either side. B'K OF WILMINGTON, Wilmington, N. C. Indian female.	50 Die.
C Female and eagle, shield	100 One Hundred. B'K OF WILMINGTON, Wilmington, N. C. C One Hundred C	ONE HUNDRED
3 Female grain and sickle.	BANK OF YANCEYVILLE, North Carolina. Vig. Interior of a tobacco factory	3 Male portrait
4	BANK OF YANCEYVILLE, North Carolina. Vig. Same as 3s. IV	4 Male portrait.
V5V Mechanic and tools.	BANK OF YANCEYVILLE, North Carolina. Vig. State arms of North Carolina; ship on right; bridge and cars on left.	5 Washington.

Left end	Centre	Right end
X Male portrait.	BANK OF YANCEYVILLE, North Carolina. 10 Vig. Female, sickle and grain; farm house in background; cars crossing bridge on left.	TEN
20	Faust, Gutenburgh, and Schoeffer; manufacturing. Portrait of Washington. BANK OF YANCEYVILLE, N. C.	XX Male portrait
L Mechanic and mechanical tools.	BANK OF YANCEYVILLE N. C. FIFTY.	50 Male portrait
Two males and one female; males are carrying the female. THREE	Female reclining; eagle, shield, safe, key, scales, &c.; ship on right; cars on left. COMMERCIAL BK., Wilmington, N. C. Female and shield.	3 Female erect; scales, sword, &c.
THREE Male portrait. THREE	COMMERCIAL BK. OF WILMINGTON. North Carolina. Liberty and plenty; ships and trees in distance.	3 Sailor.
4 Sailor.	Title of Bank. Vig Same as 3s. Red 4 Red 4	4 Male portrait
Male and large figure four extending across the note.	4 Female, shield, eagle, &c. 4 COMMERCIAL BK., Wilmington, N. C. Female and shield	Female erect; scales and large figure four extending across the note.
FIVE Female seated and large figure Five. FIVE	Female, eagle, shield and figure Five. Ornamental V each side. COMMERCIAL BK., Wilmington, N. C. Female and shield.	FIVE Female seated and figure Five. FIVE
Ship and house. 10 Negro at work.	Water scene and female representing Liberty in a car; steamship in distance on right; boat in distance on left. COMMERCIAL BK., Wilmington, N. C. Female, shield, &c.	10 Female, car of corn and letter X.
20 Two females.	Indian Queen, shield, &c.; steamship on right. Female, anchor, &c. Title of Bank.	20 20

Left	Centre	Right
50 Two females; one seated, the other standing. 50	Female looking over rocks elsewhere, etc; canal and city in distance on right. COMMERCIAL BK., Wilmington, N. C.	50 Female, eagle, shield, &c.
100 Ship under way	Sailor reclining; roll of rope, anchor, windlass, spy-glass, &c.; vessel on left. 100 COMMERCIAL BK., Wilmington, N. C.	Sailor and blacksmith. Flag and anchor.
3 Girl's head	FARMERS' BANK of North Carolina. Men, cattle, sheep, hogs, etc 3 3	3 Boy's head.
3 Eagle, liberty, starry drapery and shield	FARMERS' BANK, Elizabeth City, N. C. Vig. Three females.	3
4	Two negroes on load of cotton drawn by 4 mules; negro on ground driving. Title Female, column, steamer, etc.	4 Female portrait.
IV	FARMERS' BANK, Elizabeth City, N. C. 4 Two sailors and female with spy-glass in boat. IV	4
Title. Girl's head. FIVE	Several mill doors; man, horse, cart, wheel, boys on bridge, etc.	5 FIVE
FIVE Two Indians	FARMERS' BANK, Elizabeth City, N. C. 5 FIVE	5 Female and Indian on either side of shield.
6 Male portrait	Spread eagle on limb of tree, factories on right, cars crossing bridge on left. 6 Title of Bank. SIX	6 Female with grain and sickle, farmhouses and church spires in background.
7 Eagle at top of shield anchor and female with quadrant on right.	Harvest scene. FARMERS' BANK, Elizabeth City, N. C	7 Female.

Left	Centre	Right
8 Little girl and dog.	Eagle at top of shield on either side of shield. FARMERS' BANK, Elizabeth City, N. C	8 Washington.
X Female and child also harvest scene.	State Die. Spread eagle and shield, ship on left. FARMERS' BANK, Elizabeth City, N. C.	10 Male portrait
Clay. X	Title of Bank Farmer feeding hogs; two horses, fence, etc. Calhoun. 10	10 Girl's head.
20 XX 20	Shield, view of bridge and canal female on either side representing agriculture and commerce. 20 FARMERS' BANK, Elizabeth City, N. C.	XX XX
50	Female and eagle, cars crossing bridge, city in distance. FARMERS' BANK, Elizabeth City, N. C.	50
100 Milkmaid seated with cattle.	FARMERS' BANK, Elizabeth City, N. C. ONE HUNDRED.	100 Shield, Justice and truth.
Female. THREE	3 Female seated, flag, keg, safe, and shield; beehive on left. 3 MERCHANTS' BANK, Newbern, N. C.	Female erect and large figure 3.
Large fig. 4 Female with liberty pole and cap. Large fig. 4.	Large fig. 4. Drove of cattle and sheep at a brook. Large fig. 4. MERCHANTS' BANK, Newbern, N. C. Safe and dog.	Female and shield and large fig. 4
FIVE	5 Female seated; sickle, plough, and sheaf of grain; cattle on left. 5 MERCHANTS' BANK, Newbern, N. C.	FIVE Female, scales, eagle, &c. V
Male seated; eagle, shield, &c. 10	X Female reclining with scroll, eagle, and portrait of Washington. X MERCHANTS' BANK, Newbern, N. C.	10 Male portrait 10

Left	Centre	Right
TWENTY	20 Man holding the globe on end of pole. 20 MERCHANTS' BANK, Newbern, N. C.	Two females, one in air with horn of plenty, and other seated XX
100 Female seated with sickle. 100	100 Female seated 100 with liberty pole and cap, child, eagle, anvil, wheel, &c.; ship on left. MERCHANTS' BANK, Newbern, N. C.	Female and eagle. 100
V 5	MINERS' & PLANTERS' BANK, Murphy, N. C. Indian head. Two females, seated; cars and plantation in distance. V Horse	5 FIVE V
10 Scene in a coal mine.	Plantation scene. Title of Bank. TEN X	10 Clay.
Cupid. Washington.	Title of Bank. 20 20 XX Surveying scene. TWENTY.	Cupid. 20
5 Male portrait	BANK OF CAMDEN, Camden, S. C. V Female seated on bale, child at her feet. V	5 Boy's head.
5 Med. head. 5	Male portrait. Church, monument, and tree. Male portrait. BANK OF CAMDEN, Camden, S. C. Dog's head	5 Med. head and figure 5. 5
10 Med. head. 10	Med. head and word Ten. Indian Queen, shield, bale of goods, &c.; steamship on right. Med. head and word Ten. BANK OF CAMDEN, Camden, S. C.	10 Med. head 10
10 Male portrait	Negro gathering cotton. Title of Bank. Female by shield. Steamship.	10 X Train of cars
20 Male portrait	Title of Bank. Negro, cow and calf. Sofaive	20 Calhoun

50 Male portrait	Title of Bank. Plantation scene—negroes in cotton field. 50 50 L	50 Girl's head.
100 Male portrait	Two shields, cupid at top, soldier right—female left. C Title of Bank C 100	100 Female portrait
5 Indian seated.	5 Female seated; anchor, bale of goods, rudder, &c.; ship on left in distance. 5 B'K of CHARLESTON S Carolina	Indian walking. 5
5 Male portrait	V V BANK OF CHARLESTON, Charleston, S. C. Liberty and soldier on either side of two shields; cupid at top. 5 FIVE FIVE 5 Shields and tree.	5 Male portrait
X TEN	10 BK of CHARLESTON, Charleston, S. C. Plant. Two females, owl, bales, building, vessel, etc. Palmetto tree.	10 Calhoun.
10 Cars. 10	Med. head. Title of Bank Med. head. Female seated, safe, money bags, &c.; cars on right.	10 Cars. 10
20 Portrait of Washington. 20	Two females seated, cupid and cars on right; Houses and shipping on left. 20 Eagle.	Indian Queen, shield, &c. 20
Female with pole. 50	BANK OF CHARLESTON, Charleston, S. C. 50 Naval vessels attacking fort. 50 50 Palmetto tree. 50	Female with pole. 50
Statue of female. 100	BANK OF CHARLESTON, Charleston, S. C. Soldier and female either side of two shields with motto es surmounted by eagle with trumpet. Medallion head either side. Palmetto tree.	Statue of female. 100
Male portrait	500 Palmetto tree. 500 BK OF CHARLEST'N, Charleston, S. C. D D	Male portrait

5 Portrait of Jefferson.	Surrender of Lord Cornwallis. BANK OF CHESTER, Chester, S. C. Palmetto tree, cotton on each side of it.	5 Portrait of Washington.
10 Male portrait.	BANK OF CHESTER, Chester, S. C. Portrait of John C. Calhoun. Same as Fives.	10 Male portrait.
Sailor holding American flag; female in sitting position; casks, anchor, bale of goods, horn of plenty. TWENTY	Train of cars. BANK OF CHESTER, Chester, S. C. Same as Fives.	20 Portrait of female.
50 Female.	Horses; buildings in the distance. BANK OF CHESTER, Chester, S. C. Same as Fives.	50 Portrait of W. R. King.
100 Portrait of female.	Capitol at Washington. BANK OF CHESTER, Chester, S. C. Same as Fives.	100 Eagle.
5 Male portrait.	Large V, female therein. BK of GEORGETOWN Georgetown, S. C.	5 Portrait of a Girl.
Figure 5 with a cupid on either side. Female portrait.	BK. OF GEORGETOWN. Georgetown, S. C. V State Arms.	FIVE 5 Dollars.
10	BANK OF GEORGETOWN, Georgetown, S. C. X	10 Female portrait.
10 Girl's portrait.	Large letter X in center; Med. Heads of Washington and Franklin on either side supported by four cherubs. BK OF GEORGETOWN, S. C.	10 Indians, trees surrounded by barrels, bales, wheel, &c.
5 Cupid.	BANK OF HAMBURG S. C. Man and negro sharpening scythe; men at work in distance. Title each side. V V	5 Cupid.

5 Train of cars. 5	B'K OF HAMBURG, Hamburg, S. C. Eagle. Female seated; cars in distance on left. Eagle.	5 Steamboat and two Indians in canoe. 5
10 Female supporting state arms. TEN	Two oxen, plow and yoke, figure leaning against an ox. Male portrait. Female seated on bale of goods, spinning wheel beside her. B'K OF HAMBURG, Hamburg, S. C.	10 Military figure supporting state arms. TEN
TEN on X. X	BK OF HAMBURG, Hamburg, S. C. Farm scene—male, female, children, well, dog and horse; man watering horse. Ten Dollars on red lathe strip.	10 X
20 XX	Title of Bank. Shield on which is a tree; eagle at top, female on either side; bridge and cars in distance on right; ship and steamboat on left.	20 XX
20 Female with pitcher. 20	Farm house, wagon and team, men and trees. B'K OF HAMBURG, Hamburg, S. C.	20 Man shearing a sheep, horse behind him. 20
Female holding sheaf and sickle. 50	50 Train of cars; hills, houses, and steamboat in distance. 50 B'K OF HAMBURG, Hamburg, S. C.	Female with cornucopia. 50
50	BK OF HAMBURG, Hamburg, S. C. State Arms, eagle at top, horse each side; steamboat in distance on right; cars and factories on left.	50
100 and C in red.	BK OF HAMBURG, Hamburg, S. C. Head of Liberty surrounded by stars.	100 and C in red.
100 Milkmaid C	Figure of Liberty. Ship taking in freight from boats; bridge; steamboats to left. Figure of Liberty. B'K OF HAMBURG Hamburg, S. C.	C Reaper and dog. 100
5 Male portrait	Vig. Train of cars and group of seven persons; on right, in distance, is cabin and trees; on left, men loading wagon. BK OF NEWBERRY, S. C. Tree.	5 Female portrait.

Left	Center	Right
Male portrait. 10	Vig. Three females and cupid floating in water. BK. OF NEWBERRY, S. C. Tree.	10 Female with sheaf of grain on shoulder.
20 Female with basket of flowers.	Vig. Male, apparently a soldier, female and child; houses, &c. on right and left. BK. OF NEWBERRY, S. C. Tree.	20 Male portrait.
FIFTY 50	Vig. 50; on the left is soldier and female either side of shield; on right negro on cart drawn by two horses. BK OF NEWBERRY, Newberry, S. C.	FIFTY 50
100 Palmetto tree	BK. OF NEWBERRY, Newberry, S. C. 100 Red C 100	100 Negro with cotton; field hands, etc.
5 Med. head FIVE	V Eagle standing on a rock, ships on left. V BK. OF SOUTH CAROLINA, Charleston, S. C.	FIVE Med. head 5
5 FIVE FIVE	Two females erect, male bust and shield in centre; female on right holds Liberty pole and cap; one on left a wreath; ship on right; sheaf of grain on left. 5 BK. OF SOUTH CAROLINA, Charleston, S. C. Tree, &c.	Cotton bales, anchor, &c. Portrait of Calhoun. Train of cars.
Female standing with scales and sword. 10	Eagle, shield and figure 10, BK. OF SOUTH CAROLINA, Charleston, S. C.	Female standing with scales and sword. 10
10 Male and female figures. Steamship.	Steamship under way, shipping on right, shipping on left 10 BK. OF SOUTH CAROLINA, Charleston, S. C. Trees.	Statute of Calhoun erect. TEN
TWENTY	20 Female seated on an anchor; shield and words Twenty Dollars; sheaf of rice on right; ship on left. 20 BK. OF SOUTH CAROLINA, Charleston, S. C. TWENTY TWENTY	TWENTY
FIFTY Female seated. 50	50 Female erect, with spear and right hand resting on a shield and word Fifty. 50 BK. OF SOUTH CAROLINA. Charleston, S. C.	50 Female seated. FIFTY

Left	Center	Right
100 Pillar of a building, and words One Hundred. HUNDRED	Female standing with a sickle in right hand; rocks, vase, &c. The title of the Bank is on either side of vig., in a scroll.	100 Pillar of a building, and words One Hundred. HUNDRED
Statue of J. C. Calhoun erect.	Male Portrait. Workmen at work on a dock; shipping, bales of goods, &c. B'K OF THE STATE OF S. CAROLINA.	ONE Palmetto Tree.
J. C. Calhoun erect.	1 Vig. Cars. B'K OF THE STATE OF S. CAROLINA. Tree, &c.	1 Cotton field.
ONE Female erect with sickle. ONE	1 Female reclining with liberty pole and cap. 1 B'K OF THE STATE OF S. CAROLINA.	Female erect and large fig. 1, extending across the note.
Two on med. head. Locomotive. TWO	Portrait of J. C. Calhoun, and two females seated. B'K OF THE STATE OF S. CAROLINA. Tree, &c.	TWO DOLLARS.
TWO Female erect with sickle, &c. TWO	2 Two females, shield, &c., globe and cars in distance on right, and sheaf of grain on left. 2 B'K OF THE STATE OF S. CAROLINA.	Female erect, and large figure 2.
2 Male portrait.	View of the intended State House at Columbia, S. C. B'K. OF THE STATE OF S. CAROLINA.	TWO Portrait of Calhoun.
3 Female with sickle. 3	3 Farmers eating dinner; dog on left, also other farmers at work. 3 B'K OF THE STATE OF S. CAROLINA.	Female standing and large fig. 3.
Large figure 4. Male portrait.	View of Fort Moultrie. B'K OF THE STATE OF S. CAROLINA.	Large figure 4. Male portrait.
5 Male portrait. 5	5 General Marion inviting a British officer to dinner. 5 B'K OF THE STATE OF S. CAROLINA.	5 Male portrait. 5

Left	Center	Right
10 Female, liberty pole and cap. 10	Male portrait. Male portrait. Vessels of war sailing in the water. B'K OF THE STATE OF S. CAROLINA.	10 Female, scales, and eagle. 10
XX Female, sickle, &c. XX	20 View of a cotton wharf, cars, steamboat, slaves at work, &c. 20 B'K OF THE STATE OF S. CAROLINA	XX Negro plowing. XX
50 Med. Head. 50	50 Two females seated, one holds liberty pole and cap, the other shield and spear; cars on right in distance, steamboat, &c. B'K OF THE S[illegible] OF S. CAROL[illegible]	50
100 C 100	C Female erect, two cherubs, eagle and war generally; ship on right in distance, cars on left in distance. C B'K OF THE STATE OF S. CAROLINA.	[illegible] Hundred [illegible] Dollars.
5 Bust of male. 5	5 Two females, one seated at the feet of the other; grain and farming tools in rear of one, ship in rear of other. 5 COMMERCIAL BANK Columbia, S. C. State arms.	5 Bust of male. 5
X Washington's bust. X	10 Arms of South Carolina, surmounted by spread eagle, a female on either side. 10 COMMERCIAL BANK Columbia, S. C.	X Lafayette's bust. X
20 Male bust in uniform. 20	20 XX surmounted by eagle; female, bale of cotton, water, and sloop on left; female, barrel, water, and schooner on right. 20 COMMERCIAL BANK Columbia, S. C.	20 Male bust in uniform. 20
50 Head of male 50	Female with left hand resting on an urn; an eagle before her resting upon the clouds. COMMERCIAL BANK Columbia, S. C. State arms. 50	
100 Female seated on bale, her left hand on a harp. 100	100 Two female figures, the right hand one standing, the left hand one seated, is almost and holds a wreath in her left hand; water in the distance in the rear, in front a standard, globe, &c. 100 COMMERCIAL BANK Columbia, S. C.	100 Female with sword and scales. 100
Male portrait. 5	EXCHANGE BANK OF COLUMBIA, S. C. Bust of Calhoun, and female seated.	5 Female portrait.

Left	Centre	Right
Portrait of Calhoun. 10	Female seated, with liberty pole and cap in right hand; left hand resting on shield. EXCHANGE BANK OF COLUMBIA, S. C.	10 Female portrait.
Three female figures grouped around an anchor. TWENTY	Female seated; on her right, city in the distance; on the left, rail road in distance. EXCHANGE BANK OF COLUMBIA, S. C. Fire Engine	20 Male portrait
50 [illegible] anchor and chain, bales, and bale of cotton.	Engine and train of cars. EXCHANGE BANK OF COLUMBIA, S. C.	50 Male portrait
100 Portrait of female.	Three graces and a cupid. EXCHANGE BANK OF COLUMBIA, S. C. Farming tools.	100 Female [illegible]
5 Male portrait	Six oxen drawing a load of cotton, negro driver; in distance, house and trees, and negroes picking cotton. FARMERS AND EXCHANGE BANK. Charleston, S. C.	5 Portrait of Calhoun
10 Male portrait	FARMERS' AND EX. BANK, Charleston, S. C. River scene; ships steamers, etc.; houses, &c, in distance.	10 Negroes picking cotton; houses and trees in the distance
20 [illegible] of cotton, two negroes on top; man in front, cart and horse, mule, trees, &c.	FARMERS AND EXCHANGE BANK, Charleston, S. C. XX	20 Portrait of Washington.
50 Same as 20s.	FARMERS' AND EXCHANGE BANK, Charleston, S. C. L	50 Webster.
C Vessels, &c.; small boat in front of a ship.	C FARMERS AND EXCHANGE BANK. Charleston, S. C.	100 Female seated with rake; haymaking in background.
Statue, building & &c.	FIVE Angel flying 5 above shields, female on left; oldest on right. MERCHANTS' BK., Cheraw, S. C.	V Cars, shipping, etc.

Left	Centre	Right
10 Calhoun.	MERCHANTS' BANK of South Carolina, Two females with reel, bale, anchor, &c., ocean scene on left; buildings, etc., on right. Yellow X either side. Cheraw, S. C.	10 Sailor with nautical instruments.
10 Male portrait 10	Steamboat and crocodile. Train of cars. MERCHANTS' BANK Cheraw, S. C. Cherub astride deer	X Ox team. 10
XX OF SOUTH Female portrait.	MERCHANTS' BANK Female on either side of [illegible]; buildings in distance. Cheraw, S. C.	20 CAROLINA Cars, bridge, etc.
FIFTY Sailor, State Arms, [illegible] FIFTY	THE MERCHANTS 50 Negroes picking and carrying cotton. Bank of South Carol'a Cheraw, S. C.	50 Cotton weighing scene.
V FI V VE V	Cattle scene; steamboat in distance. PEOPLES' BANK OF S. C.	5 Male portrait
Word Capital and figures 1,000,000, supported by three females as a pedestal. TEN	PEOPLES' BANK OF S. C Blacksmith beside an anvil, right hand holding hammer, left resting on cog wheel.	10 Female figure, head partially covered.
Female seated with sickle. 20	20 PEOPLES' BANK OF S. C. Portrait of W. R. King of Ala.	20 Stone mason at work, tools, &c., at his feet.
50 Two female figures seated, surveying a cotton field and negroes at work with railroad [illegible] in distance.	PEOPLES' BANK OF S. C. Portrait of John C. Calhoun.	50 Blacksmith standing beside his anvil, hand resting on the handle of his sledge. Anchor and cog wheel near him.
Childe's [illegible] [illegible] full head of steam and [illegible] in distance C	C PEOPLES' BANK OF S. C Game cock crowing.	100 Male portrait
Ceres. FIVE	Cotton, bale and Planter on horseback, negroes picking cotton. PLANTER'S BANK of FAIRFIELD, S. C. Palmetto	5 Portrait of a female

Left	Centre	Right
X Drove of Cattle.	Agricultural device, with a female, sickle in her left hand; coat of arms. PLANTER'S BANK of FAIRFIELD, S. C. Plow.	10 Train of rail road cars.
20 Goddess of Liberty.	PLANTER'S BANK of FAIRFIELD, S. C. Palmetto, cotton bales, wheat, plow, &c.; railroad cars in the distance on the left, steamship in the distance on the right.	20 Washington on horseback
25 Two females and cotton field.	PLANTER'S BANK of FAIRFIELD, S. C.	25 Portrait of Calhoun.
50 Ceres sitting on a sow.	PLANTER'S BANK of FAIRFIELD, S. C. Bust of Calhoun. Cotton Stalk in Bloom. Coat of Arms. Female with a wreath.	50 Portrait of Jackson.
C Portrait of Washington.	Capitol at Washington. PLANTER'S BANK of FAIRFIELD, S. C.	100 American Eagle and shield.
5 Car. FIVE	PLANTERS' & MECHANICS' BANK, Charleston, S. C. Female, globe and eagle. Dog's head	5 Figure 5 and word Five. 5
FIVE	Two Cupids seated; one drawing, the other reading; sheaf of grain, bee-hive, &c.; ship on left in distance. Double Med. head. Title of Bank. Eagle and portrait of Washington.	Med. head and figure 5 FIVE Med. head and figure 5
5 V FIVE	PLANTERS & MECHANICS B'K, Charleston, S. C. FIVE on 5 Female, globe and eagle. DOLLARS on 5. Dog's head.	5 V 5
10 Male portrait 10	Med. head, and figure 10. Barrel, half of cotton, sheaf of rice, farming implements, and cotton plant. Med. head, and figure 10. Title of Bank. Arm and hammer.	TEN
TEN Med. head. TEN	10 Title of Bank 10 Large eagle on limb of a tree; cask on right. Arm, anvil, wheel, hammer, &c.	TEN Med. head. TEN

S. CAROLINA.

TEN — Female with chickens. — TEN
10 PLANTERS' & MECHANICS' BANK. 10
Charleston, S. C.
X Spread eagle on limb of tree. X
Arm and hammer.
TEN — Female. — TEN

20 — Male portrait — 20
Eagle, shield, and ornamental figure 20.
PLANTERS' & MECHANICS' BANK, Charleston, S. C.
Sword, scales, &c.
Male portrait. — 20 — Male portrait.

Male portrait — FIFTY DOLLARS
50 Three females, eagle, and ornamental fig. 50. 50
Title of Bank.
Portrait of Wm. Penn.
Male portrait — Fifty

Portrait of Franklin.
100 Male portrait. Two females; one seated, and one standing; one on right holds sickle, &c; sheep on the ground and ship on left in distance. Male portrait. 100
Title of Bank.
Portrait of Washington

POST NOTE
Farming implements and sheaf of grain. Title of Bank.
Mechanical implements.
500
500 DOLLARS

Coat of Arms of S. Carolina. — 5 — Coat of Arms of Kentucky.
5 Locomotive and tender with portion of a car. 5
SOUTH WESTERN RAIL ROAD BANK, Charleston, S. C.
Ship under full sail.
Coat of Arms of N. Carolina. — 5 — Coat of Arms of Tennessee.

Coat of Arms of S. Carolina. — 10 — Coat of Arms of Kentucky.
10 Locomotive and tender with portion of a car. 10
SOUTH WESTERN RAIL ROAD BANK, Charleston, S. C.
Ship under full sail.
Coat of Arms of N. Carolina. — 10 — Coat of Arms of Tennessee.

Coat of Arms of S. Carolina. — 20 — Coat of Arms of Kentucky.
20 Ship under full sail. 20
[illegible] in foreground, a perspective of Charleston in background left of ship.
SOUTH WESTERN RAIL ROAD BANK, Charleston, S. C.
[illegible]
Coat of Arms of N. Carolina. — 20 — Coat of Arms of Tennessee.

Coat of Arms of S. Carolina. — 50 — Coat of Arms of Kentucky.
50 Vig. Same as 20. 50
SOUTH WESTERN RAIL ROAD BANK, Charleston, S. C.
Locomotive train.
Coat of Arms of N. Carolina. — 50 — Coat of Arms of Tennessee.

Coat of Arms of S. Carolina. — 100 — Coat of Arms of Kentucky.
100 Vig. Same as 20. 100
SOUTH WESTERN RAIL ROAD BANK, Charleston, S. C.
Locomotive and train.
Coat of Arms of N. Carolina. — 100 — Coat of Arms of Tennessee.

S. CAROLINA.

5 — Cars — 5
Med. head and letter V. Male portrait. Med. head and letter V.
STATE BANK, Charleston, S. C.
Two angels in a boat.
5 — Cars — 5

V
STATE BANK, Charleston, S. C.
View of the State Bank in Charleston, corner of East Bay and Broad sts.
5 — V

10 — Female seated. — X
X Cars, trees, &c. 10
STATE BANK, Charleston, S. C.
Male portrait.
X — Female seated. — 10

10 — Female sheaf of wheat. — 10
View of harbor, shipping, &c.
STATE BANK, Charleston, S. C.
10 — TEN

Portrait of Franklin.
20 Water scene, female seated in a car. 20
STATE BANK, Charleston, S. C.
Farming implements.
Portrait of Washington.

50 — Man seated drawing.
STATE BANK, Charleston, S. C.
Indians, shield, cotton plant, female and child, real globe, sheaf of wheat on right.
Female in water.
50 — Steamboat under way, and men in small boat.

Portrait of Washington.
C Female erect and sheaf of grain; man ploughing on right. Figures 100 and cupid.
STATE BANK, Charleston, S. C.
C
100

CHARLESTON.
5 Two females seated on bales; factory in distance. 5
UNION BANK OF SOUTH CAROLINA.
Male bust.
S. CAROLINA.

FIVE
5 Female seated holding sickle; bird, and ship in distance on right; sheep in distance on left. 5
UNION B'K of SOUTH CAROLINA, Charleston, S. C.
V.
SO. CAROLINA.

TEN
X Female seated holding liberty pole; ship on right. X
UNION B'K of SOUTH CAROLINA, Charleston, S. C.
TEN DOLLARS.

GEORGIA.

TWENTY
20 Female seated with sickle, a scroll, and word twenty; vessel on left. 20
UNION B'K of SOUTH CAROLINA, Charleston, S. C.
XX
SOUTH CAROLINA

ONE HUN.
100 Female reclining; man ploughing on right; ship and sheep on right. 100
UNION B'K of SOUTH CAROLINA, Charleston, S. C.
C
ONE HUNDRED

1 — ONE
AUGUSTA INS. & BANKING CO., Geo.
Female head
Boy, horse, girl, etc., at trough.
1 — 1 — 1

ONE — Two lovers — ONE
Interior of blacksmith's shop, with men at work. 1 on med head on either side.
AUGUSTA INS. AND BANKING CO., Augusta, Geo.
ONE — 1 on med. head. — ONE

2 — Washington. — TWO
2 Horse and train of cars; houses in background. 2
Title of Bank.
Portrait of Clay. Liberty in figure 2; cars and factory on left.

2 — Female and dove.
Farmer and horse; wheelwrights at work on wagon body.
Title of Bank.
2 — Liberty and State Arms

FIVE — Male portrait — FIVE
Title of Bank.
Med. head and fig. 5. Med. head and fig. 5.
Two females on a rock; cars on right; vessels on left.
V V
FIVE — Female with cornucopia. — FIVE

5 — Cooper, barrels, etc.
Title of Bank.
Male and female either side of State Arms on shield; steamboat, cars, etc.
5
5 — Girl's head.

Cupid with sheaf. — 10 — Male portrait.
Title of Bank.
Negro with white and black horse; wagon, horses, cotton field, etc.
Eagle.
Cupid and cornucopia. — State Arms.

10 — Male portrait — 10
Med hd and fig. 100. Spread eagle on shield; vessels on left. Med hd and fig. 100.
Title of Bank.
X Dog's head. X
TEN — Female with sword and balances. — TEN

Left	Centre	Right
20 Washington. 20	Med. head and figures 20. Med. head and figures 20. Signing the Declaration of Independence. Title of Bank. 20 20	20 Female seated with book; village in background. DOLLARS
XX 20	Title of Bank. Shield, female with sword and balances, seated on merchandise; cars crossing bridge on left. TWENTY.	20 Man plowing with two horses.
50 50	Title of Bank. Female. Shield on either side a female.	50
100 C	United States Capitol. Title of Bank.	100
Elk. Factory.	1 Female seated, bales; steamship in distance. BANK OF ATHENS, Athens, Geo. State Arms.	1 ONE
2 Female with sheaf and sickle.	Load of cotton bales, drawn by two horses; houses, trees, &c. BANK OF ATHENS, Athens, Geo. Ducks.	2 Male portrait.
V	Men harvesting. Male portrait. BANK OF ATHENS, Athens, Geo. Dog.	5 FIVE 5
10 Negro with basket of cotton.	BANK OF ATHENS, Athens, Geo. Female seated with mechanical implements; factory and train of cars in distance. Ducks.	10 State Arms.
Word twenty running across [illegible] XX	Four females at work on cotton machine. State Arms. BANK OF ATHENS, Athens, Geo. Dog.	20 XX
Dis. Sheep shearing.	L Shield, surmounted by eagle; Justice on right, Liberty on left. BANK OF ATHENS, Athens, Geo.	50 Male portrait.

Left	Centre	Right
C 100 C	Cattle and sheep. BANK OF ATHENS, Athens, Geo. State Arms.	100 Female reclining on bales.
ONE Female and three children. ONE	Three females reclining, eagle, &c. BANK OF AUGUSTA, Augusta, Ga.	1 Train of cars.
Female erect, Med. Head, &c. TWO	2 Female seated; sheaf of wheat, &c. BANK OF AUGUSTA, Augusta, Ga.	TWO 2
5 Female. 5	FIVE Female seated holding an eagle; female on left. FIVE BANK OF AUGUSTA, Augusta, Ga. Female.	5 Beehive. 5
10 Portrait of Franklin.	Female seated holding vase of flowers; shipping on right; town factories on left. BANK OF AUGUSTA, Augusta, Ga. State Arms.	10 An old man seated, partly supported by a staff reading a book.
20 Male portrait. TWENTY	Shield with a miniature view of sunrise, mountain scenery, water, small sail vessels, &c.; a female seated on either side of shield, locomotive and steamboat in distance. Title of Bank. State Arms.	20 Train of cars. XX
20 Male portrait. XX	XX Train of cars crossing a bridge. XX BANK OF AUGUSTA, Augusta, Ga. Key.	Military Gen. seated holding a book. XX
50 Portrait of Washington. FIFTY	Large spread eagle; sail vessels on either side. BANK OF AUGUSTA, Augusta, Ga. State Arms.	Male portrait. 50 Male portrait.
ONE Portrait of Boy.	BK OF COLUMBUS, Columbus, Geo. Wagon loaded with cotton—six mules before it; another wagon drawn by oxen.	1 Female with sickle and sheaf. 1
TWO 2	Title of Bank. Local view; river, bridge, steamboat, locomotive, trees, &c.	2 2

Left	Centre	Right
V 5 V	Cars passing under bridge with people, horses and carriage on it. Title of Bank. State Arms.	5 Washington.
TEN Girl seated.	Title of Bank. Female seated with infant; child offering birds nest; dog lying; man and woman at work in field. Ducks.	10 State Arms.
XX Female seated resting left hand on ledge; right foot on pail.	Local view; cotton factories on river bank; six mules before wagon load of cotton. Title of Bank. Ducks.	20 Scene in a cotton field; man working; man on horseback. XX
L	Title of Bank. Vig. in lower left corner of note—Local view on river; steamboat, bridge, &c.; cars in background. State Arms.	50 Washington.
100 Figs. 100 across words "One Hundred." C	Title of Bank. Vig. in large ornamental C; Hunter seated, warming his hands at fire, dog on right.	100 Figs. 100 across word Dollars. C
500 Female portrait.	B'K OF COLUMBUS, Columbus, Geo. Bust of Washington on shield; female, two Indians, soldier, etc. Has part of Title either side.	500 Portrait of female.
1 Negro with basket of cotton.	Ship—scene at sea. BK OF COMMERCE, Savannah, Geo. Dog.	1 ONE 1
TWO	2 Blacksmith shop—men at work; man plowing in distance. BK. OF COMMERCE, Savannah, Geo. Ducks.	2 Girl.
V Girl.	BK OF COMMERCE, Savannah, Geo. Shield on which is State Arms—female bust at top, on right soldier and war-like implements; on left female. Female bathing.	5 FIVE 5
X TEN X	BK OF COMMERCE, Savannah, Geo. Steamship. State Arms.	10 Indian.

GEORGIA.	GEORGIA.	GEORGIA.
20 — B'K OF COMMERCE, Savannah, Geo. — 20 Raft of timber floating down the river; boat, men, women and children on it; other rafts in distance. View of cattle, telegraph, railroad, etc. Woodman with axe, trees, logs, &c.	2 — BANK OF FULTON, Atlanta, Geo. — 2 Tobacco plantation, two men and bale. Female with spear. Locomotive.	5 — Portrait of Washington with female on either side; sickle, sheaf and locomotive on right; on left shipping. — 5 Title of Bank. Cars passing under arch; load of hay on top.
50 — B'K OF COMMERCE, Savannah, Geo. — 50 Farmer and drover bargaining for ox; farm yard scene, &c. Ship, steamship and brig; city in distance; Cotton plantation.	Hunter loading rifle, deer at his feet. — Female reclining, eagle, drapery, &c.; city, train of cars, bridge, &c., in distance. — 5 BANK OF FULTON. Atlanta, Geo. 5 Portrait of female.	TEN — Female seated with shield, pole, cap and eagle; rising sun in distance. — 10 Title of Bank. Male, female, boy, girl, dog and chickens. Woodman felling tree; another seated.
C — B'K OF COMMERCE, Savannah, Geo. — 100 Large C; and words one hundred dollars. Five females in the clouds One Hundred Male portrait	Female and Indian either side of X. — BANK OF FULTON, Atlanta, Geo. — 10 Train of cars; city, river, etc. 10 Soldier and seaman. Male portrait	XX — Title of Bank. — 20 TWENTY DOLLARS Female. Indian female and child.
FIVE HUNDRED Goddess of Liberty, erect. BK OF COMMERCE, Savannah, Geo. Ship to circular die.	Train of cars — BANK OF FULTON, Atlanta, Georgia. — 10 X and Ten Two males erect and a female seated; buildings, &c. X	50 — BANK OF MIDDLE GEORGIA, Macon, Geo. — 50 Reaper reclining. 50 on three red dies. Cupid. Sailor seated.
ONE — BK OF THE EMPIRE STATE, Rome, Geo. — 1 Female seated with State Arms; pole and cap in her left hand. Man seated beside river; quadrant, &c. at his side. Docks. Female portrait.	Female gathering wheat. — Title of Bank. — 20 Male portrait. XX Blacksmith, anvil, &c., and city in distance.	100 — Title of Bank. — 100 100 and words one hundred dollars on three red dies. Three females; cars and city in distance. Two Indians, canoe and deer.
Washington. — Steamboat "Pennington" country in background; men in boat. — 2 Sailor erect beside female seated. Title of Bank. Justice.	Drover and cattle. — Spread eagle. — 20 Title of Bank. XX Temple. Clay	500 — Title of Bank. — 500 Five Hundred on red lathe work. Five cupids, globe and anvil. Five cherubs, with cake and tablets.
5 — Title of Bank. — 5 Female seated with infant; child offering her bird's nest; man and woman at work in field. Indian on cliff viewing the progress of Civilization Docks. State Arms.	50 — Two females seated with view of sunrise on shield. — 50 Title of Bank. Bank building Male portrait FIFTY	Liberty beside column. — 1 — Shipping scene. — 1 BK. OF SAVANNAH, Savannah, Geo. Female portrait.
X — Title of Bank. — 10 Farmer seated; girl and horses on his left; boy and dog on right. Female seated. State Arms. TEN	100 — Title of Bank. — 100 Sailor, female and mechanic seated; buildings, etc., on right; shipping scene on left. Portrait of girl. Anchor on shield. Letter C enclosing bust of female & sheaf.	Goddess of Liberty. — ONE — Vig. Steamship. — 1 BK. OF SAVANNAH, Savannah, Geo Bust of female. ONE
Vig. 20 across female seated on either side of State Arms; train of cars. — 20 XX Title of Bank. Docks. Clay.	Man watering three horses at trough; sheep, goat and kid; trees and house. — 1 BANK OF MIDDLE GEORGIA, Macon, Geo. 1 Justice seated; dog.	Sailor — Three negroes at work in field. — 2 Title of Bank. 2 Cotton plant.
1 — BANK OF FULTON, Atlanta, Geo — 1 Farm scene; farmer and drover bargaining for ox. View of cattle, telegraph and railroad. Woodman felling a tree; another seated.	TWO — State Arms with female on left, and Indian on right. — 2 Title of Bank. Female feeding chickens. Four horses before wagon.	Sailor. — Med. Head. — Female seated with pole and cap, and shield; spread eagle on right. — 2 Cotton plant &c. TWO — BK. OF SAVANNAH, Savannah, Geo. — TWO

Three females holding aloft, frame on which is letter V. FIVE	5 Two females seated; on right, cotton plant, wagon and two mules; on left, vessel and steamboat. BK. OF SAVANNAH, Savannah, Geo.	5 FIVE 5
10 Indian Princess seated, with pole, cap and shield. TEN	Female portrait. Ship, steamship, &c., in distance; on left, view of ship, &c. BK. OF SAVANNAH, Savannah, Geo.	10 Female with sheaf of wheat. TEN
20 Justice with scales and sword.	Vig. Spread eagle, with a ship each side. BK. OF SAVANNAH, Savannah, Geo.	20 Bust of Webster.
50 Bust of Gen. Cass. 50	BK. OF SAVANNAH, Savannah, Geo. Female bust.	FIFTY Washington on horseback. FIFTY
100 Genius of Liberty, with liberty pole and cap; rays of light radiating from the head.	Vig. Coat of Arms of Georgia; on the right, a plough and agricultural products; on the left, female reaper, with sheaf and railroad view. 100 BK. OF SAVANNAH, Savannah, Geo. Spread Eagle.	ONE HUNDRED
1 Female. ONE	1 Female Indian, shield, merchandise, compass, artists' tools, etc.; ship on right. 1 BK. OF THE STATE OF GEORGIA.	Female with cornucopia. ONE
1 Female head.	B'K OF THE STATE OF GEORGIA. Two females seated; train of cars, negroes in field, &c.	1 1
TWO Female Indian, artists' tools, merchandise &c. TWO	Med. head and Two on it. Med. head and Two on it. Female on either side of a shield. BK. OF THE STATE OF GEORGIA.	2 Female with sword and scales in figure 2. TWO
2 Negro picking cotton.	B'K OF THE STATE OF GEORGIA. Four females on globe. 2 2	2 2
Liberty resting left hand on shield.	5 Floating female with cornucopia. BK. OF THE STATE OF GEORGIA.	5 Canal and bridge. 5

View of building, trees and monument. 5	BK. OF THE STATE OF GEORGIA. Red die. Savannah, Geo.	5 Squaw.
X Red work.	Title of Bank. Vig. Same as on left of 5s.	10 Red work.
TEN Ship. TEN	10 Female seated on merchandise, holding scales; cars, wharf and ship on left; houses in background. BK. OF THE STATE OF GEORGIA.	X Liberty, eagle and shield.
TWENTY Female with wand, seated on merchandise. 20	20 Spread eagle; farm scene on left; light house and vessels on right. BK. OF THE STATE OF GEORGIA.	20 Female, grain and sickle.
XX Red work.	Title of Bank. Vig. Same as left of 5's.	20 Red work.
Female with cornucopia. 50	BK. OF THE STATE OF GEORGIA. Words Fifty Dollars, and figures 50.	50 Sailors' head.
C Female, grain, and sickle.	BK. OF THE STATE OF GEORGIA. Words One Hundred Dollars, and figures 100.	100 Vessel.
ONE DOLLAR	[Old Plate.] Eagle and figure 1. Railroad scene; engine and train of cars. CENTRAL RAIL ROAD AND BANKING CO. OF GEORGIA. Savannah, Geo.	1 Blacksmith' arm holding a sledge-hammer.
1 Engine and cars.	[New Plate.] Stone Quarry; one man seated and two standing. Title of Bank.	1 Female seated.
2 Two blacksmiths striking upon an anvil.	Engine and train of cars. Title of Bank.	2 Female seated with wheel.

Three females one above another with anchor. FIVE	Title of Bank. Train of Cars.	5 Watch dog. 5
[illegible] Schooner under full sail. 5 Engine and cars.	[Old Plate.] 5 View of rising sun surmounted by an eagle; on right, female seated with cap of liberty; on left, female erect with scales. 5 Title of Bank.	Steamboat. 5 Ship under full sail.
5 FIVE 5 FIVE	General scene at depot on arrival of cars. CENTRAL R. R. AND BANK'NG COMPANY Savannah, Geo.	5 FIVE 5 FIVE
10 Female seated. 10	Old Plate.] X Train of cars X Title of Bank.	10
10 Sailor leaning on capstan & bale. TEN	[New Plate.] Title of Bank. Engine and passenger car.	10 Gen. Washington on horseback. TEN
Liberty beside column on which is word TEN.	10 Spread eagle on shield. Title of Bank.	X 10 X
20 Female standing, holding scales. 20	[Old Plate.] XX Engine and cars. XX Title of Bank.	XX
Three females—one above the other, and anchor. TWENTY	[New Plate] 20 Eagle. Title of Bank.	20 Engine. 20
20 Negro carrying cotton; two others picking.	Title of Bank. TWENTY DOLLARS.	20 Female with flowers.
Group: Vulcan, Ceres, and Mercury. 50	L Engine and cars. L Title of Bank.	50 Engine and cars on a bridge. 50

GEORGIA.	GEORGIA.	GEORGIA.
50 — Female with cornucopia. CENTRAL R. R. & BANKING CO. Savannah, Geo. Train of cars; trees, houses, sloop and large chimney. Dog's head. 50 — Millard Fillmore.	100 Female soaring in clouds with eagle, sword, balances, &c. Letter C with word ONE above and word HUNDRED below it. Title of Bank 100 — Three females, one above the other; one leaning on anchor.	TWO 2 Old-fashioned train of cars. 2 Title of Bank. TWO
ONE HUNDRED 100 Engine and cars. 100 Title of Bank. ONE HUNDRED	1 1 FAR. & MECH. B'K, Savannah, Geo. Two females seated by anvil; factories in distance. Female erect with sword and shield. 1 Boy's head. 1 ONE	2 — Female portrait. 2 Large figure 2, with Mercury seated on left; figure of Justice erect, on right. Title of Bank. TWO — Female seated, leaning on her left hand.
100 — Trees, wagon, train of cars crossing bridge; city in distance. CENTRAL R. R. & BANKING CO. Savannah, Geo. Three females in clouds. Locomotive. 100 — Ship; city in distance.	2 — Cattle, trees and children. 2 Title of Bank. 2 Locomotive. 2 — Cotton plantation scene.	V — Female seated leaning on shield, on which is plow and harrow. Med figure 5. Man plowing with two horses. Med figure 5. Title of Bank. Cupid astride a deer. V — Drover, cattle and sheep. V
500 Title of Bank. Three females in clouds; one crowning bust. 500	5 — Girl's head. Title of Bank. 5 Statue of female erect. 5 FIVE FIVE 5 — Boy's head.	5 — Train of cars. V Med head and figure 5. Country inn of two stories with piazza to each; tree on right; train of cars in front. Med head and figure 5. Title of Bank. Locomotive and tender. FIVE
Indian on rock, gun by his side. 1 Boy reclining watching flock of sheep; village in distance. CITY BANK, Augusta, Ga. Dog's head. 1 — Female portrait.	10 — Female, column; ship in distance. Cows in water; children by tree. Title of Bank. X TEN X 10 — Calhoun.	FIVE 5 FIVE Modern train of cars; a building with Grecian front in the distance. Title of Bank 5 — Figure of Justice with scales and sword.
TWO — Hunter with dog and gun. St. George and the Dragon. CITY BANK, Augusta, Ga. Dog's head. 2 — Indian princess seated.	Cupid with sheaf. Sailor and mechanic; shipping, etc. 20 State portrait 20 FARMERS' & MECHANICS' BANK, Savannah, Geo Cupid with cornucopia. Female portrait.	TEN Female med. head. Train of cars; on left house and trees. Female med. head. Title of Bank. Locomotive and tender 10 — Cupid's die. 10
Word five in part circle. 5 Word five in part circle. Large building surrounded by trees; man on horseback. CITY BANK. Augusta, Ga. [illegible]	50 — Female, column, etc. Sailor reclining on anchor, boat, etc.; steamship in distance. Title of Bank. 50 L 50 50 — Female with State Arms.	Indian warrior holding in left hand, in right bow and arrows. TEN TEN Eagle on limb of tree; canal scene and train of cars in background. Title of Bank. 10 — Indian squaw holding ear of corn in right hand; left hand resting on X.
Female blowing horn for farmers to return to [illegible]. CITY BANK, Augusta, Va. Ten X Dollars. 10 — Male gathering fruit; baskets, &c.	100 — Negro with two horses. C Title of Bank. C HUNDRED 100 HUNDRED 100 — Female, bale, shipping, etc. C	10 — Female seated and leaning on shield of Rhode Island. 10 Med. X. Steamboat with two upper decks; alligator in foreground. Med. X. Title of Bank. Steamboat. X
20 XX 20 Two oxen before load of straw; man with fork walking by the side, and man asleep on top of load. CITY BANK, Augusta Ga. Ducks. 20 — Three Dogs. XX	ONE 1 Old fashioned train of cars; building with cupola, and other buildings in distance. 1 GEO. R. R. & BANKING CO. Augusta, Geo. ONE — State arms. ONE	TWENTY XX State arms. XX Title of Bank. Steamboat. 2 — Female holding scale with right hand; shield on left, surmounted by an eagle. 20
50 — Dog's Head. L CITY BANK, Augusta, Ga. Spread eagle on globe; names of a few States on flags, &c. 50	1 — Bust of young female. Female with arm over eagle's neck; cornucopia of fruit and flowers; eagle on shield. 1 Title of Bank. ONE — Female figure erect.	20 — Mercury seated, figures 2 and 0. TWENTY Female seated with pole and cap in hand, on right an eagle; near her is a shield, on which is fig. 20. Title of Bank. 20 — Female with left hand on anchor; on right cornucopia.

Left	Centre	Right
FIFTY	L Old fashioned train of cars and a five story house. L Title of Bank. Old fashioned train of cars	L State arms. 50
Female Indian with bow and spear in hand, quiver on her back. FIFTY	50 Bust of Washington above the shield of the U. S., with female on either side, the one on left, placing a wreath on his brow. Title of Bank.	50 Portrait of Mrs. Washington.
ONE HUNDRED	100 Old fashioned 100 train of cars. Title of Bank.	ONE HUNDRED
100 Sailor with left hand on capstan.	Female seated, holding shield which is resting on a cornucopia; ship in distance. Title of Bank. Cogwheels and other machinery.	100 Female holding [illegible] flag; three naked infants near [illegible]
5 Bust of a Female. FIVE	INTERIOR BANK, Griffin, Geo. Farm scene, plowman, &c; on the right in distance train of cars, on left, house, etc.	FIVE Female feeding horse.
1 Female.	Portrait of Washington. Spread eagle on shield, ship on left. LAGRANGE BANK, Lagrange, Geo.	Word ONE and fig. 1. Square and compass
2 Female Head.	Single female with sword and balance seated on merchandise, cars crossing bridge on left, cotton plant and basket on right. LAGRANGE BANK, Lagrange, Geo.	2 Female in fig. 2. Female giving eagle drink.
FIVE Female.	Two females representing Commerce and Agriculture. Train of Cars. LAGRANGE BANK, Lagrange, Geo.	Word FIVE, fig. 5, and letter V. Female with scroll and scales seated on merchandise cars on left.
Figure of Justice. TEN	10 Liberty and eagle. LAGRANGE BANK, Lagrange, Geo.	10 X 10
ONE Man on horse	MARINE BANK OF GEORGIA. Portrait of Female. One.	1 ONE

Left	Centre	Right
2 Boat and anchor, two sailors one with spy glass.	MARINE BANK OF GEORGIA, Male Portrait. TWO	2 2
FIVE Group of figures, liberty, &c.	MARINE BANK OF GEORGIA. Male Portrait. FIVE	FIVE 5
MARINE B'K OF GA X 10	Male portrait. Jasper rescuing the American prisoners. MARINE BANK OF GEORGIA TEN	10
20 XX	MARINE BANK OF GEORGIA. Vig. Coat of arms; male figure on either side.	20 Male portrait.
50 L	MARINE BANK OF GEORGIA, Vig. General Oglethorpe in council with the Indians. Male portrait.	50
Title of Bank. 50 Sailor, barrels, bales, etc.	MARINE BANK, OF GEORGIA. Male portrait	50 Indians and white men
Title of Bank 100 State Arms	Title of Bank. Large red C with male portrait at bottom.	100 Male with trident gazing on town and vessels.
100 C	MARINE BANK OF GEORGIA. Male figure with trident; view of ocean and ship; city in distance. Male portrait	100
ONE Portrait of Washington. ONE	Spread eagle on limb of tree, train of cars and buildings in distance. 1 MECHANICS' BANK, Augusta, Ga. Mechanic's arm, anvil, &c	ONE
TWO Female portrait TWO	2 Mechanic seated, left arm on anvil. 2 MECHANICS' BANK. Augusta, Ga. Eagle.	TWO

Left	Centre	Right
5 Female at spinning wheel. V	Female reclining on fig. 5; medall. Head on either side; plow and buildings in distance. MECHANICS' BANK, Augusta, Ga. Mechanic's arm.	V Female with rake and twig 5
10 Indian seated 10	Eagle on trunk of tree. Medall. Head on either side; steamboat on left. MECHANICS' BANK, Augusta, Ga. Mechanics arm.	X Indian seated X
20 Female; ship in distance. XX	Female in car drawn by two horses on water; Medall. Head on either side; ship's masts in distance. MECHANICS' BANK, Augusta, Ga. Mechanic's Arm.	XX Same as 5's. 20
Two males and one female anvil and hammer 50	L Train of cars. L MECHANICS' BANK, Augusta, Ga. Mechanic's Arm.	Steamboat, snake in form of a circle inside of which is building with three pillars and man. 50
Nude female erect, standing in smoke, fig. in clouds; horses in water. 100	100 Vig. Same as 50's. 100 MECHANICS' BANK, Augusta, Ga. Mechanic's Arm.	100 Male in car drawn by two horses, a figure soaring in clouds. 100
ONE and 1. Franklin.	MER. & PLANTERS' BANK, Savannah, Geo. Wagons loaded with cotton. State Arms.	ONE and 1. Train of cars.
2 Washington.	MER. & PLANTERS' BANK. Savannah, Geo. Men harvesting wheat. State Arms.	2 Portrait of Martha Washington
3 THREE 3	MERCHANTS' AND PLANTERS' BANK. Savannah, Geo. Steamship; city and vessels in distance. State Arms.	3 Clay.
5 V	State Arms; female on either side. Steamboat. Title of Bank. Ducks.	5 Train of cars V
TEN Male portrait	Title of Bank. Female seated; houses, trees, &c. in distance. Dog.	10 State Arms.

GEORGIA.

20 — Title of Bank. Shield with female on either side; ship and train of cars in distance. State Arms. — 20. Man on horse. Shipbuilder; ship on stocks.

50 — Title of Bank. State Arms; black horse on right; light house on left; eagle at top. Ducks. — 50. Sailor and implements of warfare. Justice.

Female seated by side of State Arms. — Female seated; man plowing, and factories in distance. C. Title of Bank. Ducks. — Sailor seated on bale. 100. 100.

NORTH WESTERN BANK, OF GEORGIA, Ringgold, Geo. Male portrait on either side. 10. — Indian reading of viewing progress of civilization. — 10. Train on large X; milkmaid, barn, cars, &c.

Female soaring in clouds with sprig and dagger. — Title of Bank. Female with fig. 2 on left and 0 on right. Clasped hands. — Female in clouds with flowers. 20. 20.

1 — Farmer and sailor; ship in distance. PLANTERS' BANK Savannah, Geo. ONE 1 ONE — 1. Male portrait. Girl's head.

2 — Female portrait. Title of Bank. Boy on horseback with another horse by trough, female, etc. 2 — 2. 2. Cupid.

FIVE Med. head. FIVE — Med. head and U. S. — Liberty and Agriculture on either side of fig. 5; view of village on right and left. — Med. head and fig. 5. PLANTERS BANK OF the STATE of GEO. Savannah, Geo. — FIVE Female. FIVE

5 — PLANTERS BANK OF GEORGIA. Savannah, Ga. Man and negro at grindstone, farming scene. Eagle. — 5. Female portrait. Female head.

TEN Med. head, TEN — Title of Bank. Med. head and Ten. Two females, with pole and scroll; cars on right; vessels on left. Med. head and Ten. — X Female. 10

GEORGIA.

10 — PLANTERS B'K OF GEORGIA. Savannah, Ga. X 10 X Child's head. — 10. Boy's head. Female with dove.

20 — Title of Bank. Med. head and fig. 20. Female Indian reclining on shield; steamship on right; implements and artists' tools around her. Med. head and fig. 20. — 20. Washington. 20. Female. 20.

50 — Med. head and figures 50. Two females, Agriculture and Commerce. Med. head and figures 50. Title of Bank. — Female with cornucopia. Med. head. 50. 50.

100 C Spread eagle on branch of tree. C Title of Bank. — Med. head. 100. Female erect with liberty pole and cap.

1 — Men on horseback; negroes tapping pine trees. TIMBER CUTTERS' BANK, Savannah, Ga. — 1. Negroes in cotton field. Sailor reclining on bale.

2 — 2 Negro with hoe and tobacco leaves. 2 Title of Bank. — 2. Girl. Sailor boy.

Female soaring above buildings, river, cars, steamboat, etc.; country scene on upper right. — Title of Bank. Raft scene on Western river; steamboat. — 5.

10 — Two females with spinning wheel; buildings and cattle in background. TIMBER CUTTERS BANK, Savannah, Geo. — 10. Female portrait. 10 inverted.

20 — Title of Bank. Corn gathering scene. — 20. Female with dove. Female with sheafs.

Farmer, boy, girl, dog, houses, etc. Train of coal cars. Title of Bank. — 50. 50. Girl's head.

ALABAMA.

1 — Cupid rolling silver $; train of cars, &c., in background. UNION BANK, Augusta, Ga. — 1. Female with basket of flowers. ONE. Female figure with left hand resting on shield and surrounded by names of the States.

2 — Two Cupids and two silver dollars. UNION BANK. Augusta, Ga. — 2. Portrait of Female. Sailor with quadrant, casks, &c.

Female and two cows. 5 — Female Portrait. UNION BANK. Augusta, Ga. — 5 FIVE 5.

TEN X — Two females; between them a shield on which is a cotton plant and a horse's head for a crest, horn of plenty, bale, &c. UNION BANK. Augusta, Ga. — 10. Female [illegible] and bust.

20 — Train of cars. UNION BANK. Augusta, Ga. — 20. Head of Washington. Female with pole and cap, shield, &c.

50 — State Arms surmounted by an eagle; on either side a female, motto "Independence." UNION BANK, Augusta, Ga. — 50. Sailor with quadrant, bales, &c. Female with maps, books, compass, &c., around her.

100 — Female reclining against bales; behind bales, an eagle with U. S. shield suspended from neck by a chain, motto "E Pluribus Unum," in distance steamboat with masts and ship. UNION BANK, Augusta, Ga. — 100. Female seated on anchor. State Arms, Indian on left and sailor on right, ship masts in distance.

500 — UNION BANK, Augusta, Geo. 5 0 0 FIVE HUNDRED DOLLARS — 500. Female in clouds with cornucopia. Female in clouds with quadrant.

5 — Male portrait. Two females reclining; cars, train, and canal on right; shipping on left. Male portrait. BANK OF MOBILE, Mobile, Ala. Steamship. — 5. Portrait of Washington. Med. head.

10 — Portrait of Washington. Sailor reclining, holds American flag; bale of goods, &c.; ship on left. Portrait of Jefferson. BANK OF MOBILE, Mobile, Ala. Shipping. — 10. Female. Female, scales, eagle, &c.

Left	Centre	Right
Neptune. 10	Female reclining, and eagle with head of Washington on its breast; figs 10 on left of vignette. BANK OF MOBILE, Alabama. Lion.	10 Half eagel. 10
20 Two vessels.	Steamboat, vessels, harbor, docks, &c. BANK OF MOBILE, Mobile, Ala. Dog's head.	20 Cotton plant
TWENTY	Female seated holding balances, etc.; Lion with his paw on a key.; XX on either side BANK OF MOBILE, Alabama.	TWENTY
50 Female seated. 50	Female, eagle and horn of plenty; letter L on either side. BANK OF MOBILE, Alabama. Indian and Canoe.	FIFTY
50 Steamboat.	BANK OF MOBILE, Mobile, Ala. Angel sounding trumpet; globe, eagle, &c.	50 Cotton plant
Indian erect, with bow and arrow. 100	100 Female standing with scales. 100 BANK OF MOBILE, Mobile, Ala. Eagle.	Male erect 100
ONE HUNDRED 100 Sailing vessel.	Two females representing Agriculture and Commerce; on right figures 100. BANK OF MOBILE, Alabama. Sailing craft.	ONE HUNDRED
Med. head and figures 500. 500 Med. head and figures 500.	BANK OF MOBILE, Alabama. Female seated on bale of merchandise, figures 500 on right of vig.	Same as on right end.
Med. head and figures 1000. 1000 Med. head and figures 1000.	BANK OF MOBILE, Alabama. Neptune seated in a car; schooner; figures 1000 on left of vig.	Same as on right.
Compt's Die. One Dollar, in parr circle 1	B'K OF MONTGOMERY, Alabama. Female seated, eagle, train of cars and bridge on right, city and harbor on left in distance.	1 ONE 1

Left	Centre	Right
2	B'K OF MONTGOMERY, Alabama. Three females, one in center holds a sickle, ship on right, bridge and cars on left. Compt's Die.	2
3 Compt's Die.	Three men erect, one holds a staff, and represents a farmer. B'K OF MONTGOMERY, Alabama.	3 Cotton plant, barrel, &c.
5 State Arms. 5	B'K OF MONTGOMERY, Alabama. Group of three females, globe, scroll, building, &c.	5 5
Word ten and letter X. Man seated; scythe on tree.	BANK OF MONTGOMERY, Ala. Compt's Die. Large red die with figures 10 on it.	10 Female portrait.
XX Justice seated, city in distance.	BANK OF MONTGOMERY, Ala. Compt's die. Large red die with figures 20 on it.	20 Two males standing and female seated.
5 Compt's die.	Steamboat—others in distance. BANK OF SELMA, Selma, Ala. 5 FIVE 5	5 Negro gathering cotton
10 Clay.	Title of Bank. Scene on landing—cars, steamboat, etc. TEN 10 TEN	10 Compt's die.
20 Train of cars.	Girl's head Title of Bank. Girl's head. Compt's die.	20 Four mules, three negroes and loaded truck.
1 Female portrait.	Load of cotton; slave with two baskets of cotton and cars on right. CENTRAL BANK OF ALABAMA.	1 ONE
Word one and figure 1. Female instructing children.	Female knitting. One and figure 1. Vig. Justice with sword and scales, bridge and cars left. CENTRAL BANK Alabama	1 Agriculture

Left	Centre	Right
TWO	Train of cars and station house; train of cars and bridge on right. CENTRAL BANK OF ALA.	2 TWO
2 TWO 2	Vig. Gathering sugar cane. CENTRAL BANK, Alabama.	2 Gathering cotton; vessels in distance.
THREE	Portrait of Jackson. Indian hunter behind a rock watching two deers. CENTRAL BANK OF ALA.	3 THREE 3
V	CENTRAL BANK OF ALA. Two white men and one colored, one of the white men is seated on a barrel, the other is reclining against an anvil; steamboat on right; a city on left.	V
FIVE Female with shield seated on figure 5.	Vig. Battle of New Orleans CENTRAL BANK, Alabama.	Word five and letter V. View of cattle, telegraph and railroad. FIVE
X TEN	Slaves at work in a cotton field; house in background. CENTRAL BANK OF ALA.	10 Portrait of Washington.
10 X 10	Vig. Female reclining; eagle on left; cars crossing bridge in distance. CENTRAL BANK, Alabama.	10 X 10
20 Female artist.	XX Liberty and eagle. CENTRAL BANK. Alabama.	20 Cars.
20 Portrait of Franklin.	20 Large spread eagle and American flag. CENTRAL BANK OF ALA	XX Indian queen and tent. XX
L Slave with basket of cotton; others in the distance.	CENTRAL BANK OF ALA. Female reclining with liberty pole and cap; shield, scroll, &c.	50 Female reclining.

C 100 C	Indians in a canoe; trees and hills in background. CENTRAL BANK OF ALA.	ONE C HUNDRED
500 Male portrait	An oval tablet containing Title of Bank, with words Five Hundred Dollars below. CENTRAL BANK of Alabama. White 500.	500 Washington.
Cupid and fig. 1. Anchor.	COMMERCIAL B'K. OF ALABAMA, Selma, Ala. Head of Wm. R. King.	Cupid and figure 1. Bee hive.
2 Sailor with quadrant.	Title of Bank. Two male portraits.	2 Female figure of Commerce; bales and shipping.
3	Title of Bank. Three male portraits. THREE DOLLARS	3
Male portrait 5	Title of Bank. FIVE DOLLARS Train of cars passing through new country; group of backwoods men.	5 Female with glass.
10 Female, shield and State Arms.	Steamboat loaded with cotton. Title of Bank.	10 Male portrait
20 Continental soldiers and drummer boy.	Male head. Steamboat landing and Railroad depot, city view, etc. Title of Bank.	20 20
Sailor with flag, and female figure of Agriculture.	Title of Bank. Two females supporting State Arms; on right, vessels at sea; on left water works.	50 Male portrait
100 Portrait of King.	Title of Bank.	100 Three sailors; shipping in distance.

1 Cotton bud.	EASTERN BANK OF ALABAMA, Eufaula, Ala. Man buying paper of boy; bales, barrels, etc.	1 Eagle.
2 Female portrait.	Female seated with eagle and shield. Title of Bank. 2 2	2 Calhoun.
3 Negro carrying cotton.	3 Gen. Marion inviting a British officer to dine with him in the swamp. Title of Bank.	3 Franklin.
Washington.	Mules before loaded wagon of bales. EASTERN BANK, Eufaula, Ala.	5 Men weighing cotton.
10 Negro picking cotton.	Negro loading wagon with bales, mules, cars, steamboat, etc. Title of Bank.	10 Female with dove.
20 Female seated with sword and scales.	General railroad scene at depot. Title of Bank.	20 Eagle on shield.
1 Parents playing with child.	NORTHERN BANK OF ALABAMA. Female portrait.	1 Portrait of Jefferson.
Catching a wild horse. 2	NORTHERN BANK OF ALABAMA. Female portrait.	2 Portrait of Adams.
5 Portrait of W. R. King.	NORTHERN BANK OF ALABAMA. 5 Spread Eagle. 5	5 Portrait of J. C. Calhoun.
10 Portrait of Henry Clay. TEN	Bridge over a river, locomotive and train of cars having crossed. NORTHERN BANK OF ALABAMA.	10 Portrait of Webster. TEN

20 Portrait of Jackson.	NORTHERN BANK OF ALABAMA. Two females viewing the Huntsville Springs and water works.	20 Portrait of Gen. Taylor.
Indian with gun on right leg. 50	Negro driving four oxen with a load of cotton, cotton field in the distance with pickers. NORTHERN BANK OF ALABAMA.	50 Portrait of M. Fillmore.
Portrait of B. Franklin. 100	Capitol at Washington with the extension. NORTHERN BANK OF ALABAMA.	100 Portrait of Washington.
Female and sailor, bales, harbor, etc. FIVE	5 Train of cars SOUTHERN BANK of ALABAMA. Eagle.	5 on shield Cotton plant
Three females—Arts and Sciences. TEN	Large spread eagle; figure 10 on left. SOUTHERN BANK of ALABAMA. Indian bust.	10 Schooner.
20 Female representing Commerce.	SOUTHERN BANK of ALABAMA. Steamship and other smaller vessels. Cars.	20 Female representing Commerce.
50 Vessels.	Three females—Justice, Commerce, etc. SOUTHERN BANK of ALABAMA. Dog's head.	50 Sailor seated on bales of merchandise.
100 Female seated on bale of goods; hoe, etc.	Female seated on bale of goods; bbls., buildings, etc. SOUTHERN BANK of ALABAMA. Bee-hive.	100 Blacksmith, anvil, sledge, cog wheel, etc.
Female, eagle and globe. 500	SOUTHERN BANK of ALABAMA. Steamship.	500 Washington on horseback.
5 Cowper's ills. FIVE	Spread eagle. BK OF AMERICA, New Orleans, La. Half of Globe.	5 Men shearing sheep.

10 TEN Compt's die.	Spread eagle. Title of Bank. Half of Globe.	10 Cars passing over and male under arch.
TWENTY 20 Compt's die. TWENTY	Spread eagle. Title of Bank. Half of Globe.	TWENTY 20 Two females.
Cattle. 50 Compt's die.	Title of Bank. Spread eagle. Half of Globe.	Train of cars 50 Vessels on stocks.
100 Compt's die. Boy and girl with grapes.	Title of Bank. Spread eagle. Half of Globe.	100 100
FIVE	5 Large figure 5, ten females, cupid, eagle, etc. 5 BK. OF LOUISIANA, New Orleans, La.	FIVE
TEN	Female erect leaning on shield; ship in distance; 10 either side. BK. OF LOUISIANA, New Orleans, La.	TEN
Steamboat. 10 Steamship.	10 Two females with pole, cap and shield; portrait of Washington, bales, bbls., and ship on right; sheaf of grain, &c., on left. B'K OF LOUISIANA, New Orleans, La. Bank building.	10 Indian female with ear of corn and letter X
TWENTY	Man on horseback, going at full speed; 20 on either side. BK. OF LOUISIANA, New Orleans, La.	TWENTY
FIFTY	Female reclining by a grave; 50 on either side. BK. OF LOUISIANA, New Orleans, La.	FIFTY
50 Bank building. FIFTY	Female seated, representing Commerce; bales, bbls., &c.; shipping in distance. B'K OF LOUISIANA, New Orleans, La. Shield.	50 Two females representing Justice and Wisdom.

ONE HUNDRED	Two females; 100 on either side. BK. OF LOUISIANA, New Orleans, La.	ONE HUNDRED
100 Indian female with bow, arrows, and spear.	Train of cars; factories on left; steamboat on right. B'K OF LOUISIANA, New Orleans, La. Bbls., bales, &c.	100 Female erect with hand on capstan.
Die. Portrait of Washington. Die.	Female reclining. Eagle and a shield, and sheep. Female and figures 500. BK. OF LOUISIANA, New Orleans, La.	FIVE HUNDRED
500 Female seated with shield, horn of plenty, pole and cap. $500	View of New Orleans from opposite side of river; ships in distance. B'K OF LOUISIANA, New Orleans, La. Safe.	500 Portrait of female. $500
ONE THOUSAND	1000 Sailor seated against bales; ships in distance. B'K OF LOUISIANA, New Orleans, La. Bank building.	1000 1000
Auditors die. Figure 5 surrounded by five females.	Indian female, western hunter, sailor—three cupids, and five gold dollars. BANK OF NEW ORLEANS, La. Safe.	5 Female portrait. FIVE
TEN Female erect with pole, cap and shield. 10	Auditors die. Female seated with sheaf of wheat, cornucopia of flowers and coin, compass, quadrant, etc., laying around; in distance factories, bridge, train of cars, ships, steamboats, &c. BANK OF NEW ORLEANS, La. Two sheep.	10 Blacksmith, etc. TEN
Auditors die. Mercury seated on bale of cotton, right arm resting on 2, and left hand supporting 0 on knee. TWENTY	Train of cars; steamboat and depot in background. BANK OF NEW ORLEANS, La. Agricultural implements.	20 Figure of Hope erect, left hand on anchor. TWENTY
50 Marine God and Goddess with dolphin tails. Auditors die.	State arms of N Jersey with female on either side, motto "Prosperity and Liberty." In background factories, steamship, train of cars etc. BANK OF NEW ORLEANS, La. Deer.	50 Head of Franklin. FIFTY
100 Neptune in a shell on the sea; steamboat in distance. One Hundred	Auditors die. Steamboat under way with the name Crescent City, on the wheel house. BANK OF NEW ORLEANS, La.	100 Female seated on plow, with sickle, sheaf of wheat, fruits &c. One Hundred

500 Justice seated. Five hundred	Auditors die. Female seated on bale of goods with eagle, ship and steamer in the background. BANK OF NEW ORLEANS, La.	500 Head of female. 500
5 Portrait of Washington. 5	CANAL BANK, New Orleans, La. Large figure 5 surrounded by five females; figure 5 on either side.	5 Portrait of Lafayette. 5
Large V, with two females and three males. 5	5 Local view in New Orleans; vessels, houses, wharfs, &c. CANAL BANK, New-Orleans, La. Bales and wheels.	Large V, with five females entwined. FIVE
10 Spread eagle with shield, &c. TEN	View of large public building; houses, &c. 10 CANAL BANK, New-Orleans, La. Steamship.	TEN Figure of female, with pole, cap and shield, inside of a wreath around which is names of all the States. 10
10 Columbus. 10	Large letter X, medallion heads of Washington and Franklin; four cupids. CANAL BANK, New Orleans, La.	10 Male portrait. 10
10	Spread eagle. CANAL BANK, New Orleans, La.	10
20 Male portrait. 20	Figures 20, two angels and cupid; figures 20 on either side. CANAL BANK, New Orleans, La.	20 Female portrait. 20
Ornamental figure 20 supported by 2 marine figures. Steamship.	Three females representing agriculture, commerce and manufactures. 20 CANAL BANK, New-Orleans, La. Bales, barrels, &c.	Eagle. Goddess of Liberty. TWENTY
50 Jackson. 50	Female, figures 50, bales, shipping, etc.; female portrait on either side of vig. CANAL BANK, New Orleans, La. Eagle.	50 Lafayette. 50
50 Female seated on a barrel; ship and steamship in background. FIFTY	Female figure representing manufactures, seated on bale, with arm resting on barrel; bale of goods, anchor, ships, &c. CANAL BANK. New-Orleans, La. Pelican feeding her young.	Female with sword and balances. 50

100 Franklin 100	Sailor seated on bale of merchandise; shipping, etc.; figures 100 on left. CANAL BANK, New Orleans, La.	100 Washington 100

100 Portrait of Washington.	C Scene on a levee, loading steamboat drawn with bales, unloading wagon, &c.; locomotive, horses and wagons; numerous male figures; trees, &c. CANAL BANK, New-Orleans, La. Steamboat.	100 Female seated on chest, with cap and pole; also, cornucopia.

500	Two females conversing; shipping on left; cars on right. CANAL BANK, New Orleans, La. Steamship.	500

500 Portrait of female, supported by two marine figures.	Sea view, with steamship in front; another steamship on left, and a ship on right. CANAL BANK, New-Orleans, La. Steamboat.	500 Cherub on sea monster 500

1000	CANAL BANK, New Orleans, La. Spread ea le. Head of Washington.	1000

1000 Female seated, with helmet and breast-plate on, arm resting on shield; spear in one hand; scroll in the other.	Arms of the U. S., with female on either side, representing liberty and plenty; boxes, &c., cars and steamship on right; man plowing, and factories on left. CANAL BANK, New-Orleans, La.	1000 Steamship. 1000

FIVE	5 Female with pole and cap, left arm resting on shield. 5 CITIZENS' BANK, New Orleans, La. Pelican.	CINQ

Five on 5. Male portrait.	Title of Bank. Two females seated; factories on left. Green 5 either side. 5	Five on 5. Female portrait.

5 Girl's head. FIVE	CITIZENS BANK, of La. V Sailor, farmer, boy, dog, cotton bales, etc. V	5 Male portrait CINQ

TEN	DIX Vig. Same as 5s. CITIZENS' BANK, New Orleans, La. Phoenix.	TEN X TEN

10 Washington.	CITIZENS' BANK of Louisiana. Sailor reclining on beach; steamer and vessels in distance.	10 DIX Female portrait. TEN

X Male portrait	Storm at sea—steamers, vessels, etc. CITIZENS' BANK of Louisiana. X	10

10 Male portrait	CITIZENS' BANK, of Louisiana. Old man, child and bust. Letter X either side. 10	10 Female seated with pole and 10 on shield.

20 Sailor with flag, barrel bale, anchor, etc.	CITIZENS' BANK OF Louisiana. XX Male portrait. 20	20 Female with sword and shield.

20	Female with pole and cap; left arm on shield. CITIZENS' BANK, New Orleans, La. VINGT	20 Phoenix. XX

FIFTY Female, anchor, steamer and light house in distance.	Title of Bank. L Female pouring water [illegible] sheep drinking. L	50 Male portrait

50 Sailor and capstan.	Title of Bank. L Three females and eagle on globe. L	50 Female with dove. FIFTY

50 L	CITIZENS' BANK, New Orleans, La. Pelican.	Goddess of Liberty. 50

100	C Female with liberty cap and pole; cornucopia, &c. C CITIZENS' BANK, New Orleans, La. Phoenix.	Cent Piastres. 100 Cent Piastres

100 Female portrait.	Title of Bank. Three females and bust. Green C each side.	100 Male portrait

500 Pelican 500	CITIZENS BANK, New Orleans, La.	Goddess of Liberty. 500

1000	1000 Goddess of Liberty. 1000 CITIZENS BANK, New Orleans, La. Pelican.	1000

5 Three males, two females and large V.	Compt's die. Indian family seated contemplating city, &c. CRESCENT CITY BK, New Orleans, La. A crescent.	V Five females entwined in fig. 5.

10 Blacksmith and forge; cars on right.	Compt's die. Nine cherubs making offering to female; ten gold dollars, &c. Title of Bank. A crescent.	10 Female portrait. TEN

TWENTY Female feeding fowls.	Compt's die. 20 Negroes picking and carrying cotton. Title of Bank. A crescent.	20 Martha Washington. TWENTY

Compt's die. Girl. FIFTY	50 Female seated on either side of anvil; buildings on right. Title of Bank. A crescent.	50 Weighing cotton. FIFTY

100 Compt's die. Two cherubs 100	Drove of wild horses. Title of Bank. A crescent.	100 Female portrait. 100

5 Female holding sickle in right hand. FIVE	LOUISIANA STATE BANK. New Orleans, La. Female seated, right arm resting on a bird.	5 Eagle in the act of flying away from a vase on which is a shield.

Female figure seated.	5 Steamship and other vessels. Title of Bank. Pelican.	5 Sailor, steam ship in the distance.

V	Harbor scene—steamer, steamboats, sail vessels, etc. Female portrait below between lines of Bank. LA. STATE BANK, New Orl ans, La.	5

10 | Steamboat loaded with cotton; raft on right. | 10
LA. STATE BANK, New Orleans, La.
Cotton Bales.

10 Male bust. 10 | X Female seated, left arm resting on an escutcheon. | Roman senator in robes with casque. TEN
Title of Bank.

10 Female seated with spear and branch | Triton in his car conducting a female. | 10 Ship.
Title of Bank.
Farmer leaning on plough.

20 View of the Cathedral and adjoining buildings in N. O. TWENTY | 20 2 Female. 0 | 20 Female seated between 2 and 0.
Title of Bank.

20 Female bust. 20 | Title of Bank. | XX Female seated, pail at her feet.
Female seated, bale, cask, &c.; view of city in distance.

FIFTY A bust. 50 | L Child seated holding an escutcheon; [illegible] around him. | FIFTY Roman bust. 50
Title of Bank.

50 Female bust. | Female seated resting left arm on an escutcheon; on right the head of a [illegible] appearing; cornucopia by her side. | 50 Female seated and three children playing around her.
Title of Bank.
Steamboat.

50 Beehive. | LOUISIANA STATE BANK, New Orleans, La. | 50 Female reclining with chart, compass, globe, etc. FIFTY
Female seated on bale with sword and liberty cap; shield with scales at her feet; ship and steamship in distance.

100 Female with scroll; child at her feet. | Five men, boy, dog, anchor, boat, barrel, etc.; ship in distance. | 100 Female.
Title of Bank.

100 100 | c Three ships under sail, with all sail set. c | 100 Female with pole and cap. 100
Title of Bank.

LOUISIANA.

100 Public building. 100 | Head of Washington surmounted by an eagle, with female on either side, city, steamboat, &c., in distance. | 100 View of town and steamboats. 100
Title of Bank.
Pelican.

Two men bearing a female on their shoulders. 500 | 500 Portrait of 500 Mrs. Washington. | Female seated holding basket of flowers; at her feet the letter D. 500
Title of Bank.
Pelican.

Figures 1000 supported by two nymphs. Portrait of Washington. | Sea view—steamship and three ships. | 1000
Title of Bank.
Pelican.

5 Auditor's die; pelican feeding her young. 5 | FIVE Mechanic seated and resting arm on anvil, holding in left hand a sledge; factories and a stream of water in the background. | 5 Female with a sheaf. 5
MECH. & TRADERS' BANK. New Orleans, La.
Steamship.

10 Train of cars. TEN | Auditor's die. Female seated, globe on her right; in distance sea, ship, and steamship. | 10 Female seated.
MECH. & TRADERS' BANK, New Orleans, La.
Mechanical implements, &c.

20 Sailor boy holding the end of an oar. XX | Auditor's die. Female seated on a rock; cupids sporting with a dolphin. | 20 Portrait of Franklin. XX
MECH. & TRADERS' BANK, New Orleans, La.
Plow, sheaf, &c.

50 Sailor with spyglass. FIFTY | Auditor's die. Mechanic seated with hammer and chisel in hands; in background men at work on boiler; foundry; vessel on right. | 50 Female seated, left arm on a screw wheel. 50
Title of Bank.
Mechanic's arm and hammer.

Auditor's die. Female seated. 100 | 100 Female seated on an eagle in full flight. | 100 Vulcan with sledge. 100
Title of Bank.
Interior of a blacksmith's shop; anvil, screw wheel, and the hand of a mechanic with hammer.

V Temple's die FIVE | Female seated with wand pointing at ship on left; cornucopia on right. | 5 Female portrait.
MERCHANTS' BK. New Orleans, La.

TEN Temple's die X | Title of Bank. | 10 Female portrait.
Female seated beside grain; ship on left; lighthouse and promontory on right.

LOUISIANA.

State Arms. TWENTY XX | Two females seated; eagle, anchor, globe, etc.; temple of Fame and steamship in distance. | 20 Female portrait.
MERCHANTS' BK., New Orleans, La.

Temple's die. Female portrait. FIFTY | 50 Female figure representing winter painting of steamer on left; mirror, scale, grain cornucopia, &c. on left. | FIFTY Statue of Justice with sword and scales.
Title of Bank.

FIVE State arms. 5 | 5 Figure 5 surrounded by five females; houses, cars, and ships in distance. | FIVE 5
SOUTHERN BANK, New Orleans, La.
Plough and sheaf.

10 Male with quadrant, globe, &c., and ship. | State arms. Whites trading with Indians; wigwams in distance. | 10 Portrait of female with flowers in hand. TEN
SOUTHERN BANK. New Orleans, La.
Man seated with sledge; steamer in background.

20 XX Female seated with pole and cap. | State arms. Spread eagle; public building on right; steamship on left. | 20 Female in a reclining posture, pair of scales in her hand. TWENTY
SOUTHERN BANK, New Orleans, La.

FIFTY State arms. Two sea monsters. | 50 Female with pole and cap, and flag partly around her; eagle over her right shoulder, and globe over her left; ship and steamship in distance. | 50 Head and bust of Washington. 50
Title of Bank.
Cornucopia, bale, &c.

State arms. Male head and bust. 100 | Female reclining on a box; plough before her; on right two females and two cows; on her left steamer and other evidences of civilization, foundry, ship, &c., a cluster of fruits partly over the woman. | 100 Indian woman seated with child. 100
Title of Bank.
American shield.

500 Head and bust of a female. | State arms. Female and eagle soaring in the air, horn of plenty, the contents of which she is scattering; shield in claws of eagle. | 500 Steamship, ship in background.
SOUTHERN BANK, New Orleans, La.

5 FIVE State arms. | Eagle on shield. 5 | Figure 5 and full length portrait of Washington.
UNION BANK of LA. New Orleans, La.
5

10 State arms. Ten Dollars. | View of a Western steamboat loaded with cotton. | TEN Female feeding an eagle. 10
UNION BANK of LA. New Orleans, La.

Female with spear. State arms. Signing Declaration of Independence. XX
UNION BANK of LA. New Orleans, La. Bust of a female.
TWENTY Eagle. 20

50 State arms. Marion dining with the British officer. 50
Female figure. UNION BANK of LA. New Orleans, La. Farmer seated with sheaf of wheat by his side.
Female seated. FIFTY

100 View of the Capitol at Washington as enlarged. 100
UNION BANK of LA. New Orleans, La. Spread eagle and shield.
State arms. Figure of Justice seated. 100

Figure of Justice and a female seated at her side. State arms. Female with pole and cap crowning an eagle with wreath, shield, anchor, and a portrait of Washington. 500
Female with sickle and sheaf.
UNION BANK of LA. New Orleans, La.
$500 Sailor seated. 500

Woman and three little children on left. B'K OF COMMERCE, Cleveland, Ohio. Girl, lamb, &c., man shearing sheep.
ONE Male portrait. One dollar in part circle.

3 Male Portrait. 3
Man, Woman and two children, Grape dance making wine. BK. OF COMMERCE, Cleveland, Ohio. 3

Figure 5, and man drinking from brook. B'K OF COMMERCE, Cleveland, Ohio. V
Male portrait. Library scene: Calhoun and Webster talking. FIVE

Group of ten, fig. male and female. Male Portrait. TEN
B'K OF COMMERCE, Cleveland, Ohio. X

1 Map of Ohio, Indian seated on left, female on right; wigwams, building, cars, etc., in distance. 1
Figure of Justice. BK OF DELAWARE, Delaware, Ohio. Male portrait.

3 Female holding map of State of Ohio, with cupids on right. 3
Title of Bank.
Male portrait. Two children and butterfly.

5 Map of Ohio, with three females and eagle on right; Indian squaw and white man on left. 5
Agricultural implements and products.
Female portrait. Title of Bank. FIVE

10 Battle scene; white men, Indians, etc. 10
Title of Bank. Map of Ohio.
Two girls with grain. TEN

20 Male portrait. Female seated between 2 and 0. 20
Arms. Title of Bank. Male portrait.
20 Man on plow. 20

1 Male portrait. Female with sickle and sheaf, plow, &c., canal boat in ground. 1
Female portrait.
State Arms. Male portrait.
ONE BANK OF GEAUGA, Painesville, Ohio. 1

3 Female portrait. Male portrait. Female portrait. 3
State Arms. BANK OF GEAUGA, Painesville, Ohio. Male portrait.
THREE THREE

5 Portrait of Clay. 5 Female. 5
State Arms. BANK OF GEAUGA, Painesville, Ohio. Male portrait.
FIVE Female. FIVE

10 Male portrait. 1 Female with sheaf. 0 10
State Arms. BANK OF GEAUGA, Painesville, Ohio. Male Portrait.
TEN Sheaf, plow, &c. TEN

Mother and three children and grape vine. Male portrait; Girl with pet lamb and man shearing sheep on right. 1
ONE B'K OF MARION, Marion, Ohio. One Dollar, in part circle.

3 Male portrait. 3
Wine harvest. B'K OF MARION, Marion, Ohio. 3

FIVE BANK OF MARION, Marion, Ohio. 5
Hunter drinking from brook; ram by his side. Male portrait. Library scene with J. C. Calhoun seated and D. Webster erect.
FIVE FIVE

Four Male and six Female figures representing the Arts and Sciences. Male Portrait. X
B'K OF MARION, Marion, Ohio. TEN 10

1 1 Child seated on rock, steamboat in distance. 1
B'K OF OHIO VALLEY, Cincinnati, O. ONE DOLLAR with scallop.
Bust of child. ONE DOLLAR on ONE

3 Child seated on rock. B'K OF OHIO VALLEY, Cincinnati, O. 3 THREE
Head of girl with cap. THREE DOLLARS on THREE

5 B'K OF OHIO VALLEY, Cincinnati, O. 5
Child seated on rock, steamer in distance. FIVE Female erect, with torch, pointing with right hand, books at her feet. DOLLARS. Male portrait.

10 surrounded by small 1os. B'K OF OHIO VALLEY, Cincinnati, O. 10 surrounded by small 1os.
Male portrait. TEN Child seated on rock, steamer in distance. DOLLARS TEN

1 Indian and female either side of map of Ohio. 1
CHAMPAIGN CO. BK. Urbana, Ohio.
Girl's head. Washington.

3 Female and four cupids with map of Ohio. 3
Title of Bank.
Washington. Girl's head.

V CHAMPAIGN CO. BK. Urbana, Ohio. FIVE
Hunter drinking out of his hand. Male portrait. Library scene: Webster and Calhoun.
FIVE

Male portrait. X
Six females and four males. CHAMPAIGN CO. BK. Urbana, Ohio.
10

1 Female with sheaf, sickle and plow; female head on right, male head on left; town in distance. 1
State Arms. CITY BANK, Cleveland, Ohio.
ONE Male portrait.

3 State arms. THREE | Male head in centre; female head on each side. CITY BANK. | 3 Male head. THREE

5 State arms. FIVE | Title of Bank under vig. Head of Henry Clay on the left; female head on the right. Female medal. | 5 Portrait of Webb. FIVE

10 State Arms. TEN | CITY BANK, Cleveland, Ohio. Male portrait. Female seated, sheaf of wheat between figures 1 and 0. Farming Implements | TEN Portrait of Harrison. TEN

10 State arms. TEN | CITY BANK, Cleveland, O. Male portrait. Vig. Female seated with sheaf of wheat, wreath, &c. Agricultural implements. | 10 Portrait of Harrison. TEN

CITY BANK, Columbus, Ohio. For a description of the notes of this, see those of any of the Ohio Independent Banks, they all being nearly alike.

COMMERCIAL BK., Cincinnati, Ohio. For a description of the notes of this, see those of any of the Ohio Independent Banks, they all being nearly alike.

Female and three children. 1 | Male portrait. FOREST CITY BANK, Cleveland, Ohio. | Female and dog, farmer shearing sheep, cars in distance. ONE DOLLAR

3 Man, woman and two children, grape scene, making wine. | Male portrait. FOREST CITY BANK, Cleveland, O. | 3 3

V Man drinking from brook. | Male portrait. FOREST CITY BANK, Cleveland, O. | 5 Webster and Calhoun conversing. FIVE

Group of ten figures, male and female. | Male portrait. FOREST CITY BANK, Cleveland, O. | 10 10

1 | Vig. Male portrait; on right, female and three children; on left, lady and lamb, man shearing sheep, and train of cars in distance. FRANKLIN BANK, of Portage Co., Ohio. | 1 One dollar in semi circle.

3 Wine harvest—men, women and children. | Male portrait. FRANKLIN BANK, of Portage Co., Ohio. | 3 3

FIVE V FIVE Hunter on his knees, drinking out of his hand. | FRANKLIN BANK, of Portage Co., Ohio. Male portrait. | V Library scene; Webster and Calhoun talking. FIVE

Males, females, spinning wheel, and agricultural and other implements. | Male portrait. FRANKLIN BANK, of Portage Co., Ohio | TEN 10

V Man drinking from a brook. | IRON BANK, Ironton, Ohio. Male portrait. | 5 Calhoun and Webster conversing. FIVE

Group of 10 figures, male and female. | Male portrait. IRON BANK, Ironton, Ohio. | 10 X

1 State Arms. ONE | Male head. Female with sheaf and sickle, plough, &c.; train of cars on a viaduct. MAHONING CO., BK, Youngstown, Ohio. | 1 Male head.

3 State Arms. THREE | Female head. Male head. Female head. MAHONING CO., BK., Youngstown, Ohio. | 3 Male head. THREE

5 State Arms. FIVE | Head of Clay. Female head. MAHONING CO., BK., Youngstown, Ohio. | 5 Head of Corwin. FIVE

10 State Arms. TEN | Male head. Female with sickle and sheaf of wheat, shield; steamboat in distance. MAHONING CO., BK., Youngstown, Ohio. | 10 Male portrait. TEN

1 Wharf scene; men, horses, barrels, etc. | MARINE BANK, Toledo, Ohio. 1 Vessel at sea. | 1 Building

5 Building | Harbor scene; steamship, steamboats, and vessels, etc. MARINE BANK, Toledo, Ohio | 5 Clay.

10 | Vessels at sea. Building MARINE BANK, Toledo, Ohio. | 10 Male portrait

MERCHANTS BANK, Massillon, Ohio. For a description of the first plate of the Merchants' Bank see Springfield Bank, Ohio

Woman, and three children on left. 1 | Male portrait. Female and dog, man shearing sheep; also cars MERCHANTS BANK, Massillon, Ohio. | One dollar in part circle.

3 | Man, woman, and children; grape scene—making wine. Male portrait. MERCHANTS BANK Massillon, Ohio. | 3 Three and figure 3.

V 5 V Man drinking from brook. | MERCHANTS BANK, Massillon, Ohio. Male portrait. | Five and letter V Calhoun and Webster conversing together. FIVE

Group of ten figures, male and female. Male portrait. MERCHANTS BANK, Massillon, Ohio. | X 10

ONE on 1 | Cows in brook; boy, girl, &c. MOUNT VERNON BANK. ONE DOLLAR. Mount Vernon, Ohio. 1 | ONE on 1 Female Portrait.

3 Two children. | Two children at foot of tree; cows, sheep, &c. MOUNT VERNON BANK. THREE DOLLARS Mount Vernon, Ohio | 3 Dog and safe.

Left	Centre	Right
FIVE on 5 Female seated in letter V	MOUNT VERNON BANK. Farmer gathering FIVE corn. DOLLARS. Mt. Vernon, Ohio.	FIVE on 5 Girl's head
10 Farmer and dog.	MOUNT VERNON BANK TEN Girl's head DOLLARS Mt. Vernon, Ohio.	10 Cooper at work.
1	Male Portrait on left. Female with three children, on right Female with lamb; man shearing sheep. Railroad cars in distance. PICKAWAY CO. B'K., Circleville, Ohio.	1 ONE DOLLAR in semi-circle.
3 Scene, Wine Harvest.	Male Portrait. PICKAWAY CO. B'K., Circleville, Ohio.	3 3
5 Hunter kneeling by brook drinking from his hand.	PICKAWAY CO. B'K., Circleville, Ohio. Male Portrait.	V Library scene Calhoun seated, Webster standing by his side. FIVE
Harvest scene, group of ten figures.	Male Portrait, PICKAWAY CO. B'K. Circleville, Ohio	X TEN
1 State arms. ONE	Male portrait. Female, sheaf of wheat, &c. Female portrait. SANDUSKY CITY BANK. Sandusky, Ohio.	1 Male Head.
3 State arms. THREE	Female portrait. Male portrait and large figure 3. Female portrait. SANDUSKY CITY BANK, Sandusky, Ohio.	3 Male portrait. THREE
5 State arms. FIVE	Portrait of H. Clay. Five and large figure 5. Female portrait. SANDUSKY CITY BANK. Sandusky, Ohio	5 Male portrait. FIVE
10 State arms, TEN	Male portrait. Female seated; sickle and sheaf of wheat. SANDUSKY CITY BANK. Sandusky, Ohio	X Male portrait. TEN

Left	Centre	Right
1 ONE on 1	Female milking cows. SPRINGFIELD B'K, Springfield, O.	1 Female portrait.
2 TWO on 2	Eagle on shield. 2 SPRINGFIELD B'K. Springfield, O.	2 Female, spinning wheel, factory, &c.
3 Portrait of Henry Clay.	SPRINGFIELD B'K. Springfield, O Old man and child, bust of Washington on table.	3 Female leaning on pillar, torch in hand, &c.
5 FIVE Cattle and sheep.	[First Plate.] Female on either side of shield, on which is a view of rising sun, &c., surmounted by an eagle; steamer, train of cars, landscape man ploughing, &c., in distance. Title of Bank. Name as ones.	5 FIVE Train of cars
5. Hunter kneeling by stream to drink; woodland scenery.	SPRINGFIELD B'K. Springfield, O. Male portrait.	V Vig. Webster and Calhoun conversing in a library; books, globe, papers, &c. scattered around. FIVE
10 Spread eagle TEN	[First Plate.] Female on left of shield, on which is a view of rising sun, steamboat, &c.; steamboats, steamer, ships, train of cars, &c. Title of Bank. Same as ones.	10 Spread eagle TEN
Group of males and females, ten in number.	[Second Plate.] Male portrait. SPRINGFIELD B'K. Sprigfield, O.	10 X
5 Man drinking from a brook	STARK CO. BANK. Canton, Ohio Male portrait. Webster and Calhoun conversing together.	V FIVE
	Ten figures, male and female. Male portrait STARK CO. BANK, Canton, Ohio	X TEN
Four males and one female. 1	STATE BANK OF OHIO. Male portrait.	1 ONE

Left	Centre	Right
1 Male portrait ONE	State Arms; sailor on right; two men on left one is seated. STATE BANK OF OHIO.	ONE Full length female.
1 Portrait of Washington 1	State Arms; farmer reclining with sickle; sheaf on right. STATE BANK OF OHIO, Dog's head.	ONE Full length female. ONE
Webster. 2	STATE BANK OF OHIO.	2 Two horses, two men, canal scene, railroad, etc.
2 Male portrait 2	Shield; Indian and female on either side STATE BANK OF OHIO. Dog's head.	TWO Female TWO
2 Male portrait	STATE B'K OF OHIO. TWO on 2 Females gathering grapes from vine. TWO on 2	2 Male portrait.
THREE Male portrait THREE	3 Group of four females; spinning wheel &c. STATE BANK OF OHIO.	3 Male head.
3 Male portrait 3	Shield; Indians on right, females on left. 3 STATE BANK OF OHIO. Mutual Liability.	THREE Female sitting THREE
3 surrounded by small 3s. 3 on THREE	STATE B'K OF OHIO. Two females, one pointing to wheel, two others in background. Male portrait. Male portrait.	3 surrounded by small 3s. 3 on THREE
Same as on right. Male Portrait.	STATE BANK OF OHIO. Group of five male figures.	Figure 5 and words FIVE DOLLARS underneath. Male head
5 Franklin. 5	Shield; on right two Indians, on left three females; city in distance 5 STATE BANK OF OHIO.	FIVE Full length figure. FIVE

FIVE Female seated within large V. 5	Franklin. Large ornamental fig. 5, surrounded with cupids. STATE BANK OF OHIO. Wheat, &c.	5 5
10 Male portrait 10	Letter X on shield; female on right; farmers, train of cars on left. STATE BANK OF OHIO.	TEN Female with sword and balance. TEN
10 Male Portrait. TEN	Two females, shield, plow and steamboat; female on right is seated and holds grain; on left factory and ship in extreme distance. STATE BANK OF OHIO.	X Male portrait. TEN
10 X on TEN. 10	STATE BANK of Ohio. Three men—smith, student, farmer; tools, etc. TEN	10 Male portrait
10 Harrison. 10	State Arms; Indians on right on horseback; on left woodchopper and hunter; man plowing, cars, &c., in distance. STATE BANK OF OHIO. Dog's head.	TEN Full length female. TEN
20 Clay.	STATE BANK OF OHIO.	Female with spinning wheel; steamboat in the distance. 20
20 Male portrait. 20	State Arms, with female on right and horses in distance; on left man on horseback. STATE BANK OF OHIO. Dog's head.	20 Female Indian representing liberty. XX
50 Male head 50	State Arms; female on left and steamboat in distance; on right Indian in canoe and figs. 50. STATE BANK OF OHIO. Dog's head.	50 Female artist seated. 50
1 State arms. ONE	Male portrait. Female seated, with sheaf and sickle; train of cars, &c., in distance. Female portrait. WESTERN RESERVE BANK. Warren, Ohio.	1 Male portrait.
3 State arms. THREE	Female portrait. Male portrait in top of large figure 3. Female portrait. WESTERN RESERVE BANK, Warren, Ohio.	3 Male portrait. THREE

5 State Arms. FIVE	Portrait of Clay. 5 Female portrait. WESTERN RESERVE BANK, Warren, Ohio.	5 Male portrait. FIVE
10 State arms. TEN	Male portrait. Female seated, with sickle between ornamental figure 1 and 0; steamboat, shield, &c. WESTERN RESERVE BANK. Warren, Ohio.	10 Male portrait. TEN
Word Five and 5 V	Female, eagle and shield, steamer in distance. BANK OF CORYDON, Corydon, C. H. Ind.	Word Five and 5. V.
1 ONE	BANK of ELKHART, Elkhart, Ind. Portrait of Washington and words "one dollar" at top.	1 ONE
5 FIVE	BANK of ELKHART, Elkhart, Ind. Female bust. Buck.	5 FIVE
ONE Auditor's die	BANK OF GOSHEN, Goshen, Ind. Vig. One dollar in circular die. Spread eagle.	ONE ONE
3 3	BANK OF GOSHEN, Goshen, Ind. Circular die. Auditor's die. Circular die.	3 3
5 V	BANK OF GOSHEN, Goshen, Ind. Auditor's die and five circular dies in semi-circle below it.	5 V
X TEN	Ten dies in semi circle. Auditor's die. Title of Bank.	X TEN
1 ONE	Cupid and gold dollar; train of cars, steamboat and village in the back ground. BANK OF MOUNT VERNON, Mount Vernon, Ind., Man mowing.	A large figure 1 and goddess of Liberty.

THREE Portrait of Henry Clay.	Three females and figure 3. BANK OF MOUNT VERNON, Mount Vernon, Ind., Man plowing.	A large figure three with female, small 3, and word Three.
State Arms. Letter V surrounded by five human figures.	Large 5 surrounded by five human figures; ships and factory in distance. BANK OF MOUNT VERNON. Mount Vernon, Ind., 5	Large 5, Washington and word Five thereon.
State Arms Portrait of Martha Washington. TEN	BANK OF MOUNT VERNON, Mount Vernon, Ind TEN X DOLLARS	10 Portrait of Washington. TEN
1	Cupid rolling silver dollar; cars in the distance. BANK OF PAOLI, Paoli, Ind.	1 Female portrait. ONE
5	Five cherubs and five silver dollars. BANK OF PAOLI, Paoli, Ind.	Female holding sheaf of wheat seated in large V.
2	Two cupids and two silver dollars; cars in distance. 2 BANK OF SALEM, New Albany, Ind.	TWO Female leaning on bale of goods.
Female holding grain seated in large V. 5	Five cupids and five silver dollars. Title of Bank. Hog.	5
1 Male portrait.	BANK OF THE STATE OF INDIANA One Dollar across circular die. 1 ONE 1	ONE 1 Male portrait.
3 Male portrait.	Title of Bank. 3 Three across large die. 3 Three.	3 Male portrait.
5 Male portrait.	Female seated, sheep, horses, sloop, etc. BK. OF THE STATE OF INDIANA.	5 Male portrait.

Left	Center	Right
10 Male portrait	Four male figures seated; city in distance. BK. OF THE STATE OF INDIANA.	10 Male portrait
20 Male portrait	BK. OF THE STATE OF INDIANA. Sailor, cattle and dog; sheep in distance.	20 Male portrait
50 Male portrait	BK. OF THE STATE of Indiana. Male portrait. Three men; one seated.	50
100 Male portrait	Title of Bank. Two males and two females.	100 Male portrait
5 Male Portrait.	Vig. Female resting in clouds, eagle, shield, &c. CAMBRIDGE CITY BANK. Cambridge City, Ind. Eagle.	5 Male Portrait.
5 Male Portrait. 5	5 Farmer feeding hogs in pen; two horses looking over bars. CAMBRIDGE CITY BANK. Cambridge City, Ind.	5 Male Portrait. 5
FIVE Male Portrait. FIVE	5 Vig. Female seated on barrel, holding a pitcher; mechanical implements laying around; ships on right in distance. 5 CAMBRIDGE CITY BANK, Cambridge City, Ind.	FIVE Male Portrait. FIVE
10 Male Portrait. 10	10 Vig. A large X with portraits of ten of the Presidents of the United States thereon. 10 CAMBRIDGE CITY BANK. Cambridge City, Ind. Eagle.	10 Male Portrait. 10
1 Farmer in basket of corn.	Boy on horse, girl, dog, two men, mill, chickens and female crossing bridge. EXCHANGE BANK, of Attica, Ind.	1 Sheep, house, etc.
FIVE Female and child feeding fowls.	Cars crossing bridge; drover and cattle coming down hill. Title of Bank.	5 Female with flowers.
Word one and fig. 1. Milkmaid with tub.	EXCHANGE BANK, Greencastle, Ind. Circular die with portrait of Henry Clay, and words one dollar in half circle over his head; large figure 1 with the word one twice on each figure.	Word one and fig. 1. Auditor's die.
FIVE Two males erect, one leaning on capstan; two females seated drawing; city in distance.	EXCHANGE BANK, Greencastle, Ind. V Auditor's die.	5 Male figure erect, and two females seated on the ground; dog, cattle, sheep, &c.
Female head. State arms.	INDIANA BANK. Madison, Ind. Harvest maid, with sickle, in reclining posture; railroad train crossing a bridge in distance.	1 Flower girl.
Female head. State arms.	INDIANA BANK. Madison, Ind. Milkmaid and cows.	3 Figure 3 and three cupids.
Head of Fillmore. State arms.	INDIANA BANK. Madison, Ind. Locomotive and railroad train; town or city in distance.	5 Figure 5 supported by a female figure.
Head of Gov. Wright. State arms.	INDIANA BANK. Madison, Ind. Railroad trains crossing the Susquehanna River in Pennsylvania. Railroad bridge.	10
5 Med. head FIVE	Cars, horses, trees, large chimney and shop. INDIANA FARMERS BANK, Franklin, Ind. Quails.	5 Washington
10 Female with sheaf of wheat. TEN	INDIANA FARMERS BANK, Franklin, Ind. Milkmaid seated with pail; cows, etc. Eagle.	Male on medallion head. Franklin.
1 ONE	ONE ONE KENTUCKY STOCK BANK, Columbus, Ind. ONE DOLLAR.	1 State arms.
5 5	KENTUCKY STOCK BANK, Columbus, Ind. Coat of arms.	5 5
10 Three dies. TEN	KENTUCKY STOCK BANK, Columbus, Ind. Ten dollars Ten dollars Train of cars; two dies on either side.	10 Three dies. TEN
20 Three dies. TWENTY	Female portrait; three dies on each side. Title of Bank. Twenty Twenty Still; four dies each side.	20 Three dies. TWENTY
Indian lying behind rock watching two deers. ONE	ONE Woodman cutting a tree, buffalo. LA GRANGE BANK. Lima, Ind.	ONE Portrait of Female.
TWO Two females holding aloft sheaf of grain and sickle.	Vig. Man with sheaf of grain on shoulder, boy leading a sled to which a horse is attached; on right stacks of grain, and on left house. LA GRANGE BANK. Lima, Ind.	2 Woodman felling a tree, buffalo.
V FIVE	LA GRANGE BANK. Lima, Ind. Vig. Cattle and sheep on right steamboat in distance, on left in distance cattle and house.	5 Same as on Twos.
2 Female portrait. TWO	Farming country, ox in foreground. PARKE CO. BANK, Rockville, Ind. Canal lock.	2 Male portrait TWO
3 Portrait of Gen. Scott.	Cattle and sheep. PARKE CO. BANK, Rockville, Ind. Hog.	3 Portrait of a female.
5 Female portrait. FIVE	Cattle scene and milkmaid. PARKE CO. BANK, Rockville, Ind. Anvil and cornucopia.	5 Male portrait FIVE
10 Female portrait. TEN	Stone quarry. PARKE CO. BANK, Rockville, Ind. Loading hay.	10 Portrait of Gen. Scott TEN
1 Male Portrait.	Vig. Train of Cars; on left in distance village; on right steamboat and sloop. PRAIRIE CITY B'K, Terre Haute, Ind.	1 Woodman in the act of cutting buffalo.

Female with sheaf of grain on right shoulder.	Vig. Man seated on trough; three horses, one drinking; girl feeding animals; houses in background. PRAIRE CITY B'K. Terre Haute, Ind.	2 Same as Ones.
3 Female with flowers.	Vig. Three [illegible] of [illegible], [illegible], &c. on right, [illegible] of [illegible], [illegible] boat, &c. PRAIRE CITY B'K. Terre Haute, Ind.	3 Same as Ones.
Male Portrait. 5	Vig. Steamship and four ships under sail. PRAIRIE CITY B'K. Terre Haute, Ind.	5 Same as Ones.
Three females, one above the other; anchor, sheaf of grain, &c. TEN	Vig. [illegible] and three [illegible], [illegible] of [illegible], &c. PRAIRIE CITY B'K. Terre Haute, Ind.	10 Same as Ones.
1 State Arms.	SALEM BANK, Ind. Female portrait in circle, with words "one dollar" at top.	1 Female with sheaf of wheat; ships in distance.
Portrait of a girl; words two dollars on the upper margin of the circle. 2	SALEM BANK, Ind. Female with sheaf of wheat on her shoulder.	Same as on left.
5 V 5 V	Female and two cows; in the distance, fence and country scene. SALEM BANK, Ind. Female bathing.	5 State Arms.
V 5	Indian; two Squaws and papoose in canoe. SALEM BANK, Ind.	5 State Arms.
1 head of Washington. ONE	Indian reclining on left side; another Indian coming out of a canoe. SOUTHERN BANK. Terre Haute. Ind. Secured, &c.	1 State Arms. ONE
2 head of Clay. TWO	Train of cars; depot, steamboat, &c., in distance. SOUTHERN BANK. Terre Haute, Ind. Secured, &c.	2 State Arms. TWO

Large figure V, in background, train of cars, water fall, Indian, &c. FIVE	Portrait of Webster; Cupid on either side; flowers and scroll. SOUTHERN BANK, Terre Haute, Ind. Secured, &c.	FI 5 VE State Arms FIVE
State Arms. Female X TEN	SOUTHERN BANK, Terre Haute. Ind. Word ten, and figures 10, across. Traveler on horse, watering him at trough; herdsman, sheep, cows &c. Secured, &c.	10 Indian looking on a tree ship in the lands.
1 Auditor's die ONE	Capitol at Washington, eagle, steamer, &c. 1 ALTON BANK, Alton, Ill. Steamboat.	ONE Female standing with shield, &c.
TWO Sailing, wind lass, &c.	Auditor's die. Female and eagle; railroad and steamboat in the distance. ALTON BANK. Alton, Ill. Horn of plenty and anvil.	2 Female portrait.
THREE Large fig. 3, with mechanic, sailor and farmer. Auditor's die	Eagle on top of a shield, with a female figure sitting on each side; men plowing, ships and steamboat, and [illegible] in the distance. ALTON BANK. Alton, Ill. Bull.	3 Female portrait. THREE
5 Female portrait. FIVE	Auditor's die. Female and eagle. ALTON BANK. Alton, Ill. Dog	FIVE Large figure 5 with five females.
10 Female seated on safe with scales and sword.	ALTON BANK. Alton, Ill. State Arms on large X.	10 Train of cars.
Scene in a mill; carrying out grain ONE	B'K OF BLOOMINGTON, Illinois. Compt's die.	1 Male portrait.
2 Compt's die.	B'K OF BLOOMINGTON. Girl's head.	Cupid supporting figure 2. Farmer and boy ploughing with horse.
3 Surveyors measuring ground.	B'K OF BLOOMINGTON. Girl's head. Farmers loading hay. Girl's head.	3 Compt's die.

5	B'K OF BLOOMINGTON. Scene in the arctic regions; men pushing boat off of ice. Compt's die.	5 James Buchanan.
1 Portrait of Franklin.	BANK OF GALENA, Galena, Ill. Two drovers with cattle and hogs.	1 State arms.
State arms. TWO 2	BANK OF GALENA, Galena, Ill. Locomotive and cars.	2 Female portrait.
3 Cattle, drovers, load of hay, &c.	Female. 3 Man with sickle and bundle of grain. BANK OF GALENA. Galena, Ill.	3 State arms.
5 Female portrait.	Female with arm resting on bale; right of vignette, load of hay. State arms. BANK OF GALENA. Galena, Ill.	5 Portrait of Webster.
1 Portrait of Washington.	BANK of NORTHERN ILLINOIS, Waukegan, Ill. Three horses, with farmhouse and grounds in background.	1 Compt's die.
Compt's die. TWO	BANK of NORTHERN ILLINOIS, Waukegan, Is. Four sea nymphs bathing.	2 Portrait of female.
1 Auditor's die.	CITY BANK, Ottawa, Ills. Milkmaid with stool in left hand, leaning on cow; cows, sheep, &c.	1 Female portrait.
Fig. 5, with word Five on each side.	Indian hunters overlooking deer; squaw and wigwam in background. Aud. Die. CITY BANK, Ottawa, Ills.	5 Child and rabbits.
1 State Arms.	GRUNDY COUNTY BANK. Scene in yard; man, horses, &c. ONE DOLLAR. Morris, Ill.	ONE 1 1

Left	Centre	Right
GRUNDY Cows from 5	COUNTY BANK. feeding hay stack. FIVE Morris Ill. FIVE DOLLARS.	5 State Arms.
Auditor's die ONE Cattle; cars passing over arch.	Female seated by safe, shield, etc.; on left men, locomotive, shipping, etc, on right females and cows. KANE COUNTY BK., Geneva, Ill.	1 Male portrait
2 Girls with sheafs.	Auditors' die. Milk-maid, cows, dog, pail, etc. Title of Bank.	2 Men washing sheep.
Auditors' die Jackson.	Agricultural scene—men seated—others cradling and loading wagon; farm-house, steamboat and vessel in distance. Title of Bank.	3 Female, churn; cow and barn in distance.
Auditors' die FIVE Washington.	Drover, cattle and sheep. Title of Bank.	5 Liberty with fig. 5.
ONE Man standing with American flag; barrel, bale, &c.	[Old Plate.] Vig. Ships at dock, warehouse, &c. MARINE BANK, Chicago, Ill. Steamboat.	1 State arms.
American eagle, two mermaids. Steamship.	[New Plate.] 1 Vig. Train of cars building, &c. MARINE BANK, Chicago. Ill. Barrel, bale, &c.	Figure 1, with one running across it.
Male with American flag; female, bale, anchor, &c.	MARINE BANK. Chicago. Ill. Vig. Ships at sea.	2 State arms.
3 Female standing in side of circle; shield, &c.	American eagle. Vig. Neptune riding in car, sea nymphs, &c. MARINE BANK, Chicago. Ill. Safe.	3 Female portrait. THREE.
Three female figures, &c. FIVE	[Old Plate.] Vig. Steamship, ships, &c. at sea. MARINE BANK, Chicago. Ill.	5 State arms.

Left	Centre	Right
FIVE Indian standing with spear, &c.	[New Plate.] American eagle. Vig. Two females standing, male in centre barrel, bale, &c.; ship on right; sheaf of wheat, &c. on left. MARINE BANK, Chicago, Ill. Dog.	FIVE Five female figures encircled with large figure 5.
American eagle. Two mermaids. Steamship.	10 Vig. Steamship, ships, &c. at sea. MARINE BANK, Chicago, Il. Female writing.	10 Sailor standing, barrels, &c.
ONE Drovers, oxen, and sheep. ONE	Harvest scene, laborers (with women and children) reaping; dog in front; load of grain and horses in distance. 1 McLEAN CO. BANK, Bloomington, Ill. Hog.	ONE Ox. Auditor's die.
2 Spread eagle and shield. Auditor's die	Drove of cattle and sheep; man on horseback. McLEAN CO. BANK, Bloomington, Ill. Pig.	TWO Female figure, with small mirror.
1 Boy, girl, child, horse &c.	MECHANICS' BANK, Hardin, Ill. Female with basket of flowers.	1 Aud. die.
2 Boy.	MECHANICS' BANK, Hardin. Ill. Man and negro at grindstone; men, barns, &c.; red 2 each side	2 Aud. die.
3 Aud. die.	MECHANICS' BANK. Hardin, Ill. Boy, child, cattle, sheep, trees, etc.	3 Girl, deer and 2 dogs.
Five on V Aud. die.	MECHANICS' BANK, Hardin, Ill. V Old man, child, & bust of Washington.	5 Dollars.
ONE Female and 1. ONE	REAPERS' BANK, Fairfield, Ill. Farmer in field whetting cradle and scythe.	1 Auditors' die.
TWO Men gathering corn. TWO	Title of Bank. Large TWO in front of two females; building, squaw, scene, etc., in distance.	TWO 2 Auditors' die.

Left	Centre	Right
Boy and girl. 3	Man on horse conversing with farmer, another on ground. Title of Bank. Three gold dollars.	3 Auditors' die.
5 FIVE Female with 5 on shield.	Patent reaping machine at work in field; city, &c. in distance. Title of Bank.	5 Auditors' die.
ONE on 1 State Arms. ONE	Children at foot of tree; mowers, sheep, &c. Child's head. SYCAMORE BANK, Sycamore. Ill.	1 Fowls.
V Female figure seated. FIVE	5 Female with sickle and grain. 5 SYCAMORE BANK, Sycamore, Ill.	V State Arms. FIVE
1 Figure of Justice with sword and shield. ONE on 1. 1	ONE on 1 State Arms. ONE on 1 TRADERS BANK. 1 on ONE. Chicago, Ill.	1 1 Girl's head. 1
Female reclining on sheaf of grain; mowing scene in distance. 1	Auditors' die UNION BANK, Benton, Ills.	Men and sheep. 1
2 Auditors' die	Title of Bank Female beside column; steamer, etc. in distance.	2 Sheep.
ONE across 1 Farmer gathering corn.	Female figure surrounded by agricultural products, &c. BANK OF ASHLAND, KENTUCKY, Ashland.	ONE across 1 Mechanic at work.
5 Continental soldier charging bayonet.	Girl's head. Five men at work in Iron Foundry. Girl's head. BANK OF ASHLAND Ashland, Ky. Machinery.	5 Female portrait.
TEN	BANK OF ASHLAND Ashland, Ky. Male and female on either side of a shield on which is a head; two females on left.	10 Female head.

Train of cars another train crossing bridge in distance 20	BANK OF ASHLAND Ashland, Ky.	20 Clay.
ONE Two men standing, two women sitting	Woman swimming. Portrait of H. Clay. Woman swimming. ONE ONE B'K OF KENTUCKY.	ONE Man standing, two women sitting.
5 Clay FIVE	Portrait Female sitting on a bale, holding sheaf of wheat; man with wagon load of hay; in the distance locomotive and cars. Portrait of Jefferson. B'K OF KENTUCKY. Dog's head.	5 Washington. FIVE
Henry Clay. Male figure sitting with scroll in left hand.	B'K OF KENTUCKY. 5 Hunting scene—hunter, game, &c. 5	Portrait of Shelby. Female figure.
10 Washington 10	Portrait of Boone. Globe with eagle on top, Indian on one side, female on the other. Portrait of Shelby. 10 B'K OF KENTUCKY Dog's head.	10 Clay. 10
10 Daniel Boone hunting	B'K OF KENTUCKY. Woman in a chariot drawn by three horses.	Indian in a canoe. 10
20 Webster.	B'K OF KENTUCKY. Marion offering the British officer sweet potatoes; camp in distance. Dog's head.	20 Male portrait
Portrait of Shelby. Female figure Boone.	20 Female in the woods holding flowers in the left hand; ship in the distance. 20 B'K OF KENTUCKY. Agricultural implements and grain.	Med. head. Female figure.
Female portrait. 50	Marion offering the British officer sweet potatoes, &c. B'K OF KENTUCKY. Dog's head.	50 Male portrait
100 Male portrait 100	Male portrait. Two females sitting; bbl., anchor, &c.; steamboat in the distance. B'K OF KENTUCKY. Horse's head.	100 Portrait of Boone. Washington. 100

FIVE HUNDRED	500 Indian queen with bow in right hand surrounded by a circle composed of the arms of the different States, flags, drums, &c. 500 B'K OF KENTUCKY. 500	FIVE HUNDRED
Fig. 1 inverted. Female portrait ONE	B'K OF LOUISVILLE, KY. Female seated in front large ornamental ONE; barrels, ships, &c., in background.	1 Female with figure 1.
ONE	1 1 B'K OF LOUISVILLE, Kentucky. Female sitting on a bale.	ONE Full length portrait of Clay in a speaking attitude. ONE
2	2 2 B'K OF LOUISVILLE, Kentucky. Female leaning on a pedestal sitting.	TWO Female with shield. TWO
FIVE Female sitting in letter V. 5	5 Eagle with wings extended. 5 B'K OF LOUISVILLE, Kentucky. Locomotive under headway.	FIVE Female sitting in figure 5. 5
5 V	B'K OF LOUISVILLE, Kentucky. 5 Woman, boy and girl. 5	5 V
5 Justice V	Med. head on figure; female seated on either side. BANK OF LOUISVILLE, Ky.	V Justice. 5
5 Female with shield, etc.	BANK OF LOUISVILLE, Ky. Male portrait. 5	5 Female representing Manufactures.
Washington. Female portrait, with reaper and grain. Boone.	10 Female sitting on a bale, pointing to a ship in the distance; light house in the background. 10 B'K OF LOUISVILLE, Kentucky. Eagle with extended wings.	10 Female portrait. 10
10 Female figure spinning. X	Med. head. Female sitting, with pole and Liberty cap in right hand; river and steamboat in distance. Med. head. B'K OF LOUISVILLE, Kentucky.	X Female spinning. 10

10 Woman, boy, child.	BANK OF Louisville, Ky X	10 Boy with baton.
10 10	BANK OF LOUISVILLE, Ky. Female, eagle, shield, etc. Webster on right, Clay on left.	10 10
20 Indians hunting buffaloes.	BANK OF LOUISVILLE, Ky Female portrait.	20 Man felling a tree, oxen, children, houses, etc.
20 Washington.	Two female figures with ships and river in the distance. B'K OF LOUISVILLE, Kentucky. Agricultural implements and grain.	20 Med. head with helmet
50 Female with horn of plenty. 50	Female figure. Female kneeling with sickle in hand; flowers around her. Female figure. B'K OF LOUISVILLE, Kentucky.	50 Female with horn of plenty. 50
HUNDRED Med. head and helmet HUNDRED	Female with wings, blowing a trumpet; globe and eagle. 100 100 B'K OF LOUISVILLE, Kentucky. Indian with quiver of arrows.	HUNDRED Med. head and helmet HUNDRED
100 Female with rake, etc. C	Med. head. Female reclining on bale with spear; steamboat in distance. Med. head. BK OF LOUISVILLE KENTUCKY.	C Female with rake, &c.
ONE on 1. ONE ONE on 1.	Map of Kentucky with State arms on upper corner; on right, hunters in canoe; on left, ship &c. COMMERCIAL BK. OF KENTUCKY. Bull.	1 Female with dove.
Female and figure 1. 1	Rafting scene; male, female and child. COMMERCIAL BK. OF KENTUCKY. Words "State of Ky.," on shield.	Female with figure 1. 1
ONE Steamboat on stocks. ONE	Wood chopper with axe; horse, trees, and dollar gold piece. COMMERCIAL BANK OF KENTUCKY. State Arms.	1 Male portrait ONE

Left	Centre	Right
2 Female portrait.	Vig. Same as above ones. Title of Bank. Dog.	TWO TWO TWO
3 Boy and rabbits.	Vig. Same as above ones. Title of Bank. Canal lock.	3 Youthful figure with cap.
THREE Male portrait THREE	Three men sitting; Farmer, Sailor, and Mechanic; 5 one dollar gold pieces. COMMERCIAL BANK OF KENTUCKY. State Arms.	3 Steamboat on stocks. THREE
5 Male portrait FIVE	Indian woman, three cupids and hunter, and 5 gold dollar pieces. Title of Bank. State Arms.	FIVE View of Harrodsburg Springs. FIVE
FIVE V two females and large seals	5 Five females, fig. 5; factory, locomotive and tender on right; steamer, etc., on left. COMMERCIAL BK. OF KENTUCKY. State Arms.	FIVE Pierce. 5
10 Male portrait TEN	Steamboat running; small one in the distance. X on right. Title of Bank. State Arms.	TEN Harrodsburg Springs. TEN
20 Harrodsburg Springs. TWENTY	Woman reclining; locomotive and vessels, woman and cows in distance. Title of Bank. State Arms.	XX Clay. TWENTY
XX Male portrait TWENTY	Woodcutter seated, oxen, horse, etc., on right, men hauling on left. COMMERCIAL BK. of Kentucky.	XX Steamboat on stocks. TWENTY
50 Clay. FIFTY	50 Female reclining holding liberty pole and cap in left hand; eagle and globe; ships in the distance. Title of Bank. State Arms.	50 [illegible] FIFTY
100 Male portrait 100	100 Traders and Indians. Title of Bank. State Arms.	100 Male portrait 100

Left	Centre	Right
1 1	FARMER'S BANK, of Kentucky. Corn gathering scene. Male and female portrait. Beehive.	1 1 1
1 Male portrait ONE	Pasture; two horses running, negro boy and dogs, mules standing and reclining. FARMER'S BANK OF KENTUCKY. Bee Hive.	1 Female Portrait. ONE
2 Female Portrait. TWO	FARMER'S BANK OF KENTUCKY. Indian on horseback; Prairie Buffaloes in distance. 2 Bee Hive. 2	2 Male Portrait TWO
Man and boy plowing with two horses. V	Title of Bank. Male and female portrait. Beehive.	5 5
5 Male Portrait 5	Drove of cattle and hogs, 1 Drover and dog, river, covered bridge, rail road bridge, cars in distance. FARMER'S BANK, OF KENTUCKY. Bee Hive.	5 Female Portrait. 5
10 Male portrait	Female with sickle by harrow; negroes at work and steamboat in distance. Title of Bank. Beehive.	10 Man gathering corn-stalks.
10 Male Portrait 10	Female reclining against hogshead; tobacco plant, 2 negroes sitting in barn, wagon on left and steam boat on right in distance. Female Portrait. FARMER'S BANK, OF KENTUCKY. Bee Hive.	X TEN 10
Female Portrait. Male Portrait	20 White man standing by two horses grazed, mule, negro breaking hemp; hemp stock in background, cabin, locomotive and cars in distance. FARMER'S BANK OF KENTUCKY. Bee Hive.	20
Female portrait. Male portrait.	20 Two men, two horses, cart, cane, hat, etc. FARMERS' BANK of Kentucky. Beehive.	20
Three female figures on rock with anchor in the centre.	50 Portrait in frame, on the ground on each side agricultural implements. FARMER'S BANK OF KENTUCKY. Bee Hive.	50 Male Portrait 50

Left	Centre	Right
100 Male Portrait 100	Three female figures, steamboat and town in distance. Female Portrait. FARMER'S BANK OF KENTUCKY. Bee Hive.	ONE HUNDRED
Head of Clay. 1	Female figure sitting; city in distance, cows, &c. Female head. NORTHERN BANK OF KENTUCKY, Lexington, Ky.	1 Head of Washington
1 Boy's head.	NORTHERN BANK of Kentucky. Drovers, cattle, Sheep, etc.	1 Girl's head.
5 Head of Clay. 5	Title of Bank. 5 Same as ones. 5 Dog and safe.	5 Head of Washington. 5
X 10 X	Head of Washington. Same as ones. Head of Clay. Title of Bank. Dog and safe.	X 10 X
50 Head of Washington. 50	50 Same as ones. Title of Bank. Dog and safe.	50 Head of Clay 50
100 Head of Washington. 100	Same as ones 100 Title of Bank. Dog and safe.	100 Head of Clay 100
1 Farmer seated under tree; scythe hanging on limb.	Tobacco plantation; two men, one holding leaf of tobacco; hogshead, etc. PEOPLES BANK, Bowling Green, Ky.	1 1
2 Female portrait.	TWO TWO Female seated in fig. 2; farming scene on right and left. PEOPLES BK OF KY.	2 Boy and girl
THREE Female portrait. THREE	THREE THREE Female seated on plow with sheaf, sickle; cars and canal scene in distance. Title of Bank.	3 Female portrait.

KENTUCKY.

Left	Centre	Right
5 V	Farmer and drover bargaining for ox. PEOPLES BANK, Bowling Green, Ky.	5 Female.
X Female portrait.	TEN TEN Female seated between 1 and 0; farming scene on right and left. Title of Bank.	10 Man plowing.
20 Head of Washington 20	20 Same as cuts. 20 Title of Bank. Dog and safe.	20 Head of Clay 20
20 Female with cross.	TWENTY TWENTY Female with car's, pole, cap and motto "Excelsior" above. Title of Bank. 20 on red tin.	20 Clay.
ONE	Negro boy holding donkey; man and woman gathering corn. Girl's portrait SOUTHERN BANK of Kentucky.	1 Sheep.
1 Female figure seated and word "One."	SOUTHERN B'K OF KENTUCKY, Russelville, Ky. Vig. Female with dividers, &c., mechanical implements around. 1 each side.	1 Indian. ONE
2 Female with flowers. TWO	[Old Plate.] Spread eagle. 2 Title of Bank. Agricultural implements.	Female figure of Justice. TWO
2 Cattle and drovers.	[New Plate.] Vig. Milkmaid, cows, &c. Title of Bank. Plough, rake, shovel, &c.	2 Two cherubs
2 Female train by column; steamer. TWO	Female portrait. SOUTHERN BANK of KY. Husking scene; males, female, donkey, fence, hogs, house, &c.	2
3 Washington.	Child's head. Vig. Same as above twos. Title of Bank. Ox[illegible].	3 3

TENNESSEE.

Left	Centre	Right
3 Washington.	Negro boy watering horses, male and female gathering corn. Girl's head. Title of Bank. Rooster.	3 3
3 Female head. 3	Vig. Female, eagle, globe, &c. Title of Bank. Steamboat.	3 Three female figures. THREE
5 Female head. 5	Vig. Man on horseback with negroes at work. Title of Bank. Eagle.	5 Female figure.
5 Portrait of Clay.	Barn yard scene; negro with two horses, one drinking; woman seated on door step with infant. SOUTHERN BK. OF KENTUCKY, Russellville, Ky. Female bathing.	V Girl seated.
10 Female seated.	Woman churning; child beside her running toward wagon with hay coming up in background; negro playing with child. Title of Bank. Ducks.	10 Female seated holding hammer in left hand.
10	Vig. Female figure with ears of corn, plough, &c. Title of Bank. Female head.	10
Sailor, flag, female figure &c.	20 Vig. Farmer, tobacco hhd., &c. Title of Bank.	20 Female head. 20
50 Hunter, gun, and dog.	Title of Bank. Vig. Female head.	50 Female figure, with flag, shield, &c.
100 Washington on horseback.	Vig. Female head, with wreath, scythe, &c. 100 Title of Bank.	ONE HUNDRED
1 Farming implements. ONE	Vig. Train of cars. BANK OF CHATTANOOGA. Chattanooga, Tenn. Steamboat.	1 Female with sword and balances.

TENNESSEE.

Left	Centre	Right
2 State die. 2	Vig. Female on either side of a male portrait—representing commerce and agriculture; locomotive on right; vessel on left. BANK OF CHATTANOOGA, Chattanooga, Tenn. Temple.	2 Commerce and Agriculture. TWO
3 View of telegraph and bridge, cars passing through.	Vig. Steamboat. BANK OF CHATTANOOGA, Chattanooga, Tenn. Female bathing.	3 View of cattle, telegraph and railroad.
Female with hand holding shield, on which is med. head.	BANK OF CHATTANOOGA, Chattanooga, Tenn. Vig. Three females. 5 Locomotive.	5
X Group of five female figures, one holding liberty pole.	BANK OF CHATTANOOGA, Chattanooga, Tenn. TEN	10 Gathering cotton.
10 X	Train of cars. BANK OF CHATTANOOGA, Chattanooga, Tenn. 10	10 Words "Redeemable at Bank of [illegible]," &c. red tin.
Cupid. 20	Title of Bank. Steamboat; others in distance. Same as on right of 10s. TWENTY in red.	20 Female portrait.
TWENTY	Title of Bank. Vig. Mechanic, sailor and two females; city and lighthouse on right. 20	20 Two females seated, one with sickle, one holding fork, dog at his side, cattle and grain on left.
Female [illegible] 50	BK OF CHATTANOOGA, Chattanooga, Tenn. 50 Female with a dove. 50	50 Female with cornucopia.
50 Same as right of 10s.	Title of Bank. Negro driving three yoke of oxen in farm truck; plantation scene in distance. FIFTY L FIFTY	50 Male portrait.
C Male portrait. C	Title of Bank. View of Battle of New Orleans. ONE HUNDRED in red.	100 Same as on right of 1s.

Left	Center	Right
100 Female with shield and eagle.	BANK OF CHATTANOOGA, TENN. Words one hundred dolls and figs. 100.	100 Female portrait.
Female with cornucopia. 5	Sailor reclining on coil of rope; nautical instruments, etc.; ships in distance. B'K OF COMMERCE. Nashville, Tenn. 5 5	5 View of steamer Fa- side.
1 ONE Male portrait.	Three Females seated, with compass, &c. [illegible] anchor on right, cornucopia [illegible] two on left. B'K OF MEMPHIS, Memphis, Tenn.	1 Female with left hand on shield.
Secured, &c. TWO Male portrait.	Train of cars. B'K OF MEMPHIS, Memphis, Tenn.	2 Female with globe in right hand, bird perched upon it; spear in left resting on ground.
Secured, &c. Little girl and dog.	FIVE, letter V, and figure 5. female giving eagle drink. BANK OF MEMPHIS, Memphis, Tenn.	5 FIVE
Secured, &c. 10	BANK OF MEMPHIS, Memphis, Tenn. Female reclining; eagle on right; view of cars crossing bridge and city in distance.	X Male portrait
Secured, &c. Male portrait	20 Public building. BANK OF MEMPHIS, Memphis, Tenn.	20 Spread eagle on shield.
Secured, &c. ONE DOLLAR in part circle 1	Truth [illegible] and sheep on right. BANK OF MIDDLE TENNESSEE, Lebanon, Tenn.	1 ONE Artist and tools.
Secured, &c. 2	Indian and sailor on either side of shield; eagle at top, ship on right. BANK OF MIDDLE TENNESSEE, Lebanon, Tenn.	2 Washington.
Secured, &c. Male portrait	3 Spread eagle on shield ship on left. BANK OF MIDDLE TENNESSEE, Lebanon, Tenn.	3 Male portrait

Left	Center	Right
FIVE Secured, &c. FIVE	Portrait of Clay. Eagle on rock with shield; ship on right and ship and steamboat on left. BANK OF MIDDLE TENNESSEE, Lebanon, Tenn.	5 Male portrait
10 Secured, etc.	Man watering horses from trough by the side of well; sheep, lambs, goats, house, trees, &c. BANK OF MIDDLE TENNESSEE, Lebanon, Tenn.	10 Male portrait
20 Man seated; scythe on tree.	Tobacco field and two men, one holding tobacco in his hand; hhds, &c. BANK OF MIDDLE TENNESSEE, Lebanon, Tenn.	20 Secured, &c.
1 Double R. R. track, locomotive and cars.	An Indian with a long spear and horse; railroad cars in the distance. BK. OF NASHVILLE. Nashville, Tenn.	1 Two women, one in a stooping position, with a reap-hook in one hand and sheaf of wheat in the other.
Word Two, and figure 2. Two men loading a wagon with sheafs of wheat; two oxen and a horse attached.	Large western steamboat, mountain scenery in the distance. BK. OF NASHVILLE, Nashville, Tenn.	2 TWO
3	River, with several steamboats in view, and a magnificent view of the Nashville suspension bridge. BK. OF NASHVILLE. Nashville, Tenn.	3 Goddess of Justice, with scales in right hand; a woman sitting by her side, playing on a harp.
5 Man with spade, female with sheaf, two children with lamb.	Justice with sword and scales in circle; locomotive crossing bridge in distance. BK OF NASHVILLE, Nashville, Tenn.	5 State Arms and Chapt's die
Two females, one erect with spear, the other kneeling with sheaf.	X Spread eagle. 10 BK OF NASHVILLE, Nashville, Tenn.	Female with a small ball, bird and staff.
1 Sailor with flag, anchor, etc.	BK. OF TENNESSEE. 1 Two females seated; ship, buildings, cars, etc., in distance. 1	1 Female with grain.
1 Boy's head.	Indians hunting buffaloes. BK OF TENNESSEE.	1 Female portrait.

Left	Center	Right
2 Female portrait.	BK. OF TENNESSEE. Apotheosis of Washington; continental soldier on left; female and two Indians on right.	2 Male portrait
2 Female seated with sword and scales	Cattle and hogs; village in distance. BK OF TENNESSEE.	2 Liberty erect
5	Mechanic, sailor and farmer; city in distance. Male portrait. BK OF TENNESSEE.	5 Med. head.
5 Female leaning on a monument. V	Female seated on left of shield; cars and steamboat in distance. BK. OF TENNESSEE.	5 Female with scales, eagle, etc.
10 Male portrait	BK OF TENNESSEE. Jackson.	10 Male portrait
20 Taylor. 20	Three females representing Justice, Peace and plenty. 20 BK OF TENNESSEE. Beehive.	Justice. TWENTY
50 State Arms. 50	BK OF TENNESSEE. Female offering drink to eagle on shield.	50 Washington 50
500	BANK OF TENNESSEE, Nashville, Tenn. Boy's head. D Female with cotton bud. FIVE HUNDRED DOLLS.	500
Female portrait. 10	Title of Bank 1000 on die. M ONE THOUSAND M	Portrait of female. 00
1 Female.	B'K OF THE UNION, Nashville, Tenn. American flag and shield, with female, three children and globe on right, male and female Indian and child. Coach.	ONE Bridge; train of cars and sloop. ONE

Left	Centre	Right
Female on [illegible] in figure 5; shield. FIVE	B'K OF THE UNION, Nashville, Tenn. Male portrait; war implements around it. 5 5	5 Female, eagle, ship and ship. FIVE
X X	B'K OF THE UNION, Nashville, Tenn. Two men plowing with two horses. Girl's head on upper right. TEN Horse. 10	10 Male portrait.
20 Clay.	Title of Bank. Female seated with implements of commerce; cars and shipping in distance. 20 20	20 Female portrait.
1 Female and fig. 1; shield, etc.	BANK OF WEST TENNESSEE, Memphis, Tenn. Cupid riding silver dollar; cars, etc., in distance	1 Squaw with bow and fig. 1; falls, etc., in distance. One Dollar
2 Milkmaid; house in distance. TWO DOL.	Title of Bank. Two Cupids in combat, two silver dollars; cars, etc., in distance.	2 Man seated with rake, plow, etc. TWO DOL.
5 Sailor arms. Five Dollars	Title of Bank. Five Cupidons curious with five silver dollars.	FIVE Figure 5 surrounded by five females. Five Dollars
10 Hunter with gun, dog, etc.	Title of Bank. Female reclining on bale; cornucopia, bird, etc.; shipping, railroad, canal, etc. in distance.	10 Squaw with corn and X. TEN DOL.
20 Mechanic seated with implements; factories in distance. Twenty Dol	Title of Bank. Western steamboat loaded with cotton.	20 Female seated, money bags, bird, and growing tobacco. Twenty Dol
50 Mermaid and merman. Steamship Fifty Dol	Title of Bank. Female reclining on bales with cotton plant, bird, spinning wheel, etc.; factories in distance.	50 Female erect surrounded with banner on which is the names of the States. 50
100 Washington One Hundred	Title of Bank. Capitol of the United States.	100 Liberty seated. One Hundred

Left	Centre	Right
FIVE Male, boy, female, girl, dog and chickens.	BUCK'S BANK, McMinnville, Tenn. Hunter loading rifle; deer at his feet.	5 Male portrait
1 Male portrait	Shield and view of all the State Arms of the Union; female on either side. CITY BANK, Nashville, Tenn. Dog's head with word Fidelity.	1 Male portrait
V Male portrait	Female in clouds with pole and cap; eagle in front of her; rising sun and motto Excelsior at her back. CITY BANK, Nashville, Tenn. Same as cuts.	Word five and figure 5. Male portrait 5
Male portrait 10	Hunters, game, horse, dog, fire, trees, etc. CITY BANK, Nashville, Tenn. Eagle.	10 Male portrait
Cupid. Male portrait	20 20 Negro with white and black horse. Title of Bank. 20 Indian princess. 20	Cupid. Male portrait
50 Female with chickens.	Title of Bank. Man erecting breastworks; male portrait either side.	50 Boy and rabbits.
1	COMMERCIAL BANK Memphis, Tenn. Three females. State die. ONE	1
2 State die.	COMMERCIAL BANK Memphis, Tenn. Two females with anvil, liberty pole, and cap; cars on right; steamboat and vessels on left. 2 Vessel and building.	2
State die.	COMMERCIAL BANK Memphis, Tenn. Two sailors and female in row boat; female with spyglass. Large letter V and word five.	5 5
V Female portrait.	Train of cars, depot, passengers, etc. COMMERCIAL BK, Memphis, Tenn.	5 Female with flowers.

Left	Centre	Right
10 Female portrait.	Spread eagle on shield. Title of Bank.	10 Female portrait.
X TEN	COMMERCIAL BANK Memphis, Tenn. Female teaching child; little girl running to meet her father, dog barking at him. Shield.	10 State die.
XX Girl's head. Compt's die.	COMMERCIAL B'K, of Tenn. Memphis. 2 Female portrait. 0 20 Two females seated; cars in distance. Eagle.	20
Mill in the distance; man on horseback, driving flock of sheep, assisted by a dog. ONE	Portrait of Judge White. FARMER'S BANK OF TENNESSEE	1 Female portrait; left hand resting on shield.
2 Bucket and well, with female drawing water.	FARMER'S BANK OF TENNESSEE. Man ploughing in distance; group of cows, &c.	2 Female binding grain. 2
Female with flowers in her apron.	FARMERS' BANK OF TENNESSEE, Knoxville, Tenn. Sailor and farmer on either side of a shield.	5 FIVE Word five, letter V, and figure 5.
1	View of harbor of New York, with steamer and ship. ONE MERCHANTS BANK, Nashville, Tenn.	ONE
5 Male portrait	MERCHANTS BANK, Nashville, Tenn. Word five, letter V, and figure 5 on either side.	5 View of sail, the telegraph and railroad
XX 20	Female portrait; female beside column, steamer, etc., on right; female in shell, vessels, etc., on left. MERCHANTS' BANK Nashville, Tenn.	XX 20
Word one and figure 1. Female seated with child; farmers binding grain, cabin and trees in distance.	Female Indian seated; with shield, bow and arrows, tomahawk, cotton bale, etc. 1 NORTHERN BANK of Tennessee.	Word one and figure 1. Female erect with pole, shield and eagle. ONE

2 TWO 2	Vig. Puddling in an iron mill, rolling, &c. NORTHERN BANK of Tennessee. Kegs, lead, shingles, &c.	2 Female seated with sheaf of grain, &c.	20 Female. XX	Three females representing Liberty, Agriculture and Commerce. PLANTERS' BANK OF TENNESSEE, Nashville, Tenn.	20 Locomotive and cars.	V Female kneeling with sheaf and sickle.	Male portrait. Indian hunter crouching behind rocks watching two deers. SHELBYVILLE BK. Shelbyville, Tenn. Dog.	5 Reaper with bundle of grain.
5 Male portrait	V Five boys; three supporting staff with cap of liberty, with a shield; one boy holding sickle, grain, etc. V NORTHERN BANK of Tennessee. Anvil, &c.	5 Male portrait	50 Med. head. 50	Med. head. Woman with distaff; steamboat in distance. Med. head. PLANTERS BANK OF TENNESSEE.	Same as the other side.	TEN Man on horseback.	Male portrait. Milkmaid, pail on her left arm; cows, chickens, &c. Title of Bank.	10 Washington.
Three females seated around a shield, eagle on top, ship in distance. 5	FIVE on medallion shield. PLANTERS BANK OF TENNESSEE.	5 Medallion head.	50 Three male figures; anvil, flag, capstan and wheat.	PLANTERS' BANK OF TENNESSEE, Nashville, Tenn. Male portrait.	L 50 FIFTY	Female seated at work on bed. XX	Title of Bank. Cattle and sheep. XX Agricultural Implements.	20 Jackson.
5 V	PLANTERS' BK OF TENNESSEE. Three females seated; one playing harp. Locomotive.	5 Female seated holding medallion in right hand; shield and Am. flag in background.	100 Three females representing Arts, Commerce and Science. 100	Med. head of Franklin. Farmer's boy sleeping; sheaf of wheat, yoke, &c. behind him. Med. head of Franklin. PLANTERS BANK OF TENNESSEE.	Same as the other end.	1 Figure 1, and words one dollar in oval circle.	TRADERS' BANK, Nashville, Tenn. Shield surmounted by an eagle; miniature view of cars, etc.; female on either side; ship in distance.	Word one and figure 1. 1
Med. head. FIVE Medallion head.	FIVE Wagoner and dog. FIVE PLANTERS BANK OF TENNESSEE. Small head.	Same as other end.	100 Washington	C State arms, two females; 100 factories on right, train of cars on left. PLANTERS' BANK OF TENNESSEE, Nashville, Tenn.	ONE HUNDRED	5 Blacksmith, anvil, forge, etc.	TRADERS' BANK, Nashville, Tenn. Drove of cattle, man on horseback, etc.; some of the cattle drinking; farmhouse, trees, etc., in the background.	5 V 5
Two female figures, one reclining	10 Female with a basket seated on a log; steamboat on right; house on left. PLANTERS' BK OF TENNESSE	10 Cotton plant, barrel, &c.	5 FIVE	Two negroes and a white man at work, pressing cotton with machinery. RIVER BANK, Memphis, Tenn.	5 on FIVE.	Med. head. FIVE Med. head.	Medallion head. UNION BANK, Tenn. 5	Med. head. FIVE Med. head.
Med. head. TEN Med. head.	10 Farmer and girl talking, loading wagon with hay in background. 10 PLANTERS BANK OF TENNESSEE. Indian head.	Same as the other end.	10	Hunter shooting a deer; deer, train and stream of water. 10 RIVER BANK, Memphis, Tenn.	X TEN	5 Female with tablets, child at her feet.	UNION BANK OF TENNESSEE, Nashville, Tenn. Large V, fig. 5 and word Five on die.	5 Female portrait.
10	Female reclining supporting a shield; Indian reclining behind shield. PLANTERS BANK OF TENNESSEE. Medallion head	10	20 Liberty surrounded by stars.	RIVER BANK, Memphis, Tenn. Figs. 20 and words Twenty Dollars on three red dies.	20 Two cherubs bearing distaff and sheaf.	10 X 10	Title of Bank Three men loading dray with cotton bales. 10 Horse. 10	10 X 10
20 Med. head. 20	20 Large Med. head. 20 PLANTERS BANK OF TENNESSEE.	Same as the other end.	ONE Female feeding chickens.	Drove of cattle and drover; boy in water, trees, and house in distance. SHELBYVILLE BK. Shelbyville, Tenn.	1 Indian female and child; trees, &c.	10 Female. X	Med. head. Female seated with right arm resting on figure 10. Med. head. UNION BANK, Tenn.	X Female. 10
Manufactures and Commerce, two females sitting on ground, sailor and mechanic standing behind; city in the distance.	20 Med. head. PLANTERS BANK OF TENNESSE.	20	2 Man seated with child on his knee, female, boy, dog, hen and chickens.	Train of cars; factory, large chimney, shop and hill in distance. SHELBYVILLE BK. Shelbyville, Tenn.	2 Two males seated, and female seated, house, &c.	Med. head. TEN Med. head.	10 Female feeding an eagle in a goblet. 10 UNION BANK, Tenn.	Med. head. TEN Med. head.

Med. head. 20 Double med. head.	Med. head. Med. head. Med. head. UNION BANK. Tenn.	Med. head. 20 Double med. head.
20 Female with distaff in hand. 20	(Imitations of this plate.) Two females, large eagle, &c.; steamboat on either side. UNION BANK. Tenn.	20 Female with a distaff. 20
20 TWENTY	Title of Bank. Female portrait; XX on Twenty each side.	20 TWENTY
50 Cherub.	Scene in Arctic regions; men in boat attacked by bear. L each side. Title of Bank. Fifty Eagle Fifty	50 Cherub.
50 Steamboat. 50	Head of Indian. Female portrait; wheel behind her; bridge in distance. Head of Indian. UNION BANK. Tenn.	50 Steamboat. 50
100 Full length figure of Justice. 100	Female resting on a globe, cupid in front and steamboat on right and left. UNION BANK. Tenn. Steamboat and bridge in distance.	Same as the other end.
100 Girls head.	Title of Bank. Scene on cotton plantation; dray loaded with bales drawn by six mules. C either side and figures 100 under title.	100 Child's head.
500 Plant.	UNION BANK of Tennessee. Small view of cars.	500 Female portrait.
Plant 1000	UNION BANK of Tennessee. Child's head.	1000 Steamboat.
ONE	Female on ground, globe, books, chart, &c. BK OF THE STATE OF MISSOURI. St. Louis.	1

2 State Arms.	Steamboat. BK OF THE STATE OF MISSOURI. St. Louis.	2 Dog & safe.
Female, wheel, &c. THREE	Negro beating hemp. B'K OF THE STATE OF MISSOURI. St. Louis.	3
5 Male portrait	B'K OF THE STATE OF MISSOURI, St. Louis. Scene in the arctic regions; men pushing boat off ice.	5 Male portrait
X Male portrait X	10 Steamboat Pike running, sloops &c.; indian hunting, and white men in the foreground. 10 BK OF THE STATE OF MISSOURI.	X Male portrait X
Male portrait Eagle Male portrait	20 Two females sitting, iron sheaf; steamboat in distance. 20 BK OF THE STATE OF MISSOURI.	Male portrait Eagle Male portrait
50 Hunter with dog and gun.	B'K OF THE STATE OF MISSOURI. Female sitting; bridge, rail cars, houses, ships, hills, &c. in distance.	Female holding portrait of Washington 50
100 Indian portrait. 100	100 Indian on horse back shooting a buffalo, hunters and buffalo in distance. 100 B,K OF THE STATE OF MISSOURI.	Male portrait 100 Male portrait
1 Female head.	Indians hunting buffalo BANK OF ST. LOUIS, St. Louis, Mo. ONE DOLLAR on ONE	1 Dog and safe.
2 Head of child.	White and black horse alarmed by lightning; cattle in stream. BANK OF ST. LOUIS, St. Louis, Mo. TWO DOLLARS on TWO	2 2
5 BANK OF Female head 5 Missouri.	St. Louis. Man with bag horse, cart, mill, two boys on bridge, etc. Eagle on shield.	5 in red. FIVE

X Female head.	Steamboat, city, etc., on left; flat boat on right. Title of Bank.	10 Male portrait
X Men dressing leather.	View of steamboat landing. BANK OF ST. LOUIS, St. Louis, Mo. TEN	10 Male portrait
XX Male portrait	Portrait of Washington with female, scythe, ears sheaf, etc., on right; female, men, horse, bale, and steamer on left. BANK OF ST. LOUIS, St. Louis, Mo. 20	20 Female portrait
20 Children and butterfly.	Title of Bank. Man and boy plowing with two horses. Figs. 2 and 0 blended either side.	20 Girls' portrait.
FIFTY Female with battle axe and shield. Compt's die.	Title of Bank. 50	FIFTY Female and anchor.
5 Male portrait	EXCHANGE BANK of St. Louis, Mo. Local scene; view of iron mountain; mule team, locomotive, cars, men, trees, etc., in foreground.	5 Female portrait.
10 Shepd. girl seated; dog; female bey.	Title of Bank 10 Male portrait. 10 TEN	10 Bank building.
20 Male portrait	Men at work on iron furnace. Girl seated at table. Title of Bank.	20 Male portrait
50 Male portrait	Female seated on either side of shield, enclosing ornamental L with spread eagle at top; river and steamboat on right; cars on left. Title of Bank.	50 State Arms.
Full length floating female; city and country, locomotive, river, etc., in background.	Male portrait; letter C either side. Title of Bank. 100	100 Bank building.

Corn husking scene. negroes wheelbarrow, &c. 1	1 Eagle on rock. FARMERS' B'K OF MISSOURI, Lexington, Mo. ONE DOLLAR on ONE 1 ONE	ONE on 1 Female bust
Two cows lying down, mill, stream, &c. 2	2 Dog and safe. FARMERS' B'K OF MISSOURI, Lexington, Mo. TWO 2 TWO	TWO Female with wreath on head.
5 Portrait of Boy.	Two females seated; factories on right; cows, sheep, etc., on left. FARMERS' BANK OF MISSOURI, Lexington, Mo. Dog.	5 Washington.
10 Male portrait	Six mules before load of cotton; negro reclining on one of them. Title of Bank. Docks.	10 Indian seated
20 Male portrait	Title of Bank. Frame containing bust of Washington; male seated on right, locomotive &c; female seated on left, steamboat, &c. XX XX	20 Female portrait.
Female seated with sickle in right hand, left resting on portrait of girl. FIFTY	Two men conversing; one reclining on anvil; the other has his right hand round little boy at his side. Title of Bank. L L	50 Female portrait
100 Male portrait	River scene—steamboat; three men in small boat. Title of Bank. C C	100 Justice.
1 1 1	Figure of Liberty leaning on a column with cap, pole, and cornucopia, with fruit at her feet. Eagle clutching arrows, shield and olive branch. ONE DOLLAR MECHANICS' B'K, St. Louis, Mo.	1 surrounded by "cogs." Portrait of Henry Clay.
FIVE	MECHANICS BANK St. Louis, Mo. Scene in a blacksmith shop. Girl's head. FIVE	5 Farmer carrying corn.
[illegible] seated. TEN	MECHANICS BANK. 10 TEN	Cupid. Mechanic's arm and hammer.

20 Boy and girl.	MECHANICS BANK, Public buildings, fountains, pedestrians, horses, carriages, etc. St. Louis, Mo.	20 Male portrait
50 Clay.	Three females and bust of Washington. Title of Bank.	50 Steamboat discharging.
500 in center of black die with red border. Missouri.	MECHANICS' BANK. FIVE Male portrait St. Louis,	HUNDRED
5 5 in red.	Negroes rolling hogshead, pigs of lead, bales, etc.; man and dray on left; steamboat on right. V MERCHANTS BANK, of St. Louis, Mo. FIVE FIVE	5 Portrait of a Boy.
10 Portrait of girl.	Title of Bank. X in red. Vig. Same as fives.	10 in red.
20, inverted. TWENTY 20	Portrait of girl. Title of Bank. Vig. Same as 5s. Twenty in red.	20 in red. DOLLARS 20
Title of	Bank. 50 FIFTY in red. Vig. Same as fives. 50 in red	50 in red. Male portrait
Male portrait C in red.	Title of Bank. Figs. 100 in red and words One Hundred across in black. Vig. Same as fives.	100 C in red.
Female resting on pillar holding torch in hand, &c. ONE	ONE on 1 SOUTHERN B'K OF ST LOUIS. St. Louis, Mo.	ONE on 1 Female portrait.
TWO Female, wheel, anvil, screw, &c.	SOUTHERN B'K OF ST LOUIS, St. Louis, Mo. 2	2 Female seated resting on wheel

FIVE Male portrait	SOUTHERN BANK, St. Louis, Mo. Steamship.	5 Female seated pointing to pillar on which is inscribed "Union."
10 Girls head.	SOUTHERN BANK, St. Louis, Mo. X Man tanning leather.	Men working at beach.
Female seated. TWENTY	20 Engineers surveying land. SOUTHERN BANK, St. Louis, Mo. Eagle.	20 20 TWENTY
100 C	Title of Bank. State Arms; sailor on right and Indian on left. Girls head.	100
ONE Negro boy beating hemp. ONE	UNION BANK OF MISSOURI. St. Louis, Mo. ONE DOLLAR and ONE on oval ornamental die.	1 Female head.
2 2 Female with pen and scroll, child at her feet. 2 2	UNION BANK OF MISSOURI, St. Louis, Mo. TWO DOLLARS and TWO on ornamental die.	2 Indians gazing on waterfall.
5 Male portrait	UNION BANK of Missouri. Indians attacked by wild animals.	5 Man, woman and child.
Full length statue on a dark ground.	Cupid and 10. Title of Bank. Male portrait; steamboat, masts, etc.	10 and Cupid. TEN on red X
20 Female head XX	Chas. Webster. Title of Bank. Hunters, horses, game, dogs, fire, woods, etc.	20 Child's head. XX
50 Clay.	Title of Bank. Two females erect crowning female seated; buildings in distance.	50 Indian head.

Left	Centre	Right
C	Title. Apotheosis of Washington; female, soldier, and two indians. Female, eagle, shield, etc. Game cock.	100 Fillmore.
1 1 Female seated on rock, with grain in hand.	1 WESTERN BANK OF MISSOURI. St. Joseph, Mo. Man beating hemp. 1	1 1
2 2 Female portrait. TWO	WESTERN BANK OF MISSOURI. St. Joseph, Mo. Two females.	2 Female portrait.
5 Deer either side of frame and motto at bottom. 5	WESTERN BANK OF MISSOURI. Cattle, sheep, stream, &c.	5 Child's head.
10 Portrait of female.	Train of cars, steamboat, horses, canal boat and men. Title of Bank. X	10 Female feeding fowls.
2[illegible] Beavers.	Title of Bank. Hunters killing buffaloes. 20	20 Male portrait.
Deer. State arms. Deer.	1 Vig. Female reclining. FARMERS' AND MECHANICS' BANK. Detroit, Mich. Steamboat.	1 Eagle and shield.
Deer. State arms. Deer.	2 Vig. State arms. FARMERS' AND MECHANICS' BANK, Detroit, Mich. Steamboat.	2 Female with sword and balances.
Deer. State arms. Deer.	3 Vig. Woodland scene, water, deers, canoe in water, &c. 3 FARMERS' AND MECHANICS' BANK Detroit, Mich. Steamboat	THREE Female figure with bow and arrow, quiver at her back. THREE
FIVE	[Old Plate.] 5 Vig. Large figure 5 with female either side; three cupids. 5 FARMERS' AND MECHANICS' BANK, Detroit, Mich. Steamboat.	Deer. State arms. Deer.

Left	Centre	Right
Deer. State arms. Deer.	[New Plate.] 5 Vig. Large figure 5 with female either side; three cupids 5 FARMERS' AND MECHANICS' BANK, Detroit, Mich. Steamboat.	Deer. State arms. Deer.
Deer. State arms. Deer.	10 Vig. Female, eagle, and shield. FARMERS' AND MECHANICS' BANK, Detroit, Mich. Steamboat.	10 Female sitting under canopy. TEN
FIFTY	50 Cupid sharpening knife on grind-stone. FARMERS' AND MECHANICS' BANK, Detroit, Mich. Arm and hammer.	FIFTY Steamboat, vessels, bales of goods, &c. 50
ONE HUNDRED	100 Vulcan, sledge, and anvil; nude female seated on his left; another figure in background. Title of Bank. Beaver.	100 ONE Male portrait HUNDRED. 100
ONE Female ONE	[Old Plate.] Vig. Female sitting on a log; steamboat on right; house in distance on left. 1 MICHIGAN INS. CO. Detroit, Mich.	Female standing 1
1 Words one dollar, and figure 1 under.	[New Plate.] MICHIGAN INS. CO. Detroit, Mich. Vig. ONE, with ornamented work.	1 Words one dollar, and figure 1 under.
TWO Male resting arm on shield, &c. TWO	[Old Plate.] TWO on Medallion head. Vig. Two females sitting, bale of goods, &c., ship on right. MICHIGAN INS. CO., Detroit, Mich.	2 Female resting her arm on figure 2; cars &c.
2 TWO 2	[New Plate.] MICHIGAN INS. CO., Detroit, Mich. Vig. TWO DOLLARS, with ornamented work.	2 2 TWO
Female. 3	3 on Medallion head. Vig. Men, women, children, &c. MICHIGAN INS. CO., Detroit, Mich. Female.	3 Portrait of Washington.
Indian in full costume. FIVE	[Old Plate.] 5 Vig. Farmer plowing; dairymaid and house in distance. MICHIGAN INS. CO. Detroit, Mich. [illegible]	5

Left	Centre	Right
5 V with word five running across it.	[New Plate.] Secured by individual liability. Vig. FIVE, with ornamented work. MICHIGAN INS. CO. Detroit, Mich.	5, V, Five FIVE
Female standing with pole, liberty cap, &c.	10 Vig. Female reclining, &c. MICHIGAN INS. CO., Detroit, Mich. Eagle.	TEN Full length female.
Female. Portrait of Franklin. Female.	20 Vig. Portrait of Washington, with female on either side, &c. MICHIGAN INS. CO., Detroit, Mich. Fish.	20
Female standing with pole, liberty cap, shield, &c.	50 Vig. Three females reclining, &c. MICHIGAN INS. CO., Detroit, Mich.	50
1 Bale goods, barrels, &c.	Two females reclining with eagle and shield; cars on right; steamboat on left. PENINSULAR BANK Detroit, Mich. Plow, sheaf of wheat, &c.	1 Vessel under full sail
2 Two female portraits.	Female reclining, sheaf of wheat, country scene, &c. PENINSULAR BANK Detroit, Mich.	2 Female sitting. TWO
THREE Female, pole, liberty cap, &c.	Female sitting, barrels, &c.; ship on right; cars and factory on left. PENINSULAR BANK Detroit, Mich. Safe.	3 Floating figure. THREE
FIVE 5 FIVE	Female reclining on bale of goods, barrel, &c.; eagle on right; cars on left. PENINSULAR BANK Detroit, Mich. Safe.	5 Female sitting; male with sickle; figure 5, safe, &c.
TEN Indian standing with bow and arrow.	10 Female sitting, pole, liberty cap, spread eagle, &c. PENINSULAR BANK Detroit, Mich. Plow, sheaf of wheat, &c.	TEN Ship and pigeons. TEN

THE STATE BANK OF MICHIGAN.

These notes are printed on what is known as "Lyman's Protection," which consists in grading the section of the bill covered by the vignette proper according to the denomination of the bill, thus:—
1s, one third the length of the paper.
2s, one half the " " "
3s, two-thirds the " " "
5s, three fourths the " " "
and are also done in colors.

IOWA.

Left	Centre	Right
1 Two children and butterfly	Title of Bank. Eagle on shield; deer either side; steamboat on right, oxen on left.	[illegible] Detroit [illegible] on BANK State Bank of Michigan. One Dollar.
Red 2.	Title of Bank. Indians spearing buffaloes.	2
Female portrait. White word Three.	Title of Bank. Large white 3.	3 Man carrying corn stalks.
5 on red die. 5	Steamboat 5 Title of Bank.	5 Anchor, bales, barrels, etc.
ONE	Farm scene—man leaning on gate, woman milking; farm house in distance. Male portrait. STATE BANK of IOWA.	1 Man carrying corn.
2 Military scene—officer, men with implements.	Drovers, cattle, sheep, and hogs. Title of Bank.	2 Boy's head.
Female THREE	Husking scene. Title of Bank.	3 Deer crossing stream.
5	Title of Bank. Emigrant train.	5 Portrait of Antoine Le Claire.
10 Cars crossing bridge.	Map of Iowa with steamer "Iowa," farming implements, etc., on left, and female, factory, etc., on right. Title of Bank. Building.	10 Male portrait.
1	STATE BK OF IOWA Iowa City. Figure of Justice with sword and scales. ONE DOLLAR.	1

WISCONSIN.

Left	Centre	Right
Female leaning on column on which is word Two.	11 STATE BK OF IOWA Iowa City. Henry Clay.	2
3	Man plowing with two horses; house in distance; STATE BK OF IOWA Iowa City.	3 Male portrait
V	STATE BK OF IOWA Iowa City. Washington.	5 FIVE
X Webster.	STATE BK OF IOWA Iowa City. Three females; one crowning bust of Washington; shield, etc.	10 Ten Dollars
	The plates of the branches of the State Bank of Iowa, are the same as those of the Principal Bank.	
1 Female seated with arm uplifted on bale, bbl. &c., ships in distance. ONE	Boy reclining watching flock of six sheep, in distance. Compt's die on fig. 1. BANK OF BELOIT, Beloit, Wis	1 Female erect with flag and shield.
2 2	Four males seated and reclining; female with child, basket, &c, in distance man leading wagon with boy, two oxen before wagon; horse &c. Compt's die on fig. 1. Title of Bank	2 Washington on horseback.
Three females one above the others; an arm on which top most female has right hand THREE	3 St. George fighting the Dragon. BANK OF BELOIT, Beloit, Wis	3 Compt's. Die
5 Compt's Die.	Female seated with sheaf of grain within a large ornamental V. BANK OF BELOIT, Beloit, Wis.	5 Female within a figure 5.
Female portrait.	10 Spread eagle; cars, city and shipping in distance. 10 BANK OF BELOIT, Beloit, Wis. Horse.	Compt's die.

WISCONSIN.

Left	Centre	Right
1 Washington.	Landing of Columbus. B'K OF COLUMBUS, Columbus, Wis.	1 Compt's die.
2 Male portrait	B'K OF COLUMBUS, Columbus, Wis. Men at work surveying.	2 Compt's die.
5 Indian on a horse.	Two males, two females and child, dog and Indians. B'K OF COLUMBUS, Columbus, Wis.	5 FIVE Compt's die.
ONE inverted 1	Shield—on which is Am. shield, shovel, plow, arm, pick and motto "E Pluribus Unum," surmounted at top by weasel; mechanic on right; sailor on left. Bank of Compt's die. Fox Lake, Fox Lake, Wis. Figure 1.	Indian, female and fig. 1. Male portrait
2 Farmer sharpening scythe.	Female on either side of an eagle and words "Two Dollars" between. BANK OF FOX LAKE Fox Lake, Wis. Cornucopia, bales, etc.	2 Compt's die
V	Cattle, sheep, etc. Female portrait. BANK OF FOX LAKE Fox Lake, Wis. Anchor, bales, bbls, etc.	5 Compt's die.
ONE	Male, female boy, girl, dog, etc. 1 E. R. HINCKLEY & CO.'S BANK OF GRANT CO., Platteville, Wis.	1 Compt's die.
2 TWO	Title of Bank. 2 Drove of cattle and sheep; boy in water; man on horseback; house in distance.	2 Compt's die.
5 Compt's die.	Men at work in mine. Title of Bank.	5 5
X Compt's die.	Title of Bank. Man plowing with two oxen.	10 Agricultural implements. TEN

Left end	Centre	Right end
Female portrait. Compt's die.	Cars. BK. OF GREEN BAY, Green Bay, Wis. Man seated at lunch, two horses, plow, etc.	1 Female portrait
2 Compt's die.	Corn gathering scene. Title of Bank. Female beside shield, on which is anchor and word "Forward;" vessels in distance.	2
1 Girl with basket.	Man, two horses and pig at pump; cattle and barn in distance. BK of the INTERIOR Warsaw, Wis	One on 1 Compt's die
Two on 2 Compt's die.	BK of the INTERIOR Warsaw, Wis Milk-maid and cows.	2 Dog & safe.
Female seated in chair, FIVE	BANK OF THE INTERIOR, Wausau, Wis. Compt's die. Female with eagle, and "America" on globe.	5 Female, cow, calf, sheaf, &c.
10 Compt's die. Wisconsin.	Title of Bank. Girl's head. Farmers at lunch under a tree; female, horses, etc.	10 Portrait of Girl
1 Female seated; cow, sheaf, sickle; etc.	Compt's die. Indians surprised at appearance of white men. BK OF JEFFERSON, Jefferson, Wis.	1 Farmer cleaning scythe; mill, canal and railroad scene in distance.
2 Compt's die.	Indians welcoming white men in boat. Jefferson Title of Bank.	2 Farmer carrying corn stalks.
1 Soldier loading gun, drum at his feet.	B'K OF LA CROSSE, La Crosse, Wis. Female with grain and sickle. ONE DOLLAR.	ONE on 1. Compt's die
3 surrounded by small 3's. Compt's die	B'K OF LA CROSSE, La Crosse, Wis. 3 Old man seated, holding child, pointing to bust of Washington on table. 3 THREE DOLLARS	3 Female erect holding torch.
1 Dog and dog.	BANK OF MADISON, Madison, Wis. 1 Female with sword and scales. 1	1 Compt's die.
2 Compt's die.	Title of Bank. 2 Cow calf and sheep. 2	2 Male portrait
1 Deer.	BK OF MANITOWOC, Manitowoc, Wis. Horse at depot and on wharf. Bust of Washington on right and Franklin left. ONE ONE	1 Compt's die
2 TWO Compt's die.	BK OF MANITOWOC, Manitowoc, Wis. Horse and cart, two boys, man with bag of grain, bridge, falls, etc. TWO	TWO Female seated representing Commerce.
5	BK OF MANITOWOC, Manitowoc, Wis. Female portrait and V. Male and female on either side of shield, on which is a horse, man, boy and steamboat in distance	5 Compt's die Wisconsin
1 Man leaning against a tree with a crowd; two sitting on a log, others in background.	Vig. Three females in water; Cupid, &c. BK. OF MILWAUKEE, Milwaukee, Wis.	1 State arms.
2 Man with a gun, trees, dog, &c.	Three females—one with balances; two ships on right, &c. BK. OF MILWAUKEE, Milwaukee, Wis.	2 State arms
5 State arms.	Vig. Children in bed asleep; Santa Claus with toys on his back. Large figure 5 encircled with title of the Bank.	5 Female portrait.
V Compt's die.	BANK OF MONEKA, Viroqua Wis. Indians viewing train of cars on prairie.	5 on Five. Indian female.
X Compt's die.	Female seated on cliff, city, cars, locks, etc., below. Title of Bank.	10 Squaw and papoose.
Hunter loading rifle; deer at his feet. ONE	Drover and farmer bargaining for ox; farm yard scene. BANK OF MONROE, Monroe, Wis.	1 Compt's die ONE
Male, female, boy, girl, dog and chickens. TWO	Portrait of Washington; milk maid and cows on right; two females on left. BANK OF MONROE, Monroe, Wis	2 Compt's die.
Female feeding chickens. THREE	Drover and drove of cattle, boy in water; trees and house in distance. BANK OF MONROE, Monroe, Wis.	3 Compt's die. THREE
Female gathering wheat. 5	Man watering three horses from trough; sheep goats, trees and house. BANK OF MONROE, Monroe, Wis.	5 Compt's die
1 Deer.	B'K OF THE NORTH-WEST, Fondulac, Wis. Man, woman, and child.	1 State die. ONE
2 State die. TWO	B'K OF THE NORTH-WEST, Fondulac, Wis. Raft scene.	2 Female with grain on her shoulder.
3 Female with spyglass seated on merchandise vessel on left.	Train of cars, group of male and female figures. B'K OF THE NORTH-WEST, Fondulac, Wis.	3 State die. THREE
5 State die. FIVE	Cattle and sheep, buildings in background. B'K OF THE NORTH-WEST, Fondulac, Wis.	5 Farmer sharpening his scythe.
3 Female THREE	BK OF OSHKOSH, Oshkosh, Wis. 3 Loaded wagon, two boys and two oxen.	3 Compt's die.
FIVE V Female and fig. 5.	Compt's die. BK OF OSHKOSH, Oshkosh, Wis. 5	5 Two men plowing with two horses; dog, etc.

Left	Centre	Right
ONE Comp't's die.	Steamboat Prairie du Chein and St. Paul. 1 BANK OF PRAIRIE DU CHEIN, Prairie du Chein, Wis. Cars.	Indian ONE
2 Two children	Wild horses. Title of Bank. Dog.	2 Comp't's die.
3 Comp't's die.	Rafting scene. Title of Bank. Dog's head.	3 Farmer.
5 Farmer.	Title of Bank. Comp't's die. Load of hay, cars, city and bridges.	5 Two females
1 Country road with man's load of hay &c.	BANK OF RACINE, Racine, Wis. Vig. Man watering horse, female feeding pigs; house &c., in distance.	1 State arms.
2 Female Portrait. 2	Vig. Locomotive and train of cars; steamboat on right; city in distance on left. BANK OF RACINE, Racine, Wis	2 State arms.
3 Three cupids encircled with large figure 3	BANK OF RACINE, Racine, Wis. Vig. Men watering horse; dogs, pigs, child, &c.	3 State arms.
5 Washington. FIVE	Vig. Harvest scene; wagon, loading grain; female with child, men, basket, pitcher, &c. State Arms. BANK OF RACINE, Racine, Wis.	5 Male portrait FIVE
1	Four cows and three sheep. Girl's head. BANK OF RIPON, Ripon, Wis. Farming utensils.	1 Comp't's die.
2 Comp't's die. &c	Train of cars; city and town. BANK OF RIPON, Ripon, Wis.	2 Female feeding fowls.

Left	Centre	Right
5 Farming utensils.	Female portrait. Men at work surveying. BANK OF RIPON, Ripon, Wis	5 Comp't's die.
1 Comp't's die	BK OF SHEBOYGAN Sheboygan, Wis. 1 Blacksmith, hammer, anvil; city in distance. 1	1 Woodcutter.
TWO TWO TWO 2 Locomotive.	Yacht scene—various male and female figures on the beach. BK OF SHEBOYGAN Sheboygan, Wis.	2 Comp't's die. TWO TWO TWO
3 THREE 3	3 Ship yard scene; men at work. BK OF SHEBOYGAN Sheboygan, Wis.	3 Comp't's die
5	American shield: on right female instructing children; house in distance; on left Indian, squaw and child. 5 BK OF SHEBOYGAN Sheboygan, Wis	5 on FIVE Comp't's die.
1 Comp't's die. Wisconsin.	Indians on horseback fighting wild animals. Child's head. 1 BANK OF SPARTA, Sparta, Wis.	1 Female feeding fowls.
Cupid and fig. 2. Man, horse, dog, pigeons, etc.	Boy on horse, pony, female, ducks, trough; houses, &c., in distance. Title of Bank.	2 Comp't's die. WISCONSIN
Soldiers of the Revolution. THREE	3 Man and boy plowing with two horses. Title of Bank.	3 Comp't's die. WISCONSIN
FIVE	Title of Bank. Surveyors at work, &c. Portrait of boy.	5 Comp't's die WISCONSIN
Female bust 1	BANK OF WATERTOWN, Watertown, Wis. Vig. Female reclining in a sea shell; water scene.	1 Comp't's die

Left	Centre	Right
TWO Female figure erect.	BANK OF WATERTOWN, Watertown, Wis Vig. Indian and female reclining on globe, spread eagle between them. 2	2 Comp't's die.
3 Comp't's die.	Vig. Man on horseback, boys, sheep, and load of hay in distance. BANK OF WATERTOWN, Watertown, Wis.	3 Three Cherubs.
5 5	Vig. Two farmers inspecting drove of cattle. Female bust. BANK OF WATERTOWN, Watertown, Wis.	5 Comp't's die
1 Female portrait 1	BANK OF WEYAUWEGA, Weyauwega, Wis. Hunters, fire, horses, game, dogs, etc.	1 Comp't's die.
2 Two Dollars Comp't's die.	Man whittling stick; horse, cow, sheep; boy on gate; man in distance. Title of Bank. 2 2	2 Two Dollars Dog and game.
1 Comp't's die.	BANK OF WHITEWATER, Whitewater, Wis. Farmers at work, mowing and loading wagon—one in foreground resting. ONE	1 Boy and girl.
Three on 3. Comp't's die.	Title of Bank. Female seated with dog and pail, cows, etc. THREE	3 Cars
1 Male portrait	BK OF WISCONSIN, Madison, Wis. ONE Battle scene—old man and female, soldiers in distance. ONE ONE ONE	1 Comp't's die.
2 Male, female and child.	BK OF WISCONSIN, Madison, Wis. Comp't's die. Horse and colt, man and child, barn, etc.	2 TWO
5	BK OF WISCONSIN, Madison, Wis. Arctic regions—men firing bears; dogs, ship, etc. 5	5 Comp't's die.

ONE on 1. Boy and girl at well.
BATAVIAN BANK, La Crosse, Wis. Girl's head. 1 Girl's head. ONE DOLLAR.
ONE on 1. Compt's die.

Female with pen and tablet, child at her feet. FIVE
V Female reclining with chart, compass, and quadrant. V BATAVIAN BANK, La Crosse, Wis. FIVE DOLLARS.
5 surrounded by small 5's. Compt's die.

1 Compt's die. 1
Female surrounded by fruit and corn; in distance trees, river, shipping, village, &c. CENTRAL BANK OF WISCONSIN, Janesville, Wis. Locomotive.
1 Portrait of female. 1

2 Compt's die. TWO
Farm scene, man watering three horses at a trough; female feeding pigs; buildings in distance. Title of Bank. Steamboat.
2 Female with folded hands. 2

3 Compt's die. 3
Title of Bank. Train of cars. Agricultural implements.
3 Portrait of Washington. 3

1 Indian fishing.
ONEIDA BANK, Berlin, Wis. Two men grinding corn; children, dog, horse, etc. Beehive.
Fig. 1; Indian on left, female on right. Compt's die.

2 Two children.
Indian viewing the progress of civilization. Title of Bank. Game.
TWO Compt's die. 2

THREE Female head on a 3. Compt's die.
Title of Bank. Eagle and fig. 3. Oxen before sled drawing load of wood, man and boy; houses and men skating in distance. Indian.
3 THREE

5 Man seated, female standing, boy, horses, etc.
Title of Bank. Compt's die.
5 Indian, dog, squaw, canoe, etc.

1 Compt's die. ONE
Vig. Indian and horse on right, buffaloes, train of cars, &c. CITY BANK, Kenosha, Wis. Arms.
1 Indian female seated and child.

2 Compt's die. TWO
Vig. Large public building, men and women, horses and carriages, &c., in front. CITY BANK, Kenosha, Wis.
2 Locomotive and tender.

THREE Female seated with quadrant, spread eagle, standing on [illegible]
3 Vig. Indian and her trading house; Indians seated on left. CITY BANK, Kenosha, Wis.
3 Compt's die. THREE

Blacksmith at forge. ONE
1 Justice seated; eagle, shield, etc.; cars, bridge, village and shipping in the distance. CITY BANK OF PRESCOTT, Wis. ONE
1 Compt's die. ONE

2 Three men—one on horseback watering horse from trough; straw, hay wagon, etc.
Title of Bank. Compt's die. 2 Eagle.
2 Two horses, boy, girl and duck by trough.

3 3
Cars. Justice. Title of Bank.
3 Compt's die.

V 5
Title of Bank. Cattle and sheep, water, trees, houses, etc. Girl's head. FIVE
5 Compt's die. FIVE

1 ONE State arms.
COLUMBIA CO. BK. Portage City, Wis. Railroad train.
ONE Portrait of [illegible]

2 State arms.
Rural scene—cattle, sheep, land, water. COLUMBIA CO. BK. Portage City, Wis.
2 Female.

5 State arms. FIVE
Chariot of the Sun. COLUMBIA CO. BK. Portage City, Wis.
5 Train of cars.

ONE Compt's die. Milkmaid and cows.
COMMERCIAL BANK, Racine, Wis. Farmer, horse and dog. Blacksmith, anvil and forge.
1 Sailor with implements.

1
COMMERCIAL BANK, Racine, Wis. Wharf scene—cars, drays, males, females, shipping, etc. Girl.
1 Compt's die.

2 Female.
COMMERCIAL BANK, Racine, Wis. Train of cars, men, trees, etc.; cars, bridge and hills in distance.
2 Compt's die.

3 Female portrait.
COMMERCIAL BANK, Racine, Wis. Female portrait. Compt's die.
3 Female portrait.

Female portrait. 1
1 Female representing Commerce with implements. CORN EX. BANK, Waupun, Wis.
1 Compt's die.

Male portrait. 2
Spread eagle and shield. 2 CORN EX. BANK, Waupun, Wis.
2 Compt's die.

Compt's die. 3
Three females and fig. 3; factories in distance. 3 CORN EX. BANK, Waupun, Wis.
3 Male portrait.

5 Female portrait.
CORN EX. BANK, Waupun, Wis. Farmers, etc., in corn field.
5 Compt's die. FIVE

Female blessing dinner horn, table, etc.
CORN PLANTER'S BANK, Waupaca, Wis. Large red tinted 5. Compt's die.
5 Female with bell, [illegible]; open gate, etc.

Two men in corn field. X
Title of Bank. Two men, wagon, mill, horses drinking at trough, chickens, etc.
10 Compt's die.

ONE Compt's die.
DANE CO. BANK, Madison, Wis. Female reclining upon a rock viewing lake with city on opposite side; train passing around lake shore. 1
1 ONE

Left	Centre	Right
TWO Compt's die.	DANE CO. BANK, Madison, Wis. Two females; cars on the right and steamboat on left in the background. Safe.	TWO 2
3 Compt's die.	DANE CO. BANK, Madison, Wis. Three females joining hands. 3	3
FI5VE Compt's die.	Indian, squaw and child; female and child; between them a shield with word five thereon. DANE CO. BANK, Madison, Wis. Eagle.	5 Med. head
X Compt's die.	View of church, buildings and trees. DANE CO. BANK, Madison, Wis.	10 Med. head.
TWENTY Female with shield. Wisconsin.	DANE CO. BANK, Madison, Wis. 2 Female portrait. 0	TWENTY Compt's die.
1 Compt's die. ONE	ELKHORN BANK, Elkhorn, Wis. Elk's head. ONE Cupid. ONE Cupid.	1 Female and figure 1.
TWO Female portrait. Compt's die.	ELKHORN BANK, Elkhorn, Wis. Lovers at a well; barn in distance. Man.	2 Elk's head.
THREE Female portrait. Compt's die.	ELKHORN BANK, Elkhorn, Wis. Train of cars; hills and village in distance. Beaver.	3 Elk's head. THREE
1 Farmer seated; scythe hanging on limb of tree.	Shipping, ships, steamboat, pilot boat and city. EXCHANGE BANK OF DARLING & CO., Fond du Lac, Wis. Capital $50,000.	1 Compt's die. ONE
2 Compt's die.	Western steamboat; hills, &c. Title of Bank. Capital $50,000.	2 Squaw.

Left	Centre	Right
Hunter loading gun; deer at his feet. THREE	Indian portrait; female instructing children on right; house in distance, on left squaw and papoose. Title of Bank. Capital $50,000.	3 Compt's die.
1 Compt's die. 1 1	Farm scene, horses drinking from trough, man, cows, poultry, hogs, &c.; barn in background. FARMERS' BANK, Beaver Dam, Wis. ONE DOLLAR.	1 1 Female seated, flowers at her feet. 1
Compt's die. 5	5 Cattle eating from haymow; pitchfork, birds, &c. 5 FARMERS' BANK, Beaver Dam, Wis. FIVE DOLLARS.	5 Dog and safe.
Man with bag on back; horse, cart, mill; two boys on bridge. 1	FOND du LAC, The Farmers and Mechanics' Bank, ONE DOLLAR ONE ONE	1 Compt's die Wisconsin.
FARMERS TWO	and MECHANICS' BK Man seated with horse; wheelwright at work. Portrait of Bay. FOND du LAC, TWO	2 Compt's die Wisconsin.
1 ONE Head of Henry Clay.	Female sitting down; cars and load of hay in background. FARMERS' & MILLERS' BANK, Milwaukee, Wis. Eagle.	1 State Arms.
Portrait of female. 2	Two men reposing under a tree; hay field in the background. FARMERS' & MILLERS' BANK, Milwaukee, Wis.	2 State Arms.
5 Locomotive. 5	FARMERS' & MILLERS' BANK, Milwaukee, Wis. Female sitting down by a shield; State House in background.	5 State Arms.
1 Compt's die.	FOREST CITY BANK Waukesha, Wis. Load of hay, man, horses, barn, etc. Dog's head.	ONE 1
2 Compt's die.	FOREST CITY BANK Waukesha Wis. Liberty, eagle and shield on half globe. Shield.	TWO Female and fig. 2.

Left	Centre	Right
Compt's die. 3	FOREST CITY BANK Waukesha, Wis. Ship and other vessels at sea. Hands.	3 Sailor at wheel.
Female seated holding shield on which is V and 5. Compt's die.	Two men, child, anvil, wheel, etc. FRONTIER BANK Stevens' Point Wis.	5 Sailor seated with pipe.
Female soaring above houses, cars, steamboat, etc.; on right upper is cattle, houses, etc.	Compt's die. Title of Bank.	10 Mechanic at bench.
ONE Mower with scythe seated.	Female seated; dog and pail on right, cows on left. GERMAN BANK, Sheboygan, Wis.	1 Compt's die.
TWO Compt's die.	Women at work on cotton machines. GERMAN BANK, Sheboygan, Wis.	2 Train of cars.
Compt's die. Word three and fig. 3.	GERMAN BANK, Sheboygan, Wis. Three females; ship in distance.	3
5 Steamboat.	GERMAN BANK Sheboygan, Wis 5 Compt's die.	FIVE
ONE Soldier with gun.	Indians hunting buffaloes. GREEN BAY BANK, Oconto Wis.	1 ONE Compt's die.
TWO 2 Compt's die.	Backwoods scene—men at work clearing. GREEN BAY BANK, Oconto Wis.	2 Female; sow and calf.
ONE	HUDSON CITY BK, Hudson, Wis. Wharf scene—cars, drays, mules, &c., Female mules, shipping, etc. portrait.	1 ONE Compt's die.

2 Farmers hoeing.	HUDSON CITY BK. Hudson, Wis. Compt's die.	2 Farmers, pig, horse and sheep.
5 Sailor and captain.	HUDSON CITY BK. Hudson, Wis. Men at work surveying. Pigs.	5 Compt's die.
Compt's die. 1	IOWA CO. BANK, Mineral Point, Wis. Female portrait.	ONE DOLLAR Sailor, farmer, boy, dog, captain, grain, &c. 1
3 Compt's die.	THREE on 3. Female erect with sword and shield. THREE on 3. Title of Bank.	3 Dog & game.
Compt's. Die. Harvestman sharpening cradle.	1 Indian and white man, with upright shield between. JEFFERSON COUNTY BANK, Watertown, Wis. Bull	1 Blacksmith.
3 THREE Indian warrior.	Compt's. Die. American citizens Indian Chiefs in council. JEFFERSON COUNTY BANK, Watertown, Wis. Female.	3 Indian squaw and child sitting.
5 Large V, with group of male and female figures.	Compt's Die. Locomotive and train of cars. JEFFERSON COUNTY BANK, Wa ertown, Wis. Cornucopia	5 Washington. FIVE
1 Indians on horses, hunting buffaloes.	JUNEAN BANK, Milwaukie, Wis. Large Male portrait.	1 Compt's die. Wisconsin.
5 Two men at work; wheel, sledge, etc.	JUNEAN BANK, Milwaukie, Wis. Male portrait. Compt's die and 5.	5 Female feeding fowls.
X White men in boat; Indians on shore. TEN	JUNEAN BANK, Milwaukie, Wis. Large male portrait. TEN DOLLARS	10 Compt's die

1 Steamboat.	Vig. Female seated State holding a dagger Arms and supporting a silver dollar. KENOSHA CO. BANK Kenosha, Wis. Capital Stock, &c.	1 Female holding large figure 1.
Vig. River scene, Indian, squaw and child in a canoe. 2	State Arms. KENOSHA CO. BANK Kenosha, Wis. Capital Stock, &c.	Female holding large figure 2. TWO
1 Compt's die.	LACROSSE CO. BK. LaCrosse, Wis. Man feeding pigs; pigeon, chickens, etc. Locomotive.	1 Female holding fig. 1
2 Compt's die.	LACROSSE CO. BK. LaCrosse, Wis. 2 Horse, cows, bridge, cars, water, etc. Boat.	2
3	LACROSSE CO. BK. LaCrosse, Wis. White female showing Indian the progress of civilization; cars, city, etc. 3	3 Compt's die.
FIVE	LACROSSE CO. BK. LaCrosse, Wis. Eagle within V. Compt's die.	5 Reaper, cattle; men loading wagons in distance.
5 Large 5, two Indians, water fall, cars and bridge	Lumber, loading wagon, &c., sled, men and woods falls in distance. LUMBERMANS' BK., Viroqua Wis. Shield.	5 Compt's die. FIVE
10 Hunter seated, dog at feet.	Indian reclining; another in distance. LUMBERMANS' BK., Wis. Woodcutter.	10 Compt's die. TEN
Fig 5 inverted Compt's die.	Man with white and black horse; cars, water scene, building, etc. MONROE CO. BANK, Sparta, Wis. Indian.	Fig. 5 inverted. Female seated with pail cows, church etc., in distance.
1 Compt's die. ONE	Vig. Factory, train of cars, horses, canal boat, bridges, trees, &c.; in the distance a train of cars crossing aqueduct. NORTHERN BANK Howard, Wis. Capital $50,000, &c.	1 Indian princess seated figure 1, rainbow, clouds &c.

2 Compt's die. TWO	Vig. Drove of cattle and sheep, drovers, horse, and dog. NORTHERN BANK Howard, Wis. Capital $50,000, &c.	2 Two Females erect.
3 Compt's die. THREE	Vig. Harvest scene, farmers at lunch, female and children, boy climbing, dog, &c. in distance man, 4 horses, and load of hay. NORTHERN BANK Howard, Wis. Capital $50,000, &c.	3 Figure 3 and three male figures, sailor, farmer, & mechanic.
FIVE Blacksmith with sledge, anvil, etc. locomotive and factory.	NORTHERN BANK Green Bay, Wis. Compt's die.	5 Train of cars, cars, etc., in distance.
10	Large Spread eagle. NORTHERN BANK Green Bay, Wis. Compt's die.	10
Female with cornucopia.	5 State Arms 5 OAK WOOD BANK. North Pepin, Wis.	Female gathering wheat
1 Compt's die. ONE	Man watering three horses from trough by side of wall; goat, kid and sheep, cattle and house in distance. OSHKOSH COMMERCIAL BANK, Oshkosh, Wis.	ONE Female seated with shield.
2 Farmer's family scene.	Title of Bank. Indians on horseback hunting buffaloes.	2 on TWO. Compt's die. TWO
3 THREE	Indian family contemplating the progress of civilization. Title of Bank around Compt's die.	Fig. 3 on DOLLARS Female with flowers in her apron.
5 FIVE Compt's die.	Title of Bank. Prairie scene—Indians and horse; train of cars, buffaloes and rising sun in distance.	5 on FIVE Squaw and papoose.
2 Two children	PRAIRIE CITY B'K. Ripon, Wis. Boy and dog; house in distance.	2 Compt's die TWO

3 — Compt's die. | Title of Bank. 3 Cattle, children and trees. 3 | 3 — Dog and safe.

ONE — Goddess of liberty with spear in left hand. | State arms. RACINE CO. BANK. Racine, Wis. Portrait of Washington cupid on either side. | 1 — Female child with basket

TWO — Little girl. 2 | State arms. RACINE CO. BANK, Racine, Wis. Two females and male reclining, the female on right has sickle in right hand and sheaf of wheat in left, anvil, sledge, &c.; train of cars on left, vessel on right. Clasped hands. | 2 — TWO

3 — Sailor with left hand on rudder block. | State arms. RACINE CO. BANK. Racine. Wis. Female seated, with blacksmith on right and sailor on left. In distance on left ship; city on right. | 3

FIVE — State arms. 5 | RACINE CO. BANK, Racine. Wis. FI 5 VE Three cows standing in water, train of cars, farm house, &c. | FI 5 VE — Blacksmith, sailor and farmer.

1 — Man erect with drum, two others seated, one with pipe. | Blacksmith shoeing horse; man seated and one erect. ROCK COUNTY B'K, Janesville, Wis. | 1 — Compt's die

Portrait of boy. Compt's die. | Man gathering ears of corn; horse, colt, cart and dog. ROCK COUNTY B'K, Janesville, Wis. Dog, key and safe. | 2 — Portrait of female.

Head of girl. Compt's die | Group of persons viewing and applauding train of cars, in distance, farm house, cart, &c. ROCK COUNTY B'K, Janesville, Wis. Dog's head. | 3 — Female seated with sheaf and sickle.

5 — Compt's die. | Cattle, hogs, &c.; town on right. ROCK COUNTY B'K. Janesville, Wis. | 5 — Henry Clay. 5

1 — Country road, wagon, horses, load of hay, man, &c. houses, &c. in distance. | Vig. Man and female on either side of a shield on which is inscribed figure 1, and word one; on left blacksmith, and on right, drover, drove of hogs and a negro. ROCK RIVER BANK. Beloit. Wis. | 1 — Compt's die.

2 — Indian with gun seated on rock. | Vig. Man, woman and child, gun leaning against a rock, house and trees on right, houses, trees and a stream on left. ROCK RIVER BANK, Beloit, Wis. | 2 — Compt's die.

Female seated holding figure 3, sheaf of wheat on left. Compt's die. | ROCK RIVER BANK, Beloit, Wis. Portrait of female. | Female seated holding figure 3; masts and bbls., bales, &c. on right. 3

5 — Female portrait. 5 | ROCK RIVER BANK, Beloit. Wis. Vig. Female seated, shield, &c., in background falls, &c. | 5 — Compt's die

Cupid with sheaf. 2 | ROCKWELL & Co's BANK, Hunter with gun and dog. Fig. 2 to right and cupid with cornucopia above. Compt's die. Two Dollars. Elkhorn, Wis. | 2

Portrait of female. | 3 Title of Bank. Female, column, steamer, etc. Sheep. | 3 — Compt's die.

1 — Compt's die. Wisconsin. | SAUK CITY BANK, Sauk City, Wis. ONE DOLLAR | 1 — Female reclining with shield, pole, cap, eagle &c.

2 — Portrait of girl. Wisconsin. | Title of Bank. Compt's die. Man on load of hay in front of building, man in window; horse, colt, sheep, etc. Dog's head. | 2 — TWO

ONE — Compt's die. ONE | SAUK COUNTY B'K, Baraboo, Wis. Blacksmith shop; shoeing horse; man at forge; farmer, etc. | 1 — Indian female.

TWO | SAUK CO. BANK, Baraboo Wis. Sidaid; farmer seated town, etc., on right; Indian, hills, etc., on left. 2 | 2 — Compt's die. TWO

3 — Female with lute | SAUK CO. BANK, Baraboo, Wis. Cattle, trees, stream of water, etc. | 3 — Compt's die. THREE

5 on Five. | Three females and bust. Female portrait. SAUK CO. BANK, Baraboo, Wis. | 5 on Five. Compt's die. FIVE

Compt's die One on 1 | 1 Three men, dog, machinery, etc., in grist mill. SHAWANAW BANK Chilton, Wis. | 1 — Female with flower

Compt's die 2 | Corn husking scene—males, female, negro, dog, etc. SHAWANAW BANK Chilton, Wis. TWO | 2 — Child's head.

V — Five cherubs with anvil, globe and sledge. | SHAWANAW BANK Shawanaw, Wis. Compt's die. | 5 — Five cherubs with tablet and rake.

X — Train of cars | SHAWANAW BANK Shawanaw, Wis. Compt's die. | 10 — Indian seated; plow, cabin, wheat, etc.

Compt's Die. 1 | Indian with spear and horse; train of cars. STATE BANK. Madison, Wis. | 1 — Mechanic seated; buildings in distance.

Compt's die. 2 | STATE BANK, Madison, Wis. Three females, one with lyre; another seated painting, and middle one with tablet. | 2 — Train of cars.

FIVVE — Compt's Die. FIVVE | STATE BANK, Madison, Wis. View of the Capitol building of Wisconsin. | 5 — Indian reclining; huts in background.

1 — Portrait of Webster. | STATE BANK OF WISCONSIN, Milwaukee, Wis. Vig. Farming scene at noon. | 1 — State Arms

2 — Female Portrait. | STATE BANK OF WISCONSIN, Milwaukee, Wis. Vig. Female reclining on bale of goods, barrels, &c., ship on right; factory, &c., on left. | 2 — State Arms

Left	Centre	Right
5 / 5	Vig. Three females in water, cupid, &c. Male Portrait. STATE BANK OF WISCONSIN, Milwaukee, Wis.	5 / State Arms.
10 / Male portrait	Vig. Land and water scene, train of cars running to the left, one crossing bridge in distance. STATE BANK OF WISCONSIN, Milwaukee, Wis.	10 / State Arms.
FIVE / Eagle on cliff / Compt's die.	Man propelling raft on river. ST. CROIX VALLEY BANK, St. Croix Falls, Wis. Sunset	Five on 5 / 5, Indians, cars, water falls, etc.
10 / X, female, cows, cars, etc.	Steamboat Delian. Title of Bank. Compt's die.	10 / Indian, water etc.
2 / 2	SUMMIT BANK, Milkmaid, man, ladder, house, etc. Female portrait. Oconomowoc, Wis.	2 / Compt's die. / TWO
3 / Compt's die. / THREE	Title of Bank. Man drinking; boy, horses and plow.	3 / Boy and two horses at trough.
One on 1. / Compt's die	Indians viewing train of cars riding out in distance. SUN PRAIRIE BK. Sun Prairie, Wis.	1 / Two children.
Compt's die / V	SUN PRAIRIE BK. Sun Prairie, Wis. Man, two horses, and pig at pump; cattle and barn in distance.	5 / Clay.
1 / Female feeding chickens	WALWORTH CO. BK. Delavan, Wis. State die.	1 / Man, horse and dog.
TWO / Smith's shop	WALWORTH CO. BK. Delavan, Wis. 2 Female, lots of goods; houses in distance. 2	2 / State die.

Left	Centre	Right
5 / Head of female.	Horse Market. WALWORTH CO. BK. Delavan, Wis.	5 / State die.
1 / Female seated on stone, with pail.	WAUKESHA CO. BK. Waukesha, Wis. 1 Female seated on bale beside silver dollar, anchor, trees, &c. 1 Girl's head.	1 / Compt's die.
TWO / Compt's die. / TWO	WAUKESHA COUNTY BANK, Waukesha, Wis. Corn husking scene—two males, two females, dog, fowls, etc.	TWO / Female head
ONE	Vig. same as the above 2. WISCONSIN BANK, Madison, Wis. Badger	1 / Compt's die. / ONE
TWO	Male portrait with Indian, wigwams and canoe on right; farmer, sheaves, cars, bridge, canal boat, etc., on left. WISCONSIN BANK, Madison, Wis.	2 / Compt's die. / TWO
5 / Compt's die.	Two females representing Liberty and Justice on either side of male portrait; cars, bridge, factory, steamer, &c., in distance. WISCONSIN BANK, Madison, Wis. Bell	5 / 5
10 / Male portrait	WISCONSIN BANK, Madison, Wis. Compt's die on X. Indian.	10 / Reaper, men pitching, wagon in distance / TEN
State Arms / Male standing with American flag, female sitting at his feet, anchor, shield, bar, &c.	WISCONSIN MARINE AND FIRE INSURANCE CO. Milwaukee, Wis. Vig. Female sitting, resting right arm on a shield; ships on right and left.	2 / Female Portrait.
State Arms. / Three females ... each ... the other, anchor, &c. / THREE	Title of Bank. Vig. St. George on horse and the dragon.	3 / Female Portrait.
State Arms. / Indian with gun, &c.	Title of Bank. Vig. Man, woman, and child.	5 / Female with bundle of straw on her back.

Left	Centre	Right
1 / Hunter drinking from brook.	WISCONSIN PINERY BANK, Stevens Point, Wis. Female with child in arms, boy, dog, etc.; in distance men mowing	1 / Compt's die.
2 / Hunter and dog, chased by fire in woods	Title of Bank. Compt's die.	2 / Milkmaid and cattle.
Female with sickle and dog. / Three, 3, III	Title of Bank. Mechanic, farmer, horse, buildings, etc.	3 / Compt's die. / THREE
5 / Boy and rabbits	Three females and bust of Washington. Title of Bank.	5 / Compt's die.
V / Ship.	BK OF COMMERCE, Fernandina, Florida. Vig. Small view of two females on either side of shield, on which is tree and cow.	5 on Five. / Male portrait
X / Locomotive and tender.	Title of Bank. Same as 5s.	10 / Cotton field; vessel in distance.
XX / Same as Vig. of 5s.	Title of Bank. Steamer and other vessels, and 20 on red die in square frame.	20 / Woodman.
Small 5 in 5.	Steamer, other vessels and city. BANK OF FERNANDINA, Florida.	Small 5 in 5.
10 / X / TEN	Negro with two horses carting bales. Female with cotton bud. Title of Bank.	10 / X / TEN
20 / XX / XX	Title of Bank. Train of cars.	20 / 20 / XX

Left	Centre	Right
5 Train of cars.	BK OF ST JOHNS, Jacksonville, Florida. Cotton plant.	5 Female with eagle on shield, etc.
10 Indian war-[illegible]	Hunter shooting deer crossing stream; dogs in pursuit. Title of Bank.	10 Same as [illegible]
Same as on right of 5s Female with lyre.	Steamboat "Everglade" and other sailing vessels. Title of Bank.	20 Female with flowers.
V Clay.	Six mules driven by negro before load of cotton, passing house on road; cabin in background on right. STATE BANK OF FLORIDA, Tallahassee, Florida.	5 State Arms.
10 Male portrait.	Train of cars coming around curve; steamboat and train on left in distance. Title of Bank.	10 State Arms.
Two Indians.	20 Title of Bank. Red 20. Two men gathering corn.	20 State Arms.
Do. Queen Victoria. Do.	Five Shillings. BANK OF B. N. AMERICA, Hamilton, Canada. Arms of the Bank; or sailor, husbandman, &c.	Do. Prince Albert. Do.
TEN SHILLINGS Victoria TWO DOLLARS	$2 Arms of the Bank; or sailor husbandman, &c. $2 Title of Bank.	Albert TEN SHILLINGS
ONE Female reclining. POUND	Title o. Bank. $4 Three females seated; agriculture, commerce, &c. 1£ Arms of Great Britain.	FOUR Indian Chief seated. DOLLARS
Twenty five Arms of the Bank, &c. SHILLINGS	Title of Bank. $5 Two females seated; shipping, merchandise, &c. £1. 5. 0 Arms of Great Britain	FIVE Victoria the Royal Chair. DOLLARS

Left	Centre	Right
Ten Miniature of three females. DOLLARS	Title of Bank. £2. 10. 0 $10 Large beehive, surrounded by shrubbery, etc. Arms of Great Britain.	FIFTY Miniature of plow, sheep, cattle, tree, water, &c. SHILLINGS
Portrait of Queen Victoria.	FIVE SHILLINGS BANK OF BRITISH NORTH AMERICA, Kingston, Ca. 1 Arms of the Bank; or sailor, husbandman, dove, beehive, &c. 1	Portrait of Prince Albert.
TEN Shillings. Portrait of Queen Victoria. TWO DOLLARS	$2 Arms of the Bank; or sailor, husbandman, &c. $2 BANK OF BRITISH NORTH AMERICA, Kingston, Ca.	Portrait of Prince Albert. TEN Shillings
QUATRE Indian chief seated. PIASTRES	Title of Bank. 4 Female reclining representing Commerce; bale of merchandise, anchor, shipping, &c. 4 British arms.	FOUR Female surrounded by shrubbery, &c.; [illegible] implements at her feet. DOLLARS
CINQ Victoria seated in the royal chair. PIASTRES	BANK OF BRITISH NORTH AMERICA, Kingston, Ca. 5 Two females; lion and unicorn. 5 British arms.	FIVE Indian chief seated. DOLLARS
DIX Miniature view of town or city. PIASTRES	BANK OF BRITISH NORTH AMERICA, Kingston, Ca. 10 Two females reclining; shipping, &c. X British arms.	TEN Arms of the Bank. DOLLARS
VINGT Female standing erect with spear in left hand; right hand resting on a shield. PIASTRES	BANK OF BRITISH NORTH AMERICA, Kingston, Ca. 20 Female reclining on bale of [illegible]. 20 British arms.	TWENTY Miniature view of town or city. DOLLARS
50 Miniature view of group of three females. PIASTRES	Title of Bank. CINQUANTE Female FIFTY reclining, representing Commerce, Justice and Agriculture. British arms.	50 Miniature view of Indian, canoe, tent, trees, &c. DOLLARS
One Dollar Portrait of Queen Victoria. Five Shillings	BANK OF BRITISH NORTH AMERICA, Montreal, Ca. Arms of the Bank, or sailor, husbandman, beehive, dove, cornucopia, &c.	Montreal Portrait of Prince Albert Une Piastre
Two Dollars. Arms of Great Britain or lion and unicorn fighting for the crown. Deux Piastres	BANK OF BRITISH NORTH AMERICA, Montreal, Ca. $2	Montreal Arms of the Bank. Ten Shillings

Left	Centre	Right
Four Dollars. Indian seated Quatre Piastres.	BANK OF BRITISH NORTH AMERICA, Montreal, Ca. 4 Large sail vessel; small one in background. 4 British arms.	Quatre Piastres Miniature view of female reclining, representing Commerce. Four Dollars
FIVE Monument. DOLLARS	BANK OF BRITISH NORTH AMERICA, Montreal, Ca. 5 Large sail vessel; smaller one in distance. 5 British arms.	CINQ Her Majesty seated in the royal chair. PIASTRES
$10 Tent, canoe, [illegible], &c. Ten Dollars	BANK OF BRITISH NORTH AMERICA, Montreal, Ca. Female reclining on bale of [illegible], representing Commerce; shipping, &c., in background. British arms.	DIX View of entrance to harbor; houses, vessels, &c. PIASTRES
20 View of public buildings in Montreal. PIASTRES	BANK OF BRITISH NORTH AMERICA, Montreal, Ca. VINGT Group TWENTY of figures [illegible] Agriculture, Commerce, &c. British arms.	20 Monument, houses, &c. DOLLARS
Cinquante Arms of the Bank. PIASTRES	BANK OF BRITISH NORTH AMERICA, Montreal, Ca. 50 Steamship. 50 British arms.	FIFTY View of monument, public buildings. DOLLARS
Do. Queen Victoria. Do.	FIVE SHILLINGS BANK OF BRITISH N. AMERICA, Toronto, Ca. Arms of the Bank, or sailor, husbandman, &c.	Do. Prince Albert. Do.
TEN SHILLINGS Queen Victoria. TWO DOLLARS	$2 Arms of the Bank or sailor, husbandman, &c. $2 Title of Bank.	Prince Albert. TEN SHILLINGS.
QUATRE Female seated on bale of merchandise shipping, &c. PIASTRES	Title of Bank £1 £1 British arms.	ONE Arms of the Bank POUND
QUATRE Female seated; shipping, &c. PIASTRES	Title of Bank. 4 4 British arms.	FOUR Arms of the Bank. DOLLARS
CINQ Miniature view of house, rural scenery, &c. PIASTRES.	Title of Bank. 5 5 British arms.	FIVE Female seated. DOLLARS.

CINQ Same as 5s. PIASTRES	Title of Bank. 25s. 25s. British arms.	Twenty five Same as 5s. SHILLINGS
DIX Miniature of Cataract of Niagara. PIASTRES	Title of Bank. 10 X British arms.	TEN Queen Victoria seated in the royal chair. DOLLARS
ONE Court House.	Cattle, &c. BANK of the COUNTY OF ELGIN, St. Thomas, Can.	1 Fowls
2 Male head.	Cars, &c. BANK of the COUNTY OF ELGIN, Canada.	2 Court House.
5 Male portrait.	Men, three horses, sheep, houses, &c. BANK of the COUNTY OF ELGIN, Canada.	5 Buildings, &c.
10 Male head.	Cars, men, &c. BANK of the COUNTY OF ELGIN, Canada.	10 Court House.
	B'K. OF MONTREAL AND BRANCHES, Canada. These notes all have the place from which they are issued printed in the same manner as we have shown in the second description of the ONE.	
Female in a large figure 1.	[Old Plate.] B'K. OF MONTREAL AND BRANCHES, Canada. Steamer towing. FIVE SHILLINGS. City Arms.	Female in a large figure 1.
MONTREAL City arms supported by two Indians, the female seated.	[New Plate.] B'K. OF MONTREAL AND BRANCHES, Canada. FIVE SHILLINGS. ONE DOLLAR.	Steamship and shipping, and large figure 1. MONTREAL
ONE Female portrait.	B'K. OF MONTREAL, Canada. 1 Two Indians either side of shield; beaver at top. 1 ONE	1 Female with sheaf.

Indian either side of shield. 1	BK OF MONTREAL, Canada. ONE DOLLAR	1 Queen Victoria.
TWO St. George and dragon.	Title of Bank. 2 Queen Victoria. Prince Albert. 2 2	2 Same as vig. of 1s.
Female figure in large figure 2. 2	[Old Plate.] B'K. OF MONTREAL AND BRANCHES. Canada. Female seated. 2 Female standing. TEN SHILLINGS. City Arms	Female figure in large figure 2. 2
Same as the Ones.	[New Plate.] Title of Bank. TEN SHILLINGS. TWO DOLLARS.	Female shipping and figure 2, and Horn of plenty.
4 DOLLARS Female.	Royal Arms with motto. B'K. OF MONTREAL AND BRANCHES. Canada. City Arms.	4 DOLLARS Female.
City Arms supported by two Indians, the female seated.	B'K. OF MONTREAL AND BRANCHES. Canada. TWENTY SHILLINGS. FOUR DOLLARS.	Female holding shield and sickle, bale at her feet, large 4 resting on back of another bale.
FOUR Same as vig. of 1s.	Title of Bank. 4 Male portrait. 4 FOUR	4 Female seated by bale.
FIVE DOLLARS FIVE Same as vig. of 1s.	5 Building. 5 Title of Bank. FIVE	5 Blacksmith seated.
5 Female bust. FIVE	B'K. OF MONTREAL AND BRANCHES. Canada. Large V, with female figure 5 on either side. City Arms	Bust of female. FIVE
City Arms supported by two Indians, the female seated. 5	B'K. OF MONTREAL AND BRANCHES. Canada. TWENTY-FIVE SHILLINGS. FIVE DOLLARS.	Indian scout, one seated and two on horseback in distance, and 5

TEN Female seated by bale; steamer in distance.	Title of Bank. X Male portrait. X TEN	10 Same as vig. of 1s.
10 Female. TEN	B'K. OF MONTREAL AND BRANCHES, Canada. TWO POUNDS TEN X SHILLINGS currency.	10 Female. TEN
City Arms supported by two Indians, female seated. 10	B'K. OF MONTREAL AND BRANCHES. Canada. FIFTY SHILLINGS. TEN DOLLARS	Steamboat passengers with large 10
50 Bust of Her Majesty. 50	B'K. OF MONTREAL AND BRANCHES. Canada. A large ship in full sail and gulliott. TWELVE POUNDS TEN SHILLINGS. City Arms.	50 Bust of Prince Albert. 50
100 Female figure representing Justice. 100	B'K. OF MONTREAL AND BRANCHES, Canada. Queen Victoria seated. TWENTY-FIVE POUNDS. City Arms.	100 Female representing Commerce. 100
1 Cooper at work. UNE	1 Farmer with sheaf and scythe; buildings in distance. 1 LA BANQUE DU PEUPLE, Montreal, Canada.	1 Four cherubs and fig. 1
2 Farmer sharpening scythe. DEUX	Blacksmith and ship carpenter with implements; cars and ships in distance. LA BANQUE DU PEUPLE. Montreal, Canada.	2 Boy, key and safe. TWO
Ship carpenter seated with tools.	4 Milkmaid seated; female milking cow; vessels in distance. Title of Bank. Dog's head.	4 Blacksmith at work. 4
Two females with large X. TEN	Four cherubs, X, Prince Albert, Queen Victoria. Title of Bank. Agricultural implements.	Two females with large X. DIX
20 Sailor. 20	Title of Bank. Man plowing with two horses. Steamship.	20

50 Canal scene. 50	Title of Bank. Sailor with flag reclining on bale; ship in distance. Female head.	Steamboat.
100 Female portrait. C	General view of city, wharf and shipping. Title of Bank. Arms.	100 Portrait of female. C
ONE Justice.	1 Farmer seated on grain; reapers on left; loading hay on right. BANK OF TORONTO, Toronto, Canada.	1 Indian seated, supporting fig. 1.
4 Farmers and scythe.	Three females seated representing Agriculture, Commerce, and Arts. BANK OF TORONTO, Toronto, Canada. City Arms.	FOUR Portrait of an Indian Chief.
5 Female portrait.	BANK OF TORONTO, Toronto, Canada. British Arms. City Arms.	5 Female seated, large fig. 5; bales, ships, &c.
TEN Beaver.	BANK OF TORONTO, Toronto, Canada. City Arms.	10 Train of cars.
1 Female seated on sheaf with sword and scales.	BANK OF UPPER CANADA, Toronto, Canada. ONE St. George and the dragon. ONE	1 Female with trident and shield.
1 Miniature view of lion's head. 1	BANK OF UPPER CANADA. 1 Female seated half reclining, hand resting on figure 1. 1 St. George and dragon.	1 Miniature view of female seated, dog, figure 1, &c. 1
1 Indian with bow and arrow, &c.	Train of cars and village in distance. Title of Bank. St. George and dragon.	1 Female seated.
2 Female portrait.	Sailor reclining; anchor, boat, etc.; steamship in distance. Title of Bank.	2 Female with trident and shield.

TWO Female representing agriculture 2	Title of Bank. 2 Two flying griffins, figure 2 between. 2 Same as on ones.	TWO Portrait of Female. 2
2 Train of cars TWO	Hogs, cattle, drovers, &c.; train of cars and village in distance. Title of Bank Same as on ones.	2 Milkmaid and two cows TWO
figure 4. Queen Victoria. figure 4.	Female seated holding spear, shield, &c.; lion; implements of war, &c. Fig. 4 on either side. Title of Bank Same as on ones	4 Female representing agriculture. 4
4 Female with cornucopia.	Title of Bank. Two females, Royal arms, lion and unicorn.	4 Mechanic reclining.
5 Sailor hauling rope, capstan, etc.	V Same as 4s. V Title of Bank.	5 Prince Albert
5 Queen Victoria. V	5 Lion with his paw upon a shield. 5 Title of Bank. Same as on ones.	5 Prince Albert V
5 With horse. FIVE	Title of Bank. Queen Victoria; lion and unicorn on either side. Same as on ones.	5 Dog and safe FIVE
X Female portrait.	Title of Bank. X Same as 4s. X	10 Female with trident and shield.
X Portrait of Girl.	BANK OF UPPER CANADA Two females seated, with ewe, bust, anchor, etc.; sheaf, tools on left; building, etc., on right. Toronto, Canada.	10 Cattle, telegraph, cars, bridge, etc.
TEN Miniature view of flower girl. TEN	10 Female representing the Arts and Sciences. 10 Title of Bank. Same as on ones.	TEN Statue of Minerva. TEN

10 Sailor with hand on Jack staff.	Steamship; other vessels in distance. 10 Title of Bank. Bale, bids. and anchor.	British arms.
20 Miniature view of flying griffin. TWENTY	Two female figures; locomotive, vessel, &c., in background. Title of Bank. Same as on ones.	20 Miniature of Minerva, spear, shield &c. TWENTY
TWENTY	20 Two females on either side of shield, crown at top; house and vessels in distance. Title of Bank.	20 Blacksmiths at work.
50 Miniature of cupid. 50	L Locomotive and car; shipping, merchandise, &c. L Title of Bank. Flying griffin.	Miniature view of monument, trees, shrubbery, &c. 50
50 Female figure seated; Agriculture. FIFTY	Female seated between lion and unicorn. Title of Bank. Same as on ones.	50 Female seated, armory, &c.; vessel in the background. FIFTY.
50 Agricultural implements	Title of Bank. Same as 20s	50 Female with sickle.
100 100	Same as 50s. Title of Bank.	100 Female, bale, shipping, etc.
Die. 100 Die.	100 Arms of Great Britain, or lion and unicorn. 100 Title of Bank. Flying griffin.	Miniature of monument, trees, shrubbery, &c 100
100 Miniature view of female seated.	Queen Victoria seated between lion and unicorn. Title of Bank. Same as on ones.	100 Hot head.
[illegible]	Bank building. 1 CITY BANK, Montreal, Canada. Crown, sceptre, &c.	ONE Female. ONE

ONE ONE and figure 1. Female Figure spinning; wheel and buildings in rear. ONE and figure 1. CITY BANK, Toronto, Canada. 1 Victoria.	10 Male portrait. CITY BANK, Montreal, Canada. St. George and the dragon. 10 Male portrait.	1 Farm boy standing erect, holding rake in left; bundle of grain. COM. BANK, M. D. Kingston, Ca. Female reclining; figure 1; cornucopia, &c. 1 1 Sailor standing erect.
1 Bust of William 4th. UNE 1 1 LA BANQUE DE LA CITE, Montreal, Canada. Indian with bow. UNE PIASTRE. 1 The City B'k will pay the bearer on demand one dollar. UNE	TEN 10 TEN Bank building. CITY BANK. Montreal, Canada. 10	1 Portrait of Prince Albert. 1 1 Female erect holding a rake; sheaf, &c. 1 COMMERCIAL BANK M. D., Montreal, Canada. National arms. 1 Portrait of Queen Victoria in ornamental frame. 1
TWO 2 Female figure, Agriculture and Commerce in rear. 2 CITY BANK, Toronto, Canada. 2 Victoria.	10 Bust of William 4th. 10 CITY BANK. Montreal, Canada. DIX Lion and Unicorn. 10 X La Banque de la Cite payera au porteur sur demande Dix Piastres. X	2 Fowls TWO Cattle in water, etc. Title of Bank. 2 Female feeding fowls.
2 Bank building. 2 CITY BANK. Montreal, Canada. TWO Male and female.	10 Bust of William 4th. 10 10 CITY BK. 10 Toronto, Canada. Lion and Unicorn. X Female Figure. X	2 Portrait of Prince Albert 2 2 Two females seated; cornucopia; ship on left; sheaf of wheat and plough on right. 2 COMMERCIAL BANK M. D., Montreal, Canada. National arms. 2 Same as one. 2
2 The City B'k will pay the bearer on demand two dollars. DEUX LA BANQUE DE LA CITE, Montreal, Canada. 2 Indian in canoe. 2 DEUX PIASTRES. 2 Bust of William 4th. TWO	20 La Banque de la Cite payera au porteur sur demande Vingt Piastres. XX VINGT. Bust of William 4th; Lion on right, Unicorn on left. CITY BANK, Montreal, Canada. TWENTY	2 Justice and Liberty erect COM. BANK. M. D., Kingston, Ca. Two females seated, cornucopia at their feet. 2 2 Two females standing erect, in representation of Agriculture and Commerce.
4 Victoria with crown. 4 4 Bank building. 4 CITY BANK, Montreal, Canada. ONE POUND.	20 Female Figure. XX 20 Bust of William 4th, Lion and Unicorn 20 CITY BANK. Toronto, Canada. TWENTY	4 Female portrait. QUATRE Locomotive and train of cars; city in the background; trees, houses, head of bay, &c. COM. BANK. M. D., Kingston, Ca. 4 Female portrait. FOUR
Lion and Unicorn. 5 Figure sustaining the globe with a lever. CITY BANK Toronto, Canada. V Bust of William 4th. V	Female. XX 20 Bank building. CITY BANK, Montre.l, Canada. 20	5 Portrait of Prince Albert V Two females, cupids, and three ornamental 5s. COMMERCIAL BANK M. D., Montreal, Canada. National arms. 5 Same as one. V
5 Bust of a female. FIVE City arms supported by two Indians. 5 Bank building. CITY BANK, Montreal, Canada. 5	50 Bank building. CITY BANK. Montreal, Canada. 50	FIVE Portrait of Queen Victoria. 5 Large figure 5 encircling female, the whole surrounded by four cupids. 5 COM. BANK, M. D. Kingston, Ca. British arms. FIVE Portrait of Prince Albert.
5 Male portrait FIVE Group of persons viewing train of cars. CITY BANK, Montreal, Canada. 5 Male portrait FIVE	100 Prince Albert. Bank building. CITY BANK, Montreal, Canada. 100 Queen Victoria.	5 Engineers surveying land. FIVE Farming scene; cars and city in distance. Title of Bank. 5 Man with pickaxe, shovel, &c.
CINQ Lion and Unicorn. PIASTRES 5 Figure sustaining the globe with a lever. 5 CITY BANK, Montreal, Canada. V Bust of William 4th. V	1 Indian on rock. ONE COMMERCIAL BK OF CANADA, Kingston, Ca. Farming scene; cars and city in distance. 1 Female Indian. ONE	V 5 Mercury seated, representing Commerce, Justice, &c., lion at his feet. COM. BANK, M. D. Kingston, Ca. 5 Portrait of female.

10 Portrait of Queen Victoria.	X Female seated in position to divide the figures 10, supporting cornucopia and key. X COM. BANK, M. D., Kingston, Ca.	10 Portrait of Prince Albert
X	10 Vaulting female. COM. BANK, M. D., Kingston, Ca.	10 Miniature view of shipping.
10 Portrait of Queen Victoria.	COMMERCIAL BANK M. D., Montreal, Canada. National arms.	10 TEN
10 Queen Victoria.	Title of Bank. Three sailors, anchor, bales, sea; ship on right.	10 Female portrait.
20 Portrait of Queen Victoria.	Female seated dividing the figures 20, rake in her right hand. COM. BANK, M. D., Kingston, Ca.	20 Portrait of Prince Albert
Portrait of Queen Victoria surrounded by the lion and unicorn.	COM. BANK, M. D., Kingston, C. 50	50
100	Miniature of female, representing the Arts and Sciences. C COM. BANK, M. D., Kingston, Ca.	1[illegible]0 British arms. 100
ONE HUNDRED	COMMERCIAL BANK of Canada. C View of large building, pedestrians, etc.	100 Female portrait. $100
1000	Title of Bank. M Male portrait M	ONE THOUSAND
1000	COMMERCIAL BANK M. D., Montreal, Canada. Portrait of the Empress of France.	ONE THOUSAND

ONE Queen Victoria.	EASTERN TOWNSHIP BANK, Sherbrook, Canada. Falls, mills, bridge, buildings, etc.	Indian on [illegible] ONE
2 Queen Victoria.	EASTERN TOWNSHIP BANK, Sherbrooke, Canada. Cattle, pigs, and men on horseback; cars and bridge in distance.	2 Prince Albert
4 Male portrait.	Fall, bridge, mills, etc. EASTERN TOWNSHIP BANK, Sherbrooke, Canada	4 Male portrait.
5 Female with book.	Man with sack on back; mill, horse, colt, wheel; boys on bridge. Title of Bank.	5 Man cleaning scythe.
TEN Hunter by fire, dog, etc.	Boy watching sheep. Title of Bank.	10 Cars; buildings in distance.
XX Female, wheel, building, etc.	Man plowing with two horses; man harrowing, city, etc., in distance. Title of Bank.	20 Female with spear and XX on shield.
Ornamental work. 1 Ornamental work.	1 Large building, and arms of Great Britain. 1 ONE ONE GORE BANK, Hamilton, Canada	Ornamental work. 1 Ornamental work.
2 Ornamental die, enclosing the words "Honi Soit Qui Mal Y Pense." 2	Two females seated between the lion and Unicorn. TWO TWO Title of Bank.	2
ONE POUND 4 FOUR DOLLARS	4 IV Arms of Great Britain, or lion, unicorn, &c. Title of Bank.	4 FOUR DOLLARS 4
TEN Miniature view of shipping; bales of merchandise, &c. TEN	X Miniature view of a man mounted on horseback, spearing a dragon. 10 Title of Bank.	TEN

1 Male figure seated.	Female seated with branch and shield; fort in distance. Fig. 1 on ONE either side. LA BANQUE NATIONALE. Quebec, Canada.	1 Male figure.
2 Two females.	Same as ones with fig. 2 on word DEUX either side. Title of Bank.	2 Male portrait 2
5 Agricultural implements.	V Two men plowing with two horses. V Title of Bank.	5 Female with flowers.
10 Boy with sheep.	Locomotive and train of cars, men, etc.; steamboat in distance. Title of Bank. X TEN X	10 Female seated with spear and shield.
Female seated, holding figure 1, sheaf of wheat. 1	MOLSON'S BANK, Montreal, Canada. Vig. Steamship and other vessels.	Female seated, holding figure 1; bales, bales and ships masts; 1
ONE Female portrait. ONE	MOLSONS BANK, Montreal Canada. 1 Female resting with fig. 1 1	1 Sailor.
TWO Portrait of female.	Title of Bank. Two females seated by fig. 2. 2	TWO Female and two fig. 2s.
Large figure 2, portrait of Prince Albert, and two figure ones.	MOLSON'S BANK, Montreal, Canada. Vig. Female seated; on right men loading hay, train of cars, houses, &c.	2 Portrait of Queen Victoria.
Three females, with anchor, sheaf of wheat, &c. CINQ.	5 MOLSON'S BANK, Montreal, Canada. Vig. Female seated, with tub, two cows, one lying down; in distance cows trees, house, &c. Agricultural implements.	5 FIVE 5
10 [illegible] DIX	MOLSON'S BANK, Montreal, Canada. Large X and three Cupids. Steamboat.	10 Female portrait. TEN

20 Indian in frame. TWENTY | Vig. Steamship and five vessels, all under way. MOLSON'S BANK, Montreal, Canada. Man on horseback. | 20 Man, wheat, with whip; house and steamboat in distance.

50 Country road, drove of cattle, load of hay, horses, men, &c. | MOLSON'S BANK, Montreal, Canada. Portrait of Queen Victoria. 50 | 50 Train of cars, village in distance.

1 | View of Niagara Falls. 1 NIAGARA DISTRICT BANK, St Catherines, Ca | Five Shil's 1

1 Milkmaid. | Register's die. Lion and unicorn on either side of the crown. NIAGARA DISTRICT BANK, St. Catharines, Ca. | 1 ONE

Head of Queen Victoria. 2 | NIAGARA DISTRICT BANK, St. Catherines, Ca. Ship on stocks; female reclining on sofa on left; on right sheaf of wheat and sheep. | 2 Locomotive and tender.

2 Prince Albert. | NIAGARA DISTRICT BANK, St. Catherines, Ca. Register's die. 2 | 2

FOUR Male portrait. | NIAGARA DISTRICT BANK, St. Catherines, Ca. View of N. Y. harbor with steamship and ship | 4 Ship in canal; trees, houses, &c.

5 Male portrait. | NIAGARA DISTRICT BANK, St Catherines, Ca Three men looking at sheet on a stone; ship on stocks, shipping and city. | 5 and word five. Royal Arms.

5 Ship building | NIAGARA DISTRICT BANK, St. Catharines, Ca. Portrait of the Queen of England. | Register's die. 5

ONE Agricultural implements and products ONE | 1 Ox, sheep, horse, etc. 1 ONTARIO BANK, Bowmanville, Canada ONE | 1 ONE Man shearing sheep.

TWO Mechanic with sledge, anvil, locomotive, etc. | Two and 2. Female seated, hat on lap, dog, cows, etc. Title of Bank TWO | 2 TWO 2

FIVE Male portrait. Five and green V. | ONTARIO BANK, Bowmanville, Canada Five and fig. 5. Man sharpening scythe. 5 and Dollars | 5 and green V FIVE Bull's head.

10 and green X. Canal and railroad scene. | Indian with shield on which is canal scene, sun, steamer, man plowing, etc.; bison on right; deer on left. Title of Bank | 10 and green X. Cattle, cars, telegraph, bridge, etc.

20 Female reclining on sheaf. 20 | 20 on green die. ONTARIO BANK, Bowmanville, Canada | 20 Boy and sheep. Prince Albert. XX

Female with sickle. 50 | ONTARIO BANK, Bowmanville, Canada 50 Male portrait. 50 | 50 Female with flowers.

100 Male portrait | Female either side of anvil; factories in distance. ONTARIO BANK, Bowmanville, Canada | 100 C

1 Anchor, bales, bble, &c | Men chopping trees; cabin, horse, &c., in background. QUEBEC BANK, Quebec, Canada. St. George and the Dragon. | 1 Five Fives surrounded by flowers.

1 Medallion head with one on it. 1 | 1 Vig. Indians hunting buffaloes. 1 QUEBECBANK. Quebec, Canada. 1 | Large figure 1 and female on it.

1 ONE 1 | 1 Vig. Two females on either side of a shield, surmounted by a crown and lion, train of cars in distance. QUEBEC BANK, Quebec, Canada. 1 | 1 ONE 1

TWO | 2 British coat of arms. 2 QUEBEC BANK, Quebec, Canada. | 2 Female portrait with helmet. 2

2 Female erect with spear, globe, &c. | Vig. Male and female seated, male with scroll in right hand and rod in left. QUEBEC BANK, Quebec, Canada. 2 | 2 Female with pail.

Female portrait with helmet. | 4 Vig. River scene, ships, steamboat, city, &c. 4 QUEBEC BANK, Quebec, Canada. Female and dolphin | Female portrait with helmet.

5 Farmer and agricultural implements. 5 | 5 Vig. Two winged monsters on either side of a shield on which is a boy. 5 QUEBEC BANK, Quebec, Canada. | Portrait of Queen Victoria.

5 Female with shield on which is figure 5. 5 | 5 Vig. Two males on either side of a shield on which is a bull; ship on right; and schooner, train of cars, &c., on left. 5 QUEBEC BANK, Quebec, Canada. | 5 Three cupids. 5

10 Sailor at Capstan. | QUEBEC BANK, Quebec, Canada. TWO POUND TEN. Yoke of Oxen—man sleeping and two children. | 10

10 Medallion head. | Vig. Naval scene, ships of war, &c. X QUEBEC BANK, Quebec, Canada. | Portrait of Queen Victoria.

XX Ships, &c. 20 | QUEBEC BANK, Quebec, Canada. 20 Vig. Three figures, 2 males and 1 female; village on left, and man on horseback on right. 20 | XX Yacht. 20

50 Wharf scene, steamboat, ships, &c. 50 | 50 Vig. Female seated and two others soaring in the air; griffin on eagle; bids, boxes, &c on right. 50 QUEBEC BANK, Quebec, Canada. | 50

100 Wharf scene, steamboat, ships, &c. 100 | C Vig. Male and female figures seated in a car drawn by sea horses. C QUEBEC BANK, Quebec. Canada. | 100 Ship in full sail. 100

Five shillings. Figure of Justice with sword and scales. One dollar. | BANK OF BRITISH NORTH AMERICA, St John, N. B. Word dollar and figure 1. Arms of the Bank, sailor, farmer, &c. Word shillings and figure 5. Royal arms. | One dollar Female Five shillings

Left end	Centre	Right end
Ten shillings. Female seated. Two dollars.	Title of Bank. Word dollars and figure 2. Female reclining on bale of merchandise. Word shillings and figure 10. Royal arms.	Two dollars. Group of three persons. Ten shillings.
One pound. Arms of the Bank, sailor, farmer, &c. Four dollars.	Title of Bank. £4 Sail vessel. £1 Royal arms.	Four dollars. Female erect representing Commerce. One pound.
FIVE Queen Victoria. POUNDS	Title of Bank. £5 Two females representing Commerce, &c. £5 Royal arms.	FIVE Female reclining; vessel in background. POUNDS
Head of Queen Victoria. $40	Title of Bank. Arms of the Bank, sailor and farmer, eagle mounted on beehive, &c.; motto, "Via e gita fecion." New Brunswick.	FORTY 40 DOLLARS £10
Figure of Minerva	Five shillings. Vig. Group of three females in representation of three kingdoms, arts and sciences. Five shillings. BANK OF NEW BRUNSWICK, St. John, N. B. Two children.	FIVE SHILLINGS
Figure of Minerva.	ONE ONE Same as five shillings. BANK OF NEW BRUNSWICK, St. John, N. B Two children.	ONE
Figure of Minerva.	1 Group of three females in representation of three kingdoms, arts and sciences. ONE DOLLAR THE BANK OF NEW BRUNSWICK. St. John, N. B. Two children.	ONE DOLLAR
Figure of Minerva.	TWO TWO Same as five shillings. BANK OF NEW BRUNSWICK, St. John, N. B. Two children.	TWO
Figure of Minerva.	V 5 Same as five shillings. BANK OF NEW BRUNSWICK, St. John, N. B. Two children.	FIVE
Figure of Minerva.	5 FIVE DOLLARS Vig. same as in THE BANK OF NEW BRUNSWICK. St. John, N. B.	FIVE DOLLARS
Figure of Minerva.	TEN TEN Same as five shillings. BANK OF NEW BRUNSWICK, St. John, N. B. Two children.	TEN
Figure of Minerva	TEN DOLLARS 10 Same as 1's THE BANK OF NEW BRUNSWICK. St. John, N. B.	TEN DOLLARS
Figure of Minerva.	20 Same as 1's 20 THE BANK OF NEW BRUNSWICK, St. John, N. B.	TWENTY DOLLARS
Figure of Minerva.	25 25 Same as five shillings. BANK OF NEW BRUNSWICK. St. John, N. B. Two children.	TWENTY-FIVE
Figure of Minerva.	50 Same as 1's 50 THE BANK OF NEW BRUNSWICK. St. John, N. B.	FIFTY DOLLARS
Word shillings and figure 5 across. Sail vessel; lighthouse in distance. Word shillings and figure 5 across.	FIVE British coat of arms, or lion and unicorn fighting for the crown. FIVE COMMERCIAL BANK OF N. B. St. John, N. B. Lion.	Same as on left. View of two persons; harvest scene. Same as on left.
Seven and sixpence. Female seated with vase of flowers, &c. 7 | 6	7/6 Check. British coat of arms, &c. 7/6 Check. 7/6 7/6 Title of Bank.	7 | 6 CHECK. 7 | 6
ONE Sail vessel. ONE	£1 currency. 1 British coat of arms, &c. 1 Title of Bank. Lion.	ONE
2 Same as ones. 2	£2 currency. TWO British coat of arms, &c. TWO Title of Bank. Lion.	TWO
FIVE Female seated, holding spear, shield, &c.; vessel in distance. FIVE	£5 currency. 5 British coat of arms, &c. 5 Title of Bank. Lion.	FIVE
TEN Full rigged vessel. TEN	£10 currency. 10 British coat of arms, &c. 10 Title of Bank. Lion.	TEN
25 Same as tens. 25	£25 currency. 25 British coat of arms, &c. 25 Title of Bank. Lion.	TWENTY-FIVE
$1 Ship under sail. ONE	ONE on 1 British coat of arms, or lion and unicorn fighting for the crown. ONE on 1 COMMERCIAL B'K OF N. BRUNSWICK. St. Johns, N. B. Lion on crown.	ONE DOLLAR.
TWO DOLLARS.	Same as $1 note. TWO on 2 TWO on 2 COMMERCIAL B'K OF N. BRUNSWICK. St. Johns, N. B. Lion on crown.	$2 Ship on stocks. TWO
4 Barrels, ship, &c. FOUR	Same as $1 note. FOUR 4 COMMERCIAL B'K OF N. BRUNSWICK. St. Johns, N. B. Lion on crown.	FOUR DOLLARS.
Globe. EIGHT 8 DOLLARS. Two Pounds.	Same as $1 note. 8 or DOLLARS. 8 or DOLLARS. COMMERCIAL B'K OF N. BRUNSWICK, St. Johns, N. B. Lion on crown.	8 Female with basket
$20 Steamboat.	Same as $1 note. TWENTY 20 DOLLARS TWENTY 20 DOLLARS COMMERCIAL B'K OF N. BRUNSWICK. St. Johns, N. B. Lion on crown.	$20 Man at wheel.
50 FIFTY DOLLARS 50	Same as $1 note. $50 $50 COMMERCIAL B'K OF N. BRUNSWICK. St. Johns, N. B. Lion on crown.	50 Female, barrel, quadrant, &c.
100 ONE HUNDR'D DOLLARS 100	Same as $1 note. 100 100 COMMERCIAL B'K OF N. BRUNSWICK, St. Johns, N. B. Lion on crown.	$100 Fishing vessel.
1 Male portrait	Scene in Arctic regions. ST STEPHENS BANK New Brunswick 1 ONE 1	1 Sailor boy.

ONE
Vessels, steamboat, &c. 1 ONE
ST. STEPHENS' BK., St. Stephen, N. B. ONE DOLLAR.
Female Indian seated, with bow and arrow.

V 5 Two Indians; one seated and smoking; the other reclining; a fire, trees, waterfall, &c. 5 V
Steamboat and other vessels and hills. 5
SAINT STEPHENS' BANK. St. Stephen, N. B. FIVE DOLLARS.
River scene; men in boats, &c.
Male in field, with sheaf and sickle. 5

20 TWENTY
Female sitting; scroll in left hand; right resting on shield; spear laying upon shoulder.
Title of Bank.
Vig. Female holding a hay-rake in right hand; left hand resting on figure 0, which, with figure 2 at her right hand, is wrought in fancy lettering.
Crown.
20 DOLLARS
Female sitting; balances in right hand; rod in left.

2 TWO 2
Ships on and before the wind. 2
ST. STEPHENS' BK., St. Stephen, N. B. TWO DOLLARS.
TWO Female and domestic utensils. TWO

10 Beehive.
Title of Bank.
X Sailor with trumpet. X
10 Royal Arms.

ONE Mariner with quadrant.
Vig. Ship yard; two vessels on the stocks, &c.
WESTMORLAND BK. Bend of Petticodiac, New Brunswick
Lock and hole.
1 Portrait of Queen Victoria. ONE

THREE
Harvest scene; male and female reapers. 3
ST. STEPHENS' BK. St. Stephen, N. B. THREE DOLLARS.
THREE Steamboat. THREE.

10 X 10
Indian in canoe; in background, vessels, men, hills, &c.
SAINT STEPHENS' BANK. S. Stephen, N. B. TEN DOLLARS
Eagle.
10 Ship on stocks. 10

TWO Indian erect; bow and spear in right and left hand; plumed to his head.
Vig. Locomotive and train of cars.
Title of Bank.
Two horses standing.
2 Ship under fore and top sail.

5 Two men, shipping, bales, etc.
V Lion with shield. V
Title of Bank.
FI V VE
5 Female portrait.

X Beehive, X
10 Same as five pound note. Figures 10, and word Ten pound above, and word Currency below.
ST. STEPHENS' BK., St. Stephen, N. B. TEN POUNDS.
Dog, safe and boy.
TEN

Victoria. Five Pounds
£6. 5. 5. STERLING.
British Arms. Fig. 5 above word POUNDS either side.
Title of Bank.
Prince Albert Five Pounds
£5. 0. 0. STERLING.

UNITED STATES TREASURY NOTES.

Crawford's statue of America.
"E Pluribus Unum" at the base.
(Demand bill, 1861.)
UNITED STATES TREASURY NOTE
FIVE DOLLARS across large 5.
(Printed in green tint.)
5 Male portrait.

Washington.
Large spread eagle on rock.
100
UNITED STATES
100 One hundred dollars.

50
(7 3-10 per cent., 1861.)
Large spread eagle on rock.
UNITED STATES TREASURY NOTE.
FIFTY DOLLARS. on 50
50

Portrait of Abraham Lincoln.
(Demand bill, 1861.)
10 Spread eagle with shield and olive branch. 10
UNITED STATES TREASURY NOTE.
TEN DOLLARS.
(Printed in green tint.)
Female erect, with brushes, pallet, &c.

50 on die. Portrait of Andrew Jackson
[6 per cent., 1861.]
UNITED STATES TREASURY NOTE.
Female seated, with sword and scales.
FIFTY DOLLARS.
50
50 on die. Portrait of Salmon P. Chase.

C 100
[7 3-10 per cent., 1861.]
C Large portrait of Winfield Scott. C
UNITED STATES TREASURY NOTE
ONE HUNDRED.
C 100

TWENTY DOLLARS 20
(Demand bill, 1861.)
2 0
UNITED STATES TREASURY NOTE.
Full length figure of America, with sword and shield.
TWENTY DOLLARS
(Printed in green tint.)
20 TWENTY DOLLARS

Female with liberty cap and pole, leaning on cotton cornucopia at her feet.
[6 per cent., 1861.]
100 Spread eagle on shield, clutching arrows and olive branch.
UNITED STATES TREASURY NOTE.
ONE HUNDRED DOLLARS.
C

500 Female seated on iron safe, with scales and sword.
[7 3-10 per cent., 1861.]
Portrait of Washington
UNITED STATES TREASURY NOTE.
FIVE HUNDRED DOLLARS.
500 Female seated, wheel and smoking urn beside her.

The $5, $10, and $20 New Treasury Notes are same as the old, excepting a red stamp on face of bill, containing motto: "Thesaur Amer. Septent Sigil," and, on the back of bill, die containing the words: "This Note is a Legal Tender for all debts, &c.

500 Sailor with bundle.
[6 per cent., 1861.]
UNITED STATES TREASURY NOTE.
Oval portrait of Winfield Scott in frame of stars.
FIVE HUNDRED DOLLARS.
500 Farmer seated on fence, holding scythe.

1000
[7 3-10 per cent., 1861.]
UNITED STATES TREASURY NOTE.
One Thousand Dollars on 1000
Portrait of Sal. P. Chase.
One Thousand Dollars on 1000
1000

50
UNITED
Portrait of Alexander Hamilton.
Washington.
STATES.
FIFTY DOLLARS
50

1000 on die.
Portrait of Washingt'n
1000 on die
(6 per cent., 1861.)
UNITED STATES TREASURY NOTE.
ONE THOUSAND DOLLARS.
Full length figure of America with shield, olive branch, and bundle of rods.
ONE THOUSAND DOLLARS.
1000 on die.
Treasury building, Washingt'n
1000 on die.

5000 Female erect, with sword and scales.
(7 3-10 per cent., 1861.)
Indian female seated, bow in left hand, eagle and shield beside her.
UNITED STATES TREASURY NOTE.
FIVE THOUSAND DOLLARS
5000

www.ingramcontent.com/pod-product-compliance
Lightning Source LLC
Chambersburg PA
CBHW031338070726
47496CB00017B/1281
* 9 7 8 3 7 4 2 8 0 0 9 7 8 *